THE FRANCES GARROOD BOXSET

Cassandra's Secret

Women Behaving Badly

Ruth Robinson's Year of Miracles

THE FRANCES GARROOD BOXSET

Published by Sapere Books.

11 Bank Chambers, Hornsey, London, N8 7NN,
United Kingdom

saperebooks.com

Copyright © Frances Garrood, 2018
Frances Garrood has asserted her right to be identified as the author of this work.
All rights reserved.

No part of this publication may be reproduced, stored in any retrieval system, or transmitted, in any form, or by any means, electronic, mechanical, photocopying, recording, or otherwise, without the prior written permission of the publishers.
This book is a work of fiction. Names, characters, businesses, organisations, places and events, other than those clearly in the public domain, are either the product of the author's imagination, or are used fictitiously. Any resemblances to actual persons, living or dead, events or locales are purely coincidental.

BOOK ONE: CASSANDRA'S SECRET

One

October 2001

Outside the hospital window, a maple tree sheds golden leaves into the autumn sunshine.

'We ought to be able to die like that.' Her eyes follow the leaves as they drift downwards. 'Beautifully.' She pauses, her hands whispering over the sheets like small frightened animals. 'Not like this, all thin and ugly.'

'But Mum, you're not thin and ugly!'

'I'm not stupid either.' Bird-like eyes challenge me out of a face which has become gaunt almost beyond recognition. 'Not stupid, Cass. You can't fool me.' She sighs, and the sigh is so slight that it scarcely lifts the crisp white sheet covering her. 'The cancer may have eaten my body, but it hasn't got my brain.' A sudden smile; a glimpse of the old Mum. 'It wouldn't dare.'

I smile back, and take one of her hands in mine. It feels unbelievably tiny and fragile, and I hold it like a small precious thing which I must be careful not to break. All of her is precious now; now that I am about to lose her. Her smile, the blue of her eyes, her sense of humour, her total unselfconsciousness, her incorrigible optimism. I find myself studying her greedily, absorbing every detail, for although she is so changed, I don't want to forget a single thing about her.

'I wasn't a very good mother.' Her voice is pensive. 'I never really meant to be a mother. I'm not sure — not sure what I meant to be.'

It may have been true that, at the time, my mother wasn't sure how she had managed to produce children, but she certainly made up for any ignorance of her own by trying to ensure that the same fate never befell my brother or me. The fact that she furnished us with the information at an age when it was of no use to us whatsoever was neither here nor there; my mother had, in her own words, 'done her duty'.

This duty took the form of her (again to use her own words) 'gathering' us to her, and telling us the facts of life.

'I believe in being frank,' she informed us, years later, and with some pride. 'I think children should know these things as soon as they can understand them.'

But my brother and I didn't understand them at all. Bewildered by her inventive use of props (an egg from the larder and a jam jar full of tadpoles) and baffled by her garbled tale of eggs and passages, of body hair and bleeding, poor Lucas had nightmares for weeks, while the whole episode (apart from the tadpoles — how I longed to be allowed to keep those tadpoles!) passed me by completely. It seemed to bear no relevance whatsoever to my own narrow childish life, and so I filed it away at the back of my brain (retrieval later on was to prove tricky) and forgot all about it. Long after my brother had stopped waking in the night, screaming with fear, I was still blissfully ignorant of where I'd come from, nor did I care. I had more important things to think about.

Two years later, I was to have my first real encounter with, as it were, the facts of life in action.

Awakened one night by what sounded like cries of pain coming from my mother's room, I ran into her bedroom to find her apparently writhing around under the bedclothes with her new friend, the (as I realized, years later) aptly named Mr Mountjoy.

'Mum! What's happening?' I stood panic-stricken in the bedroom doorway. 'Are you — are you hurt?'

My mother, who was rarely lost for words, emerged from under the covers, pink and dishevelled, and came up with an inventive if baffling explanation.

'We were looking for a button.'

Mr Mountjoy stifled a kind of choking noise, and my mother gave a rather odd little smile and sat up in bed. While she was careful to pull the counterpane up with her, I couldn't help noticing that she didn't appear to be wearing any clothes.

'It's all right, darling. There's nothing for you to worry about. Mr Mountjoy is ... helping me.'

Mr Mountjoy, apparently intent on continuing the search, disappeared under the bedclothes again and my mother waved her hand in the direction of the door.

'Go back to bed now, angel. Everything's going to be fine, I promise you.'

But I didn't think that everything seemed fine at all. My brother and I had never known our fathers (we had one each, our mother had told us, as though that were something to be pleased about), and I for one wasn't used to finding strangers in her bed. Certainly, she had had men-friends, but if she had slept with them (and I must now assume that she had), I had never had any knowledge of it.

'That Mr Mountjoy was in Mum's bed last night,' I told Lucas as we walked to school together the following morning. 'What do you suppose they were doing? She said they were looking for a button, but they weren't wearing any clothes.'

'Honestly, Cass! What do you *think* they were doing?' Lucas, with his full two years of seniority, was apparently better informed than I was.

'I don't know,' I said crossly. 'I wouldn't ask if —'

'OK, OK. I'll tell you then.' Lucas paused portentously. 'They were having sex, of course.'

'Having sex,' I repeated. 'I see.'

But of course, I didn't see. In fact I remained totally ignorant of all matters sexual until a biology lesson at school several years later, in the course of which the hapless Miss Wilson took us on a whistle-stop tour of reproduction, moving seamlessly from the buttercup, via the rabbit, to sex in human beings.

'You didn't tell us any of it! *Any of it!*' I accused my mother, when I got home from school. 'Everyone else knew, but me. And all that about buttercups and rabbits — you never mentioned buttercups or rabbits!'

'I don't know anything about buttercups and rabbits, but I did tell you about people. I told you everything.' My mother looked bewildered. She had been playing Beethoven's Emperor Concerto on the ironing board. It was one of her favourites, and the record player was turned up so loud that we could hardly hear each other speak. 'I told you when you were five,' she shouted, obviously referring to the gathering together of Lucas and me. 'I told you all you needed to know.'

'But I didn't need to know it then. I needed to know it for now,' I shouted back. 'So as not to look silly in front of everyone else!'

'You must have forgotten. How was I to know you'd forget something so important?' Mother's fingers began to move up and down across the back of one of my school shirts, and she had a dreamy expression on her face.

'And I wish you'd listen,' I yelled. 'I wish — I just wish I had a normal mother!'

This was certainly true. While I loved my mother dearly and was not on the whole a conventional child, I didn't always appreciate her many eccentricities. She was one of those people who conduct their lives with no apparent reference to the rules of normal behaviour. The piano-playing was only the tip of the iceberg, and in fact apart from when I was trying to talk to her, or when I had friends round, I didn't mind it too much. But she seemed incapable of editing the thoughts as they floated into her head, and this could lead to fearful misunderstandings. If someone was looking ill, or tired, or, worst of all, just plain ugly, my mother wouldn't hesitate to tell them so. In shops and cafes, on buses and in the school playground, she was an endless and rich source of embarrassment.

Conversely, she would pay outrageous compliments to total strangers, and this could be almost as embarrassing.

'Did you know, you have the most wonderful eyes?' she once informed a rather forbidding-looking young man on a train. 'Sort of treacle toffee, with a touch of —'

But before she could finish her sentence, the young man had got up and moved to another compartment.

'Well!' said Mum, much annoyed. 'How rude! Can you imagine why anyone would want to be so rude?'

Both Lucas and I could well imagine why the young man had found our mother's company less than congenial, but we wisely kept our counsel.

And then there was the somewhat eccentric domestic setup in which we passed our childhood. True, the rambling and dilapidated Victorian house (a legacy from a long-dead aunt) was spacious, and the jungle of a garden offered plenty of scope for our imaginations, but the place was a social minefield. There was the Lodger in the basement (always referred to as the Lodger, although the actual individual enjoying this title changed so frequently that we had trouble keeping up with who was supposed to be living there). Up in the attic, there was my mother's Uncle Rupert, who had been with us for as long as I could remember. He was a rather fey, ineffectual man of wispy appearance and indeterminate age, who lived off the dole and spent his time inventing things. Thinking of things for Uncle Rupert to invent was a regular family pastime, and so he was never short of ideas, but he rarely came up with anything which could be considered even remotely useful.

Mum, however, wouldn't hear a word against him.

'Rupert's so clever,' she would say, ironing his shirts (between piano concertos). 'He could have gone a long way, you know.'

Lucas and I often wished Uncle Rupert would do just that, for his lengthy occupations of the only bathroom, the pacing of his heavy boots across the floorboards above our bedrooms, the smell of his clothes (aniseed balls, stale sweat and tobacco) and, as I approached puberty, his covert appraisal of my developing body (never enough to complain to Mum about, but certainly enough to inspire a healthy revulsion) did nothing to endear him to us.

'Does Uncle Rupert have to live with us?' I asked once. After all, none of my friends had resident uncles. Theirs were the kind of uncles who were only seen on family occasions, and if they did visit, they came sweet-smelling and wholesome, bearing gifts of toffee, and if you were lucky, money.

'Of course Uncle Rupert has to live with us,' replied my mother, shocked. 'You must understand, darling. He has nowhere else to go.'

Other people who often had nowhere else to go were, variously, my mother's friend Greta, an exile from her native Switzerland who spoke little English and cried a lot; a tramp called Richard, who played the ukulele outside Woolworths and for whom my mother had a soft spot ('Not a tramp, Cass,' she chided me once, 'Richard's a Homeless Person.' 'But he calls *himself* a tramp,' I objected. 'That's different,' said Mum); an actor called Ben, who had fallen on hard times but had once had a walk-on part in *Coronation Street*; and the nice man from the chemist (Mum's words) who kept falling out with his landlady. These people didn't all come to stay at once, of course, but they turned up at regular intervals to spend a few nights on the put-u-up in the living room and join the queue for the bathroom. Whether, like the Lodger, they paid my mother anything towards their keep, Lucas and I never did find out. Nor did we discover whether any of them were into hunting for buttons. But we did resent their regular intrusion into a household which was at best disordered and at worst chaotic, for what our mother seemed to forget was that we, too, had nowhere else to go, and that moreover, this was our home. Quite often it felt more as though we were all living in a hostel.

What I didn't realize until years later was that my mother was desperately lonely, and that her greatest dread was to wake up one morning and find that she was no longer surrounded by people. If there was no Lodger, she would visibly droop (I thought at the time that this was due to lack of revenue), and would send Lucas and me several times a day to our corner shop to ask if anyone had enquired about the advertisement she had placed in their window. If the phone was silent, she would fret that it might be out of order ('nip round to the phone box and give us a quick ring, Cass, there's a pet'). If no one called round, she immediately assumed she must have done something wrong. Flighty, insecure, by turns manically happy or beset with a sadness bordering on despair, she was not a restful person to live with.

But it was by no means all bad, and in fact my friends envied me my haphazard upbringing, for I was given the kind of freedom they could only dream of. We climbed trees and constructed tunnels underneath the hay bales in the local farmer's barn, and our mother turned a blind eye. We stayed up late with her, listening to unsuitable programmes on the wireless, and went trick-or-treating at Halloween long before the custom had caught on this side of the Atlantic. When Lucas remarked once that raw cake mixture tasted so much better than the finished article, and couldn't he have an uncooked birthday cake, Mum said what a lovely idea, and of course he could. The cake was consumed with spoons out of bowls, and while several of the party were ill that night, all agreed that it had been worth it. Their parents, however, evidently did not think the exercise had been worth it, and at least two of Lucas's friends were banned from our house for some time afterwards.

'We did have fun, didn't we?' It's as though she is reading my thoughts. 'Do you remember the time I sent a note to school and we went picking primroses?'

'Oh yes!'

A blue and white spring day, a dapple of bright new leaves, and the primroses like stars in the chalky soil, their faces turned to the sun. We picked the slender pink stems, sniffing the perfume of the flowers, and filled a basket with them, then sat on our coats on the ground ('Don't sit on the wet grass; you'll get piles.' 'Piles of what?' 'Never you mind.') to eat our picnic lunch of crisp rolls and ham and apples. It never occurred to me at the time to question what we were doing. My mother always reasoned that we were her children, and if she wanted us out of school for a day, then that was her right.

'What did you say in the note?'

'What note?'

'The note you wrote to the school on the primrose day.'

'I forget.' Her eyes start wandering again, then return with a snap. 'Oh yes! I said you had your period!'

'Mum!' I was ten years old at the time, my chest as flat as a board, my body smooth and hairless as a plum.

'Well, what did you expect me to say?' And of course, as usual, there is no answer to that.
'And Deirdre and the cowpat. Do you remember that?'

Blowing up cowpats with Lucas and his friends in the field behind our house, choosing a nice ripe one ('crisp on the top, with a squidgy middle,' advised Lucas, the expert); our excitement, watching the smouldering firework, waiting for the explosion; and the sheer joy when a particularly messy one erupted in a fountain of green sludge, splattering the blonde ringlets and nice clean frock of prissy Deirdre from next door. Oh, Deirdre! If you could see yourself! We rolled in the grass, kicking our heels, convulsed with mirth, while Deirdre, howling and outraged, ran home to tell her mummy what bad, bad children we all were.

'What'll your mum say?' one of Lucas's friends asked anxiously.

'Oh, Mum'll laugh.'

Mum laughed. She tried to tell us off, but was so proud of the inventiveness of Lucas, and so entertained at the fate of prissy Deirdre, that she failed utterly. But she promised Deirdre's mother that we would all be 'dealt with'.

'Whatever that means,' said Mum, dishing out chocolate biscuits and orange juice. 'Poor child. She doesn't stand a chance, with a mother like that. But I suppose she had it coming to her.'

'I wonder what happened to her?' she muses now.

'Who?'

'Prissy Deirdre.'

'Married, with a nice little semi with net curtains, a Peter-and-Jane family and a husband who washes the car on Sundays.'

But Mum is no longer listening. She is drifting away from me again, her eyes wandering, her fingers plucking at the sheets.

Mum rarely, if ever, told us off, and not only appeared to trust us implicitly but often sought our advice. We were always invited to be present when she interviewed prospective Lodgers, and although these meetings were rarely the formal, fact-finding missions she fondly imagined them to be, she always listened to what we had to say. As we grew older, she would even seek our views on her latest man-friend, although in this she tended to disregard our opinions and go her own way.

'Can't you see he's just after somewhere to stay?' Lucas exclaimed on one occasion (the gentleman in question had no job and no visible means of support).

'So that suits us both, doesn't it?' Mum cried gaily. 'He can live here with us!'

'But Mum! He's just using you!'

'And I, my sweet, am using him.' She patted Lucas on the head. 'One day, you'll understand.'

Money, or rather, the lack of it, was an ongoing problem, and to this day I'm not sure what we lived on. True, there was the Lodger, and Mum did have a variety of odd jobs, but she quickly became bored with them, and was out of work more often than she was in it. In this as in every other area of her life, there would be sudden bursts of industry, where she would appear to be holding down several jobs at once. Then her maternal conscience (a flighty thing at the best of times) would kick in, and she would be at home for weeks on end, baking amazing cakes from recipes of her own invention and making strange-looking garments on her ancient Singer sewing machine. The cakes were always different and always odd-looking — sometimes burnt round the edges, often flat as pancakes — but they were invariably delicious. The garments — usually made from, and looking exactly like, old curtains — we hid at the backs of drawers and cupboards until she had forgotten about them. Sometimes she worked from home, as on the occasion when she took a job packing bottles of cheap perfume in little boxes. The perfume-packing regularly fell behind schedule, and the whole family, plus the Lodger and sundry hangers-on, would end up helping her out. The smell of that perfume — 'Gardenia' — haunted me for years afterwards.

On one memorable occasion when finances were particularly bad, Mum decided that she would capitalize on Lucas and me, and to that end she decided to take us along to a modelling agency.

'You're both good-looking children,' she told us, as she scrubbed and brushed us into shape. 'I'm sure they can use you for a catalogue or something.'

I was enormously excited. It would never have occurred to me to think of myself as model material, but perhaps Mum knew something I didn't. With high hopes of fame and glamour, not to mention days off school, I allowed myself to be dressed in a hideous flowery frock passed on to me by a friend of Greta's, and off we set. But the woman at the agency shook her head.

'No, no. Not the girl,' she said, after I had paraded in front of her. 'I'm afraid she's not suitable. The boy, now ... The boy we can certainly use.'

At the time, it seemed desperately unfair, but when I look back now, I can see that Lucas's high forehead, clear complexion and dazzling combination of blond hair and brown eyes must have made him an exceptional candidate. But to Mum's credit, she turned the offer down. If the woman wouldn't accept us both, then she shouldn't have either of us.

'They come together,' she said grandly, as though we were some sort of double act. 'I can't allow you to have Lucas without Cassandra. It just wouldn't be right.'

Lucas, it has to be said, appeared to be much relieved at these tidings. He had been worrying for days about what his friends would say if he were to turn up in their mothers' favourite magazines advertising cutesy children's clothes, but I was bitterly disappointed. I think it was the first time in my life that I realized my looks were unexceptional. Never a particularly vain child, I had nonetheless hitherto been quite pleased with what I saw when I looked in the mirror. Mum had always told me I was pretty; I had therefore had no reason to believe otherwise. Now, it seemed, I must accept that there was room for doubt, and I never quite regained the cheerful confidence in my appearance which I held in those early years.

Was my childhood a happy one? As with many childhoods, the memories are so tinged with nostalgia that it is hard to be objective, but there were certainly some wonderful moments, and there is no doubt that I was much loved.

But when I was fourteen, everything was to change.

Two

May 1961

Up until that time, while I was of course aware of my essential femaleness, I had given little thought to myself as a sexual being. Puberty may have been well on the way, but I was not particularly impressed by its manifestations, and had I not had to put up with the regular leerings of Uncle Rupert, I probably would have ignored it altogether. My breasts at that stage were poor little things, barely disturbing the surface of my chest and certainly not requiring the services of a bra; and any other bodily changes were not sufficiently interesting to exercise my mind more than fleetingly. I knew that I was turning into a woman, and I was quite pleased about that, but unlike many of my friends I was in no hurry. I had the good sense to recognize that childhood doesn't last forever, and that I should enjoy its advantages while I could.

Even now, after all these years, I still find it astonishing that innocence can be destroyed so quickly and so thoroughly in just a few brief minutes. One day, I was an ordinary child when I got up in the morning (as ordinary as it was possible to be in our household), but when I went to bed that night, I was someone else altogether. And yet nothing had actually been done to me. I had suffered no physical harm. I suppose, when I could bring myself to think about it objectively, I had been lucky. I had had a lucky escape. But at the time, lucky and escape were two words which seemed to have little connection with what happened to me on that awful day.

Apart from Uncle Rupert, who had gone to bed early, I was on my own in the house. My mother was out pulling pints at the local pub (a new job, and one which she appeared to be enjoying enormously), Lucas had gone to the pictures with his friends, the put-u-up was temporarily out of commission, and even the Lodger was away for the weekend. The only sounds were the ticking of the grandfather clock in the hall (a funny lopsided tick, strangely comforting in the silent house) and the occasional swish of tyres as a car drove up the road past the house. I never minded being on my own — after all, I had never had any reason to — and I felt relaxed and happy. The weekend stretched invitingly before me, and if I could get my homework done now, I would be free until Monday morning.

I don't know how long Uncle Rupert had been watching me, but it could have been for some time. I rarely closed my bedroom door, as one of my mother's more sensible house rules was that no one was allowed into anyone else's room without permission, and I had been fully absorbed in what I was doing. So it was with some shock that when I looked up I found him standing behind me, looking over my shoulder. He had a habit of shuffling silently round the house in his slippers, appearing unexpectedly in odd places, so his arrival in itself was not particularly disconcerting. But his rather odd demeanour together with the fact that he had entered the room unannounced immediately rang alarm bells.

'Hello.' Uncle Rupert placed an unwelcome hand on my shoulder. 'How's it going, then?'

'Fine. It's going fine.' My hands were clammy and I wiped them on my grey school skirt. 'I — I'm doing my homework,' I added, more for something to say than anything else, as it must have been perfectly obvious what I was doing.

'You're growing into a very attractive young woman,' Uncle Rupert said, as though I hadn't spoken.

'Am I?'

'You know you are.'

There followed a pause, in which Uncle Rupert appraised my body unashamedly. I felt as though he were peeling the clothes off me garment by garment with his pale, fishy eyes, and I tried to stand up.

'No. Stay where you are.' Uncle Rupert squeezed my shoulder. 'I like looking at you sitting there.'

Why didn't I just get up and leave the room? Why didn't I at least move away, as my instincts told me to? But it was as though I were suddenly paralysed, unable to move or even speak. To this day, I can still see the books spread out on my desk, the maths problem, with the rectangle half-drawn and my pencil and ruler lying across the page, the tiny fragments of rubber where I had erased a false start. I can smell the woody scent of pencil sharpenings, and hear the wheezy, unsavoury breaths of Uncle Rupert as he stood, as motionless as I was, his hand still on my shoulder.

My eyes met Uncle Rupert's, and there was something in his gaze which I had never seen before; something sinister and predatory; something which sent prickles of fear up and down my spine.

'I need — I need to finish this.' My mouth was dry, my heartbeats pounding in my ears. 'Before — before Monday.'

'Plenty of time for that,' Uncle Rupert said. 'After all, it's the weekend, isn't it?' He reached behind him and closed the bedroom door. 'I thought you and I could play a little game, while we're on our own. Just the two of us.'

'What — game?' I had never in my life known Uncle Rupert play games, and couldn't think what he meant.

'Just a little game. A little secret game. You'll see.'

'No, please —'

'Now Cassandra, you know me.' He had never called me by my full name before. 'There's no need to be afraid of me. No need to be afraid of old Uncle Rupert.'

'Please. I — I need to get a drink.' I made as though to get up.

'Later. You can have a drink later. After our little game.' He pressed me back into my chair with surprising force. 'Be a good girl. Be a good girl and everything will be fine.'

By this stage, I was beginning to panic. Uncle Rupert was gripping my shoulder more firmly now, effectively anchoring me to my chair, and I knew I didn't have the strength to push him away. There was no one else in the house to respond if I were to call out. The bedroom window was open, but I doubt whether anyone outside would have heard me, and even if they did, what could they do? I had no choice but to stay where I was and hope beyond hope that he would soon tire of this game of his and leave me alone.

But Uncle Rupert had only just begun.

He moved closer. I could smell the stale tobacco on his breath as he stooped over me, and feel his leg pressing against my own. The rough material of his sleeve brushed my cheek as he took my hand in one of his.

'I have something for you,' he said. 'Something special. I think you're going to like it.'

I tried to pull my hand away, but he held on to it firmly. His own hand was unpleasantly damp, and I could feel his untrimmed fingernails digging into my palm.

'Look on it as a little present. A present from me to you. A very special present.'

Slowly, very slowly, he began to pull my hand towards him.

'There's a good girl.' His voice was soft, conspiratorial, and there was a faint smile on his face as he drew my hand inside the folds of his dressing gown.

For a moment, I didn't know what it was that I was feeling; a toy, perhaps, or some kind of practical joke. But only for a moment. Then, I knew. I was innocent and I was totally unsuspecting, but as he covered my hand with his own and began to move it gently back and forth, I realized with a horror beyond any horror I had ever felt before what it was that I was holding; what it was that Uncle Rupert was doing.

'There. Isn't that nice?'

Nice? *Nice*? I was speechless. Nothing could have prepared me for this. *Nothing*. Not my mother with her cosy chats, not Miss Wilson with her tales of rabbits and buttercups, not the innocent body of Lucas, remembered from the shared bathtimes of our early childhood — none of these things could have prepared me for anything so utterly, hideously, appalling.

For a moment I was so shocked I could barely breathe. Then, at last, I found my voice. And screamed.

Summoning up all my strength, I pushed Uncle Rupert away. Taken by surprise, he stumbled backwards, giving me the chance to get to my feet and throw the door open. I tore down the stairs, half-sobbing as I screamed, stumbling on the loose piece of stair carpet, tripping over Lucas's school shoes lying in the hallway. I pulled open the front door and fled down the garden path, out of the gate and along the road. I had no idea where I was going; I only knew that I had to get away. I had to put as much distance between myself and Uncle Rupert as was humanly possible, and I had to do it fast.

I don't know how far I would have gone had I not fallen, literally, into the arms of Greta, who was apparently about to surprise us with one of her unscheduled visits.

'Cassandra!' Greta dropped her suitcases and pressed me to her bosom. 'The matter is what?' (Greta's English had improved over the years, and while it was still somewhat eccentric, it was at least comprehensible, if only in parts.)

'Uncle Rupert!' I sobbed into the collar of her ancient overcoat.

'Iss ill?'

'No. Not ill. Horrible!' I raised my streaming face. 'Uncle Rupert is horrible, horrible, *horrible*!'

'Iss horrible?' The tears, which were never far away, welled sympathetically in Greta's pink-rimmed eyes. 'Why iss horrible?'

'I can't tell you.'

'Uncle Rupert iss nice man, I think,' said Greta, stroking my hair.

'No! Uncle Rupert is not nice man! Uncle Rupert is disgusting old man! I hate him!'

'No hate Uncle Rupert,' Greta admonished (she had always, inexplicably, had a soft spot for him). 'You make mistake, I think?'

'No! No mistake!'

But of course I couldn't tell Greta what had happened. At that moment, I couldn't have told anybody, and besides, in a situation such as this, the language barrier would have proved too great. I didn't know the German for what Uncle Rupert had done, and Greta was unlikely to understand the English, even if I could have brought myself to say the words.

'We go home, yes? Nice-cup-of-tea?' Greta didn't herself like tea, but she had learnt that this was what the English resorted to in times of stress, and she was obviously anxious to remove me from the street before I made more of a spectacle of myself.

'No! We can't go home! Uncle Rupert's there!'

'Uncle Rupert no hurt,' said Greta firmly, taking my arm in a surprisingly strong grip and steering me back down the road in the direction of the house. 'I take care.'

What could I do? I had nowhere else to go, and no money, and it was getting dark. I wasn't sure where my mother worked, and even if I had known, I could hardly burst into a crowded pub with my unwelcome tidings. Besides, I would probably be safe with Greta there. Something told me that Uncle Rupert was unlikely to stage a repeat performance in her presence.

As it happened, by the time we got home, there was no sign of Uncle Rupert. The house was quiet, and his bedroom door was firmly shut. Greta set about putting the kettle on and hunting for the teapot while I sat at the table and shivered. I shivered with cold, I shivered with fear, but most of all, I shivered with shock. Up until now, home had been safe; it had been a haven. The people who came and went were a disparate lot, but they were basically OK, and I had certainly never felt remotely threatened by any of them. But now, all that was spoiled. My room — my own bedroom — had been the scene of Uncle Rupert's ghastly activities. Would I ever be able to go in there again?

Just then, we heard my mother's key in the front door, and she came into the kitchen.

'Why, Greta! How nice!' Mum embraced her. 'Well, this is a lovely surprise, isn't it Cass? Cass?' She looked at me closely. 'Whatever's the matter?'

'She no like Uncle Rupert,' said Greta, pouring boiling water into mugs. 'She run away.'

'You ran away? Cass? What's all this about?'

'Uncle Rupert — Uncle Rupert — he —' I burst into tears again.

My mother turned pale, and it was at that moment that I understood. My mother knew. She knew what had happened, and that meant that she knew something about Uncle Rupert that none of us had known; something she should have warned me about; something she should have protected me from. I had always been aware that there was some dark secret in Uncle Rupert's past, and had hitherto assumed that it was in the nature of a personal tragedy. Now I realized that it was something far more sinister, and something which my mother should have taken a great deal more seriously when she invited him into our home all those years ago.

I stood up from the kitchen table and faced her.

'You haven't — you haven't asked me what happened,' I said, and my voice suddenly seemed distant and separate, as though it were coming from a long way away.

'My poor darling.' Mum tried to put her arms round me. 'You tell me all about it, then.'

'You know all about it.' I pushed her away. 'You *know*!'

'I couldn't have — I didn't — oh, Cass! What did he do? Did he — did he touch you?'

Just for that moment, all my hatred and my anger was directed at my mother; my mother, whom I suddenly held completely in my power. Because while I didn't fully understand the significance of her question, I suspected that if I were to tell her that yes, Uncle Rupert had touched me, she would have been dreadfully punished for what she had failed to do.

'Tell me, Cass! Tell me at once! What did Uncle Rupert do to you?' Mum gripped me by my shoulders and half shook me. 'You have to tell me!'

'Nice-cup-of-tea?' suggested poor Greta. 'Make better feel, no?'

'Shut up, Greta!' shouted Mum, still holding on to me. 'Can't you see this is a crisis?'

'Let me go!' I cried, trying to push her away. 'You let me go!'

'But you must tell me,' Mother said, more gently now, relinquishing her grip. 'You must tell me what happened. What did Uncle Rupert do?'

'But you already know —'

'No. I don't know. I know Rupert has one or two ... strange habits, but I don't know exactly what he did to you, Cass. You have to believe me. I would never have left you on your own with him if I'd thought — if I'd thought you were in any sort of danger.'

I hesitated. I knew my mother loved me; I knew that she would have protected me with her own life had she been required to do so. But it was also clear that she knew Uncle Rupert was capable of posing some kind of threat. I was still angry with her, but I also desperately wanted her to know what had happened. I ached for her sympathy, for her indignation on my behalf, and most of all, for the familiarity and safety of being held in her arms.

I looked round the kitchen. We were on our own now, Greta having made a tearful and reproachful exit some minutes ago. I sat down again at the table.

'What did he do, love? Please tell me.' Mum sat down beside me and took my hand. 'I can't do anything about it if I don't know, can I?'

'He came into my room,' I began slowly. 'He didn't knock or anything. He just came in.'

'And?' Mum prompted.

'And then — and then he — he made me — touch him.'

For a few moments, my mother didn't say anything. She just sat there, stroking my hand, and when I glanced at her, I was surprised to see that she too had tears in her eyes.

'Did he — did he do anything else?' she asked. 'Anything at all? Did he touch you?'

I shook my head.

'He forced me. He made me do it.' My scalp crawled at the memory. 'But I ran away. Greta found me.' I hiccoughed. 'Oh, Mum! It was horrible!'

'I can imagine,' Mum said grimly. 'Horrible. Quite horrible. My poor, poor darling.'

And then, quite suddenly, she too seemed overwhelmed by rage.

'Where is he? Where did he go?' she shouted. '*Where is Rupert?*'

'I'm not sure. In his room I think.'

'Right. You stay here, Cass. You hear me? Stay right here till I get back.' And she stormed out of the room and up the stairs.

A moment later, I heard her banging on Uncle Rupert's door, and I crept guiltily out into the hallway. After all, I reasoned, this was my disaster, not my mother's. I had a right to hear the outcome.

Muffled shouts came from (presumably) Uncle Rupert's room and I listened breathlessly. I had rarely seen my mother angry, and never as angry as this. What would she do? Would she kill Uncle Rupert? Should I call an ambulance, or the police, or maybe a neighbour? Supposing Uncle Rupert attacked Mum? Should I try to rescue her?

As I stood dithering, I heard Uncle Rupert's door open again, and my mother's voice on the landing.

'You promised!' I heard her cry. '*You promised*! I trusted you. I took you into my home, I left you alone with my children. And look how you've repaid me! I want you out of here first thing in the morning. Do you hear? First thing in the morning!'

It was a very long time before I heard of Uncle Rupert again. I was packed off to a friend's house early the following morning, and by the time I returned home, every trace of him had gone. His room was clean and empty. Even the curtains had been removed from the windows. It was as though he had never lived in our house at all.

Three

The months following Uncle Rupert's departure were difficult for all of us. I was still traumatized by my experience, and yet old enough to reason that it didn't make sense to mind so deeply about what had happened. After all, I had suffered no harm, I hadn't been attacked, the source of my upset had been removed. Life could and should go on as normal. And yet everything had changed.

Worst of all was the feeling of being unclean; of being *soiled*. That was the only way to describe it. Something had been dirtied; something that no amount of washing and bathing (and I did plenty of both) could reach. Something clean and wholesome and good had been taken from me, and young as I was, I knew that I could never have it back.

Nowadays, no doubt, I might have received counselling, but my mother knew nothing about psychology, and it certainly wouldn't have occurred to her to seek that kind of help. She did, however, recognize the depth of my distress, and tiptoed round my feelings with great tenderness, offering me little treats, letting me off household chores (much to Lucas's disgust) and generally treating me with kid gloves. She cooked my favourite meals, bought me the expensive coat I longed for (I never did find out how she managed to pay for it) and, in a bizarre moment of inspiration, sent a note to the school to excuse me from PE.

I have no idea how this was supposed to help, or indeed what she told the school, but I was delighted. I was not an athletic child, and I did not — and still do not — have the slightest idea how the ability to climb up ropes or do handstands could possibly equip anyone for life.

I'm not sure what my mother told the rest of the household, but they too seemed to treat me with new consideration in the weeks that followed. Lucas, the only one who knew the whole story, made an effort to be nice to me, although I could see that he couldn't understand what all the fuss was about. Greta made soothing noises whenever she saw me, and gave me presents of the Swiss chocolate sent to her by her cousin. Having apparently finally run out of alternative refuges, she was now permanently installed in Uncle Rupert's bedroom, which she set about embellishing with flowery curtains and pink wallpaper and faded photographs of her family (usually against a chocolate-box backdrop of hygienic-looking cows and snow-topped mountains). She invited me up to see her handiwork, and I admired it from the doorway, but I wouldn't go in, and she seemed to understand.

'Poor you little girl.' She patted me kindly. 'Better soon I think?'

The nice man from the chemist brought me violet bath salts and a new hot water bottle, and even the Lodger, a bespectacled college research student with enormous feet and acne, offered me chewing gum and asked after me when our paths happened to cross.

Taken up as I was with my own problems, I still couldn't help noticing the effect Uncle Rupert's departure had had on my mother. I had never thought her especially fond of Uncle Rupert. Although, as I later discovered, he was more a distant cousin than a proper uncle, she had known him all her life, and he had lived with us for almost as long as I could remember. While they had led largely separate lives, and I had never seen any signs of affection between them, there was no doubt that Mum missed him sorely.

On several occasions I caught her going into his room and just standing there, gazing out of the window between Greta's fluttering pink curtains, an expression of great sadness on her face. The music she played on the ironing board was sad and pensive; a Brahms intermezzo, Chopin's funeral march, Beethoven's Moonlight Sonata. The music poured out plaintively from our ancient record player as mother's hands moved slowly up and down pyjama legs and blouses and the ridiculous frilly apron Greta wore in the kitchen. Not much actual ironing got done in the weeks following Uncle Rupert's departure, but no one complained. Mum too was suffering, and without actually saying anything, everyone seemed to understand.

'Where is Uncle Rupert?' I asked her one day.

She looked at me blankly. 'Uncle Rupert?'

'Yes. Where is he? Where's he living?'

'He's gone away. A long way away. You don't need to worry about him any more.'

'Are you — are you very cross with him?' I ventured.

'Yes. Well, I was. I was very cross indeed. But you know, Cass, some people do things they can't help. It's — it's a bit like an illness.'

But try as I might, I couldn't see that what Uncle Rupert had done could possibly have had anything to do with his health. Years later, I wondered what my mother could have been thinking of, harbouring an ageing paedophile in the same house as her children. But then Mum had always been trusting, and if, as I gathered, Uncle Rupert had given her his word that he wouldn't misbehave, it was typical of her to have believed him. Trust was second nature to my mother. I never knew her to turn away a stranger or lock a door, and it was little short of a miracle that in a house with four outside doors, all of them unlocked, we were never once burgled. The only occasion upon which someone entered the house illegally, they crawled in through the larder window, and Mum was so entertained by the thought of the effort they must have gone to (it was a very small window) that she refused to report the intruder.

'After all, he only took a bottle of wine. Not a very nice wine at that. He's welcome to it!' she said. And the doors remained unlocked.

In addition to my other problems, Uncle Rupert's bewildering performance had done nothing to foster in me a positive image of the opposite sex. In the street or on buses, in shops and even at school (it was an all-female establishment, but we did have two male teachers and a caretaker), I was constantly and fearfully aware that every man had the same equipment as Uncle Rupert, and that presumably they were all capable of the same dreadful antics. How could any woman want the body of a man near her, let alone have close physical contact with it? Mother's searches for buttons took on a whole new meaning, and I shuddered.

'I shall never have sex,' I told my mother. She was lying in the bath, and I was sitting on the edge. I always found that this was the best time for confidences, partly because her nakedness made her somehow more accessible, and also because being locked in the bathroom with her made me feel safer.

'Of course you will. Why ever shouldn't you?' Mum's milky limbs shimmered under the water as she turned on the hot tap with her toe.

'Because of — you know. I just couldn't. It's *horrible*!'

'Actually —' my mother picked up a flannel, and began slowly soaping her arms — 'it's rather nice. You'll enjoy it when your time comes, Cass. Believe me.'

'No, I shan't. I can't understand how anyone can enjoy *that*.'

'When you love somebody, it's the most wonderful thing in the world.' Mum's voice was dreamy. 'Lying together, feeling so close. You wait, Cass. You'll be surprised.'

'Did you love all the people you had sex with?' I asked curiously.

'Oh, Cass! What a question!' Mum laughed.

'Well, did you?' I persisted.

'Probably not,' she confessed, pausing with the flannel in mid-thigh. 'I should have, but no. I didn't always.'

'Then why did you do it?'

'That's a good question.' Mum stepped out of the bath and reached for a towel. 'I suppose I wanted to feel needed.'

'But we need you! Lots of people need you! You don't have to have sex to be needed.'

'There's a particular sort of needed that I want to be.' She laughed again. 'You'll understand one day, I promise you. Anyway, you don't want to bother yourself with any of this now. You're much too young.'

But whereas a few weeks ago I might have agreed with her, now I no longer felt too young to think about sex.

I look back on that time now as one of the loneliest of my life. Kind as she was, my mother soon appeared too preoccupied with her own worries to pay more than passing attention to mine. Lucas was increasingly out with his friends, and seemed to think it was time I put Uncle Rupert out of my mind. And my friends, through no fault of their own, were unaware of my problem. I spent a lot of time lying on my bed, listening to music, or playing with the mangy and recalcitrant dog Mum had recently acquired ('*Dog found tied to railway line*', the headline in the local paper had screamed, followed by a phone number for anyone who might like to rehouse the unfortunate animal. My mother had found this invitation quite irresistible, and had responded without hesitation). The Dog (like the Lodger, he never acquired a name of his own) seemed as disturbed and preoccupied as I was, and we were probably good company for each other.

'That's good,' said Mum approvingly, watching me encouraging him to fetch an old slipper from behind the sofa. 'It'll bring him out of himself. You too, Cass.'

The Dog and I looked at each other in a moment of complete understanding. My mother might fantasize all she liked, but we both knew that it would take more than a slipper to sort out our problems.

But I had underestimated my mother, for unbeknown to me, she was taking my troubled state more seriously than I could ever have imagined. And had I known what she was planning, I would have put up with any amount of neglect rather than face the ordeal which was to come.

Four

'Boarding school! You want to send me to *boarding school*!' I could hardly believe my ears when my mother disclosed to me what she obviously considered to be a truly inspirational idea. 'Whatever for?'

'It will do you good to get away,' Mum said.

'I don't want to get away! Why should I want to get away?'

'After — what's happened. You need a change. You may not want to go now, but you will when you see the school. It's a lovely place, all green and wooded and —'

'You mean you've seen it?'

'Well, not exactly.' Mum looked sheepish. 'But I've seen the brochure and heard all about it and it sounds just perfect. You and I can go and see it together, Cass. It'll make a nice day out for us. And they want to meet you, of course. And they'll need you to do a little test.'

'What sort of little test?'

'Oh, a bit of maths and English. Nothing too difficult. You'll sail through, Cass. It's just a formality.'

'But I don't want to go! Mum, please don't make me! I'm happy here, and —'

'But Cass, you're not happy. Anyone can see that. And the doctor says —'

'The doctor? You mean to say you've been talking about me to the doctor?' My mother seemed to have been taking her parenting duties to unusual lengths. 'And you've told him — oh no! You haven't told him about — about Uncle Rupert!'

'Well, I did mention there'd been a spot of bother at home. I didn't tell him exactly what had happened, though.' It seemed to me extremely unlikely that the doctor would recommend boarding school as a cure for a 'spot of bother', but I was too upset to challenge my mother on this particular point. All I could see was that I, an innocent victim, was being punished for the disgusting behaviour of Uncle Rupert, and that it all seemed terribly unfair.

'And Lucas? What about Lucas? Is he going to boarding school too?'

'Of course not. There's nothing wrong with Lucas.'

'But there's nothing wrong with me!' I wailed.

'Oh, there is,' Mum said, patting my knee fondly. 'And you're the one who needs a bit of special attention.'

In vain did I weep and wail. In vain did I alternately rail against my mother and sulk in my room behind a loudly slammed door. Her mind was made up.

The day out to visit the boarding school involved a long and sticky journey in the ancient Rover belonging to the nice man from the chemist, who was the current occupier of the put-u-up in the living room. Of all the people who came and went in our household, he was the only one to own a car, and he obligingly offered his services as chauffeur for the day. It was his day off, and he fancied a day out in the country, he told us. Wasn't that lucky?

Naturally I was relegated to the back seat, where I sat and sulked for much of the journey, annoyingly aware that since the two grown-ups had their backs to me, my sulk was largely wasted. I was hot and uncomfortable, and the too-small girly-pink frock which my mother had insisted I wear strained across my developing chest. The sulk forbade my partaking of the picnic lunch Mum had brought and which she and her companion ate sitting in a field while I remained in the car, feeling desperately thirsty.

I remember lying on my back along the seat (no seat belts in those days), my knees drawn up, watching the tops of trees and flashes of blue sky skimming past, and thinking that I would never forget this journey or this awful day. The interior of the car had an antiseptic smell — perhaps something to do with the professional calling of its owner — and it reminded me of hospitals and the terrifying occasion when I had been wrenched screaming from the arms of my mother to have my tonsils removed, and this did nothing to improve my humour.

Now of course I realize that I was behaving like a spoiled brat; that had I reasoned with Mum rather than screaming at her, she might well have listened to me and let me stay at home. But my furious outbursts had only served to fuel her conviction that there was something seriously wrong with me, and her eccentric reasoning had persuaded her that boarding school was the perfect answer.

At the time I never thought about the sacrifices she was prepared to make. Lucas and I were all she had; she mightn't have been the most consistent of mothers, but she adored us, and looking after and providing for us was her life. Too bound up with my own misery and my dread of being away from home, I never spared a thought for her feelings and how much she would miss me. As for the money involved, that never entered my mind. School had always been free, and I assumed that the same applied to boarding school. It wasn't until years later that I discovered my mother had put by what she thought of as an emergency fund for me and Lucas, and that most of this had now been earmarked to pay the majority of my school fees. I also failed to notice that a small watercolour — the only really valuable item in the house, and one I later discovered to have been by a well-known Victorian artist — suddenly disappeared. I know now that Mum hoped for a bursary, but she wasn't banking on it. She had learnt the hard way never to bank on anything. It was to her considerable credit that she made no reference to bursaries when she spoke of the test I was to take. She had told me it was a mere formality, but to her it could mean the difference between relative comfort and real hardship.

Towards the end of our journey, there was much discussion and consulting of maps, in the course of which Mum and the nice man from the chemist nearly came to blows.

'You said you'd do the navigating. I'm just the driver,' he pointed out, as they pulled into a layby to take stock.

'It was fine while we were going north. North is easy,' Mum said.

'What do you mean, north is easy?'

'You don't have to turn the map round, with north. South is much more difficult. Everything's upside down.'

'Oh, don't be ridiculous! Nothing's upside down. It's perfectly straightforward. You're just being a typical woman.'

'How dare you patronize me!' Mum cried.

'And how dare you shout at me in my own car!'

'Perhaps you're forgetting that you are currently living in my house,' my mother rejoined.

'And perhaps you are forgetting the advantages that arrangement brings you.'

Advantages? What advantages? I longed to ask, but didn't want to disturb my sulk.

'And perhaps you are forgetting who's in the back of the car!'

'Oh don't mind me,' I said, relieved to be able to break my silence without sacrificing the sulk. 'You two just carry on fighting. I hope we do get lost, then I shan't ever have to go to that horrid school.'

The arguing dwindled to curt little exchanges, the navigational problems appeared to settle down, and much to my disappointment, we arrived at the school fifteen minutes early.

'Sit up, Cass,' Mum said, as smooth tarmac gave way to crunchy gravel. 'We're here. Look! Isn't it lovely?' She seemed quite carried away. 'Imagine being part of all this!'

In spite of myself, I sat up and looked. But what I saw was very far from lovely. The dark mock Gothic building, turreted and menacing, looked like something out of a horror film. Bleak ivy-clad walls and small sinister windows did nothing to soften the effect, and the surrounding conifers and laurel bushes all added to an impression of deepest grey-green gloom. I almost expected to hear the howling of wolves and see the dark shapes of bats flitting round the chimney pots. It didn't help that the sun had now gone in and rain clouds were gathering above the shiny slate roofs.

'It was built by the Earl of something in 1890, apparently,' Mum continued. 'He wanted something unusual; something *different*. I believe he committed suicide in the end,' she added cheerily.

The interior of the school was cool and dim, redolent of floor polish and disinfectant and cabbage. In the main hallway were four huge leather armchairs with a polished wooden table in the middle. There were portraits on the walls, a vase of wilting lilies in a kind of niche, and a glass cabinet containing a collection of fossils. The only movement came from the motes of dust dancing in the shaft of daylight from the window halfway up the curved staircase. Of human life there was not a sign.

'Should we sit down, do you think, Cass?' Mum asked, still apparently overawed (the nice man from the chemist had wisely gone off to park the car and do his crossword). 'Or — ring something?'

'There doesn't seem to be anything to ring,' I said, too wretched to continue my sulk.

'We'll sit down, then.' Gingerly, Mum lowered herself into one of the chairs. She looked very small and vulnerable in her best summer frock, surrounded by all that creaking leather, and suddenly I felt sorry for her. Poor Mum. She was probably trying to do her best for me, but even I hadn't imagined that a school could be anything like this. My only ideas of boarding schools had come from my long-ago acquaintances with such jolly romps as 'Fiona of the Fourth Form' and 'Penny against the Prefects', and while I personally had never hankered after midnight feasts and pillow fights in the dorm, I could see that for some it might be fun. But I couldn't imagine anyone having fun in this joyless place.

'Ah! Mrs Fitzpatrick, I presume, and this must be Cassandra.' A tall thin woman with a wispy bun of greying hair appeared as though from nowhere, and we both jumped. After a brief struggle, Mum managed to extricate herself from her armchair, and we all shook hands. 'I'm Mary Armitage. Headmistress. Do come this way.'

She led us into a small office (more portraits, but no fossils), and after the briefest of conversations, sat me down at a desk laid out with paper and pens.

'Just a few simple questions, Cassandra,' she said, handing me a question paper. 'I'm sure you won't have any trouble. Your mother and I can go next door and have a cup of tea. I'm sure you could do with one after your journey, Mrs Fitzpatrick?'

Left to my own devices, I realized for the first time that this was of course my opportunity — my only opportunity — to rescue myself from the fate which was closing round me. All I had to do was fail the test! Why hadn't I thought of it before? If I failed the entrance test, the school would presumably no longer want me, otherwise there would be no point in having a test at all. At last my future was in my own hands. Joy and relief flooded through me. I could stay with Mum and Lucas and everyone else. I could play with The Dog and see my friends and I would never have to leave home again. I would show them! Of course, Mum would be disappointed, but she'd get over it.

I smiled and picked up a pencil. For the first time in my life, I was going to fail an exam.

But I had reckoned without my pride.

I paused, pencil poised, agonizing over my decision. To fail or not to fail. Fail. Failure. Such miserable, condemning, dismissive words. I looked again at the first maths question. It was temptingly easy. How could I — how could *anyone* — get such a simple question wrong? I sighed, and picking up a ruler, I set to work and drew a neat triangle.

Five

When news of my scholarship arrived, my mother was beside herself with pride.

'The top scholarship, Cass. Just think! *The top scholarship* for St Andrew's, and you've won it. I just knew you had it in you!'

This last was almost certainly untrue, for no one could have anticipated that I would acquit myself with such distinction. It was true that I was reasonably bright, but *that* bright? My only (private) conclusion was that the other pupils at this illustrious establishment must be particularly dim if someone like myself was able to shine among them.

Mum set to work at once to make preparations for the celebration party. In our household, modest as it was, any event was an excuse for a party, since my mother's idea of heaven was a houseful of people, and what better way to fill a house with people than to throw a party? While others might worry about gatecrashers, my mother welcomed them with open arms ('such a wonderful way of meeting new people, Cass'), and while lesser mortals concerned themselves with the possibility of spilt drinks and stained upholstery, my mother cared not a jot.

Of course, I didn't want a party at all. All I wanted was to be left in peace to grieve over my fate, possibly gaining a little sympathy in the process, but it seemed that the preparations for what was after all *my* party could go ahead quite comfortably without any reference whatsoever to me.

Mum spent days planning and baking, and everyone connected with our household was recruited to help. Greta made wonderful Swiss confections; Richard, it transpired, had a special recipe for sausage rolls (how on earth did a homeless person, never mind a tramp, come by such a thing, I wondered? but I knew I would be considered to be indulging some sort of unspeakable prejudice if I voiced my doubts); the Lodger was commandeered to put fiddly little things on cocktail sticks; and the nice man from the chemist had promised to open bottles and hand things round.

The guest list included everyone from distant cousins (most far too distant to be expected to attend) to ex-Lodgers and some of my own school friends. These last I declined to invite. It was bad enough having to leave them for what they would almost certainly see as posher environs than any they could hope to aspire to; to be seen to be celebrating the fact would be crass in the extreme. My own special gang of lively miscreants would disapprove of what they would certainly see as snobbish aspirations, and little Sally Mayfield, who dreamed of academic opportunities which could never be hers, would be jealous.

'What about Myra?' Mum asked. 'Surely you'd like to have Myra.'

I thought of the girl who had been my best friend since primary school; fiery, red-headed, naughty Myra, who had taught me to smoke when I was nine years old and with whom I had played dubious games of doctors and nurses at the bottom of the garden; Myra, who was privy to all my secrets (except Uncle Rupert), who despite my efforts to dissuade her was already a seasoned shoplifter, and who lived in a run-down house on the most notorious council estate. Not for the first time, I wondered whether my mother ever had any sense of what was appropriate.

'Myra wouldn't understand,' I said.

'What's there to understand? A party's a party. It'll be fun. *Fun*, Cass. Sometimes I think you've forgotten what it's like to have fun.'

In this, she was probably right. But then, was it entirely appropriate for someone my mother's age to spend so much of her time in pursuit of fun? In those years of my early teens, there were times when I felt that I was the adult and she the child, and that because of this unnatural and premature reversal of our roles, I sometimes had to be doubly sensible to make up for my mother's immaturity.

The party was a success. All my mother's parties were successes, as she didn't hesitate to remind me. It seemed as though everyone I had ever known was packed into our house, eating and drinking and laughing, some of them smoking strange-smelling cigarettes, others making uninvited use of the bedrooms to further their new-found friendships.

Richard had brought his ukulele; Greta sang along to an old gramophone record, accompanied by Mum on the ironing board; someone I had never seen before had brought bagpipes; The Dog sat in the cupboard under the stairs and howled. The noise was indescribable.

I found Lucas sitting on the stairs drinking a pale liquid out of a bottle.

'Vodka,' he explained briefly. 'Want some?'

I nodded and took the bottle from him.

'It doesn't taste of anything,' I objected.

'It doesn't have to,' Lucas grinned. 'Have some more.'

I had some more, and soon discovered that Lucas was right. It didn't matter in the least what vodka tasted like; it was the effect that mattered. Very soon I was singing along to the nearest instrument (the bagpipes, as it happened; not an easy instrument to sing along to, but as I discovered, I simply had to open my mouth and the vodka did the rest).

At half past eleven the neighbours started to bang on the door and talk about disturbed sleep and work in the morning. Mum smiled and apologized and invited them all in, and some of them even went home to fetch more bottles to replenish our diminishing stocks.

'Just think,' I said to Lucas, as we walked unsteadily towards the kitchen in search of more food, 'any of these people could be our fathers.'

'So they could.'

We rarely discussed our fathers, partly because there was nothing much to discuss, but partly because I think we each minded more than we let on how much we missed having another parent, but didn't like to tell the other how we felt.

'I hope mine wasn't a Lodger.' This was something I dreaded, because Lodgers — even the nicest and best Lodgers — somehow seemed to belong to an inferior species. This may have been because they inhabited the basement, or simply because I would have preferred my father to be at the very least a homeowner, not reliant on anyone else to put a roof over his head.

'Or Uncle Rupert,' Lucas said.

'Oh, no.' I shuddered at such a dreadful thought. 'Mum never fancied him, I'm sure. Besides, he's an uncle. A relation. You can't — you're not allowed to, well, do it with a relation, are you?'

'What's there to stop you?' Lucas grinned unkindly. 'Besides, he's only a very distant kind of uncle; probably not really an uncle at all. And Mum was very fond of him, wasn't she?'

'Not that kind of fond,' I said. 'Besides, we don't look like him, do we? I'd rather it was a Lodger — any Lodger — than Uncle Rupert!'

We sat on the floor eating slices of Greta's apple strudel, contemplating the mysteries of our paternity. I was feeling dizzy from the vodka, and depressed by the (albeit unlikely) theory that I might have been a product of the scrawny loins of Uncle Rupert.

Much later, when most of the guests had departed (some were still lingering in odd corners, and at least two were in my bed) and I was being very sick in the bathroom, my mother came in. She appeared cheerful and only mildly tipsy, and smelled strongly of the odd cigarettes.

'Oh, Cass. You're drunk. Poor you.' She sat down on the edge of the bath and held my head while I deposited the rest of my party food down the lavatory. 'You need to drink lots of water and then go to bed.'

'I can't.' I wiped my face and rinsed out my mouth. 'There are people in my bed.'

'How tiresome.' Mum stroked my hair. 'Never mind. You can come and share mine.'

It was years since I had slept in my mother's bed. In my early childhood it had been a place of refuge when I was ill or unhappy. When I had chickenpox, when I had flu, when my pet hamster died, I had sought — and been given — consolation between those sheets, and I can still remember the musky scent of my mother's skin and the sweetish spicy smell of the perfume she used to wear.

'Well, did you enjoy the party after all?' Mum asked, when we had undressed — I was wearing one of her nighties as I didn't like to disturb the occupants of my bedroom — and I had settled myself in what I had come to think of as the visitors' side of the bed (my mother always slept on the left).

'Yes. I suppose so.'

'Good. I thought you would.'

'Mm. Mum —' I hesitated — 'was Uncle Rupert my ... my father?'

'Uncle Rupert?' Mum let out a peal of laughter. 'Good heavens, no. Whatever gave you that idea?'

'Something Lucas said.'

'Then I shall have to have a word with Lucas, the bad boy,' said Mum fondly.

'Then who? Who was my father? I really need to know.'

I had never pressed my mother on this subject before; she had always been so odd and evasive that I hadn't liked to. But a combination of vodka and the intimacy of sharing her bed had given me new courage.

'Why do you need to know?'

I felt that Mum was playing for time. 'I need to know where half of me comes from. I don't feel whole only knowing about your side.'

But when I came to think about it, I didn't really know that much about Mum's family, either. Her father had been something in the Foreign Office, but had succumbed to a heart attack when she was small. Her mother had been neglectful, and had more recently developed some form of dementia and, after Mum's vain attempts to keep her with us, been committed to an institution some distance away. I knew Mum felt bad about this, and she did contrive to visit my grandmother regularly, but she returned from these visits guilt-ridden and depressed. Her mother no longer knew her. She must have been one of the few people who really did think she was Napoleon (presumably since she was sufficiently deranged to imagine herself to be a French emperor, then the addition of a sex change was a minor detail), and obviously someone like my mother was considered far too insignificant to be granted an audience of any length with anyone so important. Apart from my grandmother (whom we never saw now as Mum thought it might upset us), there was only a sprinkling of cousins, most of them distant, and an aunt in New Zealand doing interesting things with sheep. Ours was not what you would call a close family.

'I think feeling whole is more about being at home and comfortable with who you *yourself* are,' Mum said now. 'I'm not sure it has much to do with your parents.'

'I'd still like to know.'

'Well, I never really knew my father, either.' Mum stroked my hair, her voice pensive.

'That's not the point, Mum. You knew *who he was*. I want to know who *my* father was.'

'Well, there's a bit of a problem there.'

'Why?'

'The thing is, Cass, that I don't know who he was, either.'

'How?' I sat up in bed, shocked. 'How can you not know who he was?' It seemed to me inconceivable that anyone should perform that incredibly rude act and not know with whom they were doing it.

'There were several men —'

'Lodgers?' Oh, please not Lodgers.

'No. We didn't have Lodgers then. Just men. People I met. People I got close to.'

'Oh, Mum!'

'I know. I didn't behave very well, did I?'

'So — so you've no idea at all?'

'It was a long time ago, Cass. I did wonder — of course I did — but then life became a bit hectic, and it went out of my mind. I know this may sound odd to you, but I had you, my beautiful little girl, and I reckoned we could all get by without fathers. After all, I did.'

At this point, I'm sure anyone with an ounce of spirit, any real heroine, would have declared that that was the moment when she decided to track down her real father; that nothing would stand in the way of her discovering his identity; that if necessary she would devote her life to the search for this errant — and probably completely unaware — parent. But while I certainly did want to know who my father had been, I was on the whole content with my family, albeit small. My experiences of men hadn't been particularly positive, and I tended to agree with my mother that we probably didn't need one in our lives. What did shock me, and probably drove any other thoughts from my mind, was my mother's undoubted promiscuity. For while I knew she must certainly have slept with a number of men, I had no idea that her behaviour extended so far back into the past and that her memory of her encounters could be so scanty.

We must have drifted off to sleep after this, because I don't recall that we discussed the matter any further. In fact, the subject of my father was not to be addressed again for many years, and by that time I was able to understand a bit better why my mother had behaved as she had.

We awoke the next morning to find several dishevelled partygoers in the kitchen looking for aspirins and breakfast. Mum was in her element, and spent a happy couple of hours frying bacon and ministering to hangovers. One or two people even stayed on to help with the clearing-up, and I was allowed the day off school.

Six

Mum was packing my school trunk, the uniform list at her side, piles of clothes scattered over the bed.

'Skirts, navy, two. White blouses, five. Five white blouses? Whatever do you need five blouses for? Three should be plenty.' She ticked them off her list. 'Long grey socks, six pairs. Six pairs of socks? You've never possessed six pairs of socks in your life. What can they be thinking of? I'll send four.'

We had already been through all this in the uniform shop, so I didn't take too much notice. After all, no one was ever teased for having only four pairs of socks.

The knickers were another matter.

Typically, my mother had refused to buy underwear at the uniform shop where, it has to be said, the prices had been craftily hiked up to match the prestigious standing of the school. Knickers and vests could be bought anywhere, she reasoned. There was no point in paying the earth for knickers and vests.

'I'll get them, Cass,' she'd said. 'No need for you to come with me this time.'

She had returned in triumph.

'Really cheap, Cass. A bargain, and good quality, too. One hundred per cent cotton.' She tipped out her purchases onto the kitchen table. 'How about that?'

To this day, I shall never know how my mother managed to find royal blue knickers. School knickers, as everyone knows, come in bottle green, grey or navy. No one wears royal blue knickers. No one (as far as I know) even *sells* royal blue knickers.

'But Mum — they're the wrong colour.'

'Blue. They're blue. Nice bright blue knickers.'

'But the list says navy! I can't wear those. I'll get into trouble.'

'Don't be ridiculous, Cass. Of course you won't. Who's going to see them, anyway?'

'Everyone!' I wailed. 'Everyone will see them. I'll have to do gym in them. It says so on the list.'

'Oh, gym!' said Mum dismissively. 'What does it matter what you wear for gym? It's not as though you're going out in them.'

'The knickers are nice, I think?' Greta, slicing carrots, was as usual trying to pour oil on troubled waters and, as usual, completely missing the point. Normally I could cope with her well-meaning interventions, but on this occasion I could cheerfully have strangled her.

'I don't want nice knickers. I want navy knickers!' I raged. 'Is it so much to ask? I've got the wrong colour or number of everything else. Can't I even have the right knickers?'

But Mum was adamant. She had paid good money for those knickers, there was nothing wrong with them, and she certainly wasn't taking them back.

And then there were the name tapes. I had wanted proper name tapes with my name embroidered on them in swirly blue writing. But no. Mine had to be hand-written with a laundry marker on pieces of tape. Mum, usually so generous, also loved a bargain, and home-made name tapes, she assured me, were a marvellous way of saving money. Some were in my writing, some in Mum's, and a few in Greta's strange foreign-looking script. Even Lucas did a couple ('to remind you of me, because I'm not much good at writing letters'). Everyone complained about the length of my name.

'Cassandra Fitzpatrick,' grumbled Mum, writing it out for the umpteenth time. 'Why couldn't you have had a shorter name?'

'You gave it to me,' I pointed out. Personally, I would much prefer to have been called Jane. Even Susan would have been preferable to Cassandra.

'I didn't think. At the time.' Mum reached for another piece of tape. 'Besides, the Fitzpatrick bit wasn't my idea.'

'My *father* might have had a shorter name. He might have been Smith.'

'I never slept with anyone called Smith,' Mum said (fortunately we were alone together when this exchange was taking place). 'There was a Jones once,' she added thoughtfully.

'Could it have been Jones?'

'Too long ago.' Mum sighed. 'Oh dear. Isn't life complicated, Cass?'

I forbore to remind her that some of her life's complications were of her own doing, since I knew she was only too aware of the fact. Besides, by this time I was beginning to realize that the idea of my going away was as disturbing for her as it was for me, and I didn't want to risk upsetting her further. I myself was now resigned to my fate. It mightn't be as bad as I imagined, and my mother could even be right. A change might do me good. After all, as she frequently pointed out, I wasn't particularly happy at home these days.

'Two terms, Cass. Give it a couple of terms,' she'd told me. 'If you really don't like it after that, then you can come home.'

'Promise?' I wanted to make absolutely sure where I stood.

'Promise.'

'OK. I'll give it a go. But I really need to know I can come home if I want to.'

'Of course you can.' Mum had kissed the top of my head. 'This is where you belong. I'm just — well, I'm just lending you to boarding school. This will always be your home.'

At last the preparations were over and I was ready for my new life, with my second-hand trunk, my four pairs of socks, the dreaded blue knickers and all the other impedimenta of a new boarding school pupil. Most of my uniform and other belongings were not quite regulation, since my mother seemed incapable of following what were, after all, fairly simple instructions. Thus, my shoes, though black (regulation) bore an interesting little motif on the sides; my hockey boots looked suspiciously like football boots; and my towels ('two large, two small, white') were three medium-sized and blue. But apart from the knickers (of which more later) I didn't mind too much. I'd been raised as a non-conformist in matters of dress and habit, and there seemed no reason why boarding school should make any difference.

When the time came, I was given quite a send-off. Lucas lent me Blind Bear, his treasured childhood companion (its eyes had been removed by a vicious little boy in his class at infant school, a crime which Lucas had never quite managed to forgive); Greta contributed two of her favourite bars of Swiss chocolate to my tuck box (Mum's contribution was a jar of peanut butter, two packets of rich tea biscuits and an enormous box of Turkish Delight); and the Lodger pressed a ten-shilling note into my willing hand. As for the nice man from the chemist (we had now been invited to 'call me Bill' — inevitably, the name had stuck, and he was Call Me Bill until our acquaintance ended many years later), he presented me with a pretty little box of toiletries. I suspected that these were left over from last Christmas, since the soap smelled musty and the talcum powder refused to sprinkle, but it was a kind thought. Even Richard turned up with a battered copy of an Agatha Christie novel ('to take your mind off things') and Ben (who was, in his words, 'on location' filming an advertisement for socks) sent a card to wish me luck.

My transport consisted of a battered white van loaned for the occasion by an ex-Lodger. My driver was Mum.

'Are you sure?' I asked anxiously, when this arrangement was explained to me. 'Are you sure you know how to drive a van?'

'Of course I do.' Mum laughed merrily. 'Car, van — what's the difference? Just gears and brakes and a steering wheel. They're all the same when it comes down to it.'

But I wasn't so sure. My mother was an occasional and erratic driver (she had never actually owned a car) with — as in other areas of her life — her own rules. I was an unwilling passenger at the best of times when she was in the driving seat, and to my unpractised eye the van didn't look at all the same as a car.

'You can't see out of the back,' I objected. 'There's no window.'

'Wing mirror,' said Mum. 'That's all you need, really. A wing mirror. We'll be fine, Cass. Trust me.'

I longed for Call Me Bill and his Rover, but the Rover was out of commission with engine trouble, and in any case, my mother was evidently eager to chauffeur me herself.

'It's the least I can do, Cass,' she said. 'We'll take a picnic, like last time, and The Dog can come too. It will make a change for him.'

In the event, it made an unwelcome and terrifying change for all of us. The van rattled and bounced all over the road, ricocheting off kerbs and verges; Mum, trying to drive and map-read at the same time, cursed and fumed; and The Dog whimpered miserably in the back as he scrabbled back and forth in his attempts to avoid the wildly slithering and very heavy trunk. As for me, I clung to the edges of my seat and closed my eyes, praying for this horrible journey to end as soon as possible.

We were too late to have our picnic, and in any case, I doubt whether either of us could have eaten anything; and when we eventually arrived at the school, the skies opened up as though on cue and welcomed us with a spectacular thunderstorm.

Seven

It is hard now to recount my initial experiences of boarding school. Everything was so new, and so entirely different from anything I had ever known, that my memories of those first few weeks are a jumble of mixed-up impressions and emotions, all of them tinged with an appalling homesickness.

I had never in my life been homesick simply because I had never been away from home. Very occasionally I had stayed overnight with a friend, but I much preferred my friends to come to me, and in this they were more than happy to concur. For my friends adored Mum. No one had a mother like mine, apparently; a mother who appeared unshockable and one to whom they could talk about anything (frequently, inevitably, sex — my friends had a voracious curiosity when it came to matters sexual, and my mother was always happy to answer their questions; no question ever fazed her, and if she didn't know the answer she would make one up). My mother would also allow us all to stay up half the night eating unsuitable food and giggling and listening to Radio Luxembourg ('turn out the lights, when you're done, Cass, and try not to make too much noise'). Even in her more depressed moments, Mum was unfailingly hospitable and kind, and would put herself out to make sure we all had a good time.

So homesickness was an entirely new experience. Of course I had expected to miss my home and family, but nothing had prepared me for the physical pain and the sheer wrenching grief which overwhelmed me, usually at bedtime, but often suddenly, unexpectedly, during the day. Some little thing — a word, an image, a small imagined unkindness — would set me off, and the pain would surge up through my chest, threatening to choke me. I tried not to cry, and usually succeeded, but I shall never forget how it felt. At night in bed, I would hug Blind Bear to me, chewing on his ears (one eventually came off altogether) to stifle the ache in my throat, thinking of Mum and Lucas and everyone else carrying on with their lives without me. I would imagine Mum bending over to kiss me goodnight, ruffling my hair as she pulled the blankets up under my chin; the pencil of light from the passage shining under my bedroom door; the cosy familiar sounds of someone running a bath, milk bottles being put out on the doorstep and The Dog being let out for a final run (three times round the lawn, a quick pee against the gate post, a triumphant yap and back in again).

From my initial impression of the school on that first visit, I had half expected it to incorporate the combined elements of a horror film and *Tom Brown's Schooldays* (a story I loved, but not one in which I would like to have taken part), but in fact it was not unpleasant. The teachers were kind on the whole, and my fellow-pupils reasonably friendly. My name blended in perfectly with the Fionas and the Camillas and the double-barrelled daughters of the higher echelons (I think it was the first time in my life that it hadn't been singled out for censure and accusations of snobbery), and I was enough of a chameleon to be able to disguise the hint of Norfolk lilt which was part of my heritage. Of course, by no means all my peers were either posh or wealthy — and some, like me, had earned their places through scholarships and bursaries — but they were in such contrast to the girls in my previous school that at times it felt as though I were living with the combined female offspring of the entire aristocracy.

Next to the homesickness, my biggest problem was having to conform to set rules. Of course my previous school had had its rules, but the classes were large, the pupils a disparate lot and discipline a problem, so most of us managed to get away with all kinds of deviations. Thus, our uniform varied considerably from girl to girl, badly executed (or hastily copied) homework was often overlooked, and our meals (most of us took packed lunches) were of our own choosing. Besides, we were only at school between the hours of 9 a.m. and 4 p.m. After that, our day was our own.

Not so boarding school. Every minute of every day was regulated. Apart from a few brief hours at the weekend, we had little time to ourselves. Ruled by the clock and the school bell, we were shunted from one activity to another; from bed to breakfast, from supper to prep, from piano practice to PE; we were like army recruits scurrying round a barracks, always under pressure and often (in my case) late.

Bedtime was particularly hard for me (in bed by 8.30, lights out at 9) as I had never in my life had a bedtime. Of course I had heard of bedtimes — most of my friends had bedtimes — but I had never had to abide by them myself. My mother reasoned that if we were tired, we would go to bed, and in this Lucas and I were fairly sensible. It may have been because we had never had a bedtime to conform to that we had no reason to rebel, and in fact we were usually in bed in good time. To be told to go to bed at a particular time was a different matter altogether, and seemed a terrible infringement of my freedom. Deprived of my customary hour of reading, I was often unable to sleep, and would lie in the dark listening to the regular breathing of my companions, clutching Blind Bear and longing for home.

Likewise, meal times. In our household, these were rare, not least because my mother was often at work. There was always food around, and we were encouraged to help ourselves when we were hungry. Sometimes Mum cooked for us, but often we (or whoever else happened to be around) prepared our food. Lucas and I were quite accomplished cooks, used to combining whatever ingredients we found in the larder, and we both enjoyed experimenting with new dishes. Some of these may have seemed odd to an outsider (Lucas's sardine omelette was a favourite), but to us it was just the way things were done. If you were hungry, you prepared yourself something to eat. It was as simple as that.

At school, the meals were regular, overcooked and bland. From the breakfast toast (limp and leathery) through lunch (usually some kind of meat, always liberally anointed with the same lumpy gravy and accompanied by sad-looking boiled-to-death vegetables) to supper (something on toast followed by cake or biscuits from our tuck boxes; mine was empty by the end of the second week) there was a sameness in our diet which took away all the pleasant anticipation I had hitherto associated with food.

Throughout all this, although thoughts of Uncle Rupert himself were mercifully beginning to fade, I was often haunted by fears and nightmares. Sleeping in an unlocked dormitory with seven other girls I felt exposed, but I tried to console myself with the thought that perhaps there was safety in numbers. I might not be able to secure the door, but should an intruder strike, there were more of us to choose from, and my bed was furthest from the door.

My favourite moment of the week was the hour on Sundays that was allocated for us to write our letters home. Most of my schoolfellows found this a terrible chore, and sat chewing their pencils and gazing out of the window, but for me this was the nearest I got to talking to Mum, and I made full use of it.

My own post (given out at breakfast) was meagre. Mum, it is true, endeavoured to write to me once a week, but often these letters were short and scrappy, written in odd moments at work or while waiting for potatoes to boil or a cake to be cooked, sometimes scrawled on the backs of envelopes or bills (on one occasion I received my news from home on the back of a bloodstained butcher's bill; not an epistle I felt tempted to cherish for long). What she wrote was often entertaining, but I felt cheated that she didn't devote more effort to her correspondence with her exiled daughter; that I obviously wasn't the priority I had expected to be. Lucas, true to his word, rarely wrote, and although Greta made an effort, her written English was so much worse than the English she spoke that her letters were often very difficult to understand.

Myra sent me the occasional note, but I think she was probably dyslexic (no one had heard of dyslexia in those days) and it would sometimes take me days to unscramble the hotchpotch of blots and characters her letters comprised. Altogether, my post bag tended to be a disappointment, and a disappointment at breakfast is not a good start to the day.

I kept all my letters in a box in my bedside locker, and together with my letters home, which Mum saved and which I still have in my possession, they make poignant, even nostalgic reading. Going through them now, I recall the pains I went to to avoid too much mention of the homesickness which dominated those early weeks, as I knew how much distress it would have caused. I was not an especially stoical child, but I recognized my mother's vulnerability, and tried my best to avoid adding to her problems. Yet when I read those letters now, and remember how I felt when I was writing them, I feel that pain almost as fiercely as I did then; and in spite of the many trials and tragedies that were to take place in the years which followed, I still think that the aching, solitary suffering of homesickness was one of the hardest things I have ever had to endure.

Eight

St Andrew's School
10th Sept. 1961

Dear Mum,

This place is all right but not as nice as home. My bed is a bit like a hospital bed, with a locker, but no flowers of course. I sleep next to someone called Susannah who actually snores (I thought only men snored) although she says she doesn't. There are only nineteen girls in my class, so the teacher always knows what's going on, and no one is allowed to sit at the back (Myra and I always sat at the back so that we could write each other notes during class). We play a most peculiar game called lacrosse, and I've got to have my own lacrosse stick (it looks just like a fishing net) and I'm very bad at it.

I think I've got a best friend, although I'm not sure how she feels about me. Anyway, we get on well and make each other laugh. Her name is Helena (quite a sensible name for this school) and she lives in a big house in Derbyshire. She is new too, which helps, but she is much better at lacrosse than I am.

The blue knickers are a disaster. I told you they would be. Our PE teacher is an enormous woman in a green tracksuit, and she has a very loud voice.

'What colour do you call those knickers, Cassandra?' she bellowed at me the first time we did PE, and I thought that was a pretty silly question, so I said 'red', and she put me in detention for being cheeky. But I really really do need navy ones, Mum. I'm not being fussy, and I don't mind looking a bit different, but those knickers make me look very different indeed. Helena calls them 'blue-mers', which she thinks is very funny, but then she's got navy ones so it's OK for her to laugh.

The other girls are quite nice on the whole, although there's a gang who are a bit stand-offish and stay with each other in the holidays and make private jokes and tease poor little Monica, who is fat with sticky-out teeth and red hair. I try to be nice to her, but she's an awful wimp and very greedy. I offered her my biscuits and she took three.

Work is fine. I came second in a maths test, and my last essay was read out in class, but I got into trouble for setting fire to my lab coat when we were doing chemistry. I can't see the point in boiling things up in test tubes, although some of the colours are interesting.

Must go. Supper time.

Love from Cass xxx

PS Please ask Lucas to write to me. I wrote to him every day when he was in hospital.

Hazelwood House
13th Sept.

Darling Cass,
It was lovely to get your letter with all your news. I read it to everyone at breakfast, and they were all very interested. Call Me Bill said boarding school was obviously doing you good. Is it? Are you happy? You don't say, but I really want to know.

All is much as usual here. I think The Dog misses you as he keeps going up to your room and snuffling under the bed. Call Me Bill is sleeping in it at the moment, but of course I'll turn him out and give your room a good clean before you come home at half-term.

I hope you don't mind, but it's turned very cold and Richard is sleeping in the living room. They say you can't have too much of a good thing, but if a ukulele is a good thing, then I assure you that you can. I almost prefer Lucas on the violin.

We've got a new Lodger. We found him in the local paper. He's a weasely little man with tufty hair and eyes like tiny black beads, and he seems to be out at night a lot. Lucas thinks he's a cat burglar because he's the right size for climbing through windows and always seems to have plenty of money. I don't really care what he does as long as he pays the rent and cleans the bath after use. But I don't think I'll get fond of him. It's odd, isn't it, that there are the kinds of Lodgers one can be fond of, and those one can't. I don't think he's especially fond of us, either.

I'm sorry about the knickers, and can't understand why everyone's making such a fuss. I'll try to get some more when I have time. I haven't much time at the moment as I've got a new job as a waitress. Such fun, Cass, and I get lots of tips. Greta thinks it's beneath me, but what does she know? I don't think she's ever done an honest day's work in her life, or any other sort, come to that. But then she's got Private Means.

Lucas has a girlfriend! She is small and mousy, with a stammer. I wonder what Lucas sees in her. Maybe she makes him feel masterful. Masterful or not, Lucas's hormones aren't helping his school work. He seems to come bottom in everything.

Got to go. Making gingerbread men.
Love, Mum xx
PS I hated chemistry too. I think it's a boy thing.

(This was the first and longest of Mum's letters. I think she must have been missing me, or perhaps writing me letters was a novelty. If that was the case, the novelty was very shortlived.)

St Andrew's School
17th Sept. 1961

Dear Mum,

Who were the gingerbread men for? Isn't everyone too old for gingerbread men now? Lucas certainly is, if he's got a girlfriend. Talking of which, I don't suppose he'll ever write now. I wonder what they do together. I can't imagine Lucas kissing anyone. What's her name?

I'm OK, but I seem to get into an awful lot of trouble. There are so many rules and regulations, and I often can't remember what I'm supposed to be doing.

I'm either late, or in the wrong place, or I've forgotten some important piece of equipment. Talking of which, I REALLY need those navy knickers. Matron looked out a pair that had belonged to someone who left, but they are enormous and look even more ridiculous than mine. The elastic has gone all floppy, and I have to hold them up with my tie. Even then, I don't dare do too much leaping about in case they fall down. This may not seem very important to you, but at the moment I can't think of anything that would make me happier than some of my own which actually fit me. You asked me if I was happy, and the answer is not very, but the right knickers would be a start. PLEASE, Mum.

Does Call Me Bill have to sleep in my room? I don't like the idea of him poking around among my things, and I certainly don't like the thought of him in my bed. Why can't he get a place of his own? As for Richard, I always thought he rather took pride in being a Homeless Person. If he's living in our home all the time then he can't call himself one any more, can he?

He certainly shouldn't put his HUNGRY AND HOMELESS notice round his neck. It's not fair on the people who give him money. The Agatha Christie he gave me has fifteen pages missing, so I shall never know what happened in the library.

The new Lodger sounds awful. Couldn't you find a better one? If you really think he's a burglar you could try going through his stuff when he's out. There might be a reward, and then you could stop being a waitress. It's time our family had some proper money. Helena is very rich and lives in a big house and has a horse of her own. She wants me to stay with her for half-term.

I came bottom in a chemistry test. I've never been bottom in anything before, but if I had to be, then I think I'd choose chemistry to be bottom in. Tell that to Call Me Bill. He might not like to sleep in the bed of someone who comes bottom in chemistry.

Love from Cass xxx

Hazelwood House
21st Sept.

Darling Cass,

The gingerbread men were for Richard. He says they remind him of his childhood. And of course he's homeless because he hasn't got a home of his own. I'm surprised at you, Cass. I always thought you were such a kind child.

Call Me Bill saw your letter and took umbrage and has gone back to his landlady with a bunch of flowers. So you've managed to upset him too, and you're not even here! I miss his car. It was useful for shopping and the doctor.

Lucas's girlfriend is called Millie. Rather a silly name, I thought. And I've no idea what they get up to but I've told Lucas all about condoms, so they should be fine.

I went to the market to try and buy your knickers, but they only had pink or white frilly ones.

Greta is having Spanish lessons.

We've decided the Lodger isn't a burglar after all as he's got quite a posh voice and washes a lot.

Please don't go somewhere else for half-term. We'll really miss you.

Love, Mum xxx

(I must have been very irritated by this letter of Mum's, for my reply had a waspish edge to it.)

St Andrew's School
24th Sept. 1961

Dear Mum,

I'm doing OK still, though I haven't cracked the chemistry yet. Miss Cole keeps me behind after everyone has gone to explain things all over again, but I still don't understand it. She says I don't concentrate. How can anyone concentrate on anything so boring? Yesterday we boiled up potassium permanganate in a test tube and then filtered it. What possible use is that to anyone? I spilt mine down my front and had to go and change.

Your last letter was very odd. For instance, what makes you think that someone with a posh voice who washes a lot isn't a burglar? I'm sure there must be clean burglars as well as dirty ones. Having said that, I never thought he was a burglar in the first place (although I've never met him).

Call Me Bill should never have read my letter. My letters home are PRIVATE. If he read it, then he deserves to go back to his landlady. I hope she gives him a hard time.

Don't bother about the knickers. Helena was so sorry for me that she wrote to her mother to say she had lost hers, and her mother sent some more, so I've got those (I'm not sure how you lose six pairs of knickers, but her mother didn't ask any awkward questions). Of course the market don't have navy ones. They have cheap and nasty common ones. I would NEVER buy knickers from the market.

As for Richard, he's using you. It seems to me that everyone uses you, and you just don't realize it. And what does Greta want to learn Spanish for? She needs to have English lessons first. I hope she's still helping with the cooking.

Helena really wants me to stay for half-term. She says I can ride her horse. She's got an older brother, and acres of garden. I'm not usually jealous of people, but sometimes I'm a bit jealous of Helena.

I don't think I want to hear about Lucas and Millie.

Love from Cass xxx

Hazelwood House
5th October

Darling Cass,

I thought this picture postcard of the town hall would remind you of home. The Dog's been knocked down. Stitches in leg, but otherwise OK. Call Me Bill's landlady's allergic to flowers and threw him out again so he's back. Greta knitting you a cardigan. Please come home for half-term. Sorry this is so short — no room for more.

Love, Mum xxx

Nine

My mother moves restlessly on her pillow, her fingers plucking at the sheet, her lips moving soundlessly.

'Are you in pain, Mum?'

'Pain,' she nods. 'Oh, such pain!'

I ring the bell and a nurse — one my mother particularly dislikes, all bosom and bustle and shiny badges — comes in with a syringe on a little tray.

'Roll over, dear.' My mother claws her way to the edge of the bed, exposing her painfully thin bottom. The nurse stabs with a practised flick of her wrist. 'There we are. All done. Time to sleep now.'

'"Roll over, dear,"' mimics my mother, as the nurse whisks out of the room. 'Like the bloody lottery. Silly cow.'

We exchange glances and smile. Oh Mum! I love you so much. Have I ever told you just how much I love you?

'Love you, Cass.' Mind-reader. Becoming drowsy. Beginning to drift off now, on a tide of drugs.

'Love you too, Mum.'

At this moment, I would give everything I have to spare my mother her suffering, and yet over the years, she and I have caused each other much pain, one way or another. That, I suppose, is the price of love. But often I didn't realize how much I was hurting her.

I must have hurt her badly that first half-term, and yet at the time, I barely gave it a second thought.

For I did go to Helena's for half-term. I think that postcard of Mum's clinched it. I had missed her so much, and imagined her missing me. I had pictured us rushing into each other's arms when I returned home, my favourite meals being cooked, perhaps even one of Mum's famous parties to welcome me home. I had already gathered that life at home was progressing quite nicely without me, and I could just about handle that. But I had hurried to fetch my post that morning, and all I had received was that one lousy postcard. Up until then, I had never even noticed the town hall, and I certainly didn't need a cosy little reminder of its continued existence.

How I regretted sparing Mum all my tales of woe; the homesickness, the nights spent weeping into my pillow, the touching, cherished services of Blind Bear. Selflessly, I had spared her feelings by not bothering her with emotive accounts of my misery, and she had repaid me by letting Call Me Bill into my bed and sending me a postcard instead of a proper letter. However much information you put on a postcard (and there was very little on this one), there is something careless and impersonal about a piece of correspondence which is open for anyone to read.

One of our Lodgers, a snob and a name-dropper, who had so many letters after his name that they took up more room than his address (Mum thought he had made most of them up), used to send us what Lucas called boastcards. These would arrive from various distinguished venues where he disported himself in the company of those whose names he so frequently dropped, and were obviously intended to be read by — and to impress — as many people as possible. They were usually just addressed to Mum, but they fooled no one.

Thus, with that postcard, my mother had put paid to her chances of having me home for that first precious exeat. If she was going to treat me with such cavalier indifference, then two could play at that game. Besides, the idea of spending the half-term holiday in Helena's grand house appealed to me enormously, and although I still longed to go home, I would be back at Christmas and could see everyone then. I might even send Mum a postcard.

But Helena's house was not at all what I had imagined. There was no park, no tree-lined drive, no stone steps sweeping up to the front door. The house was big, it is true, but it was modern and ugly, with unpleasant orangey-pink brickwork and pretentious black and gold gates. There were certainly statues in the large, manicured garden, but these were poor imitations of armless Greek females swathed in drapery, stooping sentimentally over seats and flower beds, and there was a vulgar little Cupid peeing into a pond.

Inside, the house was a shrine to the gods of conspicuous consumption, from the gold-plated drinks trolley in the spacious living room to the lavatory paper holder in the downstairs cloakroom, which played a merry jingle from a Disney cartoon every time you took a sheet of paper.

'Do you like it?' Helena asked, when she had shown me round the house. 'My parents had it architect-designed.'

'It's amazing,' I said with absolute truth, and fortunately this seemed to satisfy her.

'I'll take you up to your room,' she continued, picking up my suitcase. 'Come on.'

I had envisaged us sharing a room, having cosy chats into the small hours, exchanging those confidences which are best shared in the dark. This was what I had been used to at home, where any visitors I had were accommodated on a mattress on my bedroom floor. This arrangement had suited my friends and me admirably, but obviously things were done differently in Helena's household.

'Here!' Helena flung open a door. 'This is yours.'

The room was vast, with an enormous double bed and even a small sofa. Everything was fussy and frilly, decorated in what my mother used to call 'bridesmaid colours' (peach, aqua, lilac), with matching fluffy towels laid out in the adjoining bathroom. In those days, it was almost unheard of to have one's own bathroom, but while I was impressed that I should have the use of one, there was something very insular and chilling about having one's needs catered for on such a solitary basis.

But despite my spacious accommodation, I was beginning to feel stifled; stifled by the opulence and the frills, stifled by the feeling that I was supposed to react in a way which I found almost impossible, and stifled by the heat. I had never in my life experienced central heating. Home was heated by a combination of open fires and electric heaters. If we were cold, we were told to put on more clothes, and in the winter we all used hot water bottles. Here, the heat was overpowering, and although it was a chilly week in October, the only occasions upon which I wore a sweater were when we went outdoors.

Helena's parents were kind and welcoming, but they were not what I would call homely people. Her mother was immaculate in her pale slacks, low-cut blouses and stilettos, with dyed blonde hair and lots of gold jewellery; her father was quiet and dark-suited, and seemed to spend most of his time at work.

'Where do you keep your books?' I asked Helena once, desperate for something to read (I had already finished the two I had brought with me).

'Books?' She smiled vaguely. 'We haven't really got many books, though Mum sometimes goes to the library.'

So I had to content myself with old copies of *Reader's Digest* and the heavy (and obviously unread) volume of *European Art Collections* from the coffee table.

The other disconcerting thing about a visit which was less than satisfactory was the change in Helena. I suppose we all alter according to our environment, but Helena was a different person when she was at home. Gone were the giggles and the pranks we enjoyed at school, and she spent much of her time phoning her friends or shopping with her mother (I was invited to accompany them but declined, since I had no money and didn't want to be in a position where I had to borrow any). The horse, Elvis, which was kept in an adjoining paddock, was my only consolation, and although I was a timid rider (I had never been on a horse before), I enjoyed grooming him and leading him down the nearby lane to graze (the grass in his field was sparse, and so far he had declined the hay that was on offer). I think Elvis was as lonely as I was, and so the arrangement probably suited him as well as it did me.

'Aren't you bored?' Helena asked me once. 'Just standing around watching Elvis can't be much fun.'

'I'm never bored,' I said, and it was true. While the discipline at home had always been pretty lax, the one thing Mum would never tolerate was boredom. If you had a brain to think and eyes with which to read, there was no excuse, she always told us, and in this she was successful, for I don't remember either Lucas or me ever being bored.

Strangely, I felt even more homesick at Helena's than I had at school. School wasn't meant to be homely, and I had never expected it to be so. But before my visit to Helena's I had anticipated at least a little of the comfortable domesticity of home. A cosy kitchen, cooking smells, Mum in her old apron, the busy sound of the wireless (BBC Home Service), people's various comings and goings; all these helped to comprise the atmosphere which I had always called home, together with saggy, old, comfortable furniture and dusty collections of books in every corner. In contrast, Helena's house was bandbox tidy, the cushions neatly angled on their corners on sofas and chairs, the pale carpet spotless, the air fragrant with lavender furniture polish. I tiptoed round the house, terrified lest I disturb or sully any of this perfection. I was grateful that I had tucked Blind Bear at the bottom of my suitcase, for without him I don't think I would have survived at all.

The day before we were due to return to school, Helena's elder brother, Alex, returned from boarding school for his half-term holiday. I had never given much thought to the subject of Greek Gods, but seeing Alex for the first time, I knew immediately what one would look like. Tall and slim, with waving blond hair and sea-green eyes, he eyed me up and down when we were introduced and smiled a lazy teasing smile.

'So this is Cassandra.' His voice was unexpectedly deep, his handshake warm and firm. 'Well well. You never told me how pretty she was, little sister.' He turned mockingly to Helena. 'Perhaps you were jealous?'

'Oh, shut up, Alex!' Helena was obviously stung. 'Take no notice of him, Cass. He's like this with all my friends.'

'Only the attractive ones,' Alex said, unperturbed by Helena's indignation. 'And this one, Helena dear, is very attractive indeed.'

I shall never know how I got through the rest of that evening. Sitting opposite Alex at dinner, I was painfully aware of him watching me; of the teasing smile, the slightly raised eyebrow, and once, when I caught his eye, a knowing wink. I couldn't imagine that this sophisticated young man was actually still a schoolboy, having to wear a uniform and abide by rules and bedtimes just as we did. Helena had told me that he was seventeen, but to me he looked much older; certainly years older than Lucas. He seemed to treat his parents with the same levity as he did his sister, although they both obviously adored him; and if his manner towards them was more than a little high-handed, neither of them seemed aware of it. They questioned him closely, applauding his sporting achievements and exam results, laughing at his jokes, hanging on the most humdrum of his words. If they had possessed a fatted calf this would certainly have been the occasion for it to be called into service.

I glanced at Helena, and felt for her. Poor Helena. With her indifferent academic achievements and average looks, how could she compete with such a brother? Hitherto I had never given much thought to sibling rivalry. Lucas and I had always been sufficiently fond of each other and sufficiently different in our abilities for comparisons to seem unnecessary, and Mum was not one to show favouritism. But there was no mistaking who was the favourite child in this family.

Later that evening, as I was making my way up to my room, Alex stopped me on the staircase.

'I meant what I said,' he told me.

'What? What did you mean?' I pressed myself against the wall, hoping he would go past me and let the matter drop.

'You're very pretty, Cassandra. Very pretty indeed.' He turned to face me, placing his hands against the wall on either side of me, effectively preventing me from moving on.

'Please — please let me pass.' I made as though to move away, but Alex merely laughed.

'Oh Cassandra, don't tell me you're shy!'

'No, of course not. I just want — I want to go to bed.'

'Bed? Did you say bed? What a very forward young lady you are!'

'I mean I want to go to my room.' My heart was thumping inside my chest like a trapped bird, and my palms were sweating. I longed for Helena to appear, but she had already gone up for a bath, and was unlikely to come down again. 'Please. Please let me go.'

'Why? Why should I let you go?' Alex seemed to consider for a moment. 'OK. I'll let you go. But you'll have to pay.'

'Pay?'

'Yes. A kiss. One little kiss, and then you can go. A small price to pay, wouldn't you say?'

'No. I mean, I'd rather not. Please let me go. I just want to go upstairs.'

'A kiss, Cassandra. I demand it.' Alex leant forward. I could feel his breath warm on my cheek and smell the wine he had had at dinner. 'One little kiss.'

I put out my hands to push him away, but he was surprisingly strong. His hands were on my shoulders now, his face close to mine.

'No! *No!*' I managed to get the words out before his mouth closed on mine, and then I screamed. All the terror and revulsion of my encounter with Uncle Rupert came back to me, and I screamed with a strength born of desperation. On some distant level I was aware that I was overreacting; that nothing serious could happen on a staircase in a house full of people, but the screaming wouldn't stop. It was almost as though it had nothing to do with me; as though some other part of me had taken over.

'Hey! Hey!' Alex looked as frightened as I was. He took me by the shoulders and shook me gently. 'Cassandra! I didn't mean anything. It was just a joke. Come on. Stop this noise, for goodness' sake!'

From different parts of the house, I could hear doors opening and hurrying footsteps. I had to get away. Stifling my sobs, I ducked under Alex's arm and rushed up the stairs, along the corridor and into my room, where I slammed the door shut and then leant against it, my chest heaving, the tears still streaming down my face.

'Cassandra? Let me in, dear. Whatever's the matter?' Helena's mother was outside the door, trying the door handle. 'Come on, Cassandra. You must tell me what's wrong!'

Reluctantly, I moved away from the door. I had no idea what I was going to say. I knew that if I told the truth no one would believe me, for I couldn't imagine Helena's parents ever thinking ill of their golden boy. I would be branded a liar, and Helena wouldn't want me for her friend any more.

Fortunately, Alex had come up with his own version of events.

'Alex said you thought you saw a mouse. Is that true, Cassandra?' Helena's mother came into the room and put her arm round me.

'No. Yes. Yes — I'm sure I saw a mouse.' I sat down on the bed. 'I'm sorry. It — it scared me.'

'That's all right, dear, although you did give us all a bit of a fright. After all, if it was a mouse — and I sincerely hope not; we've never had mice in this house — it's nothing to be afraid of, is it?'

I shook my head, unable to speak. I was furious with Alex. Furious with him for subjecting me to his unwanted attentions, furious that he should imply that I was the kind of girl who would be afraid of a mouse, and furious that he should lie to get himself out of his predicament, secure in the knowledge that I would probably back him up. I felt stupid and humiliated and ashamed, and all I wanted now was to be left alone.

But I had to endure all the fussing attention which Helena's mother seemed to think appropriate for a deranged guest, and it wasn't until I'd had a hot bath ('leave the door unlocked, dear — just in case'), a mug of hot milk (which I hated) and a hot water bottle (which I didn't need) that I was finally left on my own.

Homesick and wretched, wishing myself anywhere but in this awful house, I eventually cried myself to sleep.

Ten

The injection is beginning to work and Mum becomes drowsy, her eyelids drooping, her twitching transparent hands loosening their grip on the sheet. I want her to sleep — of course I do — and yet we have so little time left together and I don't want to waste a minute of it. Apart from anything else, there's so much I want to ask her; so much that will die when she dies. How old was I when I took my first steps? Lost my first tooth? Stopped believing in Father Christmas? My whole childhood is sleeping with her on that pillow, and the bits I can't remember will go when she does. But how can I deny her the little respite she gets from her pain and her anxiety?

That term seemed endless. The weather turned bitingly cold, and we shivered as we scurried between classrooms, rubbing life back into our mottled thighs after games of hockey, where the only pain worse than the blow of a hockey stick against an unsuspecting ankle was a tumble onto the frozen pitch. We were always hungry, and there never seemed to be enough food. Meals were hurried (just twenty minutes for supper, before the start of evening prep), and we went to bed with rumbling stomachs.

Many relied on the contents of tuck boxes to stave off their hunger, and the arrival of food parcels — for that was what they amounted to — was greeted with great joy. Fortunate (and popular) was the girl who received a steady supply of provisions from home, but I was one of the unlucky ones, for in this respect, as in so many others, Mum proved unreliable. When I did receive a package from home it was as likely to contain something knitted by Greta (which I wasn't allowed to wear) or a book (which I didn't have the time to read) as the sweets and biscuits I craved. The navy knickers did finally arrive, tucked round two packets of peanuts, but the knickers were too late and the peanuts were musty-tasting. I suspected Mum had found them mouldering away at the back of a cupboard (no sell-by dates in those days).

My friendship with Helena resumed as though half-term had never happened. Perhaps there are some friendships which rely on a particular environment in order to thrive. No reference was made by either of us to what had been a pretty unsuccessful week, and nothing was said of Alex or mice. Had Helena questioned me on the subject of the episode on the stairs, I don't think I would have been able to dissemble as readily as I had to her mother. I suspect that, like most teenagers, Helena was not overly preoccupied with the ills of others, preferring to concentrate on her own problems (at the time, the likelihood that she would come bottom in the end-of-term exams).

My own school work was proceeding well. St Andrew's was not an especially academic school, seeming content with its small but respectable annual clutch of university places, and most of the time I hovered comfortably near the top of my class. My chemistry results were consistently abysmal, but that didn't bother me. An inability to get by in French or an ignorance of English literature might be expected to carry a stigma, but no one was ever condemned for failing to shine at chemistry.

Piano lessons were another matter.

Perhaps to make up for the fact that she had never had piano lessons herself, Mum insisted that I should have them. Not for me the record player and the ironing board; I was to learn to play a real piano properly.

'It can't be that hard,' she had told me, before I started my new school, her hands moving lovingly up and down the back of one of Call Me Bill's shirts (she had taken to doing his laundry as well as everyone else's) to the accompaniment of a Mozart concerto. 'Lots of people can play the piano.'

What she had evidently failed to notice was that lots of people play the piano very badly, and we were both about to discover that I was one of them.

'I can't. I just can't,' I sobbed during my fourth piano lesson, when once again I had failed to understand how a scatter of dots and squiggles could be interpreted as musical notes.

'But you can read, can't you?' Mr Presley, a dapper little man who came to the school twice a week to teach piano, looked bewildered. 'It's the same principle. You translate letters into words. You do the same with music, only in this case it's notes. Now dry your eyes, Cassandra, and try again.'

I tried again. And again. But to no avail. How could anyone not only interpret all those lines and dots, but do it with *both hands at once*? By the end of the term, I had failed to master even the rudiments of 'The Jolly Farmer', a horrid bouncy little piece which was the launch pad of the musical career of all Mr Presley's pupils. And at my last lesson of the term, he gently suggested that I might consider giving it up. I could have kissed him.

I looked forward eagerly to Christmas: to the chaos and bustle of a house full of Mum's waifs and strays; to the bedraggled football socks which served as Christmas stockings and which Lucas and I hung up on Christmas Eve; and to Christmas carols from an old and very scratched record (we had to help it along in the middle of 'Silent Night', where it always got stuck).

I was much exercised as to how I was to travel home, dreading a repeat of Mum and the van, but in the event I was spared, for Call Me Bill took the afternoon off to bring her to collect me in his car.

'Here we are!' cried Mum gaily, getting out of the passenger seat and sweeping me into her arms. 'Oh, Cass! You've grown, and you're so thin!'

I forbore to take this opportunity to remind her that her contributions to my intake of food had been sadly lacking. There would be plenty of time for that later. As I succumbed to her embrace, I was aware of other girls watching us. Next to the Jaguars and the Mercedes, Call Me Bill's car looked shabby and tired, and Mum, swathed in several layers of faded cardigans and sporting a bright red knitted hat (Greta's handiwork, I had no doubt), appeared out of place among the tailored and coiffed mothers of my friends, but I didn't care. I was used to — even proud of — my family's eccentricities, and after my experience of Helena's household, I was also grateful.

The Dog, anxious not to be excluded from the reunion, leapt from the open car door and threw himself at me ('He so wanted to come,' Mum later explained. 'He couldn't wait to see you.' How on earth could she tell?), and completed our little display by making a neat deposit in the middle of the lawn. It was time to get going.

That Christmas was everything I could have hoped for. Mum, inspired by a posh magazine she'd seen at the dentist's, had festooned the bannisters and mantelpieces with swags of red ribbon and ivy, and there was a colourful wreath on the front door. All this looked rather incongruous when combined with our faded paper chains and the battered decorations on the Christmas tree, but it gave the house a more than usually festive feel, and in any case, none of us was too much bothered with matters of taste.

The house guests consisted of Call Me Bill, who didn't appear to have any family, the Lodger, who had fallen out with his parents, and a friend of Greta's who was over from Switzerland. Fortunately, Greta's friend was small and shy and fitted perfectly onto the sitting-room sofa (I refused to give up my bed, reasoning that I had been without it for quite long enough, and for once Mum understood).

If I had grown, so had Lucas, who seemed to have reached overnight that spotty gangly stage so common in adolescent boys; all bony wrists and Adam's apple and wispy suggestions of facial hair, which seemed designed to put off the opposite sex rather than the reverse (which I imagined to be what adolescence was all about). Certainly, the girlfriend had apparently ditched him in favour of an older model, but Lucas appeared unfazed. There were, he told me confidently, plenty more fish in the sea. I just hoped for his sake that the fish didn't go too much on appearances.

Otherwise, Lucas seemed much the same, and we quickly settled back into our easy bantering relationship punctuated with the odd comfortably familiar squabble. His school report was as bad as mine was good, but Mum seemed entertained rather than annoyed.

'Look, Cass,' she said, holding up a report in either hand. 'They're almost mirror images of each other. If I could add all your good points together, I'd have a perfect child!'

And there was something in what she said. For while I had contrived to come either top or second in almost every subject except chemistry, chemistry appeared to be the one subject in which Lucas had if not excelled, then at least passed unnoticed. Add to this the fact that he was good at sport and passable on the violin — while my sporting record had been as bad as my piano playing — and it would appear that between us Mum had indeed produced the ingredients for one perfectly rounded child (and presumably one dismal failure as well, but she obviously preferred not to look at it that way).

But throughout Christmas and the new year — through all the feasting and drinking, the partying and singing — there was something about Mum which wasn't quite right. She seemed to be throwing herself into the festivities with a kind of desperation, almost as though she were using Christmas as a diversion from some other far more serious matter. And as the three weeks of my holiday drew to a close, I became increasingly worried. Was Mum heading for one of her famous depressions? She hadn't had one for some time, and they didn't usually last long, but I dreaded a return of those black moods; of the overwhelming sadness and the weeping and the catalogue of regrets which haunted her on these occasions. As far as I knew, nothing had happened to precipitate such a decline; she had seemed happy, Lucas and I were reasonably settled, the house was as full as even Mum could have wished. And yet I knew that something was wrong.

'Is Mum OK?' I asked Lucas one day, while we were out walking The Dog. 'She doesn't seem — right.'

'I don't know.' Lucas picked up a stick and threw it for The Dog. 'I've asked her, and she says she's fine, but she's not herself.'

'It's not man trouble, is it?' Man trouble featured regularly in our mother's life, and although she tended to keep it to herself, and Lucas and I rarely even knew the identity of the man in question, the fallout of man trouble affected us all.

'I don't think so. I don't even think there's been a man recently, though you never can tell with Mum.' Lucas paused. 'She might tell you, Cass. After all, you're a woman.'

I wanted to say that no, I wasn't a woman, I was not yet fifteen, and still anxious to hang on to what little childhood I had left, but there was no point in trying to explain this to Lucas. Lucas, with his fake ID for getting into pubs and his eager anticipation of his provisional driving licence (one year to go) wouldn't understand at all.

I tackled Mum while she was drying her hair up in her bedroom.

'What's up, Mum?'

'Up? What do you mean, what's up?' Mum lifted and shook out a thick handful of hair. She had beautiful hair, a deep rich auburn; a colour she hadn't managed to hand on to either of her offspring.

'There's something wrong, isn't there?' I sat down on the bed beside her. 'Please tell me, Mum. I need to know. I can't go back to school, leaving you like this. I'll only worry.'

She turned to me, letting her hair fall back onto her shoulders, and placed the hairdryer on the bedside table.

'Oh, Cass. I'm in a bit of a mess. I don't know what to do.'

'Mess? What sort of mess? Is it money?'

'No. Not money.'

'What, then? You've got to tell me.'

'Something — something's happened, Cass. It — it's difficult.'

'So I see. But you'll have to tell me sooner or later, so you may as well get it over now.'

'You're too young. You shouldn't have to be bothered with this sort of thing yet.'

What sort of thing? What on earth could have happened to Mum which required me to be older in order to cope with it?

'Are you ill? Is that it?' I was becoming frightened. Perhaps Mum had some incurable illness. How would I manage? How would any of us manage without her?

'No. Not ill. Oh, Cass. Promise you won't say anything to anyone else if I tell you?'

'Promise.'

'And you'll forgive me?'

'Of course.' Why shouldn't I forgive her? What on earth had Mum been up to? I took her hand and gave it a squeeze. 'Tell me, Mum.'

'Well then.' She took a deep breath. 'There's no easy way of saying this, but — oh, Cass! — I'm pregnant. I'm going to have a baby.'

Eleven

January 1962

I eased myself off the bed and walked unsteadily over to the open window to get some air.

'Cass? Cass! Please talk to me. Please say something.' Mum's voice was small, almost childlike, and I was filled with unreasoning rage. How could she do this to me; to us? What could she have been thinking of? I could imagine — just — a scenario in which I might have to confess an unwanted pregnancy to my mother, but I had never in my wildest dreams imagined that it could be the other way round. It was all wrong. She was the adult. She was the one who was meant to be sensible and responsible, and although I knew only too well that I couldn't always rely on Mum to be either of these, she was still my mother.

'How?' My voice came out in a strangled croak, and I held on to the window sill, concentrating my gaze on the lawn outside, where Lucas was playing with The Dog.

'Well, the usual way, I assume.' Mum gave a little laugh.

I rounded on her. *'How can you*? How can you laugh at a time like this?'

'No. You're right. It's not funny. I'm sorry.' She looked down, her fingers plucking at the counterpane. 'But it's not the end of the world, Cass. It might even be — fun.'

'Fun? You call this fun? You announce that you're pregnant, and you think it's going to be *fun*? You've got no husband, in case you haven't noticed, and Lucas and I haven't even got fathers. Has this — this baby got a father?'

'Well, of course it had a father —'

'*Had.*'

'Well, yes. I mean —'

'I know what you mean. You mean this poor little sod won't know its father either!'

'Language, Cass!'

'*Language*? You talk to me about language? Mum, how can you expect me to show you any respect if you — if you go around behaving like this. At your age, too. It's — it's disgusting!'

'I didn't go around behaving like anything. And I'm not even forty yet, Cass. I'm not — old.' Her voice was a whisper now, and there were tears on her cheeks.

'Old enough to know better, though.' I had the upper hand now, and the feeling was not unpleasant.

'Yes. Yes, I suppose you're right.' She wiped her eyes with the back of her hand. 'But I hoped you'd understand.'

'I don't understand. I'm not meant to understand. I don't even want to understand. I just — I just want things to be the way they were!'

'So do I. Believe me, so do I.' Mum looked up at me. 'Cass, I'm so sorry. I really didn't mean this to happen.'

'And I don't suppose you meant Lucas to happen, or me to happen. We're all your — your little mistakes, aren't we?' I said bitterly. 'After all your little talks about birth control, too.'

'Well, you needed to know.'

'No. We didn't. You're the one who needs to know, and look at you!' I moved away from the window and came towards her. She looked small and vulnerable and beautiful, and at that moment, I hated her. 'This isn't just your life we're talking about. It's mine and Lucas's and — everyone else's. This is going to ruin everything.'

'We'll be OK, Cass. We've always been OK. We'll get by. And I've never looked upon you and Lucas as mistakes. You might not have been — well — planned exactly, but you're the best things that ever happened to me. I can't imagine life without either of you. And this baby will be special too. We'll make it special.'

'We?'

I was in no mood to extend a welcome to my unborn sibling or to have any involvement in this situation. Unmarried mothers still carried a stigma, and while Mum had managed to shrug hers off so effortlessly that we were barely aware of it, I knew that people talked about us. It seemed to me that just as everyone had got used to the fact that there was no father in our household, Mum was going out of her way to remind them.

'Cass, of course you're upset. I understand that. But there's nothing more I can say or do.' She hesitated. 'Except, I suppose, get rid of it.'

'*What?*' Even I had heard unsavoury tales of gin and hot baths and women in dingy parlours armed with knitting needles. In those days before the 1967 Abortion Act, it was often the only resort for women who didn't have a very good medical reason to get rid of their unwanted babies.

'Well, I could. People do. I could — find someone to do it.'

The words hung in the air between us, serving only to fuel my anger. For with that clever little twist, Mum had somehow managed to shift her problem from herself onto me, and it felt as though she was asking me to make the decision for her; as though she was telling me that if I wanted her to get rid of her baby, she would.

'You can't ask me to do this!' I yelled at her.

'Do what? I haven't asked you to do anything!'

'Yes, you have. But I won't. I won't! This is your baby and your decision. Leave me out of it!'

'But Cass —'

'No. No more. There's nothing more to say. You got yourself into this mess, and now you've got to sort it out. I've got my own life to lead.' And I rushed from her room, slamming the door behind me.

'What on earth was that all about?' Lucas met me on the landing. 'Are you in trouble?'

'No. Not me. Mum.' I wiped my streaming eyes and leant against the bannisters. 'But I'm not supposed to tell you,' I added, remembering my earlier promise.

'Well, you'll have to now,' Lucas said reasonably. 'You can't not tell me after all that racket you two have been making.'

'Well —' after all, what had Mum done to deserve my loyalty? — 'you and I are going to have a new little brother or sister. Isn't that nice?' I paused, enjoying in spite of myself that frisson of excitement which comes with being the bearer of bad news.

'You're joking!' Lucas's expression had changed from curiosity to horror.

'Ask her yourself if you don't believe me.'

'Are you sure about this, Cass?'

'Well, that's what she's told me.'

'I can't believe it. I thought she was past all that sort of thing. Well, the baby bit, anyway.'

'Oh, dear me, no. She seems to think she's still a spring chicken. I told her it was disgusting.'

'That was a bit harsh.'

'No, it wasn't. It is disgusting to go around flaunting yourself the way Mum does, and getting into trouble like this. Some example she is!'

'Oh, Cass, you know Mum. She'll never change. That's the way she is.' Lucas sounded suddenly very weary and very grown up and it infuriated me.

'You mean you're happy to let her go on making dear little babies until — until she can't any more? Is that what you mean?'

'No, of course not. I just mean that this is — must have been — a mistake, a one-off, and I suppose we'll just have to make the best of it.'

We. That word again. Well, Lucas could join in this new cosy little game of happy families if he wanted to, but I certainly wasn't going to have anything to do with it. Hitherto, I had been dreading leaving home and going back to school, but now it offered a welcome escape. At least no one could ask me for help or advice if I wasn't here. At least at school I would have the security of being treated as the child that I still was, and not a cross between a best friend and an agony aunt to my feckless mother.

'Well, you do as you like, Lucas,' I said. 'You can see her through this — this crisis, happy event, however she likes to think of it. I'm off again in a week.'

'You mean you're still going back to school?' Lucas sounded shocked. 'Even after this?'

'You try stopping me.'

'Leaving me to — to deal with this?'

'No, Lucas. *No!* Leaving *Mum* to deal with this. This is her problem. We've got to let her sort it out herself. I'm sorry to be leaving you, I really am, but you don't have to be her nursemaid. You've just got to get on with your life, like me. She managed having you and me without any help. She's told us enough times. I'm sure Greta will make a wonderful nanny. After all, she doesn't seem to have anything else to do.'

'Does Greta know?'

'No one knows. Yet. But presumably they'll have to sooner or later.'

'Oh, Lord.' Lucas sat on the top stair and put his head in his hands.

'Quite.'

I knew I was being hard, but it was the only way I could distance myself from the situation, for I knew that once I allowed myself to sit down and really think about it, I'd feel compelled to stay at home and help. To be fair, Mum hadn't suggested that I should, and it was unlikely that she would ask me to make any kind of sacrifice for her. Mum rarely actually asked for help; she simply made everyone aware of her problems, and sooner or later someone would offer whatever support was needed. There was a fragility about Mum which was hard to resist, but I was beginning to see through it. I know she never intended to trap or deceive any of us — in fact I'm sure that nothing was further from her thoughts — but her very neediness did it for her, and even if she wasn't aware of it, it was a powerful tool in getting her what she wanted.

'Lucky you.'

Lucas sounded bleak, and I felt genuinely sorry for him. Poor Lucas. He was just finding his way out of childhood into the heady world of girls and the right kind of jeans and consideration of his future career, and Mum, albeit unwittingly, had neatly plunged him into a situation which was bound to be a rich source of anxiety and embarrassment.

Once more, I was overwhelmed with anger, for whatever I might say, however brave and independent I might sound, I knew that fate had taken yet another cruel twist, and that life at home would never be the same again.

Twelve

'Octavia, I think. Octavia Fitzpatrick. How does that strike you, Cass?' Mum was driving me back to school in the borrowed van for the beginning of the new term. Once again, my trunk was making its unstable presence known in the back, but at least The Dog had been granted a reprieve, because I absolutely refused to take him with us. I myself had little choice if Mum chose to subject me to this ordeal, but there was no need to inflict it on a helpless animal. Besides, his yelpings didn't help Mum's concentration, and on this occasion I badly needed her to concentrate.

'What do you mean, "Octavia"? What are you talking about?' I held on to my seat and closed my eyes as we rounded a sharp bend in the road.

'The baby. If it's a girl. I think Octavia's rather nice.'

'Octavia's a ridiculous name.' I was in no mood to discuss names.

'It's a very old name. A classical name. I think it's rather nice.'

'It's inappropriate,' I countered. 'It means "eighth". You have to have had seven children before you can have an Octavia.'

'Oh, don't be so silly, Cass. Of course you don't.'

'Yes, you do. Anyone can see you didn't do Latin at school.' Latin was one of my best subjects. 'In any case, isn't it time someone in our family had a normal name?'

'Lucas, Cassandra and Octavia,' Mum mused, ignoring me. 'I think they go together rather well.'

'Mum, we're not going to be travelling around together for the rest of our lives. We're not a circus troupe.'

'It would look good on Christmas cards,' Mum continued, undeterred. 'I'm not so good on boys' names, though. Have you any ideas, Cass?'

'I wish you'd just concentrate on looking where you're going.'

'Oh, Cass. What's happened to you? You used to be such fun.'

Mum may well have had a point. I still had the eerie feeling that as I grew older, she was becoming inexorably younger; while I was being asked to grow up and face my responsibilities, my mother was contriving to turn a blind eye to hers. If we continued like this, I thought, as we swerved round another corner, we might eventually pass each other; she tottering happily back towards childhood and I struggling to make my way in the world of grown-ups.

'Nappies,' Mum said, as we lurched into a lower gear. 'I got rid of all the nappies. Damn. I shall have to buy new ones.'

'Mum.' I took a deep breath. 'This is our last day together. Would you please, *please*, stop talking about babies!'

'Sorry, love. So. What would you like to talk about?'

Of course, I couldn't think of anything. Besides, I knew that whatever subject I might choose, I would be wasting my breath, for now that she had recovered from the initial shock, Mum was showing all the excitement and wonder which might have been expected of a first-time mother, and she seemed incapable of talking about anything else. Her thoughts were filled with cots and pushchairs, with the redecorating of the tiny box room ('Pink or blue, Cass? Or would yellow be safer?') and with the prospect of labour ('I know it hurt, but I can't remember how much').

Her mood might have been more muted if the reaction of the rest of the household had been less enthusiastic, but by the time she told them her news — several days after her traumatic revelation to me — she appeared to have made a miraculous recovery from the subdued and emotional state in which I had initially found her, and her excitement was so infectious that she soon had everyone thinking what a brilliant idea it all was. I almost expected them to ask why she hadn't thought of it before.

'A little baby,' whispered Greta tearfully. 'Iss wonderful, no? I look after? I help, yes?'

'Oh, yes, Greta! That would be perfect!'

Call Me Bill, although initially shocked (Lucas and I privately suspected that Call Me Bill was sexually uninitiated, and likely to remain so), soon came round to the idea, even going so far as to say that a baby in the house would 'help to keep us all young'. Richard accepted the news with equanimity, and a visiting ex-Lodger — an ageing professor with a pronounced squint which had terrified me when I was younger — was fulsome with his congratulations. As for the neighbours, while they no doubt made the most of this nice little morsel of gossip, outwardly they appeared unfazed. One couple even made a coy appearance, bearing a little packet of bibs and a bunch of flowers, and I distinctly overheard snatches of conversation including such encouraging snippets as 'think you're amazing' and 'coping on your own ... so brave'.

Lucas and I looked at each other. It was as we had anticipated. Once again, Mum had everyone on side, leaving us to struggle with any fallout.

I agreed with Lucas that, before I returned to school for the new term, we should at least attempt to establish the paternity of our new sibling. We had to accept that any trail leading us to discover the identities of our own fathers had long since gone cold, but we thought it unlikely that even Mum could have forgotten so recent an encounter as that which had resulted in her present condition.

After some difficulty finding her on her own (I suspected she had been avoiding us), we finally ran her to ground in her bedroom, sorting out socks.

'Mum. We need to talk to you.' I closed the door carefully behind us.

'Oh dear! You both look very serious.' Mum laughed, but she looked uneasy.

'Yes. We'll come straight to the point.'

'Please do.'

'Well, we — that is Lucas and I — we —'

'Who's this baby's father?' demanded Lucas, never one to beat about the bush. 'We want to know, and the baby will certainly want to know. You owe it to us.'

'Do I?' Mum absently paired a blue sock with a grey one and rolled them in a neat ball.

'Yes. You do. After all this — this *disturbance*, you certainly owe us something.'

'Aren't I allowed a bit of privacy? I don't ask you personal questions, Lucas.' Another pair of mismatched socks. 'I don't know what gives you the right to ask me this.'

'What about the baby's rights? Doesn't it have a right to know its father?' I interrupted.

Mum sighed. 'All right. I'll tell you. But you're not to tell anyone else. Is that understood?'

We nodded.

'And you're not going to like this.'

No surprises there, then.

'Well —' Mum abandoned the socks and sat down on the bed — 'it was — it was someone I met at a party.'

'Someone you met at a party,' echoed Lucas.

'And,' Mum continued, 'before you ask, no, I don't know who he was. I don't know and I don't want to know. He was having a few problems and I — well, I cheered him up. I think he may have had a beard.' The last sentence she added as though this might somehow make it sound better.

'If you had time to find out about his problems and — cheer him up, you must know *something* about him.' Lucas sounded exasperated.

'It was very dark. We'd had a lot to drink.' Mum paused. 'I know. I'm sorry. It sounds awful, put like that, but that's the way it was.'

'But — but someone must know who he was. There can't have been that number of men drifting around in the dark with beards and problems!' I said.

'There were a lot of people, we'd all been drinking. He and I fell asleep on the sofa, and by the time I woke up, he'd gone. He might even have been a gatecrasher.'

'Oh, Mum. How *could* you?'

'I was lonely, Cass. *Lonely*. I don't suppose you've ever been really lonely, have you? I don't expect you to understand. One day,' she continued, 'one day, you may understand, and you may even forgive me. I didn't mean it to happen, and I certainly didn't mean to — to get like this, but I'm going to make the best of it. I didn't want it, I certainly didn't plan it, but now it's happened I really am looking forward to it. It'll — well, it'll give me a purpose. For when you two have left home. I'll have something — someone — to live for.'

I felt totally bewildered. Couldn't Mum see that Lucas and I would always love her and need her? That her life wouldn't come to an end simply because we'd left home (in fact, sometimes our house was so full, I used to wonder whether she would even notice our absence)? Evidently not. Mum's need to be needed was such that a third illegitimate child obviously offered an unexpected lifeline, for even if our house were suddenly to empty itself of all its waifs and strays, a baby, Mum's baby, would still be there. She had guaranteed herself another eighteen years' companionship (or so she seemed to think); a further eighteen years of being at the centre of another person's life. Little wonder, then, that she was so excited.

As for the baby's father, I think that consciously or unconsciously, Mum quite simply preferred her children not to have fathers. Although I'm sure that she never set out to be a single parent (in fact, she herself had said that she hadn't intended to be a parent at all, and I'm sure that was true), I believe she wanted us to herself; and I think she would have found it very hard had she had to share us with anyone else. Besides, she herself had never had a father — or not one she could remember — and I really think she considered fathers to be largely unnecessary.

It was a miserable grey January day with a leaden sky and a hint of snow to come, and I was feeling depressed. The long spring term stretched ahead of me, promising more frostbitten days on the hockey pitch, more inadequate meals and more work. There seemed to be little to look forward to.

The daylight was failing fast, and the windscreen wipers squeaked as they battled with the first few flakes of snow. As we progressed, the headlights illuminated curtains of dancing snowflakes, and we skidded on the slippery surface. Once again, I closed my eyes and gritted my teeth. Experience had taught me that Mum drove better when uninterrupted (although that wasn't saying much) and although I wasn't looking forward to my return to school, it was preferable to ending up in a ditch miles from anywhere.

'I do love you, you know, Cass,' Mum said suddenly, leaning forward and squinting through the windscreen.

'I know. I love you too.'

'That's all right, then.' Mum patted my knee. 'We'll get by, all of us. We always do, don't we?'

'I suppose so.'

'That's my girl.' I could feel rather than see her smiling in the dark beside me. 'And I really will try to write more this term.'

'Not all about babies?'

'Certainly not all about babies.'

'And send tuck?'

'Of course.'
'Sensible tuck?'
'Very sensible tuck.'
'Thanks, Mum.'
'You're welcome.'

I found myself smiling too, for it was impossible to stay grumpy for long when Mum was in this kind of mood.

Thirteen

I fitted back into school and its routine as though I'd never been away, and although the cold and the hunger were sometimes hard to put up with, and the homesickness still tended to surface from time to time, I was surprised at how glad I was to be among my classmates again.

Possibly because of my reputation for noisy nightmares, I had been moved across the dormitory to a bed under a window, with the added bonus of a window ledge which could be used for displaying photographs and other personal possessions and which gave Blind Bear a nice view of the garden while I was having lessons. Whether the change of bed had any effect, or whether my head was so full of other things that it hadn't room for bad dreams I shall never know, but the nightmares appeared to have stopped, and unimpeded by lack of sleep I was able to apply myself to my studies with new enthusiasm.

'You are lucky,' sighed poor Helena, as she struggled with geometry and the idiosyncrasies of irregular French verbs. 'Mum and Dad were really upset with my results last term. You seem to do it without even trying. I bet your mum was proud of you.'

'I think Mum's always proud of us,' I said. 'She seemed quite pleased, but she's not too bothered about exam results.'

'I thought everyone's parents were bothered about exam results,' Helena said. 'I'd love to meet your mum. She sounds amazing.'

'Oh, she is,' I assured her. 'She certainly is.'

But I wasn't too sure about a meeting between Helena and my mother, and I certainly wasn't sure about having my friend to stay (Helena was clearly angling for an invitation). How would Helena fit into our household, with its eccentric set-up and its modest mod cons? And — more to the point — how would she react to my mother's interesting condition? I hadn't yet told my friends about Mum's pregnancy because I wasn't at all sure how I was going to go about it, and I had a feeling that Helena at least might well be shocked. While I, with my unfortunate experiences, preferred to forget about sex altogether, my friends were at an age where the subject was endlessly fascinating; an age when much speculation went on (usually in whispers after lights-out) as to what it was like and whether one's parents 'still did it'. The received opinion was that most of them were probably too old; so irrefutable evidence that my own unmarried mother not only still did it but was currently proudly manifesting its consequences was bound both to fascinate and to shock.

In the end, Mum inadvertently managed to break the news for me by sending me another postcard, this time a reproduction of a portrait of a tiny Italian princess, which managed to fall into the wrong hands at breakfast.

'I like to think your new brother or sister will look something like this,' she had written on the back. 'She looks like an Octavia, don't you think?'

By the time the postcard reached me, it had been all round the dining hall, and everyone knew about the baby. At the time, I even wondered whether Mum had done it on purpose, but then she wasn't to know that the card would be given to another girl by mistake, and besides, she would have taken it for granted that my friends already knew. Mum was never very good at secrets, and assumed that everyone else was the same.

'Gosh, Cass! Is your mum really having a baby?' Someone asked, obviously impressed.

'I thought she wasn't married,' added Helena helpfully.

'She isn't,' I said, tight-lipped and fuming.

'Well, how did she —?'

'How do you think?' I retorted rudely. 'I thought you all knew so much about this sort of thing.'

'I only asked!' Helena looked hurt.

'Then don't,' I snapped. 'I'm off to finish some prep.'

My classmates gave me a wide berth until lunchtime, when a very plump, very plain (albeit double-barrelled) girl with the unlikely name of Fern could no longer contain her curiosity.

'Tell us, Cass. You must be excited! I've always wanted a baby brother or sister.' (Fern was an only child, and my uncharitable view was that her parents, having seen what their particular recipe produced, had long since decided not to repeat the experiment.)

'Perhaps,' I said, choosing my words carefully and trying not to be unkind (people were often unkind to Fern). 'Perhaps it's different if your parents are married.'

'Ooh!' Fern's hand flew to her mouth, and her eyes widened. 'I forgot. I'm sorry!'

'Don't mention it,' I said coolly (I'd had time to calm down). 'But to answer your question, no. I'm not looking forward to it.'

'Why ever not? Don't you just love babies?'

'No, I don't.' If the truth be told I'd hardly ever met a baby, but current circumstances had not disposed me to feel kindly towards them.

'You'll be able to help with it.' Fern ploughed on, undeterred. 'Changing its nappies and feeding it and —'

'I shall do no such thing,' I interrupted. 'I want to have as little to do with it as possible.'

'You didn't really mean what you said, did you?' Helena asked later. 'I mean, about the baby. You must be — well — a bit interested in it. I'd love to have someone in my family who was younger than me,' she added with feeling.

'We're fine as we are,' I said. 'We don't need any more people in our house, and certainly not a baby. And I like being the youngest.'

'You might have a sister. Wouldn't you like a sister?'

'Certainly not!' For I had thought about this, and had decided that if the baby should be a boy (an eventuality which didn't seem to have occurred to Mum), then I would at least retain the distinction of being her only daughter.

'When's the baby going to arrive?' Helena persevered.

'I don't know.' And it was true. Amid all the excitement and the trauma, I had completely forgotten to ask this rather crucial question. 'How long do babies take?'

'I don't know. About a year, I think.'

'That's all right, then. Anything can happen in a year.' Thinking about it now, it seems strange that having been so thoroughly equipped with information regarding all the clinical details of the sexual act, no one had seen fit to tell us something as fundamental as the length of human gestation. But in my case at that stage ignorance was bliss, for having no idea of the imminence of the new arrival I was granted a brief reprieve from any immediate anxiety.

For the moment, despite frequent jolly reminders in Mum's letters, I tried to put the question of the baby to the back of my mind. For the first time since I started at St Andrew's, I was grateful that I had this separate world; a world of my own, which didn't include babies or Lodgers; a world where life was on the whole predictable and where other people — real grown-ups — made all the major decisions.

My fifteenth birthday took place towards the end of February, and was celebrated with a small but pleasing collection of presents from my friends and crowned by a surprise visit from Mum.

'Isn't this lovely?' she cried, when I was summoned to Miss Armitage's study to greet my unexpected guest. 'Miss Armitage was so kind to let me come.' (Birthday visits were not generally permitted.) 'Call Me Bill brought me. He's waiting in the car. As it's Saturday, we're allowed a whole hour together.'

'How did you manage it?' I asked, when we were alone together.

'I told her what a difficult time you'd been having. She was so understanding.'

'What difficult time?'

'Oh, you know.' Mum said. 'This and that. Now, why don't you open your presents?'

As usual, Mum's enthusiasm was so infectious and our time together so short that I decided to leave the subject of the difficult time for the moment and enjoy her visit. I took her up to the dormitory ('Oh, isn't it quaint!' cried Mum) and she laid several parcels out on my bed. There was a new wristwatch from her, a strange little china figurine from Greta, and a box of fudge from Lucas. Call Me Bill's present, she explained, was chauffeuring her here. I couldn't expect a present as well (I didn't). Best of all, there were four packets of chocolate biscuits and a huge sponge cake dripping icing and jam.

'Oh, Mum! This is great!' I put on the watch and admired the cake. 'Thanks so much.'

'And now, perhaps I can meet some of your friends.'

'I think they're all doing things. They're — busy.'

'Not all of them, surely, Cass. I've been so looking forward to seeing them.'

'Well ...'

'Are you ashamed of me?' She laughed. 'Is that it?'

'No. Of course not.'

'Well then.' She patted my hand. 'Introduce me to Helena, at least. I've heard so much about her.'

We found Helena sitting alone in our classroom, battling with the extra maths prep she had been given.

'Cass! Thank goodness! You can help me with this.'

'Helena, this is my mother.'

'Oh! I'm so sorry. I didn't see you.' Helena stood up and shook hands with Mum. 'You've come for Cass's birthday. How nice.'

'Yes, isn't it?' Mum gave Helena one of the radiant smiles she used to melt (and, I suspect, break) hearts. 'Oh, poor you,' she went on, seeing the screwed-up pieces of paper littering the floor and the pink and flustered face of Helena. 'I hated maths. Such a ridiculous subject, I always thought.'

'Me too,' Helena sighed. 'And Cass is so clever at it.'

'Isn't she? I don't know where she gets it from,' Mum said, inadvertently drawing attention yet again to my fatherless state.

Helena, seeing the connection, blushed. My mother, who had no insight into her own lack of tact, did not.

'Oh, algebra.' Mum peered over Helena's shoulder. 'All that business of x and y. I never could make head nor tail of it. Why don't you leave that and come and have a piece of Cass's birthday cake?'

'That would be lovely —' Helena began.

'I thought we'd leave it until after supper,' I said quickly, for Mum had already outstayed her hour, and I feared repercussions.

'Midnight feasts in the dorm!' Mum clapped her hands girlishly. 'What fun!'

'No, Mum. Not midnight feasts in the dorm. Something to share with my friends after measly beans on toast. Come on. We'd better leave Helena in peace.'

'Then perhaps we'll meet again, Helena. You must come and stay with us some time. I know Cass would love to have you, wouldn't you Cass?'

'Of course,' I said, but without much conviction. I liked keeping my school and home lives separate, and suspected that any mingling of the two could lead to complications.

'Oh, I'd just love to,' Helena said. 'That's so kind of you.'

'We must fix something up, then.' Mum beamed at her, then looked at her watch. 'Goodness! I ought to be going. Come and see me off, Cass, and you can say hello to Call Me Bill. Goodbye, Helena. Hope to see you again soon.'

Later that evening in our dormitory, we divided up my birthday cake with a ruler (all we could find) and served it on sheets of paper torn from an exercise book. Like all Mum's cakes, it was messy but delicious.

'I think your mum's wonderful,' Helena sighed. 'I always get birthday cakes from the cake shop; all hard and dry and tasting of cardboard. Not a bit like this,' she added, wiping jam off her chin.

I had always rather fancied a posh shop-bought cake, with icing-sugar frills round the edges and my name in pink lettering, but maybe Helena was right. At least Mum went to trouble with her cake-making, even if the end results would never win her any prizes.

Altogether, it had been a most satisfactory day, and as I licked the last sticky crumbs from my fingers, I reflected that life was on the whole pretty good. I was doing well in my studies, I had just enough friends for the maintenance of self-respect without the risk of being crowded, and I had it on fairly good authority that there wouldn't be any baby for some time yet. Maybe Mum had been right about boarding school after all. It could be that it was just what I had needed.

Fourteen

'Cass.' Mum's awake now, her blue eyes lucid, her face still free from pain.

'Yes, Mum. I'm here.' I pull my chair closer.

'About my funeral.'

'Yes.' Oh, please don't talk about your funeral. Not now. Not yet. I'm not ready for your funeral.

'About flowers.'

'Yes?'

'I don't want no-flowers-by-request.'

'You mean, you'd like to have flowers?'

'Oh yes. Lots of flowers. I'd like everyone to send flowers.'

'I'll — I'll make sure they do, Mum.'

'That's all right, then.' A little sigh, eyes closed, resting. 'You can take the flowers home, you know.'

'What, all of them?'

'Yes. I want everyone to take some flowers home. Mustn't waste them.'

'That's a nice idea, Mum.'

'It is, isn't it?' She smiles. Looks almost happy. My mother loves planning things. 'And, hymns.'

'Yes?'

'None of that lead kindly light stuff.'

'Not if you don't want it.'

'I don't.' She shifts restlessly. 'Nice jolly ones. Jerusalem. And that nice Welsh one.'

'Guide Me, Oh Thou Great Redeemer?'

'That's the one.'

'We'll have that one, then.'

'Cass?'

'Yes?'

'Where's Lucas?'

'He came last night. He'll be here later.'

'Perhaps he'll read something at the funeral.'

'I'm sure he will.'

'Do you think there'll be enough money for horses?'

'Horses?'

'To pull the coffin. I always fancied being pulled along by a team of shiny black horses.'

There isn't the money — there's never been any money — but what does it matter?

'Of course. If you want horses, you shall have horses.'

Another smile.

'*They'll all notice me then, won't they?*'

'*They certainly will.*'

Oh, Mum! Shiny black horses and lots of flowers. We can certainly manage the flowers, and perhaps we can run to one shiny black horse. I'll do my best. There must be someone who would lend us their shiny black horse.

My grandmother died suddenly that half-term. She too had wanted black horses to pull her funeral carriage. As she had explained to anyone who would listen, a team of black horses was only fitting. It wasn't every day that Napoleon was buried, and things had to be done properly. She had given her instructions in halting French, a feat which greatly impressed Mum.

'Her brain's shot to pieces, Cass, and yet she remembers that Napoleon would have spoken in French. I had to get one of the nurses to translate for me.'

Notwithstanding her damaged brain, my grandmother had managed to plan her funeral in minutest detail, although of course her grandiose ideas were out of the question. For there could be no cathedral service of thanksgiving, no grand procession, no reception for foreign dignitaries in her honour. The daughter of a Norfolk labourer, but with her position in life briefly elevated during her short marriage to my respectably middle-class grandfather, she would be buried alongside the other also-rans of the humble parish where she had spent most of her life.

When Mum received the news of her mother's death, she was distraught.

'Poor Mother. Poor poor Mother,' she wept. 'I should have done more. I should have kept her here. We'd have managed somehow.'

'We wouldn't, Mum. How could we have managed?' I reasoned. 'What with your work and — everything else.'

'But she should have come first. I ought to have put her first.' Mum reached for another handkerchief. 'What kind of daughter was I? You tell me that, Cass.'

I could have said that she was the sort of daughter who couldn't possibly have coped with an ageing incontinent Napoleon with tendencies to violence and sleepwalking, but my words would have been wasted. Mum had to grieve, and since it appeared that guilt was an integral part of the process, we had to allow this cocktail of emotions to run its course.

The funeral was fixed for the following week. Call Me Bill made most of the arrangements over the phone, since Mum was in no fit state to organize anything, and I was allowed to stay off school for a further two days in order to attend it. I myself was not especially affected by our loss, since I had scarcely known my grandmother and had had little recent contact with her. Even when I was small and she was in control of her faculties, I had been well aware that she looked upon children as an inconvenience at best, and so I had never had the chance to establish any sort of relationship with her. I did, however, wonder that a woman who appeared to be so cold and at times even ruthless could have produced a daughter as open and affectionate as my mother.

We travelled to the funeral by rail, a journey involving several hours and two changes of train. The weather was cold and our carriages unheated, and Mum alternately railed against herself and wept. Lucas and I consumed quantities of the sandwiches we had brought with us (Mum refused to eat anything) and spent our time reading or playing battleships and hangman on scraps of paper. It was not a happy journey.

The funeral itself was conducted in a small parish church by a wild-haired vicar with a beard who looked, I thought, exactly like John the Baptist. He had the appearance and the air of someone who might well have blazed a trail on a diet of locusts and wild honey, and he conducted the service with energy and humour. Our grandmother was then laid to rest in the pretty churchyard, and we all adjourned to the parish hall for tea and cakes (there had been no one to organize a proper wake, much to Mum's distress).

Here things became more interesting, because we encountered relatives whom we had barely heard of (although they all appeared to have heard of us), and for almost the first time in my life, I had a sense of family. I also got the distinct impression that Mum was the black sheep of that family, and that it was unlikely her present condition would do much to redeem her.

But as next of kin to the deceased (my mother had been an only child), Mum was deserving of some sympathy, and having miraculously recovered her composure, she milked the situation to the full.

As I watched her kissing the pale powdery cheeks and embracing the frail bodies of the friends and family members who came up to offer their condolences (why was everyone so *old*?), I was bowled over yet again by Mum's charm; her smile, the tilt of her head, the way she listened to people as though there was no one in the world she would rather be with. These were rare traits, and although they were genuine enough, she was not above using them to her advantage. This, I suspected, was how she tempted willing Lodgers into our damp basement and even more willing lovers into her bed. At her best, my mother was quite simply irresistible.

'There,' she said, after we'd taken our leave and set off on our walk back to the station. 'I think I've managed to stave off the worst of the gossip. At least for the time being. They might even manage to overlook the — well, the baby now.'

'Does it matter?' I asked, for after all, we rarely had any kind of contact with these people.

'It's a good point, Cass. But yes. It does matter. In spite of everything, I mind what people think.'

'Why? Why do you mind?' For quite often it seemed as though my mother couldn't have cared less what people thought of her.

'Because I haven't made much of a success of my life, have I? I haven't done anything particularly clever. I haven't really achieved anything. But if people like me, well, that's something, isn't it?'

'Of course people like you. Everyone likes you. My friends think you're wonderful.'

'Do they really?'

'You know they do. I've told you.'

'I don't deserve it, though, do I?'

'Oh, Mum! Of course you deserve it.'

'At the moment I don't feel as though I deserve anything.' Once again, the tears were very near the surface. My mother thrived on people and attention, and now that the attention had ceased and we were on our own again, she seemed to wilt like a plucked flower.

'Come on, Mum,' said Lucas, as anxious as I was to get her onto the train in one emotional piece. 'You've done really well today. Keep it up just a bit longer, and we'll soon be home.'

But it was too late. Once again, the tears were pouring down Mum's cheeks, landing in bright splashes on the red wool of her scarf.

'I miss her,' she sobbed, fumbling in her pocket for a handkerchief. 'I'm going to miss her so much. I know she's not been — herself for some time, but she's my mum. My poor little mum,' she repeated, stumbling on the kerb and clutching at my arm. 'And she'll never see the baby now, will she? My poor baby will have no grandparents at all.'

Somehow, we managed to get her home, steering her on and off trains, mopping her up and patting and soothing her as best we could. By the time we got home we were all exhausted.

Greta had stayed up in her dressing gown to welcome us back, although it was well past midnight.

'Nice-cup-of-tea?' she said, as Mum fell through the front door and into her arms.

And for once, I could have kissed her. Greta might have been a fusspot — she was often infuriating — but she was kind, and most of all, she was one of us; in her own way, far more a member of the family than my late grandmother had ever been.

'Oh, Greta!' I said, as I took off my coat and peeled my gloves from my frozen hands. 'What would we do without you?'

Fifteen

I made the decision to stay at home until the following week, for I was worried about Mum. She was in a bad state, and while to a certain extent this was to be expected after her bereavement, the signs were ominous. She took to her bed, eating little and subsisting on cups of tea, and when she wasn't asleep, she spent her time weeping or simply gazing out of the window, leaving her room only to go to the bathroom.

We had been down this road before. Mum never did things by halves, and her depressions were full-blown and frightening; and while they didn't usually last long, everyone dreaded them. It was these (mercifully rare) occasions that brought it home to all of us how central Mum was to the mood if not the running of the household, for everyone relied on her cheerful good humour, her hospitality, her knack of making people laugh and her sheer kindness.

The house fell suddenly quiet, and we all crept around speaking in whispers as though someone much closer than my grandmother had died. The wireless was silent; there were no noisy recitals on the ironing board; even The Dog, who it seemed could do depression almost as well as Mum, lay outside her bedroom door and whimpered miserably.

'Mum, what can I do to help?' I asked, bringing in yet another cup of tea and setting it down on the bedside table. 'There must be something we can do for you.'

Mum looked at me as though noticing me for the first time.

'Why aren't you back at school, Cass? You shouldn't be here at all.'

'I stayed on to help. I can't leave you like this.'

'But do the school know?'

'Of course they do. Call Me Bill rang and explained.' It had seemed more appropriate to ask an adult to phone on my behalf than to ring the school myself.

'But you can't miss school, Cass. You must go back.'

'I can. I'll be fine. I've got some reading to be getting on with, and I can easily catch up next week.' I paused. 'Mum, shouldn't you see a doctor? Get some — pills or something?'

'If you like.' Mum patted my hand absently. 'Though I'm not sure pills will help.'

Dr Mackenzie, a wholesome no-nonsense Scotsman who knew our family well, was duly summoned, and having run the gauntlet of The Dog — who seemed to have appointed himself Mum's guard dog — he was reassuringly down to earth.

'Now then, Mrs Fitzpatrick —'

'Miss.'

'Miss Fitzpatrick, then. What's all this about?'

Mum shrugged and gave him a wan little-girl smile. Dr Mackenzie sat down on the bed.

'You've lost your mother, and of course you're upset. But you've your new little one to think about. You can't go starving yourself and worrying your family like this.'

'I'm not starving —'

'Cassandra here says you've hardly eaten anything in the past week. Isn't that right, Cassandra?'

As Mum's female next of kin, I had thought it appropriate that I should be present at this interview, and as it turned out this was just as well.

'Just cups of tea,' I said. 'And a bit of toast.'

'A bit of toast? Have you no sense, woman?'

Mum looked startled. She wasn't accustomed to being challenged in this way.

'You may well look shocked.' Dr Mackenzie got out his instruments and took Mum's blood pressure. 'A bit on the low side,' he said. 'You need to eat, and take exercise, and get some fresh air in your lungs. What kind of a bairn are you going to produce if you go on like this?'

'I hadn't thought.' Mum looked down at her hands.

'No. I daresay not. Now, I shall be round tomorrow morning, and I want to find you out of bed and dressed.'

'No pills?' Mum asked.

The doctor patted her shoulder kindly. 'There's no pills for what you're suffering from, my dear. It has to take its time. But while it's doing that, you've a life to get on with.' He stood up and closed his bag. 'A life and a family.'

'Is there anything we ought to be doing for her?' I asked, as I showed Dr Mackenzie out.

'Yes. A good deal less than you're doing now. Wait on her, and she'll never leave that bed of hers. She's not had it easy, your mum, but she needs to get back to normal. To start functioning again. And you can help her do that.'

'Is it all right if I go back to school?'

'Back to school? Of course you should be back at school! You've your own life to lead, lassie. You need your friends, too.'

His kindness brought tears to my eyes, and I suddenly realized how tired I was.

'You're a good daughter, but don't you try to be too good a daughter. It'll not do either of you any good. Away with you to that school of yours. Get back to normal. I'll keep an eye on your mum.'

'Doctor?'

'Yes?'

'When — when's the baby due?'

'Has she not told you?'

'I suppose I just never got round to asking.'

'Oh — about June time I think. Not so long to go now.'

'*June!*'

'Aye. June.' He laughed. 'Don't they teach you anything at school nowadays?'

'Not — that. They told us all about — well, you know — but not how long.'

'Not how long, eh? Then it's a bit of a shock for you?'

I nodded.

'Don't you worry. It'll be all right. Your mum's a strong woman. She'll manage.' He looked at me and smiled. 'And so will you. But you've to remember, this is her bairn, not yours. She's done it all before. You get on with your schooling and enjoy being young, Cassandra. It doesn't last long, let me tell you. Don't you go taking on your mum's problems. You'll have plenty of your own, soon enough.'

If only he knew that I felt I had quite enough problems as it was. I would have loved to have been able to talk to this good kindly man, and I wondered what it would be like to have a father like him; someone strong and sympathetic; someone who would go out to work every morning carrying a briefcase, and come home with a nice safe pay cheque at the end of the month; someone who would protect me from people like Uncle Rupert and Alex.

After the doctor's visit, Mum made an effort to pull herself together. She got up and dressed the next day, and made arrangements to return to work the following week. She even baked a cake.

But she was not herself, and I was worried. I knew it made no sense to stay at home, but it also seemed wrong to leave Mum to Lucas and Greta. I thought of the disparate collection of relatives who had attended my grandmother's funeral, and wondered where they all were. Would any of them come to our rescue, if we needed them? I very much doubted it.

I returned to school on the Sunday afternoon by train (no car was necessary as I only had a small suitcase). Call Me Bill drove me to the station and waved me off, and while I felt uneasy at leaving everyone else to cope with Mum's precarious mental state, I also felt a guilty sense of relief. After all, Dr Mackenzie had told me to get on with my own life, and so that was what I should do.

Sixteen

The rest of that term passed uneventfully, and I managed to achieve my aim of coming top overall in the end-of-term exams. I returned home for the Easter holidays with an excellent school report and feeling more confident than I had in a long time.

Mum seemed almost back to her normal self, and insisted on organizing the annual Easter egg hunt in the garden, although Lucas and I tried to tell her that we were far too old for such frivolities.

'Nonsense! No one's too old for Easter eggs, and this makes them more fun,' said Mum, undeterred, but she invited some neighbours' children round to join in and salvage our dignity.

Mum's size had increased considerably since half-term, and it was with a kind of horrified fascination that I observed her swollen body and breasts. I had never had any close contact with pregnancy, and hadn't realized that the human body could expand so rapidly and in such an astonishing way. It did nothing to change my feelings about all things sexual, for I certainly never wanted to look like that. What must it feel like to be *inhabited*; to have someone else conducting their own small separate existence inside you, with no apparent reference to your own? There'd been a time when I had assumed that one day I would be a mother; now, I was absolutely determined it should never happen.

But Mum seemed to be enjoying her pregnancy, and was looking forward keenly to the birth of her baby. Richard had decorated the box room, and courtesy of Greta, who was in her element, the baby had enough knitwear to last it until it started school.

'Won't it be a bit hot?' I asked, fingering shawls and matinee jackets, bonnets and bootees. After all, there had to be a limit to the amount of warm clothing a June baby would require, even in the coolest of British summers.

'Do you think so?' Mum picked up a little jumpsuit knitted in a startling shade of purple. 'Maybe you're right, Cass. Perhaps I should get some cotton things as well.' She put the jumpsuit back in the drawer. 'I've forgotten what they need. It's been a long time.'

Other things Mum appeared to have forgotten included a cot and a pram, although she had purchased a plastic bath, a matching potty and enough nappies for a small army of incontinent infants. Mum's memory wasn't so much bad as selective. The rest of us did our best to help her fill in the gaps, but my knowledge of babies was scanty and Greta's non-existent. Call Me Bill was helpful in the field of fringe pharmaceuticals, and brought home liberal supplies of baby powder and nappy cream, most of them with suspiciously faded labels.

But Lucas showed little interest in the baby. Having recently shed the worst of his spots and caught up with his new bass voice and gangling limbs, he had suddenly become popular. He spent a lot of time in the bathroom doing interesting things to his hair and spraying himself with pungent smells, while the telephone was kept busy with breathy female voices asking to speak to him. He seemed unaware that the journey upon which he was embarking with such enthusiasm was the same one whose benefits — if that's what they could be called — our mother was about to reap. When it came to it, I concluded sadly, everything seemed to come down to sex.

I managed to divert Mum from her prenatal trance long enough to get her to buy me my school summer uniform of, among other things, 'blue checked dresses, four' (Mum sent me back with three), 'white ankle socks, six pairs' (I had four) and 'white tennis dresses, two' ('Whatever do you want with two tennis dresses?' Mum cried. I was grateful that she saw the point of even one tennis dress). And Call Me Bill drove me back to school for the new term.

Looking back, I remember that summer term as a magical time. In the forgiving light of early summer, the main school house seemed to shed its air of menace and looked almost inviting, while the gardens really came into their own. Smooth lawns were edged with a variety of shrubs and shaded by two large cypress trees, and beyond the main garden there was an outdoor swimming pool discreetly concealed behind a high hedge. There was also a large meadow which became a carpet of the kinds of wild flowers so rarely seen these days. Bees and butterflies busied themselves among drifts of cowslips and buttercups, which later gave way to pale purple orchids, scabious, vetch, harebells and a myriad other flowers.

Occasionally, when the weather was unusually hot, we were allowed to have our lessons out of doors, and we would sit on the grass under one of the cypresses, making notes in exercise books propped on our knees, the sound of the teacher's voice interrupted only by the calling of wood pigeons and the distant sound of a cuckoo. To this day, I shall never be able to hear a cuckoo without being taken straight back to the smell of newly mown grass and the sound of Miss Kennedy reading the poetry of Browning: 'God's in his heaven. All's right with the world.'

One evening towards the end of June, I was summoned to Miss Armitage's office to receive news of the birth of my new sister.

'Mother and baby are both doing well,' she told me. 'I'm sure you'd like to speak to your mother. You may use the office telephone when she comes out of hospital next week.'

I left the office unsure of how I should be feeling. Of course I was relieved that Mum was OK, but not especially pleased at the news, and I certainly wasn't looking forward to seeing the new arrival. Was there something wrong with me?

My friends did nothing to help my flagging self-esteem.

'Oh, how wonderful!' cooed Helena. 'You are lucky! A sister, too.'

'I already told you. I didn't want a sister.'

'You'll change your mind when you see her. I'm sure you will.'

'I wouldn't count on it.'

'Oh, Cass. You're such a misery sometimes.'

'On the contrary. I'm usually perfectly cheerful. I just don't happen to want a baby sister. Or any kind of baby, come to that.'

'A new little baby,' said Fern dreamily. 'Oh, Cass! You'll love it. I know you will. How can you not love a new little baby?'

What was wrong with everyone? I wondered crossly. Why did babies render perfectly sensible human beings all gooey and sentimental? After all, babies were only underdeveloped people, and hadn't we all started out like that? I tried to imagine Miss Armitage as a baby, or Call Me Bill. Had Call Me Bill's entrance into the world been greeted with glad cries of 'It's a boy!'? Had people once cooed and gurgled over Miss Armitage? It was hard to imagine. The whole baby thing defeated me. I could see that babies were necessary — that we all had to start somewhere — but why did everyone have to make such a *fuss*?

When I spoke to her on the telephone the following week, Mum was euphoric.

'You should see her, Cass. She's beautiful. She's got lots of hair and big blue eyes, and such tiny little fingers and toes.' It would appear that Mum had gone as daft as everyone else.

'You're not still calling her Octavia, are you?' I asked.

'Of course I am! She's always been Octavia. Why should I change my mind now? You'll come round to it, Cass. She just is an Octavia. Octavia Beatrice, after Mother. I thought of calling her Octavia Cassandra after you, but it was a bit of a mouthful. I hope you don't mind.'

'Don't mention it,' I said, relieved that at least I wouldn't have to share my name.

A few days later, I received in the post a grainy black and white photograph of Mum in her nightdress holding in her arms something tiny and swaddled. It could have been a doll, or even a small animal for all the resemblance it bore to a human being, and I hid the photograph away. If I showed it to my friends, it would be one more thing for them to swoon over, and by now I was thoroughly sick of the whole subject of babies.

End of term came, and Call Me Bill, who in the last year had become quite a member of the family (even to the extent of converting a dusty storeroom into a bedroom for himself), fetched me home in his car.

Mum greeted me in the hallway, holding a swaddled bundle.

'Meet your sister, Cass!'

Obediently, I inspected the bundle. And fell instantly in love.

Of course, I had seen babies before, from a distance, and they really did seem to me to look much the same. I tended to feel that once you'd seen one, you'd more or less seen them all. I acknowledged that their parents could no doubt tell them apart, but was pretty sure that no one else could.

But this baby was different.

'Goodness!' I said, taken aback.

'Yes. Isn't she?' Mum laughed. 'Do you want to hold her?'

I put down my bags and very carefully took the bundle in my arms. The baby stared up into my face with unblinking blue eyes from beneath a shock of dark hair, her tiny mouth pursed as though considering what to make of me, one walnut-sized fist showing above the blanket.

'Iss beautiful baby, no?' Greta was standing beaming beside Mum, as though the baby had been the result of some joint effort involving herself.

'Yes. Oh, yes.' I laid a finger against the baby's cheek, and it was like touching a petal. 'I didn't know babies could be — like this.'

Poor little Octavia Beatrice. Such a big name for such a tiny person. She was to affect our lives in a way none of us could have imagined.

Seventeen

'Cass?' She grips my hand.

'Yes?'

'I'm frightened.'

'Of course you are.' Who wouldn't be?

'It'll be all right, won't it? After all —' a small smile — 'lots of people have done it before. Lots of people have died.'

'Yes. Of course they have.'

'Shakespeare, Queen Victoria, Charlie Chaplin. They've all done it.'

'Yes.'

She moves restlessly.

'Do you believe in Heaven, Cass?'

'I don't know, Mum. I'd like to. I do feel that something of all of us lives on.'

For how could anyone as full of life as Mum cease to exist; simply stop, as though someone had turned off the ignition? Somehow, the idea of no afterlife seems even more implausible than the comforting picture of clouds and angels in the illustrated children's bible I was given as a child. I have often thought that if death were not so commonplace — if we weren't all in the same boat, heading towards that same unavoidable destination — it would simply be too outrageous to be believable.

'I've had a good life, really.' She sighs. 'I've been lucky.'

Oh Mum! How can you say that, after all you've been through? But then my mother has never been a complainer. She has known depression and disappointment, loneliness and tragedy, but while I have often seen her weeping, and sometimes desperate, I don't think I have ever heard her complain. At her best, she has been capable of the kind of happiness which is totally infectious, lighting up those around her and dispelling ill-temper in even the most curmudgeonly of companions.

Mum was certainly happy in the months following Octavia's birth. She appeared to achieve a degree of serenity I had never seen before, and the household seemed to settle down as though with a sigh of contentment, not untempered with relief.

The weather that summer was fine, and although we didn't go away (there had rarely been enough money for summer holidays, and Lucas and I had long ceased to expect them), as always we managed to enjoy ourselves. Lucas's new life largely excluded me, not least because my lack of interest in the opposite sex was equalled only by his preoccupation with it, but I was happy simply to be at home. I spent my time walking with The Dog, crying over Thomas Hardy (my latest discovery), and catching up with Myra and some of my other friends.

And then there was Octavia. Her neat round head, her peachy skin, the watchfulness of her navy-blue eyes, the feathery crescents of her lashes when she was asleep — they all combined to fascinate and enchant me, and in my enslaved state I was happy to do for her anything Mum asked. Helena and Fern would have been proud of me, for I changed her nappies, bathed her and took her out for walks, and it was I who was rewarded with her first wobbly smile.

Only one thing about Octavia bothered me. Ridiculous as it might seem, I found myself scrutinizing her for any sign, any clue, which might identify her father, for as things were, I felt as though I only knew half of her; it was almost as though that other half — the unknown half — would remain forever a stranger. There had been a time when I had done the same with my own reflected image, ruling out the features which were Mum's and building up a (probably totally inaccurate) picture of my father from the bits of me which didn't match hers.

Octavia was certainly very like Mum, with the same creamy complexion, and hair which was already showing hints of auburn, but she was a very long baby (Mum was fairly short), and I suspected that her father had probably been tall. A tall stranger with a beard and problems. It certainly wasn't much to go on, and as time went by, I abandoned my researches. I didn't know what Mum planned to tell Octavia, for she certainly seemed to remember more about this baby's conception than she had about mine or Lucas's, but that bridge needn't be crossed for some time yet, so I put the thought to the back of my mind.

Mum's attitude to Octavia was doting but scatty, and I noticed in her the same haphazard attitude to mothering which Lucas and I had experienced when we were younger. She obviously adored the baby, but was quite happy to leave her care to the rest of us if it suited her. Octavia didn't seem to have any kind of routine, and appeared not to expect any. Mum fed her when she cried, got her up if she wanted to play with her or show her off, and put her back in her crib when she had better things to do. One minute she would be all over the baby, taking her out to visit friends, playing her lullabies on a cracked record (singing along with the inevitable ironing board accompaniment), even taking her to the clinic to be weighed and crowing proudly over her progress. The next, she would be off out ('Cass, look after Octavia would you, there's a dear'), and might not return until late.

It gave me some insight into the way Lucas and I must have been treated as infants, for while I knew that our upbringing had had little structure, I had no idea this had gone as far back as our babyhood. It went some way to explain our indifference to order or routine, and — at least when we were younger — our unquestioning acceptance of the unexpected.

Although I enjoyed looking after Octavia, there were times when I couldn't help feeling taken for granted. But this rarely lasted long, for just as I was beginning to wonder whether Mum was pleased to have me home for my own sake, or more because I provided a free babysitting service, she would bake my favourite cake, or take me out to buy me a new dress she could ill afford, and I would feel valued again. I know this wasn't a deliberate ruse to keep me sweet — Mum was incapable of being that devious — but I did feel as though everything was done more on a whim than with any proper planning. She had a childlike knack of living for the moment, and while this could be infuriating if it required childcare at the drop of a hat, it could also be enormous fun if it involved a trip out or an unexpected treat.

Sometimes I worried about how she would manage when I went back to school. Greta was fine, but she tended to fuss, and while she too adored Octavia, she wasn't what I would call a natural where babies were concerned. Twice she let Octavia roll off the bed onto the floor, and on one occasion she nearly drowned her in the bath. I also caught her apparently trying to feed the baby chocolate.

'Greta! What are you doing?' I caught Greta's hand.

'Chocolate. She like, no?' Greta looked hurt.

'No! I mean, she might like the taste, but she's much too young.'

'She lick,' Greta countered.

'Of course she licked it. She licks everything. That doesn't mean it's good for her.'

'I try.' Greta's eyes filled with tears.

'Of course you tried.' I put my arms round Greta's shoulders. 'You're very kind. You're good to all of us. It's just that — well, perhaps we ought to ask Mum before we give the baby anything new.'

'OK. I ask.' Reluctantly, Greta put away her chocolate.

But as I might have known, Mum was no use at all.

'Chocolate? Of course she can have a little lick of chocolate from time to time. What harm can it do?'

I had no idea what harm chocolate could do to a young baby; all I knew was that it didn't seem appropriate. But in the event it didn't seem to affect Octavia in the least.

The summer holidays came to an end all too soon, and almost before I knew it, it was time to return to school. Lucas, who had recently passed his driving test, offered to take me in the borrowed van, and while the prospect didn't exactly thrill me, the thought of a journey with Mum plus baby and quite possibly The Dog was even worse, so I accepted the offer.

Although I was much more settled than I had been a year ago, and was looking forward to the new school year, I was apprehensive about leaving home and I knew I would miss Octavia dreadfully.

'You will take care of things, Lucas, won't you?' I said.

'Take care of things? What do you mean?' Lucas was driving much too close to the car in front, but I knew better than to interfere.

'Well, you know. Keep an eye on Mum, make sure the baby's OK, see that Greta doesn't start feeding her apple strudel. That sort of thing.'

Lucas grinned.

'We've managed a whole year without you, Cass. I'm sure we'll cope.'

'But Octavia —'

'Octavia will be fine.' Lucas pulled out to overtake, and I closed my eyes. It seemed to me that much of my time travelling to and from school was spent with my eyes shut. 'After all,' he added, as we regained our side of the road, 'you and I survived, didn't we?'

'Yes, I suppose so.'

But I wasn't convinced. There was something fragile, something almost impermanent about Octavia, and I feared for her. She was so serene, so undemanding, so obliging; she was almost too good to be true. If it didn't sound so corny I would have described her as truly angelic; almost not of this world.

Eighteen

Mum's letters that term were some of the happiest I had received from her. Granted, they were still written on odd scraps of paper — the backs of envelopes, shopping lists, the electricity bill (a red one, needless to say) — but they were busy with news and plans.

She had a new job at the dry cleaner's ('Only part-time, but such fun, Cass.' Only Mum could manage to have fun in a dry cleaner's), the autumn colours were the best she had seen for years, The Dog had learnt to 'die for the Queen' (he was probably just exhausted), and she had found a new Lodger ('Such a good-looking young man, Cass.' Oh dear). As for Octavia, she was full of smiles and Mum swore she could feel a tooth coming through. As Lucas had predicted, life at home was evidently proceeding quite happily without me.

I came home for half-term and was mortified to find that Octavia appeared to have forgotten who I was while Greta was now firmly in place as mother substitute during Mum's frequent absences. In spite of her initial misgivings, Octavia seemed happy to have me look after her, but Greta had become proprietorial and bossy (possibly in retaliation for the chocolate incident), and I had to mind my step if I wasn't to encroach on this new and treasured territory. Lucas's attention was equally divided between the latest girlfriend (a leggy blonde) and consideration of his future (A levels loomed); and Call Me Bill was preoccupied with his new hobby, compiling a slim volume of his own verse. None of us had been aware that Call Me Bill was a closet poet, and when he had coyly submitted some of his poems to our scrutiny, I think we all very much wished that that was where he'd stayed.

I remember reading a poem entitled 'Avalanche', which included such memorable lines as:

A froth and a fever of snow in Geneva,
A tumble of skis on the high Pyrenees

'It's very — original,' I said, as I handed the closely written sheet of paper back to him.

'Yes. Isn't it?' he said happily, replacing his precious creation in its folder. 'I'm so glad you like it, Cass. Especially as you're the artistic one. It means a lot to me.'

I wasn't aware that I had actually said I liked the poem or that I was particularly artistic, but I seemed to have satisfied Call Me Bill, and I was pleased about that. I also felt humbled by his appreciation, and ashamed that Lucas and I had privately giggled over lines where sense had often been sacrificed for the sake of flowery alliteration. After all, who was I (currently struggling to understand the great T.S. Eliot) to judge Call Me Bill's poems?

The new Lodger was indeed good-looking — even beautiful — and it was Lucas who pointed out that he was almost certainly gay.

'Do you think so?' Mum said, when he mentioned it to her.

'Of course he is, Mum. Can't you see? The way he dresses, the way he walks. Apart from anything else, he's too — too domestic to be anything else.'

'Oh, what a waste,' sighed Mum. 'And I've asked him to stay for Christmas, too.'

For my own part, I thought he was the nicest Lodger we'd had in a long time. He had all the characteristics I liked about men without posing any kind of threat. He was fun, intelligent, and wonderful with Octavia, and I felt happier knowing he was around to keep an extra eye on things.

The rest of the term flew by, and almost before I knew it I was home again for Christmas. Octavia had grown, and was if anything even more beautiful, with the beginnings of a head of bright auburn curls, those huge blue eyes and little pink bud of a mouth. The halls were decked, Mum was in festive mood, and there were enough jolly people around (including the gay Lodger) for Mum to feel content. There was even a dusting of snow.

But I had my own preoccupations. This was a big year for me as well as for Lucas, for I had O levels in the summer and mock exams as soon as I returned to school, as well as possible A level subjects to consider. I spent much of the holiday in my room revising, swathed in cardigans and coats (my room had only a small electric heater), eating extra strong mints and drinking coffee.

'Do come and join us,' Mum would say, appearing at my door at regular intervals. 'We see so little of you, and it's *Christmas*.'

She failed to see that my achievements, of which she was so proud, came at a price; I had to work. She seemed to think that my ability was such that all I had to do was simply turn up for examinations and spill the contents of my remarkable brain onto a piece of paper. But then by her own admission, Mum had never passed an exam in her life, and had scant understanding of what was involved.

During that spring term, I had little time to think about home. Mum's brief letters continued to arrive with their snippets of (still cheery) news, but I was absorbed by my work and thoughts of my future.

I did well in my mock exams, and there was talk of aiming for a place at Oxford or Cambridge if my O-level results came up to expectations. I was terribly excited. I had visited Cambridge once, and had been bowled over by the beauty of the older colleges, with their rosy brick and their ancient walkways, their lawns and their quaint old-fashioned courts. I could think of no greater privilege than to be a part of such a place; to form my own small link in that centuries-long chain of tradition and learning. For the first time in my life, I was imagining a life away from the confines of home or school; a life of my choosing; a grown-up life; a life which was *my own*.

When I came home at Easter, Octavia was crawling and pulling herself up on pieces of furniture. I gathered that she was well ahead of the usual milestones, but then as Greta kept pointing out, she was an exceptional child. She was also amazingly self-sufficient for one so small, and would spend happy hours examining picture books (as often as not upside down) or trying to balance one brightly coloured brick on top of another. She rarely cried, and communicated by small kittenish mewings to express happiness or displeasure. Mum maintained that she was musical, and she certainly appeared to enjoy the ironing-board recitals.

'I think *she* really will play the piano,' Mum said, in a rare if oblique reference to my own brief but failed piano-playing career. 'Someone in this family ought to,' she added wistfully.

Poor Mum. The least ambitious of parents, she had always allowed us simply to be ourselves and to develop in our own ways, but she had nonetheless made no secret of the fact that she would have loved one of us to be a musician. Over the years, she had become convinced that she herself could have been a fine pianist if she had had lessons, and that her life would then have turned out very differently.

I returned to school for the summer term and O levels. That June was baking hot, and we sat our exams in the new sports hall (discreetly positioned behind trees so as not to interfere with all that Victorian gloom), whose glass walls and polished floors encased us in a stifling atmosphere, compounded by the blistering heat and the collective anxiety of the hapless candidates inside. We sat at our carefully spaced desks, fanning ourselves with our question papers, exchanging despairing glances under the stern gaze of the invigilator. Would this summer *never* end?

The last day of the exams was marked by torrential thunderstorms, and I can still picture us all as we ran from the sports hall, whooping with joy and relief. Once outside, we dropped our pens and pencils in the mud and danced in the rain, stretching out our arms, lifting up our faces, running our ink-stained fingers through our dripping hair, revelling in the coolness and the wet and the wonderful fresh smell of damp earth and grass. No one tried to stop us as we whirled and pranced and shouted. One girl even threw off her school frock and tore across the lawn half-naked, finishing with a victory roll down a grassy bank into the bushes. The exams were over; the long summer holidays beckoned.

The very next day I was summoned to Miss Armitage's office. I went along, carefree and unsuspecting. I had done nothing wrong, so I had nothing to fear. Perhaps I was to be awarded a prize at the forthcoming speech day, and had been summoned to give her my choice of books. I had already made my decision in anticipation of just such an eventuality; I had recently discovered Elizabeth Gaskell, and would choose as many of her works as the prize money would allow. I was already anticipating weeks of joyous summer reading.

The moment I was admitted to the office, I knew something was wrong. Miss Armitage wasn't sitting in her usual chair, but was pacing in front of her desk, her expression serious.

'I think you'd better sit down, Cassandra.' She pointed to a chair. 'Please, Cassandra. Please sit.'

Wordlessly I sat down. All at once my throat was dry, my heart thumping in my chest, my stomach churning. No girl was ever invited to sit down in Miss Armitage's office. Something truly dreadful must have happened. I felt sick and empty and very afraid, and yet totally aware of everything that was going on around me; of the ticking of the clock in the corner, of the distant calling of a wood pigeon and the laughter of a group of girls passing beneath the window. I noticed that the calendar on the desk still bore yesterday's date and that the sky outside the window had darkened. Perhaps we were due for another storm.

Miss Armitage looked nervous and ill at ease, and for once, she didn't seem to know what to do with her hands. I watched as she laced and unlaced her fingers, fiddling for a moment with the buttons on her blouse, finally folding her hands firmly together as though to prevent them from escaping. She took a couple of steps towards the window, and then turned to face me again. I waited.

At last she spoke.

'I'm afraid I have some bad news,' she said. 'You're going to have to be very brave, Cassandra.'

Obediently, I continued to wait, sitting on my own hands and tucking my feet behind the legs of the chair to stop them from shaking. In spite of my fear, enough of my brain was still functioning for me to know that if I ever had the misfortune to break bad news to anyone, I would tell them straight away. No preamble, no build-up. However bad it was, I would give it to them straight. For nothing could be worse than this waiting.

Miss Armitage cleared her throat.

'It's your sister, Cassandra.'

'Octavia.' My voice seemed to come from a long way away. *Oh, please please, not Octavia!*

Nineteen

'Cass?' Mum's awake again, and I reach for her hand.

'Yes?'

'The pond. I should have had it filled in. It was all my fault.'

Not the pond again. It's years since Mum has mentioned the pond, and while I know she can't have forgotten it — how could any of us ever forget it? — I hoped that at least it had ceased to preoccupy her; that it had left the forefront of her mind and been filed away somewhere where it had come to cause her less pain.

'It wasn't your fault, Mum,' I say now. 'How could it have been your fault? And Octavia was so young. She wasn't even walking. How could you have known that she would be able to get to it on her own?'

'I should have known. I should have. It was my job to keep her safe.' A tear forms in the corner of her eye and leaks into the starched cotton of the pillowcase, and I ache for her.

'Oh Mum. It was such a long time ago. Years ago.' I hesitate. There is no point in saying that it doesn't matter; that the passage of years has lessened the significance of Octavia's death, yet I can't bear to see Mum suffer yet again for something for which she has already paid so dearly. 'And her life wasn't in vain, was it? She gave us all so much pleasure.'

'And we loved her.'

'Oh yes. We loved her.' For no one could have had more love in such a short lifetime than my little sister.

'But the pond —'

'Mum, darling mum, you have to forgive yourself for the pond, even though there's nothing to forgive. You have to let it go.'

Of course, in a way, we were all responsible.

Mum had said just after Octavia was born that we should fill in the pond; that it wasn't safe. But we managed to persuade her to leave it, at least until Octavia was walking.

That pond held so many memories for Lucas and me. Frogspawn in the spring (descendants of that first jam jar of tadpoles which Mum had used in her bewildering introduction to the facts of life) and the joy of fishing for newts with a worm tied to a piece of cotton (not forgetting the excitement when they all escaped from the tank in my bedroom in the middle of the night). Best of all, Prissy Deirdre from next door had fallen into that pond not once, but twice, and had emerged drenched and stinking and completely unrecognizable. The second occasion had confirmed all her mother's worst fears about our family, and that was the last we saw of Prissy Deirdre.

So the tragedy wasn't just Mum's fault. Lucas and I had wanted to keep the pond; even Greta had put in a good word for it ('Iss pretty, no?' No. Not really. But we knew what she meant). Besides, who could have anticipated that Octavia would manage to crawl down the back steps and across the lawn and get as far as the bottom of the garden in the time it took for Mum to answer the phone?

I have no idea how I got home that afternoon. I believe someone took me in a car — I have a vague memory of being wrapped in a blanket and of the unfamiliar smell of leather seats — but everything else about that dreadful journey passed in a blur.

The house seemed to be full of people. I remember Dr Mackenzie and some neighbours and Richard, and the gay Lodger making tea, and Call Me Bill ushering people in and out, and Greta (inevitably) weeping. I remember the pale controlled face of poor Lucas, who was being heartbreakingly brave as the Man of the House, and the whimpering of The Dog, who had a sixth sense where disaster was concerned.

And Mum.

Mum was sitting on the floor when I went into her bedroom, her arms locked round her knees, rocking to and fro. Just rocking.

'I don't know what to do. I don't know what to do. I don't know what to do.' Rock, rock, rock. 'I don't know what to do.'

Her face, when she lifted it, was completely drowned in tears, so swollen that I couldn't see her eyes, her hair and clothes were soaked in tears. I had never in my life seen anyone weep the way Mum wept.

'Cass.' She held out her arms to me. 'Oh, Cass! What am I going to do? Whatever am I going to do?'

I knelt down beside her, and we wept and rocked together, holding each other and sobbing into each other's shoulders. There was something primitive and strangely soothing about that rocking. Maybe it was to do with the automatic way mothers rock their babies, or perhaps we both felt that the swaying rhythmic movement would in some way help us to keep ourselves — and each other — alive. For at the time, I felt that if I were to let go of Mum she might simply lie down and never get up again.

Eventually, I persuaded her to sit on the bed, and we stayed there together for some time, holding each other, as dusk dimmed the sky outside and the busy comings and goings downstairs continued. People tiptoed in and out of the room, murmuring and bringing us cups of tea, and Dr Mackenzie returned to check on Mum.

'There there, my lass.' He joined us on the bed. 'My poor poor lass.' He held her hand and stroked it. Then he took a bottle of tablets from his pocket and shook two of them into his palm, offering them to her with a glass of water. 'You take these and try to get some rest.'

Mum took the tablets and pushed her sodden hair out of her eyes.

'Did she suffer, doctor?' Her voice was so low that he had to bend down so that his head was touching hers.

'Only for a wee while,' he said. 'Maybe a minute or two at most.'

I was grateful to him for being truthful; for not trying to patronize Mum with any of that stuff about not suffering at all; words which fool no one, and offer less comfort than the truth.

Mum nodded.

'Thank you,' she said.

Dr Mackenzie got up from the bed.

'Well, I'll be on my way,' he said, 'but I'll be back tomorrow.' He paused in the doorway. 'There's nothing I can say that will comfort you,' he added. 'Nothing at all. But you will get through this. Somehow, you'll get through it.'

He indicated for me to follow him out of the room, and after he had closed the door, he put his hands on my shoulders.

'Now you take care of yourself, Cassandra. Don't take too much responsibility. This is your loss, too, and you need to grieve as well as your mum. Give me a ring if you're worried about anything, or if you just want to talk.'

Yet again, Dr Mackenzie reminded me of the father I never had; his steady masculine presence brought home how much we needed a man — a proper man — in the family, especially at a time like this. I gave a brief thought to that other bereaved parent, Octavia's father, who didn't even know he'd been a father, and just for that moment, I hated him. He might have missed out on knowing his little daughter, but he had also been spared this agony, and I found that hard to forgive.

Downstairs, I found the Lodger making yet more tea, while Greta tried to concoct something for our supper (why? I couldn't imagine any of us ever wanting to eat again). Call Me Bill had had to go back to work to sort out some problem, and Richard had disappeared. Lucas was out walking The Dog. The house seemed to be full of flowers, but otherwise it felt almost normal.

'Where is she?' I asked Greta. 'Where — where is Octavia?'

'I think at hospital.' Greta struggled to open a tin of corned beef, cutting her finger.

'Did you see her?'

Greta paused, a tea towel wrapped round her hand.

'Yes. I see her.'

'What — what did she look like?'

'She look like sleeping,' Greta said. 'Just sleeping.'

'The ambulance men were brilliant.' The Lodger handed me a cup of tea. 'But there was nothing they could do. Oh, Cass. I'm so sorry.' He gave me a hug, and as I clung to him, I heard the sob in his own throat. 'I'm so very, very sorry. She was a very special little human being.'

'Yes.'

I looked round the kitchen. Some of Octavia's clothes were still drying on the clothes horse, and a woolly dog with three legs and a well-chewed tail lay where she had left it on the floor.

How were we ever going to get over this?

Twenty

During the week between Octavia's death and her funeral, life in our house seemed to stand still. Cards and letters and flowers continued to arrive, together with a succession of visitors. Food was prepared (although little was eaten) and gallons of tea were consumed. Laundry and shopping were done and The Dog was taken for walks, but otherwise nothing *happened*. We said little to each other — what was there to say? — and moved around each other carefully, politely, like awkward strangers, although of course it was tragedy that was the real stranger in the house.

Call Me Bill took the week off work to help, although there was little he could do, and the Lodger, who was currently between jobs, was a tower of strength. Poor Greta did her best to stem her weeping, aware that to outdo Mum in the weeping stakes would be inappropriate (if not impossible), and Lucas continued to be stoical.

'It's OK to cry, you know,' I said to him one evening, watching his pale still face. 'After all, everyone else seems to be doing it, and she was your sister.'

'I can't, Cass. I just can't.' He turned to me with a hopeless shrug. 'I've even tried sticking pins into myself, but it's as though I've lost all feeling.'

'Oh, Lucas.' I put my arms round him. 'What are we going to do?' I found myself echoing Mum's words.

'I don't know. Nothing seems real any more, does it?' He allowed my embrace but didn't return it. 'It's odd to think that a short time ago she didn't exist. Not at all. Not even as a tiny speck. No one wanted her or expected her. We were all quite happy without her. She just — arrived, and then she died. And now look at us all.' He paused. 'We only had her for a year.'

I had assumed that Mum's reaction would be similar to her behaviour after the death of our grandmother, but being new to the business of bereavement I hadn't realized that death has its own hierarchy, and that for Mum, Octavia's death far outweighed that of her own mother.

Almost overnight, Mum's room became a shrine to Octavia. There were photographs of her on every surface, together with her toys and books, and her small garments had all been carefully laid out on the bed, as though they were waiting for her to wear them again. In the midst of all this sat Mum, grubby and dishevelled, clutching Octavia's comfort blanket and favourite teddy, still rocking and weeping.

'What can we do?' I asked Dr Mackenzie when he called in on the third morning. I had expected him to approach Mum in the kindly but firm manner as he had last time, but he seemed to be treating her with the same kid gloves as the rest of us.

'There's nothing I can do, Cassandra. Not really. I can only keep an eye on her and give her something to help her sleep. That's all.'

'But you helped her when Grandma died. She took notice of you then.'

He sighed.

'This is different, my dear. The loss of a child is the worst thing that can happen to anyone. You lose your parents and — well, that's sad, but it happens. But not your child. No one expects to outlive their own child.'

'Isn't there anything we can do?'

'You're doing all you can, but strange as it may seem, your mum knows what's best for her. What she's doing may look a bit weird, but she's dealing with it in her own way. It won't always be like this. One day, she'll let go of Octavia's things, and one day — one day — she'll let go of Octavia. But not yet. Not for a long time. The poor lass has quite a journey ahead of her.'

'And — us? What about us?'

For I missed Mum. I missed having her around *for me*. This was the worst thing that had happened to me as well as to Mum, and yet although she responded when I spoke to her, I knew she was a long way away; that I couldn't really reach her. Ever since that first evening when we had clung together, she no longer seemed to need me. She didn't appear to need anyone. She was alone with her pain and her guilt and the ghost of her dead baby.

'Ah, poor Cassandra.' He put his arm around my shoulders. 'I know it must be so hard for you too, but there are people in this house who'd be glad to have you lean on them. Greta, for instance. She's not a strong woman, but so kind. She's longing to comfort you, but doesn't like to say so. And she needs some comfort, too. That little baby seems to have belonged to all of you. You must all help each other.'

That night, I joined Greta on the sofa, and we held each other and wept together. She wasn't the same as Mum, but I think we were able to offer each other something, and Greta had loved Octavia at least as much as I had. Octavia was probably the nearest she'd ever come to having a child of her own, and having no other family, her loss must have been all the worse for that.

Octavia's funeral was held on a perfect June day in our little parish church. We had never been churchgoers, but Mum said she wanted the best for Octavia, and none of us was going to argue with that.

I don't know what I had expected, but I found the sight of Lucas walking down the aisle carrying the tiny white coffin more heartbreaking than anything that had happened in the whole of that awful week. There had been no shortage of volunteers for this last sad task (Call Me Bill and the Lodger to name two) but Lucas had insisted. His position in the family dictated that he should be the one to carry Octavia's coffin, and that was what he would do.

The church was packed with people, many of whom I'd never seen before, but I was rapidly learning that the death of a child touches everyone, and that these people needed to be there for themselves as much as for us, even if we were never to see them again. The wispy grey relatives of my grandmother's funeral were mercifully absent — they probably didn't even know what had happened — and for that I was grateful.

The church smelled of cool air and polish and roses, and there was complete silence as Lucas laid down his small burden in front of the chancel. It was as though we were all holding our grief in check, waiting for the permission that only Mum could give. But she remained silent; she probably had no more tears left to weep. So the rest of us had to contain ours as best we could.

I remember envying those people whose cultures allow them to stamp and howl and rage around a grave or funeral pyre; who can express their grief physically, who can embrace and console each other while screaming their outrage to the heavens. It seemed so much more natural than our stiff upper lips and rigid self-control, and the robed ritual and musty prayers of the Church of England.

Octavia was buried in the churchyard. There had never been any question of cremation, for Mum said she found it unthinkable that anything should be done to damage her small body even further. It was far better that she should lie among the ancient gravestones and the yew trees, where we could visit her. I know now that Mum needed a grave to tend; a place where she could go to nurse her grief. I myself have always favoured the gentleness of burial over the violent destruction of cremation, and on more than one occasion have been reminded of the comforting words at the end of Wuthering Heights:

I lingered ... under that benign sky; watched the moths fluttering among the heath and harebells, listened to the soft wind breathing through the grass, and wondered how anyone could ever imagine unquiet slumbers for the sleepers in that quiet earth.

There mightn't have been any heath or harebells in our churchyard; rather the ubiquitous daisies and the brazen faces of dandelions. But I derived some small comfort from the thought of Octavia slumbering — such a deeply peaceful, consoling word — in the gentle environment of grass and trees and sky.

I remember little about the rest of that day. I know people came back to the house with us, and we must have offered them some kind of refreshment, but all I can recall is the feeling of utter exhaustion. Too tired to talk, too tired to cry, too tired even to think, all I wanted was to go to my room and curl up under the blankets in my old familiar bed, and sleep and sleep.

Twenty-one

I didn't go back to school that term. Call Me Bill collected my trunk and the rest of my stuff, and returned with a car full of my belongings together with a box of kind little notes and messages from my friends and teachers. Miss Armitage had already sent me an uncharacteristically warm letter of sympathy, closing with the injunction to 'be brave, but not too brave'. I got the feeling that it wasn't the first occasion upon which she had had to write such a letter to one of her pupils, and I have never forgotten that wise advice.

Grief is a strange thing. There were moments, even days, when I felt almost happy again; when I would read a book or go for a walk or see a friend, and everything would seem normal. Then some little reminder — a baby in a pram or a small head of auburn hair — would set me off again, and it was as though everything had happened only yesterday.

For the first time ever, the summer holidays seemed too long. As we moved from July into August, one drab sultry day merged into the next, the dusty leaves seemed to wilt on the trees and in the hedgerows, and flowers and weeds drooped together in our neglected garden. I think we were all painfully aware of the contrast with the previous August, when the house had been alive with the cries and the new presence of Octavia, but none of us said anything. We were each of us cocooned in our own sadness and our own memories, and while we did our best to help one another, I think that for each of us the journey was a different one.

Mum still spent much of her time in her room, but while she had gradually relinquished Octavia's clothes, she kept the teddy and the blanket in her bed with her. Sometimes I found her sniffing them, as though she were trying to extract from them the last traces of Octavia, and one day towards the end of August, I found her in tears.

'I can't smell her, Cass. Her smell's gone. I can't smell her any more. I shall never smell her again!'

I knew what she meant. I myself had paid covert visits to the bathroom where a tin of Johnson's baby powder was still sitting on the window sill, and had sprinkled it onto my hand and sniffed it, causing the tears to well up yet again as I remembered Octavia's bath times and her warm baby smell.

Why do we do these things? Why do we put ourselves through such painful experiences again and again, when there is no need? Is it simply hanging on, or is there more to it? Could it be that by pouring salt into our wounds we are in some way trying to purge them? Or perhaps we are testing ourselves, just to see if it still hurts as much as it did last time, like poking one's tongue into the gap left by an extracted tooth.

The aloofness which had come over Mum before Octavia's funeral had gone, and she became pathetically dependent and afraid of being left on her own. Each time she heard a door open or close, she would call out, and if any of us left the house she would question us closely as to where we were going and how long we'd be away.

'Where are you going, Cass?' Her voice followed me wherever I went, and I found it increasingly hard to be patient. Of course I needed my family, but I also needed my friends, and some time to myself to sort out my own feelings; to come to terms with what had happened and to think about my future. Because whatever anyone else might do, I had to make plans. I couldn't allow my life to come to a full stop because my sister had died, tragic though that was. Sooner or later, I had to move *on*.

When my exam results arrived I had done even better than anyone had expected, and for a few precious hours things seemed to return to normal as everyone rejoiced with me. Mum was terribly proud, and spent a happy morning with the telephone and her address book, phoning anyone and everyone to tell them how clever I was. Normally I would have found this embarrassing, but I was so pleased that she had found something to be happy about — that she was still capable of happiness — that I would cheerfully have consented to a full-page announcement in a national newspaper if that would have prolonged the atmosphere of celebration.

Lucas's A-level results, on the other hand, were abysmal, but then, as he himself pointed out, he didn't deserve good results since he hadn't done any work. He had recently decided to join the police, and they didn't seem to mind too much about his academic prowess. I suspected then — and still do — that Lucas got in on charm, since that has always been his greatest asset, although when I suggested it I was told very firmly that that was not what the police were looking for. Privately, I thought the police force could do with a bit more charisma to ginger up their image, and Lucas might be just what they needed. No doubt my idea of a policeman's role was naive, but I could see Lucas consoling the victims of burglaries or talking potential suicides off bridges and rooftops, and was quite sure he would be a success. As for Mum, she was so taken with the idea of having a policeman as a son that the failed A levels barely registered with her at all.

'It'll be so *useful*, Cass,' she confided to me, in one of her bewildering twists of logic.

I knew better than to challenge her. If she wanted to dream of a lifetime's immunity from the law, then that was fine by me.

As the end of the holidays drew nearer, I began to feel anxious. There had been no mention of my going back to school; no half-hearted replacing of outgrown uniform or grumbling over the price of hockey sticks. I didn't like to bring the subject up as it seemed heartless to be thinking of leaving home at such a difficult time, but the new term was almost upon me.

'Mum?' I found her sitting in the kitchen, absently brushing The Dog and gazing into space. 'About — well, about school.'

'What about school?' Mum removed a burr from The Dog's tail, and examined it as though it were suddenly of great interest.

'Going back, I suppose. We — I — haven't done anything about it, and the term starts next week. I need — well, I need new things.'

'New things,' mused Mum. 'What new things?'

'My skirts are terribly short, although Greta's let them down as far as they'll go, and my blouses —'

'You mean boarding school?'

'Well, yes. Of course, boarding school.'

'Oh. I didn't think.'

'What didn't you think, Mum?' I sat down beside her.

'I suppose I didn't think you'd be going back. But you must go back. Of course you must.'

'Yes.'

'If you really want to.'

'Well, yes. In any case, they're expecting me. I can't just not turn up.'

'No, of course you can't.' She gave The Dog a final pat and pushed him away.

'Well then?'

'Well then,' she repeated, and took my hands in hers. 'Oh, Cass. What am I going to do without you?'

'Mum, you've got everyone else, and I'll soon be home again. I'll write lots, and I expect they'll let me phone.'

But I knew. Perhaps in a way I had always known. I wouldn't be going back to boarding school. For even if Mum could bear to part with me — and this seemed doubtful — how could I leave her like this?

'I shouldn't be doing this to you,' Mum said. 'It's all wrong.'

'You're not doing anything to me, Mum.'

'Yes, I am. I'm putting pressure on you. I don't mean to. I want you to have your own life, of course I do. And I don't want to — hang on to you. It's not fair. Especially with you being so clever.'

I laughed.

'Oh, Mum! What's my being clever got to do with it?'

'Opportunity, I suppose. It's the least I can do, to let you have your opportunities. You could go far, you know, Cass. You could even be a doctor.'

To Mum, being a doctor represented the pinnacle of achievement.

'Mum, I don't want to be a doctor. The thought's never even crossed my mind.'

'Ah, but you could be. If you wanted.'

'Almost as good as being a policeman?' I teased her.

'Even better than being a policeman,' Mum said, giving me one of her increasingly rare smiles.

I got up and walked across to the window. There was already an autumnal light in the sky, and the bushes were festooned with those pretty jewelled spiders' webs which seem to appear towards the end of summer. The grass was thick with dew, and swallows were beginning to line up for their autumn journey. This time of year always reminded me of blackberry-picking and the glossy brown of newly hatched conkers, of sharp pencils and clean white rubbers, and the inviting smell of shiny new exercise books. Most people see spring as the season for new beginnings, but for me it has always been the autumn.

But not this year. This year, I wasn't looking forward to autumn at all.

'I won't go back, Mum,' I said, turning away from the window. 'I'll stay at home with you.'

'Oh, you must go, Cass. Of course you must,' Mum said, but I could see the relief already beginning to dawn in her face, and I knew she wouldn't need much persuading.

For a few moments I was filled with anger. I had been packed off to boarding school with no reference to my feelings and through no fault of my own, and now, when I was really settled, I was being compelled to leave. It wasn't fair. Whatever might or might not have happened, it simply wasn't fair.

But my anger was short-lived. I looked down at Mum, who had aged ten years in the past few weeks; at the empty high chair which was already gathering dust in the corner of the kitchen, and at poor lonely Greta, who had just come in with a basket of clothes to iron, and I sighed.

Of course it wasn't fair, but then life wasn't fair. How could I ever have expected it to be?

Twenty-two

My old school had been the local secondary modern, for in order to remain with my friends when we left our primary school, I had taken pains to ensure that I failed the eleven-plus. I had enjoyed my time there, where the company was convivial, the discipline lax and such talents as I had as yet undiscovered. Now, however, it appeared that I was High School material, and if my education were to continue, I had little choice but to enrol.

The local High School was prestigious, and proud of it. It had a good record of Oxbridge entrants (the honours board in the assembly hall glowed with the collective triumphs of the girls who had passed through its classrooms), and it was very soon made clear to me that in the fullness of time, my own name was expected to appear among them. To this end, pressure was applied at every turn; pressure to work hard, pressure to conform, pressure (it seemed to me) to sacrifice any pleasure I might have found in my studies in the interests of better examination results. And I was not accustomed to pressure. So, before I had been there a term, I switched off.

In vain did my teachers lecture me on wasted talent and the importance of my future. In vain did they talk of present frustration and future regret. I was deaf to them all. If my future really was my own, then presumably it was up to me what I did with it, and as to future regret, well, that too would be *my* problem.

I'm sure that much of my lack of co-operation was due to the effects of Octavia's death (something which my teachers seemed to disregard, although they were all aware of it), but I had always had an obstinate streak too. Apart from Mum's decision to send me away to school (and for that, I had long since forgiven her), I had always been consulted as to what I wanted to do, and I saw no reason why that should change.

At the beginning of my second term Miss Carrington, the headmistress, sent for Mum, but if she had any hopes of getting parental co-operation from that quarter, she didn't know my mother.

'Silly cow,' Mum said, on her return from this interview. 'I see what you mean, Cass. I don't think I'd want to do anything that woman told me, either.' She paused. 'But think about it, Cass. You are clever, and you don't want to waste it.'

This was the nearest Mum came to trying to influence me, and I did think about it. But since Octavia's death, the dreaming spires of academe had lost much of their appeal. I was probably being foolish, but nowadays I found it hard to contemplate any kind of future beyond the life that I had at the moment, and in any case, leaving home seemed an impossibility. Mum needed me, of that I was certain, but I was becoming increasingly aware that I also needed her and the familiarity of home. It wasn't just the loss of Octavia itself which had made me insecure; it was the realization that nothing could be relied upon any more; that you could wake up one morning expecting everything to be as usual, and go to bed the same evening with your world in tatters.

Mum, finally acknowledging that all of us were suffering to some degree, was wonderfully kind to me, and it seemed that once more we had slipped back into our original roles; she was the mother, and I very much the child. I think it probably did her good to realize how much she was still needed, and it may well have been some small help to her on her long road to recovery. There were still occasions when she would cling to me, but as the months went by, there were reassuring glimpses of the old mum, and I began to hope that perhaps there might eventually be life after Octavia for all of us.

Meanwhile, we had a fresh diversion, for just after Christmas (and I shan't even attempt to describe that first aching Christmas following Octavia's death), there occurred an unexpected development in our household when, quite out of the blue, Call Me Bill took Mum aside, presented her with flowers, and made her a proposal of marriage.

While obviously shocked, Mum also appeared to be both touched and entertained by this unexpected offer, and quite at a loss as to how she should deal with it.

'Just imagine,' she said, when she told Lucas and me about it. 'Just imagine Call Me Bill proposing! Proposing to me! Me and Call Me Bill *married*!'

Lucas and I tried to imagine, but neither of us could manage it. Call Me Bill married was enough of a challenge in itself; Call Me Bill married to Mum was something that not even our lively imaginations could begin to address. Apart from anything else, Lucas and I had long since decided that Call Me Bill wasn't interested in sex, and the thought of Call Me Bill in bed with my worldly wise mother must surely be out of the question. Perhaps he was planning a celibate relationship; one of friendship and mutual support. But if that was the case, how would he cope with Mum when she returned to her normal philanderings?

'He's probably sorry for me,' said Mum.

'Mum, everyone's sorry for you at the moment, but they don't all come round with offers of marriage,' I said.

'True. But what on earth shall I say to him?'

'You mean you haven't given him an answer?'

'I said I'd think about it.'

'That was a bit of a cop-out,' Lucas remarked.

'Well, I couldn't just turn him down, could I? It would have been so unkind.'

'So you're not planning to turn him down,' Lucas said.

'Of course I am!'

'Well, then. The sooner you tell him, the better. It's even more unkind to leave him in suspense.'

'I suppose so.' Mum sighed. 'I didn't think Call Me Bill was the marrying kind,' she went on. 'I suppose this'll change everything. He'll be upset and move out, and nothing will be the same.'

'Perhaps he could marry Greta?' I suggested, but without much hope.

'Greta's certainly not the marrying kind,' Mum said.

'It would seem,' said Lucas, 'that no one in this house is the marrying kind.'

'So. What are you going to say to him?' I asked.

'Well, I shall say how honoured I am, and grateful. That sort of thing. And then I shall say I hope we can still remain friends and —'

'Oh, for goodness' sake, cut to the chase, Mum,' Lucas said.

'All right. I shall tell him — I shall say I'm, well, I'm —'

'Not the marrying kind,' we finished for her.

'Something like that.'

'You'd better get on with it, Mum. He's been waiting nearly twenty-four hours,' I said. 'Better get it over with.'

In the event, Call Me Bill took Mum's decision with the kind of stoicism we had come to associate with him. Lucas and I privately thought he might even have been relieved. It was more than possible that he'd thought he was doing the right (rather than the sensible) thing in offering marriage to Mum; that her vulnerability had finally got to him, virtue had temporarily triumphed over common sense, and by now he could well be regretting his actions. Whatever his motives, Mum needn't have worried about his future plans. It appeared that Call Me Bill had no intention of moving out of the house, and nothing was going to change. And if Lucas and I noticed a new lightness in Mum's step, and a lift in her mood, we knew better than to mention it. If she had received a boost from Call Me Bill's proposal, then that was all to the good.

'What iss happen?' Greta wanted to know, sensing that something was being withheld from her. 'Something iss happen. I know this.'

I hesitated. Should I tell her? It wasn't really my news to tell, and yet Greta was one of the family. It didn't seem fair to keep secrets from her.

'Call Me Bill asked Mum to marry him,' I told her.

'Oh.' Greta's face fell.

'Don't worry,' I patted her shoulder. 'She's said no, and he's taken it very well.'

For a moment, Greta didn't seem to know what to say, but I noticed that the tear which had been threatening to fall had disappeared.

'It's OK to be pleased,' I assured her. 'I'm pleased, too. So's Lucas. There's been enough change round here recently. I think we're all much better off as we are.'

Still Greta hesitated, then she smiled at me.

'Nice-cup-of-tea?' She had obviously decided to return to safer and more familiar territory.

'Nice-cup-of-tea would be lovely, Greta,' I told her.

Even after all these years, when I think of Greta, I always picture her in her flowered pinny presiding over our ancient blue-and-white teapot. She still never touched tea herself, but it was Greta's tea which fuelled our family in times of crisis and which gave me my life-long tea habit.

Twenty-three

It is now almost dark, and the unlit room fades to monochrome as I continue my vigil by my mother's bed. I hear the supper trolley rattle past the door, but it doesn't stop. There will be no more suppers for Mum, for she can no longer eat. She exists on sips of tea and water, and the occasional teaspoonful of the brandy I have brought for her. I am exhausted and hungry and I could do with a shower and a change of clothes, but I daren't leave her. Mum saw me into the world; it seems only right that I should see her out of it and do all I can to ease her journey.

Lucas visits, in a hurry. Lucas is always in a hurry. He has an important job and a demanding wife, and he is afraid of death. I don't really blame him. He brings grapes she can't eat, and the wrong sort of flowers; garage flowers, wrapped in crackly cellophane. But she seems pleased. Mum has always adored presents, and never seems to mind if they are not what she wants.

A young nurse comes in to check on her.

'She looks very peaceful,' she whispers to me.

'I'm not dead yet,' retorts Mum, making the nurse start.

'Oh, dear. I didn't mean to upset her.'

'I'm not deaf, either.'

'That wasn't very kind,' I say, when the nurse has gone. 'She's doing her best.'

'I know.' Pause. Her breathing's a bit more laboured now, and it's an effort for her to speak. 'I'm sorry.'

Mum's eyes close, but her hands start to move over the bedspread. Her right hand rocks rhythmically back and forth, and I recognize Beethoven's Moonlight Sonata.

'Sing it for me, Cass.'

So I hum, and Mum plays, and it all seems perfectly natural. I remember all the other works mum has played over the years on the ironing board, her ancient record player belting out the music.

'I could have been really good, you know, Cass.' The Moonlight Sonata comes to an abrupt halt, and she gives a little hopeless gesture with her hands. 'Really good. If only I'd had the lessons.'

'I know, Mum. I know.'

Oh God, if there is a God, make it all right for her. Be there to welcome her when she arrives, and fill her heaven with suitable men, dependable Lodgers and a Steinway grand for her to have her piano lessons on. And look after her. Please look after her. Because my mother has never been much good at looking after herself.

In February, Mum quite suddenly returned to her ironing-board recitals. She played sad, pensive pieces — pieces she had played after her mother died — but we all took it as a good sign. Greta, who had been heroically doing all the ironing in the aftermath of Octavia's death, must have been particularly relieved, for between recitals Mum managed to get quite a lot of it done. For myself, I took it as another indication that we might eventually return to normality, and I was ridiculously cheered. To anyone outside the family, ironing-board recitals must have seemed — and I'm sure on occasion, were — quite absurd, but to us, they were part of life and very much a part of Mum.

A few weeks later, the gay Lodger left to set up house with his partner (at least, that is what we assumed; he had always been very discreet about his private life). While we mourned his going — he had been a wonderful support over the past months, and a good friend to our family — finding a replacement gave Mum something to focus on.

'We've had an application from a woman, Cass,' she told me. 'Imagine! A woman Lodger!'

I couldn't see the problem myself, although our Lodgers had always been men. A woman might make a nice change. But Mum would have none of it, and adjusted her advertisement accordingly.

Unusually, we had several applicants, and Mum settled on a hunky Charlton Heston look-alike with a Ph.D. in bats.

'Bats!' Mum cried gaily. 'Now isn't that interesting, Cass?'

I had never found bats especially interesting, and suspected that it was the Charlton Heston aspect rather than the bats which had appealed to Mum. But provided he didn't bring his bats with him, if he was going to help reawaken her interest in the opposite sex, then I certainly wasn't going to argue.

The bat-loving Lodger appeared to bring Mum a new lease of life. They stayed up late into the night talking, they went for long walks together (ostensibly looking for bats, but even I knew that bats are in short supply at two o'clock in the afternoon), and from the covert padding of feet on floorboards and the opening and closing of bedroom doors in the middle of the night, no doubt engaged in other activities as well.

If Call Me Bill was hurt by Mum's activities so soon after his proposal, he didn't show it, and the rest of us were relieved that yet another aspect of Mum's life appeared to be returning to normal.

'Do you think we ought to talk to her about — well, about birth control?' Lucas asked me, when this had been going on for about a fortnight. 'We don't want another — another —'

'Octavia?' I said.

'Well, yes. I mean Octavia was lovely, but I just couldn't bear to risk going through all that again.' It was almost the first time Lucas had referred to his own feelings about Octavia's death, and I was touched.

'You're right. I'll speak to her.'

When I mentioned our conversation to Mum, she didn't appear to mind at all.

'Oh, Cass! There are these dear little pills you can take now, which take care of all that. Isn't it wonderful?' She rummaged in her bag and brought out a small pink packet. 'One pill for each day, and bob's your uncle!'

'Are you sure?' This sounded to me a bit too good to be true.

'Quite sure.' Mum beamed at me. 'Dr Mackenzie gave them to me ages ago. Wasn't that kind?'

'You won't forget to take them?'

'Of course I won't forget to take them. Now stop fussing, Cass, and run along. I've got a lot to do.'

Not for the first time, I thanked God for Dr Mackenzie.

Meanwhile, at school, I continued to plod. I listened in class, did my homework and generally toed the line, but I put no effort into anything I did. In a less able child this would have passed unnoticed, but it continued to frustrate my teachers, who all knew I could do so much better. The only teacher who seemed to understand at all was Mrs Harvey, the kindly woman who taught us English.

'What's this all about, Cass?' she said one day, when I had stayed behind to help her tidy up the classroom. 'You have outstanding O levels and an excellent brain. You could go such a long way if you wanted to. What are you planning to do with your life?'

'I don't know.' I put down the blackboard rubber and dusted my hands on my skirt. 'I honestly don't know. I did know, once, but now life's so — so muddled, I'm not sure of anything any more.'

'In what way, muddled?'

'Mum, Octavia —'

'Octavia?'

'My little sister. She — she —'

'Yes, I know. It must have turned your world upside down.' She sat down on the edge of her desk. 'And your mother?'

'Mum needs me. Us. She needs us all to be together. I couldn't leave her even if I wanted to.'

'And do you want to?'

'No. Well, sometimes I suppose I do, but I feel — safer at home.'

'And you think that by producing mediocre work — and it is mediocre, Cass — you're guaranteeing yourself a permanent place at home?'

'Maybe.'

'If you work hard and do well, you'll still have a choice. Just a wider choice than the one you'll have if you carry on as you're doing at the moment. You can still choose to stay at home if that's what you really want, but you can also go to university if you change your mind.'

'I'm not so sure about that. Does anyone in this place really have a choice? It's just — *assumed* that we'll all go to university if we get good A levels. No one even bothers to ask us if it's what we want.' I slammed the lid of my desk shut. 'Well, not me. I'm not going to be pushed around.'

'I can see that.' Mrs Harvey sighed. 'But don't cut off your nose to spite your face, Cass. It would be such a waste.'

'Perhaps.'

'And it's not too late, you know. You could easily catch up.'

'I'll be fine,' I said. 'Don't worry about me.'

'But I do worry about you, Cass. You're a lovely girl with a really bright future ahead of you, there for the taking. And no,' she said, seeing that I was about to interrupt, 'I don't just mean university. You could do anything you wanted if you wanted it enough. Anything.'

'Well, at the moment I just want to be left alone,' I said unkindly.

'That's your choice, too. And you have the right to make it,' she said, ignoring my rudeness. 'But think about it. And if you ever want a chat — about work or jobs or anything at all — I'd be more than happy to help.' She stood up and picked up her briefcase. 'You know where to find me.'

Of course, I should have taken Mrs Harvey up on her offer. After all, I had nothing to lose, and probably a great deal to gain from talking to someone outside the family who was willing to listen; someone who obviously liked me (no one had ever called me a lovely girl before) and cared about my welfare. Looking back now, I think I was probably quite depressed, for while Mum was still supportive, she was obviously beginning to feel a bit better and expected the same to apply to everyone else. That we all dealt with Octavia's death in our own ways and at our own pace didn't seem to occur to her; there was light at the end of her tunnel, and she assumed it was the same for the rest of us.

However, she was still often overcome by great waves of grief and crushing fits of weeping, when she would once more take to her bed for a day at a time, berating herself for that moment of inattention which had contributed to Octavia's death, and mourning the loss of her little daughter. But she would recover from these bouts quite quickly — especially since the arrival of the new Lodger — and often failed to notice that the spirits of the rest of the household didn't necessarily keep pace with her own. I resented the Lodger; not so much because of Mum's relationship with him, but because I feared he was taking her attention away from me.

Spring gave way to summer, and the first painful anniversary of Octavia's death. At Mum's suggestion, we marked the occasion with a party in her memory, but instead of being the celebration of her life which Mum had envisaged, it turned into a maudlin all-night binge, at which Mum got hopelessly drunk and eventually passed out draped over the ironing-board where she had been giving a tearful rendition of 'Rock-a-Bye Baby'.

'It was too soon,' I panted, as Lucas and I hauled her unconscious body up the stairs to her room. We could have done with Charlton Heston, but he had mysteriously disappeared. Call Me Bill had long since taken himself off to bed, tutting with disapproval. Sundry guests were lying in unhelpful heaps all over the house. 'We should never have let her do it. I mean, a *party*, for goodness' sake! Whatever can she have been thinking of?'

'No one,' said Lucas grimly, hitching Mum's legs over his shoulder, 'stops Mum when she's decided to do something. You of all people should know that.' He too was very drunk, and being drunk always made him disagreeable.

I put Mum to bed in her clothes, too exhausted to be bothered with trying to undress her. I felt lonely and miserable and hopeless. It had been altogether a horrible day; I had just received my exam results, which were every bit as bad as I deserved, and I had a splitting headache from a disgusting vodka mixture of Lucas's.

Returning to the kitchen, I found the gay ex-Lodger making coffee, and fell weeping into his arms.

'Everything's awful, I've got no one to talk to and I'm an utter failure,' I sobbed into his shoulder. 'Whatever am I going to do with my life?'

Twenty-four

At the beginning of my final school year, the pressure to pull my academic socks up was really on, so in order to get my teachers off my back, I told them I was going to be a nurse.

I should explain that in my particular educational establishment, there only ever appeared to be three career options. If you were in the A stream, you went to university; and if you were in the B stream, you either went to teachers' training college or you became a nurse. Since both professions were supposed to be vocations, it seemed strange (not to say convenient) to me that those who were under-equipped for the academic life should be automatically assumed to have a calling in one or other of these directions. Since I felt that by this stage I had had enough of teachers and their profession to last me several lifetimes, I opted for nursing.

I don't think that at the time I had any real intention of carrying this through — apart from anything else, I still wasn't ready to contemplate leaving home — but the reaction of the teaching staff, who did everything in their power to dissuade me, proved irresistible.

Mum, needless to say, gave me her full backing.

'A nurse!' she said dreamily. 'How worthwhile. You a nurse, and Lucas a policeman! Oh, Cass! I'm so proud of you both!'

Dear Mum. Her reasoning, as ever, was flawless. How could anyone fail, with a nurse and a policeman in the family? Crime and disease would be forever kept at bay, and she need never worry again. Within twenty-four hours, she had us both promoted, and was happily anticipating her role as mother to a Chief Detective Inspector and a Hospital Matron. Never mind that Lucas was at the very bottom of his career ladder (with his lowly qualifications, there were to be no short cuts for Lucas) and I was still at school; in Mum's eyes, we were both consummate successes. And Lucas had a uniform. Mum had always had great respect for uniforms, and even I had to admit that Lucas looked rather fetching in his.

But if I thought that getting into a nursing school was going to be easy, I was badly mistaken. Many of the better hospitals had waiting lists, with no chance of getting a place for at least two years, and the two interviews I did have went badly.

'Why do you want to be a nurse, Miss Fitzpatrick?' asked the tightly upholstered, hatchet-faced matron of the first hospital I went to.

Such an obvious question, you would have thought, but it hadn't occurred to me to prepare an appropriate answer.

'Well, I couldn't really think of anything else,' I confessed. 'And —' remembering Mum — 'it's so worthwhile, isn't it?'

'Is it?' Her penetrating gaze seemed to pin me to my chair like a helpless insect.

'Well, yes. I mean, looking after sick people ...' My voice trailed away uncertainly.

'Nurses certainly look after sick people,' my tormentor continued, in the kind of tone one might use to a very small, very stupid child. 'But I think you'll find there's a little more to it than that. You obviously haven't given the idea a great deal of thought, have you? I expect you imagined that you'd just put on a pretty uniform and float about doing good works?' She folded her hands together on the desk and waited.

This was almost exactly what I'd thought, and I blushed.

'Hm. I thought as much.'

By this stage, all I wanted was to escape into the fresh air, away from this stuffy office and this awful woman.

'I'd still like to be a nurse,' I said feebly.

The matron pursed her lips and consulted a sheet of paper on the desk in front of her. I recognized the school's headed writing paper, and my heart sank.

'Your head teacher doesn't seem to think you are particularly suited to the job of nursing, and I'm inclined to agree with her.' She rose from her chair, indicating my dismissal. 'You will be hearing from us in due course.'

I escaped into the sunny street outside, seething with anger; anger at myself, anger at that horrible woman, but most of all anger at Miss Carrington who, for reasons best known to herself, seemed hell-bent on sabotaging any chances I might have of (to use her own words) 'making something of myself'.

For my second interview, I was better prepared. I read everything about nursing I could lay my hands on, from the life of Florence Nightingale (who turned out to be more pioneering battleaxe than ministering angel) to the present day, garnering in the process enough information to fill a fairly hefty manual.

But the second matron appeared to be no more impressed than the first.

'Miss Fitzpatrick, you seem to have swallowed an encyclopaedia,' she observed. 'Just tell me what it is about nursing that appeals to *you*.'

I was ready for this, too.

'I'd like to be at the cutting edge of modern hospital care. I'd like to contribute to the standard of that care, and make a difference,' I spouted recklessly, aware that I sounded more like a government white paper than a candidate at an interview, but somehow unable to stop. 'I'd like to —'

'Hold on, Miss Fitzpatrick.' The matron held up her hand, sparing my further efforts. 'I simply want to know what it is you think you have to offer us. Personal qualities, for example. What personal qualities do you have which might make you a suitable applicant?'

'I think I'm kind,' I said desperately.

'That's certainly a start.'

'And — and my sister died.' I burst into tears.

I have no idea what made me say that, but perhaps I detected beneath that starched bosom and stern expression a hint of the sympathy I still craved. The matron didn't look in the least surprised at my outburst, but I detected a softening of her features as she leant forward and handed me a spotless handkerchief.

'Tell me about it,' she said.

I started talking, and once I'd started, I found I couldn't stop. I told her about Octavia, about the terrible day when she had died and about leaving boarding school. I told her about Mum and our unusual family set-up, and I told her about the pressures I had received from school and the real reasons I had applied to be a nurse. I was sure I'd scuppered any chances I might have, but I no longer cared. I was carried along on a tide of words and emotion, and by the time I'd finished, I felt better than I had in a long time.

There was a long pause.

'I see.' The matron straightened the papers on her desk, and looked at me over her spectacles.

'Miss Fitzpatrick, do you think you are ready to be a nurse, even if it is what you want? Do you think you can deal with the problems of others when you have recently had so many of your own?'

'I don't know. I hadn't thought about it.'

'Well, do. Do think about it. Nurses have a great deal to cope with. They see people in pain, people dying, and they can't always make everything better. They have to be strong. Not hard-hearted, but emotionally tough. I think at the moment you are too fragile to take on a job which will drain you both physically and mentally.'

'So that's — it,' I said, feeling more disappointed than I would have imagined.

'Not necessarily.' She smiled at me. 'I like you, Miss Fitzpatrick. You are sensitive and honest and intelligent, and it may surprise you to know that I think that, given the right circumstances, you might be a good nurse. But not yet. Not for a while.' She paused, as though assessing my reaction. 'Take your A levels — you're going to need them, even for nursing — and come and see me again, and we'll have another talk.'

'But the waiting list is so long,' I wailed. 'It'll be years, even if you decide to accept me.'

'I have ways of opening doors,' she said, 'to the right candidates. I can't promise we'll take you next year, but if things have settled down at home, and you're feeling stronger, well, we'll see. That's all I can say at the moment. I'd like to give you a chance, but I can't make any promises. Fair enough?'

'Fair enough.' I summoned up a smile. 'And thank you.'

'Oh, Cass! You've been crying! What's that dreadful woman done, to make you cry?' Mum, who had travelled up with me for the interview, was waiting for me outside the door.

'Mum, you haven't even met her. She's actually rather nice,' I said.

'Poor Cass,' Mum appeared not to have heard me. 'Doesn't she want you?'

'Perhaps. But not yet.'

We proceeded to walk together back down the corridor.

'Not yet? What can she be thinking of?' cried Mum. 'The woman must be mad.' She sniffed. 'Anyway, there are plenty of other jobs you can do. You don't need to be a nurse. Just look at them,' she added, as we passed a group of nurses. 'Look at them, with their black-stockinged stalks of legs and their smug little nurse faces! I think you're well out of it, myself.'

'Well, you've certainly changed your tune.' I couldn't help laughing. Mistress of the volte face, Mum could execute a speedier change of direction than anyone I knew. 'And you haven't let me explain. She was actually very kind, but she thinks I need more time. She's prepared to see me again next year. I think she's probably right,' I added. 'And I'd like to come here. It feels — right.'

'Oh.' Mum's anger subsided as quickly as it had arisen, but I felt sorry for her, for I knew she was disappointed, for herself as well as for me. She had been looking forward to telling people about my new vocation, and now she would have to wait.

As we took our seats on the train for the journey home, I gave Mum an edited account of my interview, and she seemed to accept it.

'You could try somewhere else, Cass,' she said. 'There are plenty of other hospitals.'

'I know. But I like St Martha's, it's one of the best and it's in London.' (I had set my heart on London.) 'And the matron was right. Perhaps I do need a bit more time. I could even have changed my mind again by next year.'

'I suppose so.'

'Don't look so sad, Mum. I'll get a job sooner or later, and I promise I'll do my very best to make sure it's one which requires a uniform!'

'Am I that pathetic?' Mum asked.

'No. Not pathetic at all. I know you want the best for me, and you've never tried to push me. You're the best sort of mother to have.'

'Are you sure?'

I thought of my peers, many of whom were threatened or bribed into getting the best grades; whose parents' aim seemed equally divided between trying to relive their lives through their children and boasting about the academic achievements of their brilliant offspring. And then I thought of Mum, who had praised and encouraged me every step of the way, however good or lowly my achievements, and whose unconditional pride in me had come to mean so much.

I gave her a hug.

'Quite sure,' I told her.

As our train drew out of the station, and we passed the terraces of grim, sooty houses with their defiant lines of bright washing flapping in their cluttered back gardens, my spirits lifted. A woman picked up a screaming child and carried him indoors, a black and white cat sat washing itself in a patch of sunlight, an old man filled a bucket from a heap of coal.

I was determined that one day — one day quite soon — I would be back.

Twenty-five

I was by now nearly eighteen, an age at which clothes and make-up and, above all, boys might be expected to feature prominently in my life, but while I certainly liked nice clothes, and even occasionally wore make-up, my interest in the opposite sex remained non-existent.

Not so my classmates, whose conversation was now dominated by the fascinating subject of who was going out with whom, what they had been up to and, most pressing of all, whether or not they had *gone the whole way*. One girl who had certainly gone the whole way was the hapless Pamela Adams, who started to put on a suspicious amount of weight, was observed by our PE teacher, interviewed (with her parents) by Miss Carrington, and left in tears. We never saw Pamela again. The Sixties may well have been swinging, but not yet for us, and certainly not in our school.

My only experience of boys my own age (apart from Lucas and his friends, and my disastrous encounter with Alex) had been the challenging ordeal of a term of ballroom dancing classes, in the lower sixth form, with the boys from the Grammar School. These were entirely voluntary, taking place after school, and I was persuaded by my friends (and much against my better judgement) to give them a try.

The classes would commence with a ritual that could have been a precursor of the car boot sale, with a touch of the cattle market thrown in. The girls huddled self-consciously on one side of the school hall, while the boys regarded them critically from the other. Then the more streetwise of the boys would swoop, carrying off the beautiful, the confident and the downright sexy for a faltering hour of quicksteps and waltzes, with more than a smattering of flirtation thrown in, while the luckless remainder would trail across and pick up the remnants: the shy, the plump, the spotty or the downright plain.

I don't think that I was unattractive. Photographs of me at that age show a serious-looking girl with wide-apart eyes, a ponytail of dark hair and a nice if hesitant smile. I was reasonably slim, had as much bosom as I felt I needed, and my legs, as I recall, were quite respectable. But I was always one of the last to be chosen, and the humiliation stayed with me for a long time.

I wasn't normally shy. In our household, where people came and went and strangers were often entertained as a matter of course, I had long been accustomed to meeting — and getting on with — new people. But this was different. Here, I was being judged according to a whole new set of criteria, and the experience was disconcerting, to say the least.

Oh, the agony of standing there waiting, of undergoing the scrutiny of the equally wretched also-rans among our male counterparts, and praying the desperate prayer of the wallflower: don't let me be chosen last. Oh, please don't let me be the last!

Thanks to the presence of a short fat girl named Alice, and an equally unfortunate classmate with a squint and a speech impediment, I never was the very last, but on more than one occasion, I came dangerously close.

'Why do we do this?' I whispered to Alice on one occasion, as we stood together awaiting our fate.

Alice shook her head miserably.

'My mother wanted me to come,' she said. 'She says it will give me confidence.'

'And has it?' I asked curiously, wondering what sort of mother Alice must have. At least my mother had had nothing to do with my own decision.

Alice shook her head.

'I hate it,' she admitted. 'But I don't want to let Mum down. Besides,' she added, 'she collects me late on Tuesdays because of my sister's violin lesson, and there's nothing else to do.'

I could think of plenty of other things to do, which begged the question of why wasn't I doing any of them, but I think there must have been something in me that was refusing to be beaten. I'd signed up for the dancing, not the boys, and I wasn't going to give up simply because of a few minutes of blushing discomfort.

In fact I felt I could have enjoyed the classes, given the right partner, but that partner rarely came my way, and so I had to put up with fumbling fingers and equally fumbling apologies as we made our uncertain way round the dance floor. By the end of the hour, I don't know which were more bruised; my feelings or my feet.

After half-term, however, I was picked by a boy who if not good-looking was certainly quite pleasant, and what was more, he could dance. We both learnt fast, and after two sessions we were selected to show the rest of the class our tango. Miss Mason (PE teacher turned dance instructor) was obviously impressed.

'Very good, Cass. Excellent — er, what's your name?'

'Daniel, Miss.'

'Yes. Well done, Daniel.'

My friends were also impressed, but not so Daniel's colleagues. He had to put up with their mincing imitations all the way home, he later told me, and acquired the new nickname of 'Dancing Danny'.

'I don't mind, though,' he said, as we waltzed carefully round the room. 'It's worth it, to — to dance with you.'

'Thank you.' I was trying to concentrate on the music (one-two-three, one-two-three).

'Can I — could I walk you home?'

'But I only live ten minutes away.' The point of being walked home completely passed me by. Whatever did he want to walk me home for, especially as he lived in the opposite direction?

'I — I like you,' Daniel said lamely, as we swept round a corner (one-two-three).

'Oh. OK, then.'

Daniel smiled and blushed and we got out of step. Whatever was the matter with him? I thought crossly, as I tried to put things to rights (one-two-three). We were here to dance, not to have this kind of silly conversation.

For the next three weeks, Daniel walked me home, but I found our walks awkward and uncomfortable, since without the dancing, it appeared that we had little to say to each other. I soon realized that Daniel's interest in me went beyond my prowess as a dance partner, and on several occasions he tried to take my hand (I solved this problem by thrusting my hands into my pockets, pleading cold fingers and chilblains).

'How do you tell a boy you don't like him?' I asked Mum, our willing source of information on such subjects.

'Oh, Cass! Have you got a boyfriend? How sweet!'

'No,' I explained patiently. 'I haven't got a boyfriend and I don't want one. That's the whole point.'

'Well.' Mum sat down on her bed. 'What's he said to you?'

'Nothing really. He just walks me home after dancing and tries to hold hands.'

'And you really don't like him?'

'He's OK I suppose.'

'Good-looking?'

'Not bad.'

'Well then.'

'What do you mean, well then?'

'When I was your age, I always used to think that any boyfriend was better than none,' Mum said. 'Someone to go out with, do things with. You know.'

'No. I don't know.' I was beginning to get cross. I had my own friends to go out with. I didn't need a boy in order to have fun. 'And I don't suppose you ever had to go out with anyone you didn't fancy, did you?'

'Well, no. That's true.' Mum's face took on a dreamy expression. 'I was rather lucky, as it happens.'

'And you liked boys.'

'Oh, I certainly liked boys.'

'Well, I don't like boys. I've never liked boys. I probably never shall.'

'Don't be ridiculous, Cass!'

But I couldn't see that there was anything ridiculous about the way I felt. Since I certainly didn't want to get married and had never been especially keen on the idea of having children, there didn't seem to be any need for me to have anything to do with men at all, other than on a casual basis. I had always rather liked the idea of a future where I had a place of my own; a small flat or cottage somewhere, with my own things in it; a place where everything stayed where I had put it, any guests came by invitation (my invitation), and when the phone rang, I would know it was for me.

It wasn't that I disliked men. I was fond of Call Me Bill, and had formed comfortable relationships with some of our Lodgers. Many of the men who passed through our house — friends, visitors, and what Mum liked to call her Special Friends — were pleasant enough. But I didn't want a man of my own. In my experience, if you excluded Call Me Bill and the gay Lodger, men were on the whole poor helpless creatures, who forgot birthdays and couldn't find their socks.

In the end, Mum was of little help when it came to the question of how to discourage Dancing Danny, so I withdrew from the dancing classes pleading a sprained ankle (the ankle also got me out of games, so something good had come out of the experience, even though I had to remember to hobble for three weeks).

Nearly a year later, I was still as indifferent to boys as I had ever been, and if I felt the occasional stirrings of interest when confronted by a nice smile or an appraising pair of eyes, I quickly stifled them. As for Mum, she wisely let me be. I know now that she hoped I would train as a nurse and go on to fall in love with a doctor, and reasoned that if I were to get involved with someone while I was still at school, neither of these eventualities might take place.

Twenty-six

August 1965

My final school year passed uneventfully. I did just enough work to gain the A levels required by the nursing school while ensuring that they fell comfortably short of the standard I would need to gain a place at a decent university. And to my delight, after a further interview and some uncomfortably searching questions from the matron, I was offered a place at St Martha's for the following November. Matron said that while she was still concerned that I might find the whole experience harder than I imagined, she thought that I'd matured since she had last seen me, and had 'managed to come to terms with the family bereavement'.

I had once heard Dr Mackenzie tell Mum that the pain of bereavement never goes away, but that over time, it changes from a wound into a scar. This seemed and still seems to me the best description of a pain which is in many ways beyond description; a mental pain which is also physical, tearing at the solar plexus, the very centre of one's body. I remember during those first months after Octavia's death Mum doubling up over her own pain, clutching it to her, almost nursing it, curling herself round it and rocking it as though it had a soul of its own.

There had been no party to commemorate the second anniversary of Octavia's death; even Mum realized that this had not been a good idea, and that something sombre and reflective might be more appropriate. So this time, we had all trooped down to the churchyard with armfuls of roses from the garden and scattered them on her grave. It was a beautiful June day; the best kind, with a blue and white sky and air alive with the sound of birdsong; the kind of day which can so easily exaggerate emotions and rekindle joy or grief.

After the scattering, no one seemed to know what to do. Had we been religious, we would no doubt have prayed, but as it was we just stood in silence, covertly watching each other, waiting for a cue from Mum as to what was to happen next. Beneath my lowered eyelids, all I could see was feet: Mum's unsuitable high-heeled shoes, already sinking into the wet grass, and the childish round-toed shoes favoured by Greta; the crisp turn-ups of Call Me Bill's trousers and Richard's ancient brogues neatly laced with string. Lucas's shoes were black and highly polished as Mum had requested that he should come in his uniform, and the more sensible among us had come in stout shoes or boots. In Lucas's *Scouting for Boys*, a book over which he and I used to howl with mirth, we had read that one could tell a lot about a person from his footwear, and for once I could see it might well have a point.

I am ashamed to say that my thoughts were preoccupied not so much with Octavia but with the unwelcome presence of the Charlton Heston Lodger, whose attendance both Lucas and I thought quite inappropriate. After all, he had arrived after Octavia's death, and any feelings he had were inevitably centred around Mum. I noted with satisfaction that when he placed a protective arm around her shoulders, she shook it off and moved away from him. Perhaps she too felt that while this relative newcomer might be accepted into her bed, he was not welcome at the graveside of the baby he had never known.

But that was back in June, and now it was August, a month I was accustomed to look forward to as the one time in the whole year when I could please myself. This year, however, was different, and while I was still glorying in my new freedom from the world of school and examinations, I realized that I couldn't just sit around at home doing nothing for the next three months, so I took a job at the local cinema as an usherette.

At first I was rather pleased with myself. For the first time in my life, I had regular money of my own (Mum's attempts at distributing pocket money, although doubtless well meant, had been sporadic and unreliable), the work was undemanding, and I had a torch to read by. But by the time I had seen *Seven Brides for Seven Brothers* twenty-nine times and sold enough ice cream to put me off the stuff for life, I thought I would go mad, especially as it was very soon made clear to me that reading books by torchlight was not in the job description.

'Give it up and do something else,' advised Mum, whose easy-come easy-go attitude to the world of work seemed to have done her little harm. But I liked to think that I was made of sterner stuff and so I stuck it out, much to the entertainment of Lucas and his friends, who regularly heckled me from the back row between their amorous gropings. I have never felt quite the same about the cinema since, and am always particularly nice to the usherettes.

Meanwhile, I was eagerly looking forward to November. The doubts which had been sown as to my suitability as a nurse had only served to fuel my enthusiasm, and while a year ago I had never even considered nursing as a career, now I couldn't believe that I had ever thought of doing anything else. I knew I was intelligent, I believed that I was caring, and while I liked to think that I had taken on board the matron's warnings of the pressures of hard work and emotional stress, I was in no doubt that I could cope with them when they arose. As for leaving home, London was only an hour and a half away by train, and there was always the telephone. Mum was still preoccupied with Charlton Heston, Lucas was living at home, and Greta and Call Me Bill were there to help hold the family together. They would hardly notice that I was gone. As I stood for long hours in the darkened cinema, with nothing but my thoughts and the noise and dazzle of yet another all-too-familiar film to occupy my mind, I built up such a delightful fantasy of my new life that I am surprised I could have been so gullible as to believe in it.

The reality, when it came to it, was of course totally different.

For a start, I and the others in my group were stationed in a nurses' home some distance from the hospital for eight weeks of classroom training. I had to share a bedroom with a girl called Angela, who looked as though she had come straight off the set of a *Carry On* film; all long legs and pouting lips and fluttering mascara. Angela and I disliked each other on sight, and this made for a difficult few weeks.

Then there was the Home Sister, a redoubtable woman of the old school, whose mission in life seemed to be to ensure that military discipline was maintained at all times, and that during the hours of darkness we were kept in and anyone of the opposite sex was kept out. This last group included Lucas, who came to visit me, and Angela's father (at least, she said he was her father but he looked a great deal too young and glamorous to be anyone's father — in this, I was on the side of the Home Sister).

Those eight weeks seemed interminable. The drone of the tutor's voice induced in me a kind of torpor, and the only relief came from our brief forays into the practical room, where we practised our hospital corners and bandaged one another's arms and legs, and the one afternoon a week when we were allowed onto the hospital wards, where we felt more like spare parts than proper nurses.

And, to my surprise, I was homesick. It was the first time I had been away from home since Octavia's death, and I felt suddenly vulnerable and insecure. Octavia had died while I was at St Andrew's, and in some part of my mind there was the illogical thought that if I had been at home, it might never have happened; that my presence at home was necessary in order to keep everyone safe. I knew this made no sense, and that it was more about my needs than those of my family, but I couldn't get away from it. I worried and fretted if I hadn't heard from home, and when Mum's letters did come, they were as irregular and scatty as the ones I had received at boarding school, and all the more poignant for that, for they reminded me of a time when our family was still untouched by tragedy. As for phone calls, the evening queue for the only pay phone was long, and I rarely had more than a few minutes to talk.

'You're all right, are you, Mum?' I would ask. 'You're sure you're all OK?'

'Of course we're OK,' Mum would reply, sounding amazingly cheery, and she would grab hold of the nearest person to endorse her reassurance (on one occasion, the only family member available was The Dog, and I was subjected to a costly minute of snufflings and lickings which offered no consolation whatsoever). 'Have you seen any operations yet?'

'No, Mum. I keep telling you. I shan't see operations for ages. I'm still in school, remember?'

'Oh yes.' She sounded disappointed. A nurse who hadn't seen any operations obviously didn't really count.

'But I shall. We have to. We all have to do a spell in theatre.' I hesitated, trying to think of something which would interest her. 'We did see a brain in a bucket,' I offered.

'A brain in a bucket! Fancy!'

The brain in question had been brought in to illustrate a session on the nervous system. It looked grey and pickled and very dead, and yet all I could think of was that that brain represented a *whole person*; all of someone's life and thoughts and memories were in that bucket, together with their talents and abilities, their sadnesses and their triumphs. When it came to it, I reflected, only your brain was really *you*; other parts of the body were mere trappings in comparison with that amazing organ. I found the whole experience quite unnerving, and while the other girls appeared to be torn equally between disgust and hilarity, I found my encounter with the bucket and its grisly contents very sobering.

Twenty-seven

Mum is asleep now, drifting on a gentle tide of morphine, gradually bobbing away from me. Before long, she will be out of reach. She will have embarked on that part of her journey where I can't be with her. Soon, I shall no longer be able to talk to her.

I'm glad that she is at peace, but at the same time I want to say to her: 'Don't go! Stay a little longer! Please don't leave me. I'll be lost without you.'

Another memory. I am about five years old, and have become separated from my family in a London park. Everything seems enormous — huge trees, vast expanses of grass, a lake as big as the sea. I feel very tiny and very lost and absolutely terrified. What if they never find me? What if I have to stay here all night? What if the swans come and get me ('They can break a man's arm, you know,' my mother had helpfully informed me only minutes before). And worst of all, what if I get carried away by a Stranger?

They eventually find me, filthy and sobbing, hiding under a bush only yards from where I last saw them. Mummy! Oh, the joy of being folded into that familiar bosom, petted and soothed, and comforted with strawberry ice cream in a cone.

Drifting in and out of sleep, I wonder in my wakeful moments whether in some strange way her mind and mine might join together in our separate states of unconsciousness; whether her sleep can merge with my own, and she can find some comfort in the companionship of my dreams. For these dreams — tiny little vignettes now — are all about my mother. I see her running down a hill on a bright summer's day, arms outflung, laughing; decorating a cake for my birthday, the letters melting into each other, the C of my name running down the side of the cake; weeping over the intransigence of a particularly difficult Lodger.

And appearing, totally out of the blue, at visiting time, sitting by the bed of a patient in what was only my second week as a proper signed-up member of the nursing staff on my first ward.

'Mum! What on earth are you doing here?' I hissed, looking around to see if anyone had noticed her.

'I had to come up and see you, Cass. In your uniform.' She beamed. 'I thought it would be a lovely surprise for you. You don't have to take any notice of me,' she added. 'Just you carry on. I shan't be any bother.'

I hesitated. On the one hand, Mum looked much like any other visitor, and might well pass as one provided she behaved herself. On the other, try as she might to make it otherwise, 'bother' of some kind or another tended to accompany Mum wherever she went.

'What about your job?' I asked her. 'Shouldn't you be at work?'

'Oh, that!' Mum laughed. 'I phoned in with the flu. And don't look so disapproving, Cass. This is important. I couldn't let you down, could I?'

If being let down involved not being visited by Mum at work, I felt I could have coped with it all too easily, but I knew that she would never understand. To Mum, not coming to see me in my new uniform would have been the same as not coming to see me in the school nativity play when I was five.

'You will be good?' I pleaded, aware of the ward sister watching me from behind her desk.

'Good as gold,' Mum promised. 'This lady hasn't any visitors, so I can keep her company. She comes from Bromsgrove,' she added, turning to her new friend. 'I had a cousin who lived in Bromsgrove,' she told her. 'Now isn't that a coincidence?'

It was also, as far as I knew, untrue, but if Mum did nothing worse than enliven someone's dull afternoon with fictitious tales of her past, I wasn't going to stop her, so I returned to my work. When Mum left at the end of visiting time, I breathed a sigh of relief. She had made her inspection, and that, as far as I was concerned, was that.

But I had underestimated Mum, for two weeks later, she was back.

'Mum, you can't keep doing this,' I muttered, making as though to straighten a pillow. 'Or if you must come, you could at least warn me.'

'That would spoil the surprise,' Mum said.

'I don't want surprises.'

'Don't be so ungrateful, Cass. I don't know what's got into you.'

'What's got into me,' I said, 'is that I have just started on a busy surgical ward with a dragon of a sister, and I want to make a good impression. Having my mother following me around does not make a good impression.'

'Nurse Fitzpatrick! I thought I told you to do the temperatures!' The booming voice of the dragon interrupted our little dialogue.

'Temperatures!' murmured Mum, pink with pride. 'Fancy!'

These visits of Mum's — always unannounced but always at visiting times, and on one occasion, she even came accompanied by a friend — continued sporadically until the day when she was found feeding grapes and chocolate to a patient who was supposed to be fasting in preparation for an operation.

'Who is that woman?' demanded the sister. 'She's a blessed nuisance. I'm sure I've seen her before.'

But none of the other staff knew, and I certainly wasn't going to say that the blessed nuisance had anything to do with me. To Mum's credit, she allowed herself to be soundly reprimanded and escorted off the ward without so much as a glance in my direction, although she did make her feelings clear when we met for tea afterwards.

'I think it's disgraceful, starving a poor old woman like that. She hadn't even had any breakfast!'

And try as I might to explain why this was necessary, Mum simply couldn't see it. If someone was hungry, then it was her duty to feed them, just as it was her duty to house the homeless (increasingly, I suspected, in my room, since I was no longer around to defend it).

But in those early months, there were other and worse surprises than Mum's visits. I learnt, among other things, that the decibels generated by a trolley's worth of gleaming metal bedpans cascading onto the floor rivalled the kind of sound one might expect if a high-speed jet ploughed into an iron foundry; that a carelessly spilt pint of blood could make a bed — not to mention its hapless occupant — resemble a battlefield; and that an apparently sick and frail little old lady could, when confused, throw an amazingly powerful punch (I had the bruises to prove it).

I also learnt, for the first time in my life, what it felt like to be totally exhausted — physically as well as mentally.

'How do you do it?' I asked Angela, who was preparing for yet another night out on the town (I was becoming quite attached to Angela, possibly because we no longer had to share a room). 'Where do you get the energy?'

'Priorities, Cass. Priorities.' Angela applied another layer of mascara to her bat-black lashes. 'After a day in the sluice, a girl needs to remind herself what it's like to have a good time.' She applied a generous dose of lacquer to her hair. 'It wouldn't do you any harm to come with me.'

'No thanks.' I was lying on her bed, watching her get ready. 'A hot bath and bed for me.'

'You're old before your time, Cassandra.' She shook her sleek peroxide head at me and bent to squeeze her feet into a pair of needle-sharp stilettos. 'What you need is a bit of fun.'

'Am I so boring?' I asked her.

'Not boring.' Angela shrugged her bare shoulders into a faux fur coat borrowed for the occasion. 'It's just that you never seem to let your hair down. You always look so — serious. You don't go to parties or out on dates —'

'I went to that party last week!'

'Yes. And stood in a corner looking miserable. That nice boy tried to chat you up, and you behaved as though he was trying to abduct you.' She gave a final twirl in front of the mirror and grinned at me. 'I wouldn't have minded being chatted up by him, I can tell you.'

After Angela had left on a waft of cheap perfume, I returned to my own room and thought about what she had said. It was true that I didn't like parties. All that getting-to-know-you small talk, usually conducted against a background of ear-splitting music; embarrassed shuffles round a smoky dance floor followed by the fighting-off of unwanted advances; the solitary walk home, leaving my friends still part of that vibrating, hormone-charged, inebriated mass of partying humanity.

Later on, lying in the bath, gazing at the twin humps of my breasts, ribcage, hip bones, knees and toes, rising like pale hillocks from the steamy water, I acknowledged for the first time my fear of the opposite sex. Hitherto, I had rationalized my feelings, putting them down to disinterest rather than anything stronger; thinking that I was independent-minded enough to plan — even to want — a future without the encumbrance of husband and children. But now at last I saw what had been staring me in the face for some time.

I was afraid of men.

Twenty-eight

I suppose I must have imagined that Uncle Rupert had, if not ceased to exist, then at least been expunged from our lives. After that day when Mum had unceremoniously thrown him out of our house, I had assumed that she'd also thrown him out of her life. It never for a moment occurred to me that she might have kept in touch with him.

But of course I should have known better.

Incoming calls were received by the payphones situated on each floor of the nurses' home, and if no one felt like making the pilgrimage to the end of the corridor, they often went unanswered. But on this occasion, I had a feeling that the call might be for me, and so it was I who answered it.

'Oh, Cass!' Mum sounded breathless. 'I'm so glad it's you. Something awful's happened.'

'What? What's happened? Is it Lucas?'

'No. Not Lucas.'

'Well, who? Who then?'

'Uncle Rupert.'

'*What?*'

'Uncle Rupert.'

'Uncle Rupert.' My voice sounded very faint, drowned out by the thumping of my heartbeats, and I felt the blood rush to my face.

'Yes. He's in prison.' There was a catch in her voice. 'Oh, Cass. I didn't want to have to tell you, but there's no one else I can talk to about it.'

'And what exactly do you expect me to do?' I began to feel seriously angry. 'Feel sorry for him? Bake him a nice Victoria sponge with a chisel in it? If that disgusting old man's ended up in prison, then it's probably high time, and no more than he deserves.'

'I know it's terrible, Cass. I know that. But in a way he can't help it. That's the way he is. He's just, well —'

'Hang on a minute. Are you telling me that he's done something like — like what he did to me — again? Are you saying he was *free* to do it again? Is that what's happened?'

'Well, yes. I mean, he hasn't actually harmed anyone. Not really.'

'Oh, sure. Just paraded around naked, or showed his disgusting appendage to some poor innocent schoolgirl. Nothing to worry about, then. No harm done.'

'Something like that. He was in this park, and —'

'Mum, I don't want to hear about it. I really, really don't want to hear about it.'

'No. Of course you don't. I'm sorry.'

'That's OK.' My anger evaporated as quickly as it had arisen. I was never able to stay cross with Mum for long, and now I took pity on her. 'Look, Mum. I know you were fond of him. I know he's your family. But you've got to understand that this has come as quite a shock to me. I thought he'd — disappeared a long time ago. I'd no idea you were still in touch with him.'

'Well, I wasn't. Not really. Just — just the odd Christmas card. That's all.'

Only my mother would send Christmas cards to the man who had abused her daughter, not to mention her hospitality. Only my mother had this extraordinary capacity for forgiveness. Only my mother could be so naive, so trusting, so *stupid*.

'*Mum!*'

'I know. I know, Cass. I've been so silly. But I really thought he'd change. He promised me, when I sent him away. He said he'd get help.'

'Where did you send him?' My curiosity got the better of me. 'Where's he been all this time?'

'He's got this cousin in Northumberland. He's a vicar or something. It sounded — safe.'

I knew very little about either Northumberland or vicars, but they sounded as though they might offer something in the way of security, if not actual redemption. But apparently not.

'And I had to tell you, Cass, in case it gets into the newspapers.'

'*The newspapers!* Is that likely?' I asked.

'You never know. The press seem to like — that sort of thing.'

'You're — you're not going to visit him, are you?'

Was there the tiniest hesitation, before Mum replied? It would be just like her to battle her way halfway across England to visit her fallen relation.

'No. I don't think so.'

'Thank goodness for that.'

'But — but would you mind if I wrote to him, Cass?'

'Why ask me? It's nothing to do with me.'

'It is. You know it is. If you don't want me to, I won't.'

'Oh, no. You're not doing this to me, Mum. I'm not taking responsibility for what you do or don't do. This has to be your decision.'

'But I wouldn't want to upset you, Cass.'

'Mum, you *are* upsetting me. This phone call's upsetting me. I didn't ever want to hear — *that man's* name again, and now here it is, out of the blue, and you're asking my permission to write him comforting little notes in prison!'

'Perhaps I'll just not tell you. How would that be?' Mum said, after a moment.

'OK. Don't tell me. But the thought of you even thinking about him after all this time — well — it's horrible. I don't want to talk about him or think about him ever again. You do whatever you have to do, but please leave me out of it.'

'I'm so sorry, Cass.'

'Yes.'

'Shall I ring off now?'

'Perhaps you'd better.'

'Goodbye, then.'

'Goodbye.'

When I'd returned to my room, I wondered if I hadn't been a bit hard on Mum. I sat down on my bed and tried to unscramble my thoughts. Sheets of paper with my notes on the digestive system surrounded me (we were supposed to be revising for a test), and I shoved them to one side. My own digestive system was making threatening noises, and for a moment I thought I was about to be revisited by the rather unappetizing hospital supper I had just eaten. I took some deep breaths to steady it, then went over to the washbasin and splashed my face with cold water.

I must pull myself together and stop overreacting. Nothing had changed; I was perfectly safe, and Uncle Rupert was well out of reach in his prison cell. I wondered whether they'd allow him to continue inventing things, and whether there was anyone to bring him his tobacco and aniseed balls. My emotions were a mixture of anger and fear and icy contempt, but I felt no pity whatsoever. I like to think that I am, as a rule, a sympathetic person, who tries to see the best in people, but I could see no best at all in Uncle Rupert. To this day, I think he is the only person I have ever thoroughly loathed, and while years later I was able to reach a degree of understanding, if not actual forgiveness, I have been unable to summon up any real feelings of compassion.

'Are you OK, Cass?' Angela asked me at breakfast a few mornings later. 'You look as though you've seen a ghost.'

'I suppose in a way I have. Well, heard about one, anyway.' I buttered a piece of leathery toast.

'That sounds intriguing.'

'Not intriguing. Rather disgusting, actually.'

'Do you want to talk about it?'

'No. Not really. If I don't talk about it, maybe it'll go away.'

It could well be that it might have helped me if I had been able to talk about it. Not at breakfast, perhaps, but at some other more appropriate time. When Angela managed to relieve her brain of its usual preoccupations with men and clothes and make-up, she could be a surprisingly good listener, and had I been able to unburden myself even a little, it might have made all the difference.

But hindsight is a wonderful thing, and my anxiety didn't last for long. Besides, at that time I was still unaware that the legacy bequeathed to me by Uncle Rupert went a lot deeper than an unpleasant phone call, some shocking memories and a few broken nights' sleep.

Twenty-nine

Despite my mother's undoubted courage during her illness, she has not been an easy patient. Unaccustomed to being told how to behave, she did not take easily to her role as a patient, and couldn't see why she had to fit into a routine; why she was only allowed visitors at certain times, and why she wasn't allowed to smoke in bed.

'But Mum,' I tried to explain. 'It's dangerous. Can't you see that? You might fall asleep with a cigarette in your hand and set fire to yourself.'

'I never have before,' she replied.

'You've never smoked in bed before. In fact, come to that, you've hardly ever smoked at all.'

'I've hardly ever needed to. It's very stressful, this whole dying business. I just felt I needed a cigarette. What's the harm in that?'

So on several occasions, we closed the door and opened a window, and Mum smoked while I listened out for the brisk footsteps which heralded the approach of authority. When we were eventually caught out, it goes without saying that I was the one who made all the apologies, while Mum sat, cigarette in hand, mutinous and unrepentant.

The half-finished packet of cigarettes is in her locker still, hidden from prying eyes inside a toffee bag. But Mum won't be smoking any more cigarettes now, and idly I wonder what will happen to them. They will probably be handed over to me later, when she is gone, together with her other belongings. I have always hated these collections of patients' 'personal effects'; the last pathetic remnants of people's lives; the toilet articles, the handfuls of coins, the half-eaten packets of sweets or chocolate, the get-well cards which failed to bring about the hoped-for miracle.

I wept over the contents of the first bedside locker I had to clear out after its owner had died; all those little reminders of a life once lived and the small treats brought in by a family who hadn't yet come to terms with the prospect of an inevitable outcome. I remember that there were, among other things, an old newspaper with the crossword half-completed, a home-made card from a grandchild, a freshly ironed pair of pyjamas, some sweet papers, a wristwatch. What would the family do with them? I wondered. What was a newly widowed woman expected to do with a worn shaving brush and a pair of spectacles?

It was the staff nurse, a kindly woman with more understanding than I probably deserved, who took me aside and helped me see that it wasn't so much that I hadn't confronted death before, but rather that I had, and I realized she was right. Octavia's death, something which I thought I had managed to put behind me, was still very much a part of me, and as we talked, I was able to tell her about our hopelessness when we were confronted by the toys and clothes and all the other baby paraphernalia that had remained after my little sister's death.

But on the whole, I was enjoying my new career. It was exhausting and demanding, but never boring, and I developed a new respect for the courage and humour of my fellow human beings. True, not everyone suffered their ordeal in saintly silence, and there was always that tiny minority of patients who expected to be given the majority of the attention, but it was all part of the job, and if I occasionally had to retire to the sluice to take a few deep breaths (in those days, junior nurses spent a great deal of their time in the sluice), there was usually someone around to commiserate.

And so I moved from a surgical ward to the Outpatients' Department, with a couple of weeks off for lectures and study (this time a welcome break) and then on to a spell of night duty.

Working at night was like being in a different world; a world of dim lights and murmured voices and soft footsteps. There were no meals to give out, no blanket baths or dressings to administer, none of the routine maintenance of the day shift. Doctors appeared when they were needed, their hurried evacuation of their beds evident in uncombed hair or a glimpse of pyjamas under a white coat. Any rushed activity heralded a new admission or an emergency, and in the case of the latter I did my best to keep my head down. With my lack of experience, I felt I would be of little use in the event of a cardiac arrest, and while I had been trained in the arts of resuscitation, I was in no hurry to try them out on a real patient. Clarrie — the reassuringly unrealistic and limbless rubber patient we practised on in the classroom — was one thing. I was happy enough to empty my lungs into her recumbent body, or thump new life into her imagined heart. A genuine emergency was something else altogether. Fortunately, on these occasions it was usually made clear that I was surplus to requirements, and I would be relegated to 'keep an eye on the rest of the ward' while the serious business took place behind drawn curtains.

Mum's impromptu visits had ceased some time ago (no doubt the novelty had worn off), and her contact was sporadic. But when the time came for the third anniversary of Octavia's death, I received an excited phone call.

'I thought we'd all go and see *The Sound of Music*, Cass. How does that sound?'

'*The Sound of Music*. Well, it's certainly a thought,' I said carefully, wondering where on earth the inspiration for this extraordinary idea had come from.

'Yes. Octavia would have loved it —' would she? — 'and we can all go out for tea afterwards.'

'Who's we?'

'Oh, everyone. Greta — she'll love the mountains, won't she? — and of course Call Me Bill, and we'll pay for Richard, and —'

'OK, Mum. I get the picture.'

'You don't sound very excited.'

'Well, it's not easy. Getting the time off may be a problem, for a start. And how do you know it will be on?'

'I saw it advertised, that's what gave me the idea. It's such a happy family film, Cass. It'll help to cheer us all up.' She paused. 'And last year wasn't — well, it wasn't very successful, was it? I'm determined that this year will be better.'

I agreed that almost anything had to be better than last year, and a visit to the cinema was certainly a novel idea. I myself had already seen *The Sound of Music* twice, and Mum to my certain knowledge three times, but it was a nice story and the songs were tuneful and cheery. Maybe Mum was right. It could just be that *The Sound of Music* was what we all needed.

But in the event, it proved to be far from what Mum needed.

We started off happily enough as we trooped into the cinema with our bags of sweets and settled ourselves in the back row. Greta wept at the sight of the mountains, but then that was to be expected, and Call Me Bill dozed off a couple of times, which was probably to be expected too (Call Me Bill was not what you would call a romantic). But Mum seemed to be enjoying herself, tapping her feet as Julie Andrews sang and danced her way across the Alpine meadows, and humming along to 'I Am Sixteen Going on Seventeen' (much to the annoyance of the people in front of us). So far so good. But as the film progressed, I noticed that she was becoming quieter. When 'Raindrops on Roses' came round for the second time, I was aware of vague snifflings, and by the time we had reached 'The Lonely Goatherd', she was beside herself.

'What on earth's the matter, Mum?' I whispered, reaching for her hand in the darkened cinema. 'You said yourself, this is a happy film.'

'They're — all — alive,' sobbed Mum. 'All. *All alive.*'

'Of course they are. It wouldn't be a happy film if they weren't!' I squeezed her hand. 'Shh, Mum. We're going to disturb everyone else.'

But it was too late. Mum was sunk in misery, impervious to the shushings and the fierce glances of those around us, and in the end I had to take her out, with the rest of our party in reluctant attendance. We emerged into pouring rain (for which we had come totally unequipped), and hurried Mum into the nearest cafe, where we sat her down behind a potted palm and ordered strong coffee.

'Now, what's all this about?' I asked her, stirring sugar into her coffee and pushing the cup into her hand. 'Come on. Drink this up and tell us what's the matter.'

'They're all alive,' Mum said again, between sobs. 'Beautiful alive children. We should never have gone to the cinema. It was a silly idea.' She took a sip of her coffee and added more sugar.

'But we could hardly have gone to see a film about dead children,' I reasoned, beginning to get her drift. 'That wouldn't have been a very jolly thing to do.'

'No. But I didn't realize,' Mum said. 'I just didn't realize.' Poor Mum. How could she have known — how could any of us have known? — that the joyous singing and dancing of all those merry, healthy children, with their bright smiling faces and their unlikely abundance of musical talent, would be for Mum a dreadful reminder of what could never be for Octavia? Never mind that Octavia was unlikely ever to have danced or yodelled on a flower-spangled mountainside; but if she had lived, at least the possibility — however remote — wouldn't have been so cruelly snatched away.

After an uncomfortable half-hour, in the course of which we tried to cheer ourselves up with scones and cream and fruit cake (Lucas seemed to be the only person with any appetite), we escorted Mum home, where I helped her up to her room.

'Oh, Cass!' She sat down on her bed and ran her fingers through her hair. 'I thought I was over it. Over the worst of it, anyway. But I'm not, am I?'

'Poor Mum.' I sat down beside her and took her hand. I noticed that there were grey streaks in the auburn of her hair, and that new lines were forming round her eyes and mouth. 'You know you're not over it. You'll never really be over it. But these waves will become less frequent, and you'll be more — more used to it.'

'Will I?' The face turned towards mine was childlike and hopeful, as though I might have the answer; as though I might be able to make everything all right again.

'I think so. Of course, I don't know. Nobody knows. But that's the way it seems to be with most people.'

'Is that the way it is for you, Cass?'

'Well, it's different for me. She was my sister, and although that's awful, it's not the same as losing your own child, is it?'

'That's the trouble.' Mum sighed. 'There's no one to share it with. No — father.'

It was the first time since her pregnancy that Mum had mentioned Octavia's father, and I was surprised. Perhaps it had taken Octavia's death and the long journey which followed it for her to realize that another parent would have made a difference; there would have been someone else to share her bereavement in the way that only a parent can, someone who would have fully understood how she felt.

It was natural that Mum should be upset on Octavia's anniversary, but I was worried about her. Would she be all right when I returned to London the next morning? Of course Greta would keep an eye on her; and Call Me Bill, although never exactly warm, was kind and dependable. But Lucas was out a lot, preoccupied with his job and a very dishy WPC from his department, and the Charlton Heston Lodger had departed some weeks ago after an unseemly row about scrambled eggs (I never did quite get to the bottom of that) and had not yet been replaced. As far as I knew, there was no new man on the scene; no one to offer the kind of support which Mum seemed to find so essential for her emotional survival.

'You will look after Mum, won't you?' I said to Lucas that night, when Mum had gone to sleep.

'Don't I always?' Lucas leant against a kitchen worktop, drinking beer out of a can.

'Up to a point. But you're — well, you've got other interests.'

'You mean Gracie.' Lucas grinned. 'Aren't I allowed a life?'

'Of course you're allowed a life,' I said, thinking that Gracie seemed an oddly inappropriate name for a policewoman. 'I'm just asking you to look out for her, that's all.'

'It's all right for you, Cass.' Lucas put down his can and wiped his mouth on the back of his hand. 'You're never here.'

'That's not fair. I come home whenever I can.'

'Whenever you want, more like.'

'And I suppose you stay at home out of the goodness of your heart, do you? Not by any chance because it's cheap and convenient and Greta does all your laundry?'

'Probably a bit of both,' said Lucas peaceably. One of the infuriating things about Lucas is that he would never have a proper row. 'But don't worry, Cass. You know Mum. She'll be OK. And of course I'll look after her.'

'And keep me posted?'

'And keep you posted.'

But in spite of his reassurances, I felt uneasy, and when I said goodbye to Mum the next day she was still in bed, with The Dog curled at her side (never a good sign, for The Dog had not improved with age, and these days he was arthritic and not a little smelly; he occupied the bottom of the barrel where Mum's sleeping companions were concerned).

'Bye, Mum.' I kissed her cheek. 'I'm off now.'

'Goodbye, Cass.' She returned my kiss, absently fondling The Dog's ears. 'You will — you will come home again soon, won't you?'

'As soon as I can,' I promised. 'I'll come home as soon as I possibly can.'

Thirty

It was with a sense of relief tinged with guilt that I returned to London after my emotional sojourn at home. At the hospital I had my friends and my work. I had my own little world, removed from the emotional problems of home, and if my social life was unexciting, then I had only myself to blame. Here in London I could truly be myself, and while I wasn't always happy — is anyone? — my lifestyle and my choices were my own. For the first time in my life, I was beginning to feel like an independent adult, no longer defined as a daughter or even a sister. Homesickness had become a thing of the past, and while I loved my home and family, I could envisage a time in the not too distant future when I would no longer necessarily depend on them.

The situation on the boyfriend front was not improving. By now I had been out with several men, one or two of whom I had liked a lot, but I was unable to progress towards anything approaching intimacy. As soon as someone tried to kiss me or even put an arm around me, my body seemed to freeze, and with it any inclination on my part to take the relationship further. I became adept at sidestepping physical contact, and if anyone tried to kiss me, I found that gazing down at the floor often proved discouragement enough.

Of course, medical students had a reputation — Lucas had cheerily reminded me of that before I had even left home — and I found that many of them more than lived up to it. I very quickly learnt not to accept invitations back to student rooms 'for coffee' (at least one prospective seducer didn't even possess a kettle), and endeavoured to stay in mixed company at all times. The result of course was that I was usually summarily dumped after a couple of dates, and would return once again to the uncoupled state.

'What's wrong with you, Cass?' Angela asked, after I had been dropped by two men in rapid succession (by this time Angela had sampled more 'coffee' than could possibly have been good for her).

'Nothing's wrong with me. I just like being single,' I replied, trying to sound convincing.

'No one likes being single,' Angela said. 'We aren't made to be single.'

'Maybe I am.'

'Of course you're not. Come on, Cass. You're an attractive girl. You're young. You've got it all. What are you afraid of?'

'Lots of people prefer to be single,' I persisted. 'Some of the ward sisters, for a start.'

Angela snorted.

'Only the old ones, poor old trouts. Probably all lost their men in the war. In their day, I don't suppose there were enough men to go around. Nowadays, there are plenty of spare men.' She grinned at me. 'We're lucky, Cass. It's a good time to be young.'

She was right, of course. In a way, our generation had it all. Far removed from such world events as the Vietnam War (of which, I'm ashamed to say, I knew very little), we had opportunities undreamed of by previous generations, and looking back, I think I managed to be happy much of the time. I had all the Beatles records, I had even come to enjoy dancing (especially as nowadays it was no longer necessary to have any contact with one's partner; in fact sometimes one didn't even need a partner at all) and I had the right sort of legs for a miniskirt. I just wouldn't be needing the pill.

But part of me wanted a boyfriend. I wanted someone who was special to *me*; someone who was mine, if only temporarily; someone who would take me out on my birthday and send me flowers on Valentine's Day. The annual Nurses' Ball loomed, and I had no one to go with, while most of my friends had their partners already lined up and Angela appeared to have at least three candidates to choose from.

But in the event, there was to be no Nurses' Ball for me, partner or no partner, for three days before it was to take place, I received a phone call.

'Cass?' Lucas's voice sounded strained. He rarely phoned me, and I immediately sensed trouble.

'It's Mum, isn't it?' I said, after a moment.

'Well, yes.'

'Tell me, then. Don't keep me waiting.' What had Mum been up to now? A broken love affair? A bent Lodger? Or, worse, another unplanned pregnancy?

'She's depressed. She's been really bad since Octavia's anniversary, and she doesn't seem to be coming out of it. I don't know what to do.'

'But she can't be! I spoke to her two days ago, and she sounded fine. Why didn't she tell me? Why didn't you tell me?'

'I thought she'd come out of it. After all, she usually does. And besides, she didn't want you worried. She's so proud of you, Cass. You and your nursing. She said she didn't want to — to disturb you, I think she said. So we thought we'd wait —'

'We?'

'Greta and I. After all, Greta's very good with her, and she's at home all day, and —'

'But you should have told me! Of course you should. You had no right to keep something like this from me, Lucas. She's my mother, too. I need to know!'

'Do you? Do you really?'

I felt a sudden surge of resentment and anger; anger with Mum for failing to cope, anger with Lucas for being right, because of course I didn't need to know about Mum's problems, but also anger with myself for even having such thoughts.

'You want me to come home.' It was a statement rather than a question.

'Would you, Cass? Just for a few days? You're so good with her, and you're — you're —'

'A woman?' I said helpfully.

'Well, yes. She doesn't talk to me the way she does to you. You seem to understand each other.'

'Does she want me to come home?'

'Of course she doesn't. Mum thinks you're totally indispensable, and that countless lives will be lost if you desert your post for more than a day.' He paused. 'But she'll be delighted to see you, I can promise you that. And I know you'll make a difference. I wouldn't ask if I wasn't desperate, but I've tried everything, and I simply can't get through to her. Greta's out of her depth, and as for that new doctor, well, he's useless.'

Not for the first time I thought nostalgically of Dr Mackenzie, who had been so efficient at dealing with Mum. But that good man was now enjoying a well-earned retirement, and his replacement — a spotty young man with the bedside manner of a shy teenager — would most certainly be unable to handle her.

Managing the time off proved easier than I had anticipated, and within hours I had packed a bag and was on the train home.

The scene which met me was not encouraging, but I wasn't surprised, since it was always this way when Mum had one of her depressions. While she rarely actually did any housework herself or made any attempt to keep things in order, without her the whole place seemed to wilt. It was as though it required her spirit, her good cheer, to energize everyone else into making an effort. Now, the house was dusty and neglected, Call Me Bill was apparently away visiting a friend (how could he, at a time like this?) and Richard was at the kitchen table drinking coffee and reading the *Daily Sketch*. Greta was sitting beside him, knitting something long and shapeless in an unpleasant shade of green.

'Where is she?' I asked, after the formalities were over.

'Iss in bed.' Greta gave me a hug. 'Iss not well,' she added unnecessarily. 'I take you up, yes?'

'That won't be necessary.' I was annoyed with Greta, who was becoming lazy. She had enjoyed our hospitality for years now, making very little financial contribution. The least she could do now was to keep things in some sort of order even if she'd given up trying to cope with Mum herself.

I was hit by a wall of stale air as I entered Mum's room, and when my eyes became accustomed to the gloom (the curtains were drawn) I could see her curled up like a child under the covers with The Dog lying across her feet.

'Cass!' She sat up and held out her arms to me. 'What a lovely surprise!'

'Hello, Mum.' I kissed her, then went over to the window and drew back the curtains.

'Oh, don't.' Mum held her hands up to her eyes. 'It's too bright!'

'No, it's not. It's a beautiful day, and this room is disgustingly hot and stuffy.' I flung open a window, then came back and sat down on the bed. 'That's better. Now, what's all this about?'

Mum shivered and drew the covers up to her chin.

'You're being all hearty and firm,' she said reproachfully.

'Well, someone's got to be hearty and firm.' I pushed The Dog off the bed, and he slunk off into the corner, whimpering with indignation. 'Have you seen the doctor?'

'Oh, him! He's quite useless. He wouldn't give me any pills, so I told him to go away. He said that in that case he had patients who really needed him, and I haven't seen him since.'

'I'm not surprised,' I said, revising my opinion of the youthful GP.

'Well, he could have called back. To see how I was.'

'But you told him to go away!'

'I didn't mean it. I was just — testing.'

'Mum, it's no good playing silly games with the doctor. He hasn't the time even if you have. Look ...' I stood up. 'I'll go and run you a nice bath, and we can talk while you're having it.'

'But I don't want a bath.'

'Mum, you need a bath. No arguing. Then I can change the sheets on this bed and give it a good airing.'

'Is this the way you treat your patients?'

'Oh, I'm much worse with my patients.'

I ran a deep bath, and poured into it the contents of several nearly empty bottles and jars, producing a great deal of foam and an interesting but not unpleasant-smelling cloud of steam.

'Ugh.' Mum hovered in the doorway. 'What's that smell?'

'Essence of Roses, Jasmine Garden, Lemon Soufflé and Eastern Delight,' I read out the labels on the bottles. 'Who thinks up these ridiculous names? Now, in you get.'

I closed the door and whipped off her nightie. Obediently she stepped into the warm water. I noticed that she had lost weight.

'Mmm. Not bad.' Mum lay back in the bath, and there was a shadow of a smile. A sea of foam trembled up to her chin, and the sunlight filtering through the bathroom window caught the red of her hair. She looked like a tousled film star.

I reflected that it would take more than a bout of depression to cause Mum to lose her looks.

'Now talk to me.' I sat down on the bathroom stool.

'It's Octavia.'

'Of course it's Octavia. But what's brought this on now?'

'I didn't know anniversaries would be this bad,' Mum said. 'I thought this time would be better. I wanted to celebrate her, remember her, but not — not feel like this.'

I knew what she meant. We could go on trying to tell ourselves that an anniversary was just another day, but the time of year, the June sunshine, the roses in the garden — they would always be a poignant reminder of that awful day three years ago. How could they not be?

'Maybe one day we'll be able to celebrate her,' I said gently. 'But it's only been three years, Mum.'

'Oh, Cass. What am I going to do?' Her eyes filled with tears. 'Whatever shall I do?'

'You'll just go on, Mum. As you have been doing. And there'll be good days and bad, and eventually there will be more and more of the good days. Then one day you'll be able to look back and remember Octavia and smile. And be glad you had her.'

'Are you glad, Cass? Are you glad we had her?'

'Yes. Oh yes.' Funnily enough it was a question I had never asked myself, but now I found myself replying without hesitation. The baby who had been neither planned nor wanted had become central to our family, and although we no longer had her with us, her place in the family was assured for as long as we were around to remember her. 'How could I ever regret knowing her, having her for my sister? She was — she was just perfect,' I finished lamely.

'She was, wasn't she?' Mum seemed pleased.

'Of course she was. And now she can never be anything else. A perfect, happy baby.'

When Lucas got home from work that evening, he was impressed to find Mum sitting up in bed between clean sheets, eating supper off a tray. I probably should have persuaded her to get dressed and come downstairs, but I reckoned that the bath was victory enough for one afternoon.

'I knew you'd be able to do it, Cass,' he said. 'I knew we could depend on you.'

But for how long, I wondered some time later, as I took The Dog out for his late-night pee, lingering beneath the huge silent arc of a star-studded sky, smelling the scent of damp grass and flowers. For how long would I have to continue to take responsibility for my family? For my mother?

The winking lights of an aeroplane crossed slowly overhead; The Dog, mission accomplished, whined and licked my hand; Greta called from the back door that she had made me a cup of cocoa and it was getting cold.

I sighed, and turned back towards the house.

Thirty-one

'Has she come yet?' My mother's voice is as faint as the whisper of dried leaves, yet it startles me, for these are the first words she has spoken for hours.

'No. Not yet. But she will. She will come.' I take Mum's hand and stroke it. I thought she had forgotten, but once again, I have underestimated my mother. *'She's on her way. She'll be here as soon as she can.'*

Mum nods, and closes her eyes again. She doesn't have to say who she means and I don't have to ask, but I'm relieved that I know now what it is — who it is — that Mum's been waiting for. But please, please let it be soon, for even Mum can't hang on indefinitely.

It's strange how, at the end, people so often seem to have control over the timing of their death. Some, like Mum, wait for a particular person to come before they can finally let go, while others will hang on until a person close to them has gone home, or perhaps merely left the room for a few minutes, and thus spare those closest to them their last moments. Or maybe they simply want to die in privacy, claiming the last prerogative which is truly theirs, for dying can be an undignified business as well as a lonely one.

Outside the door, the ward is slowly coming to life after the relative peace of the night. A telephone rings, there is the brisk sound of daytime footsteps, laughter, the rumble of a trolley. An orderly brings in a cup of tea, then remembers, and makes to leave the room.

'Please?' I hold out my hand. My mouth is dry, my head aches and I am groggy from lack of sleep. *'Is it OK if I have it?'*

'Sorry. Of course.' She places the cup on the locker. *'Can I get you anything else? A piece of toast?'*

'No thanks. Tea will be fine.'

Dark brown, stewed hospital tea. But this morning, it tastes like nectar, and I drink it gratefully, watching as the new day washes the colour back into the room; the pale green of the walls and the darker tiles of the floor, the white sheets, the blue of my skirt. Lucas's flowers red and white and yellow, a horrible combination — are in a vase on the locker, already wilting from the stuffiness of the central heating, and outside the window the maple leaves continue to drift and swirl on their downward journey.

Mum is sleeping again, her breathing shallow, one hand twitching slightly outside the covers. Even now, it seems odd to see her within the narrow confines of a single bed. I doubt whether my mother has occupied a single bed since she was a child, and it must seem strange to her, too.

I wanted her to be allowed to die in her own bed and in her own home. I wanted to look after her myself. It didn't have to be like this, I told her.

But Mum had been adamant.

'You've your own life to lead, Cass. The least I can do is to die in hospital. Tidily. After all, lots of other people do, so it can't be that bad. You can visit me,' she had added, as though this

were a novel idea. 'You can come and see me in hospital. I've been enough trouble to you over the years. Quite enough trouble.'

But has she really been so much trouble? Or could it be that my need to take care of her has been at least as great as her need to be taken care of? I may not have seen it at the time, but I didn't have to keep running home to her. She certainly never asked me to. And she would have coped. For in a way, Mum has always been on her own, and even if she hadn't had Lucas and me, she would have got by somehow.

But in the first two years of my nursing training, I must have made at least half a dozen mercy dashes home, including the case of the thieving Lodger (who I'm pleased to say ended up behind bars), Greta's appendicitis, another of Mum's depressions and the death of The Dog.

The Dog had become increasingly decrepit over the years, and must have been quite an age, although given the circumstances under which we had acquired him, there was no way of knowing exactly how old he was. Various organs were beginning to fail, his hearing and eyesight were poor, and his bodily functions unreliable. The vet, a no-nonsense man who Mum said would have been better suited to working in an abattoir, recommended that we have him put down.

But of course Mum would have none of it. After the difficult time The Dog had had, it was only fair to 'let him die peacefully at home', as she put it.

'But Mum, he will die peacefully at home,' I told her, when she relayed this piece of information over the telephone. 'I'm sure the vet will come to the house to do it. He won't have to go anywhere. You could give him his favourite meal first,' I added, trying to soften the blow.

'You've become very hard, Cass,' Mum said, after a pause pregnant with disapproval. 'It must be this nursing business.'

Given that Mum was still enormously proud of me and my 'nursing business', this seemed hardly fair, but I let it pass.

'Not hard, Mum. Kind. I'm trying to be kind.'

'Hmm.'

'Well, what's the point of telling me about him if you don't want to hear what I think?' I asked, exasperated.

'I thought you'd be sympathetic.'

'I am sympathetic. But he's a *dog*, Mum. He's had a good innings. We've given him a fantastic life, and now I think it's time to let him go.'

But Mum refused to listen, and when a month later The Dog, on one of his increasingly rare forays into the outside world, wandered blindly into the road and was knocked down and killed, she was understandably upset.

'You'll have to come home to deal with him, Cass,' she told me, when she phoned to break the news. 'After all, you're a nurse.'

'Being a nurse doesn't qualify me to bury dogs any more than anyone else. Can't Lucas do it?'

'Lucas is away on a course. Call Me Bill says dead bodies make him sick and Greta won't stop crying. The Lodger doesn't like dogs,' she added, as though an affection for dogs were a prerequisite for anyone thinking of burying one.

'Where is he?'

'At his German class I think.'

'Not the Lodger. The Dog.'

'He's in the cupboard under the stairs.'

'Ah.' The cupboard under the stairs was warm and stuffy. Time was not on my side.

'Can you put him outside, or at least somewhere a bit cooler?'

'No one wants to pick him up. He's a horrible mess, Cass. The man wrapped him in a blanket so we wouldn't have to look.'

'What man?'

'The man who ran him over. He was awfully nice. It wasn't his fault. He was just going down to the village to buy some paint stripper, and his wife —'

'Mum, I don't need to know the domestic arrangements of this person.'

'All right. But you will come, won't you? I think you owe it to The Dog. Even if you won't do it for me,' she added.

After the hours of walks and grooming and bathing which I had lavished on this very spoilt and fortunate animal, I didn't feel I owed him anything, but I had loved him as much as anyone, and perhaps I ought to put in an appearance.

Fortunately the death of The Dog coincided with a week's legitimate annual leave. It would also get me out of a date with Neil, a charming young junior doctor with melting brown eyes and large capable hands, and the kind of bedside manner which would make being ill a positive treat. However, he also had something of a reputation, and, I suspected, another kind of bedside manner which I was all too eager to avoid.

'Ah, little Cassandra,' he sighed, when I told him I had to go home. 'Excuses, excuses.'

'It's not an excuse. It's an emergency.'

'Emergency, excuse, whatever you say. But this is the third time you've stood me up. A man can only hang around for so long.'

For a moment I hesitated. I imagined those eyes gazing into someone else's, those hands holding a hand that wasn't mine, and the thought was not pleasing. Then I thought of the distinct possibility of being invited back to his place for coffee (and I was sure that Neil had made a great deal of coffee in his time), and my mind was made up.

'I'm sorry. I have to go home. My — my mother needs me.' When I arrived home the following morning, the house seemed very quiet without the hoarse barking which usually greeted my arrival, and I was overcome with sadness.

'Oh, Cass. There you are,' Mum said as though I'd just popped in from next door. She kissed my cheek, and I couldn't help noticing that, considering the circumstances, she appeared remarkably cheerful. Occasions such as this tended to generate either deep gloom or wild celebration where Mum was concerned, and it was with sinking spirits that I sensed a party coming on.

'I thought we'd have a party,' she continued, as though reading my thoughts. 'The Dog never had a party while he was alive. I think we should give him one now.'

'A party.' I dropped my case on the kitchen floor and sat down. 'What does everyone else think?'

'Oh, I haven't told them yet. You're the first to know.' She beamed, as though this were a truly splendid piece of news. 'I've got it all planned. I thought we'd have the burial first, and then we can all come back to the house for food and drink. We can ask the neighbours, of course, and Lucas will want to bring Gracie, and Greta's got a friend over from Switzerland, and —'

'I thought Lucas was on a course.'

'Oh, didn't I tell you? It was cancelled.'

'No. You didn't tell me.' So I needn't have come home after all. I swallowed my irritation. 'Who's digging the hole?'

'The hole?'

'Yes, the hole. For The Dog.'

'I hadn't thought.'

'Well, it's not going to be me,' I said. 'If I've got to — to deal with the body, the least you can do is organize someone else to do the digging. I'm tired, Mum,' I added. 'I've just had a gruelling spell of night duty. Grave-digging duties are not part of the deal.'

Late that afternoon, the noisome and very unpleasant remains of The Dog (had he really only been in the cupboard for twenty-four hours?) were interred in a deep hole under the cherry tree (the hole courtesy of a very disgruntled Lucas, who felt that he was being shown up in front of the lovely Gracie). Tears were shed, Richard gave an interesting rendition of the last post on his ukulele (yes, it is possible, just, but I doubt whether anyone else would have recognized it), a bright wreath of marigolds was laid, and we all repaired to the house for the party. There seemed to be a lot of guests; people I'd never met in my life before, and quite a few old friends. How on earth had Mum managed to assemble them in such a short time?

She had certainly done The Dog proud. His framed photograph formed the centrepiece on the dining-room table, and around it there was enough food to feed a small army. As ever, the drink flowed, and Lucas, having recovered from his post-burial sulk, made his vodka mixture, so everyone got riotously drunk.

'What we need,' mumbled Mum, as she lay on the floor with her head in my lap some time after midnight, 'what we need is — is — is —'

'What do we need, Mum?' I stroked her hair, reflecting through a haze of alcohol that whatever might be said about Mum, she certainly knew how to throw a good party.

'What we need is —' she waved a hand vaguely in the air — 'is one of those things — you know — woof woof.' She giggled.

'You mean a dog?'

'That's the one. We need a dog. Clever Cass. A dog. A new dog. That's what we need.'

It seemed a bit soon to be replacing The Dog when we had only just come to terms with his loss, but even after she'd had time to sleep on the idea and recovered from her hangover, Mum was adamant. After all, as she explained to us, there was an open tin of dog food in the fridge. It would be a shame to waste it. Besides, a new dog would cheer us up, and would take our minds off the old one. She said that it would be best if she went to choose the new dog on her own; that way, she would have no one to blame but herself if Things Went Wrong.

Thus two days later, she set off to the rescue centre, and returned in triumph, a small bouncy black and white hearthrug frolicking at her feet. Its eyes were entirely obscured, and it seemed to be lacking something. It took me a few minutes to realize exactly what.

'Mum, do we really need a dog with three legs?' I asked.

'He doesn't mind,' Mum said gaily. 'He's used to it. Apparently he lost it ages ago. And look at it this way, Cass. He'll have only three legs whether we have him or not, so he might as well live on three legs here. And he won't need so much exercise, will he?'

'Won't he?'

'Of course not. He's got one less leg to exercise, hasn't he?'

'Where are his eyes?' I couldn't even tell which end of the hearthrug was which.

'Under here somewhere.' Mum poked about in the matted fur. 'There we are! Lovely brown eyes! We'll give him a nice bath, and he'll come up as good as new.'

Her new friend did not enjoy his nice bath, and Mum emerged some time later soaked to the skin and sporting several nasty scratches, but with her enthusiasm still intact.

'Here we are,' she said. 'Doesn't he look lovely?'

Lovely was hardly the word, but we all agreed. When Mum was in this kind of mood, we would do anything to keep her there. Besides, she now had something to look after, and Mum was never happier than when she felt needed.

We looked at each other and gave a collective sigh. New Dog had joined the family.

Thirty-two

I returned to London reassured. New Dog had settled in happily (although personally I had yet to understand what Mum saw in him), Mum was in her element ('There might be someone who could make him a new leg, Cass. Or perhaps even a little wheel?'), and things were more or less back to normal.

At the hospital, things were not back to normal. The bad news was that Matron summoned me and kindly but firmly informed me that since I had had far more than the permitted amount of leave, I would be taking my final exams four months after everyone else.

These tidings were not entirely unexpected, but I was nonetheless disappointed. I had hoped that I might scrape by — just — but what with my numerous visits home on compassionate leave, and a nasty bout of glandular fever in my first year, my luck had run out. In a few months' time I would have to bear the humiliation of seeing my colleagues promoted to the role of staff nurse, while I remained a humble student.

The good news (if you could call it that) was that the dashing Neil seemed intent on waiting for me to change my mind about going out with him, and to that end had endured a whole week without the pleasures of female company (or so he informed me).

'Come out with me, Cass.' He cornered me on the ward, where I was writing up some notes. 'Just one little date. And then if you really don't like me, I promise I'll leave you alone.'

'I never said I didn't like you.'

'Well, then.'

'It's not as simple as that.'

'Of course it's simple.' He drew a chair up to the desk and sat down beside me. 'Look at me, Cass. Look me in the eye, and tell me you really don't want to go out with me.'

'Well ...'

'Great. That's settled, then. Tonight? Shall we go out together tonight?'

'I don't know. I've got things to do. I've got to —'

'Wash your hair?'

'Well, yes. Among other things.'

'I like your hair just the way it is.'

As most of my hair was invisible under my cap, I couldn't help laughing, and Neil seemed pleased.

'You've got a sense of humour,' he said with satisfaction. 'I like a girl with a sense of humour. So that's fixed, then? You'll come out with me?'

Still I hesitated. Rationally, I could think of lots of reasons to go out with Neil. He was attractive, caring and kind, and if he had something of a reputation, well, I was a big girl. Surely I could look after myself, couldn't I? By now I had dealt with cardiac arrests and haemorrhages and all manner of emergencies; I had run the gauntlet of the great Professor Armstrong-Phillips, whose tantrums in the operating theatre would put any self-respecting toddler to shame; I had on occasion even been briefly in charge of a busy ward. What was a night out with a young doctor in comparison with any of these? So I agreed, feeling that since I had neither a valid excuse nor the ability to tell a convincing lie, I didn't have a lot of choice.

But that first date proved my misgivings to be quite unfounded. We had dinner in a little bistro in South Kensington, all checked tablecloths and candles in wine bottles and real French waiters, and we found plenty to talk about. Neil was the perfect gentleman, there was no mention of going back to his place for coffee, and he saw me home with a chaste kiss on the cheek. It was the first time I had felt completely relaxed on a date, and I was both happy and relieved. I felt as though I had finally broken through some invisible barrier. Maybe from now on things would start to improve.

After two more similar dates, I decided that I was in love. I found myself singing as I walked down the street, lying awake at night just basking in the warm feeling of being loved (or so I thought), and daydreaming as I went about my duties. I felt wildly happy and more alive than I could ever remember feeling before.

'What's the matter with you, Cass?' Mum asked suspiciously, when I phoned to ask how things were at home. 'Something's up. I can tell.'

'Nothing's up. I'm fine.'

'I know — you're in love! That's what it is.' Mum had a nose for this kind of thing. 'Oh, Cass! How wonderful! Is he a doctor?'

'Well, yes. As a matter of fact he is.'

'What's his name?'

'His name's Neil.'

'Have you been to bed with him yet?'

'I'm not prepared to say,' I replied primly.

'Oh, come on, Cass. You and I don't have any secrets from each other.'

It was true that Mum certainly didn't seem to have any secrets from me (or, come to that, from anyone else) but that was her choice. I decided that my love life was going to be just that. Mine. I wasn't going to allow it to become public property the way hers was. I could just see news spreading round the household and among Mum's friends like celebratory wildfire. For some time now, Mum had been making it clear that she thought it high time that I divested myself of my virginity (she had lost her own so long ago, she told me, that she couldn't remember the occasion or even the man in question). A doctor, as she explained now, would be just the person to do it with, since 'doctors know all about that sort of thing'.

'Mum, I don't want to talk about it,' I said now.

'Oh, Cass.' She sighed. 'Who would have thought you'd grow into such a prude?'

I thought of my friends, most of whom also went to considerable lengths to conceal their sexual exploits from their parents, but for reasons quite different from my own, and wondered for the hundredth time what it would be like to have a normal mother; one who would wait up at night for me, to demand 'What time do you call this?', or warn me against the perils I might incur from involvement with the opposite sex. But of course, I would never know.

'If there's anything important to tell you, then I will,' I said.

'You don't have to get married,' Mum continued, as though I hadn't spoken. 'I've never had a lot of time for marriage, myself,' she added (what a surprise). 'Living together is just fine.'

'Mum, I've only known him three weeks. Give me a break.'

'You could bring him home for the weekend. We'd all love to meet him. Or I could come up to London.'

'No, Mum. No.'

'Why? Are you ashamed of me?'

'Of course I'm not ashamed of you. It's just that it's too soon. It's not such a big deal. Not yet, anyway. Now can we let the subject drop, please?'

But in the event, Mum never did get to meet Neil.

By the time we reached our fourth date, Neil was obviously ready to raise the stakes and invited me back to his rooms for a meal.

'It'll be more cosy there. We've never really had time on our own, Cass,' he said.

'Yes we have!'

'No. I mean really on our own. I don't call eating in a crowded restaurant being on our own.'

Why did I feel this frisson of fear? Why wasn't I jumping at the chance of spending an evening in the company of a man with whom I imagined myself to be in love?

'Come on, Cass. I'm not such a bad cook, although I'll admit the facilities aren't up to much.'

'It's not the cooking.'

'Well what, then? What is it? Don't you trust me?'

'Of course I trust you.' I smiled at him. 'And OK, I'd love to come. Thank you.'

Neil's room in the doctors' quarters was cramped, and the kitchen in which he was operating to produce our meal even smaller. I made myself at home, as instructed, while he beavered away amid clouds of steam and the odd muttered curse. I was plied with wine and peanuts but my offers of help were refused, and since there didn't seem to be room for more than one cook to turn round, never mind do anything useful, I occupied myself by examining Neil's collection of books (mainly medical) and browsing through a copy of the *British Medical Journal* (full of dense earnest print and long words, illustrated with graphic photos of tumours and suppurating skin lesions).

We ate our meal off trays on our laps, and Neil opened a second bottle of wine. I was by now feeling pleasantly euphoric and relaxed (notwithstanding Mum's parties, I wasn't normally much of a drinker), and I was beginning to wonder what on earth I had been worrying about. The food was certainly edible, Neil was in excellent form, and I knew I was looking good in my new miniskirt and blouse.

'Come and sit beside me on the bed,' Neil said, when he had cleared away our trays. 'It's much more comfortable.'

Obediently, I did as I was told, and then, as he put an arm round my shoulders, I lay back against the pillows beside him. The Beatles thrummed from the record player ('she loves you, yea, yea, yea'. Oh yes, I thought. I do. *I do*), Neil's aftershave smelled deliciously masculine and the feel of his cheek against mine was strong and protective. I gave a little sigh.

'Enjoying yourself?' Neil asked, shifting slightly beside me.

'Mm. Yes.' The room tilted slightly and then righted itself. A poster appeared to be sliding slowly down the wall, and the books in the bookcase jiggled and blurred. I smiled, and moved closer into Neil's willing arms.

'That's better,' Neil murmured. 'I was beginning to think you didn't fancy me.'

'What do you mean?'

'Well, you've always jumped like a startled rabbit when I've touched you, and done that ducking thing with your head when I tried to kiss you. You're a cool customer, little Cassandra. I'll say that for you.' He kissed the top of my head. 'And I reckon I've been a very good boy.'

'Of course you're a good boy.' Another poster seemed to be joining its partner on their journey down the wall. I was certainly feeling very strange.

'But being good is fine, as far as it goes,' Neil murmured, placing a hand somewhere in the region of my midriff. 'I'd like to go a bit further.' The hand began to meander slowly upwards in the direction of my bosom. 'Just a tiny, tiny bit further.'

His voice was soft and caressing, like that of a parent soothing an anxious child. The posters, which seemed miraculously to have regained their former positions, now began to tilt slowly sideways, and the narrow bed swayed beneath us.

'A bit further? What do you mean?' I held on to the edge of the bed in an effort to steady it.

'I think you know what I mean.' The hand paused for a moment, and then continued on its travels upwards. 'Come on, little Cassandra. You know you want it as much as I do.'

'Want what?'

At this stage I have to say it must have seemed that I was quite extraordinarily stupid, but I was very drunk, and the civilized nature of the evening's proceedings had persuaded me that Neil's reputation was entirely undeserved. As ever, he had behaved impeccably, and I felt that he had been the innocent victim of vicious gossip from people who ought to know better. As for my own feelings, these had always been emotional rather than physical. I certainly longed for Neil, but my longing was of the children's fairy-story variety; all hearts and flowers, being gently wooed, and then perhaps carried away into the sunset like Snow White.

Of course I knew that Neil probably wanted more, but so far he had seemed so sensitive to my finer feelings that I think I had managed to persuade myself he might be prepared to wait. After all, this was love, and if he was in love with me (and why wouldn't he be?) then his feelings could be helped to transcend anything as basic as sex. If sex were ever to come into our relationship it would be in the fullness of time and when I was ready. I certainly wasn't ready yet.

So when the wandering hand, having found its way between the buttons of my blouse, finally arrived at my left breast and grasped it firmly by the nipple, I was taken completely by surprise.

'*No!*' I gripped his wrist and pulled his hand away. 'What do you think you're doing?'

'What do *you* think I'm doing?' Undeterred, the hand made its way back.

'No. Please. Please, don't!' I pulled away from him and tried to sit up.

'What on earth's the matter with you, Cass? Anyone would think I was trying to rape you!'

'Just — don't. I don't want you to — to do that.' My feet found the floor, and I stooped down and tried to put my shoes on. The room was still spinning gently and my head was pounding, but I was thinking perfectly clearly and all I wanted was to get away as quickly as I could.

'Well, you little prick-teaser!'

'I'm not!' Tears stung my eyelids. 'That's a horrible thing to say!'

'Is it?' Neil's voice was cold. 'I think you've just been leading me on all this time, Cass. I suppose you thought it was a bit of fun. You probably even told your friends, I shouldn't wonder. Had a laugh at my expense.'

'That's not fair!'

'No. *You're* not being fair. I've taken you out, I've tried to understand this — problem you seem to have. And all the time you were just stringing me along.' Neil swung his legs off the bed and stood up.

'It wasn't like that.' By now I was weeping. 'Please try to understand.'

'Oh, I understand all right. I understand perfectly. Just let me warn you, Cass. This game you're playing is a very dangerous one, and could land you in serious trouble. Not everyone's as nice as I am.'

'Well, I don't think you're being nice at all.' I hunted for my bag, trying to see through a blur of tears.

'I don't suppose you do.' Neil watched me as I struggled into my coat. 'I'm sure you'll understand if I don't see you home.'

It took me several weeks to get over Neil. I think he really was my first love, and while first loves are often insubstantial things, helped along by a combination of youthful imagination, optimism and a sturdy pair of rose-tinted spectacles, their passing can be very hard to bear.

Worse still, though, was the realization that my problem with men really was here to stay.

Thirty-three

Six months later, I took my final examinations; and after what seemed an interminable wait, received the news that I had passed. I was now a State Registered Nurse, with a shiny badge and a royal-blue uniform to prove it.

Within days, Mum paid a visit to inspect me, but this time with my reluctant permission, and with promises not to embarrass me or — more importantly — give food to the patients. Her proud gaze followed me for an entire afternoon, and while her behaviour was beyond reproach ('I'm afraid I'm not allowed to feed you,' I heard her whisper to an elderly man, as though he were an animal in the zoo), I found her presence discomfiting.

'Why don't you go and get yourself a cup of tea in the canteen?' I asked her at one point.

'Oh no. I don't want to miss a minute of this. There might be an emergency, Cass. I'd hate to miss seeing you dealing with an emergency.'

Fortunately, there were no emergencies, and the afternoon passed without incident. But while I was of course grateful for the interest Mum took in my promotion, I was also relieved to hear that there wouldn't be a repeat performance.

'It's difficult to get away nowadays. New Dog needs me,' she explained, after we'd had some supper together before she caught the train home. 'I can't leave him for long. The others — well, they don't understand him.'

I don't know exactly when I realized that I was suffering from depression. I suppose because I had always considered myself to be a reasonably sanguine person, it never occurred to me that I should fall prey to any kind of mental problem. Certainly, life had had its ups and downs, but then that was the same for everyone, and if I was occasionally sad or fed up, then I knew that sooner or later I would snap out of it and return to normal.

Of course I had long been accustomed to Mum's depressions. These were unmistakable, tending to strike suddenly out of a clear blue sky, plunging her into the depths of weeping despair, paralysing her mentally and physically and dragging everyone within her vicinity down with her. Then, just as she seemed to reach rock bottom, and we were wondering whether she was ever going to return to normal (although 'Mum' and 'normal' were not words I was accustomed to use in conjunction), she would bounce back as though nothing had happened.

My own depression was different, creeping up on me over several weeks, and so gradually that for a while I didn't realize what was happening. I was tired, certainly, but then I had been working hard. I wasn't sleeping, but I had suffered from bouts of insomnia before. I had no boyfriend, but that was nothing new, and since the unfortunate episode with Neil, I had long since managed to persuade myself that I was better off without one. And if life seemed flat and colourless, then that was probably because, what with work and the drab London winter, there didn't seem to be a lot to look forward to.

The bouts of weeping were something else. I have never cried easily, but now I found myself bursting into tears at the slightest provocation. Rudeness from a patient, a phone call from home, the prospect of an extra-long shift — any of these could induce in me a wave of despair quite disproportionate to the significance of what had triggered it. I began to dread waking in the morning, while getting up, washing and dressing — once activities carried out without a thought — now became at best chores, and at worst, almost insuperable obstacles. I know Mum suspected that something was wrong, and of course I could have told her how I felt. But what was there to tell? Nothing awful had happened, I wasn't ill, and life on the whole should have been good.

Eventually, the decision as to what to do was taken out of my hands.

'Nurse Fitzpatrick, you need help.' My ward sister, a tough woman of the old school but one with a surprisingly soft centre, took me aside.

'I'm fine,' I lied. 'Just a bit tired.'

'We're all a bit tired. It's the nature of the job.' She tilted her head, appraising me as though I were one of her patients. 'You're not yourself. You're forgetting things, making silly little mistakes, and there's obviously something the matter. Do you want to tell me about it?'

'There's nothing to tell. Really.'

'Nothing to tell, or nothing to tell me?'

I shook my head, unable to speak.

'I think you should go and see Dr Burns. Just for a chat. Take the rest of the day off, and go to his surgery this evening. I need healthy staff on my ward, and at the moment you're not really up to the job. Get yourself sorted, and then come back to me and we'll have another talk.'

Dr Burns was the medical officer in charge of our health. I don't believe student nurses have such things these days, but we were fortunate, and while the hospital worked us hard, they also looked after us well.

Some hours later, I was weeping helplessly in Dr Burns's surgery.

'I'm fine. Really I am.' I fumbled for my handkerchief.

'So I see.' He regarded me with kindly amusement over his half-rimmed spectacles, then passed me a box of Kleenex.

'I just — just —'

'Feel a bit low?'

I nodded.

'And when did you pass your exams?'

'Eight months ago.' I blew my nose.

'Did you want to be a staff nurse?'

'Of course I did! I mean, I do.'

'Are you sure?'

'Well, yes. Yes, of course.'

Dr Burns steepled his fingers and leant back in his chair. 'It's a big step from being a student. More responsibility. More demands. More people to look after.'

'What do you mean?'

'I know a bit about your history, Nurse Fitzpatrick. You've maybe had more than your share of responsibility, one way and another. From what you've told me in the past, it seems to me that you've spent much of your life looking after other people. It could just be that there's a part of you saying enough is enough. That it's time to start taking care of number one.'

'Are you suggesting I give up?' I was incredulous. It had never for a moment occurred to me that I shouldn't continue my nursing career.

'No. Not necessarily.' Dr Burns sat forward in his chair once more. 'I'm just wondering whether nursing is the right career for you. Whether it's something you really should be doing.'

'Of course it is!'

'Is it?' He opened a folder with my name on it and perused the sheaf of notes inside. 'You've had a lot of time off, one way and another.'

'But I had permission! I always had permission. I've had family problems as well as being ill.'

'I know all that. Nurse Fitzpatrick — Cassandra. No one's criticizing you. I believe your conduct has been exemplary. But Matron's recently had a word with me —'

'She had no right!'

'She has every right. She's in charge of the nursing staff, and not much gets past her, believe me. I can't tell her what passes between us. Between you and me. That's confidential. But she's within her rights — in fact it's her duty — to tell me if she has concerns about her nurses.'

'Oh.'

'She has no problems with your work, but she is concerned about how you're coping.'

'Then why didn't she say something to me?'

'I believe she was going to suggest you came to talk things over with me, but it seems you beat her to it.'

'I don't know what to do.' I took another Kleenex.

'I know you don't. That's what I'm here for.' Dr Burns regarded me thoughtfully. 'I'd like you to take a bit of time off.'

'But I've had masses of time off! I can't have any more. I want — I want —'

'What do you want, Cassandra?'

'I want to go home.'

I burst into tears again, thinking how feeble that sounded, and wondering what on earth had made me say it. A few hours ago, nothing could have been further from my thoughts, but now the thought of home, the very word *home*, made me ache with longing. The warmth of our big untidy kitchen, Greta's brews of too-strong tea ('builders' tea' Mum called it), my own familiar bedroom (provided there was no one else in it), Lucas's amused banter, and of course Mum herself — suddenly I felt I needed them all as never before.

'Then that's what you shall do.' Dr Burns took up his pen and wrote something in my notes.

'What, *now*? I can't. The ward's busy, and two people are off with flu, and —'

'And I suppose they can't possibly run the ward without you.'

'Well, yes of course they can, but —'

'No buts. You've just said it yourself. You're not indispensable. I'm not asking you, Cassandra. I'm telling you.' He put down his pen and smiled at me. 'You need to go home, get some rest, do a bit of thinking. I'm signing you off for a month.'

'*A month!*'

'Yes. A month. I'm prescribing some tablets for you. Some mild antidepressants. Get some rest, some fresh air. Relax for a bit. I'll see you when you get back, and we'll take it from there.'

'And what about Matron?'

'I'll tell Matron. Just let the ward know what's happening, and off you go. I don't want to see you for another four weeks. All right?'

'All right.'

I left the room feeling numb but oddly relieved. I couldn't remember when anyone had last taken responsibility for my welfare; made important decisions on my behalf; *taken care* of me.

As I changed out of my uniform later that evening it was with an enormous sense of relief, as though I were shedding an ill-fitting skin. But it never crossed my mind that there was any possibility that I might have worn it for the last time.

Thirty-four

February 1970

I spent the first three days at home crying. The relief — the utter relief — of being able finally to let go; to be rid of the constraints of my job, of maintaining a stiff upper lip and avoiding the watchful of eye of Sister was indescribable. I don't think I had fully realized how low I had been until I was able to give full vent to my unhappiness with the blessed release of being free to weep whenever and wherever I wanted to.

Mum's reaction was at first ambivalent. On the one hand, while she was deeply distressed on my behalf, she was also bewildered. For some years now I had been the strong one — the person upon whom she could rely for help and support when she needed it — and for me to disintegrate like this must have been hard for her to deal with. On the other hand, Mum loved looking after people, and once she had got used to the idea that this time it was I who needed her, she was in her element. She rushed up and down stairs with trays and cups of tea, she made all my favourite dishes, she even offered to read aloud to me. Entertained by this idea, I accepted her offer, and we spent a weepy afternoon together while she read me selected excerpts from *Little Women*, one of my favourite childhood books.

To her very great credit, Mum didn't ask any questions until I'd been home nearly a week. A veteran of the battle against depression (albeit her battles had been very different from mine) she knew better than to look for glib answers or easy diagnoses, and she wisely waited until I was ready before expecting me to do any talking.

'I do love you, you know, Cass,' she said unexpectedly one morning, as she brought me breakfast in bed.

'I know you do, Mum.'

'Whatever you do,' she added.

'Yes.'

'And — the nursing thing.'

'Yes?'

'I shan't — I shan't be disappointed if you don't go back.'

How I blessed Mum for that, for while I had given very little thought to my future, I knew what it must have cost her to, as it were, give me permission to turn my back on a profession of which she was so proud.

'I don't know what I'm going to do, Mum,' I said now. 'I don't feel ready to make any decisions.'

'Of course you don't.' She sat down on the bed and stroked my arm. 'You must stay at home as long as you want. There's no hurry.'

'I've got another three weeks before I have to go back. I may be feeling better by then.'

Mum seemed to hesitate, plucking at the bedspread, gazing towards the open window.

'I'm — I'm sorry I haven't been a better mother. I — well, I didn't really know how. And then somehow it was too late.'

'I suppose it's like that for everyone,' I said. 'After all, no one tells you how to do it, do they?'

'No. I suppose not.'

'In any case, you've been a brilliant mother.'

'Do you really mean it?'

'Of course I mean it. I wouldn't have you any other way.'

'You're sure?'

'Quite sure.' I sat up and gave her a hug. 'Besides, you're *my* mother. How could I possibly want any other?'

She nodded, satisfied for the time being.

'But I don't know what to do to help you, Cass.'

'I don't want you to do anything. Just be there, Mum. Just get on with things as normal. I have to sort this out for myself, but if I know I have your support whatever — well, whatever happens, then it'll make it that much easier.'

The rest of the household were equally supportive, and Greta would happily (if that's the word) have wept along with me if Mum had permitted it.

'No, Greta,' she said, as Greta reached for her handkerchief. 'This isn't your depression. It's Cass's. You can't just cash in on it like this. Go and make yourself useful.'

So poor Greta, unable to show her solidarity in the way she knew best, made a reproachful retreat to the kitchen.

Lucas, who was still besotted with Gracie, was distracted but kind; Call Me Bill bought me flowers; and two ex Lodgers called in to ask after me. In fact, the only person who thoroughly resented my presence was New Dog. New Dog and I had never really got on, I suspect because he recognized in me a rival for Mum's attention. Now that my victory was beyond doubt, he spent his time sulking in corners or snarling unpleasantly at me from behind doors. In the end, even Mum lost patience with him.

'New Dog! *Basket!*' she yelled at him, and New Dog was so astonished at this unaccustomed treatment that he stayed in his bed for a whole day.

But after a week or so, New Dog and I came to some sort of understanding, and we took to going for long walks together in the fields behind the house, New Dog hobbling with astonishing speed on his three legs and rolling in cow-pats, while I brooded on the meaning of life and what I was going to do with mine.

As the weeks went by, my depression began to lift. Without the pressure of work and the expectations of other people, I felt the knot of anxiety that had taken up residence in my stomach begin to relax and dissolve, and I began to experience moments of happiness once more. Spring was on the way, and here in the country I was able to appreciate it to the full. On fine days, New Dog and I took our walks to the accompaniment of skylarks and blackbirds, blackthorn blossomed in the hedgerows, and the woods were taking on the faintest tinge of green. Greta had started her spring cleaning — an annual ritual which she undertook alone since no one else was interested — and Mum was talking of getting a new job (a sure sign that the year was under way).

I had forgotten how much I missed home, and began to wonder what had been the attraction of London and my independent life there. The familiar routine, from the sound of Greta's feet on the creaky staircase as she went down in the morning to put the kettle on to New Dog's last trot round the garden at night — all these things had been woven into the fabric of my life for so long that I found myself settling back in as though I had never been away.

When the time came to go back to London to see Dr Burns, I was overcome by panic. I don't know what it was that I was so afraid of — after all, it had been made clear to me that I wouldn't have to do anything I didn't want to; that no pressure would be brought to bear upon me — but suddenly the very thought of getting on the train for that now familiar journey, of walking through the doors of the hospital, of all those busy purposeful people, was almost unbearable.

Seeing my anxiety, Mum insisted on coming with me.

'It's all right, Cass,' she said, reading my thoughts. 'I won't talk to anyone. I'll just keep you company on the train. I won't even come into the hospital if you don't want me.' Then her eyes lit up. 'I tell you what,' she added triumphantly, 'I'll bring New Dog with me, then I can't possibly go in with you, can I? New Dog and I can have a nice walk in the park, and we can meet up afterwards and you can tell me how you got on.'

In the event, this proved to be an inspirational idea, for New Dog (who had been bathed and blow-dried by Greta before we left, and was now fluffy and sweet-smelling) kept everyone in our carriage entertained all the way to London. It would seem that having only three legs had its advantages, and New Dog, who could be very charming when it suited him, was not above exploiting his handicap to the full. In the hour and a half it took us to reach our destination, he sat on at least three different laps and was fed a variety of sandwiches and biscuits.

Three hours later, we were on our way home again.

'I'm sorry, Mum,' I said to her, as the train pulled out of the station. 'I'm so so sorry.'

'Don't be.' Mum's efforts to conceal her disappointment were heroic. 'If it's not right for you, then it's not right at all.'

I thought of the kindness of Dr Burns and especially of the final words of Matron.

'I took a gamble when I took you on, Nurse Fitzpatrick. I think we both knew that. You've given us a lot, and I hope we've done the same for you, but I think you need time at home and perhaps a change of direction.' She had smiled at me, closing my file. 'Maybe one day — one day — we'll see you back here again.'

But I think we both knew that that was not to be. I had made my last journey to St Martha's.

Thirty-five

The door opens and Greta comes in, bearing a huge basket of fruit topped with a shiny yellow ribbon.

'Iss all right I come?' she whispers, approaching the bed tentatively, her eyes already filling with tears.

Poor Greta. She has aged immeasurably since Mum's illness, and I worry about what will become of her when the inevitable happens.

'Of course it's all right.' I give her a hug. 'But she's asleep at the moment.'

Greta puts her basket of fruit on the locker and takes a chair.

'She has pain?' she asks.

'Yes. Some pain. But they're giving her stronger injections now.'

I pray that Mum's eyes remain closed, for she finds Greta's visits upsetting. Greta longs to help, but there is nothing she can do, and the distress this causes them both does nobody any good.

'How's the dog?' I ask her now. The dog — Last Dog (perhaps Mum knew something we didn't) — is an animal after Mum's own heart. He has never learnt to follow even the simplest instructions, and conducts his life with no reference whatsoever to the feelings of those who care for him. Mum adores him. Greta, however, does not.

'Dog iss very bad,' Greta says. 'He take cheese and pork pie.'

'Oh dear. Does he miss Mum?'

'Last Dog miss nobody.'

'Oh well. At least that's one thing less to worry about.'

'Your mum, she like the fruit, yes?'

'I'm sure she will.' Mum hasn't been able to eat anything for days, but it's no good telling Greta that.

For some time, we sit together in silence, listening to the tiny shallow sounds of Mum's breathing and watching the blue and gold of another beautiful autumn day in the world outside the window. I am too exhausted for conversation, and I suspect that Greta is feeling much the same.

After a while, Greta gets to her feet.

'I go. Yes?'

'Well, it's lovely to see you, Greta, but there's not really much you can do.'

'You tell her I come?'

'Of course I'll tell her.' I summon up a smile. 'Look after yourself.'

'Poor Greta,' Mum whispers, when Greta's left the room. 'Couldn't — couldn't talk to her.'

'I'm sure she'd understand.' I squeeze her hand. 'I didn't know you were awake.'

'Disappointed. Hoped it might be — you know.'

'She's on her way. She'll be here soon,' I say, praying that I'm right.
Mum nods and sighs again.
'I'll wait, then.'
Poor Mum. I think she's ready to let go, but she can't. I didn't think she'd live through the night, but I had underestimated her. Mum has unfinished business.
I undo the cellophane wrapped round the basket of fruit (not so useless after all) and help myself to a banana.

I'd now been home for three months, and while much better, I still had no idea what I wanted to do. I had become a regular visitor to the labour exchange, but jobs were in short supply locally, and I had no transport to travel further afield. I was entitled to the dole (what a dreadful word that is, sounding as it does like the tolling of a bell at a wake), but missed my monthly pay cheque and the self-respect that came with it.

In the end, I applied for — and was given — a job in a small local art gallery. The elderly proprietor, who had the unlikely name of Humphrey Hazelwood, was a man of great charm and kindness, and we immediately hit it off.

'I'm afraid you may find the work a little dull after all the excitement of hospital life,' he told me at my interview.

'I think a dull job is just what I need at the moment,' I said. 'Although I'm sure I shan't find it dull,' I added, afraid of offending him.

The gallery was housed in a half-timbered building in the High Street: sandwiched between an even older tea shop and an estate agent. It was a building of uneven wooden floors, low beams and narrow doorways, with a treacherous little staircase up to the first floor. In many ways it was totally unsuited to its purpose, since the windows let in little daylight, and despite strategically placed lighting, customers frequently had to be escorted out into the street to inspect their prospective purchases. But this being England, such inconveniences were generally considered to add to the gallery's charm, and if it would never make its owner rich, then it almost certainly afforded him a comfortable living.

The job itself was interesting without being demanding, involving meeting artists and customers, helping to hang pictures, answering the phone and doing a little typing, and it proved to be exactly what I needed.

'General dogsbody,' Lucas remarked unkindly, when I told him what I was doing.

'If you like. But it's a job.'

'If you say so.' Lucas had never quite understood how I could turn my back on a career for which I had trained so hard, and had done his utmost to make me change my mind.

'I do say so. Lucas, I need a break, and this is relaxing while still being work.'

And it was true. It was wonderful to have so little responsibility, to meet people without being expected to save their lives, and yet still to be able to have an intelligent conversation. The pressure was finally off, and I was enjoying it.

Mum seemed reasonably happy with my choice, and I heard her telling friends that I was 'working in the art world'. She herself was going through an energetic phase, and to that end had decided to train as a postwoman ('Lots of exercise, Cass. And you meet so many interesting people').

I hoped she wouldn't be disappointed, for many people were out when the post arrived, and the rest were unlikely to have the time to exchange pleasantries with the person who delivered it. She had hoped to be allowed to take New Dog with her. After all, as she explained, many of the customers had dogs, so why shouldn't she. Besides, New Dog would fend off the ankle nippers and hand-biters who plagued the lives of those who delivered the post. But the Post Office wasn't having any of it, so New Dog had to stay at home with Greta.

I remember that summer as one of the more peaceful periods of my life. While I wasn't deliriously happy, neither was I discontented. I was enjoying being at home, and had met up again with some of my friends, including Myra, whom I hadn't seen since our schooldays. Myra was now a hairdresser, with a tiny flat of her own and a shaggy boyfriend who favoured beads and kaftans. She was refreshing company, for she didn't hassle me about my future or reproach me for my past, nor did she question me on the delicate subject of my love-life. I was warmly invited to join her and the beaded boyfriend on some of their outings, and found myself having fun. It was a long time since I had had any fun.

The seventh anniversary of Octavia's death passed without incident. Since the disastrous expedition to *The Sound of Music*, Mum had stopped trying to turn it into an Event, so after taking flowers to the grave, we went out for a quiet family meal.

'It does get easier. Just a bit,' Mum admitted, over her prawn cocktail. 'But it never goes away. It's always — there. Part of me.'

'Part of all of us,' I said.

'Perhaps I should have had another.'

'Another what?'

'Baby. Another baby. After all, we'd all got used to having one around, hadn't we?'

Lucas and I exchanged glances.

'Mum, Octavia wasn't like a dog. You can't just go and replace a baby. If you'd had ten more babies, they still wouldn't have been Octavia.'

'Then I shall have to leave the babies to you and Lucas,' Mum said, spooning up that nasty pink sauce which always comes with prawn cocktails.

Summer gave way to autumn, and once more the leaves began to turn and the swallows lined up on the electricity wires outside our house in preparation for their journey south. I had now been home for seven months, and still hadn't made any long-term plans. Next year, I would be twenty-four. *Twenty-four*. Mum had had Lucas by the time she was twenty-four, and while she was hardly a shining example of how to lead a life, it could never be said that hers had been without interest.

Thirty-six

I had never been especially good at art, nor had I been particularly interested. After achieving a reasonable O level in the subject, I had simply forgotten about it. But working in the gallery aroused at first my interest and then my enthusiasm. Talking to the artists, studying the different styles and mediums in which they executed their work and discussing the pictures with our customers became increasingly absorbing, and, perhaps inevitably, the question arose: I wonder if *I* could do that?

At first the answer was a resounding no. There was no earthly reason why my minimal talents should have developed, since I had neither practised nor applied them, and in any case, where and how should I begin? In the end, I discussed the matter with Humphrey, who suggested I should have some lessons. One of our artists, Edward, held evening classes, and was prepared to take me on at a discounted rate (money was still tight).

I opted for watercolours rather than oils, and my first few paintings were poor smudged little efforts. I knew in my head what I was trying to achieve, but transferring the images onto paper was a different matter. Soon, however, I began to get the hang of it, and before long I was thoroughly hooked. The gentle wash of colour over paper, the blurring of water and trees onto a background, the suggestions of light or shade, stillness or movement, the hint of a house or boat or the pale petals of a flower — all these I found deeply satisfying. I enjoyed the flowing movements of my wrist as I painted and the subtlety of the colours as I mixed them on my palette.

'You know, that's not half bad,' Edward told me, after I'd been learning for about six weeks. 'I think you could be good at this, Cass.'

I glowed with pride, and like a child who has been praised at school, I couldn't wait to get home and tell my mother.

'Why, that's great, Cass. Maybe one day you'll be a famous artist —' Mum specialized in imagining short cuts to fame and fortune — 'with pictures in a London gallery and your paintings on postcards. No one in the family's ever been good at art before. I wonder where you get it from?'

I refrained from the obvious suggestion that my artistic talents might have come from my father, since Mum disliked discussions of this kind, preferring to assume that she alone was responsible for the genetic input of her offspring. For myself, I cared little about the provenance of my new-found talent. It was enough that I had discovered it.

After a while, I brought my paints home and began working in my bedroom. It was a light, south-facing room with views over the garden and the countryside beyond. I still have some of my early attempts at portraying that garden, those trees, the fleeting cloudscapes and the jigsaw puzzle coats of the black and white cows in the fields beyond. Looking at them now, they seem amateurish and clumsy, but at the time I was delighted with them, and Mum proudly framed one for the sitting-room wall. It is in her house to this day.

After I had been painting for about six months, Humphrey suggested I might like to try to sell one or two of my pictures. We could hang them in the gallery, he said, and see what happened.

I was enormously excited. While I found great satisfaction in my painting, it had never occurred to me that anyone might like to buy my work. The idea of hanging one of my pictures in the gallery was exciting enough on its own; the thought that someone might actually want to pay for it — to live with it on their walls and make it part of their home — was beyond anything I could have hoped for.

I sold my first painting for £2, and I can still recall the pride with which I stuck the red SOLD sticker onto the frame, then went to share my news with Humphrey.

'Well, that's wonderful Cass. Very well done.' He gave me a hug. 'You know, a long time ago, I had a go at painting, but I was no good at it at all.'

'Really?' I was surprised. For some reason I had assumed that Humphrey must have started off as an artist himself.

'Really.' He laughed at my expression. 'It was disappointing, I have to confess. I can't imagine anything more satisfying than being able to create something beautiful; something which will give pleasure to other people.' His voice was wistful. 'But that was a long time ago. I accepted that it wasn't for me, so instead I learnt a bit about the art world, and went on to start up this little business. If I can't be an artist myself, then I think that what I do is the next best thing. I see myself as a kind of mediator between the creator and the purchaser.'

'You're very good at it,' I ventured, thinking of the encouragement he gave his artists and his knack of matching the right picture to its new owner (not to mention that owner's budget).

'I think the key to a satisfying life is finding something you're good at, whatever that may be, however unexpected, and going ahead and doing it.' Humphrey fumbled in his pocket for his pipe and tobacco. 'That's what I did, and while it'll never make me rich, I've had a lot of fun. So many people drift into moulds or jobs that don't fit them, and spend their working lives being miserable. And there's no need. There's a job out there for almost anyone if they look for it. One doesn't always get it right first time.'

'Is this little talk aimed at me?' I asked, after a moment.

'Take it whichever way you like, Cass.' Humphrey struck a match and lit his pipe, the smell of tobacco clouding his small office. 'I know you've been floundering a bit, but it often takes a while to find what it is you want to do in life, and sometimes that also means finding out what you *don't* want to do. You obviously enjoyed a lot of your nursing, but in the end it wasn't what you wanted to do for the rest of your life. Nothing wrong with that. And your experience will stand you in good stead.'

I thought then, and have often thought since, that I would love to have had a father like Humphrey, who in many ways reminded me of dear Dr Mackenzie all those years ago. While my fatherless state wasn't something I dwelt on a great deal, working for Humphrey brought home to me again what it might have been like to have had a father to love and support me; someone strong and wise; someone who would love me unconditionally; someone safe. I knew Humphrey had two daughters, and just for a moment, I envied them.

Over the next six months, I sold several more paintings, and as my confidence developed, so did my ability. I took to going out on my day off, taking my paints and easel and a packet of sandwiches, and spending the day painting some of the marvellous scenery of the surrounding countryside. New Dog often accompanied me, and was happy to explore the hedges and ditches or simply lie in the sun while I painted. Often walkers would come and look over my shoulder and comment on my work, and while it puzzled me that I was as it were fair game, and not apparently entitled to any privacy, I didn't mind. Their remarks on the whole were kind, and I gained at least one new customer.

Mum continued to be supportive, but was also bewildered by my solitary pursuit. Unable herself to manage more than an hour or so on her own without seeking company or reaching for the telephone, she couldn't understand that I was happy to spend whole days by myself.

'You must get so lonely, Cass,' she said, on more than one occasion. 'It doesn't seem natural.'

'It's perfectly natural to me,' I said. 'I enjoy my own company.'

'And still no boyfriend,' she continued (this was a recurring theme, and unlikely to go away). 'When I was your age —'

'I know, Mum. I know what you were up to when you were my age. You've told me often enough. But I'm different.'

'Perhaps you're a slow developer.'

'Mum, I've had one career, and I'm embarking on another. No one could call that slow.'

'You know what I mean.'

'Men,' I sighed.

'Yes. Men.'

And of course she was right. Most of my friends had boyfriends and several were now married. Even the unconventional Myra was currently assessing the beaded boyfriend as husband material. I knew that by spending much of my leisure time alone and refusing the rare party invitations that came my way I was avoiding the issue, but I didn't know what else to do. The incident with Neil had distressed and frightened me, and while I knew that my reaction had been out of all proportion to what had happened, I also knew that I couldn't face risking a repeat performance.

And so I drifted along reasonably contentedly. My pictures continued to sell steadily, Humphrey gave me more responsibility at the gallery, and life at home was, if not exciting, then too comfortable for me to wish to seek any change. Lodgers came and went, Call Me Bill suffered increasingly with an arthritic hip, and Lucas and Gracie got married.

It took some time for Mum to come round to the idea of a wedding in the family.

'A wedding? Lucas and Gracie want a *white wedding*? Whatever for?' she asked me.

'It's traditional, I suppose. It's what people do.'

'It's not what we do.'

'No. Probably not. But you're lucky, Mum. All you have to do is wear a hat and behave nicely. I've got to be a bridesmaid.'

In the event, the wedding went off very well. Gracie looked beautiful (looking beautiful was what Gracie did best), Lucas was dashing in his morning suit, and I wilted in my hideous peach frock. As for Mum, she behaved better than I'd expected, and if her enormous lime-green hat upstaged that of the bride's mother, then, as she pointed out, it certainly wasn't deliberate. The flirting at the reception, on the other hand, almost certainly was deliberate, but if one or two eyebrows were raised, then Gracie's family were going to have to get used to Mum. It was going to take more than a nice, conventional daughter-in-law to change the habits of a lifetime.

After the wedding, Mum seemed downhearted.

'I've lost him, Cass. I've lost Lucas,' she told me sadly.

'Of course you haven't.'

'They say you lose a son. When he gets married.'

'That's nonsense. You'll never lose Lucas. He's just moved on, Mum. That's what people do when they marry.'

But while I tried to reassure her, I felt that Lucas had drifted away from me, too. Some of the closeness we had always shared had gone, and Lucas had lost some of his sparkle and become ever so slightly dull. He and I no longer seemed to be on quite the same wavelength or laugh at the same things, and it was hard not to blame Gracie, who, while pleasant enough, appeared to have little sense of humour. It must have been hard for Gracie, too. Her background was so very different from ours that I'm sure she must have felt the difference between our two families as keenly as we did.

I had been working at the gallery for several years when we received some news which was to affect us all.

'Cass, I've just had a letter. From a solicitor.' Mum seemed agitated, and looked as though she'd been crying. 'And — and I don't know how to tell you this.'

'Quickly,' I suggested, with the now familiar feeling that I was about to be the recipient of bad news.

'It's Uncle Rupert. He's — he's died.'

'Oh.'

'Poor man.' She hesitated. 'He must have died all alone.'

'I'm sorry.' What else could I say? Mum was obviously upset, and I was sorry about that if nothing else. Uncle Rupert had been released from prison some two years ago, but Mum hadn't told me where he was living and I hadn't wanted to know.

'It seems he had quite a lot of money.'

'Did he?' We'd always been led to believe that Uncle Rupert was entirely without funds. Where had it been hiding all these years?

'Yes. And — oh Cass! — he's left it all to you!'

Thirty-seven

'How could he. *How could he!*' After the initial shock, I was overcome by blinding rage.

'But Cass! All that money —'

'To hell with the money! I couldn't give a damn about the money!' I turned on her. 'Mum, can't you see? *Can't you see what he's done?*'

'No. What has he done?' Mum looked bewildered.

'He's escaped, that's what he's done. He's escaped, and he's paid me off, or thinks he has. How dare he! *How dare he!*'

'But Cass, I don't understand.'

'Of course you don't understand. You never really did understand, did you? He was a wicked, evil, dirty old man, and now he's got away with it.'

'How can you say he's got away with it? He spent all that time in prison, and now he's dead. I can't see that he's got away with anything. And he's tried to make it up to you —'

'No! No, he hasn't. He's *bought* me; he's paid me off; cleared his nasty little debt. Good old Uncle Rupert. What a brilliant move. He'll never have to face the music now, will he?'

'But Cass, he's *dead*. How can he face the music when he's dead? And all that time in prison —'

'Yes. All that time in prison, and I'm sure he richly deserved it. But that was nothing to do with me. That happened when he did it to someone else. That was when he was *caught*. How many other times were there when he *wasn't* caught? You tell me that. How many other girls' lives has he cocked up?'

'But Cass, I never knew. I thought — I thought you'd got over all that a long time ago. It was years ago. You never said anything. Why didn't you tell me?'

'What was the point? What on earth would have been the point? You couldn't have done anything about it, could you?'

'I was furious with him at the time. You know I was. And I did throw him out of the house.'

'You threw him out of the house! Well, big deal. You could hardly have kept him here, could you, unless you were prepared to risk his raping me. Lucas too — why not? — while he was about it. Perhaps you would have preferred that. Perhaps you would have been happy to let him stay, if I hadn't made such a fuss.'

'Cass! That's not fair!'

'Isn't it? Think about it, Mum. You left him alone with me, knowing what he was, not even warning me. You risked my safety and you risked — you risked my life!'

'Oh, don't be ridiculous, Cass. Uncle Rupert may have been many things, but he wasn't a murderer.'

'I'm not talking about murder. I'm talking about *my life*. What he did to it. How he's — spoiled it.'

'Now you're being melodramatic. How can Uncle Rupert have spoiled your life? You have a good life. You're successful and I thought — I thought you were happy.'

'But there's something missing, isn't there?' I was beginning to enjoy myself in the way that one does when one's so angry that suddenly it seems as though there are no holds barred. And while I knew I was being cruel, I couldn't seem to stop. 'You're the one who's always bringing it up so you ought to know the answer. What is it that's missing from my life, Mum? Come on. It's hardly a difficult question.'

'Well, you haven't got a boyfriend —'

'Right. I haven't got a boyfriend. And why do you think that is?'

'I've no idea. You always told me you weren't bothered about men, and I assumed you were telling the truth.'

'Of course I'm bothered about men! I'm a normal woman, believe it or not. It's just that I can't face — I can't face the physical thing. And it's all because of Uncle Rupert. It's what he did to me; what he left me with. It's all his fault. And no amount of money can make up for that.' I burst into tears and fled from the room.

In my own bedroom I sat on the bed, sick and shaking. I had stopped weeping, but I was overwhelmed by a feeling which I can only describe as shock. Because until that minute, until that conversation with Mum, right up until the moment those words came out of my mouth I had never really known what was wrong with me.

It wasn't as though Uncle Rupert had been constantly on my mind. In fact I had hardly given him a thought in years. But now I realized that he must have been lurking there all the time, somewhere in that part of the brain which conveniently files away the distasteful or the plain abhorrent; not so much Uncle Rupert himself, but the feelings of fear and revulsion I had had when he came into my room all those years ago. It was something which had cast a shadow over my life for so long that I must have long since learnt to live with it, never thinking to question it, accepting it — albeit reluctantly — as part of what I was.

Now, it dawned on me for the first time that there was probably nothing wrong with *me* at all; that I could have had a normal adolescence and early adulthood and enjoyed normal healthy relationships. I could have partied my way through my nursing years like all my friends; I could have gone out with boys and fallen in and out of love the way everyone else seemed to (I had had plenty of opportunities), and without all that angst, all that neurosis, I could have had so much more *fun*. As it was, my trust and my innocence had been stolen from me, and something which should have been precious and special had been spoiled long before I'd had a chance to exercise my own choice and judgement. It was all such a terrible waste.

And now here I was, twenty-seven years old and living at home. I hadn't been out with a man in years, and my family and friends had already written me off as, if not yet a spinster, then a likely candidate for a cosy little place on the shelf.

Looking back now, I know I was being unfair; unfair to Mum, certainly, and perhaps even a little unfair to Uncle Rupert. I had always been naturally shy, and I couldn't blame him for that, and maybe I could have sought some kind of help. But in those days, people still tended to accept themselves and their lots as *faits accomplis*, without question and certainly without having recourse to anyone else. Hitherto, it had never occurred to me that the basis for my problem lay anywhere but within myself.

But now, at last, I had someone else to blame, and I felt literally sick with rage; a rage which was entirely impotent since there was no longer anyone upon whom I could justly vent it. Uncle Rupert was dead; the only possible target for my anger now was poor Mum.

For a week or so we avoided the subject of Uncle Rupert altogether. I was still feeling too upset and Mum was no doubt reluctant to incur another of my outbursts. Eventually, however, we had to face the problem of what to do about my unwelcome inheritance.

'It would be a shame to turn it down, Cass,' Mum said. 'Can't you forget where it came from and just enjoy it?'

'No. No I can't. I want nothing — *nothing* — from Uncle Rupert.'

'You could share it with Lucas,' she said, after a moment. 'He and Gracie are always short of money.'

I thought of Lucas and Gracie, who after much 'trying' (that expression always amuses me; it makes the whole business seem such terribly hard work) were expecting their first child.

'I don't know. It's still Uncle Rupert's money.' I hesitated. I had never had much money, and in spite of myself, I was tempted. 'In any case, where did it all come from?'

'I've no idea. He never talked about money, and since he was always saying how hard up he was I assumed he hadn't got any.'

'Did he ever pay you anything towards rent and things?'

Mum looked uncomfortable.

'Well, he did help sometimes.'

'You mean he didn't give you anything.' How typical of Mum, to house someone like Uncle Rupert, to feed him and look after him, expecting nothing in return. Typical, too, that there wasn't a hint of resentment at the revelation of Uncle Rupert's hidden assets.

'That doesn't matter, Cass. It's all in the past. I was happy to do it until — until he went.'

'What about his funeral?' I asked, with the sinking feeling that we might be expected to put in an appearance at his wake.

'All over. He died a month ago, and I only found out when I got this letter.' She sighed. 'I'm so sorry, Cass. So sorry about — well, about everything. I never realized how badly you still felt about him; how much he'd hurt you. And of course, you were right. I should never have let him live with us. He'd only been in trouble once before, and I really thought he could change. He made me a promise, and I trusted him. I don't blame you for being angry. You have every right. I just — I just never thought.'

Poor Mum. How could I stay angry with her? In some ways so worldly-wise, but in others, such an innocent; of course she'd believed Uncle Rupert when he'd promised to reform. She looked for — and usually found — the best in everybody. In Mum's eyes, even Uncle Rupert was capable of redemption.

'I know,' I said, with sudden inspiration. '*You* have Uncle Rupert's money. You've certainly earned it, and if it's mine, then presumably I can give it to whoever I like.'

'Oh no. I couldn't possibly. It's out of the question.'

'Then — then we'll share it.'

'We?'

'Yes. You, me and Lucas. I won't feel so bad about it if we share it, and heaven knows, we could all do with it.'

In the end, that was what we did. And while for some time afterwards I felt uncomfortable about the source of my inheritance, it was true that the money would be useful. I would be able to buy my own little studio; something I had dreamed of for years. Gracie would have free rein to plan her frilly little nursery, while Lucas would be able to replace his car, which for some time had kept going on a wing and a prayer, and Mum ...

'Mum? What will you do with your money?' I asked some weeks later, when everything had been arranged.

'I'm going to travel,' Mum said grandly.

'Travel? Travel where?'

'Oh, anywhere. I'll just take off, and see what happens.'

'Is that wise?'

'Of course it's not wise.' She patted my cheek. 'I can't wait. I'm going to have such fun!'

'That's what I was afraid of.'

But Mum was no longer listening.

Thirty-eight

My mother is sleeping again, her hands making tiny fluttering movements, and I wonder whether she is dreaming of flying.

'I fly in my dreams, you know, Cass,' she once told me.

'How?'

'Breast stroke. You've no idea how difficult it is to get off the ground. Doing breaststroke.'

'I can imagine.'

'Yes. You have to work at it with your arms, and then when your legs leave the ground, you have to kick like mad.'

'Goodness. It sounds exhausting.'

'Oh, it is. But so exciting, too, Cass. Except that no one seems to notice in dreams. Sometimes I call down to them "Look at me!", but no one ever does. They just get on with what they're doing, as though people fly all the time. It's so disappointing.'

'It must be.'

'Much more fun than aeroplanes. You don't really feel as though you're flying, in an aeroplane.'

'I understand what you mean.'

But Mum's disdain for aeroplanes was forgotten as she anticipated setting off on her travels, and she could hardly contain her excitement.

'Imagine, Cass! Just flying off like that. I can't wait!'

'But won't you be lonely, going off on your own?'

'Oh, I'll find people. I always find someone to talk to.'

'And where, Mum? Where are you going to fly to?'

'I don't care. Anywhere. Somewhere sunny, with sea. An island, perhaps.' She was ironing her holiday clothes — an eclectic selection of cotton skirts and blouses, some of them dating back to our early childhood — between skippy little Chopin waltzes.

'Most people,' I said, 'choose their destination before planning their wardrobe. Shouldn't you at least pick a country to start from? You don't have to stay there if you don't like it.'

'You're right. Let's choose a place. Help me, Cass.'

So we got out the atlas (which, needless to say, was wildly out of date, but as Mum pointed out, sun and sea and islands don't move around even if empires do), and after some discussion, settled on the Greek islands.

'Little white houses and blue sea,' said Mum, who had once received a postcard from Crete. 'Perfect.'

'And you can move from one to another,' I said. 'They look quite close to each other, and there are bound to be boats sailing between them.'

'Yes. And there's Athens, with all those statues and pillars and things. Do you think they speak English?'

'Bound to,' I assured her.

'I'll take a phrase book, in case.'

'Good idea.'

'And I can speak a little French.'

'That might be useful,' I said, although even my imagination had trouble envisaging my mother trying to make her way round Greece in schoolgirl French.

A fortnight later, Lucas and I took Mum to the airport.

'I hope she'll be OK,' Lucas said, when we'd waved her off. 'I hope she doesn't do anything silly.'

'Of course she'll do something silly. This is our mother we're talking about. But she'll find people to bale her out — she always does — and if the worst comes to the worst, I can always fly out and rescue her.' I lowered myself into Lucas's new and very posh car. 'But it's going to be very strange without her.'

This was certainly true, for without Mum, the whole household wilted. It was like the occasions when she had one of her famous depressions; the spirit of the house seemed to die. Everyone went about their business as usual, but — to use Mum's favourite word — the *fun* seemed to have gone out of everything. Greta went round looking tragic, the ready tears even nearer the surface than usual; Call Me Bill grumbled because he had to iron his own shirts (Greta refused); and the Lodger, a peevish little man with no sense of humour, complained that there didn't seem to be anyone in charge (there wasn't). Richard popped in from time to time 'to cheer us up' with recitals on his ukulele (these proved counterproductive); and as for New Dog (not so new now, with arthritis and an increasingly unreliable temper), he took it upon himself to guard Mum's bedroom, lying in the doorway and growling at anyone who came near him. He allowed me to step over him to change the sheets and give the room an airing, but he bit Greta's ankle when she tried to gain access.

'New Dog iss nasty cross animal,' she complained, when I escorted her to the doctor for a tetanus injection. 'Time he put down, I think.'

'I wouldn't if I were you,' I told her. 'Mum would never forgive you.'

In any case, I was fond of New Dog, and I was also sorry for him. Mum was his friend and his rescuer, his protector and his companion. As far as he was concerned, she had always been there, and he was quite naturally upset and confused by her sudden disappearance.

Over the weeks, we received a series of postcards from various parts of Greece. Some of these were of the cheery wish-you-were-here variety (although I very much doubt that she wished any of us were there; we would only have spoiled her fun); others were wistful and occasionally even homesick. But on the whole she appeared to be enjoying herself. She had, she told us, met 'lots of interesting people', she knew several phrases of Greek, and was now adept at Greek dancing.

'What is she doing?' Lucas asked, when he called in to hear news of her progress. 'There's only so much time you can spend doing holiday things. What is she actually *doing* out there? Does she plan to stay there forever, or what?'

'I've no idea. I hope not.' New Dog wasn't the only one who was missing Mum.

'Well, I think she's being very irresponsible.'

'Oh Lucas, Mum's always been irresponsible. In any case, doesn't she deserve a break? She's never really had a holiday before, and we're managing OK without her. And it's hardly affecting you. You don't even live here any more.'

'That's not the point. Besides, the baby's due in six weeks. Doesn't she care about her new grandchild?'

I imagined that few things were further from Mum's mind than Gracie's baby, but I decided not to say anything. Lucas wouldn't understand.

Meanwhile, I had been spending my own inheritance. I had found a small attic bedsit with lots of light and stunning views. It was exactly what I'd had in mind as a studio, and while it was hardly big enough to live in all the time, there was a gas ring, a shared bathroom, and room for a narrow bed. I painted it white, put up blinds rather than curtains and furnished it from a second-hand shop in the village. The effect was clean and simple and airy, and best of all, it was mine. Greta approved of it, Call Me Bill brought me a bottle of wine to celebrate, and Gracie disliked it on sight. I knew I'd done the right thing.

Mum returned after an absence of eight weeks, unannounced and unexpected, brown and cheerful and full of news, the most interesting of which was that she had blown all her money.

'What, all of it?' I asked. 'You've spent *all* your money?'

'Every penny.' Mum opened a bottle of ouzo which she'd brought home with her, and poured everyone a glass, while New Dog bounced and wagged at her feet in a frenzy of delighted welcome.

'But Mum, that was your chance to save something for — well, for —'

'Exactly. For what? No, Cass. I wanted to enjoy it, and I have. I never expected it or asked for it, I've had a wonderful time, and now it's gone. I'd probably have wasted it anyway.' She grinned. 'You know I've never been any good with money.'

'I don't know what Lucas will say.'

'Then we shan't tell him.' Mum knocked back her ouzo. Obviously she'd been practising. Personally, I thought it was revolting.

'At least you're back in time for the baby.'

'Oh yes. Gracie's baby. How is she?'

'The same.'

'Iss fat,' said Greta helpfully.

'Is she still making a fuss?' Gracie had been making very heavy weather of what had been on the whole a pretty uneventful pregnancy, and Mum had little sympathy with her.

'Oh yes. You'd think that no one had ever had a baby before.'

'Poor Lucas.' Mum grimaced. 'And you, Cass. How've you been?'

'I've bought this gorgeous studio! You've got to come and see it.'

The next day, Mum visited my little attic.

'A garret. A real garret. Oh, Cass! How romantic!'

'Yes. Isn't it?'

'You're not leaving home, are you?' Mum said, eyeing the bed.

'Not exactly. But I can sleep here if I need to; if I want to work late. It'll be a bolt-hole if I need one.'

'That's all right, then.' Mum looked relieved. 'I'd hate you to leave home, Cass.'

'I know you would. But Mum, I'll have to go one day. I can't live at home forever.'

'Why not?'

'Because — because people just don't. I shall be twenty-nine next year. *Twenty-nine*. It's time I was a bit more independent.'

'I don't see why.'

'Mum, I'm an adult, with my own friends, my own career. With my pay from the gallery and the sales of my paintings, I may not be rich but I make enough money to live on my own. I don't know anyone else of my age who lives with their mother.'

'Are you ashamed of me? Is that it?'

'Don't be ridiculous, Mum. It's got nothing to do with being ashamed. It's to do with — with how I feel about myself.'

'And about me?'

'Well, yes. Perhaps. I think you and I maybe depend on each other more than we ought to. I love you, Mum. You know I do. You're my best friend. But we need to — separate a bit.'

'We separated when you were nursing. You were miles away then.'

'Yes. But I did keep coming home, didn't I?'

'To sort me out.' Mum's voice was bleak.

'Well, yes. Sometimes. But also to sort myself out.'

'So what are you going to do?' Mum asked, after a pause.

'Nothing at the moment. I've got my studio, and that's a start. And I'll just see what happens.'

But of course nothing would happen unless I made it happen, and I could see myself living at home forever unless I took some kind of initiative. Although life on the whole was good, I was feeling increasingly trapped by my situation. On the one hand, there was Mum, who undoubtedly did need me. Even if she felt free to take off to Greece for a couple of months, she did so in the knowledge that I would still be there when she got back, to support her as I had always done. But there was also that other problem; the problem I had carried with me all my adult life and which I felt powerless to address.

Given my circumstances, I suppose it was inevitable that when a man finally did make an appearance, he was to be much older than I was.

And, perhaps also inevitably, married.

Thirty-nine

I have often wondered about that phenomenon by which two people can know each other for some time, and then, quite suddenly, be struck by the same powerful spark of mutual attraction. But so it was with Edward and me.

My art classes had ceased a while ago, but we still saw each other from time to time when he came into the gallery with his paintings. We always passed the time of day, and he was generous with his encouragement when it came to my own work, but it certainly couldn't be said that we knew each other well; we were acquaintances rather than friends.

He was a softly spoken, gentle man, attractive rather than good-looking, with the stooping demeanour so often adopted by the very tall. Later on, I found it hard to imagine that I had failed to notice anything special about him, although I'd certainly admired and even envied his ability. He favoured oils rather than watercolours, and his stormy skies and blazing sunsets always reminded me of the seascapes of Turner. While my own style was very different, I would have given a great deal to be able to produce paintings as good as Edward's.

It was Humphrey who observed what was happening almost before I was aware of it myself.

'I think Edward is becoming rather attached to you,' he remarked, assembling matches and tobacco and beginning the complicated ritual of the pipe-smoker.

'And I like him.' We were having a leisurely cup of coffee in the course of an unusually quiet morning.

Humphrey eyed me thoughtfully.

'You know what I mean.'

I lowered my eyes, blushing.

'I thought so.' Humphrey took a puff of his pipe, and leant back in his chair. 'Be careful, Cass. That's all. Just be careful.'

'What do you mean?'

'I think you know what I mean.'

'Do I?'

'Yes, Cass. You do.' He looked at me over his half glasses. 'I'm very fond of you. I always have been. And I worry about you.'

'There's nothing to worry about. I'm fine.' My voice sounded bright and brittle, and even as I spoke, I knew it would take a lot more than I could manage to pull the wool over Humphrey's eyes.

'If you say so. But you're a vulnerable young woman, and Edward's — well, let's just say that there are complications in his life. He's also a lot older than you. I don't want you to do something you'll regret. Either of you.'

'I haven't done anything.'

'Yet.'

'I — we — haven't done anything,' I repeated. 'And there's no reason why we should.'

'If you say so.'

'I do say so.'

'That's all right, then.'

'Yes.'

'But you can always talk to me, you know.'

'Yes. I do know. Thank you.'

Afterwards, I thought about what Humphrey had said, and wondered exactly what it was that he had observed. Edward and I had spoken to each other no more than usual, and had spent no time at all on our own together. And if I had recently become acutely aware of his physical presence, of his smile and the tone of his voice when he spoke to me, then I found it hard to believe that anyone else could have noticed. Whatever it was that had developed between us was certainly there, but up until now it was as though it had been lying in wait, unacknowledged, biding its time until one of us should take notice and do something about it.

It wasn't until a week later that Edward asked me out. 'Would you care to come for a cup of tea and a bun before you go home? There's — a picture I'd like to discuss with you.'

'Yes. Thank you. I'd love to.'

It had been as simple as that. And while I knew that this had nothing to do with a picture and everything to do with Edward and me, it seemed the most natural thing in the world that we should get together like this.

'Thank you for coming,' Edward said, over tea and iced buns in the tea shop next door. 'I thought you might say no.'

'Why would I say no?'

'Because — because there's an attraction between us, and I thought you might think it unwise, I suppose.'

'There's nothing unwise about tea and buns,' I said, licking icing sugar off my fingers.

'You know what I mean, Cass.'

'Yes. I suppose I do.' After all, why else would we have chosen a corner table when the best tables — the ones in the window — were free?

'You probably don't know, but I'm married,' Edward said, after a long pause.

'I thought you might be, but I wasn't sure.'

'So I shouldn't be doing this at all.'

'Probably not. But then I suppose neither should I.'

'Things are — complicated.' Edward broke his bun into tiny pieces, and arranged them neatly round the edge of his plate. 'I do care very much for my wife.'

'Yes.'

'And I will never tell you she doesn't understand me.'

'Good.' I had never accepted that so many wives didn't understand their husbands. It had always seemed to me more likely that they understood them only too well.

'In fact, I shan't talk about her at all. Except to say that, in a way, we are already separated.'

'In a way?'

'I can't talk about it at the moment. Not yet. But can you just accept that anything — anything we do, you and I, can't hurt her. That I would never do anything which could cause her pain.'

'But surely —'

'Trust me on this, Cass. Please.' He picked up a fragment of his bun and placed it carefully in the middle of his plate. 'My wife is — unwell, and in a way, she still needs me. I will always be there for her. She hasn't anyone else. We have no children.' He looked up at me, and there was a deep sadness in his face. 'But we still need to be — discreet, you and I. There are people — family, friends — who might talk. Who might be upset.' He pushed his plate away. 'I don't want this to be spoiled by other people's gossip. You deserve better than that. I think even I deserve better than that.'

Looking back, it seems extraordinary that Edward and I could have been so frank and taken so much for granted at this early stage in our relationship. But that was one of the things I liked about him. There was no game-playing, no subterfuge, no pretending things were other than they were. He was very fond of me, he wanted a relationship, but he was married; and despite his mention of some kind of separation between him and his wife, the implication was that he and I could probably never be together. He had laid his cards on the table, and it was up to me to decide what I should do about it.

And yet in a way there was no decision to make. It was as though a path had been mapped out for us, and we were compelled to follow it. Right from the beginning, we both accepted it almost without question, together with the complications and problems that it might entail. There was no rosy mist obscuring the future; no feeling of live now, pay later; none of the blind, careless passion which I had been led to expect if ever I were to find love. I believe that we both knew that our relationship would not come without a cost, and that right from the start, we were prepared to pay it.

But of course, although it may not have felt like it at the time, I did have a choice, and I have often wondered how my life would have turned out if I had chosen a different course. Would I have met someone else? Would I ever have found the happiness and fulfilment that was to come? And perhaps above all, was I justified in committing an offence against a woman I had never met and who had certainly done me no harm, even if that woman were to be unaffected by it, as Edward had implied? I shall never know. We make decisions, and we live with the consequences. All I know is that I have never had any regrets.

On our second meeting, Edward drove me out into the country in his battered Morris Minor. It was a beautiful summer's evening, and we walked along the river bank and stopped at a pub for a drink. Edward didn't take my hand, and the only contact we had was when I nearly slipped in some mud, and he placed a hand on my arm to steady me.

We sat outside with our drinks, watching the ducks and swans drifting by among the reeds, and the reflections of the pale green boughs of willow arching into the water. I stole glances at Edward's big capable hands cradling his beer glass, his profile turned towards the river, the crinkle of tanned skin around his blue eyes, the slightly too long hair lapping his collar.

'We know very little about each other, Cass.' He turned and smiled at me, and for a moment it was as though that smile held everything I'd ever wanted.

I smiled back at him.

'What do you want to know?'

'Anything. Everything.' He laughed. 'Where do we start?'

'I don't know. I've never — done it like this before.'

'Neither have I.' He took a draught of his beer and wiped his mouth on his handkerchief. 'Maybe we'll just have to make up the rules as we go along.'

'So long as that's all we make up,' I said.

'So long as that's all we make up,' he agreed, and at last he reached for my hand. 'You have beautiful hands,' he said, turning mine over in his and examining the palm, then replacing it gently on the table in front of me like some small, precious object. 'Artist's hands.'

'And nurse's hands.' My skin still tingled where his hand had touched mine, and I was almost afraid to move my hand, as though I might break the spell created by that first moment of physical contact.

'Really? You're a nurse as well?'

So I told him all about my failed academic career, my years as a nurse and my subsequent breakdown. I told him about Mum and Lucas, about our eccentric domestic set-up and about the life and death of Octavia. I talked until the sun began to set behind the hills and the midges hovered in clouds over the water, and the tiny forms of bats streaked to and fro across the darkening skyline. And all the time, Edward listened. It was years since anyone had really listened to me like that, and it was almost like a drug. Only with difficulty did I finally manage to stop.

'Goodness. I don't usually talk like that,' I said. 'I'm sorry.'

'Don't be. I'm interested.' Edward smiled. 'Poor Cass. You haven't had it easy, have you?'

'Haven't I?' I'd never thought of my life as so very different from other people's, and certainly no worse.

'Well, you seem to have been through the mill. One way and another.'

'Maybe.' I fingered the stem of my glass. 'But I've been lucky, too. I have a wonderful family and some good friends, and I enjoy my job. Many people would envy me.' I drank the last of my wine. 'But what about you? Tell me about you.'

'Me.' Edward paused, gazing into his empty glass as though he might find in it the answer to my question. 'It should be easy, shouldn't it, but I've always felt happier listening than talking, especially when it comes to talking about myself.' He pushed the glass away and put his elbows on the table, resting his chin in his hands. 'I guess I'm a pretty ordinary sort of bloke; a middle-of-the-road artist, although I love what I do; not particularly well off, but then I've never minded much about money; with a banger of a car, a dilapidated cottage and a cat. No kids, though. I would have liked children.' He seemed about to say something else, then hesitated.

'Go on,' I said.

'And — and too old for someone as young as you.'

'Can I ask —?'

'Forty-five. Well, forty-five next week. And you are, what, twenty-five?'

'Twenty-eight.'

'That's still pretty young.'

'Not too young, though.'

'Don't you think so?'

'No. It's such a cliché, but really age isn't that important.'

Edward gazed out once more towards the river.

'You know, I can't believe this is happening. I've never done anything like this before. I never expected it, and I certainly wasn't looking for it.'

'No.'

'But you. It's different for you. You must have been looking for — hoping for someone to come into your life, Cass.'

'Not really.'

'Why ever not? You're young and beautiful. You must have had lots of boyfriends in the past. You must sometimes think about marriage and children. Don't all girls?'

'Perhaps,' I admitted. 'But then you see, my life's a bit — well, complicated, too.'

'Do you want to tell me about it?'

'Not now. Not tonight. It's — well, it's too soon.'

Edward nodded.

'There are no-go areas in my life, as you know, and you're entitled to yours. Never think you have to tell me everything, Cass. Just so long as we're honest with each other. I think that's all that matters.'

But of course I knew that if we were to have a relationship — an affair, even (how I hate that word, along with all its sordid connotations) — sooner or later Edward would have to know the secret which had darkened my life for so long, and I had no idea how I was going to go about telling him.

But just for the moment, just for the duration of that magic summer evening, with the last of the daylight staining the sky crimson and Edward once again reaching across the table for my hand, I would allow myself to be happy.

Forty

Our courtship — if an adulterous affair can be said to have such a thing — was slow and measured and tender. We behaved as though we had all the time in the world, pacing ourselves, basking in our developing love, and for the time being, asking little more than simply to be in each other's company.

Of course affairs, by their very nature, have their problems, the greatest of these being when and where to meet. I have never found subterfuge easy, and have always thought of myself as being a pretty straightforward and honest person, so it was hard having to take unnecessary bus rides so that Edward could pick me up in the next village, or smuggle him up to my studio when no one else was around (I had talkative neighbours).

And then there was Mum.

'What are you up to these days, Cass?' she asked me, after our third meeting. 'There's something you're not telling me.'

I hesitated. I had never lied to Mum, and yet I didn't want to tell anyone about Edward. Not yet, anyway. It was too soon, and I was still finding my way and getting used to the idea of him myself. Having to cope with Mum getting used to him as well was more than I could deal with, especially as she was bound to want to know every detail of our relationship. I would tell her one day, I decided, but not yet.

'I'm not up to anything,' I told her, 'or at least, nothing you need to know about at the moment.'

'Ah!' Mum's tone was triumphant, her radar as accurate as ever. 'A man! I knew it. How exciting! Tell me all about him. Where did you meet him? What does he —'

'Mum, please. Just don't ask. Not yet. I need — time. If you let the subject drop, I promise I'll tell you everything when I'm ready. If there's anything to tell,' I added, remembering that even the best affairs tend to have a sell-by date.

'If you insist.' Mum looked disappointed. Her own love life had recently run into problems (in the form of an avenging ex-wife), Greta was away, and Lucas and Gracie were preoccupied with their new baby daughter (Mum's take on grandmotherhood was ambivalent). She had evidently been hoping for a diversion in the form of my new romance, and now this was not to be. 'It's so boring of you, Cass,' she sighed. 'It's ages since you had a man, and now you won't even tell me who he is.'

'No, I won't. But I shan't tell anyone else, either —' Mum could be jealous where my confidences were concerned — 'and if anything exciting happens, you'll be the first to know.' And she had to be content with that.

Only two things clouded my happiness. The first, obviously, was the fact that Edward was married. I had never considered myself to be the kind of person to have an affair with someone else's husband, and while Edward had made it clear that our relationship wouldn't interfere with his marriage, I still felt uncomfortable with the idea that somewhere out there was a woman whose happiness or stability might be compromised for the sake of my own.

And then there was the knowledge that sooner or later Edward was going to want more than just holding hands or a hug, and I had no idea how I was going to deal with this eventuality. I was twenty-eight years old, and had never even been kissed properly; how would he react when he found out? And what was I going to do? I gave much thought to the idea of sex with Edward, and a part of me longed for that closeness, that intimacy, that oneness which I had yet to experience with another human being. I found him physically very attractive; his smile and the touch of his hand had an effect I'd never experienced before; but my over-riding fear was greater than my desire, and the second he showed signs of taking things any further, something within me seemed to freeze.

For a while, Edward showed no sign that he was aware of any problem, and we had been seeing each other for some weeks when he finally brought the subject up.

'I think it's time we talked about this — this difficulty of yours, Cass.' We were lying companionably on the bed in my studio, sharing a bottle of wine.

'Yes.'

I could have asked what he meant; I could have prevaricated; there were lots of things I could have done to give myself more time. But Edward had been patient, and I owed him some kind of explanation.

'You know what I'm talking about, don't you?' He stroked my hair off my face and smiled down at me.

'Yes. Yes, I do.'

'But it's hard to talk about?'

'Very hard.' I brushed away a tear. 'I — I don't know where to start. And it's all so silly. You'll think me such a fool.'

'I won't. If something has caused you this much distress, how can you imagine I would ever think you a fool?'

'I know, I know. I'm not being fair.' I put down my glass and sat up on the bed, drawing my knees up to my chin, gazing out of the window at a sky stippled with tiny clouds. 'I suppose just finding the words is difficult. I've never told anyone before. Mum knows about it, but we don't talk about it any more. I suppose she feels guilty, and in any case, there's nothing she can do.'

'Perhaps there's something I can do.'

I laughed. 'That's the problem.'

'I thought it might be.' Edward sat up and pulled me to him. 'Try me, Cass. Just try me. What have you got to lose?'

'You,' I whispered into his chest.

'I don't think you'll lose me, however hard you try.'

'OK. I'll tell you. But do you mind if I don't look at you while I'm doing so? I think I'd find it easier.'

'You do what's best for you.'

I climbed off the bed and curled up in a small armchair facing the window, with my back to Edward. I fixed my gaze on the clouds, the blue of the sky, the vapour trail of a distant aircraft, and I began to speak.

'I was fourteen,' I said, and paused. I had never had to put my experience into words before, and even finding those words was difficult.

'Go on,' Edward said. 'Just tell it as it happened. Try to forget I'm here.'

'We had this — cousin of Mum's living with us.' I swallowed. A chattering flock of starlings flew past the window and somewhere a door slammed. I heard the faint sound of Edward shifting his position behind me, and the louder sound of my own heart thumping in my chest. 'We called him Uncle Rupert. I never liked him very much.'

As I talked, the words seemed to flow more freely, as though they were gradually becoming disentangled from that part of my brain where they had been stored for all those years, and I found myself reliving the events of that dreadful afternoon. I did what Edward had suggested and imagined I was on my own, telling my story as though I were telling it to myself, omitting nothing, wondering at how every detail was still imprinted on my mind. Smells and sights and sounds which had remained hidden for years emerged as though I had experienced them only yesterday, and when I finally finished my story, I found that I was sobbing.

For a moment, time seemed to stand still, and I wondered what Edward was thinking. Would he think I was making a fuss about nothing? Or worse, would he think I was exaggerating or even inventing my story as some kind of excuse? I dared not turn round and look at him for fear of what I might read in his expression.

Then I heard the bed creak as Edward stood up and I felt the wool of his sweater against my cheek as he folded me into his arms.

'Oh, Cass.' His voice was muffled by my hair. 'You poor darling.' He fished a handkerchief out of his pocket and wiped my streaming eyes. 'I'm so so sorry. I don't know what to say.'

I shook my head, taking the handkerchief from him and blowing my nose.

'You don't have to say anything. What's there to say? It happened, it was a long time ago, and I should have got over it. In fact, until he died, I thought I had.' I looked round my bright little room; at the books and pictures, the easel set up in the corner, the simple furniture. 'He — he gave me all this. I should be grateful. But something stops me. Something was left behind, and I can't get rid of it. Something was — *spoiled*.'

'Cass, you do know I love you, don't you?' Edward said, after a moment.

'Yes. Yes, I do.' He'd never actually said it before, but I suppose I'd known from the beginning that he loved me.

'Well, in that case, you have to trust me. Somehow — *somehow* — we'll sort this thing out together.'

'Do you think we can?'

'Well, I don't know for sure. Of course I don't. But I do believe that if you love me half as much as I love you, we'll get through this somehow.'

'How?' I asked fearfully.

'We'll take things very very slowly,' Edward said, kissing the top of my head. 'And you must trust me.'

'I do. Of course I trust you.'

'That's a start.' He took my hand and helped me to my feet. 'But let's leave it for now. I think you've had quite enough emotion for one day. Now, what did we do with that bottle of wine?'

Forty-one

Very gradually, with infinite patience and great tenderness, Edward began to lead me along the path to physical love. He refused to call it sex. Sex, he said, was for kids; kids who knew no better, who referred to 'having sex' as though they were having a cigarette or a drink and who looked upon it as just another form of recreation, like going out for a meal or to the cinema. Sex between loving adults was something quite different; something special. Edward had no time for the loveless couplings of the bike shed or the parked car, and while he admitted that he hadn't always been this idealistic — and confessed that few experiences were more disconcerting than waking up to find the wrong head on the pillow beside you — I gathered that for him such adventures had happened many years ago in his youth, and while not necessarily regretted, were certainly never to be repeated.

I thought of Mum, whose sexual activities, I knew for a fact, had taken place in all manner of venues, frequently with little or no love, and rarely with any regret. What would Edward have to say if he knew about her adventurous *modus vivendi?* And what would he think of her if they were ever to meet? In the end, I decided that it didn't much matter. What mattered was that Mum had found her way, and I was finding mine. I would never — could never — behave as Mum did, but neither could I judge her.

'Of course, in a way, our lovemaking has already started,' Edward told me some days later, as we walked hand-in-hand along our favourite river bank. 'It's about talking and listening as well as the physical part, and you're already so good at that, Cass. The rest will come naturally, I'm sure.' He turned to face me, taking both my hands in his. 'I will never do anything you don't want me to; anything to frighten or alarm you. All you have to do is trust me.'

A few days later, Edward kissed me. At first my body froze, and my ready response with it, but as he caressed my neck and shoulders and his lips gently traced my throat and cheek and forehead, I found myself relaxing in his arms. When the kiss finally came, I was more than ready for it, and I melted into it as though it was something I had been waiting for all my life.

'There. That wasn't so bad, was it?' he said.

I shook my head, too happy and relieved to say anything.

Edward laughed at my expression.

'In that case, perhaps we ought to do it again.'

And this time I didn't hesitate.

After that first kiss, Edward encouraged me to lead while he followed, taking his cues from me, picking up on the small shy hints I gave as to what I wanted him to do. Sometimes, he almost seemed to be making me wait, as though he wanted to be absolutely sure that he had read my signals correctly, and when one hot night in August we finally did make love, I felt that if I had had to wait another second, I would have been unable to bear it.

'We did it! We did it!' I exulted, wrapping a sheet round my naked body and dancing round the room.

'Very romantic, I'm sure,' Edward remarked wryly, observing me from the bed.

'But can't you see what this means?' I sank down beside him. 'I'm OK. I'm normal. Everything's going to be all right.'

'I told you so.'

'Mr Smug!'

'Mr Smug seems to have made you pretty happy, and that can't be bad.'

'Oh, Edward! I still can't believe it. There's nothing — *nothing* — wrong with me. I'm a proper, whole woman.'

'I never doubted it for a minute.'

'Don't tease.' I lay back on the pillows. 'It's something people take for granted, isn't it? Like eating or breathing. I've looked at my body so many times and thought, if I can't use it — use it properly — give it to someone I love — then what's it all *for*?'

'Well, now you know.' Edward propped himself on his elbow and smiled down at me. 'And may I say, for a beginner, you were pretty amazing.'

'Do you think we ought to do it again? Just to make sure?'

'I think that's an excellent idea. We've got a lot of time to make up.'

I'd like to be able to say that from that moment I never looked back, and while in a way that's true, I still had disconcerting flashbacks and moments of something akin to panic. And I still couldn't look at Edward's body.

'I shouldn't worry too much about that,' he told me. 'It's not what it was.'

'Maybe not, but it's yours, and I ought to be able to accept it — all of it — because it's all of you.'

'Undress me, then.'

'*What?*'

'Undress me. Take my clothes off. You can do it in any order you like, stop if you want to, put things back on again if you want to. Imagine I'm a — doll.'

We were in my studio again, and Edward was sketching me. I was half-turned towards him, but couldn't see his expression.

'Do you mean that?'

'Yes. Why not? I've undressed you often enough. I know the male body isn't as beautiful as the female. Well, not to me, anyway. And mine certainly isn't beautiful. But if it helps you to feel that you're in control, then maybe it won't be quite so alarming.'

'It's certainly an interesting idea.'

'You've moved your head!'

'Of course I've moved my head! It's not every day I get an offer like this.'

'Turn your face back a little to the left, chin down a bit — yes, that's fine.' Edward continued to draw, the strokes of his pencil making soft sweeping sounds across the paper. 'Well? What do you think?' he asked, after a few minutes had passed.

'It sounds a bit — artificial.'

'Can you think of anything better?'

'Not really.'

'Well, then.' He stood up to examine his drawing, then sat down and took up his pencil again.

'Won't you mind?'

'Mind? Why should I?'

'I don't know.' I shrugged. Maybe it was I who minded; my own reaction, rather than Edward's, that I feared.

So that evening, I undressed Edward, while he lay on the bed reading aloud from the instruction manual for my new steam iron.

'This is crazy,' I said, unbuttoning his shirt.

'"Ensure that the plug is correctly fitted." Carry on Cass.'

'But —'

'No buts. If I think about what you're doing, I cannot answer for the way my wicked body will react, and then the whole point of this operation will be wasted. This very boring leaflet is an excellent distraction. Now, where was I? Ah, yes. "Always use distilled water when filling your iron." Well, fancy that. "Turn iron to correct setting ..."'

'I love your hairy chest.'

'Good. "Stand iron on its end when finished ..."'

'I can't get your shoes off.'

'Try undoing them first. "Before seeking help, please consult the following checklist for problems. Is your iron switched on?" They must think people are frightfully stupid. "Check the fuse —"'

'Gosh. Purple socks! I never thought you were the kind of person to wear purple socks.'

'They were a present. Cass, will you please, please get a move on? I can't manage to keep up my boredom levels if you don't. And will you please stop talking. How can I concentrate on this if you're prattling away all the time? "For address of your nearest stockist please phone ..."'

It took a long time, but eventually I managed to remove all Edward's clothes. And of course, he was right. There was nothing to be afraid of. Edward's body, unlike Uncle Rupert's, was all of a piece; I hadn't been suddenly presented with one disembodied (and uninvited) part of it; he had already given me all of it, together with all of himself. His was the body of the man I loved, and yes, it was beautiful. How could I ever have thought it might be otherwise?

'I'd like to draw you,' I said, standing back and admiring him. 'If you just stay like that —'

'Don't you dare!' Edward leapt to his feet and pulled me back onto the bed. 'And now, if it's all right with you, I think I deserve some kind of reward.'

Forty-two

It's some hours now since my mother opened her eyes or gave any indication that she knows what's going on, and I'm reluctant to disturb her. The nurses have washed her and brushed her hair, but she looks desperately thin and frail, and has aged ten years in as many days. She would hate to know that she has been reduced to this dry fragile shell.

'Don't let just anyone see me when I'm dead,' she told me, only last week. 'I shan't be looking my best, when I'm dead. I don't mind you, Cass. And Lucas, if he wants. But not Greta. She'll only be too upset. And not Gracie. I don't want Gracie to see me. Being dead is — well, it's private, isn't it?'

I agreed that death was certainly private, and promised that all unwanted visitors would be kept away. She had seen Lucas's two daughters, who had visited her a few days ago, and had made it clear that she had said her goodbyes to them. And Mum has never seen eye to eye with Gracie. But there is still that one person; the person she so desperately wants to see. Every time someone opens the door, I hope it will be her, but despite several messages (missed trains, a lost mobile phone), she still hasn't arrived. I know she will never forgive herself if she's too late, but the matter is out of my hands. All I can do is hope.

Mum always minded about her appearance. She wasn't vain in the conventional sense, and spent little money on clothes or make-up, but she was proud of her luxuriant hair, her slender legs and enviable figure, and as she grew older, she mourned their inevitable deterioration.

'It's so unfair, being a woman,' she once said to me. 'It's as though nature is saying you don't need to look good any more, so everything starts to go downhill. It's different for men. Men seem to grow better-looking as they grow older.' She sighed. 'Of course, it's all about babies.'

'What on earth do you mean?' I asked her.

'Droopy boobs, saggy tum, grey hair, wrinkles. If you can't make babies, then you don't need to attract someone to make babies with any more, do you?'

'Oh, Mum, don't be ridiculous. You still look fabulous, you know you do. Besides, you don't want to make any more babies, do you?'

'No,' she admitted. 'But I'd still like to have the choice.' Mum had looked on the menopause as an unwelcome intruder into her life, and she grieved for the passing of her fertility. It must have seemed especially poignant that it had come at a time when I was finally discovering myself as a sexually functioning woman, and while she rejoiced for me, it brought it home to her that she wasn't getting any younger. Of course, she still had relationships, and it appeared to me that she was as attractive to men as she ever was, but some of her gay confidence was lost, and recently there had been some interesting, not to say colourful, additions to the bottles and jars on her dressing-table.

I had told Mum just enough about Edward and our relationship to keep her happy, without disclosing those aspects I wanted to keep to myself. I have always been a private person, and while I didn't mind Mum telling me about her love life, I didn't always want to exchange her confidences for those of my own.

'When are we going to meet him?' was a question she asked increasingly often, and one which was becoming more and more difficult to deflect. The fact that he was married didn't work at all, since Mum had scant regard for marriage (although she had rarely had affairs with married men herself). I tried telling her that Edward felt awkward about his married state, but that didn't work either.

'What's to feel awkward about?' Mum asked. 'We're not here to judge him. Besides, didn't you say he was separated?'

I recalled Edward saying all those weeks ago that 'in a way' he and his wife were already separated, and while I had been reassured by his words, they inevitably raised more questions than they answered. But while I did ask him several times if he couldn't explain what he meant, he always refused.

'Don't you trust me?' I asked him once. 'Is that it?'

'Of course I trust you.'

'Then please tell me, Edward. Please. I feel as though I'm being — excluded from an important part of your life. I've told you all about me. Things I've never told anyone.'

'But this isn't just about me, is it? Someone else is involved. You'll understand one day, Cass, I promise. I have — I have my reasons for keeping it to myself for the time being, but I will tell you.'

'Is she abroad? Is that it?'

'No. I only wish she was — could — go abroad.'

'A long way away, then?' I persisted.

'No, not a long way away. Not a long way away at all.' He smiled, but his eyes were full of such enormous sadness that I couldn't bring myself to question him further. If Edward had promised me he would tell me what I wanted to know, then he would keep his promise. Meanwhile, I would just have to wait. As for Mum, she would have to wait, too. And while it would have been wonderful to celebrate our love publicly, to be seen out and about together without subterfuge and to be able to acknowledge openly our coupled state, secrecy seemed a small price to pay for my new-found happiness.

And so I remained in ignorance until the day when, quite by chance, I saw Edward's wife.

It was my half-day, and I had gone into town to do some shopping. I was waiting at the bus stop for my bus home when I saw coming towards me a wheelchair, pushed by a tall and very familiar figure. Edward was leaning down, speaking to the woman in the wheelchair, but even from a distance I could see she was only half aware that he was talking to her. It was like a flash photograph. In those few seconds, I took in Edward, the wheelchair, the woman huddled beneath a rug, with glazed unseeing eyes, the awkward angle of her head, the twisted hands. And then I turned and fled, before either of them should see me.

When I got back to my studio, I sat on the bed and wept. I wept for Edward and for the woman who was so cruelly crippled, but I also wept for myself. For if Edward really loved me, why hadn't he let me in on this part of his life? Why hadn't he trusted me to listen and to support him? That I had assisted in betraying a wife was bad enough. Doing it to someone ill, someone handicapped, someone at such a terrible disadvantage, seemed unforgivable.

When Edward came round that evening, I told him what I had seen.

'You could have told me. You *should* have told me. How could you have kept something this important — this *painful* — to yourself? What does that say about me? About our relationship?'

Edward shrugged helplessly.

'Please, Edward. Tell me all about her. You have to tell me now; now that I've seen her. I want to understand.'

'I don't know where to start.'

'Well, the beginning would be a good place.'

Edward sat down, gazing at the floor, his hands between his knees.

'We'd only been married five years,' he began.

'Go on.'

'We were going to a wedding. I was driving. There was — an accident.'

'And?' I prompted.

'She — Vanessa — was terribly injured. They didn't think she'd make it through the night, but she survived. Oh, Cass. It would have been so much better for her if she hadn't.' He took out a handkerchief and blew his nose. His head was bent and I couldn't see his face, but I believe that he was crying. 'She was so beautiful, Cass. Vibrant, happy, full of life. And now — well, you've seen her. Sometimes she recognizes me, but most of the time she's no idea who I am. I tried looking after her myself, but in the end I couldn't manage, so she lives in a home. They're very good to her, very kind, but there's not much anyone can do. I visit her once or twice a week; sometimes her family come and see her. Today was the first time I've taken her out in ages. I thought it might help, but I don't think she even realized she was outdoors.' He looked up at me and attempted a smile. 'So there it is. Now you know.'

'Oh, Edward. I'm so so sorry.' I knelt down by his chair and took his hand. 'But why didn't you tell me? Wouldn't it have helped, to tell me?'

'I didn't want you to feel sorry for me, I suppose. Or sorry for Vanessa. I didn't want you to be tied to me by pity, or because you felt you had to support me. And Vanessa ... She has so little dignity left, and to be pitied by my lover — and you are bound to pity her, Cass; how could you not? — is so degrading, somehow.'

'The accident ...' I hesitated. 'Was it — was it your fault?'

Edward shook his head.

'A lorry came out of a side road and didn't see us. It hit the car on the passenger side.' He ran his hands through his hair. 'But I still feel responsible. I know there was nothing I could have done — goodness knows, I've replayed it over and over in my head — but there are all those "if onlys". If only I'd filled the car up the day before and we hadn't had to stop for petrol, if only we hadn't been running late, if only we hadn't been going to that wedding at all — we nearly didn't. If only.'

'How long ago did it happen?'

'Seven years.'

'How terrible. How absolutely terrible, for both of you.'

'Yes. Though I don't think Vanessa is aware of anything very much at all, which I suppose is a blessing. She likes her food, and seems to enjoy music. Sometimes I read to her, but I don't think she takes it in. It's such a waste, Cass. Such a tragic waste. I lost the woman I loved on the day of the accident. The Vanessa who's left is someone quite different. But I owe it to her to visit her, to make sure she's well looked after. To do the little I can.'

'And — her family?'

'Her parents are dead, but she has two sisters. I get on with them both, and they made it clear some time ago that if I — well, if I found someone else, they would understand, but they'd rather I kept it quiet. At the time, I never imagined that would happen, so I didn't give it much thought. But now there's you.' He sighed. 'I hate keeping it a secret — you and me — but I feel in a way it's the least I can do. To divorce Vanessa would seem unutterably cruel, when she's done nothing to deserve it.'

'But don't people round here know? They must have heard of the accident. News like that usually travels pretty fast.'

'We lived in Surrey at the time, but I couldn't bear to stay on in the house, so I moved up here where nobody knows us. I brought Vanessa with me and found her a place to live so I could still visit her.' He got up and walked over to the window. 'No one here knows about her, and it's best that way. I don't want sympathy for her or for me. You can have too much sympathy, you know, Cass. I think in a way I was trying to get away from that, too. I didn't want to be "poor Edward" any more. I just wanted to get on with my life.'

I think that at that moment I loved Edward more than I had ever loved him; for his caring, his loyalty and his integrity. And I ached for his loss and for the seven lonely, agonizing years which had followed.

'Humphrey told me that you — well, that you had problems,' I said now. 'How much does he know?'

'Humphrey knows everything. He's the only person I've told, and he's been such a good friend to me. He was probably trying to protect you, Cass; warn you off. He knows I can't offer you what you want.'

'How does he know what I want?'

'Well, I suppose it was an assumption. But he probably assumes you want marriage and children. Don't most women?'

'Not this one. Not necessarily.' I joined him by the window and took his hand. 'I've never been particularly interested in marriage. I suppose it's because I've never lived in a married household. Mum never wanted to get married, and she's managed all right. Of course, I'm not really like her. One relationship is enough for me. But marriage? To be honest, I've never really thought about it.'

'And now?'

'And now what?'

'What — what do you want to do? Now you know about Vanessa.'

I sighed.

'It's a difficult one. I hate to feel I'm taking advantage of her in some way. On the other hand, you say she can't really be hurt by anything we do.'

'I love you so much, Cass. I'm not sure I could cope without you now I've found you.' Once more, Edward's eyes filled with tears.

'Can I sleep on it?' I asked, after a moment.

He nodded. 'Of course. And I'll respect whatever you decide to do.'

But when it came to it, there wasn't really any decision to make. I think my mind was made up even before Edward left the room.

Forty-three

Living with a secret is never easy, but I probably coped better than many people because I've always been quite good with secrets. I had friends, but none of them particularly close, and except for Myra (who was very understanding and could be surprisingly discreet), I didn't tell any of them about Edward.

It was with some reservations that I finally told Mum about Edward's situation, having extracted from her a promise of absolute secrecy. Her reaction was typical.

'Oh, the poor man! How perfectly dreadful for him. I wonder if there's anything I can do to help. Perhaps I could go and visit his wife? Or even take New Dog to see her? They say people like that often respond to animals rather than humans. And New Dog is handicapped too, isn't he, so they've got something in common. I could go on the bus —'

'No, Mum. No!' Whatever Vanessa's state of mind, I was sure that there were few things she needed less than New Dog.

'Why ever not? Honestly, Cass. You're such a wet blanket sometimes.'

'Mum, I'm not telling you about this so that you can do something about it. I'm telling you because you're my mother and you wanted to know. There's nothing you can do for Vanessa. In fact it doesn't seem there's much anyone can do for her.'

'I could make her a cake. Most people like cake.'

'Mum, please. Just leave it, will you?'

For a moment, Mum looked crestfallen, then she brightened.

'But you can introduce me to Edward, can't you? There's nothing to stop you now. And after all, I do introduce you to my men-friends.'

This last was not strictly true, for while I had certainly met most if not all of Mum's lovers, it was as often as not when they were scantily clad *en route* to the bathroom, or in the kitchen waiting to be fed (usually by the long-suffering Greta). Mum rarely bothered with formal introductions.

'Well ...' I hesitated. I had become accustomed to keeping my two lives separate, and wasn't sure how well they would mix. Edward was my refuge as well as my lover. Our life together was an oasis of peace in a generally troubled world. Would all that change if I were to bring him home?

'Oh, come on, Cass. I'll behave beautifully, I promise. I won't let you down.'

'It's not that. And I do want you to meet him, of course I do. But Mum, I don't want the others around. Not yet.'

'But Greta and Call Me Bill are family,' Mum protested. 'We don't have any secrets from them.'

'You may not have secrets from them, Mum, but I do. I'm very fond of both of them, you know I am. But I don't want them knowing all about my personal life. I don't even want Lucas to know at the moment.'

'Oh, Lucas.' Mum sniffed. 'He's become so stuffy. I blame Gracie.'

It should be explained that Mum tended to blame Gracie for everything where Lucas was concerned, and this was not entirely fair on Gracie. For while she would never be the kind of daughter-in-law Mum would have liked (given her feelings about marriage, she would probably have preferred to have no daughter-in-law at all), Gracie was a perfectly nice girl; just a bit ordinary, and somewhat lacking in imagination. But she was a good wife and mother, and she seemed to suit Lucas, and that was really all that mattered.

I brought Edward home for tea and one of Mum's cakes, and they took to one another immediately. Edward thought Mum was 'so refreshing', and Mum considered Edward to be 'very charming, and so good-looking, Cass' (to my shame, I experienced a frisson of alarm, for Mum had been known to take up with younger men, and Edward was nearer Mum's age than mine). New Dog greeted him in a frenzy of leaping and licking, and true to her word, Mum appeared to have banished the rest of the household from the premises.

'Your mother is amazing,' Edward said to me on the way home. 'I've never met anyone quite like her.'

'I don't think there is anyone quite like her,' I said.

'And the way she talked about Vanessa. As though it was the most natural thing in the world for her daughter to have a married lover with a handicapped wife.'

'She wanted to go and see her.'

'Who? Vanessa?' Edward looked alarmed.

I laughed.

'Don't worry. I told her Vanessa was off limits. But Mum's like that. She looks for people to look after.'

'Does she look after you?' Edward asked.

'What a strange question.' I thought for a moment. 'No. Not really. She's best with sick people and animals, waifs and strays, that sort of thing. I don't think I count. When we were children, she tended to treat Lucas and me more as friends, except when we were ill. I think that's one of the reasons you make me so happy. I've never felt really looked after before.'

And it was true. If I thought about it, I don't think I had ever felt protected the way I did when I was with Edward. He was strong and sensible, calm in a crisis and good at making decisions. I could rely on him totally, and while I would happily have looked after him had the occasion demanded it, it was wonderful to have a relationship in which this was not a dominant factor. We never talked about it, but I'm sure we both recognized an element of father-daughter in our relationship, and

I believe it was something we both needed. I had never had a father, and Edward was no longer able to look after Vanessa as he wanted to do. We had each found in the other something much more than simply a lover — although that was wonderful in itself — and I think we both helped one another to grow emotionally stronger.

My painting, too, improved greatly after I met Edward. Before, there had been a hesitancy, almost a shyness about my work. My paintings were nice enough, and people seemed to like them, but they had a self-effacing quality which reflected my own personality. Now, they became bolder, more assertive, and I was developing a real style of my own. I started experimenting in charcoal and pen and ink, and produced some pleasing sketches of Lucas's children (which I sold, since they were not to Gracie's taste). People began to commission drawings of their own children, and occasionally their pets, and I was happy to oblige. It made a pleasant change to be invited into people's homes to do my work, and I made several good friends in the process. I continued to work for Humphrey, who was beginning to talk of retirement and increasingly left the management of the gallery to me. For the first time in my life, I was fulfilled on all fronts, and happier than I had ever been.

And so the years passed. In time, I was able to buy my own small terraced house and convert the dining room into a studio, while Mum consoled herself for my absence by installing a new Lodger in my old bedroom. Edward and I spent as much time together as either of us needed (two artists living together doesn't always work), and an increasing amount of my work now involved commissioned drawings of babies and children.

It was almost my thirty-fourth birthday when Edward brought up the subject of children.

I was putting the finishing touches to a sketch of a sleeping baby. The child had adopted that position typical of babies, lying on its front with its knees drawn up. The soles of its feet peeped out from under a well-padded bottom, and one dimpled fist was visible beside the curve of a plump cheek.

I was pleased with the drawing and was leaning back to admire it, when I became aware of Edward standing behind me.

'Cass,' he said, putting his hands on my shoulders. 'Would you like one of those?'

'One of what?' I reached for a pencil to sign my drawing.

'A baby of course. Cass, I think it's time you and I thought about having a baby.'

It may seem odd now, in an age when women clamour for the right to have babies with or without a partner, but Edward and I had never discussed the matter of children. Of course, I had thought about it from time to time; imagined what it would be like to have Edward's child; what it would be like to be a mother. But children had never featured very strongly in my plans and I had never been especially maternal. As a child, such dolls as I had were more likely to be used in games of cowboys and Indians, or subjected to bloodthirsty surgical procedures, than mothered in the conventional sense. And while I liked small children, I had never really considered having one of my own. So Edward's question took me by surprise.

'A baby? You and me?'

'Why not?' Edward sat down beside me.

'Do *you* want children?'

'Well, I certainly did, when Vanessa was — well, before the accident. Then I more or less said goodbye to the idea. But now — well, yes. I would like a child. Your — our child.'

'What's brought this on?'

'*Anno Domini.*' Edward laughed. 'Since I hit fifty, I realized that doors were beginning to close; doors that couldn't be reopened. There are so many things I'll never do now; paint a masterpiece, climb Everest, learn to tap-dance ... well, you know what I mean. But a baby — that's something I can do. Something we can do.' He spread his fingers. 'I haven't been able to do much for you, Cass. I haven't given you marriage or a home together, the usual things. But I can — could — give you a baby.'

'Goodness!' I was more taken aback than I would have imagined.

'I know. I think I'm even surprising myself. But just think about it. I know it's a big decision, especially for you. Between us, we can afford a baby, and I'll play my part. I'd be a good father.'

'I know you would. But it's not that easy, is it? I mean, what would people say?'

'You mean the unmarried thing?'

'No.' I laughed. 'With a mother like mine, the unmarried thing is hardly likely to be a problem, is it? No, I mean Vanessa, her family, people who don't know about us. Wouldn't I and my illegitimate offspring be a bit of an embarrassment?'

'I think we could get round it. After all, Vanessa's been ill for a long time, and I think her family have more or less guessed about you. They might even be pleased for me.'

'A baby. Our baby. It's certainly a thought. Can I think about it?'

Suddenly the streets were full of women with pushchairs, pregnant women, parents towing reluctant toddlers along busy pavements. No doubt they had always been there, but so far they hadn't been part of my agenda. Now, I found myself taking notice of them, surreptitiously peering into prams and even straying into shops selling baby clothes, where I would finger tiny dresses and sleep suits and try to imagine buying them for my own baby.

'What's that you've got?' Edward asked, when I was unpacking some shopping about a week after our baby conversation.

I held up a small fluffy blue rabbit.

'I couldn't resist it,' I told him.

'Is that — is that by any chance a present for Cass junior?'

'Or baby Edward. One or the other.'

'Oh, Cass! I'm so pleased!' He hugged me. 'I can't tell you how pleased.'

'Me too.' I put down the rabbit and returned his hug.

'When shall we start?'

'No time like the present. But not in front of the rabbit.' I replaced it carefully in its paper bag.

Forty-four

I hear footsteps flying along the corridor, coming towards us. I remember my nursing days, and the strict injunction never to run unless there was a fire or a dire emergency, but I know those footsteps, that breathless speed, even from behind a closed door. And when the door is flung open, I am not disappointed.

'Gran! Oh Gran!' Tavvy flings herself onto the bed, then turns to me. 'I'm not too late, am I? Dad met me and brought me straight here. Please tell me I'm not too late!'

'You will be, if you crush her. For goodness' sake be careful, Tavvy!' I stand up and pull her back off the bed, laughing in spite of myself, and then give her a huge hug. 'Oh, I'm so pleased to see you! You've no idea how pleased. She's been waiting for you for days. I didn't know how much longer she could hang on.'

'She looks so — so breakable. There's nothing of her.' The tears run down Tavvy's cheeks. 'Poor, poor little Gran. She doesn't deserve this.' She sits down by the bed and takes Mum's hand in hers. 'Darling Gran. It's me. Tavvy. I'm here now.'

Mum's eyelids flutter, and there is the faintest ghost of a smile.

'I knew — knew — you'd — come.' Her voice is barely audible, and Tavvy leans down to catch her words.

'Of course I came. How could you think I wouldn't?' Tavvy strokes Mum's hand, then lifts it to hold it against her own cheek. 'I wouldn't let you do — do this without me, would I?'

Mum closes her eyes again, but the smile is still there, hovering, as though reluctant to leave her lips.

Tavvy weeps, noisily, helplessly, her mane of auburn hair — Mum's hair — falling forward over her face, her shoulders heaving with her sobs. Poor Tavvy. She and Mum have always been close, and I know she has had an appalling time trying to get here. I haven't seen her for nearly a year, and I scan her greedily, taking in the mass of freckles on her bare arms, her torn jeans and Save the Walrus (Walrus?) T-shirt, her sandaled (and far from clean) feet. She has lost weight, and I could swear she's grown a couple of inches. I hate to have had to interrupt her precious gap year, and yet I am so glad she is home and safe.

'Why didn't you call me before?' she asks now. 'You know I would have come.'

'I'd no idea it would be so quick. Besides, I wasn't to know you'd go off trekking into the jungle! Anyway, you're here now, and that's all that matters.'

It was my idea to name our daughter Octavia. Mum never actually suggested it, but I knew it was what she wanted, and it is after all a pretty name. She had tried to persuade Lucas to give it to one of his children, but he (or more likely, Gracie) was having none of it. And when the girls turned out to be as pleasantly ordinary as their mother, Mum felt vindicated.

'Anne and Sarah! I ask you! With names like that, what do you expect?'

However, I'm pretty sure that it wasn't so much the children themselves who bothered her as the fact that they had made her a grandmother, and that was something she told me she wasn't ready for yet.

'It sounds so *old*, Cass. Grey hair and lavender water and those enormous knickers with elastic.'

'And a shopping trolley,' I teased her.

'That too.'

'And flannel nighties.'

'Don't mock, Cass. It's not funny, growing old.'

But by the time Octavia came along, Mum had become used to her grandmotherly status, and was even heard to boast about it to disbelieving suitors ('No, really? You can't be! You look much too young!' was the response she expected and, as often as not, received). Nonetheless, I hoped that she would form a better relationship with my baby than she had with Lucas's, for while Lucas's children had a legion of grandparents, uncles, aunts and cousins courtesy of Gracie's family, Edward and I had few relatives.

But I needn't have worried, for Mum was besotted from the word go with the small bohemian who was our daughter. Refusing to wear the clothes other children wore, or play with the same toys, Tavvy went her own sweet way, and while she wasn't deliberately disobedient, nor even especially naughty, rules puzzled her. Whether she was talking to a stranger or picking flowers in someone else's garden, she quite simply didn't understand what she was doing wrong. 'But Mummy, I didn't know' was her oft-repeated refrain. The 'stranger' hadn't been strange at all; he was very nice. If she had a garden, she would be quite happy for someone to come and pick her flowers. What was the problem?

Beautiful, eccentric and imaginative, she spurned friends of her own age ('They just want to *play*, Mummy') but loved adult company and made a wonderful companion. She never needed to be entertained, and provided she had pencils and paper, was rarely bored. Her drawings from an early age were prodigious in quality as well as quantity, and if her school work was neglected in favour of her art, she came up with such plausible excuses that it was difficult to argue with her.

Edward adored her, and played a full part in her upbringing. We took it in turns to care for her, with help from Mum when the need arose, and she divided her time between our two homes. She never questioned this arrangement, seeming to enjoy the freedom and flexibility it engendered, together with her two bedrooms (not to mention the two cats — Tavvy loved cats). Whatever happened during the week, Edward and I always tried to spend the weekends together, and the three of us would have breakfast in bed on Sunday mornings; Edward and I with coffee and toast and the Sunday papers, and Tavvy in the middle with her boiled egg and soldiers.

It wasn't a conventional upbringing, but it worked, as I tried to explain to Lucas on the one occasion when he took it upon himself to question our childcare arrangements.

'It's not normal, Cass. To live in two houses, the way you do, and push the child back and forth like a — like a tennis ball.'

'Tavvy's not pushed anywhere! She wouldn't put up with it, for a start.'

'And that's another thing. She's in very real danger of being spoiled,' Lucas said, as though being spoiled were on a par with being trapped in a burning building.

'Is that what Gracie thinks?' I asked mildly.

'Gracie did happen to mention that you might have problems later.'

'Well, do thank Gracie for me. I'm sure she'll be able to advise me if that ever happens.'

'There's no need to be sarcastic, Cass. We're only trying to help. After all, we have been at this game a lot longer than you.'

I thought of my two well-behaved nieces, who had probably never in their lives made a mud pie or climbed a tree (activities much favoured by Tavvy) and smiled. It was true that Sarah was beginning to show signs of rebellion, which Mum considered to be a promising start, but Anne appeared to be a lost cause. Gracie may not have been a particularly forceful character, but her genes more than made up for it.

'Of course you have, Lucas,' I said. 'I'll bear it in mind.'

Despite Lucas's warning, we had little trouble with Tavvy, and even her teens passed largely uneventfully. True, she could be wayward and moody, but no more than most teenagers, and as for the multiple piercings of her ears and the ring in her belly button, I thought they looked rather nice (the pierced eyebrow lasted only two days because Tavvy said it was too painful).

When Tavvy was sixteen, Vanessa died. Unsurprisingly, Edward was deeply saddened at the ending of a life which had been so cruelly cut off, and much angered by those who expected him to feel relief at what they imagined to be his long-awaited freedom. 'Now you and Cass can get married' was the often repeated refrain (our relationship had long ceased to be a secret), but we felt strangely reluctant to upset the status quo. We had lived separately for so long that the idea of such a major change was unsettling.

We asked Tavvy what she thought.

'Whatever do you want to get married for?' was her response.

'Isn't it what most people's parents do?' Edward asked.

'Most people!' scoffed Tavvy. 'No. We're all much better off as we are. Trust me. Besides, you two couldn't possibly live together. It wouldn't work.'

And I think she was probably right. We could manage the upkeep of our two modest homes, and we had our own routines and habits (not to mention the two by now ageing cats, who would no doubt fight). One day, maybe we would think again, but for the time being we were content. As for Tavvy, she flitted to and fro at will, as often as not staying with Mum. By now, Call Me Bill had died, and Greta was in poor health, so what with caring for her and seeing to sundry Lodgers, Mum had her hands full. Tavvy liked to go round 'to help', although I suspect that the two of them spent most of the time drinking tea and gossiping.

Humphrey was by now in his eighties, and had retired some years ago, but I stayed on as manager of the gallery. I continued to sell my paintings, but I had had to accept that I would never be good enough to make a living from my work, as Edward did.

But while Edward was undoubtedly good, Tavvy was better. Her paintings — wild, colourful and full of life, like Tavvy herself — delighted her teachers, and even before she left school several of them had sold. Many were exuberant abstracts in bright colours; bold swirls of paint interweaving or dancing across the canvas. Some were reminiscent of the French Impressionists (Tavvy particularly admired Gauguin), but there was a wildness and originality which were all her own. There was nothing shy about Tavvy's work; she had the courage I had lacked, and once she discovered oils, there was no stopping her.

'So you're going to be an artist, like your parents?' people would ask her, and Tavvy was always surprised.

'Just because I can paint doesn't mean that's what I'm going to do as a *job*,' she told me, exasperated at what she saw as a ridiculous assumption. 'No. I'm going to travel and have fun. Then I'll decide what I'm going to do.'

'Quite right,' said Mum, who had called in to see us. 'Aren't people silly?'

'Well, you've had to drop your other A levels, so your options are a bit restricted,' I suggested. 'Art seems the obvious direction, doesn't it? At least for the time being. You don't have to do it forever.'

My mother and Tavvy exchanged despairing glances.

'Dear old mum.' Tavvy patted my shoulder.

'She's just trying to be sensible,' my mother said, and they both rocked with laughter. They say the apple doesn't fall far from the tree; I think the apple that was my daughter had skipped a generation.

But even Mum had to agree that travel must be paid for, so when Tavvy got her one A level, she had to work to earn her gap year. Like Mum, she was not good at holding down a job, and managed to get through four within the first three months.

'People are so stupid,' she said, after three weeks as a chambermaid. 'Do they really think we don't find what they hide under their mattresses? I handed this customer his magazine, with a perfectly straight face, and said "I believe this is yours, sir", and he complained to the manager, and I was sacked.' She laughed, 'Oh, Mum. You should have seen it! All those naked bodies! And you've no idea what they were doing to each other. Men and women, two or three at a time, too. I wish I'd been able to keep it. Gran would have been fascinated!'

Eventually Tavvy found her niche, helping out at a day nursery, and while the manager frequently questioned some of the more unusual games she invented to entertain the children, her small charges and their parents thought the world of her.

After several months, Tavvy had saved up enough money for her expedition, and my house began to fill up with all the impedimenta of the backpacker. Wherever I went, I seemed to trip over camping equipment and hiking boots, insect repellent and mosquito nets. Typically, she had refused the services of gap year organizations or anyone else who might have been of assistance, preferring to plan her own itinerary. Her plans were typically vague, involving little more than, as she put it, 'taking off and seeing what happens', and were more than a little reminiscent of Mum's famous holiday.

'On your own?' I asked fearfully, when Tavvy told us of her intentions. 'Is it safe to go on your own?'

'Oh, Mum. Lots of people do it. I'll be fine.'

'I'd feel much happier if there was someone with you.'

'I did ask around, but no one wanted to come. Anyway, it'll be more fun on my own. I can do what I like.'

'Don't you always?' Edward asked mildly.

'Oh, Dad! Don't be so stuffy! In any case, isn't that what you love about me?'

'Surely you ought at least to have some sort of itinerary,' I said.

'Why? This will be much more exciting,' Tavvy said. 'I'll start with Peru, and see where that takes me. After all, if Peru was good enough for Paddington Bear, it's good enough for me.'

'Paddington Bear left Peru and came to England,' Edward pointed out. 'Perhaps he knew something you don't.'

'More fool he. Anyway, that's where I'm going. I've decided. And Gran thinks it's a great idea.'

'Gran would,' I replied, silently cursing my mother. For while she would no doubt be sleeping soundly in her bed while her granddaughter cavorted around the world, I was pretty sure I would lie awake worrying for weeks to come.

And so it was that one freezing November afternoon, Edward and I found ourselves waving our daughter off at Heathrow airport.

'She'll be all right,' Edward said, squeezing my hand, as we watched Tavvy making her way through into the departure lounge. 'She's nearly twenty, and she knows how to look after herself.'

'Yes,' I whispered, fighting back the tears, trying not to think of all the potential hazards lying in wait for the lone female traveller.

Tavvy looked back a last time; a slight figure weighed down by an enormous backpack and a cloud of bright hair under a battered straw hat. She grinned broadly and blew us a final kiss before disappearing from sight.

It seemed like the last curtain in the wonderful drama which had been Tavvy's childhood.

Forty-five

October 2001

Another evening, another dusk, perhaps another night of waiting. Now, Tavy and I sit on either side of Mum, holding her hands. There have been other visitors — Lucas, Greta, Edward with a flask of soup and some sandwiches — but Tavy and I will stay here together until the end. It's what Mum would have wanted.

My mother sleeps. She hasn't stirred since Tavy's arrival, but the faint smile still lingers on her face, and I believe she is at peace.

I tell Tavy about her funeral plans.

'Black horses, Tavy. Imagine. Where on earth are we going to find a black horse?'

'I know someone who's got a brown pony,' Tavy says, after a moment. 'Would that do?'

'A brown pony ... Oh, why not? I'm sure a brown pony will do nicely. Can it pull a cart?'

'I expect so,' says Tavy, who knows nothing at all about horses. 'If not, we'll teach it.'

I think of all the things that will need to be done when Mum dies, and mentally add to the list teaching the brown pony to pull a cart.

'And flowers. She wants lots of flowers.'

'I should think so,' says Tavy. 'A funeral wouldn't be a funeral without lots of flowers. Not wreaths, though. They're too — too —'

'Funereal?'

'That's probably it.' We both laugh.

'I'll miss her so much,' Tavy says, after a moment, and begins to weep again. 'The world won't be the same without Gran.'

'I know.'

We sit on, chatting quietly, laughing, crying. Mum's breathing becomes increasingly shallow and erratic, and once again I find myself clinging tightly on to her hand, as though a part of me is still trying to hang on to her. When I look across the bed, I see that Tavy is doing the same.

'We must let her go, Tavy,' I say, reaching across to take Tavy's hand in mine. 'We have to let her go.'

'Do you think she'll speak again?' Tavy asks, through more tears.

I shake my head.

'There's no need. I think she's said all she wants to say. Now you're back, there's nothing to keep her.'

More time passes, a doctor looks in, a nurse asks if we're all right and brings us hot chocolate. Eventually, Tavy and I both doze off, curled uncomfortably in our hospital chairs.

I must have fallen into a deeper sleep than I intended, for when I awake I am quite stiff and, for a brief moment, disorientated. But I know even before I open my eyes that Mum has gone.

There is a stillness in the room; a silence which wasn't there before. The hand I hold in mine is still faintly warm, but my mother is no longer here. It's like coming into a room just after someone has left it: the embers are still glowing in the hearth; the seat of a chair still retains the warmth of the person who was occupying it; but there is no longer anyone there.

Tavy wakes with a little cry.

'Oh, no!' *She clutches at Mum's hand.* 'She's gone! She didn't even say goodbye!'

'She did. When you arrived. That was her goodbye.'

Tavy's head is bent and I know she's crying, but soundlessly this time. My own tears seem locked in my throat as though waiting for permission before they can be released. Somewhere, a church clock strikes, and an ambulance makes its noisy response to someone else's emergency; perhaps someone else's tragedy.

Eventually, Tavy lets go of Mum's hand and stands up, gazing down at the small, still figure in the bed.

'So that's — it.' *She sounds surprised.*

'Yes. That's it.'

'So quiet for such a dramatic thing. The end of someone's life. You expect — oh, I don't know. A fanfare or something. Something more — important.'

'I know what you mean.'

'She didn't suffer, did she?'

'No. Not too much.'

'That's good. And you, Mum. You've lost your mother.' *She comes and puts her arms around me.* 'Poor old mum.'

'I'll be all right.' *I return her hug.*

'You've still got me. And Dad.'

'Of course I have.'

Tavy moves away, and stands silhouetted against the light coming in from the corridor. Although she is so thin, her stomach has a gentle and unmistakable curve, and she places her hands over it protectively, as though challenging death to seek out another victim. Catching my gaze, she gives a small helpless shrug.

'I was going to tell you, Mum.' *Her voice has the same tone as it did when she was a little girl and was afraid I might be cross with her.* 'I did love him, you know. He said he said he'd stay with me. He promised to look after me.'

'But he didn't.'

'No. He didn't.'

The words hang between us, as though waiting for some kind of resolution.

I take Tavy in my arms again and hold her close.

'Poor Tavy.'

'Oh, Mum. I've wanted you — needed you — so much.' *She sobs into my shoulder.* 'I've been so stupid. How could I have been so stupid?'

'It happens. These things happen. But we'll manage,' *I say, stroking her hair.* 'It'll be all right.'

'Will it?' She lifts a tear-stained face to mine.

'Of course it will.'

'And — Dad?'

'You leave Dad to me.'

We stand there for a long time, holding each other, and I draw comfort from the warmth of my daughter's skin, her hair against my cheek, the small catch of her breath.

Outside the window, another dawn is lightening the sky; a new day is beginning; the last leaf detaches itself from a branch of the maple tree, and begins to spiral slowly towards the ground.

BOOK TWO: WOMEN BEHAVING BADLY

Prologue

The Catholic Church has always had a problem with sex, and never more so than with that of the extramarital variety.

A certain Catholic bishop reflected gloomily upon the problem of adultery in his diocese (it was a large diocese, and there was a lot of adultery), and after much thought and some heartfelt prayers, he hit upon an idea: a self-help group for adulterers! Why had no-one thought of it before? There were self-help groups for drug-users and alcoholics, so why not for those who were slaves to their illicit passions? It was a wonderful idea, and he knew just the person to lead the group.

Father Cuthbert O'Donnell was not pleased. He was a shy man, he had never led a group before, and he had enough problems on his own doorstep without extending his boundaries any further. When the Bishop approached him, he prevaricated and he reasoned — he even cited his asthma attacks — but to no avail. The Bishop was insistent. The meetings must obviously take place somewhere away from the big towns where people might know one another, and Father Cuthbert's little village was just the place. Money would be provided for tea and biscuits, and the Bishop himself would put in motion the business of recruiting people to attend, making as sure as was possible that the individuals concerned did not already know one another.

"And how will you do that, Your Grace?" Father Cuthbert enquired boldly.

The Bishop tapped his nose and smiled. "I have my ways."

"But —"

"No buts, Father. I'm sure you will carry out this duty as conscientiously as you do all your others."

"Adulterers Anonymous?" hazarded Father Cuthbert, accepting defeat.

"No, *no*, Father. *Theology*. We will call the meetings Basic Theology for Beginners, to preserve confidentiality, and avoid embarrassment."

And that was the start. To Father Cuthbert's surprise, the group went well. The members seemed to enjoy the opportunity to discuss their problems with their fellows, and gradually, some of them came to see the error of their ways.

Within six months, of the ten original group members, just three were left. Five had broken off their irregular liaisons, one had resorted to divorce, and one, tragically, had killed himself, thus (as Father Cuthbert sadly informed his fellows) further compounding his tally of mortal sins.

Notwithstanding the fine example of some of their fellows and unmoved by the suicide, the three remaining members of the group — all women — seemed unwilling to mend their ways, and after consulting with the Bishop, Father

Cuthbert informed them that it was with much regret that he had decided that he could no longer extend to them his hospitality (not to mention the coffee and biscuits) at the presbytery. If they wished to continue their meetings, they would have to make alternative arrangements.

Alice, Mavis, and Gabs decided to do just that. This is their story.

Part One

Alice

Alice hurtled round Tesco's, throwing things into her trolley, with one eye on the time. In half an hour, she was due to pick up Finn from football practice, and then she had to get him home and feed him before she left for her meeting. Baked beans, biscuits, cereal — what kind was Finn into these days? It seemed to change from week to week. Something crisp and chocolatey would probably do. Washing powder, socks — would Finn mind Tesco socks? Probably not. After all, socks were socks, weren't they? Alice threw in a couple of packs. She would take off the labels, and Finn probably wouldn't even notice.

At the checkout, Alice realised she'd forgotten the milk. Well, they'd have to make do with what they had. If necessary, they could always borrow some from next door. The woman who lived there kept cats and always had plenty. Alice disliked the cats, who came over the fence and killed birds and dug up her one flower bed. Their owner was sympathetic but said there was nothing much she could do. Cats would be cats. Alice had heard once that in the eyes of the law, cats weren't possessions; they were "free spirits." In other words, they could more or less do what they liked. The title somehow exonerated the owners from any responsibility.

If only the same could be said of teenagers.

Finn was fifteen, the age of the 'great ennui' as a friend of Alice's (and mother of three sons) put it. Everything — school, holidays, television, some of his friends and most of hers, even life itself — everything was "bore-*ring*." Wherever he was, his gangling frame seemed to fill the house, his boat-size trainers tripped her up in the hallway, his music blared from the open door of his bedroom. He languished across armchairs or along the sofa, his bare (and none too clean) feet dangling, his jaws slowly masticating gum, his eyes either closed or glazed over. He slept for twelve hours at a time and ate enough to feed a small third-world village. The smell of toast would waft up the stairs long after Alice had gone to bed (how was it that a *smell* could wake one up?), and they were always running out of food. As for his room… well, to use an awful cliché, don't even go there (Alice didn't).

But he made her laugh. No-one had ever made Alice laugh the way Finn did. He was an excellent mimic, told wickedly funny stories, and his bagpipes act (an upside down kitchen stool and a very rude "Scottish" song) could make her cry with laughter. His quick ripostes, the little notes he left her ('out of bread, peanut butter, and chill pills for Mum'), his bear hugs (he was very affectionate), and on good days, his companionship, all made it worthwhile.

Alice would look at this huge, towering boy-man and remember with horror how she very nearly got rid of him.

Finn was an accident. Alice had known his father just three hours (or was it four?). They'd met at a party and ended up in the summerhouse on a heap of rather smelly cushions with a bottle of cheap wine (Alice had been just sober enough to know that the wine was disgusting, but too drunk to care).

Alice was not the kind of person to have one-night-stands. She was organised, disciplined, focused and ambitious. At thirty-one, she had been fully occupied in developing her career as a journalist and wanted nothing to get in her way. A husband and children — especially children — had never been part of the plan. Alice liked men and enjoyed sex, but her relationships, like her work life, were organised, with secure boundaries. She never went out on a date if she had a deadline to achieve, she didn't sleep with a man until she knew him pretty well, and she never went out with anyone from work. But it had been a difficult week, she'd been tired, the party had offered a welcome diversion (Alice wasn't usually a party-goer), and Finn had been the result.

It had taken Alice a month to decide what she was going to do. She wrote down all the reasons why she should and shouldn't continue with her pregnancy; she listed all the pros and cons; she consulted her closest friend. In the end, she decided to go ahead and have the baby. As a friend said, people often regretted getting rid of babies, but rarely regretted keeping them. She might even grow to like her child. Stranger things had happened.

To her great surprise, she adored Finn from the start. Never having had much time for babies before, she put her feelings down to hormones and waited for them to wear off. But the love increased as Finn developed from what looked like a rather surprised baby hedgehog into a plump, sunny human infant, who slept through the night, ate all the right things, and was quite happy to be handed round and looked after by anyone to whom his mother gave him.

Of course, a baby was not the greatest of career moves. The local newspaper for which she had been working was male-dominated, and while she wasn't exactly discriminated against (that wasn't permitted), little allowance was made for her new status as a mother. Alice had made her decision, and she would also have to make such arrangements as were necessary to look after her child.

So Alice juggled. She had read about mothers juggling children and careers but had never realised how hard it could be. Even when she was able to work from home, Finn and his needs were a constant distraction, and despite the services of an excellent childminder, things could go wrong. Besides, children didn't always go according to plan. They could be sick in the night, springing sudden alarming fevers; they could have accidents, the aftermath of which required the presence of a parent. Later on, there were school sports days, speech days and school plays. Finn wasn't much of an actor or a sportsman, but had still been given small parts requiring a maternal audience (a tree in a nativity play; a reserve for the school second football team), and since Alice was a perfectionist and this now extended to motherhood, life became complicated. But after fifteen years, Alice would have been the first to admit that having Finn had made her a better person. She no longer fretted over a dirty kitchen floor or an unironed shirt, or whether fish fingers twice in a week would permanently damage Finn's health. There simply wasn't time. She became more relaxed over her own minor shortcomings and more tolerant of those of other people.

"Welcome to the real world, Alice," said her mother.

It had taken Alice two years to decide to contact Finn's father. It had been quite a job tracking him down (the friend of an acquaintance of a friend — that sort of thing) and had required a lot of courage to phone him. At first, he'd been disbelieving, then shocked, and then angry.

"*Two years*? All this happened *two years ago*, and you didn't think to tell me? *If* I am this child's father, which I very much doubt. As for you, I can't even remember your name, never mind your face."

Alice refrained from reminding him that it probably wasn't her face that had preoccupied him at the time, and explained who she was.

"A *journalist*? I don't trust journalists. How do I know you're not going to sell your story to some sleazy little newspaper?"

"I wouldn't dream of it. This is strictly between you and me."

"Well, I'll need DNA of course. Proof. You can't just go around telling someone you met two years ago that they fathered your child, and not expect him to want proof."

"Of course you can have proof. I expected you'd want it, and you can have it."

"What's it like, this child?"

"He. He's a boy."

"He, then."

"Blond. Blue-eyed. Very sweet."

"I've got brown eyes." The voice was indignant.

"Well, I've got blue eyes."

"Brown eyes are dominant. Everyone knows that. If it — he — was mine, he'd have brown eyes."

Alice had sighed. "Let's just do the DNA thing, shall we? Then we can talk about the colour of his eyes."

Finn's father turned out to be an artist of mediocre talent and minimal means. Known to his friends as Trot (something to do with an interest in Trotsky as a boy), he was, Alice thought, pleasant enough, although when they met, she didn't recognise him at all. He was not exactly what she would have chosen as the father of her child, but she could have done a lot worse. Once the DNA was sorted out (eye colour notwithstanding), he seemed to warm to the idea of fatherhood, and while he made it clear that financial support would not be forthcoming (Alice never asked for any), he did take an interest in Finn. Trot was bad at birthdays and Christmas, but good at exciting trips and occasional surprises, and he and Finn got on remarkably well. Finn never called him Daddy or Dad, and nobody asked him to. He was just Trot. Alice privately thought that Finn preferred to think of Trot as a mate, and that was fine. At least he had a father. What he called him was immaterial. Trot remained single, and this seemed to please Finn, although Alice wasn't quite sure why.

Now Alice loaded her groceries into the back of her car and started the engine. If she hurried, she would just about make it to the school in time. Finn was a poor timekeeper and was probably still changing out of his football gear or gossiping in the changing rooms. He disliked football but was fond of the master in charge, and the second team was short of players. Alice reflected that in spite of his shortcomings, Finn had a very kind side to him. She hoped very much that he had had a shower.

While she was preparing their meal, Alice asked Finn about his plans for the weekend.

"Fishing with Trot," was the somewhat unexpected answer.

"*What?*"

"Yeah. Trot's taken up fishing, and wants me to go with him. He's picking me up from Kenny's in the morning." Finn was spending the night with Kenny, a friend of whom Alice didn't altogether approve.

"Is this another of his crazes?" Trot was given to sudden enthusiasms, which as often as not fizzled out before they'd had a chance to get going. To date, he'd clocked up, among other things, birdwatching (he got bored), horse riding (he fell off and lost his nerve), motorbikes (ditto), and visiting steam railways (Alice suspected that the necessary travelling involved too much effort). Finn frequently accompanied his father on these forays into new, if not always fascinating, territory, and never seemed to mind if they didn't last. Trot was fun to be with, and Finn enjoyed the fun, if not always the activities.

In some ways Alice was envious of their relationship. While she'd never wanted or expected any help with Finn's upbringing, she couldn't help feeling that Trot had all the fun of parenthood with none of the responsibility. She had borne him an intelligent and on the whole rather nice son, and Trot was free to pop in and out of Finn's life at will, taking him out when he felt like it and yet sometimes not bothering to contact him for weeks on end. Oddly enough, Finn didn't seem to mind, possibly because Trot had always been like that and he didn't expect anything else, but Alice found herself minding on his behalf. On his last birthday, Finn had only received four cards (theirs was a small family), and Alice had felt for him. It wouldn't have hurt Trot to make the effort; he certainly knew when Finn's birthday was. But as Trot himself had said, he'd never been good at birthdays.

"Birthdays, smirthdays…" he'd mocked when Alice had mentioned it some years ago. "Who cares?"

"Children care," she'd told him. "Birthdays mean a lot to a child."

"They didn't to me."

"Well, you had a mother and father, and as far as I can recollect, grandparents. I doubt very much whether you went short on your birthday. Would it be so difficult just to send a card?"

"He might expect to find money in it. I'd hate to disappoint him."

"Well, money in it wouldn't be such a bad thing," said Alice, infuriated. "After all, you spend money on him at other times."

"There you are, then," Trot said. "I am a good daddy after all."

"No, you're not. You're just another kid. That's why you and Finn get on so well."

"I rest my case."

But fishing sounded like a good idea. It would get Finn away from his computer and out into the fresh air, and as she was behind with her current deadline and was going to have to put in some extra work, they wouldn't be missing time together.

"Oh, I forgot. Trot asked if I could bring some lunch with me," Finn said.

"Now you tell me!"

"Just a few sandwiches. I'll make them."

"We're nearly out of bread. I do wish you'd told me this earlier."

"Sorry. I forgot."

"And I suppose Trot intends you to feed him, too." Trot's domestic arrangements were haphazard.

"As a matter of fact, he did ask. He's had a busy week."

"And I haven't?"

"He's got an exhibition coming up."

"When?"

"Well, not for a few weeks, but he's busy getting it organised."

"Well, I'm busy trying to earn enough money to keep you in peanut butter and cornflakes."

"Twisty Chocolate Honey Flakes," Finn said. "I like those."

"Okay, whatever. The point is that I work, Finn. *Work*. Does that mean anything to you?"

"All right. Keep your hair on."

"And," Alice said, trying very hard to keep her temper, "*Trot is not busy*. Or certainly not as busy as I am. He's his own boss, he's got no one else to think about, he can work when he wants, and... and... go fishing when he wants. And make his own bloody sandwiches!" She dumped a pile of folded laundry on the kitchen table. "I wish I had time to go fishing!"

"He's bringing the drink," Finn said.

"What drink?"

"Oh, just a few cans."

"Finn, you are underage, and Trot will be driving."

"We won't have much, and it'll have worn off by the time we come home. Trot doesn't do drink-driving."

"Well, if you say so. But you know how irresponsible he can be. You'll have to try to be the sensible one."

"Aren't I always?" Finn, who had been foraging in cupboards, piled packets of crisps and Kit-Kats, a bag of tomatoes, some apples, and a large packet of cheese on the worktop. "There. One picnic lunch. I'll just hard boil a few eggs, and that should do us."

Alice looked at what amounted to a large proportion of their weekend supplies and bit her tongue. After all, it wasn't Finn's fault if he had a feckless father, and a feckless father who was in touch was better than no father at all.

"Do you think Trot would like to come back for supper afterwards?" she asked.

"Really?" Finn beamed. He loved it when the three of them got together, and it rarely happened. "I'll ask him."

"It'll probably have to be something simple as I've got this article to finish, but that's okay, isn't it?"

"No problem."

Later on, as she set off for her evening with Mavis and Gabs, Alice wondered whether she and Trot could ever have made a go of their relationship. He was personable, amusing, and intelligent, and she could certainly have done a lot worse. But no, it would never have worked. Quite apart from the fact that he wasn't her type, Alice knew that Trot would have driven her mad within days. It would have been like having another child.

Besides, there was Jay.

Only the members of the Basic Theology group knew about Jay, and of course Father Cuthbert (who no longer counted), but none of her family and friends knew, not even Finn. Especially not Finn. The affair had been going for nearly four years now, and while Alice accepted that there was no future in it, she couldn't bring herself to let go. She didn't so much mind not being married to him or living with him; she could cope with that. What she found difficult was the secrecy.

Before their affair had begun, Alice had had no idea how many pitfalls awaited those engaged in an illicit relationship. A car parked in the wrong place, the risk of bumping into someone they knew, the difficulties involved in arranging any time together — there were times when the problems seemed insurmountable. Weeks would go by when they scarcely saw each other, and had to make do with the odd snatched phone call or brief unsatisfactory meeting. And yet in some ways, it was the risk — the excitement, perhaps — that kept the relationship fresh, for it was hard to grow tired of someone when you hardly ever saw them.

Alice had met Jay on a crowded train. Jammed up against each other (there was standing room only), they had struck up a conversation. The train was slow, and Jay was a good listener — attentive without being intrusive — and by the time Alice reached her destination, she realised that she had spent most of the time talking about herself, and that she knew virtually nothing about her companion.

"Gosh. I'm sorry. I haven't stopped talking, have I?" she said as the train began to slow down. "What must you think of me?"

"Does it matter what I think of you?" Jay had asked her. His tone was teasing, but his expression was serious.

They had held each other's gaze for a long moment before Alice blushed and looked away.

"Yes. Yes, it does," she said, wondering that she should mind so much about the opinion of a stranger.

"That's good. Because — because I'd like to see you again. That is, if you don't mind."

And that was how it had started. Afterwards, Alice often wondered at the coincidence of their meeting. If it hadn't been one of her London days (her job on a Sunday colour supplement enabled her to do most of her work from home); if she hadn't missed the earlier train; if she had been able to find a seat... all those ifs. But they had met, and before she left the station that evening, Alice knew that her life was about to change.

Their first meeting took place in a discreet coffee bar halfway between their homes (they lived some distance apart), and there was none of the awkwardness that Alice had feared.

"I'm afraid I did nearly all the talking last time," she said. "Now it's your turn."

"What do you want me to say?" Jay had asked.

"Tell me about yourself. After all, you already know quite a lot about me."

"Well, I live in town, I support Manchester United, I have two black labradors, and I'm allergic to shellfish. Will that do?"

"Hardly. For a start, I want to know what you are, what you do for a living."

"I'm a medic."

"That doesn't tell me much! What kind of medic?"

"Oh, this and that. Nothing particularly interesting."

"Is that it?"

"Not quite. But I suppose I've got out of the habit of talking about it, partly to avoid people asking my advice. If you tell anyone you're a doctor, you're considered fair game, even at social gatherings. So I try to avoid it. Sometimes I just tell them I'm an accountant. It seems that no-one's interested in accountants."

Alice laughed. "So you won't tell me any more? Even if I promise never to ask your advice?"

"I hope you'll never need it. I'm an oncologist." Jay smiled at her expression. "Cancer," he explained. "I work at the District General, and I also look after the local hospice."

"Isn't that a bit depressing?"

"People do get better, you know. More so now than ever. And if they don't, well, at least I can help to make things a bit easier. Make a difference."

Looking at Jay — at his dark, serious eyes and warm, sympathetic smile — Alice could well imagine that he would make a difference. She had only spent a couple of hours in his company, and he was already making a considerable difference to her.

"You wear a wedding ring," she said now. "You're — married?"

"Yes, I'm married."

"And?"

"And we will talk about it, but not now."

"Children?"

"No children."

Alice nodded. A waitress whisked past carrying a tray; two women at a corner table were discussing a party they'd been to. Alice picked up her bag from the floor, and then put it down again. The seconds ticked by.

"I don't — do this kind of thing," she said, after a moment.

"Neither do I." Jay touched her hand. "I've never 'done this kind of thing,' as you put it, before."

"Then — why…?"

"I think you know why."

"Yes. Yes, I do."

For the attraction between them was overwhelming; something Alice had rarely felt before and had almost given up hope of finding again. And while she realised, even at that early stage, that the way ahead would almost certainly be both difficult and painful, she felt powerless to stop.

One of Alice's rules had always been never to date married men, but she had been completely swept away by Jay, and their affair had developed rapidly from there. Because of the distance they had to travel (given Jay's work, that was probably just as well), meetings between them were infrequent and not easy to arrange, but they saw each other when they could, and phoned often. It wasn't ideal, but it had to be enough. Alice considered that it was a price worth paying, and so, apparently, did Jay.

Over time, Alice discovered that Jay was something of an expert in his field, but while he did sometimes discuss his work with her, he was dismissive of any accolades.

"It's just a job," he would say. "I'm fortunate to be doing something I love." And he would leave it at that.

"Am I allowed to be proud of you?" she had asked him on one occasion, when he had been invited to open a new wing of the hospice.

"What do you mean?"

"Well, if I were — related to you, I'd be proud of you. Of what you do. All those people you help; all those families. Are mistresses allowed to be proud?"

Jay had laughed. "You can be proud if you want to be. Of course you can. But I just do my job. As you do yours."

Alice knew that Jay's marriage was an unhappy one, but they never discussed it. It was bad enough to betray another woman by sleeping with her husband; to ask questions about her seemed almost worse. Fortunately, Jay seemed to feel the same way, so Angela remained an unknown quantity. All Alice knew was that after many shared years of trying (and failing) to produce children, Jay felt that the least he could do was to stay with his wife. As he said, if he allowed himself to be free, he might be tempted to find someone with whom he could have a family, and that would be unforgivably hurtful. So in that respect, Alice was a reasonable solution. She didn't want more children even had she been young enough to have them, and she made very few demands.

Of course, one of the hardest things to bear was that she and Jay could never go public as a couple. Alice had to put up with the pitying comments of married — or at least, coupled — friends. One or two even asked her why she had never married, as though her age had put any marriage prospects firmly in the past. Occasionally, friends would probe, suspicious at her continued single state and apparent lack of interest in the opposite sex, and one or two had even hinted that she might be gay. Alice had fended off any questions as politely as she could, but found their intrusiveness puzzling. Why was it apparently perfectly acceptable for people to ask about her sexual proclivities when they would be unlikely to question her politics? On several occasions she had been tempted to confide in a close friend, but she knew only too well that a secret shared is all too often a secret spread, and she couldn't afford to take that risk. One day, when Finn was older, she would tell him. But not yet. He was too young to understand, and besides, what with exams and spots and the alarming surges of testosterone that went with being fifteen, she felt that he had enough to cope with.

So she and Jay continued as best they could, snatching the odd meeting, phoning often, and trying to live in the moment. Because that was all they had, wasn't it? A relationship such as theirs didn't have a future, or not the kind that could be planned or worked towards. They loved, they laughed, they had rows, and when they could manage it, they had great sex. It had to be enough.

But of course, it wasn't. Or not always. There were times when Alice ached for Jay's company, for the feeling of his arms around her, for his smell and the sound of his voice. She longed for the luxury of a night together or simply the exchange of news at the end of a busy day — the ordinary things that so many couples took for granted. Flowers and candlelit meals no doubt had their place — and goodness knows, she'd had few enough of those — but they were fripperies compared with the day-to-day stuff of marriage.

Oddly enough, while she was rarely jealous of Angela, Alice did occasionally envy Jay's patients. She knew this made no sense, but when she thought of the amount of time he spent with them — talking to them, touching them, *looking after* them — she couldn't help experiencing the odd pang. For while Jay did his best to dissemble, she knew how much he cared about them, and she hoped they realised how fortunate they were in having him.

Alice tried not to share these thoughts with Jay. Things were hard enough for him as it was, without her whinging. Besides, their time together was precious, and she didn't want to squander it on complaints and if-onlys. She had gone into the relationship with her eyes open, she had known the risks and the difficulties, and she had never been one to waste time on regrets.

Did she feel guilty? At the beginning she had certainly felt very guilty, and more than once she had thought of ending the relationship. But as time went on and she became accustomed to the situation, the pangs of guilt became less frequent. Angela had her husband and her home and her career as a solicitor (that much Alice did know), and provided she never found out about the affair, little harm would be done. In a way, they were all three of them victims, and while Alice didn't try to absolve herself from her own responsibility, it could have been worse. She could have been younger, more demanding, wanting marriage and children. As it was, all she asked for was what she suspected Jay and Angela could no longer give to each other; love, intimacy, and a little happiness. It could even be that her relationship with Jay was helping to keep his marriage together.

Alice was glad that she wasn't dogged by the Catholic guilt that had beset her fellows in the "theology" group. But then, Alice was not a Catholic. Her attendance had begun purely coincidentally when she had been invited to write a piece on marital infidelity and had been put in touch with Father Cuthbert. Under conditions of strict confidentiality and with the permission of the group members, Alice had been allowed to attend a single meeting, but she had been so taken with the freedom they experienced in being able to discuss their relationships that she had asked — and been permitted — to carry on attending. She suspected that Father Cuthbert saw her as another opportunity for bringing about redemption — and, who knows, even introducing a new convert to the One True Faith — but for Alice, the meetings had been, quite simply, a life-saver. The opportunity to talk about Jay to people who would neither judge nor dissuade her (she didn't count Father Cuthbert; it was his job to judge and dissuade) was a revelation, as well as an indescribable relief, and she quite quickly realised that she was becoming dependent on the meetings. She would save up little anxieties and other aspects of her relationship with Jay to share with the other members, and she invariably received the understanding and sympathy she longed for.

But now they were on their own, the three of them: Alice, Gabs, and Mavis. Three very disparate women who all shared a very big secret. They had agreed to meet every two months, taking turns to host the meetings, and tonight's would be their first one.

Alice smiled to herself. Quite apart from the fact that it might provide material for a most entertaining article, she was looking forward to her evening.

Mavis

Mavis Wetherby knew enough about men to know that left to themselves, they were perfectly capable of choosing their own clothes, but give them a wife or girlfriend, and the job was invariably delegated. This particular wife was taking an inordinate amount of time to choose a shirt and tie for a birthday present, and Mavis was anxious to get away on time in order to prepare for her meeting.

"I think the blue shirt and the striped tie…?" the woman said, but without conviction. "On the other hand, stripes look so like school ties, don't they? Perhaps spots would be better."

"Or this nice paisley?" Mavis held up another tie. "This one's very popular, and it's pure silk."

"It doesn't quite match the shirt."

"Perhaps a different shirt, then? It's easier to find a shirt than a tie, I always think."

"Maybe you're right. I suppose I could always get him socks, but they're so boring, aren't they? Everyone gives him socks." The woman laughed. "And then one sock always gets lost in the wash."

Mavis had often heard about the missing sock phenomenon, but never having lived with a man and rarely wearing socks herself, she had not come across it.

"Hankies, perhaps? We have some lovely Irish linen hankies, gift-boxed."

"He uses Kleenex."

"A cashmere scarf, then? You can't go wrong with cashmere." She fetched one from a drawer and laid it out on the counter. "Pure cashmere, and a lovely gift."

"Cashmere always bobbles, I find."

"Our cashmere never bobbles." Mavis bridled. "If it does, you can bring it back for a full refund."

"Oh, I don't know…"

"Perhaps you'd like to think about it?"

"His birthday's tomorrow. I've left it rather late." The woman looked wildly round the shop, as though seeking inspiration. "Do you have any Swiss Army knives? He's always wanted one of those."

"No, I'm afraid we don't." If Mavis had been married to a man who had always wanted a Swiss Army knife and if she'd cared for him at all, she would certainly have made sure that he had one by now.

"Oh — I'll have the scarf, then," said her customer with the reckless air of someone who was about to bungee jump off a cliff.

"Any particular colour?"

There followed a further fifteen minutes of discussion, in which everything from the husband's eye colour and personal preference to the wife's own taste were taken into consideration, and she finally left the shop with a neat parcel containing a cashmere scarf in a rather insipid shade of green.

On her way home, Mavis reflected upon this conversation and the many similar conversations she had had over the years and wondered, not for the first time, how it was that she had got herself into this particular job. She had had a good secretarial training in the past and had started her working life as a PA, holding several responsible — not to say interesting — posts, and she was not unintelligent. But following an unpleasant incident of what would now be called sexual harassment, she had fallen into this job almost by chance. It had come at just the right time, the pay was reasonable (her secretarial skills were taken into consideration and even, on occasion, used), and for the first time in a while, she felt appreciated.

Ten years on, she was stuck with the job, and knew that at her age, she was unlikely to get another. Besides, she had since taken responsibility for her elderly mother, and Mr. Strong (such an inappropriate name for such a dapper little man) was a reasonable if rather fussy employer. A further advantage was that she lived only ten minutes' walk away, so she could always pop home if her mother had one of her little crises. The job was, above all, *convenient*.

In a funny way, she'd come to believe in the shop and what it stood for. Gentlemen's outfitters were a dying breed, and she shared some of Mr. Strong's pride in keeping this one going. It wasn't so much the gentlemen or even the clothes; it was more the idea of the survival of a small business under the threat of mass-market competition, of not allowing the old traditions of personal service and individual attention to be sacrificed on the twin altars of progress and profit. She liked the old-fashioned handwritten till receipts and the brown paper parcels in which the goods were despatched, and so, it seemed, did the customers, for enough of them continued to patronise the shop to justify its continued existence. The whole experience reminded her of a bygone age of courtesy and decorum, which was, for the most part, long gone, and although she wasn't quite old enough to remember a time when this kind of service was the norm, she still felt a sense of nostalgia. She experienced similar feelings when she heard the voice of Vera Lynn or the speeches of Winston Churchill, or the Pathé News giving bulletins of the war effort in its clipped, oh-so-British accent. Nostalgia for a Britain long gone, a Britain that was unlikely ever to return.

Some time ago, a friend had told Mavis that she had been "born to serve," and she had been unsure how to take what had probably been intended as a compliment. It made her sound like something between an army officer and a doormat, and since she had never imagined herself in either role, she hadn't managed to take it in quite the spirit in which it was meant. But now, she rather liked the idea. Service. To be of *service*. That had to be good, didn't it? Serving her customers, helping them to choose exactly the right gift or garment; the job had its compensations, and people often came into the shop asking particularly for Mavis's assistance.

Another recipient of her services was, of course, her mother.

Mavis loved her mother and was prepared to do her duty by her (she was an only child), but when the old lady could no longer manage on her own, it was with some reluctance that she had welcomed her into her own home. Never having married or lived with anyone since she was a girl, she had initially found it hard to have to sacrifice a downstairs room, as well as her independence and much of her privacy. But in the end, the deed had been done with minimal fuss, and Mother had duly moved in, together with a few bits of furniture, an enormous and very dusty rubber plant, and a bad-tempered cat, who had been bought from a rescue centre and who rejoiced in the name of Pussolini (the name had been Mavis's idea, and her mother, failing to make the necessary connection, had thought it rather sweet). The plant had mercifully died, but Mother (and the cat) lived on, and five years on, Mavis could no longer imagine life without her.

Old Mrs. Wetherby was an uncomplaining soul. She was good-natured, cheerful, and continent; she ate what she was given and slept a great deal. But she was becoming unsteady on her feet and had had several falls, and she was also becoming alarmingly forgetful.

"Alzheimer's?" Mavis had asked the doctor fearfully the last time he'd called.

"Oh no, I don't think so. It's just her age." The doctor was young and spoke with the careless insouciance of one for whom old age was still a long way off, and only happened to other people and patients. "Make sure she has plenty of mental stimulation, and she'll be fine."

But it is hard to stimulate someone who refuses to leave the house when you yourself have to be out all day, and Mother, with nothing but daytime television and the cat for company, continued her slow decline. A kindly neighbour used to pop in once or twice during the day to see that all was well, and Meals on Wheels had been delivered by the cheery ladies of the WRVS, but the neighbour had moved away, and the WRVS ladies had made their excuses after one of them had been ambushed and bitten by the cat, so once again, everything was left to Mavis.

Mavis reached her own front door and took out her keys. On her way home, she had purchased wine and cheese straws and crisps, and a small fillet of plaice for her mother. As she passed through the hallway, dodging the malevolent advances of Pussolini (Pussolini was a one-woman cat, and sadly, that woman was not Mavis), she went in to check on her mother.

"All right, Mother?"

"Fine, dear." Her mother had a particularly sweet smile, and the kind of blue eyes whose colour becomes increasingly striking as the face around them ages. "I've just been to Mass."

"No, Mother. I don't think so. It's Friday."

"Is it, dear?"

"Yes." Mavis kissed her papery cheek. "I'll take you to Mass on Sunday."

"That's kind." Her mother paused. "Isn't it time I went to confession?"

"You went last week, remember?"

Her mother loved confession. Mavis had no idea what this gentle woman could have to confess, since she never went anywhere, met no one, and was invariably kind to the few people she did come across. She even managed to help a little round the house, peeling potatoes or doing a spot of dusting. What sins could she possibly conjure up out of the recesses of her increasingly muddled brain, even if she were able to remember them? Mavis suspected that she simply rehearsed old sins of long ago, and she would love to have been a fly on the wall when these sins were recounted, but she would have to remain in the dark. Her mother would leave the confessional with a contented smile, do her penance (three Hail Marys), and then they would come home together.

Mavis herself eschewed the confessional. There had been a time when she too used to like going to confession: the quiet murmuring of the priest, the whispered sins (the more serious sandwiched between the milder, so as to escape notice), the familiar rhythm of the prayers of penance, and the feeling of a slate wiped clean, with everything forgiven and forgotten. But that was a long time ago. That was before Clifford.

Mavis had met Clifford over twenty years ago, when she was a young woman and he a middle-aged married man. Alas, she was no longer young, and Clifford, who was now retired, remained married, but they were still together. Like all these things, it was a long story.

At the time, Mavis had been engaged to be married. Tim had been a nice Catholic boy, and she had been fond of him — perhaps even a little bit in love. But then she had met Clifford, and he had shown her that while there was nothing wrong with nice Catholic boys, a mature, sophisticated man had other, better things to offer. At the time, Mavis was both naïve and inexperienced. Flattered by Clifford's attentions and overcome by a surprisingly strong physical attraction, she had broken off her engagement, and the affair had started. It had been going on ever since.

Mavis would have been the first to admit that it was Clifford's looks that had first attracted her. He wasn't conventionally handsome, but he had fine eyes, an endearing, almost apologetic smile, and at the time, a good physique for his age. Also (and Mavis considered this to be almost as important) he was kind, and a perfect gentleman. He opened doors, walked on the outside of the pavement, pulled out her chair for her in restaurants, and pampered her with flowers and chocolates and expensive silk underwear — all the things that young men of her own age no longer seemed to bother with. Mavis's late father had been just such a gentleman, and Clifford had reminded her of him. That perfect gentlemen didn't sleep with people other than their wives and that her father would most certainly have been deeply shocked had he known about the affair were facts that Mavis chose to ignore. Love, as everyone knows, can be astonishingly blind.

From the start, Clifford told Mavis that he had long outgrown his marriage — a marriage that, he said, no longer gave happiness to either party — and that he would leave Dorothy to be with her. Not yet — never yet — but one day, when the time was ripe. But as the years rolled by and the time remained as unripe as it had been at the beginning, Mavis gradually lost first hope, and then, oddly, the inclination to take Clifford away from his wife and family. For what she slowly came to realise was that, contrary to what she might have expected, in this relationship she was the strong one, while Clifford was weak, and without the secure backdrop of a conventional marriage — without that little stake in society — he would find it hard to carry on his day-to-day life. This didn't make her love him any the less — if anything, it increased her affection for him, for she liked feeling needed.

Clifford needed her reassurance, both as a man and as a lover, and she was able to give it to him. This was all the more surprising since Clifford had been a successful businessman and should have had every reason to feel confident, but outside his field of expertise, he remained strangely diffident. As for their sexual relationship, Mavis had had little experience of sex before they met, while Clifford, with all those years of marriage under his belt (so to speak), might be expected to know his way around the female body and be able to give as well as to receive pleasure.

This proved not to be the case. Clifford had been a clumsy lover — hesitant, shy, and amazingly ignorant when it came to lovemaking. Here, Mavis came into her own, surprising even herself. Clifford's shyness gave her a confidence she could never have hitherto imagined, and before long, she was not only taking the initiative, but also discovering and sharing new ways to make love.

Of course, this delighted Clifford. Mavis was too tactful to enquire about what had been going on in his marriage bed all these years, but it didn't take long for her to suspect that the answer would almost certainly be, not very much. He had told her that he and Dorothy rarely made love, and she believed him. His hunger for her body, her hands, her mouth — as well as her company — increased as their relationship progressed. Mavis's looks had never been remarkable, but she had inherited her mother's clear eyes and soft dark hair. Her breasts were the kind often described as "pert," and she had good legs. Clifford thought — and frequently told her — that she was beautiful. Mavis herself was totally without vanity, but as she often said to herself, if one man thought she was beautiful and if he was the right man, what did it matter what she, or anyone else, thought? With his endearments, his attention, and his increasing skill at lovemaking, he managed to make her *feel* beautiful. What more could a woman ask for?

Mavis knew that when Clifford said that he would eventually leave Dorothy to be with her, he meant it, even after all these years. She also knew that he felt guilty that their relationship had deprived her of the chance to have a family of her own. Often, in the early days, he had asked her whether she shouldn't leave him to find someone who could give her what he thought all women should have: a home with a husband and babies. But Mavis didn't need a husband, and she didn't want babies. She had never been maternal, and when that particular door finally closed with the onset of the menopause, she had no regrets.

"I would like to have given you children," Clifford had said again quite recently. "Or perhaps just one child."

"You know I never wanted children," she told him. "We went through all that years ago."

And this was true. When Mavis was approaching her fortieth birthday — that final alarm call from the body clock — Clifford had offered to father her child.

"I would pay for its upbringing, keep in touch, be a proper father to it," he told her. "We'd manage somehow. And then when I leave Dorothy —"

"No." Mavis had smiled. "No. It's a lovely idea, but it wouldn't work. I'm fine as I am. And you have your own children. Let's just carry on as we are."

No one knew about Mavis's involvement with Clifford. While she did have friends, none of them were close, and she suspected that her mother would have been distressed and scandalised if Mavis had chosen to confide in her. Father Lucian at the local Catholic church knew of course, for on the rare occasions when she went to confession, Clifford naturally had to be mentioned, and while she herself no longer felt particularly guilty about him, she also felt that it would be dishonest to leave the confessional without mentioning him.

"You see, we're not hurting anyone," she told Father Lucian when he gently upbraided her for her adultery. "No one need ever know."

"*God* knows," said Father Lucian (originality was not Father Lucian's strongest point), "and besides, you're damaging yourself and your immortal soul."

Mavis thought about her immortal soul, and considered that on the whole, it was in fairly good shape.

"What if we don't have sex anymore?" she asked, genuinely interested. "Suppose we go on seeing each other, but keep the relationship platonic?"

There was a long pause while Father Lucian (presumably) took sex out of Mavis's relationship and considered it anew.

"Oh no," he said after a while. "It still wouldn't do."

"Because?" Mavis prompted.

"Because of your feelings for each other."

"We'd still feel the same, even if we never saw each other again," Mavis told him.

"That's different," said Father Lucian. "That's quite different."

It was Father Lucian who had contacted Mavis about the Basic Theology classes, having himself been approached by the bishop (the bishop was having some difficulty in recruiting enough sinners to make the classes worth his — or more to the point, Father Cuthbert's — while). Mavis had initially been curious rather than enthusiastic. She knew very well that the agenda would be the return of sheep to the Catholic fold rather than actually helping those sheep to come to terms with their difficulties, but it would be interesting to meet other people in the same position as herself, and she was entertained at the subterfuge of Basic Theology classes. Father Cuthbert's parish wasn't far, and she could put Mother to bed early (her mother loved being in bed, and so that was never a problem), and so she agreed. Apart from anything else, she was aware of Father Lucian's disappointment at being unable to persuade her to see the error of her ways, and she thought that maybe this would go some way towards appeasing him.

Clifford, on the other hand, was appalled.

"You're going to leave me," he said. "You're — you're breaking it off between us!"

"Of course I'm not," Mavis said. "Don't be so ridiculous."

"But why, then? Why are you doing this?"

"I suppose because it would be — it would be nice to talk to someone."

"About us?"

"Yes. About us."

"But *I* don't talk about us to anyone. I don't need to talk about us."

"Well, I do," Mavis told him.

"But why? After all this time, why? Why now?"

"Because there's an opportunity, I suppose. And because I'm a woman. Women like to — no, *need* to — talk about personal things, and I've never had anyone before. Now there's this, and I think it might help."

"Do you need help?" Clifford asked her. "Because you know I will leave Dorothy. I will. I'll do it soon if you want me to."

"No, that won't be necessary." Mavis patted his hand as though she were soothing a small child (it sometimes occurred to her that perhaps Clifford represented the child she'd never had). "You have to stay with Dorothy."

"Oh, Mavis. I know I've promised and promised, and you've been so good. I *can* leave her, you know. I don't even think she'd mind all that much now. We're so — apart. We seem to have been apart for years, since even before I met you."

Mavis turned to him and smiled. A lesser woman would have been irritated at the repetition of what might seem by now to be an empty promise, but Mavis knew better. She knew that every time Clifford promised to leave Dorothy, he meant it. Whenever it was going to be — when the children were older, when his younger daughter had left home, when he could afford to run two homes, when Dorothy had had her hip operation — Clifford really intended to leave her and be with Mavis. Often she had wondered how it was that she could see what he could not — that he was deceiving himself, and that for some time, he had managed to deceive her too. But perhaps in a way Clifford needed to believe that she and he would finally be together; he needed to believe that one day he would be able to make this very difficult decision.

"What will you say?" he asked her. "What will you tell them?"

"I don't know." Mavis had asked herself the same question. "I'll see what everyone else says."

"You won't tell them about the — *you know*."

"No, I won't tell them that." Mavis thought of the discreet cardboard box under her bed and the interesting little device inside, and how surprised people would be if they thought that she knew about, never mind used, such a thing. She smiled again. "No one will ever know about that."

Clifford returned her smile. "It's given us a lot of fun, hasn't it?"

"It has. Oh, it certainly has."

Later, after she had tucked her mother up in bed, Mavis tidied her small sitting room and laid out the snacks, the wine and glasses, and some apple juice. She felt quite excited. It was a long time since she had entertained anyone, and she was looking forward to it. Her mother hadn't questioned her when she'd said she was having some friends round. With the self-centredness often found in the very old or the very young, she was happy for Mavis to do as she wished, provided her own needs were met first, and this suited them both.

Arranging a small vase of early daffodils on a side table, Mavis wondered what it would be like for the three of them to meet up without Father Cuthbert's anxious, solicitous presence. Would they miss his apologetic interruptions, his gentle rebukes, and his awkward fumblings with the coffee and the biscuits?

On the whole, she thought that they would not.

Gabs

Gabs looked at her watch, and then at the half-naked man who was crawling round the room on his hands and knees, barking like a dog.

"I'm afraid our time's nearly up," she told him.

The dog stopped barking and looked up at her mournfully. "Just five more minutes?" he asked.

"No. I'm sorry. You've got to get dressed, and so have I." She put down her whip and began easing herself out of her gymslip and tie. "And I have an appointment."

"Another — client?" He sounded jealous. It was odd how so many of them were jealous, when they knew very well what the deal was.

"No, not another client. I've got a meeting this evening, and I don't want to be late."

"You don't look like the sort of person who goes to meetings."

"There's a lot of things I don't look like," said Gabs, undoing her pigtails and pulling her hair back into a ponytail. "There's a lot you don't know about me."

"But I'd like to. Really I would. I'd love to — to get to know you better."

"No. Sorry. It's not in the terms."

"Well, then, just one little kiss? Just a tiny one?"

"That's not in the terms, either. You know that, Gerald. No kissing. No blow jobs."

"Oh, I'd never ask for — for one of those." He looked shocked.

"Well, that's okay, then."

"Next week?" Gerald stumbled to his feet and shook himself (he really did look just like a dog). "Shall I see you next week?"

"Next week," Gabs agreed.

"Same place?"

"Sure. You're paying." The hotel was a nice one, and the room service excellent.

"I'll see you then." Gerald fumbled in his wallet and counted out money from a bundle of notes. "Is this all right?"

Gabs checked the money carefully and picked out a ten-pound note. "You've overpaid me," she said, handing it back to him.

"No, no, that's fine. You're worth it."

"Thanks." Gabs pocketed the money. "Have a good week."

As she walked through the hotel foyer, Gabs attracted a certain amount of attention. No doubt the hotel staff were unaccustomed to someone of her appearance (long pink hair, a tiny denim skirt, high-heeled cowboy boots, and multiple piercings of ears and face), but Gabs met their stares with a cool, level gaze.

"Someone going to open the door for me, then?" she enquired of no one in particular.

A uniformed flunky moved reluctantly forward.

"My money," said Gabs, waving a twenty-pound note at him (but taking care not to let go of it), "is as good as anyone's." And she flounced out into the street.

Gabs was a Catholic and a tart. Not an easy combination, it is true, but as many have found before her, once a Catholic, it is very hard to escape from the Mother Church. And once a tart… well, that remained to be seen.

Of course, Gabs didn't normally describe herself as a tart. The few to whom she'd confessed her preferred occupation were informed that she was "a high-class escort," but in the end, it amounted to much the same thing.

Gabs herself would have disagreed, since she had strict guidelines and firm boundaries, and woe betide the gentleman who overstepped the mark. Besides this, she expected to be taken to respectable houses or (even better) posh hotels such as this for her liaisons; she had expensive tastes in food and wine (champagne and lobster were high on the list) and was happy to accompany clients on the occasional trip abroad. Her standards were high, it is true (if she can be said to have had such things), but she was rarely disappointed. For once a man had had a taste of Gabs (so to speak), he was usually enslaved, and he almost invariably came back for more.

Of course, not every man favoured the facial piercings and the pink hair, but both could be removed if the occasion required it. Her own hair was short and spiky and usually blond, but she tended to favour wigs for work, depending on her client's taste. She could scrub up to look divine in a ball dress, or dumb down to resemble, well, a tart. Gabs was nothing if not flexible. She charged a lot for her services, but her clients got their money's worth, and she received few complaints.

Gabs' day job was a part-time care worker for a private agency — an odd type of work for someone of her calling, one might have thought, but Gabs was very soft-hearted and adored (and was adored by) the elderly people with whom she worked. The kisses that she refused her clients were generously bestowed upon her patients, and the former would have been astonished (not to say disappointed) to see the tenderness and empathy with which she carried out her duties. Many a time Gabs was urged to take up a full-time post, and even offered promotion, but her need to be free at short notice in case she was required by her clients precluded any kind of permanent commitment. This suited Gabs perfectly.

Now Gabs tap-tapped her way down the high street in her very high heels, ignoring the admiring glances and the whistles. She barely noticed the attention she attracted, for she was used to it. Gabs wasn't beautiful — you couldn't even have described her as pretty — but with her petite figure, her generous breasts, her huge green eyes, and her air of feminine vulnerability (in fact, there was nothing vulnerable about Gabs, but no one was to know that), she had the kind of sex appeal that men found totally irresistible. They wanted to gather her up and take her away with them; to protect her and look after her; and while there were few things Gabs needed less, she was happy to go along with the idea if it increased her clients' delusions of masculine strength and dependability.

Gabs wasn't vain. She liked the way she looked, and she made the most of it — apart from anything else, it paid the bills — but otherwise she took it for granted. She had never understood women who agonised over their faces or their figures. She realised that she was probably fortunate, but had always thought that had she been favoured with a different appearance, she could have coped quite happily. She would just have had to find a different job.

An hour later, she arrived back at her flat.

"Hi! I'm back." She eased off her boots and threw her wig into a corner of the living room. "Steph? Are you in?"

"In my bedroom."

Gabs followed the voice and found her sister sitting on the bed, trying to do something with her hair.

"Going out?" Gabs asked.

"Yes. But *my hair...*" Steph wailed. "It goes all frizzy in this weather."

"Borrow one of my wigs," Gabs said, sitting down beside her. "Much less trouble than trying to sort out your own. I've got this great auburn one —"

"But everyone knows I haven't got auburn hair!"

"Of course they do. And they'll know you've borrowed mine. Does it matter? It would suit you."

"Gabs, you don't understand. I like to look *real.*"

"And I don't?"

"No — yes — oh, you know what I mean. You don't *mind.*"

"That's true." Gabs looked at her sister critically. "That top doesn't suit you. It's too — black."

"How can anything be too black?"

"Quite easily. I've got this turquoise one — it's quite new — it would look great with those jeans."

Steph turned to face her. "Gabs, will you stop trying to make me look like you? I'll never have your figure, and I'll never be as — sexy as you are, but I like to choose what I do to make the best of what I've got. I don't need your clothes or your wigs or —"

"Okay, okay. Keep your hair on."

"Is that supposed to be funny?"

"No. But it was quite funny." Gabs laughed. "Lighten up, Steph, for goodness' sake. Tell you what. Let me straighten your hair for you, and then I'll do your make-up, shall I?"

"Oh, would you?"

"Course. And before you say anything, I'll do nice conventional make-up. Less is more and all that."

"No funny colours?"

"Absolutely no funny colours."

Half an hour later, Steph was transformed. The frizzy hair had been straightened and lay obediently on her shoulders, and her face had been made up in tasteful shades of soft browns and corals, with just a hint of shimmer on the cheeks.

"There," said Gabs. "How's that?"

"Wow! That looks great. Thanks." Steph turned to her. "You know, you could do this for a living. You're brilliant at it."

"No, thanks," said Gabs. "I prefer the job I've got."

"Jobs, you mean."

"Okay. Jobs, then."

"You know, Dad still has no idea what you do."

"Good. Let's keep it that way, shall we?"

"Gabs —" Steph took Gabs's hand — "it's not — it's not *good* for you, you know."

"It's very good for me." Gabs pulled a handful of banknotes out of her pocket. "Look. Can't be bad for a day's work, can it?"

"You know what I mean."

"Yeah. I know what you mean. But give it a rest, Steph, will you, and stop doing the older sister thing? You and I will never agree. And I accept what you do, don't I?"

"But I'm an estate agent!"

"Exactly."

"You're impossible!"

"Quite probably."

Steph turned back towards the mirror and put on a pair of pearl earrings. "Have you got your meeting this evening?" she asked.

"Yep. Should be fun."

"It's not meant to be fun, is it?"

"Well, it wasn't when poor old Father Cuthbert was in charge, but it could be now the pressure's off."

"What pressure?"

"The pressure to change and become good little Catholics once more."

"Good little Catholics can have fun too, you know," said Steph, who was herself a very good little Catholic — Mass every Sunday, confession once a fortnight, the works.

"I'm sure they can. Just not as much fun."

"So what will you do now? What will you talk about?"

"I've no idea. We'll probably have a good old gossip, get rat-arsed, and come home again."

"I wish you wouldn't talk like that!"

"That's probably why I do it."

"And I wish you'd stop teasing."

After her sister had left for her date (if that's what it was), Gabs wondered how it was that the two of them managed to coexist. She knew that Steph disapproved of almost everything she did, and for her part, she couldn't imagine a more boring existence than that led by her sister, but maybe that was it. They complemented each other. Personalities apart, Gabs was tidy, while Steph seemed incapable of putting anything away; Gabs' cooking consisted of things-on-toast (or other things out of packets), while Steph could knock up a soufflé or a risotto at a moment's notice; Steph had always been the good girl and Gabs the bad girl. Even their looks were so different that people had difficulty in believing that they were sisters. Gabs' face was gamine, her figure (apart from the breasts) tiny, while Steph fought an ongoing battle with her weight and her mouse-coloured frizzy hair. But once they'd got their childhood out of the way (for sixteen years, they'd fought like cats), they had become good friends, and while they had — and regularly aired — their many differences, on the whole they managed to get along pretty well.

The Basic Theology classes had been Steph's idea. She'd heard about the scheme via someone from church, whose daughter had been invited (but refused) to attend, and had immediately thought of her errant sister. Of course, Gabs would almost certainly say no, but it was worth a try.

To her great surprise, Gabs said yes, and after only minimal hesitation. The idea of the Basic Theology class both entertained and intrigued her, and while she was going for all the wrong reasons (Steph knew her sister too well to have any illusions on that score), at least she was going.

"Basic theology for fallen women!" she'd cried delightedly.

"Well, I wouldn't put it quite like that," Steph had said.

"You couldn't have put it as *well* as that," countered Gabs rather unkindly.

"Besides, there'll be men too, I expect," Steph reminded her.

"So much the better," Gabs said. "I know. You could come with me. You could hold my hand."

"Since when have you ever needed your hand held? Anyway, I don't need the course," Steph replied, with justification (Steph was, incredibly, still a virgin).

"*I* don't need it, but it might be fun."

"Everything you do seems to be fun."

"Too right. Otherwise what's the point?"

So far, Gabs had rather enjoyed the meetings, although they would certainly have been more entertaining if the members had included at least one kindred spirit. As it was, everyone was terribly earnest, and there had been confessions and tears and a great deal of Catholic guilt. When it had come to her turn, Gabs had been unrepentant and had shocked her fellow members with her frank disclosures of her goings-on.

"You don't — you don't actually get *paid* for doing that?" one member had asked when Gabs had "confessed" to a particularly bizarre practice (mercifully, Father Cuthbert was out of the room at the time).

"It's my job. Course I get paid. You get paid for doing your job, don't you?"

"Then why are you here?" someone had made bold to ask.

"Because," said Gabs, "you never know. I just might have something to learn."

It was clear from the start that poor Father Cuthbert didn't know what to do with Gabs. He couldn't really ask her to leave, since she behaved nicely, waited her turn, and listened attentively to what everyone else had to say. On the other hand, he obviously thought she was a bad influence, and her lack of any kind of conscience bothered him.

"Have you thought what this is doing to the marriages of these — these men?" he'd asked.

"Not my responsibility," Gabs had replied. "After all, I don't ask them to come. *They* come looking for *me*. And if it wasn't me, it would be someone else. Someone not nearly as good," she'd added in an undertone.

"What was that?" Father Cuthbert was rather deaf.

"Nothing," said Gabs, reaching for the last chocolate digestive.

But now there would be just the three of them. Despite what she'd said to Steph, Gabs wasn't at all sure why she'd agreed to meet up, and she wasn't sure about Alice and Mavis, either. True, they both seemed pleasant enough, and Alice at least appeared to have some sense of humour, but they were both so *serious*. Of course, they probably had reason to be, since they both claimed to be in love with other people's husbands, but without Father Cuthbert to tease, Gabs thought the meetings might be a bit flat.

Gabs herself had never been in love. While she had been violently attracted, many times, she was wise enough and experienced enough to suspect that there was a considerable gulf between sexual attraction and real love. But of one thing she was sure. When she did meet the right man — and she was sure that sooner or later this would happen — her days as an escort would be over. Others might have disagreed, but Gabs had her principles, and among these, loyalty had always been one of the foremost.

Had she known what it was to be in love, it is doubtful whether Gabs would ever have taken up her unusual calling. As it was, she fell into it more or less by accident.

The accident was called Gavin — an uncouth young man, ill-favoured in appearance, with few social skills and no sexual experience whatsoever. Gabs had taken pity on him at a party, one thing had led to another, and she had ended up introducing him to the kind of riotous, glorious, and unconventional sex that most men can only dream about. Gavin's thanks had been profuse, and his words had remained in Gabs' mind long after Gavin himself had left it: *"You are so so good at this! You've changed my life!"*

Gabs wasn't accustomed to being good at anything. While Steph had been to university, she had left school at sixteen with no qualifications and little hope of earning any kind of decent living, and had drifted aimlessly from job to job, earning just enough to get by. But now she had it on authority that she was actually good at something. Admittedly Gavin had had no one to compare her with, but she knew that what he'd said was true. She was good at sex. When she came to think about it, she *felt* good at sex. Totally unembarrassed, completely confident, and perfectly happy in her own body (which in itself was a considerable asset), it suddenly seemed that she was made for the job. All she had to do now was to find her clients.

This of course took time. No one can set up in Gabs' line of business overnight, and she depended on word of mouth rather than scrappy advertisements in phone boxes (and since the advent of mobile phones, phone boxes themselves were in short supply). Besides this, Gabs didn't want anyone to have any illusions about the services she provided, and to that effect she produced her list of terms, which clients were required to read before they'd so much as taken off their shoes. But once the rules were read and understood, she proved both generous and inventive, and that, together with her growing collection of props, contributed to her success. At the time of the theology lessons, Gabs had as much business as she needed and was making a very comfortable living.

Now Gabs made herself a sandwich and changed into jeans and a sweater. She ran her fingers through her hair, touched up her eyelashes, and applied a crimson slash of lipstick.

It was time to go.

The First Meeting: February

Mavis waited in her living-room. It was a very long time since she had invited anyone to her house, and she was surprised to find that she was feeling quite apprehensive. She wanted — no, she *needed* — the continued contact with Alice and Gabs, but wasn't at all sure that the friendship (if that was what it was) would survive beyond the safe, if rather stifling, confines of the presbytery. Like a plant removed from its pot, it could just crumble away at the roots, leaving the three protagonists to flounder on their own once more.

It wasn't that Father Cuthbert had been particularly hospitable or that she had enjoyed his obvious disapproval, but he had taken control of the meetings, and on the one or two occasions when feelings threatened to run high, it had been Father Cuthbert who had sorted things out.

Would that be her job now, Mavis wondered. Did that responsibility belong to the host, as well as the provision of the crisps and the wine? She hoped the wine would be acceptable (Mavis knew very little about wine) and that the crisps weren't stale. She tried one, and it seemed fine. Cheese and onion flavour. Of course, not everyone liked cheese and onion. Perhaps she should have bought some salt and vinegar as well, or plain. Plain would have been safer. But there was no time now to go shopping for plain crisps.

She checked the room once more and closed a small gap in the curtains. There was a clean hand towel in the bathroom, and Mother was tucked safely up in bed. She hoped very much that the house didn't smell of urine, as she suspected it sometimes did. She herself was so used to the smell of her own home that it was hard to tell.

The cat put his head round the door. For once, his expression was obsequious, pleading. He probably sensed that he was not welcome (he wasn't) and that it would be better to approach with tact rather than his usual belligerence. Mavis shooed him out and shut him in the kitchen, where she left him snarling unpleasantly.

Alice arrived first. For a few moments, the two women hesitated, as though wondering whether or not to embrace. Nowadays people tended to greet one another in a kind of kiss-fest — mwah, mwah — one cheek and then the other, but Mavis had never felt comfortable with this. They hadn't kissed at Father Cuthbert's, but then it would hardly have seemed appropriate. In the end they shared a brief, self-conscious half-embrace, and Mavis took Alice's coat and led the way into the living room.

"This is cosy." Alice sat down in a corner of the sofa. "You — you live with your mother, don't you?"

"Yes. Mother's in bed." Mavis started to open a bottle of wine, but her hand was shaking and the corkscrew slipped.

"Here. Let me," said Alice, taking the bottle from her. "I've had a lot of practice with corkscrews. Too much practice, my doctor would say."

Mavis smiled. "Thank you. I rarely drink. Not that I don't like it," she added quickly. "It's just that drinking on your own isn't much fun, and Mother's not supposed to drink. It doesn't agree with her pills."

"Don't you drink with your — with your —"

"With Clifford? Yes, we do sometimes. But there's not much opportunity. He's usually driving, for a start. But we share a little hamper at Christmas and on my birthday."

"And I guess your mother has another early night?"

"Yes. And I'm afraid I give her an extra half sleeping pill. Is that awful of me?"

"Not awful at all. The name of this game is survival, isn't it?" Alice poured wine into two glasses. "I'd give anything to share a little hamper with Jay, but we don't even seem to have the time for that."

Both women were relaxing and beginning to talk more freely when Gabs arrived. Gabs had no problem with kissing, and embraced them both warmly.

"Fucking cold, isn't it?" she said cheerfully, throwing her coat over a chair and making for the small gas fire. "Real brass monkey weather."

Mavis was slightly shocked by Gabs' language and had never understood the connection between brass monkeys and cold weather, but she tried to take it in her stride. She offered wine, and Gabs accepted a glass of white. "Right. Where do we start? Not the same without poor old Father Cuthbert, is it? Who's in charge?"

"I don't think anyone's in charge," Mavis said uncertainly.

"Tell you what," Gabs said. "I'll be Father Cuthbert." She lowered her voice. "Now, dears, have you all been *thinking*?"

The other two laughed.

"Gosh! You sound exactly like him," Alice said. "But you forgot the prayer."

"*Let us pray*," Gabs intoned. "No, on second thought, let's not. Let's get down to the gossip. Much more interesting. Who'll go first?"

Alice and Mavis looked at each other.

"Oh, I'll go first, then," Gabs said. "Well, I'm not changing my ways, that's for sure. For a start, I've got a living to make."

"But you told Father Cuthbert that you were seriously thinking about it," Alice said.

"Poor old soul, I had to let him think he was doing some good. But no. No chance."

"How do you — how can you — I mean, what makes you do it?" Mavis asked. She had been longing to ask this question.

"Well, funnily enough, I quite enjoy it. I know that sounds odd, but it's a fact. Oh, I don't mean I enjoy it *sexually*. No orgasms or anything like that. Perish the thought." She laughed. "But I'm good at it, and my clients enjoy themselves, and it pays well. What's not to enjoy?"

Mavis could think of lots of things not to enjoy about having sex with strangers, but she didn't like to say so. Fortunately, Alice had a question.

"How do you find your — clients?" she asked. "Where do they come from?"

"Word of mouth, mostly." Gabs got a pack of cigarettes out of her bag, looked at them longingly, and put them away again. "Reputation. That's the best way. The least risky, too."

"I suppose it can be dangerous," Mavis said. "On your own with a strange man?"

"Yep. It can be. But I'm pretty good at looking after myself."

I'll bet you are, Mavis thought, not without admiration. "I could never do what you do," she said. "Not in a million years."

"Oh well. Each to her own."

"Do the same people come to you regularly?" Alice asked.

"Oh yes. I've plenty of regulars."

"Do you ever get women?"

"No."

"And would you? Do — something with a woman?"

Gabs laughed. "No. Definitely not. Never thought about it till now, but no. 'Fraid not."

"I suppose you have to have health checks," Alice continued (another question Mavis wouldn't have dared to ask).

"Oh yeah. My doc knows me well. I'm clean. And I'm very careful. Plus, all my clients have to have a shower first. I insist on that."

"So if you enjoy your work and the Catholic guilt thing hasn't kicked in, why did you go to Father Cuthbert's little gatherings in the first place?" Alice asked. "It seems like a waste of time for you. And for him, come to that."

"Good question. It was my sister's idea, and she was so chuffed when I said I'd think about it, I didn't like to let her down. Besides, it's been a laugh, hasn't it?"

A laugh? Those long evenings at Father Cuthbert's *a laugh*? Mavis had experienced many emotions during her visits to Father Cuthbert, but never mirth. But then Gabs was one of those people in whose lives "having a laugh" seemed to feature quite largely. Mavis herself couldn't remember the last time she had, so to speak, had a laugh.

"Don't look so worried, Mavis," Gabs said. "And don't mind me. Steph says I don't take life seriously enough, and she's probably right."

This was a Gabs Mavis hadn't seen before. At the presbytery she had tended to keep her counsel, listening rather than talking, paying due respect to Father Cuthbert without actually agreeing with him. She had never sworn, and she certainly hadn't talked of orgasms. Mavis herself had never said the word to anyone, even Clifford (there'd never been any need), and once again found herself admiring Gabs' refreshingly direct approach. And Gabs' spiky dyed-blond hair, her scarlet lips, her bat-black eyelashes, the studs in her nose and eyebrows, and the hint of a tattoo snaking up her neck from under her collar — these all added up to someone who behaved and dressed as she wished, letting others think what they liked.

And Alice. Alice too appeared confident; at home in her own skin. She was certainly not as outspoken as Gabs and appeared generally more conventional, but she had a certain poise. Yes. That was the word. *Poise*. She was older than Gabs, of course. Mid-forties, perhaps? Mavis wasn't good at guessing people's ages, and nowadays it was so hard to tell. People coloured their hair and everyone seemed to wear jeans, so they were all becoming increasingly similar. Mavis herself had never worn jeans, feeling that she hadn't got the right shape for trousers. Besides, Clifford liked her in skirts, and she found herself dressing to please Clifford, even when he wasn't there.

Mavis reached for the wine bottle. "More wine, anyone?"

Alice felt herself unwinding. She was tired, and the combination of the warmth from the fire and the wine (not very nice wine, but it did the trick) was making her sleepy. She watched with amusement as Mavis tried to conceal her embarrassment. Was Gabs being deliberately provocative, or was she just being herself at last, free from the confines of Father Cuthbert and the presbytery? Time would tell. Whatever Gabs was playing at, Alice couldn't help liking her. She was fresh and unselfconscious and different. In Alice's world, people were always trying to create an impression, but as often as not the effort involved masked any genuine characteristics. With Gabs, her act — if that's what it was — seemed effortless. Idly, she wondered whether Gabs would do an interview — it would certainly make an interesting feature — but decided not to ask her. Not yet, anyway.

"What about you, Mavis?" she said now. "Tell us how your — relationship is going."

"It just — carries on," Mavis said rather lamely. "It's been going on for so long that it's part of my life."

"A bit like a marriage?"

"A marriage, and not a marriage."

"Does his wife know?"

"Oh no." Mavis looked shocked. "Of course not."

"How do you know?" Gabs asked her. "She may have her own bit on the side, for all you know. The fact that you're fucking her husband might suit her nicely."

"I don't think Dorothy's the type," Mavis said after a moment.

"Well, you don't look the type, either," Gabs said. "When you think about it, very few people do, but most of them are at it in one way or another." She laughed at Mavis's expression. "Oh, I know *I* look the type."

"Do I look the type?" Alice asked, interested in the view of someone who was evidently an expert.

Gabs considered her carefully. "Possibly. You're quite a private person, aren't you? Not as private perhaps as Mavis — sorry, Mavis — but I reckon you keep your personal life to yourself."

"I have to," Alice said. "We all have to, don't we? Isn't that why we're here?"

"Yeah. But a lot of women can't help themselves. They just have to tell a couple of friends, and then word gets out. My guess is you haven't told anyone at all. Am I right?"

Alice agreed.

"Not even the son? What's his name?"

"Especially not the son, whose name is Finn, and who would be extremely interested."

"Teenagers, eh?" said Gabs, whose own teenage years couldn't have been that far behind her.

"Teenagers indeed," Alice agreed. "I'll tell him one day — I'll probably have to — but not yet. Apart from anything else, he's too busy coming to terms with his own hormones."

"All the hormones and none of the sense," said Gabs, who was showing a remarkable degree of insight for one so young.

"Too right."

"I never wanted children," Mavis said. "Just as well, really."

"Well, I didn't exactly *want* one," Alice said. "It just happened."

"But you're glad you've got him?"

"Oh yes."

"Who's his dad, then?" Gabs asked. "Not your feller, I gather."

"Not my feller. Finn happened long before that. It was an irresponsible artist called Trot."

"You still see him?" Gabs asked.

"Yes. Because of Finn."

"How civilised. Mostly they just bugger off."

"That's true." Alice had at least two friends whose partners had buggered off, leaving them holding their respective babies.

At that moment, the door opened, and an elderly woman appeared, wearing a flowery nightie and carrying a strange yellow bag. She was without either slippers or teeth.

"Someone has locked poor Puss in the kitchen," she said, ignoring the visitors. "Would you let him out, dear? He's making a terrible noise."

"Mother, you know we can't have him around when we've got company."

"He'll be fine now I'm here." Mavis's mother sat down in a rocking chair, cradling her yellow bag in her arms. A clear plastic tube appeared to connect the bag with her nether regions, and it wasn't difficult to guess what it was. "A glass of white for me, dear. And some of those nice crisps."

"Oh dear." Mavis looked around her in desperation, then lowered her voice. "I'm not sure what to do. She can be a bit aggressive when she's had her sleeping pill."

"Let her stay," Gabs said. "You'd like to stay, wouldn't you?" she said to Mavis's mother.

"Of course. This is my house. Mavis only lives here." She held out her hand, smiling sweetly. "I'm Maudie. How d'you do?"

Gabs took the proffered hand. "You're lucky to have one of those." She pointed to the bag. "They save so much bother, don't they?"

"Oh yes," Maudie said, patting the bag. "You don't have to wait for help. I wouldn't be without mine. You can just pee all night without even thinking about it. You should try it."

"I don't think I could do my job with one of those," Gabs said, winking at Mavis. "But there's a lot of my old people could do with one, but the authorities won't let them have them."

"Why ever not?"

"Risk of infection, they say. But I just think they want our lives to be as difficult as possible."

"My dear, I do so agree with you," Maudie said.

"How did you manage to get yours?"

"Mavis persuaded them. Mavis is a very good persuader. She said she couldn't manage me without. I think she was just being lazy. But it suits us, doesn't it, Mavis?"

Mavis was obviously uncomfortable with the way the conversation was going, but there wasn't much she could do about it.

"They tickle a bit at first," Maudie was saying, "but you get used to it. And look —" she gave her tube a hefty tug — "they stay in, whatever you do."

"So they do," said Gabs.

"Mother, don't you think you should go back to bed?" Mavis said, desperation in her voice. "We're having a meeting."

"Are you, dear? That's nice. No, I think I'll stay. I like talking to — what's your name, dear?"

"Gabs."

"What a very odd name."

"Mother!"

"It's okay, Mavis; I don't mind," Gabs said. "It's short for Gabriel. My mother was religious."

"Are you religious too?" Maudie asked, scattering half-chewed fragments of crisps.

"Not very, no," Gabs said. "Are you?"

"Well, I go to Mass. I like Mass," Maudie confided, "but church sometimes *gets in the way*, doesn't it?"

"It certainly does," Gabs said. She leaned forward and whispered something in Maudie's ear, and they both laughed uproariously.

Alice felt sorry for Mavis, with her unfashionable sixties hairdo and her sensible shoes. She was obviously a nervous host, and now her mother had gatecrashed the proceedings and was forming this unlikely alliance with Gabs. Gabs appeared to be enjoying the situation, and it was also clear that she was good with old people.

Good with old people. How patronising that sounded. As though the elderly were somehow different, separate, and could all be lumped together so that others could be good with them. Alice herself would have hated to be classified with people all her own age (forty-seven) and expected to behave in a uniform manner. But no one claimed to be particularly good with people of forty-seven.

"More wine, anyone?" Mavis had apparently given up the unequal task of guiding the meeting back onto the rails and was once again struggling with the corkscrew.

"No, thanks. I'm driving," Alice said, aware that she was probably already over the limit.

"Why not?" Gabs held out her glass. "I came by taxi," she explained. "It's been a good week, and so I can afford a little luxury."

"How much do you charge?" Alice asked. "That is, if you don't mind my asking."

"It's complicated," Gabs said. "I have a sort of sliding scale."

"Do you now? That sounds exciting." They both laughed. Mavis, on the other hand, merely looked confused, and was obviously worried about the continued presence of her mother. But she needn't have worried.

"We've got some kitchen scales, but Mavis dropped them," said Maudie, helping herself to more crisps. Someone (Gabs?) had poured her a glass of wine, and she was becoming merry. "Not sliding scales. Smashed scales." She seemed pleased with her little joke. "Shall we sing something?"

"I think she's confusing this with the day centre," Mavis said. "No, Mother. We can't sing anything. This is a meeting."

"*Keep the home fires burning*," warbled Maudie, spilling wine on her nightie and dropping her plastic bag on the floor. "Where's the bloody cat?"

Gabs was enjoying herself more than she had anticipated. The evening, lubricated by cheap wine and the timely arrival of Mavis's mother, was looking up, and while she felt sorry for Mavis (poor cow; where *did* she get that skirt?), she couldn't help being amused at her discomfort.

"My guess," she said, taking another swig of her wine, "is that the 'bloody cat's' shut up somewhere. It's making the dickens of a noise."

"Let him out, Mavis," said Maudie. "Poor puss. Poor, poor pussy. All by himself. *Ding dong bell, pussy's in the well*." She started singing again.

"All right. I'll let him out. But on your own head be it, Mother. Remember what happened last time?"

"Bollocks," said Maudie cheerfully when Mavis had left the room. "She does talk a lot of — what was that word I just said?"

"Bollocks?" Gabs said.

"That's it. Bollocks."

Mavis returned, accompanied by a huge tabby cat, which wound itself into the room with tail stiffly upright and a wary, malevolent gaze.

"What's his name?" asked Gabs, who was fond of cats.

"Puss — Puss — what's he called, Mavis? I've forgotten," Maudie confided.

"Pussolini," said Mavis.

"What a great name! Does he live up to it?" asked Alice.

"Oh yes. He lives up to it all right," Mavis assured her.

The cat strolled up to Gabs, sniffed her ankles, and then jumped onto her knee.

"Goodness!" said Mavis. "He never does that."

"He knows I like cats," said Gabs, who had been surprised at the glimpse of humour from Mavis. Maybe there was more to Mavis than she'd initially thought.

"No one likes Pussolini," said Mavis, with more feeling than she'd shown all evening. "Except Mother, of course."

Gabs stroked the cat and wondered where the rest of the evening was going. Since the advent of Maudie, some of the point had been lost, and she for one couldn't remember what they'd been talking about.

"Where were we?" she asked now.

"Sliding scales?" said Alice.

"Oh yes. Sliding scales. Perhaps I'd better save that for next time?" She glanced towards Maudie, who appeared to be listening attentively. She might not have her own teeth, but there was nothing wrong with her hearing.

Maudie reminded Gabs of her own great-grandmother, a redoubtable woman who had lived to be ninety-eight. Adored by her numerous descendants, she'd managed to stay on in her own home until the very end, regardless of the gloomy prognostications of her family, who were concerned that she would have falls and forget to eat properly. Considerate to the last, she had died in her sleep two years ago on Boxing Day, leaving her relatives with happy memories of a riotous final Christmas and the reassuring thought that she had died in her own home (the fact that they had done their best to remove her from it was conveniently forgotten). Gabs still missed her, for she herself was the black sheep who'd skipped a couple of generations, and she hoped that she would be able to carry on the same feisty heritage of nonconformity.

"Would you ever marry?" Alice asked her suddenly.

"Yeah. I guess so."

"It might interfere with your livelihood."

"I'd give it up," Gabs said. "It was only ever a stopgap. I sort of fell into it; I can fall out again — no problem. There's plenty of other things I could do. I've got my care work, for a start. But if I do marry, it'll be someone rich. My old gran always used to say, 'Don't marry for money, but marry where money is.' I think she had the right idea."

"And did she? Marry where money was?" Mavis asked.

"No." Gabs laughed. "My granddad hadn't got a bean. But I gather it wasn't for want of trying. What about you two? Would you marry your fellers if you could?"

"Good question," said Alice. "But yes, I think I would. Well, I'd live with him, anyway. I love Jay, and I think we'd make a good couple. What about you, Mavis?"

Mavis glanced at Maudie, who appeared to be asleep. "I don't know," she said. "Once, I certainly would have. But he kept on promising to leave his wife, and I kept pretending I believed him, and now I think I've accepted things as they are. I have my home; he has his. He's got his kids, and I never wanted any. It's odd, but I think we're best off as we are. Provided Dorothy never finds out."

"What about if something happens to him?" Alice asked.

"Yes, that's always bothered me. No one knows about us, so I'd probably be the last to hear. And then when I did find out, there'd be no one to offer a shoulder to cry on."

"That bothers me, too," Alice said. "We're the invisible ones, aren't we? There's no place in the pecking order for mistresses. We sort of hover on the outskirts of other people's families — skeletons in cupboards, secrets that have to be kept. I often wonder what I'd do if anything happened to Jay. That's one of the reasons I'll eventually have to tell Finn. He and I are pretty close, and I'd really need him."

Listening to them, Gabs felt some sympathy, but she also couldn't help thinking they were both mad. There must be a moment between attraction and falling in love, and if the guy was married, that was surely the moment to stop. This had nothing to do with ethics and everything to do with practicality. Gabs had no compunction about sleeping with other people's husbands, but she had no intention of falling for one. That way lay endless complications, and Gabs preferred her life to be straightforward.

"How do you manage to live like that, year after year?" she asked. "Secret meetings and phone calls and never being able to be seen out with your man?"

"That seems odd, coming from you," Alice said, but without malice.

"Oh, I'm different. I don't get involved," Gabs told her.

"How? How do you not get involved?" Mavis asked.

"It's a job. You don't get involved with all those socks and ties you sell, do you?"

"That's not at all the same," Mavis objected, although she couldn't help laughing. "No one ever fell in love with socks and ties."

"True. But it's the same idea. You approach your job in one way, your social life in another."

"Well, I couldn't do what you do," Mavis said, not for the first time.

Gabs tried to conjure up a mental picture of Mavis stepping out of her sensible skirt and old-fashioned court shoes and preparing to entertain an eager (and paying) client, but failed. "Horses for courses," she said. "You've got your socks and ties; I have my clients."

"And I," said Alice, consulting her watch, "have to go. I've got a piece to finish this weekend, and I haven't even started it."

"Me too. Early start tomorrow," Gabs said. "No days off in my job. I'll just phone for a taxi."

Alice and Gabs gathered up their coats and bags and prepared to leave. As they stood in the hallway saying their farewells, Maudie's voice could be heard coming from the living room.

"Bad girls," she called after them cheerily. "All of you. Bad, bad girls."

Mavis looked shocked, but Gabs laughed. "She's right," she said. "No flies on your mum. We are bad girls. After all, that's why we're here, isn't it?"

Part Two

Alice

On the evening after the meeting, Trot and Finn returned home filthy and late.

"Really kind of you to ask me for tea," Trot said, pecking Alice on the cheek. "I've brought wine." He deposited a bottle of Liebfraumilch on the kitchen table. Alice reflected sourly that this seemed to be a weekend for cheap, nasty wine, but tried to accept the offering with good grace.

"Did you catch anything?" she asked, stirring Bolognese sauce.

"Trot caught an old watering can, and I caught a very small fish. I put it back," Finn said. "We threw away the rest of the maggots," he added. "I didn't think you'd want them hanging around."

"How kind," murmured Alice.

Finn opened a cupboard and brought out a box of cereal. "Want some?" he asked Trot.

"Yeah. Why not?" Trot said, taking off his jacket and flinging it over a chair.

"Well, one reason is that I'm serving supper any minute," Alice said. "And it'll —"

"Spoil our appetites," chorused Finn and Trot, giving each other high fives and fetching bowls and spoons. Alice noticed that Trot could always locate anything connected with food or drink, but never knew where to hang his coat.

After supper, they played Monopoly. Trot and Finn, who for some reason loved the game, wrangled and fought, and finally formed a syndicate, winning handsomely. Alice, who loathed it, happily admitted defeat. She had spent much of the game in jail (despite having a "get out of jail free" card), working on her article, and neither of the others had even noticed. Games of Monopoly with Trot had been known to last into the small hours, and she needed to get some sleep.

Afterwards, Finn asked whether Trot could stay the night.

Alice looked at Trot — at his filthy jeans, his unshaven face, and his socks, which were more hole than sock. Trot followed her gaze.

"I'll have a shower," he said.

"And I'll lend him some clean boxers," Finn told her.

And I, thought Alice wearily, will have to make up the bed, provide clean towels, and afterwards do the necessary laundry.

"Please?" Finn said again, making puppy eyes at her.

"Oh, all right," Alice said. "You'd better sling your things into the washing machine — both of you. I'll put a wash on now."

"You're an angel." Trot patted her on the head. "Isn't she, Finn? Isn't your mother just the best?"

"Don't push your luck," Alice warned, tidying up the Monopoly money and wishing that Trot was equally good at making the real kind. For if he were, some of it might — just might — come Finn's way, and at the moment, keeping Finn was not cheap.

Later, lying in bed, listening to the distant chug of the washing machine and the sound of cars swishing down the road outside the house, Alice was unable to sleep. She'd had a disturbing phone call from Jay that afternoon and couldn't get it out of her mind.

"We need to talk," Jay had said.

"We are talking," Alice said, aware that she was deliberately missing the point, but nervous about what that point might be.

"No. Talk properly. Face-to-face," Jay said. "The phone is — difficult."

"Tell me about it," said Alice. "Jay, we've been conducting our relationship mainly over the phone for four years now. I know the phone's difficult. But it's better than nothing."

"Well, I still need to see you."

"You're — you're going to dump me." Alice had a sudden terrifying glimpse of a scenario in which she was despatched from Jay's life in the course of a conversation in some distant pub, or worse, a lay-by.

"Of course I'm not!"

"Well, what then?" For Alice couldn't think of anything more serious, and certainly nothing that couldn't be discussed over the phone.

"Trust me, darling. This is something I need to talk about when we're together. When I can see your face, and you can see mine."

"Do you love me?"

"You know I do."

"Then tell me. Please. You can't leave me waiting like this."

"Let's make it soon, then. Can you meet me for lunch on Monday? I've got a good registrar. He can do my ward round, and I can catch up with him later."

"Possibly. But I've got a deadline. I've got to get some work done on Monday." That Jay was prepared to miss a ward round did nothing to reassure Alice.

"I'll come over then, shall I?"

"You can't come here! You never come here."

"That's precisely why I can come, just this once. Presumably Finn will be at school."

"Well…"

"That's fixed, then. I'll come to your place at one o'clock on Monday. I'll park round the corner and walk the last few yards. No one will see me. Trust me, Alice. It'll be fine."

"What? You parking round the corner, or whatever it is you've got to say to me?"

"Both, I hope. And don't worry."

Why is it that when someone tells you not to worry, it's almost invariably because there's something to worry about? Alice tossed and turned, going over the possibilities in her head. Perhaps Jay was ill. Maybe he had some dread disease — *the* dread disease (what an irony that would be!) — and that was what this was about. Or perhaps Angela was ill. Or could it be that Jay was tired of the lies and the duplicity, and if not exactly dumping her, was planning to tail off their relationship gradually. How would she feel about being tailed off? Alice decided that she would prefer to be dumped. At least that would be final, unequivocal. She would know where she was.

Sunday dragged. Trot took himself off as soon as his clothes were dry, muttering about having arranged to see someone. Alice knew that this would probably involve a long and jolly afternoon in a pub somewhere, and she felt for Finn, who was obviously disappointed. Finn rarely referred to Trot when he wasn't around, but was oddly jealous when he was. Trot had never had official "access" to his son; he'd just arranged meetings when he felt like it. So he'd never been a weekend father, and Finn knew better than to expect to have him to himself for two days at a stretch. But Alice guessed that the invitation to stay the night had been issued in the hope that they'd be able to spend another day together, and now that was not to be.

"Never mind," she said when Trot had said his goodbyes. "He'll be back."

"Who said I minded?" Finn said. "I don't care what Trot does."

"If you say so. Shall we get a DVD this evening? We could make some popcorn."

"I'm not a kid anymore, Mum."

"No one said you were. But I like popcorn even if you don't, and you can choose the film."

The DVD was not a success, being one of those incomprehensible American cops and robbers films, where it's hard to tell who's on which side, and everyone had such deep southern accents that it was impossible to understand anything they said. Both Finn and Alice had an early night.

On Monday morning, Alice couldn't concentrate on her article. It was the product of an interview she had been granted by an ageing pop star whom she had never heard of and who had been both recalcitrant and rude, and she was in a quandary as to how she was going to manage to write something that wasn't libellous. She decided that she was in the wrong frame of mind to solve the problem, and so she caught up on some housework instead. The deadline would have to be stretched, she thought mutinously, finding one of Trot's socks behind the radiator (how could he have missed a sock when he had presumably come with two?) and rescuing his sodden towel from under the spare bed. Alice had never met Trot's parents, who lived in Spain, but she had often thought that he must have been overindulged as a child. At least Finn was reasonably well trained, if you discounted his bedroom.

The hands of the clock in the hallway crawled towards one, and Alice went upstairs to change. She put on fresh jeans and a pretty top that showed off her breasts to good effect. She wasn't sure why she was doing this, since Jay had never been particularly observant, but she felt as though she were arming herself for some kind of conflict, and looking good made her feel somehow stronger.

Jay arrived promptly at one, bearing a huge bouquet of flowers. This was not a good sign, since they had long ago agreed that flowers would attract questions, and therefore should be given only very occasionally (and when Alice could invent an acceptable donor).

"Oh dear," she said, accepting the flowers and a kiss.

"Why? Don't you like them?"

"Of course I like them. It's just that you and I don't do flowers."

"Well, we do today."

"I'll put them in water." Alice walked through into the kitchen to look for a vase. "I've made soup," she said.

"Lovely." Jay sat down at the kitchen table and watched her fetching bread and butter and putting out plates and cutlery. "You're avoiding looking at me."

"What do you mean?"

"No eye contact."

Alice sighed. "I suppose I'm worried what I might see if I look at you properly. Look," she said as she sat down beside him, "can we get this — this whatever it is — out of the way before we eat? I couldn't face lunch at the moment."

"All right." Jay took her hand and held it between his. "There's no easy way of saying this, but —"

"Just say it. Please."

"Angela's pregnant."

"*What?*"

"Angela's pregnant. I know," Jay hurried on, "I know it's a shock. It's a shock for us, too. We never thought it would happen — never thought it *could* happen — but it has."

"But — but how? I thought she — you — couldn't have children. You had all those tests, all that treatment. You told me you'd both given up hope. That you'd got used to the idea of not having children."

"Well, we had. But now it's happened." Jay shrugged. "Angela's having a baby. After all this time."

"But — isn't she too old? I thought all that was in the past."

"She's forty-four. Well, she will be when the baby's born."

"You mean she's going to have it?"

"Well, of course she's going to have it! What did you expect? She's always wanted children. You can hardly expect her not to have this baby after everything she's been through. I thought you'd understand that. After all, you've got Finn. You know how much it means to a woman to be a mother. You once told me he was the best thing that ever happened to you."

"That makes it all right, then, does it? The fact that I've got Finn makes it okay for you to go and — and make babies with Angela? I didn't even know you were still having sex!"

"I never told you we weren't."

"No, but from the things you've said, I assumed that that side of your marriage was over."

"Well, it's not. Not quite, anyway. We don't do it often."

"How can you do it *at all*? How can you leave me and then go home and make love to Angela? How can you be such a *hypocrite*?"

"I have to. Don't you see? If I stopped making love to Angela, then she really would get suspicious."

"Oh, very convenient. You just do it for me. Well, thanks very much." Alice picked up a knife and stabbed at the tablecloth. "And of course, you don't enjoy making love to Angela. It's just a duty you have to perform. Poor old Jay. What a chore it must be, keeping two women satisfied."

"Alice. Darling. Please don't do this."

"Don't do what? I haven't *done* anything! I've been the nice, undemanding mistress — always there if I'm wanted, but prepared to step down if you're needed at home. I'm a little sideline, a hobby. An *extramural activity*."

"Oh, Alice, I was afraid it would be like this. It's one of the reasons I wanted to tell you face-to-face. At least when I'm here you can't slam the phone down on me."

"Jay, that's not fair. I have never, ever slammed the phone down on you (or anyone else, come to that)!"

"No. It wasn't fair. I'm sorry. But Alice, you're not being entirely fair either. Anyone would think I'd planned this, when in fact nothing could have been further from my mind."

The argument raged on, the soup burnt, and they ended up for only the second time ever in Alice's bed, making violent, desperate love.

"I can't bear it," Alice sobbed afterwards, as she lay with her head on Jay's chest. "I probably ought to be pleased for you, but I simply can't bear it. Angela's got everything. She's got you, she's got marriage, and now she's having your baby."

"Sweetheart, I've told you. It's you I love; you I'll always love. We can still be together. Still see each other. This doesn't change anything."

"It changes everything! Can't you see that? You'll be a family man, with new responsibilities. You'll love the baby, of course you will, and you'll want to spend time with it. Which will leave even less time for us. How will you possibly fit me in when you're a new father?"

"I just will." Jay sighed. "Because you're too important to lose. We'll find a way. We've always found ways up until now."

"We've never had anything like this before." Alice reached for a tissue and blew her nose. "How — how is she? How is Angela?"

"A bit stunned, very surprised, but pleased of course."

"And — and you? How do you feel about it?"

"Oh, Alice, I just wish the baby was yours. Ours. For years I wanted children with Angela. I would have done anything to have them. But things changed between us, and now I don't know how I feel. Trapped, I suppose. Before, I had the choice. I chose to stay with Angela because of everything we'd been through, but there was always the other option, like a door I could go through if I really needed to. Now that door's closed. Now I don't have any choice, do I?"

When Jay had left, Alice sat at the kitchen table and wept. Of all the things she had feared might happen to her and Jay — and she must have considered most eventualities — she had never in her wildest dreams envisaged this. Angela, who was unaware that she was involved in any kind of power struggle, had unwittingly made the best move she could possibly have made. With marriage and a baby on her side, how could she fail?

Alice struggled through the next couple of weeks, worn out with worry and lack of sleep. On the surface, nothing had changed between her and Jay. They managed to meet once, and spoke almost daily on the phone. The subject of babies was not mentioned. A couple of times, Finn asked her whether she was all right, but seemed satisfied — even sympathetic — when she said she was just a bit under the weather. Yet again, she wished there was someone she could talk to, but of course there was no one. It occurred to her that she could have phoned Gabs or Mavis, but she didn't feel she knew them well enough yet to burden them with this, so she kept her grief to herself.

In the end, rather surprisingly, it was Trot who came to her rescue.

Trot had recently moved house and now lived only a few miles away. He'd said at the time that he was downsizing, but Alice suspected that it was so that he could be nearer Finn. Whatever the reason, he'd taken to popping in from time to time, usually when Finn might be expected to be at home, and almost invariably unannounced.

"I've come for my sock," he told Alice, taking off his shoes and placing them neatly on the doormat.

For possibly the first time in days, Alice actually laughed. "Your *what*?"

"My sock. I left it here. It's one of a lucky pair."

After a brief search, Alice produced the sock.

"I can't believe you want this back," she said. "It's full of holes."

"Ah, but I do." Trot regarded it fondly. "It — they — were given to me by a girlfriend after I'd taken her to this fabulous hotel. We had a four-poster bed and lovely fluffy bathrobes, and —"

"Too much information, Trot," Alice said, thinking that socks were an odd way of saying thank you and wondering how Trot could afford to stay in fabulous hotels.

"You're right. Too much information." Trot stuffed the sock in his pocket. "So, what's wrong with you?"

"What do you mean, what's wrong with me?"

"You look terrible."

"Thanks a lot."

"You know what I mean."

"Yes, I probably do."

"Well, are you going to tell me?"

Alice hesitated. For the first time that she could remember, she was tempted to confide in Trot. He was often childish, frequently irritating, and always irresponsible, but there was something basically nice about Trot, and she was pretty sure that he could keep a secret.

"It's a man. It's got to be a man," Trot said.

"What do you mean, it's *got* to be a man?" Alice bridled. "I do have other things in my life, you know."

"Yes. But you're the strong type. I guess not much gets you down. But man trouble would. You've got a soft heart, Alice, even though you like to pretend you haven't." He settled himself comfortably on the sofa. "Now, are you going to tell me or not?"

Alice sat down opposite him and thought about it. "I suppose it would be nice to talk. But, Trot, this is confidential. It has to be confidential."

"A married man, then," said Trot with satisfaction. "I thought as much."

"Trot, if you're going to be like this, I shan't tell you anything."

"Okay. Sorry. But you so rarely let me in on your life that I can't help feeling… well, not pleased exactly, but — I don't know — privileged perhaps. And of course, your secret's safe with me. Apart from anything else, who could I possibly tell? You and I don't exactly move in the same circles."

So Alice told him. She told him about meeting Jay, about their affair, and finally she told him about the baby.

"Goodness. That's a bit of a bugger, isn't it?" Trot said when she'd finished.

"You could say that. Yes."

"What are you going to do?"

"I honestly don't know. I've thought about it and thought about it, and all I know is that I can't live with the idea of Jay's wife having a child, but I can't live without him, either."

"You could marry me," Trot said after a pause.

Alice looked up, expecting to find that he was teasing her, but his expression was serious.

"Oh, come on, Trot! That's a ridiculous idea!"

"Thanks very much."

"I'm sorry, but you know what I mean. You and I? Married? It would never work."

"It might. And we make nice babies. That's a start."

"We made one nice baby, and that was a very long time ago."

"True."

"Besides, we don't love each other."

"Don't we?"

"Okay. Let me put this another way. Do you love me, Trot?"

"Well, not love exactly, but —"

"There you are, then."

"You're right," Trot said. "It was a silly idea. But just for a moment, it seemed to make sense. And Finn would love it."

"But it wouldn't solve anything, would it?" Alice said. "I'd still love Jay, and you'd still want your freedom."

"I guess so."

After Trot had gone, Alice thought about his proposition (it could hardly have been called a proposal). She didn't doubt that for a few moments, he had meant what he'd said, but she also suspected that in those few moments, the prospect of a bigger house, with a cook-housekeeper thrown in, must have had a certain appeal. As for Finn, she didn't think he would be particularly pleased at the idea. He had never mentioned the possibility of his parents being married, and Alice suspected that things suited him very nicely the way they were. He liked having Trot to himself, and if she and Trot were married, he would have to share him.

Alice sighed. It wasn't really marriage she wanted; it was Jay. And if she was to keep Jay, it would have to be on his terms (or the terms dictated by his situation).

But then, wasn't that the way it had always been?

Mavis

The morning after the meeting with Gabs and Alice, Mavis was still wondering whether she'd imagined Maudie's comments the previous evening. "Bad girls," she had called them, and that could only mean one thing. Somehow Maudie had found out about Clifford.

"But how long have you known?" she asked Maudie. "However did you find out about — about my man friend?"

"Always known," Maudie replied. "Have you seen my teeth anywhere?"

"They're behind the clock on the mantelpiece, where you left them yesterday. Mother, I really need you to tell me. How did you know about Clifford?" For if her mother had managed to find out about her affair, then maybe other people had, too. Perhaps she hadn't been as careful as she had imagined.

"Told you. I've always known. Oh — there they are. That's better." Maudie gave Mavis a gleaming porcelain smile. "Am I going to confession?"

"Mother, you went last week. There's no need to go again yet. Now, about Clifford."

"Oh, him." Maudie sniffed.

"Yes. Him. How do you know about him?"

"I hear things," Maudie said enigmatically. "Got my hearing aid, haven't I?"

"Then why didn't you say anything before?"

"What's to say?" Maudie shuffled over to her favourite armchair, dragging her catheter bag behind her. "Anything on the telly?"

"I shouldn't think so. It's only eight o'clock."

"That problem woman. She'll be on. I like her. She does DNA and all sorts."

"It's Saturday. I don't think she's on on Saturdays. It'll probably be cartoons."

"Those'll do." Maudie sat down. "Have I had breakfast?"

"You had porridge."

"I don't like porridge."

"Well, you ate it."

"Without my teeth?"

"You said you didn't need teeth for porridge."

"Did I? What did I have on it?"

"Brown sugar. Look, Mother, it's really important to me, I need to know how you found out about Clifford, and I want to know how much you heard."

"When?"

"Last night. When those — those friends of mine were here."

"You had a party," Maudie said. "Didn't ask me, did you? Nice people, though. I liked that — that what's her name? With all the rings and things."

"Gabs?"

"That's the one. The tart."

"Mother!"

"Well, that's what she is. She told me so herself. Turn the telly on, would you, dear?"

"I'll turn the telly on when you answer my question," Mavis said.

"What question?"

"About Clifford."

"Who's Clifford?"

Mavis sighed. Conversations with her mother frequently went like this. One minute Maudie would remember things quite clearly; the next, they'd be forgotten again. Mavis could never be entirely sure whether her mother was playing games; she was quite capable of feigning forgetfulness if it suited her. But now, she could tell from Maudie's expression that the conversation of a few minutes ago had been forgotten and that to persevere would be a waste of time.

Mr. Strong's Gentlemen's Outfitters, being an old-fashioned shop, closed after lunch on Saturdays, so after Mavis had made Maudie a sandwich and settled her for her afternoon nap, Clifford picked her up in his car for one of their rare afternoons out together.

She could tell straight away that there was something bothering him.

"What's the matter?" she asked as soon as they were out of sight of the house.

"Well, I don't suppose it's anything much really, but I've been getting this pain in my chest."

"Have you seen a doctor?"

"Not yet. I've made an appointment for next week. But chest pain's always worrying, isn't it?"

Yes, thought Mavis wearily. And so is a persistent cough, pain in the legs, lassitude, and headaches, all of which had afflicted Clifford in the last few months. Since his retirement, Clifford had become a hypochondriac. Whether it was because he no longer had enough to occupy his mind or because several of his friends had recently died, Mavis didn't know. But while she tried to be sympathetic, Clifford's preoccupation with his health was beginning to get just a tiny bit boring.

He spent a great deal of time on the internet looking up various diseases and had self-diagnosed, among other things, heart disease, cancer, brain tumours, and a rare condition with a long German name that even he couldn't remember. All these fears had proved groundless, and Mavis was beginning to lose patience. They had little enough time together as it was, and now much of that was taken up with Clifford and his health concerns.

"Yes," Clifford continued, warming to his subject. "My great-uncle died of a heart attack, so you see it runs in the family."

Mavis doubted whether the illness of a single great-uncle (who probably smoked, because in those days, didn't everyone?) could be said to constitute a risk to the rest of his family for all time, but decided not to say so.

"I'm sure you'll be fine," she said lamely.

"No one can be sure," Clifford told her.

"Well, no one can be *sure* of anything. But your blood pressure's okay, isn't it? And your cholesterol?"

"That's no guarantee."

"Of course not. But you're pretty fit —" Clifford had recently bought a rowing machine— "and you eat all the right things."

"But," said Clifford, who was not to be deterred from the matter in hand, "you read about people dropping dead when they've just run a marathon, don't you? You just can't tell."

"Cliff, can we talk about something else now? After all, there's nothing you can do about it at the moment, and this is our precious afternoon together."

"Aren't you concerned, then?"

"I'd be concerned if there really was something wrong with you, but we don't know yet, do we?"

"I'd be concerned if it were you," Clifford said rather plaintively.

"Yes, I'm sure you would."

But Mavis wasn't sure. It occurred to her, not for the first time, that Clifford was becoming increasingly self-centred. She realised that this was partly her fault. She had always given in to him, letting him have his own way and allowing him to make the decisions, simply because it was easier. But there were times when she too wanted attention, when she also would like her feelings to be considered. Such occasions were becoming increasingly rare.

She decided to change the subject.

"Are we going to Dennis's?" she asked. Dennis was a friend of Clifford's who worked abroad for much of the year. In his absences, Clifford kept an eye on his flat for him. While she had never met Dennis, Mavis suspected that Dennis knew exactly what purpose the flat was used for in his absence, but chose to turn a blind eye. Clifford, who could be very naïve, maintained that Dennis had no idea. They didn't tend to use the flat except for the purposes of lovemaking because it was some distance away. It was also very cold.

"I'm sorry, darling," Clifford said now. "I don't think that would be a good idea. Until we know my heart's all right, I think we should lay off for a while."

This had happened during both the cancer and the brain tumour scares, and Mavis was both annoyed and disappointed.

"You do understand, don't you?" Clifford continued. "It would be awful if something went wrong, wouldn't it?"

Mavis had a brief and horrifying image of herself and Clifford, locked together in that most embarrassing of clinches, being loaded onto a stretcher to be disentangled (and in Clifford's case, treated) in the hospital. But it only lasted a few seconds.

"I think it's worth the risk," she said boldly.

"Mavis, I can't believe you said that." Clifford pulled into a side street and switched off the engine, turning a reproachful gaze upon her. "You must see that my health is important. To both of us."

"A bit too important," Mavis said, surprising even herself. "What about me? What about my health?"

"Why? What's wrong with you?"

"Well, nothing at the moment, but —"

"There you are, then. There's nothing to worry about, is there?"

"Maybe not. But I'd like to feel you were just a bit interested."

"Of course I'm interested!"

"Well, at times it certainly doesn't feel like it."

"Funny. That's what Dorothy said."

Mavis felt a brief moment of solidarity with Dorothy. If it was difficult having an affair with a hypochondriac, it must be even harder being married to one.

"So, what are we going to do?" Mavis asked.

"Well, I thought perhaps a walk? The fresh air might do me good."

It was a cold, damp day, the billowing grey clouds pregnant with rain, and there was a bitter wind.

"Well, it wouldn't do me good," Mavis said. "And I haven't got the right shoes." Only the right knickers, she thought bleakly. New French knickers, bought specially for the occasion as a treat for Clifford, who had a fondness for such things (Mavis herself found them rather draughty). "If that's all you can suggest, I think you'd better take me home."

"What, already?"

"Yes. Already."

Mavis knew she would probably regret her decision, for she was scotching the possibility of salvaging anything pleasurable from the wreckage of their afternoon, but she was seriously annoyed.

"Well, this is great, isn't it?" Clifford said as they drove off again. "I make the time to come all this way over to pick you up, and you ask to be taken home again just because I won't — because we can't go to Dennis's. What a waste of an afternoon!"

"I'd rather be at home than walking about in the cold listening to you going on about your health," Mavis said.

"Oh, that's how you feel, is it? Well, I wish you'd told me before!"

"So do I," said Mavis with feeling.

"What are you trying to say exactly?"

"I'm *trying to say* that I'm sick and tired of hearing about your health problems. For years I've accepted that I have to come second to your wife and family, but I will not play second fiddle to an imaginary heart condition!"

"Oh, so it's imaginary, is it?"

"Quite probably."

"You're an expert, then?"

"Not on heart conditions, no. But I know you pretty well."

"That's what you think," said Clifford, swerving violently. "Now look what you made me do! I nearly ran over that cat!"

"It's not my fault if you aren't looking where you're going."

"So you're an expert driver, as well?"

"I would be if you'd let me."

This was a sore point. When Clifford and Mavis had first got together all those years ago, he'd promised to teach her to drive. Like so many of his promises, it had come to nothing, and Mavis had never got round to making alternative arrangements. This of course was largely her fault; she could easily have obtained driving lessons elsewhere. But the fact that she was responsible for her nondriving status served only to inflame her resentment, for there are few things more infuriating than finding that you are to blame for the situation in which you find yourself.

"You're probably too old now, anyway," Clifford said.

"Too old for what?"

"Too old to learn to drive."

"Clifford, that was a horrible, cruel thing to say!"

"The truth hurts," said Clifford comfortably.

"Oh, so the truth hurts, does it? Well, try this for truth." Mavis was getting into her stride. "You are becoming an old, fat bore. You seem to think of nothing and no one but yourself. And I've had enough of it!"

There was a stunned silence.

"Did you say I was old?" Clifford said after a moment.

"Yes, I did. You're a lot older than I am, and you say I'm too old to learn to drive. That definitely makes you old."

"And fat?"

"Yes. Just look at your beer belly!"

"And a bore?" There was a dangerous note in Clifford's voice.

There is a moment in a row — especially one that has been building up for some time — when suddenly there are no holds barred. All the ammunition comes out of the arsenal, and to hell with the consequences. The satisfaction for the combatants is as brief as it is deep.

Mavis was aware of all this, but there was no going back now, and so she might as well enjoy the moment (if *enjoy* was the right word). It was years — literally — since she and Clifford had had a row, and this one was long overdue.

"Yes. Just listen to yourself. Headaches, chest pain, indigestion… There's always something to complain about. Have you any idea how deeply boring it is having to listen to you?"

"It must be, for someone with your sparkling personality," said Clifford, driving much too fast. "And there's your dazzling career, of course, too. We mustn't forget that. And if we're talking about looks, you're perfect, I suppose? You haven't a grey hair on your head, have you? And you probably think you've got the body of a supermodel, too. Lucky me. What have I done to deserve you?"

"How dare you!" Mavis cried. "You've enjoyed my body for years — you've said so often enough — and as for age, well, you — you *stole* my youth, didn't you?"

"Oh, please! Don't be so bloody melodramatic. I never stole anything. You gave yourself to me of your own free will. I always promised to leave Dorothy —"

"Oh, Dorothy! Yes. I forgot. All those empty promises. How many years is it now? You were never going to leave Dorothy, were you? You were lying all along!"

The row raged all the way back to Mavis's front door, where Clifford drew up with a screeching of brakes. He didn't get out to open the car door for her (Clifford's manners were usually impeccable), and so Mavis had to make her exit unaided. As she straightened up, an icy little breeze found its way up her skirt and into the French knickers, reminding her of past treats and present disappointment and further fuelling her anger. She slammed the door.

"So that's it, is it?" Clifford yelled through the open car window.

"That's it," said Mavis, getting out her house keys.

For a moment, their words hung suspended like breath in the cold air between them, waiting for someone to reach out and rescue them, to make everything all right again. Mavis knew that this was a make-or-break moment, but she couldn't bring herself to climb down, and she was pretty sure that Clifford wouldn't, either.

"Goodbye, then," said Clifford.

"Goodbye."

As she stood on the doorstep feeling the first fat drops of rain down the back of her neck and watching Clifford's car sweep off down the road, Mavis thought that she might be going to cry, but she was relieved when the moment passed. It would be a shame to risk red swollen eyes and a headache for Clifford. He wasn't worth it.

Her mood was not improved when she found that in her absence, Maudie, most unusually, had got out of bed and had been busy in the kitchen. This had happened only once before and was possibly due to the after-effects of last night's wine, but today it was the last straw. Much of the kitchen and Maudie herself were covered with flour and jam and butter, and several items of crockery appeared to have been smashed. The cat, who was rarely discomfited, had taken refuge on top of a cupboard.

"What *are* you doing?" Mavis demanded.

"Making a little pie, dear. Your father likes a little pie when he comes home from work."

"Mother, Father has been dead for eighteen years."

"Has he, dear?" Maudie's eyes filled with tears. "Why did no one tell me?"

"They did tell you. There was a big funeral. Remember?"

"Did we have cooked meats afterwards?"

"Yes, we had cooked meats afterwards." Mavis fetched a dustpan and brush and began clearing up the mess.

"And flowers?"

"And flowers."

Maudie cheered up a little. "Well, that's good."

"Yes." Mavis tipped the last shards of china into the bin and filled a bowl with soapy water.

Maudie shuffled towards her, leaving floury footprints in her wake. "Is it time to go to confession?"

"*We are not going to confession*! I am going to clean you up, and this mess, and then you are going to go and watch television while I make supper."

Maudie's face crumpled.

"You shouted at me," she said in a bewildered little-girl voice. "Mavis, you shouted at me!"

"Oh, Mother, I'm sorry." Mavis immediately regretted her outburst. "I'm so sorry. I've just had an awful afternoon. I shouldn't take it out on you."

"Is it because of Father?" Maudie asked.

"No. It's because of — Clifford."

"Who's Clifford?"

"My man friend."

"What man friend?" Maudie licked raspberry jam off her fingers and then wiped them on her cardigan.

"Oh, never mind." For it seemed that the existence of Clifford had still not returned to Maudie's befuddled brain.

Mavis was surprised to find that she was disappointed. For if Maudie really did know about Clifford, then it would have been nice to talk about the afternoon's row, to gain a little sympathy and, if not some understanding (understanding was not Maudie's strong point these days), at least a little support. But this was obviously not to be.

That night, after she had put her mother to bed, Mavis was once more overwhelmed with rage and grief. How could Clifford have said all those awful, hurtful things? How *could* he? After all she'd done, all she'd been through for him, all she had sacrificed. She thought of the years she had given to Clifford, of her youth and such physical attributes as she had once had; all, *all* had been Clifford's. Her body had been entirely his, for she had had no other lover, and she very much doubted whether anyone new would want it now. Her fertility, too. That had been wasted on Clifford. As she undressed for bed, she took off the pretty camisole, the stockings, the suspender belt — all garments that had been bought to please Clifford rather than herself. The knickers were a particularly cruel reminder of the events of the afternoon, and in another moment of fury, Mavis ripped them to shreds and stuffed the filmy pink fragments in her wastepaper basket.

But while she tried to keep her anger stoked up with memories of Clifford's faults, his many virtues kept creeping into her mind to spoil her mood. Clifford's chivalry, his compliments, and his loyalty — all these came to the surface of Mavis's mind. For she knew that the things he had said had been spoken in anger and that he probably hadn't meant them. And if he had been unreasonable, she had undoubtedly been the one to start the row.

Was it for her, then, to seek a reconciliation? It was still not too late to do something about it. Several times, her hand reached for the phone so that she could contact the mobile that Clifford kept especially for her messages, and on each occasion, she withdrew it. Despite her part in the afternoon's events, she wasn't ready yet to step down and apologise. She would wait and see what happened.

But nothing happened. A week passed, and Mavis received no word from Clifford. In all the years of their relationship, they had never been out of touch, and Mavis began to be seriously worried. It had been all right to have the row — understandable even to part on such bad terms — but no contact at all? It was unheard of.

Gradually pride was replaced by fear. For what if she were to contact Clifford, only to be told that he no longer wanted her in his life? How would she cope with that? It was sobering to discover that she had come to identify herself as much by her illicit relationship as she would have by marriage. Without Clifford, she was — what? A rather ordinary, fifty-something spinster who lived with her mother and sold socks and handkerchiefs. How dull. How terribly *ordinary*.

And yet, did she love Clifford? Did she truly love him as she once had? Certainly in the beginning, she had been very much in love with him, but over the years, things had changed, and now she wasn't so sure. Mavis's heart had never been broken; now she wondered whether it was in Clifford's power to break it. Certainly if he were no longer a part of her life, he would leave a huge gap, and she would miss him sorely. But was that the same as love? Or was there also an element of fear that if he were to go, no one else would ever want to fill the vacancy that he left behind him, that no other man would ever *want* her?

By the end of the second week, Mavis had almost resigned herself to her situation. She would have to concentrate on her job and looking after her mother, and get used to a life without Clifford — a life that would be without interest, without the little outings that punctuated her otherwise humdrum existence, and above all, without sex. She got out the little box from under her bed and looked longingly at the device inside. Would it ever be called into service again? She knew that women used these things on their own — Clifford had told her that that was what they were designed for — but the very thought made Mavis blush. No, she couldn't possibly do that. Besides, the Catholic Church had strong views on the subject of solitary sex, and old principles die hard. She climbed into the loft and hid the box in an old trunk, where it would waste away over the years among the cobwebs and the dead flies and the dust.

The very next day, Clifford phoned.

"Shall we go to Dennis's?" he asked as though nothing had happened. "Would you like me to take you to Dennis's?"

And forgetting all her doubts, Mavis replied without a moment's hesitation.

"Oh yes!" she said, her whole being glowing with relief. "Yes, please!"

Gabs

Gabs had a problem.

She had always prided herself on a relatively trouble-free existence, for she was not by nature a worrier, and such problems as she did have, she tended to keep to herself. On this occasion, however, she decided to confide in Steph.

"I think I'm falling in love," she said, leaning on a kitchen worktop and watching her sister stirring something complicated in a saucepan.

"*What?*" Steph dropped her wooden spoon and hugged Gabs. "Thank heavens for that! Oh, Gabs! I'm so happy for you! I knew it would happen eventually, and now of course everything will change, and you'll have to —"

"Steady on. Not so fast," said Gabs, pushing Steph gently aside and rescuing the spoon. "I haven't told you everything."

"Well, go on, then. Tell me. Who is he?"

"Are you ready for this?"

"Of course."

"Well, it's Father Augustine."

There was a very long, very shocked silence.

"But you can't!" Steph cried when Gabs' news had sunk in. "Gabs, you can't. You just can't!"

"Oh, but I can." Gabs dipped her finger in the saucepan and licked it.

"No, you can't. He's a priest, *our curate*. He's only just arrived; he's hardly had time to settle in."

"And he's celibate," said Gabs helpfully.

"And he's celibate. Besides — oh, Gabs — he's so young!"

"Yes, isn't he?" Gabs grinned. "Bloody gorgeous, too."

"Gabs, this isn't a game. You can't do this to him. It isn't fair."

"I'm not doing anything to him," Gabs said. "Not yet, anyway."

"How did you meet him? You never come to church."

"He sat in on one of Father Cuthbert's meetings once. Heaven knows why. Probably some mad idea of the bishop's. Anyway, I've seen him around, and we nodded to each other. Then I bumped into him in Boots the other morning, and I just knew."

"But you don't *know* him at all."

"Maybe not. But I intend to."

"Have you even spoken to him?"

"I asked him the time."

"How original."

"Steph, don't try to be sarcastic. It doesn't suit you."

"You can't suddenly decide you're in love when you barely know the other person. It's ridiculous!"

"Ah, but I know *men*. I'm a very good judge of men. And trust me, Steph, this one is special."

"*I know he's special*," Steph wailed. "We all think he's wonderful. So please, Gabs, keep your hands off him. For my sake, if not for his."

"I would if I could," Gabs said, and there was genuine regret in her voice. "But he's the one. I'm certain of it. It's just tough that he happens to be a priest."

"Not tough. Off limits. Absolutely off limits."

"No one," said Gabs, "is off limits."

"Married men are. You always said you'd never pinch another woman's husband."

"True. But this is different."

"No, it's not. He's married to the church. He's a bride of Christ."

"Oh please, Steph. Don't be so pompous."

"I am not being pompous! It's the truth. It's what he's been training for all these years. He has a vocation. But of course, you wouldn't know anything about vocations, would you?"

"If he decides that his vocation is the most important thing in his life, I shall certainly respect it," Gabs said. "Don't worry. I shan't make him do anything he doesn't want to do. That's a promise."

"I don't trust you," Steph said. "I don't trust you one little bit."

"And I don't blame you." Gab sighed. "I'm not sure I trust myself."

To be fair to Gabs, despite her words to her sister, she did try to put Father Augustine out of her mind, but as everybody knows, the harder you try not to think of something, the more it keeps edging its way back into your thoughts. As she led Gerald round on his lead, as she spanked Anthony (never Tony; always Anthony) and frolicked on a waterbed with a well-known cabinet minister, she thought of Father Augustine. His fresh young face, his clear and surprisingly deep voice, his dark hair and eyes, and (strangest of all) his transparent integrity — all of these haunted Gabs' thoughts by day and her dreams by night. There seemed to be no getting away from him.

"You're not yourself today," Gerald grumbled as he squatted on the floor barking.

"Sorry. I'm just a bit tired." Gabs shook herself (the dog thing seemed to be catching).

"Do you mind if I die for the queen? That's one of my favourites."

"Go ahead," said Gabs dreamily.

"But you've got to watch," Gerald said. "It's not the same if you don't watch."

Gabs watched.

"And — and tickle my tummy?"

Gabs tickled his tummy. But her heart wasn't in it, and Gerald was upset.

"I've paid extra for today, and it's not — I'm not —"

"Getting your money's worth?"

"Well, yes. I mean, you're very good and everything, and I don't know anyone else who'd do what you do, but still…"

"You're right. I'm sorry." Gabs smiled and patted his head. "Come on, then, good dog. Good dog, Gerald. Walkies? Shall we go for nice walkies?"

"That's better." Gerald beamed. "I'll go and fetch my lead."

On her way home, Gabs told herself that Steph was right. She was being ridiculous. She hardly knew Father Augustine, and besides, there were lots of other men out there. She should know. If Steph was annoyed that she had "picked on" a Catholic priest, Gabs was even more so. Of all the men she'd come across — many of them very nice, intelligent, presentable — why this one? What was it about him that she found so irresistible? After a long, honest look at her feelings, Gabs decided it was largely due to his unavailability that Father Augustine's charms outshone those of any other man she'd met. Those men she came across were mostly by definition available, at least for most purposes, and if she was honest, Gabs had to admit that there was a part of her that despised them for that. Father Augustine was different. He also represented a challenge. Gabs had never been one to turn her back on a challenge.

But it wasn't just Father Augustine's lack of availability or even his physical charms that had got to her. There had been a moment at Father Cuthbert's when she'd caught his eye, and she had been struck by something in his expression, which was a mixture of attraction and reproach. And looking away, Gabs had done something she'd hardly ever done in her life before. She had actually blushed.

The emotion behind that blush hadn't lasted, but the effect of Father Augustine had, and for the first time, she had a glimpse of what it might be like to bridge the gap between sexual attraction and real love, to have a relationship that was based on something more important than sex. She had had a moment's insight into a depth of feeling between a man and a woman that was greater than anything she had known, and while up until now she had cheerfully done without it, suddenly she knew that it was the only thing that would complete her, the one experience that would make her fully a woman.

So what should she do? Of course, she knew what she ought to do; Gabs did have a conscience even if she generally chose to disregard it. But supposing — just supposing — she had what it took to offer Father Augustine the chance to share an experience such as the one she dreamed of? Would it not be wrong to deny it to him? Of course he could well already know what it was to be in love; vows of celibacy didn't bring any guarantees of immunity. But Gabs felt — no, she *knew* — that she could give him something he had never experienced before, and it wasn't just sex, either.

She spent several days brooding and plotting, and eventually she came up with a plan. She would start by going to Mass.

This wasn't easy, as she didn't want Steph to find out, and her sister was an assiduous churchgoer. Sundays were definitely out as there were always so many people and she would be sure to be noticed. She would have to risk going on a weekday.

The first time was a disappointment, as the service was conducted by the parish priest himself, Father Pat, a dour old Irishman with no sense of humour and a penchant for threats of hell and damnation. But a judicious phone call confirmed that the Wednesday morning Mass would be taken by Father Augustine, and so Gabs went along.

Part of her had genuinely hoped that the attraction would have worn off, that seeing Father Augustine in his priestly robes would have a deterrent effect on her burgeoning affections, and she could forget about him and get on with her life. But of course, it had quite the opposite effect. Not to put too fine a point on it, Father Augustine looked divine. How could it be, Gabs wondered, that a man could look so enchanting, when to all intents and purposes what he was wearing was simply a long frock? Gabs had never liked men in kilts, and this wasn't so very different, was it? It was. The robes suited Father Augustine down to the ground in every sense. Idly, Gabs wondered what he was wearing underneath. She knelt down and closed her eyes, the better to aid her imagination.

Father Augustine conducted the service slowly and thoughtfully (Father Pat tended to race through the Mass as though it were some kind of competition), he smiled at the congregation (Father Pat rarely smiled), and he shook hands with everyone as they made their way out.

Awaiting her turn, Gabs felt ridiculously nervous. Would Father Augustine recognise her from his visit to Father Cuthbert's? Quite possibly not. She had removed all the rings and studs from her face, borrowed a subdued jacket of Steph's, and was without make-up. She might just get away with it.

The woman in front of her had some kind of problem, and it seemed that Gabs would have a lengthy wait. She wiped her sweating palms on her skirt (she must give a dry handshake) and resisted the temptation to adjust her hair. She looked up at the ceiling (red brick; the church was a modern one) and across at a statue of the Virgin Mary. She counted to ten, and then she counted backwards. And she waited.

Finally her turn came.

"Good morning." Father Augustine's handshake was firm and cool. "I haven't seen you here before, have I?"

Good. He hadn't recognised her.

"My sister's the churchgoer," Gabs said, as though that gave her some kind of licence to be made welcome, like borrowing someone else's membership card. "She's Steph."

"Ah. Steph." Father Augustine smiled. "A great worker in the vineyard."

Gabs experienced a stab of jealousy. "I'm Gabs," she said, resisting the temptation to say that hers was a different vineyard, with far sweeter grapes.

"Well, it's very nice to meet you, Gabs. Shall we be seeing you again?"

"We" rather than "I." What a difference a single word could make. Gabs' heart sank a little. "Oh, I expect so," she said.

"I'll look forward to it."

"Yes. Me too."

And that was that.

Reflecting on the meeting on her way home, Gabs decided that Father Augustine seemed to be everything she had imagined, and more. It was true that his manner had been just a little cooler than she might have hoped, but presumably in his position, he had to be careful. It was more than likely that she wasn't the only girl to have noticed his remarkable personal qualities, and he might even have had to fend off other approaches.

But there was something else about him, something that she hadn't noticed before. Gabs imagined that she had detected a sadness behind the smile, as though he carried some secret burden that he was attempting to conceal, and she thought that she recognised that look. It was loneliness. Father Augustine was lonely. Well, of course he was, living as he did with Father Pat and the sour-faced housekeeper, who guarded the presbytery against unnecessary visitors and untimely phone calls. It was unnatural for a young man to live like that, with no one of his own age and no fun. Fun played a big part in Gabs' life, and she found it hard to imagine how others contrived to conduct their lives without it. Father Augustine needed some fun in his life, and who better to provide it than Gabs herself? But first, she needed a one-to-one encounter with him, and she knew just how to arrange it.

The following Saturday, she went to confession.

"Bless me, Father, for I have sinned," she whispered, perching on the small and very uncomfortable seat provided for penitents. She could see through the gauzy partition of the confessional the outline of Father Augustine's features, his brow resting on his hand, his eyes closed in concentration, and she wondered whether he would recognise her voice.

"How long is it since your last confession?" he asked her.

"Oh, ages," said Gabs. "Absolutely ages."

"I see."

No, you don't, Gabs thought sadly. *You don't see, and you'd be appalled if you did.* There followed a short silence. Father Augustine coughed encouragingly.

"I haven't really come to confess anything," Gabs said. "Well, not at the moment, anyway."

"We all have sins to confess," said Father Augustine. "You could make your confession while you're here, couldn't you?" He remained silent for a few moments. "Take your time."

Gabs hadn't expected this.

"Oh, no!" she said.

"Why not?" Father Augustine lifted his head and shifted in his seat. "Perhaps you're struggling with your faith at the moment?"

Gabs reckoned that more or less summed it up, but decided not to say so.

"It's complicated," she said.

"Yes?"

"I just thought — well, I thought it would be nice to get to know you a bit better."

"Ah." There was a long, thoughtful pause. "And why is that?"

"Well, we met at — at Father Cuthbert's a few weeks ago, and I was at Mass last week. I'm — I'm Gabs."

"*Ah!*" A different sort of "ah" this time.

"You — you remember me?"

"Yes, I remember you."

"And?"

"What do you want me to say, Gabs?"

"I don't know." This was not going the way Gabs had hoped (although she had little idea of what she had expected).

"Well, something must have brought you here today. What is it that you want from me?"

I want *you*, thought Gabs wildly. I want your body, your mind, *all of you!*

"Just to have a little chat, I suppose," she said.

"Well, that can be arranged, of course, but not here. I'm here to hear confessions."

"Yes. Of course you are. I'm sorry."

"That's quite all right. Would you like a blessing?"

"Yes. Yes, please."

Father Augustine gave Gabs a blessing. But still she didn't move. It was as though she had been glued to her seat.

"Is there anything else I can help you with?" asked Father Augustine. "Because I think there may be others waiting."

"Yes. Yes of course."

"And if you want to talk at any time, just ring the presbytery."

Two days later, Steph accosted Gabs in the bathroom.

"I gather you've been going to Mass," she said.

"Yes." There was no point in denying it. "You've used up the last of the toothpaste."

"Don't change the subject."

"Okay. So I went to Mass. What's the big deal?"

"The big deal," said Steph, "is that you never go to Mass."

"Well, I do now."

"So, you've returned to the fold, have you?"

"I think that's my business." Gabs applied a pair of very long false eyelashes and gave them an experimental flutter.

"So you'll be giving up your — your *work*."

"No."

"I see."

"No, you don't. You're just being prudish and sarcastic, and you don't understand at all!"

"What's to understand? You're a tart in pursuit of an ordained priest. It seems simple enough."

"Goodness! You really do mind about this, don't you?" Steph had never called Gabs a tart before.

"Of course I do. I care about Father Augustine — he's a good man trying to do a difficult job in a pretty godless world — and I can't bear the idea of you making his life even harder than it is already. And believe it or not, I care about you, too. Because you're trying to do something that would be a hideous mistake and that could mess up your life as well as his."

Gabs sat down on the edge of the bath. "Steph, I can't help it. I've tried to forget him, I really have, but I can't."

"*Of course you can help it*. Don't be so ridiculous, Gabs. You're the one doing the chasing; you're the one who's started going to Mass. I gather you've even been to confession. So you're the one who can stop all this. *Now!*"

"My goodness! Word certainly gets around!"

"Well, what did you expect?"

"A bit of privacy? A little less gossip?"

"You don't deserve privacy. Father Augustine belongs to his church and his congregation. What you're doing is like stealing. And that's everyone's business."

"You seem to have a great deal of faith in my powers of persuasion," Gabs said mildly.

"Oh, I know what you can do," Steph said. "You once told me you could have any man you wanted, and it seems to have worked pretty well so far. And a priest is in a vulnerable position, especially a young one like him."

"I've barely spoken to the man yet. And he does — he would have a choice in the matter."

"That's what you say."

"Hm." Gabs looked at her sister. "You're not just a tiny bit jealous, are you?"

"No. Of course not!" Steph hesitated for a moment. "Well, okay then, perhaps I am sometimes. Just a little. I haven't had much success in the boyfriend department. I haven't got your — assets. But I'm certainly not after Father Augustine; and besides, this isn't about me."

"No, it's not. And now if you'll excuse me, I have an appointment."

While she understood Steph's viewpoint, and in a more reasonable mood might even have agreed with it, Gabs was so infuriated by what she saw as Steph's prudish interference that it made her all the more determined to succeed in her mission. She was not stupid; she knew that what she was doing was at the very least ill-judged, but she reasoned to herself that it was also her business and her life, and she could do what she wanted. As for Father Augustine, he wasn't some naive child, as Steph seemed to imply; he was a grown man, perfectly capable of making his own decisions. He certainly didn't need Steph to look out for him.

Gabs smiled grimly to herself. Steph had done more to damage her own cause than she could have imagined.

The Second Meeting: April

Hosting a meeting with Gabs and Mavis was proving more difficult than Alice had anticipated. For a start, there was Finn.

"What's this meeting about?" he'd asked her when she told him that she'd like to have the house to herself.

"I told you. It's a reading group."

"But you don't read," Finn said reasonably.

"I do when I have time."

"Okay then. You don't have time. So what's the point in joining a reading group?"

"The discussion will be interesting."

"No, it won't. How can listening to people discussing a book you haven't read possibly be interesting?"

"Finn, this is my house, these are my friends, and what we do or what we talk about is none of your business."

"And you want me out of the way?"

"Correct. Anyway, I thought you were seeing Trot."

"He called it off. Something about seeing a man about a dog."

Alice knew that this probably meant seeing several men about a pint, but refrained from saying so.

"You don't go out when I have friends," he pointed out.

"You have your own room to take them up to," Alice said.

"Well, why can't you —"

"Entertain people in my bedroom? I don't think so, Finn."

"It's an age thing, is it?" Finn asked.

"I suppose you could say that."

"Okay. Here's the deal," said Finn after a moment's thought. "I'll ask Kenny round, and we can play computer games in my room. We won't make any noise, and we won't interfere with your meeting. How does that sound?"

"I suppose it sounds all right," Alice said doubtfully.

"And Kenny can stay the night."

"Who said anything about staying the night?"

"I did." Finn kissed the top of her head. "Thanks, Mum."

Now Alice did a quick tidy round the living room. She scooped up Finn's trainers and sweater and deposited them at the bottom of the stairs, and rescued a bag of dirty PE kit from the hallway. She cleared away a pile of books, plumped up some cushions, and brushed a few stray crumbs under a chair. The house would never be as tidy as Mavis's, but it'd have to do.

Gabs arrived first.

"Sorry to be early," she said, dumping an enormous holdall on the floor and sinking down on the sofa. "I came straight from work. It wasn't worth going home first."

Alice fetched a bottle of wine and glasses.

"Will red be okay? I haven't any white."

"Anything would be wonderful." Gabs kicked off her shoes. "Ooh. That's better. What a day! This man — he's a real creep, but rich, you know? — he actually asked me to… Oh, never mind. I just want to forget him. Cheers!"

The door opened, and Finn came in.

"Hi," he said, seeing Gabs.

Alice introduced them.

"Hi, handsome." Gabs grinned at him.

"Enjoy the book, did you?" Finn asked her.

"What book?"

"The reading club book." Finn winked at Alice, who could cheerfully have killed him.

"Oh, that book!" said Gabs cheerily. "Loved it. Just couldn't put it down."

"What was it again?" Finn asked.

"*War and Peace*." Gabs didn't bat an eyelid. "You should try it sometime."

"Finn, did you want something?" Alice asked.

"Nope. Just checking."

"Well, that sounds like Kenny at the door."

"Yeah." Finn dragged his eyes away from Gabs, beneath whose tiny skirt there was a tantalising glimpse of suspender.

"You going to answer it?"

"Yeah."

"Well, go on then."

"Nice boy," said Gabs when Finn had left the room.

"He has his moments," Alice told her.

A moment later, Finn was back.

"It wasn't Kenny," he said, ushering Mavis into the room. "And this lady has brought her mother with her."

"I'm so sorry," Mavis said. "In the end, I couldn't leave her on her own. She's been getting up to things, and the friend who sometimes sits with her is busy."

"I've come in a taxi," said Maudie, beaming. She was bundled up in several layers. There was no sign of the plastic bag.

"Have you read *War and Peace* too?" Finn asked Maudie.

283

"Don't mind if I do. Two sugars," said Maudie, unwinding coats and scarves.

"I've turned down her hearing aid," Mavis explained.

"Isn't that a bit cruel?" asked Finn.

"Finn, will you please leave us now?" Alice said.

"Isn't there anything I can fetch?" Finn looked longingly at Gabs.

"No, there isn't. You can go and make up a camp bed for Kenny."

"Right."

"Off you go then."

"Yeah. Okay."

"Aren't they just darling at that age?" said Gabs after Finn had left.

"No." Alice had had enough of Finn for one evening, and she wasn't sure that she trusted Gabs. She poured wine for Mavis and herself, and sat down.

"What about me?" Maudie said.

"Tea?" Alice asked her.

"I'll have what you're having."

"Just give her a drop," Mavis said. "Last time was a bit of a disaster."

"And I'll have some of those crisps. I've brought my teeth." Maudie fumbled in the pocket of her cardigan. "Here they are." She picked some bits of fluff off them and popped them in her mouth. "What's on telly?"

"That's an idea," Mavis said. "If we sit her over in that corner by the television, she'll be quite happy, and she won't be able to hear what we're saying."

Alice had not been looking forward to this evening. She'd had a terrible few weeks, she was exhausted, and now she was going to have to spend another evening with Gabs and Mavis and Mavis's mad mother. In addition to this, she'd lied to Finn, and Finn knew it. She would have liked nothing better than an early night with something soothing on the radio and a large glass of whisky, and instead, she was going to have to listen to tales of Mavis's lover and the unsavoury antics of Gabs. She reflected that there were few things that made one less inclined to listen to the problems of other people than being preoccupied with one's own. To her surprise, she burst into tears.

"Gosh. I'm sorry," she said between sobs. "I don't know what's the matter with me."

"Don't you?" Gabs fished a large and very male-looking handkerchief out of the holdall and passed it to Alice. "Course you do. Come on, Alice. Tell us."

So Alice told them. She told them about Angela's baby, about her fears and Jay's assurances, and her desperate insecurity. She even told them about Trot's proposal.

"Bloody hell! You have had a time of it, haven't you?" Gabs moved across to Alice and rubbed her back sympathetically.

Alice nodded. "And I wanted his baby. *I* wanted his baby," she wept. "*I wanted Jay's baby!*"

Jay's baby? Where on earth had all that come from? Occasionally she had thought it might be nice to have a baby with Jay, but obviously she must have felt more strongly about it than she'd realised. It had always been an impossibility, and so she thought she had put it out of her mind.

"Of course you want his baby," said Gabs, refilling Alice's wine glass.

"How awful for you," said Mavis.

"Yes. But it's the waiting that's the worst. The not knowing what it'll be like, what it will do to Jay. Angela may have quite a long wait, but I feel I've been lumbered with one as well. Before, I imagined we'd just carry on as we always have. Not ideal, but manageable. This is quite different. This is unknown territory."

"Clifford has children," Mavis said, "but they've always been there, so they haven't really affected us. If he'd had one after we'd started seeing each other, I don't know what I'd have done."

As Gabs and Mavis discussed her situation, Alice was soothed by their interest and their understanding, and she was glad she hadn't call the evening off, as she'd been tempted to. She was also grateful that neither had suggested that she should end her relationship with Jay. It was the obvious solution — if it could be called such a thing — but already they knew her well enough to see that at the moment, it was not an option.

"And the proposal?" Mavis asked. "No chance there, I suppose?"

Alice shook her head. "Trot's not marriage material. He's a good father to Finn; well, a good friend, anyway. But no. It wouldn't work. Besides, I don't think he really meant it. He was feeling sorry for me, that's all."

"And you don't love him."

"There is that."

They all laughed, and Alice found herself relaxing. The evening was going better than she had expected, despite her emotional outburst, and Maudie seemed happy enough in her corner, tutting over a makeover show in the course of which some poor woman appeared to be having her breasts rearranged. At least I have nice boobs, she thought. I should be grateful for small (if a B cup could be called small) mercies. She poured everyone another glass of wine.

Mavis hadn't wanted to come this evening. The prospect of dressing her mother up and persuading her out into the night and into a taxi just so that she could spend an evening with people she hardly knew was not an appealing one, but a sense of duty had prevailed. Now, after a glass of wine and Alice's outburst, she was feeling a great deal better. There was nothing quite so cheering as talking to someone who was worse off than yourself, and Mavis didn't envy Alice one bit. Alice might be younger and more attractive than she was (Mavis had no illusions about her appearance) and she might have that rather nice-looking son, but she wouldn't be in her shoes for anything. She had no idea whether Clifford and Dorothy still had a sex life and she didn't want to know, but to have indisputable evidence that the sex life was not only ongoing but had, so to speak, borne fruit would be unbearable.

"You said Clifford had children," Alice said. "Have you ever seen them?"

"A couple of times. The first was a long time ago. I did that hanging around the playground thing, trying to guess which ones they were."

"And did you? Guess, I mean."

"No. I asked another child which ones they were."

"And?"

"They weren't at all what I'd expected. I suppose I thought they'd look like Clifford, and they didn't at all. One even had red hair."

"How did you feel?" Gabs asked.

"Nothing. I felt nothing."

It had taken three bus rides and an entire morning for Mavis to get to the school, and then she'd had to hang around until the children came out into the playground after lunch. It was pouring with rain by the time she got there, and she'd forgotten to bring an umbrella. She'd taken shelter under a tree, anxious that if the weather continued like this the children wouldn't be allowed out at all, but fortunately the rain eventually stopped, and as soon as the bell rang, they poured out into the playground, laughing and shouting, dauntingly similar in their red and grey uniforms. She had spent some time watching them, trying to pick out two that might be Clifford's.

What was she looking for? Even all those years ago, Clifford's figure was moving comfortably from well-built but distinguished towards plump and balding. She could hardly have expected his two little girls to resemble him. And of course, they didn't. When they were finally pointed out to her (one was with a friend, practising handstands; the other was standing on her own eating an apple), she waited to see how she'd feel, and was surprised when she found that she had no feelings about them at all. They were quite nice-looking little girls, but they could have belonged to anyone.

"I think I expected to feel *related* in some way. I know that sounds ridiculous, but because I was so close to Clifford, I expected to feel something for his children. It was a relief in a way when I didn't. I had been so afraid that I'd — oh, I don't know — that I'd *want* them."

"And you didn't," said Gabs.

"No. I didn't."

"Did you speak to them?"

"I didn't get the chance. A teacher came over and asked me what I wanted. I think she thought I was planning something sinister, and so I left."

"How are things now?" Alice asked, and Mavis realised that it was her turn to speak.

"Up and down. We had a falling-out, and had no contact for nearly three weeks."

"What was that about?" Gabs asked.

So Mavis told them.

"A hypochondriac," mused Gabs. "I don't think I could put up with that."

"I'm not sure I can, either," Mavis said. "But the trouble is that this time, he was right. He's got angina."

"Oh dear."

"Yes. Actually, he seems rather pleased about it. He's got this little puffer thing he uses and some pills to put under his tongue, and he's making a bit of a meal of it."

"You don't sound very sympathetic."

"That's what Clifford says. But I think I'm running out of sympathy. The brain tumour and the cancer sort of drained me."

"So?" Gabs asked.

"So we just carry on. I still love him — well, I think I do — but I refuse to worry. He's got a good specialist. He and Dorothy can do the worrying." Mavis realised that she sounded hard, but she'd had to toughen up recently, and the experience had been rather invigorating.

"What about sex?"

"We've done it once."

"And?"

"He was fine, although he wanted... he insisted..."

"Yes?"

"He insisted that I should — be on top." Mavis blushed. She'd never talked about this kind of thing before, and while she and Clifford had tried many positions in their time, it was not something she had ever imagined herself discussing with anyone else. Besides, this particular position was not one that showed her in a flattering light. Straddled across Clifford on Dennis's bed in Dennis's icy bedroom, she'd been too aware of his view of her dangling breasts and less-than-firm stomach to enjoy the experience.

"Not a bad position," mused Gabs, the expert. "Although I could suggest —"

"No. No, thanks. On top is fine. For the moment."

"And the French knickers?" Alice asked.

"I bought another pair. A kind of peace offering."

"And did they go down well?" Gabs smirked.

"Yes, they did." Mavis saw that Gabs had made some kind of joke, but was not sure what it was.

The more she saw of Gabs, the more aware Mavis was of her own naivety, and she felt oddly ashamed. She was probably old enough to be Gabs' mother, and yet where matters of sex were concerned, Gabs could make her feel like a mere child. Gabs discussed sex with the ease of someone who assumed a similarly relaxed attitude on the part of her listener, and Mavis simply couldn't do it. Sex had always been private, personal, *secret*. Otherwise, she reasoned to herself, what was the point? For Mavis, one of the great attractions of sex had always been its *rudeness*. It was a childish expression, she knew, and redolent of the games of doctors and nurses that her friends had played as children (Mavis had not been invited to join in), but one that best expressed how she felt. Of course, that was only part of it; there was the closeness and the reciprocity that accompanied the sex she had with Clifford. But she still privately delighted in (and wondered at) the fact that grown people with respectable lives and jobs and positions in society could do this incredibly rude thing without it seeming remotely abnormal. It could be because sex had never been a part of her everyday life; appointments had to be made, venues found, and limits placed on the amount of time she and Clifford could allow themselves to do it in. They had only twice enjoyed the luxury of actually sleeping together — sharing a bed for a whole night, waking together, breakfasting together — things that most couples took for granted. Sex had always been, as it were, taken out of context. Couples who lived together could presumably make love whenever they felt like it. She and Clifford had to do it when they could, which wasn't necessarily the same thing at all.

Alice appeared to understand Mavis's unease, for she turned to Gabs.

"Come on, Gabs. Your turn now. Tell us what you've been up to."

"Okay." Gabs took a sip of her wine. "Well, I've had a bloody few weeks. My favourite patient died, my boss at the agency's being an absolute cow, and I've fallen in love with a priest. My sister is being all disapproving and holier than thou, and the priest isn't having any of it."

"Oh, not a priest!" Mavis said. "That's — that's awful!"

"Awful for who?" Gabs demanded.

"Well, just awful, I suppose."

"More awful than shagging someone else's husband?"

"Well, no. Yes. I don't know. It just seems so — so *extreme*."

"Who is he, Gabs?" Alice asked quickly.

Gabs explained about Father Augustine.

"Gosh. I remember him," Alice said. "Dark. Good-looking. He sat in a corner at Father Cuthbert's looking embarrassed. I felt quite sorry for him."

"Gorgeous, isn't he?" Gabs sounded proprietorial.

"There must be other gorgeous men around who are more available."

"Oh, not you as well! I've had enough of all that from my sister. I thought you two at least would understand."

"But I've never — I'd never dream of going after a priest," Mavis said.

"You went after someone's husband. Isn't that worse? Father Augustine doesn't belong to anyone else. And don't say he belongs to the church because I've heard all that, too. He wouldn't be hurting another human being."

"I never *went after* Clifford," Mavis said.

"Well, what, then?"

"We just — met. We weren't looking for one another."

"Well, I wasn't *looking* for a priest." Gabs refilled her glass. "You could say that we just met, as well."

"It just doesn't seem right," Mavis said.

"Bloody hell, Mavis! None of us are doing what's right, as you put it! That's why we're here, isn't it?"

"Perhaps," said Alice, "this is different because it's happened after the Father Cuthbert meetings. Mavis and I had our — our lovers long before we all met. You're *planning* a relationship and expecting us to give you our backing. Isn't that it?"

"I suppose," Gabs said. "But whatever you think about what I'm doing, there's no one else I can talk to about it."

"You say you're in love, but do you really know him?" Alice persisted.

"I feel that I do."

"Couldn't you stop now, before…?"

"Before anyone gets hurt?" Gabs sighed. "Yeah, I could. We could all stop now, couldn't we? But this feels like a chance. An opportunity. I really think I could make him happy."

"Oh, Gabs! For heaven's sake! How do you know he's not happy already being — *married* to the church?" Alice seemed to be losing patience.

"He doesn't look happy. He looks — lost, I suppose."

"So you've no intention of giving up on this?"

"Nope. I can't."

"Of course you can," said Mavis.

"No, Mavis, I can't. You can't give up your Clifford, and I —"

"Of course I could give Clifford up! But what we have suits both of us, and since Dorothy doesn't know, no one gets hurt and nothing changes. If you succeed in seducing a priest, think of what he's got to lose!"

"Ah, but think of what he's got to gain," said Gabs, who was feeling angry and unrepentant. She had been looking forward to being able to discuss her feelings about Father Augustine, and Mavis and Alice were turning out to be almost as prudish as Steph. "Hang on a minute —" she glanced round the room — "Mavis, where's your mum?"

Everyone looked towards Maudie's corner, but apart from some fragments of crisps, there was no sign of Maudie herself.

"She can't have gone far," Alice said as Mavis rushed into the hallway.

They searched all over the house, but there was no sign of Maudie.

"The back door's open!" Alice called out. "She must have gone out that way."

"Can she get into the street?" Mavis asked.

"I'm afraid she can. And it looks as though she has. The garden gate's open, too."

Alice called up the stairs. "Finn! Can you and Kenny come and help us? We seem to have lost Mavis's mother."

The two boys clattered down the stairs. They didn't appear to be taking the exercise particularly seriously, but they could move fast, which would be a help. They dashed down the street in one direction, and Mavis and Alice went in the other. Gabs was asked to search the garden.

As she poked about among the bushes and investigated a rickety garden shed, Gabs had pangs of guilt. This emergency could well be her fault. Unbeknown to Mavis, she had topped up Maudie's wine glass when no one else was looking, reasoning that the poor old soul didn't have much fun in her life, and a little drop more couldn't possibly do her any harm. Maudie had looked very settled and had even dozed off a couple of times. It had all seemed perfectly safe. How on earth had she managed to get up and leave the room without anyone noticing?

Gabs abandoned the garden, which was small and bore no traces of Maudie, and joined the others in the street.

"She can't have just vanished," Alice said.

"Oh yes, she can," said Mavis grimly. "She does this sometimes. The doctor says it's because she's confused, but I sometimes think she does it just to keep me on my toes."

They searched down side roads and alleyways; they went into gardens and knocked on front doors. No one had seen or heard Maudie.

"This is ridiculous," Alice said after a fruitless twenty minutes. "She doesn't move fast; she's very conspicuous, especially at this time of night. Where on earth can she have got to?" She lifted the lid of a wheelie bin and peered inside. Gabs giggled. "Not funny, Gabs."

"No. Sorry." Gabs was cold and fed up, and her guilt was rising to a dangerous level. Should she confess about the wine or keep quiet? What if something awful had happened to Maudie, and it was all her fault? Gabs liked Maudie. She reckoned there was more going on under that neat grey perm than many people imagined, and guilt notwithstanding, she would be very sorry if the old lady were to meet with some kind of accident.

Just then, a police car drove slowly up the road and drew to a halt at the kerb. A policeman got out and put on his cap.

"Good evening. We've found a — a lady, wandering on her own. She doesn't seem to know where's she's meant to be. I wonder whether you can help?"

"That'll be Mother," said Mavis. "Where is she?"

"She's in the car. She appears to have been drinking."

"Well, she's not driving, is she? There's no law against drinking in the privacy of your own home," said Gabs.

"But she wasn't at home, was she? And there is a law against being drunk and disorderly."

"*Drunk and disorderly?*" Mavis repeated. "Surely not."

"Yes, madam. She was sitting on the pavement singing a — singing an inappropriate song. She was causing offence to members of the public."

"How many members of the public?" Gabs demanded, aware that members of the public at large in the streets on a Friday night were far more likely to be drunk than a harmless old woman.

"I don't think that's any of your concern. But a gentleman complained."

"Where's your sense of humour?" cried Gabs. "If I can get drunk and sing inappropriate songs at her age, I shall be very pleased."

"We are not paid to have a sense of humour. We are paid to keep the streets free from crime." The policeman looked Gabs up and down and sniffed. "*Madam.*"

"Oh, get a life, will you? You're just —"

"Can I have my mother now, officer?" said Mavis quickly. "And I'm so sorry if she's caused offence."

"Mavis, you don't have to creep to the police! This is ridiculous!"

"Gabs," said Alice, "shut up, and help us get Maudie out of the car."

Maudie appeared to be none the worse for her little expedition, although she was very cold and her clothes were streaked with dirt. She was still clutching an empty wine glass and appeared unaware of the trouble she'd caused.

"I've had such a lovely ride," she said, holding on to Mavis's arm. "And this young man has been so kind. But he didn't like my song. Such a shame. It was one of your father's favourites, dear."

"I'm sure it wasn't," Mavis said. "Could someone give me a hand?"

Alice took the other side of Maudie, and together they half pushed, half pulled her back towards the house.

"'Roll me over, in the clover, roll me —'"

"Shh, Mother. People don't want to hear that. I think we should be going. I'll phone for a taxi. We'll go home, shall we, Mother? And you can have a nice cup of tea."

"Don't want tea. I want another little drop of… little drop of…"

"No more little drops for you tonight, Mother. You've had quite enough."

Finn and Kenny appeared from round the corner.

"Ah, you've found her," Finn said. Both boys seemed very entertained by the situation. "She's drunk, isn't she?"

"Of course she's not," said Mavis, puffing with exertion (Maudie was not light).

"What's this?" Finn asked, picking up the yellow bag that was trailing in Maudie's wake.

"Pee," said Alice firmly. "Thank you, boys, for your help. You can go and —go and get on with whatever it is you were doing."

Mavis blushed and quickly took the bag from Finn.

"Doesn't that hurt?" Alice asked when the boys had gone back into the house.

"Doesn't what hurt?" Mavis was busy securing the bag to Maudie's person.

"The bag. When it drags along like that."

"You'd think so, wouldn't you? But she never seems to mind."

"'Roll me over, lay me down, and do it again!'" warbled Maudie, tripping on the kerb and nearly taking her two helpers down with her. The wine glass rolled into the gutter and shattered.

"Mother! Be quiet."

"That's what the young man said."

"I don't blame him."

Gabs was feeling relieved on two counts. Maudie had been found and no harm done, so she could stop feeling guilty about the extra glass or two of wine. And the attention had shifted from her own doings, which weren't being very well received. But she was also disappointed. She had hoped to have a sympathetic hearing from Alice, if not from Mavis, and instead they had both turned prim and disapproving, despite the fact that they were in no position to cast aspersions on Gabs' doings. At least Steph was entitled to the moral high ground since that was more or less where she belonged. Mavis and Alice most certainly were not.

The little party broke up quickly since Mavis wanted to get Maudie home and it was getting late. Mavis and Gabs phoned for taxis, and a date was set for the next meeting.

But if Gabs had anything to do with it, there wouldn't be a next meeting. Not for her, anyway. If she wanted to be lectured, it was cheaper and easier to stay at home and listen to Steph. Sitting glumly in the back of her taxi, ignoring the rather obvious chat-up lines of the driver (who, although he didn't know it, almost certainly couldn't afford her), Gabs dreamed of Father Augustine and planned her next move.

To hell with Alice and Mavis. Gabs had a life to lead.

Part Three

Alice

Alice found the plant behind Finn's bed. It was quite large, but severely pot-bound and badly in need of water. The wilting green leaves were instantly recognisable, and Alice sighed. This was all she needed.

She tackled Finn when he got home from school.

"About your plant," she said, trying to keep her voice even.

"What plant?" Finn was foraging in the fridge. "Is there any cheese?"

"How many plants have you got? The one behind your bed, of course."

"Oh, that plant."

"Yes. That plant."

"Quite pretty, isn't it?" Finn looked shifty.

"No, Finn, it's not especially pretty. And since when have you been interested in plants?"

"Biology project?" said Finn, but without much hope.

"I doubt very much that you'd be asked to grow cannabis as a biology project."

"Oh! Is *that* what it is?"

"Stop playing games with me, Finn. I haven't got the energy."

"Okay." Finn put down the knife he was holding and folded his arms. "I'm looking after it for someone."

"Kenny?"

"No, not Kenny."

"Who, then?"

"I can't tell you."

"You have to tell me."

"I don't *have* to tell you anything."

"Finn, please. I need to know. Like it or not, you're my responsibility. And that includes knowing who gave you that plant."

"If I tell you, do you promise not to get cross?"

"It depends."

"In that case —"

"Okay. I won't get cross. But you must tell me, Finn."

"Right, then. It's Trot's."

"*Trot's?*"

"Yeah. He's gone away for a few days and didn't like to leave it."

"It's not a *pet*! What can he be thinking of?"

Finn shrugged. "He might be away a bit longer. He wasn't sure."

"How dare he! How dare he do something like this, which he knows full well could get you into trouble!"

"You said you wouldn't get cross," said Finn, picking up his knife again.

"Maybe. But this really is the last straw!"

"Well, don't blame me." Finn began cutting slices from a lump of cheese. "It wasn't my idea."

"You could have said no."

But Alice knew that this was unfair. Of course Finn couldn't have said no. Apart from anything else, she imagined that in the world occupied by her son, being asked to look after your father's cannabis plant would be considered incredibly cool. Refusal would hardly be an option.

"He's just experimenting," Finn said. "He's only got the one. You can't do much with one, can you?"

"I've no idea. But I do know that if it's found on our premises, you'll be in trouble."

"Who's going to find it?" asked Finn through a mouthful of sandwich.

"That's not the point."

"Well, what is the point?"

"The point is that you've got a stupid, irresponsible father, who ought to know better."

And to think, Alice thought later on when she'd cooled down a bit, that she had, if only for a few seconds, considered marrying this man. She must have been out of her mind.

That evening, when Finn had gone out (and despite vigorous protest on his part, the plant had been consigned to the dustbin), Alice rang Trot on his mobile.

"Where are you?" she demanded.

"In Ireland. Why? What's up?"

"What are you doing in Ireland?"

"Fishing. Not that it's any concern of yours."

"It is my concern if you decide to leave your — your pet *plant* with our son!"

"Oops."

"Yes. Oops."

"Oh, come on, Alice. There's no need to overreact. It's just a plant."

"It is not just a plant! You are growing an illegal substance, and bringing Finn into it is just not on."

"Blah, blah, blah." Trot had obviously been drinking. "Oh, Alice, you take life so *seriously*. Where's your sense of humour?"

"I'm trying to bring up a teenager. Your son. On my own. I can't always afford to have a sense of humour."

"What have you done with it?"

"Done with what?"

"My plant."

"I've thrown it away, of course."

"You can't do that!"

"I just have."

"I grew that plant from seed!"

"Well, you could say that you grew Finn *from seed*, and you don't seem to worry too much about what happens to him."

"Very funny."

"Believe me, Trot, I'm in no mood to be funny."

"But my plant," Trot wailed. "I wasn't going to use it. It's just that I've become kind of fond of it."

"Well, that's tough," said Alice, and rang off.

She was furious. This was typical of Trot, and she wouldn't have been surprised if he had done it just to annoy her. Trot and a single cannabis plant hardly constituted the basis for a drug cartel, but it was probably another of his little demonstrations to show her how young at heart and open-minded he was — another ruse to gain Finn's admiration. The sympathy and kindness he had shown her so recently were apparently forgotten, and Trot had returned to his previous preoccupations. He hadn't even asked her how she was (although to be fair, she hadn't given him much chance).

Alice got out the remains of a bottle of wine and poured herself a large glass. This was one of the occasions when it would have been nice to be able to phone Jay — to talk about Finn and Trot and their revolting plant, and gain herself a little sympathy. But Jay was probably still at the hospital, or maybe at home with Angela, cosily watching television; or, worse, looking through baby catalogues and choosing nursery furniture. Alice knew very little about Angela, but she imagined her to be the kind of woman who would have a pretty-pretty nursery, with matching everything and tinkly mobiles and a Peter Rabbit frieze.

It would all be very different from when she had had Finn. She had been living in a studio flat — the kind that was ideal for a single career woman, but almost impossible for a mother with a young baby — and while her parents had offered her a bedroom at home, it was too far from work and Alice was too independent. So she and Finn had coped as best they could, Finn sleeping in his very second-hand cot in the corner while Alice typed her articles between feeds. By the time he was crawling, things were becoming difficult, and when he could not only reach the door handle but manage to let himself out onto the landing, life became impossible. Before Alice bought her first tiny house, Finn had contrived to escape and fall down the stairs three times, and the neighbours were threatening to complain to the authorities.

While Alice tried to keep off the subject of the baby when she and Jay were together, Angela was constantly on her mind. Ever since her bout of weeping when she was with Mavis and Gabs, she had been consumed with jealousy. It was as though the green-eyed monster had been let out of the bag, and now there was no getting it back in again. Never hitherto a jealous person, she had been both astonished and ashamed at the strength of her feelings. She had never especially wanted marriage, and she certainly hadn't considered the possibility of more children, but the thought of that baby — that collection of Jay's cells — growing inside another woman was intolerable. Suddenly, the streets were full of women with babies, pregnant women, women pushing buggies. She even found herself wandering into the nursery department of a large store and fingering tiny sleepsuits, miniature shoes, and frilly little dresses.

She told herself to get a grip, that this was ridiculous. She wasn't a particularly maternal person, and while she would always be glad that she had had Finn, she wouldn't have felt incomplete if she'd never had a child. But this was different. This was about Jay, about the man she loved. And it was, quite simply, unbearable.

Would she feel better when the baby was born? When that little bit of Jay had finally exited Angela's body? Alice had no idea. But she wouldn't have that long to wait, since, as Angela had initially put her condition down to the menopause, the pregnancy had been diagnosed relatively late, and there were now only five months to go.

Two nights later she met up with Jay in one of their regular haunts — a rather shoddy pub in the middle of nowhere, with so few customers that it was a miracle that it hadn't closed down altogether. As often happened, Jay was late — some crisis at the hospital had required his attention — and Alice was kept waiting. And while she knew he couldn't help it, she couldn't help resenting the fact that as far as Jay's priorities were concerned, she always seemed to come last.

As soon as he arrived, they made their way over to "their" table (one with a good view of the door, against the unlikely event of the arrival of anyone they knew), and Jay fetched drinks from the near-deserted bar.

"What's up with you?" Alice asked him as he sat down beside her.

"What do you mean, what's up with me?"

"You seem — I don't know — more cheerful than usual," Alice said.

"Well, we've been trying out a new drug on a couple of patients, and so far the results are really promising. They're so young, these two. Only kids, really. It would be wonderful if this could work for them."

"Yes. That's great. Of course it is. But there's something else. I can tell."

"Well…"

"Go on."

"It's the baby. This morning I — I felt it move."

Alice took a very slow, very careful sip of her drink, then replaced it on its stained beer mat.

"How — how nice for you," she said. Someone had written a telephone number on the beer mat in red biro. There was a name beside it. Brett? Ben? Something like that.

"I wasn't going to mention it. After all, what was the point?" Jay said. "But you did ask."

"Yes, I did ask."

"It's hard keeping things from you," Jay said. "I'm afraid you know me too well."

"Yes."

"Oh, Alice! Please don't let this upset you. It has nothing to do with you — with us."

"Well, how do you want me to react? You can hardly expect me to be over the moon, can you?"

"Of course not. I know that would be asking too much."

"Quite." Alice wiped her hands on her skirt. "Anyway, I'd have thought that being a doctor, you'd be more matter-of-fact about — how would you put it? — *foetal movements*."

"I've never had much to do with babies or pregnancy. Not since my training, anyway. Besides, it's different when — when it's…"

"Your own?"

"Well, yes."

Fighting back her tears, Alice remembered Finn's first fragile flutterings — the tiny movements that were only of interest to her, because of course there had been no one else to share them with. Then she thought of Angela — smug, lucky Angela — with Jay's hands on her belly, with Jay to tell her how wonderful it all was, and, no doubt, how clever she was, too.

"It's no good," she said. "I can't. I just can't."

"Can't what?" Jay asked her.

"Can't be pleased, generous, nice — whatever it is you want me to be. I simply can't bear it, Jay!"

"Oh, darling! I'm so sorry." Jay took her hand. "So, so sorry."

"No, you're not. Nor should you be." Alice searched in her bag for a tissue. "Having a baby is — wonderful. Of course it is. But at the moment, it's simply too much to bear." Her throat ached with holding back the tears. "I — I don't know what to do."

"Darling, you don't have to *do* anything. Just be yourself, and we'll go on seeing each other as we've always done. I've told you and told you; this makes no difference to us. None at all."

"But it makes a difference to *me*," Alice whispered. "Can't you see? Your life's going to change, and I'm going to be even more on the outside."

"You've always been on the outside of my marriage. You've said so yourself. But you'll never be on the outside of my life. You're the woman I love, the person I think about, want to be with, *need*."

"Yes. But now you'll be a family. A proper family. I've never been — been a family."

"Of course you have. You are. You and Finn are a family, aren't you?"

"In a way. But it's not the same."

"Drink up, and we'll go and talk in the car," Jay said, downing his beer. "We can't talk properly here."

"You mean I can't cry properly in here," Alice said.

"That too."

In the car, Alice wept and wept. It seemed that nowadays, she spent much of her time weeping, and while she knew it was unfair to inflict her grief on Jay, a part of her felt that he owed her something to atone for the misery his situation was causing her.

"I can't see a way out," she said when the tears had abated.

"There doesn't have to be a way out. No one's going anywhere. Nothing's going to finish."

"Are you sure? Are you sure you're still going to want me when you've got the baby?"

"Darling Alice, I'll always want you. You may give up on me, but I'll never let you go. Not if I can help it. I'd give anything — *anything* — for this to be happening to us. For this to be *our* baby."

"Would you? Would you really?"

"Of course I would! If things had been different and if you'd wanted it, I'd love to have had a baby with you. I can't think of anything more wonderful."

"So — you've thought about this before? About us and babies?"

"Oh, Alice, what do you think? I was in what I thought was a childless marriage, with a woman I didn't — well, with Angela. And then you came into my life, and if things had been different, there would still have been time for us to have a family. Of course I thought about it. I thought about it more than you'll ever know."

"Then why didn't you say something?"

"What would've been the point? We agreed from the beginning that I couldn't leave Angela. So it would have been selfish of me to — to taunt you with what might have been. With what we could never have." He stroked damp strands of hair back from her face and kissed her. "I do love you, you know. So, so much. I wish I could prove to you how much I love you."

Alice rested her head on Jay's shoulder, and for a while they sat in silence, watching the light fading behind the trees and a swirl of rooks cawing their way home across a sky pricked with the first pale stars. Alice felt empty and sad and utterly hopeless. Was her future always going to be like this? Sitting on the edge of Jay's life, listening to him talking (or almost worse, trying not to talk) about his child, waiting, always waiting. And waiting for what? Jay would never leave Angela now, and while Alice had never really expected him to, there had always been that tiny chance that one day, perhaps, Angela and Jay would drift apart naturally, or Angela might even find someone else. But now, whatever happened, the two of them would always be connected by this child.

Scrabbling in her bag for more tissues, she wiped sooty streaks of mascara from her cheeks. She looked a mess, but in the dusk, Jay could barely see her, and Finn probably wouldn't even notice. Besides, he still hadn't forgiven her for "killing" Trot's plant.

"I had a proposal recently," she said.

"*What?*"

"Yes. Trot proposed."

"You never told me! You didn't say yes, did you?"

"Of course I didn't, and I don't think he really meant it, but it would have been a solution, wouldn't it? And you'd be off the hook." She looked at Jay. "Why? Would you have minded?"

"Actually, yes, I would have. Which isn't really fair under the circumstances, is it? But I don't think I could bear it if you... well, if you..."

"If I belonged to someone else?"

"Yes. I'm ashamed to say it, but yes. I know it's not what I deserve, but I don't want anyone else to have you."

"I know what you mean."

Jay rubbed his chin and then ran his fingers through his hair, a characteristic gesture when something was troubling him (although Jay himself was probably quite unaware of it). How well I know this man, Alice thought. I can read his moods as though they were my own; I can frequently anticipate what he's going to say next; I know his likes and his dislikes; I know the feel of him and the smell of him. She wondered whether Angela knew him as well as she did, and while she thought that this must inevitably be the case — after all, they had been married for some years — she very much hoped that it was not. If she were to have any crumbs of comfort at all from this painful situation, she would like to be the one who knew Jay better.

Jay turned to her.

"Alice, we need a night away."

"Just how are we going to manage that?"

"I've got a conference coming up. A big oncology do, with consultants from all over the country. It'll mean a night in Birmingham. Could you come with me?"

Alice considered.

"I suppose I might."

"It's the week after next. The room's sure to be a double — they always are — and it's booked anyway. It won't make any difference to the hotel if you join me."

"Won't other people notice?"

"Not if we get there before the others. It'll mean you'll have to stay in the room, and you can't really come down for meals — I'll have to bring you something — but you won't mind that, will you?"

Alice sighed.

"Yes, Jay, I will mind that. I don't want to be hidden away, using back staircases, avoiding people. I know we've done it before, and it didn't seem so bad then, but I suppose I'm getting past that kind of thing. It feels so — so shabby, somehow."

But in the early days, it hadn't seemed so bad. Unable to get enough of each other, they had grabbed even the smallest of opportunities to be together and to make love. Those occasions had been few enough but, at the time, had seemed heaven-sent. A hotel bedroom with a big, comfortable bed; the luxury not only of sleeping together but of waking up together. On the first occasion, Alice had thought that she could ask for nothing more, and the subterfuge and the lengths they had had to go to to make sure that she kept out of the way of Jay's colleagues had only added to the excitement.

"Then we'll do our usual, shall we?" Jay said.

"I suppose we'll have to."

Nowadays, on the rare occasions when they could have a few hours together, they had resorted to booking a room in some small B&B "for a night." They would usually reach their destination soon after lunch, and then in the early evening, they would pretend that they had received news of some emergency at home, necessitating their immediate departure. Although no one ever appeared to suspect them of any subterfuge — why should they? — Alice invariably felt embarrassed, guiltily aware of rumpled sheets and damp towels in the bathroom. And of course they had had to pay for the full night as arranged, not to mention breakfast, so it was a costly exercise. But as things were, it was the best they could manage.

This was only a little less sleazy than the conference scenario, but at least both of them were in it together and on an equal basis. No one was being left hiding in a bedroom, being brought sandwiches like some kind of hostage, or being let out when the coast was clear. The only problem was that they were beginning to run out of venues and were having to travel ever farther afield in search of new ones.

And then of course there were the lies she had to tell Finn. Alice hated lying to anyone, particularly her son, but it seemed that lies were another part of the adultery package; it was impossible to conduct an affair such as hers without lies.

When she got home later on, Finn was sprawled on the living-room floor watching television.

"Where've you been?" he asked. "I'm ravenous."

"Editorial meeting. I told you." Alice took off her jacket. "And I left you something in the fridge."

"I had that hours ago. By the way, Trot rang."

"Oh yes?"

"He was asking about his plant. Said could you ring him."

"Trot knows about his bloody plant! And no, I won't ring him. I've got better things to do than run around after Trot."

"That's what I told him." Finn got up and stretched. "Cup of tea?"

"Please."

Finn always ended his sulks with offers of tea, and Alice was grateful. At least one of her relationships was back on track.

"Did you know," said Finn as he dropped teabags into mugs, "that the only thing that stops us from going rotten is being alive?"

"Well, fancy that," said Alice. And she actually laughed.

Mavis

Mavis had known for some time about the wedding, but had filed the information away at the back of her mind. She knew that when she retrieved it and considered it properly, she would find it very painful, and so she had decided to postpone the pain for as long as possible.

But now, she could no longer ignore it. Clifford's elder daughter, Kate, was to be married in a fortnight's time, and the subject was, inevitably, much on Clifford's mind. If she loved Clifford — and at the moment, she thought that she probably did — then Mavis must try to be generous and allow him to talk about it.

"Is it going to be a big wedding?" she asked him, aware that this was something she might have been expected to ask some time ago.

"About a hundred," Clifford told her. "And more for the evening do."

Mavis had never understood the thinking behind "evening dos." If she were young and newly married, she would want to drive off — preferably in an open-topped car, with her hair flying in the wind (impossible, as Mavis had always worn her hair short) — leaving her guests behind, waving and cheering her on her way. But people didn't do that anymore. Instead, the dignity of the occasions seemed to degenerate gradually as the day wore on, ending sometime after midnight with a drunken bride shimmying among her guests and begging the exhausted band to stay on for just one more dance. Mavis had been to several such weddings and had reflected that, apart from anything else, the happy couple would be in no fit state to travel the next day.

"It's costing a packet," said Clifford now (Clifford could be quite mean on occasions). "I can't think why the bridegroom can't chip in."

"At least you're not having to provide a dowry," Mavis told him, picturing Clifford collecting together a small herd of cows and goats, and perhaps some gold coins as well, to be delivered to his daughter's new family.

"Well, it feels like it," Clifford grumbled.

"And the speech. Have you written that yet?" Mavis asked.

"Oh yes. I did that ages ago. I'm quite looking forward to it, actually." Clifford liked being the centre of attention.

"I hope it's not too long." Mavis hated long speeches.

"Funny. That's what Kate said. Short and clean were her orders."

"I suppose the dirty jokes are for the best man," Mavis said.

"Not if I can help it," said Clifford.

The two weeks between this conversation and the wedding proved quite extraordinarily difficult for Mavis. While she tried to keep her mind engaged with other matters, her thoughts would keep returning to Clifford and his family. Clifford himself was understandably preoccupied, and while it was obvious that he was making an effort to keep off the subject, it was inevitable that it should crop up. Meanwhile, Mavis's imagination ran riot. She pictured Dorothy (as much as it is possible to picture someone you've never met) busying herself with guest lists and table plans, with flowers and dresses and last-minute cancellations. She imagined the bride, too. How was she feeling? Were there any last-minute doubts? And how many people harbouring such doubts went through with the wedding anyway? Mavis could see that weddings gathered a momentum all of their own, and that as they accelerated towards the actual day, it must become increasingly hard to stop them. Mavis had had a friend who had called her wedding off on the actual morning of the wedding, and while Mavis had been full of admiration for what had seemed to her to be a most courageous decision, the girl's parents hadn't spoken to their daughter for months afterwards. Weddings, it would seem, didn't just belong to the couple in question; they became the property of anyone who had an interest, vested or otherwise, and as such had the potential to wound (or delight) a great many people.

On the morning of the wedding, Mavis woke early. She imagined the bride having breakfast in bed and then luxuriating in a bath full of fragrant bubbles, while everyone bustled around her doing — what? What was there to do on the morning of a wedding? Mavis had no idea, since she imagined that most of the things that needed to be done would be well in hand by now, but she was sure there must be last-minute things — a final alteration, perhaps (Dorothy kneeling on the floor, her mouth full of pins, doing something to a hem?), the attentions of a hairdresser, and perhaps someone to attend to make-up.

And Clifford, what would he be doing? Mavis imagined him bumbling about, getting in the way, before it was time for him too to get ready — perhaps doing a last-minute run-through of his speech, getting dressed, maybe asking Dorothy to fasten or adjust something. *Dorothy.* Jealousy spread through Mavis in a sudden wave, taking her by surprise (she was not normally given to jealousy). Weddings brought families closer, didn't they, so if ever Clifford was to feel close to Dorothy, it would be on a day such as this, an occasion in which Mavis could never play any part. She gritted her teeth. Just let this wedding be over, she thought. Just let it be *over.* In just twelve hours' time, the whole thing would be finished, everything would return to normal, and Clifford would be hers once more.

Afterwards, Mavis realised that she had always intended to see the wedding, although it was only during that last fortnight that she had acknowledged the fact. This was a big day in Clifford's life, and while she couldn't exactly share it, she meant to be there. She had no illusions about how she would feel; she knew that it would be difficult. But apart from anything else, she was curious. She wanted to watch the guests arriving, to see the bride, and most important of all, Dorothy. Mavis had never seen Clifford's wife, and this was the ideal opportunity. Of course, Dorothy would be looking her best — as the mother of the bride, that was her job — and in any case she was bound to be far more glamorous than Mavis herself (most women were), but Mavis still wanted to see her. She wouldn't have put it so vulgarly as to say that she was eyeing up the opposition, but that was what it amounted to.

Once before, Mavis had tried to see Dorothy. She had taken a taxi out to Clifford's home, which was some miles away, and had spent a morning hovering outside. She knew that the family weren't away and she felt sure that Dorothy must go out at some stage, but although she had waited for two hours, no one had either entered or left the building.

The house itself was a substantial Victorian building, attractive in an ugly kind of way, with what appeared to be a substantial garden. Mavis had glimpsed a washing line to one side and found herself trying to examine the garments to see if they could tell her anything about their owners. She thought she recognised a couple of shirts of Clifford's, and there were children's dresses and shorts, and a lot of underwear, including several pairs of stout, no-nonsense women's knickers. Mavis was enormously cheered by the knickers, which looked quite large. Did that mean that Dorothy was fatter than she was? Oh, please let Dorothy be fat! Even a little bit fat. Then she could be as beautiful as she liked, if only Mavis (who had always been quite slim) might be allowed the better figure.

Mavis was careful to ascertain from Clifford the whereabouts of the church where the wedding was to be held without actually seeking directions. Whatever happened, she didn't want him to guess what she was going to do, and she even mentioned plans for that weekend so that he would think she was going to be busy. By dint of asking several vague questions and then phoning the vicarage pretending that she was a guest who had lost her invitation, she managed to obtain the information she needed.

It was a grey, billowy day in early June. The forecast had been good, but the sun had yet to make an appearance, and Mavis was relieved. It meant that she could cover herself up without looking too eccentric, and to this end she dressed in an old raincoat, headscarf, and dark glasses. She must have resembled a wounded celebrity hiding from the paparazzi, but she achieved the desired effect. A careful examination of her reflection in the mirror before she left home reassured her that, short of wearing fancy dress, she was as unrecognisable as it was possible to be.

She arrived at her destination in good time and positioned herself discreetly on the other side of the road, with a good view of the church. No one appeared to pay any attention to her. People always stop to look at a wedding, and several others had paused in small groups to watch and gossip. She was just another onlooker, another outsider.

As she watched the guests arriving at the church, she was overwhelmed with a sense of such isolation that it made her catch her breath. The embraces, the laughter, the excited chatter, and the anticipation were all going on just across the road, and here she was, Clifford's lover, the woman who only a few days ago had been performing the most intimate of acts with him, feeling as though she were a spectator from another world. This was a family in celebratory mode, doing what families do best — everybody happy, any cracks carefully papered over for the occasion, and all to be photographed for posterity.

Dorothy was instantly recognisable — a great mountain of a woman, swathed in apple green silk, a complicated arrangement of tulle and feathers trembling on her head as though overcome by the importance of its role in the proceedings. Her large, rather pale face was not unlike Clifford's, and Mavis wondered briefly whether married couples, like dogs and their owners, came to resemble each other over time. Dorothy seemed to tower over the other guests, who had parted before her like the Red Sea, and when she reached the porch, she busied herself tweaking and smoothing the small bridesmaids who were waiting there, her large hands waving and gesticulating importantly. Watching her, Mavis wondered that Clifford had ever had the courage to breach the more intimate areas of such a fortress, and she felt for him. Poor Clifford. No wonder his sexual advances had been so timid in their early days together. Dorothy looked like the kind of female who would be more likely to consume her partner after intercourse than to cherish him. No wonder, too, that Clifford was such an expert in the field of male helplessness, for who would need to be capable with a large bossy Dorothy to put him right (Dorothy had always seemed to Mavis to be a particularly bossy name).

As Mavis watched Dorothy finally disappearing into the gloom of the church, she spared a thought for the bridegroom. If appearances were anything to go by, it was going to take a brave man to stand up to a mother-in-law such as this one.

But all thoughts of Dorothy instantly left her as the bridal car drew up at the church gate.

No one could describe Clifford as handsome, but he was one of those men who could look truly distinguished when the occasion demanded it, and this occasion demanded nothing less. The morning suit, the new haircut, the gold tie matching the yellow roses and — honeysuckle, was it? — in the bride's bouquet, all combined to give him a sleekness and elegance that Mavis had never seen before. As he handed his daughter out of the car, Mavis was reminded of all the occasions when he had done the same for her, and for a moment, her feelings of isolation were compounded by grief — grief for her solitary state, grief for the smiles and the affection between father and daughter, and for the first and only time, grief for the daughter she herself would never have.

Kate was tall, handsome rather than pretty, and going by the tendrils escaping from her headdress, Mavis noted that she was the redhead of the playground all those years ago. The wedding dress was nice enough, but it looked to Mavis like all wedding dresses: it was white, and there was far too much of it. Mavis had never understood why it was that brides should wear on their wedding day dresses that were, to all intents and purposes, fancy dress — something they would never dream of wearing in the ordinary run of things and would almost certainly never wear again. She recalled poor Princess Diana — such a pretty girl — emerging from her coach so enveloped in *that dress* that she looked as though she were struggling out of an enormous wedding cake. No doubt she would have had to take half a dozen attendants with her every time she needed the lavatory. It didn't bear thinking about. If Mavis had ever married (and during her brief engagement, she had had time to give the matter some thought), she would have worn something long and pretty, but definitely not white. White suited very few people, and it certainly didn't suit Mavis.

When the wedding party had disappeared from view and the church door had safely closed behind them, Mavis crossed the road, and taking her courage in her hands, she walked up the church path. The sun was struggling out from behind the clouds, bringing to life the warm stone of the church itself, and a fresh grave, still covered with bouquets of wilting flowers, was a stark reminder of another rite of passage marked within this ancient building. The churchyard seemed strangely quiet and empty after the bustle and noise of a few minutes ago, and Mavis could hear the sound of traffic from the distant motorway and the insistent call of a cuckoo.

She lingered under a window, listening to the strains of the organ, to the distant murmur of voices and the singing of hymns, imagining the solemn vows, the muted joy, the hats, the flowers. Did young couples making these promises realise how big a commitment it was to which they were pledging themselves? So often, she had heard the familiar words of the marriage service, had listened to people glibly (or so it seemed to her) promising to stay together till death should intervene, and had wondered whether the thought of death really occurred to them at all. No doubt Clifford had once made similar vows in a church such as this, almost certainly in all sincerity. Mavis hoped very much that Kate would prove more successful than her father at keeping her promises.

By the time the marriage ceremony was over and the church bells had started ringing, Mavis was safely back on the other side of the road in the shade of a plane tree (the sun was becoming quite hot). The church doors opened again, and the wedding party spilled out blinking into the sunlight, milling about, laughing and chatting, forming and re-forming in their various groups to be photographed. After a while, cars started to arrive, confetti was thrown, and guests began to move on (presumably to the reception). It was time for Mavis to go home.

That evening, making supper for herself and Maudie, Mavis tried to analyse her feelings about the day. It had certainly been painful, and she hadn't enjoyed the experience. But on balance, she was glad that she had been there. So much of Clifford's life was a closed book to her; now, at least she had had this small glimpse of that other Clifford, the husband (albeit a cheating one) and father, the Clifford whom she could never really know.

A few days later, Mavis and Clifford were speaking on the telephone.

"Well? How did it go?" Mavis asked, trying to inject some enthusiasm into her voice.

"How did what go?" Clifford's tone was surly.

"The wedding, of course."

"Well, you tell me."

"What do you mean by that?" Mavis asked.

"What do you think I mean?"

"I wish you wouldn't do this," said Mavis, infuriated.

"Do what?"

"Answer a question with a question. Speak in riddles."

"Well, let me put it this way. You are in a better position than I am to judge how the wedding went."

"Oh, don't be ridiculous, Clifford! How can I possibly —"

"You were there. You saw it. *You* tell *me*."

"Oh."

"Yes. Oh."

"I wasn't *there*. I wasn't a *guest*. You can't blame me for — for wanting to see it."

"I would call it spying. It was sneaky, Mavis. It's not what I expect from you."

"Well, what *do* you expect from me? It was a very important day in your life, and I wanted to see you. Is that so awful?"

"Yes. I'd say it is. Lurking under the trees like that."

"I wasn't *lurking* like anything! I was trying to be inconspicuous, and I think I succeeded."

"Not inconspicuous enough," said Clifford.

"Oh. So what would you like me to have done? Worn a mask? Would that have been inconspicuous enough for you?"

"A mask might have been an improvement, certainly. But what I would really have liked was for you not to have been there at all. You had no place there, Mavis. No right."

"I had every right! It's a public place. I have as much right as anyone to stand on a pavement."

"If you say so."

"Cliff, please, let's not have another row," Mavis said. "It's such a waste of time. Of *our* time."

"Well, if you will pull silly stunts like this, what do you expect?"

Since she was the very last person who could ever have been accused of pulling 'silly stunts', Mavis actually laughed.

"It's not funny, Mavis."

"No, of course not." Mavis hesitated. "Cliff, can I ask you something?"

"I suppose so."

"How did you know it was me?"

"Your shoes."

"My *shoes*?"

"Those awful old flat shoes. I'd know them anywhere."

"I'll remember that for next time," said Mavis boldly, thinking that Clifford must have amazing eyesight to be able to recognise a pair of shoes at such a distance.

"You do that."

"So, can we put this silly argument behind us now?"

"I suppose we'll have to."

"I'll take that as a yes, then." Mavis decided to change the subject. "How's the heart?"

As she knew, Clifford couldn't resist an invitation to discourse on what was currently his favourite subject, and he launched eagerly into an account of each little ache and pain, every little dose from his puffer, and the necessity of taking aspirin for the rest of his life. There followed a long (and unnecessary) account of the dangers of even the smallest amount of aspirin taken on an empty stomach, because of the risk of ulcers. Mavis knew that Clifford's stomach was rarely empty, but forbore to point this out. However, she cursed the doctor for even suggesting the possibility of yet another medical condition, since this would only add further fuel to the already flourishing fire that was Clifford's hypochondria. However, she appeared to have been forgiven (even if she considered that there had been nothing to forgive), and that at least was something.

"May I see the photographs?" she asked when they were about to ring off.

"What photographs?"

"The wedding photos, of course. I'd love to see them, Cliff. Just one or two."

"Well, yes, I suppose so," said Clifford graciously. "I don't see why you shouldn't see just one or two."

"You looked — really handsome."

"Thank you." Clifford's voice positively glowed.

"I'm looking forward to seeing you next week." Mavis hesitated. "Perhaps with the photos?"

"I'm sure there'll be some photos by next week. I'll try to remember to bring them."

Well, that was all right in the end, Mavis thought as she replaced the receiver, although Clifford was becoming very sensitive these days. It could just be that his conscience was bothering him. This happened from time to time, and on these occasions, Mavis always had to tread carefully.

She went in search of Maudie, who wasn't where Mavis had left her, and found her stuffing a pile of underwear into the fridge.

"Mother, what *are* you doing?" she asked her.

"Just putting on a spot of washing, dear." Maudie poked a vest in between two milk bottles. "But there doesn't seem to be much room in this machine."

Mavis sighed. Maudie was getting worse, and she wondered just how long she would be able to continue to look after her and whether, when the time came, she could bear to let her go into a home.

"Would you like to move sometime, Mother?" she asked casually, rescuing some stockings from behind a joint of pork. "To a nice place with lots of other people to talk to?"

Maudie eyed her beadily.

"I'm not going into a home," she said. "I like living here, with you. You like it too, don't you, Mavis?"

Mavis kissed her powdery cheek. "Of course I do, Mum. You know I do."

"That's all right, then," said Maudie comfortably. "What are we having for our tea? Are we having that nice piece of pork?"

"You mean the piece that was in the washing machine?"

"Don't be silly, dear," said Maudie. "Sometimes I wonder about you, Mavis. I really do."

Gabs

Gabs was unhappy.

This was an unusual state of mind for Gabs, and she was at a loss as to how to handle it. Normally hers was a sanguine temperament, and she could usually cope with such vagaries as life threw at her with humour and competence. But her obsession with Father Augustine was beginning to take over her life, and it was making her miserable.

At first, if she was honest, the whole thing had been a bit of a lark. Okay, she had fancied him madly and had even imagined herself to be in love with him, but if he had disappeared from her life altogether, she would have got over it.

Now, however, it was different. She had contrived to see him on several more occasions, and while he was always friendly, he was also distant. Father Augustine had his boundaries, and Gabs had not yet managed to find a way past them. And yet there was an attraction; she knew there was. Gabs' behaviour might be foolish, but her instincts were usually right, and she was sure that Father Augustine was attracted to her. On a couple of occasions, he had looked as though he were about to say something and then appeared to have thought better of it, and Gabs suspected that the words that Father Augustine had thought better of were the ones she wanted to hear. People tend to "think better" of the truth, and if the truth was that Father Augustine returned Gabs' feelings, if only a tiny bit, then Gabs wanted to hear it.

Her other problem was that there really was no one she could talk to about it. Steph was being moody and rather distant, and in any case, she had made her feelings quite clear on the subject. Alice and Mavis hadn't been exactly helpful, either. And there wasn't anyone else. Gabs had friends, but they tended to be breezy good-timers — the kinds of friends who were fine for a night out and a few drinks and a gossip, but not much use in a crisis.

Was this a crisis? At times, it certainly felt like one, but then as her mother would have said, "no one's died". (Gabs' mother had, in fact, done just that, leaving her ill-tempered and wayward husband to finish bringing up their two daughters. This he had done with minimal effort and no enthusiasm, and the girls, for once in complete agreement, had left home at the earliest opportunity.)

Up until now, Gabs had reckoned that she knew all about love and that, when it happened to her, she would know just how to handle it. What she had never realised was that it could be so unbearably painful. When she saw Father Augustine, there was an ache in her solar plexus that was physical and that (oddly) had nothing whatever to do with sex and everything to do with longing simply to be with him. She continued to attend Mass, but her attendance was irregular, since she didn't want to appear too predictable. She had also managed to arrange a one-to-one meeting at the presbytery, but this had been less than satisfactory, since Father Augustine had kept the conversation strictly to the subject of God and Gabs' soul, and since Gabs felt that she no longer had much interest in either, there had been very little to say.

"Don't you ever have doubts, Father?" she had asked, hoping to steer the conversation away from herself.

"Everyone has doubts," Father Augustine had replied. "It's part of the cross we have to bear. But prayer, Gabs — that's what helps. Prayer. I can lend you an excellent little book."

He had got up from his chair and fetched down a well-worn volume from the bookcase.

"Here. Read this. I'm sure it will help you."

Gabs had taken the book, managing to brush Father Augustine's fingers with her own as she took it from him, but he had appeared not to notice.

"Shall I — do you think I ought to come back?" she had asked him as she was leaving.

Father Augustine had smiled at her. "I don't think that will be necessary," he had said, and in that instant, she knew that he understood perfectly what her intentions had been, and Gabs, who was normally a stranger to embarrassment, had actually blushed.

But she wouldn't give up. Gabs had never yet given up the pursuit of something she wanted, and she wasn't going to start now. She would bide her time. Sooner or later, something would happen to facilitate a positive outcome to her plans, and she was prepared to wait.

Fortunately for Father Augustine (if not for anyone else), something happened to take Gabs' mind off matters of the heart, for it transpired that she was not the only one with a problem.

"Gabs, can I talk to you?" Steph asked her one evening shortly after her meeting with Father Augustine.

"Course you can." Gabs yanked off her unseasonal thigh-length boots and stretched out on the sofa. "Fire away."

"Oh, Gabs! My period's late."

"Your period's late," Gabs repeated. For most girls, a late period was serious; a late period meant trouble. But for Steph — well, a late period was just that. A late period. "What's the worry?" she asked now. She noticed a ladder in her tights and wondered whether Steph would lend her a pair. "It's happened before, hasn't it?"

"No. Never."

"Well, one thing's for sure: you can't be pregnant."

"Can't I?"

Gabs sat up and looked at her sister. Steph looked very pale and very frightened.

"Well, you tell me." Gabs laughed. "Come on, Steph. You of all people. No. You can't be pregnant."

"Gabs, can you get pregnant without — without — *you know*?"

"Well, 'you know' certainly helps if you *want* to get pregnant."

"Please don't laugh at me."

"I'm not laughing at you. But, Steph, this is ridiculous. What exactly have you done?"

Steph fiddled with the buttons on her blouse. "I guess I went a bit too far."

"Who with? When?" This was certainly news to Gabs.

"That time you did my make-up for me — remember? I got talking to this — this boy from church, and he asked me out. We've seen each other a few times since then. And then about a month ago, we went to a party. I had a couple of drinks. Well, more than a couple of drinks, actually."

"And?" prompted Gabs.

"And afterwards, in his car, he — we did things." Steph looked up. "We didn't go the whole way, Gabs. You have to believe me."

"Oh, I believe you," said Gabs, thinking that her sister must be the last person on the planet to use such an old-fashioned expression. "And it's no business of mine if you did."

"But he — he did things to me. It was my fault. I shouldn't have let him, and I did stop him before…" Her voice trailed away. "But now — now…"

"Your period's late."

"Yes."

"And he didn't use a condom?"

"Of course not." Steph looked shocked.

No. Of course not, Gabs thought furiously. Steph was a good little Catholic; she wouldn't dream of using a contraceptive, would she? After all, it was a mortal sin. Gabs was overcome with sudden rage at the boy — man — whoever he was, who would take advantage of the poor innocent who was her sister.

"Look, Steph," she said, "you have to tell me exactly what you — what he — did. We need to establish that before we can decide what to do next."

So Steph told her. Her account of the events of the evening in question was so cloaked in euphemisms that only someone who knew her very well could have had any idea what she was talking about, but when she'd finished, Gabs reckoned that she might just possibly be pregnant. If she were, she had been incredibly unlucky, but where reproduction was concerned, Gabs knew that luck very rarely seemed to play much of a part. How typical of her sister it would be if she had actually contrived to achieve that rarest of phenomena: a virgin birth.

"Have you done a test?" Gabs asked her.

"What kind of test?"

"Oh, Steph! A pregnancy test, of course."

"No. I thought I'd talk to you first."

"Well, we'll do one now."

"Can't we wait?" Steph pleaded. "Just for a day or two?"

"No. We can't wait. This needs to be sorted as soon as possible."

"But —"

"No buts. I'll give you a kit."

"You mean — you mean you've got one?"

"I've got one." Gabs forbore to point out that in her calling, it would be a foolish woman who wasn't prepared for all eventualities. "Come on. It's quite simple. I give you a little stick, you pee on it, and Bob's your uncle."

"How can you be so cheerful?"

"No point in being anything else," said Gabs, who was in fact feeling very far from cheerful. "Come on."

As Gabs had feared, the test was positive.

"Oh no, *oh no*," Steph sobbed, rocking back and forth in her chair. "It can't be. It just can't."

"It can and it is." Gabs sat down and put her arms around her sister. "But it's very early, and we'll sort it. Don't worry."

"What do you mean?" Steph raised a tear-stained face and gazed at Gabs. "How can we — sort it?"

"You'll have an abortion, of course. And don't worry about the money. I can help with that. And of course, I'll come with you."

"An *abortion*?"

"Yes. An abortion. Steph, it's the only answer. You can't afford a child — you aren't ready for one — and it's quite straightforward at this early stage. You leave everything to me."

But even as she spoke, Gabs knew that she was in for a battle, for a girl who wouldn't dream of using a contraceptive was hardly going to take kindly to the idea of a termination.

"I can't," Steph wept. "I simply can't. It's taking a life. A human life. It's — it's murder!"

"Oh, for goodness' sake! Don't be so ridiculous," Gabs said. "It's just a few cells. No more human than — than that plant over there."

Steph gazed at the rather spindly spider plant that languished, unloved and unwatered, on the sideboard, and shook her head.

"You don't understand," she said.

"Oh, I understand all right," said Gabs grimly. "You're prepared to throw your life away for something that, right now, barely exists. Something that mightn't come to anything anyway. The bloody Catholic Church has a lot to answer for."

"This isn't about the church. It's about me. My conscience," Steph said. "But of course you wouldn't know anything about that, would you? I don't think you've ever had one. A life is a life. It doesn't matter how small it is. It still deserves a chance."

The age-old argument raged back and forth, complete with all its clichés: Gabs citing the woman's right to choose and the little bundle of cells; Steph countering that size wasn't important, it was the fact that it was human that mattered.

"So," said Gabs finally, "you're going to have this child, are you? And how exactly do you propose to manage? What about your job? What about money? And the father — are you going to tell him? What part is he going to play in this — this mess?"

"Oh. I hadn't thought," said Steph.

"No. So it seems. And you didn't think when you had those drinks and got into that car and took off your knickers for this — this *man* of yours."

"I didn't take off my knickers for anyone!"

"Well, if you didn't, it'll be some kind of first. A knickers-on conception must be something of a rarity."

"Gabs, I wish you wouldn't talk like that!"

"This," said Gabs tightly, "is no time to be prudish."

"No. You're right."

"Okay. First, let's get this child's father involved. You're going to need all the help you can get."

"He's — he's not around anymore."

"What do you mean, he's not around? Has he died? Emigrated?"

"No. But we finished it. It wasn't really going anywhere."

"Well, it is now. You're going to be parents, and he needs to play his part."

"Oh no, Gabs. Please. I don't want him to know. I don't want anyone to know."

Gabs resisted the urge to shake her sister.

"Steph, this is a real situation with real problems. You can't bury your head in the sand and pretend it's not happening. If you're determined to keep this child — and I still think you're mad — then you have to tell its father. You *have* to. Now, who is he?"

"He's — it's Clive," Steph whispered.

"Great."

This really was the icing on the cake. Wispy Clive, of the lanky limbs and the frightened, helpless expression; Clive, who had grown from a skinny altar boy into an equally skinny and unprepossessing young man; Clive, with the downy cheeks that somehow refused to sprout anything resembling a proper grown-up beard, and the traces of the acne that had dogged his adolescence. How on earth had he managed it?

"I know," said Steph, reading Gabs' expression. "But I really liked him. Well, I did for a while. And I trusted him."

"But you don't like him anymore."

"No. Not really, and that makes it so much worse, doesn't it? Because I always wanted to save — *that* — for someone special."

"No good crying over spilt milk," said Gabs, thinking that spilt milk was a great deal easier to deal with than spilt other things. "I know," she said with sudden inspiration, "Father Augustine. I'm sure he'll have some ideas. He's a good listener, and he seems pretty unshockable. I'm sure it would help you to talk to a priest."

Steph looked at her suspiciously. "Are you sure it's not you who wants to see Father Augustine?" she asked.

"Oh no," said Gabs airily. "That's all in the past. A foolish aberration."

"Well, I suppose that's something."

"Yes."

Gabs wondered what it was that had led her to lie so smoothly to Steph. She certainly hadn't meant to, since despite their differences, the two of them rarely kept secrets from each other. But she knew that if Steph suspected that she still had designs on Father Augustine, she would insist on seeing him on her own, and Gabs was desperate for any opportunity that might bring her into contact with him, even if the focus were to be on someone else.

Father Augustine was very kind. He was non-judgemental and sympathetic — in fact, all the things that the Catholic Church isn't supposed to be in the face of sexual immorality or its fallout — and he listened carefully to everything Steph had to say.

"Well, Steph, this isn't going to be easy," he told her. "But you've made the right decision. Too many people just get rid of their unplanned babies these days, forgetting that there's no such thing as an unwanted child."

"But Steph didn't want this one," Gabs pointed out.

Father Augustine turned a disappointed gaze on Gabs. "Steph may not want this baby now, but I'm sure she will when it arrives. And if she doesn't, there are many families who long for children and can't have them — good Catholic families."

"Oh, *please*," muttered Gabs.

"What was that you said, Gabs?"

"Nothing. But I can't believe you expect Steph to go through all this, have the baby, and then give it away!"

"I'm not suggesting anything of the sort, but it is an option that she can consider."

"I suppose so."

"Now —" Father Augustine steepled his fingers and smiled over them at Steph — "what's the next step?"

"I don't know. That's why I came to you."

"Well, I think you should tell the baby's father. He has a right to know."

"That's what I told her," said Gabs, who could see her tally of brownie points dwindling during this interview, and wanted to give them a small boost. "He deserves to know."

Steph looked at her suspiciously, but Gabs maintained an open, sympathetic expression and refused to meet her sister's eyes.

"Well, then, that's what you should do first. And see how much support he'll give you. I'm not suggesting you marry him — not at this stage, anyway. But get him involved."

Gabs tried to imagine weedy, useless Clive being "involved" with a baby — pushing a pram, changing a nappy, and doing all the other things modern fathers are supposed to do so well — and failed utterly.

"I'm not sure he'd be a lot of help," she said.

"But he should be given the opportunity," said Father Augustine firmly. "Is he a Catholic?"

"Yes," Steph said.

"Excellent." Father Augustine smiled again.

Oh, what wouldn't Gabs have given to have that smile directed at her! So far, Father Augustine seemed to be doing his best to ignore her. And besides, why was it excellent that Clive was a Catholic? Was Father Augustine really pleased to discover that he had two fornicating Catholics on his hands rather than just one?

"Yes." Steph sounded doubtful.

"And when you've told him, the two of you can come and see me together. How would that be?"

"I don't know."

"Well, never mind. We'll leave that for the time being. One step at a time." Father Augustine stood up. "I'm afraid I have to be somewhere else in fifteen minutes, but in the meantime, you've got Gabs to help you, and that's a blessing, isn't it? And always remember: I'm here if you need me."

On the way home, while Steph prattled away about how much better she felt and how wonderful it was to have a church to turn to in times of stress, all Gabs could think about was Father Augustine: Father Augustine's words (he'd actually called her "a blessing" — had he meant Gabs herself, or the *fact* of Gabs, the fact that Steph had a sister?) and those parting words to Steph: *he would always be there if she needed him*. Oh, lucky Steph! Did she have any idea how fortunate she was? She now had carte blanche to visit Father Augustine anytime she wanted, while Gabs, who loved him so much, had no excuse at all. Briefly, she wondered whether it might even be worth getting pregnant in order to have nine months of support from Father Augustine, but she dismissed the idea. There were some sacrifices that were not worth making, even for a reward such as this one.

"I think I'll leave telling Clive for a while," Steph was saying. "Just until I've got used to the idea myself. Then perhaps we could tell him together. Would you mind doing that, Gabs? I don't think I could do it on my own, but with you there, I might manage it. Gabs? *Gabs*! I don't think you've heard a word I've been saying!"

"Of course I have." Gabs dragged her thoughts away from her reveries and patted Steph's shoulder. "And you're going to be just fine."

"You've certainly changed your tune!"

"Well, if I can't dissuade you, then I'll have to support you, won't I?"

"Oh, Gabs! Father Augustine was right. You really are a blessing."

Gabs grinned at her. "Yes, aren't I?"

The Third Meeting: June

It was Gabs who had suggested the picnic, and at the time, it had seemed a good idea. The weather was warm, and there was a pleasant park within fairly easy reach of all of them. It would make a nice change from their indoor meetings and would exonerate anyone (Gabs herself, as it happened; it was her turn) from playing host. Everyone could contribute food, and Gabs said she'd bring some wine. Mavis herself would take a flask of coffee. And, rather unfortunately, Maudie.

A friend had said she might be able to sit with Maudie, but at the last minute she phoned to say that she couldn't make it.

"I'm sorry, Mavis," she said, "but I have to be honest with you. It's that cat. He doesn't like me."

"He doesn't like anybody," Mavis said. "I'll shut him in my bedroom. He'll be fine."

"You did that last time, and your mother let him out."

"Just keep an eye on her. The cat will be all right. His bark's worse than his bite."

"That's what you say, but last time, he ruined a new sweater and scratched me quite badly. And all without, as you put it, barking."

"So that means you won't be coming anymore?"

"Oh, I'm very happy to visit you both. You know that. I'd hate to lose touch altogether. But I can't sit with Maudie anymore." There was an apologetic pause. "You know how it is."

Looking at Pussolini now, lurking at the top of the stairs and batting at imaginary prey with extended claws (should she get them cut? Would anybody dare?), Mavis had to admit that he was getting worse and that nowadays he more or less ruled the roost. He hid behind things and on top of things, and pounced on unsuspecting visitors, emitting *big cat* noises and generally finding entertainment at the expense of unsuspecting visitors. He never attacked Maudie, whom he adored, and knew better than to take on Mavis, who was responsible for feeding him, but anyone else was seen as fair game.

Mavis had tried seeking advice about his increasingly feral habits, but the vet had been no help at all.

"He must have been mistreated at some time in his life," he said. "He just needs a bit of understanding."

"Oh, I understand him perfectly," Mavis told him. "He's a thoroughly evil animal."

"I don't believe there's any such thing," said the vet.

"You'll be suggesting counselling next."

"Well, you may joke, but there are people who do that kind of thing. Animal behavioural psychologists."

"Who are very expensive, I don't doubt," said Mavis, who thought that Pussolini would make mincemeat of anyone who tried to get inside his nasty little brain.

"Quite possibly."

So Pussolini lived on, uncounselled and uncontrollable. If she had had her own way, Mavis would have had him put down, but Maudie loved him, and Mavis couldn't bring herself to do it. There was little enough in Maudie's increasingly narrow existence, and she was generally so undemanding. The least Mavis could do was put up with her cat. But this meant that soon she herself would be a prisoner in her own home, for while Maudie usually behaved perfectly when she was at work, she became particularly confused in the evenings and couldn't really be left.

So Maudie would have to come on the picnic.

Gabs and Alice didn't appear to object to Maudie's status as honorary club member, and it had been a beautiful warm day, so Mavis gathered together her contributions (sandwiches and hard-boiled eggs), dressed her mother up in suitable clothing (Maudie had recently taken to spending all day in her nightie), and phoned for a taxi. The evening might not be so bad after all.

There were still quite a lot of people in the park making the most of the evening sunshine: teenagers flirting and messing about on the swings, couples strolling hand-in-hand, men in suits on their way home from work. Mavis was the last to arrive, and Gabs and Alice had already laid out rugs on the grass and opened a bottle of wine.

"Come and have a drink," said Gabs, helping Mavis to set up the picnic chair she'd brought along for Maudie.

"Thanks." Mavis put down her bags. "I'm not quite sure what to do about Mother. There's no telly for her to watch, and it wouldn't be appropriate for her to — well, to hear what we say, would it?"

"Not to worry. She can borrow my iPod," said Gabs, fishing it out of her bag. "Here, Maudie. Have a listen to this." She removed Maudie's hearing aid and plugged her in. "What do you think?" she asked her.

"I can't hear you," said Maudie. "Someone's put something in my ears."

"It's music," Gabs shouted.

"What did you say, dear?"

"*Music!*"

"I can't hear you, dear. I'm listening to this music." Maudie helped herself to a sandwich and tapped her foot in time to whatever it was she was listening to.

"Well, that seems to be okay," said Mavis, relieved. "Thank you, Gabs."

"You're welcome."

This was always the awkward moment: the few minutes before things had warmed up, and everyone was waiting for someone else to start talking. They didn't really see enough of each other, Mavis thought, peeling an egg for Maudie. The three of them still weren't completely at ease with one another. They were all so very different, with nothing in common but their relationships. She noticed that Gabs was already on her second glass of wine, and Alice seemed rather quiet. Perhaps she should speak first?

"Well, I've had an interesting time," she began, feeling oddly shy. "Clifford's daughter got married two weeks ago."

"Oh goodness! Poor you!" Alice immediately seemed to perk up. "How did you feel about it?"

"Awful."

"I bet you did. And did you go?"

How good it was to be with people who understood, people who could see that she couldn't possibly have missed this wedding. Suddenly Mavis felt as though her mental corsets had been unlaced, and she breathed a sigh of relief. "Yes, I did."

"Did Clifford find out?" Gabs asked.

"Yes. He noticed my shoes."

"Your shoes!" Gabs rocked with laughter. "They must have been pretty special."

"Well, that's the odd thing. They weren't. In fact, he was rather rude about them."

"Silly bugger," said Gabs cheerfully.

"Yes, he is a silly bugger sometimes," said Mavis, enjoying the sound of this unaccustomed word as it rolled off her lips. "A very silly bugger."

"Language, Mavis," said Maudie, who had disengaged the iPod. Gabs popped it back in again.

"And?" Alice asked. "What did he say?"

"Oh, the usual. I was sneaky. I was spying. That kind of thing."

"Well, of course you were. You could hardly pretend to be a guest."

"That's what I told him."

"And his wife — what's her name — did you see her?"

"Dorothy. Yes, I did."

"And what's she like?"

"Very large, and absolutely terrifying."

"No threat there, then," said Gabs, feeding Maudie pieces of fruit cake.

"Well, not that sort of threat. No. Except that she is married to Clifford. But I wouldn't want to get on the wrong side of her."

Mavis recalled the spectacle of Dorothy as she left the church, dwarfing everyone around her, including Clifford. Even her handbag had been enormous — a proper *Importance of Being Earnest* handbag — and Mavis wondered again what could have been inside it. Apart from a handkerchief and perhaps a lipstick, what else would the mother of the bride need to carry with her? She pictured packets of safety pins, a spare pair of knickers, perhaps even a Swiss Army knife. The importance of being Dorothy. Mavis giggled at the thought.

"Come on, Mavis," Gabs said. "Share the joke."

So Mavis shared the joke, and was gratified to find that the others were amused (Mavis wasn't usually very good at jokes). She then went on to describe the rest of Dorothy, from the trembling headpiece down to the vast shoes (size eight? possibly even nine?), and afterwards she felt a very great deal better. All these thoughts had been tumbling about in her head since the wedding, desperate to get out, and it was the first time she'd been able to put them into words.

Maudie interrupted with an observation.

"Michael Jackson," she said through a mouthful of cake.

"You're right. It is Michael Jackson." Gabs looked impressed. "How does she know that?"

"She watches a lot of television," Mavis told her. "She picks up all kinds of things."

"They did something funny to his nose," Maudie continued. "Doesn't suit him." She hummed along, tapping her foot and cramming more cake into her mouth. Mavis was ashamed of Maudie's manners, which, like the rest of Maudie, had deteriorated recently, but no one seemed to mind.

"She's lovely, your mum," Gabs said. "Mine died when I was a kid."

"Oh, I'm so sorry." Mavis was mortified that they had known each other for all these months, and yet she didn't know that Gabs had no mother.

"Don't be." Gabs poured herself more wine. "It was a long time ago, and my dad treated her like shit, so in a way she was better off out of it. But it must be nice to have a mum. Even if, well, even if…"

"She's not all there?" Mavis helped her out.

"Yeah. But she's a sweetie. And she's right about Michael Jackson's nose."

Listening to Mavis's account of the wedding, Alice had a strong sense of fellow feeling. The two of them might be very different, but they were both living their lives in the shadows of other people's marriages, and it was an uncomfortable place to be.

"I've never seen Angela," she said now. "I did think of it — of doing what you did, Mavis. Sort of hanging around outside the house and — well, spying, I suppose. But I never did."

"But when the baby's born?" Gabs asked. "How about then? Won't you want to see her — oh, I don't know — pushing a pram or something?"

"I know I'll be tempted. I've even wondered if I might be able to blag my way into the hospital pretending to be a sister or maybe a friend, just so that I can see the baby. But they'd never let me in, and besides, what would it achieve?"

"And how is the baby?" Gabs asked.

"Moving," Alice told her.

"Oh dear."

In spite of her relative youth, Gabs seemed to understand her feelings much better than she might have imagined, and Alice was grateful.

"I love Jay, so I should be happy for him, but I simply can't be. The more excited he is, the more miserable I become." She plucked a daisy from the grass and began stripping off the petals (he loves me, he loves me not. He loves me, but is there room for me and a baby?). "I wonder whether anyone is ever really happy *for* someone else?"

"No. It's a myth," Gabs said. "It's what people say when what they really mean is 'you're happy, and I know I ought to be too, but I'm not. And if it's something I want, the happier you become, the more nasty and jealous I'll be.'"

Alice laughed. "That more or less sums it up," she said. She picked more daisies and started making a daisy chain. "Angela's having another scan next week. They'll find out whether it's a boy or a girl."

"Oh dear," Gabs said again.

"Yes."

Somehow the baby would be much more real when it had a gender; when half its options had been excluded, and it became baby-pink or baby-blue; when it began to have a real identity, and probably even a name.

"Which would you prefer it to be?" Mavis asked. "Boy or girl?"

"I don't know." Alice tried to imagine Jay with a daughter (Daddy's girl) and then a son ("my boy"—she could almost hear Jay saying the words). "I've got a son, so it would sort of even things up. But then I think I'd be more jealous of a daughter. I can see Jay going all soppy over a baby girl."

"Talking of boys, how's your gorgeous son?" Gabs asked. "And don't look at me like that. It's not my fault if he finds me irresistible."

"Finn's fine," Alice said. "We had a bit of a row about a cannabis plant, but that seems to have blown over."

"What, the row or the plant?"

"Both."

"What's cannabis like?" Mavis asked. "I've always wanted to know."

"D'you want to try some?" Gabs asked.

"Heavens, no!"

"Why not? I think I've got some somewhere." She searched in her bag and retrieved a small white envelope. "Here. I'll roll you a joint, and you can have a try."

"But I don't even smoke!"

"Doesn't matter. Just take it easy."

"Suppose someone sees me?"

"No one will see you. Trust me."

"But I've heard it's got a distinctive smell. Someone might — might —"

"Smell it?"

"Well, yes."

"Live a little, Mavis. You're a long time dead."

Alice watched in amusement as Gabs burned a small piece of resin with her cigarette lighter, collected up the resulting fragments, and mixed them with tobacco. She sealed the cigarette paper with a tongue that was pointed, almost catlike, and rolled it into a neat cigarette. Alice's own pot-smoking days were brief and a long time ago, but she remembered them with affection. Now she came to think about it, cannabis could well have played a part in the creation of Finn.

"Could I have a try, Gabs?" she said. "For old times' sake?"

"We'll all have one."

Gabs lit the first joint, took a deep drag, and then handed it to Mavis.

"There you go, Mavis. Take it slowly."

Mavis took the cigarette and sniffed it gingerly.

"Are you sure it's safe?" she said.

"Quite safe."

Mavis placed the cigarette between her lips, where it wobbled unsteadily.

"You'll have to breathe deeper than that," Gabs said. "Look. Like this."

Mavis did as she was told, and after a brief fit of coughing ("perfectly normal; it'll pass," said Gabs), she appeared to get the hang of it. The others watched her with interest.

"Well?" Gabs said after a few minutes. "What do you think?"

"Nice," Mavis beamed. "I'd no idea this would be so nice. Whoops." She dropped her joint and fumbled in the grass to retrieve it.

"I told you you'd like it, Mavis," Gabs said. "Alice? Here's yours."

They smoked their joints, and then Gabs rolled them all another. People milled around them, but apart from one or two odd glances, seemed to take little notice. A dog came up to them, sniffing curiously, and for a moment Mavis wondered whether it might arouse suspicion, but after a brief investigation, it dashed off in pursuit of a pigeon.

Alice lay back on the rug, smoking and gazing up at the evening sky through a dapple of leaves. A tiny aeroplane crossed her field of vision, leaving a vapour trail. Alice tried to say the words "vapour trail" and found that she couldn't. She also found that she didn't care. She felt her back and shoulders relaxing into the ground beneath her; she heard the chatter of birds and the hum of traffic and smelled the scent of crushed grass. She could feel the fragile feathery strands of her daisy chain between her fingers. Her senses were heightened and yet dulled. The feeling was quite delicious. She no longer cared about Jay's baby — he could have all the babies he wanted — or Angela, or the bitchy editor who'd been on her case about a late article. All she needed was this evening, this park, these lovely people.

"A piece of pipe," she said, propping herself on her elbow and taking a sip of her wine.

"What?" Gabs asked.

"A piece of pipe. No. Pipe of peace. That's the one. That's what I mean. This — " she waved her cigarette — "is like smoking a pipe of peace."

"Piece of pipe!" Mavis started to giggle. "Piece of pipe. Pipe of peace. Very funny, Alice."

"It's not *that* funny," said Gabs.

"It's hilar— hilar— very funny," Mavis insisted. Her face had gone a deep red, and she was giggling uncontrollably.

"Oh, well. If you say so."

Alice lay down again. The sky was beginning to darken, and it looked as though it might rain. "It might rain," she said. The words felt heavy as they formed in her mouth, and she had trouble delivering them. It was not so much like speaking the words as giving birth to them. She pushed them out, one by one. "It. Might. Rain." That was better.

"So you said." Gabs was pouring wine for Maudie. She seemed unaffected by her cigarette.

"Mother shouldn't have a drink," Mavis said. "She's on pills."

"Just a tiny one. One tiny one won't hurt her," said Gabs.

"Mother's ruin." Mavis hooted with laughter. "*My* mother's ruin."

"Gin's Mother's ruin, not wine," said Gabs.

"Gin. Wine. Doesn't matter."

"Mavis, I think perhaps you've had enough," Gabs said. "It doesn't mix too well with alcohol, and you've had quite a bit."

She reached out to take Mavis's cigarette, but Mavis pulled her hand away. "Spoilsport," she said, taking another deep lungful of smoke. "Gabs is a spoilsport. Gabs is a spoilsport," she chanted, looking to Alice for support.

Alice looked lazily back at her and winked. Poor old Mavis. She was probably having the best time she'd had in ages. That Clifford of hers sounded ghastly, and while Maudie was, as Gabs said, a sweetie, a confused and incontinent sweetie must sometimes make a difficult companion.

"Gabs isn't a spoilsport," she said carefully. "But she has a… she has a…"

"Point?" said Gabs.

"Yep. One of those."

Mavis pouted and muttered and poured herself more wine. Maudie, who had been asleep for some time, gave a little snore, and the plastic bag, concealed up until now, appeared to have slipped its mooring, and landed with a gentle thump on the grass beside her. Alice noticed that it seemed rather full and wondered by what means it could be emptied.

"Not my problem," she said aloud.

"What isn't?" Gabs asked.

"Maudie's bag." Alice pointed. "It's — it's *arrived*."

"Bugger," said Gabs. "Oh, well, it'll probably last until she gets home." She looked at Mavis, who was now lying down and looking rather sick. "*If* she gets home."

Gabs was becoming seriously worried. Alice was right. Rain did indeed appear to be imminent, and meanwhile she seemed to be the only one in any state to take the initiative. Maudie was still asleep, Mavis was vomiting copiously into a patch of long grass, and Alice was humming tunelessly as she helped herself to yet more wine.

And it was all Gabs' fault. She was the one who'd been topping up everyone's glasses and rolling joints, and she was the one who should have seen this coming. Gabs herself was used to headier combinations of drugs and alcohol and was largely unaffected, but she should have known better than to introduce it to the others.

"Come on, guys. Time to get going." She began collecting up the glasses and putting away the picnic things. "*Come* on, Alice. You at least can help me."

"I could," said Alice dreamily. "Of course I could, but…" She rolled over onto her stomach, resting her head on her arms. "I like it here."

"Well, you can't stay here all night. Any of you. And what about Maudie? She'll catch her death."

"How can you catch death? Such an odd expression."

"Alice! Get up!"

"What if I don't?"

"I'll pour the rest of this bottle all over you." Gabs brandished the last of the wine and was appalled to see that they'd got through nearly three bottles. "Come on. I'm not kidding."

"Go right ahead. I don't care." Alice rolled onto her back again, and Gabs emptied the bottle of wine onto her face.

"Bloody hell! What d'you do that for?" Alice sat up and wiped wine from her eyes and mouth. "You silly cow!"

"You can thank your lucky stars it wasn't red, and at least it's woken you up. That's something. Now, help me get the others on their feet. We need to get going."

"How?" Alice appeared to have come to her senses. "Can't drive, can I?"

"Not my problem."

"Well, what about Mavis?"

Gabs looked at Mavis, who was in no state to travel in a taxi, never mind take care of Maudie.

"D'you know anyone with a car?" she asked.

"I thought you had one."

"I came by taxi, because of the drinking. Don't you know anyone who might fetch us?"

Alice considered. "Well, there's Trot."

"Trot?"

"Finn's father. I told you. He prop— proposed." Alice giggled. "Trot *proposed*!"

"Never mind that. Has he got a car?"

"Well, he had a car. May have sold it."

"Could you at least phone him?"

"I suppose I *could*…"

Gabs gave Alice a little shake. "Come on, Alice. It looks like this Trot is our only hope."

Gabs was furious with herself and everyone else. If she had only herself to consider, she could just phone for a taxi and go home, but she felt some responsibility for what had happened and she could hardly abandon the others to a chilly night in the park. It seemed that it was up to her to get them home, and if Alice's friend would fetch them, so much the better.

She reached for Alice's bag and retrieved her mobile. She managed to find Trot's number without much difficulty and moved away from the others to make the call.

"Hey! Alice!" A man's voice answered after several rings. "To what do I owe this pleasure?"

"This isn't going to be a pleasure, I assure you," Gabs told him. "Are you Trot?"

"Who is this? Who's speaking?"

"Long story," said Gabs. "No time to go into it. Now, can you fetch Alice and some — some friends and take us home? We're in a bit of a fix."

"What kind of a fix?"

"Never mind that. You'll find out when you get here."

"How do I know you're not a thief who's stolen Alice's handbag, and you're trying to use me as a getaway car?"

"You'll just have to trust me."

"Mm. That's more easily said than done. I —"

"Look. This is an emergency. Are you going to help us or aren't you?"

"Why can't Alice speak to me herself?"

"She's — she's not well."

"Drunk?"

"Kind of."

"Ah." There was a lengthy pause. Gabs was dying to put on the pressure, but she didn't want to lose what might well be their only chance of a lift home. "Anything to identify her? I need to know who I'm rescuing."

"Well, she's — hang on a minute — she's wearing a plain gold chain round her neck, and a ring with a bluish stone on her little finger."

"That'll be Alice." Another pause. "I've only got a van."

"She said you had a car!"

"Sold it and bought a van. There's more room in a van."

"Yes. There would be."

"So, do you want me or don't you?"

If it was a van or nothing, then it had to be a van. "Yes, please."

"Where are you?"

Gabs explained.

"Bloody hell! That's miles away!"

"Do you want the mother of your son to die of exposure?"

"Well, since you put it like that, I suppose I'd better come and fetch you."

"That would be kind."

"Yes."

"Well, d'you think you could get going, then? It's starting to rain, and we're getting cold."

"Yeah. Okay. I'm on my way."

By the time Trot eventually arrived, they were all cold and wet. Alice still seemed largely unaware of the situation, Mavis was being sick again, and Maudie was shivering and singing "Auld Lang Syne". To be fair to Trot, he appeared to sum up the situation fairly quickly and didn't ask too many questions. Alice didn't seem particularly pleased to see him, but that, Gabs reckoned, was tough. The important thing was that they now had wheels and a good chance of getting home tonight.

Fortunately, they weren't too far from the road, and together they managed to convey Alice and Mavis to the van, where, with some difficulty, they stowed them in the back among a pile of canvases, some fishing gear, and, oddly, something that resembled a Greek urn.

Maudie was more of a problem.

"Come on, Maudie. Time to go home," said Gabs, attempting to help her out of her chair. "Give me a hand, will you, Trot?"

"Who are you?" Maudie looked suspiciously at Trot. "Not going anywhere with a stranger. Anything might happen."

"Well, if you don't let this stranger drive you home, you'll have to stay here," said Gabs.

"Shall we carry her?" Trot asked.

"I suppose we could try." There was quite a lot of Maudie.

"What on earth's this?" Trot held up Maudie's plastic bag, and Maudie gave a squeak of pain.

"Don't pull that! It's attached to her," Gabs said. "Give it here."

"But what is it?"

"For fuck's sake, what do you think it is?" Gabs took the bag, which was by now very full indeed. Gabs wondered briefly whether she should empty it, but decided against it. They needed to get Maudie out of the rain, and she didn't trust Alice and Mavis in the van on their own. "Now stop asking stupid questions and grab hold of her top half."

"Leave my tits alone!" Maudie yelled as Trot tried to get a purchase on her upper body.

"Well, can you walk, then?" Gabs asked her.

"Course I can," Maudie said. "But I'm not going with *him*."

"But you'll come with me, won't you? You know me."

"Bad girl?"

"That's me. Now, up you get — that's the way — and we'll go and find this van. You carry the bag," she told Trot, "but stay close as it pulls a bit."

"Right you are." Trot followed Gabs and Maudie, holding the bag as though it were an unexploded bomb (which by now was more or less what it was).

After some time (and more rain), they reached the van.

"She'd better go in the front," said Gabs.

Together they manhandled Maudie's substantial backside into the passenger seat, followed by her legs and the bag.

"You're good at this, aren't you?" Trot said when she was safely belted in.

"Do it for a living," said Gabs.

"What, stuffing old ladies into vans?"

"Caring for the elderly."

"Bit of a waste, isn't it?" Trot remarked.

"Waste of what?"

"Of your assets." He looked at her appraisingly.

"You leave my assets out of this. Let's get going."

The journey home was long and uncomfortable. Gabs, Mavis, and Alice were crammed together in the back of the van among the clutter and the fishing gear, bouncing around uncomfortably and toppling into one another every time the van turned a corner. Maudie, her spirits much revived, was singing something rude, and Trot was cursing the lot of them. All Gabs could think of was that soon she would be home in her own comfortable bed, and this nightmare of an evening would finally be over. The only thing she had to be thankful for was that the evening's discussion didn't get round to her, because while she had been looking forward to offloading the problem of Steph's pregnancy, she hadn't been prepared to undergo further censure over her feelings for Father Augustine.

They dropped Alice off first and watched her tottering towards her front door.

"She'll be okay," Trot said. "I'll give her a ring tomorrow to make sure."

Mavis and Maudie were next. By now, Maudie appeared to have nodded off, and Mavis was asleep with her head in the Greek urn. Gabs herself was stiff and uncomfortable and longing for a cigarette. She shuffled towards the front of the van so that Trot could hear her.

"Mind if I smoke?"

"Be my guest. I'll have one too, if you've got one to spare."

Gabs lit a cigarette and passed it through to Trot.

"Thanks," Trot said. "What do you really do?" he asked.

"What do you mean?"

"For a living. What do you really do for a living?"

"Oh, this and that. But I do look after old people as well."

"Ever thought of being a model?"

"No, thanks. Anyway, I'm not tall enough."

"Are you — have you got a boyfriend?"

"That would be telling."

"You mean, mind my own business?"

"Something like that."

"Then I apologise."

"No problem." Gabs drew on her cigarette. "So, you're Finn's dad?"

"That's right."

"He's a nice boy."

"Yeah. Finn's okay." Trot stopped at a traffic light and flicked cigarette ash out of the window. "He was what you might call a one-night-stand baby."

"So I gather."

"How did you meet Alice?"

"Shared interests," said Gabs.

"Alice never seems to have time for any interests," Trot said. "Finn says she told him she was a member of a book group, but he doesn't believe her."

"*War and Peace*," said Gabs.

"What?"

"*War and Peace*. That's the book we've been reading."

"If you say so."

"I do."

At this point they reached the road where Mavis lived, and Trot pulled up by the kerb. With some difficulty, they woke Mavis and Maudie and managed to get them out of the van. By now, Mavis was coming to her senses and had become maudlin and apologetic.

"I'm sorry, I'm so sorry," she said, wobbling up the garden path on Gabs' arm. "What — what must you think of me?"

"Never mind that," Gabs said. "Now, keys. You need your keys, Mavis."

Mavis fumbled in her bag.

"Give it here." Gabs took the bag, found the keys, and unlocked the front door. "There you go," she said.

There was a loud hissing sound, and an angry ball of fur hurled itself at Gabs and attached itself to her shoulder, biting and scratching.

"Bloody hell!" Gabs lashed out at her assailant, stabbing it with the front door key. There was an indignant yowl, and the ball of fur detached itself and streaked up the stairs. "What the fuck was that?"

"The cat. Mother's cat. So — so sorry. So sorry," said Mavis.

"So you keep saying. Sorry's all very well, but that animal's a liability. It ought to be put down before it really hurts someone." Gabs got out a tissue and wiped blood from her neck. "Fucking thing!"

She and Trot settled Mavis and Maudie in their living room and made a quick getaway.

"Thank goodness that's over," said Gabs as they made their way back towards the van. "What an evening!"

"Where do you live?" Trot asked.

"It's okay. I'll get a taxi the rest of the way," Gabs told him.

"But it's no trouble." Trot grinned. "It'll be a pleasure."

"That's what I'm afraid of. No. I'll see myself home."

"Don't you trust me?"

"Nope."

"Well, that's great. After all the trouble I've been to this evening!"

Gabs patted him on the cheek. "You've been a very good boy, and I'm grateful, but now it's time to go home."

"And I suppose I can't see you again?"

"That's right. You can't."

In the back of the taxi, Gabs stretched out her legs and breathed a sigh of relief. If she never saw Alice and Mavis again, it'd be too soon.

Part Four

Alice

Finn was gloating.

It was only very rarely that he managed to attain the moral high ground, and now that he was there, he showed little inclination to vacate it. It didn't take long for Alice to decide that a sulking teenager — which was the kind she was more accustomed to—was infinitely preferable to this new, self-righteous one.

"You were stoned!" he crowed. "My mother was stoned! How cool is that?"

"Leave it, can't you, Finn?" Two days after the event, Alice was still feeling tired and very foolish. "Okay. So I was stupid. But can we let it go now?"

"Let it go? Oh no! This is too good to let go. And Trot says that after what you did to his plant, he —"

"You've been discussing this with Trot?"

"Course I have. After all, he rescued you. If it wasn't for Trot, you'd still be staggering round that park."

"He told you that, did he?"

"Yeah. He thinks it's hilarious."

"Oh, does he?"

"He's told all his friends."

"How sweet."

"Yeah. He says he wonders whether you're fit to be a mother."

"So he's going to take you on, is he?"

"Well, he didn't exactly say that."

"I bet he didn't."

"Oh, come on, Mum. Where's your sense of humour?"

"You're beginning to sound just like him."

"Well, Trot likes a laugh. Nothing wrong with that."

"Provided it's at someone else's expense."

"I had to put you to bed," Finn said.

"Finn, you took off my shoes. That hardly constitutes putting me to bed."

"Sounds good, though, doesn't it?" Finn grinned.

"No, it does not. And now, if you'll just leave me alone, you could perhaps do some homework and I can finish this article."

Aside from her adventure in the park with Mavis and Gabs, Alice was having problems at work. The colour supplement for which she worked was struggling, there had been several redundancies, and an increasing amount of work was being given to those who remained. Alice had hitherto written features, but now she found herself in charge of 'Beauty' as well.

"Beauty? I don't know anything about beauty!" she'd said when her editor had informed her of the decision.

"Then find out. You're a journalist. Finding out's what journalists do. We're all having to adapt."

"But I like features. They're what I'm good at," Alice had wailed.

"That's just as well, because you'll still be doing features. These are difficult times, Alice. We're all having to work harder. You're lucky to have a job at all."

So Alice was now officially Beauty Editor.

Beauty. Sucking her pencil, Alice reckoned that the very least of her readers probably knew more about beauty than she did, and no doubt cared more, too. She surveyed the pile of make-up samples that had been sent by various companies for her to try, and wondered what on earth she was supposed to do with them. She herself wore little make-up, relying on her clear complexion and nice eyes (she had been told that she had pretty eyes, and it suited her to believe it) to do the work for her. As for exfoliating and facial scrubs, she had never tried either.

Who did she know who might be able to help?

Within five minutes, she was on the phone to Gabs.

"I need help," she told her.

"More weed?" suggested Gabs, who sounded in excellent spirits.

"No, definitely not more weed. But I need advice about make-up. I've got all these samples, and I have to write about them, and I haven't a clue."

"I'm your woman," said Gabs. "Want me to come round?"

"Oh, would you?"

"Sure. No problem."

"Haven't you got — work?"

"Nearly finished." There was a barking noise in the background.

"Have you got a dog?" Alice asked.

"Not exactly," said Gabs. "That's right, Gerald. Die for the queen. Good boy. Mummy's on the phone. She won't be a minute."

"You *have* got a dog!"

"It's complicated." Gabs lowered her voice. "I'll tell you later. Gotta go. I'll be round in an hour."

When Gabs saw all Alice's samples, she was beside herself.

"You got all this stuff free? You lucky cow." She picked up a lipstick. "D'you know how much one of these costs?"

"Well, I've got it written down somewhere."

"Twenty-five quid! Twenty-five quid for a lipstick! Mind if I try it?"

"In a minute. I need to do this methodically. Now, cleanser. Would you mind having a go with this?"

"Sure." Gabs sat down in front of the mirror and removed her make-up with a pinkish solution in a rather fetching woman-shaped bottle. "Mm. This is quite good. Not as good as mine, though. You got another?"

Alice handed her another. And another.

Then there were the foundations, the concealers, the blushers, the eyeliners.

"Are you writing about all this at once?" Gabs was applying navy eyeshadow, and Alice wondered idly why it was the women — herself included — always opened their mouths when applying eye make-up.

"Not all at once. This week it's skincare. But if I watch you doing it and you try them all out, then I can make notes, and I won't have to ask you back."

"Oh, don't worry about that. I'm happy to play with make-up anytime. You know, this would suit you." She showed Alice a shimmery green eyeshadow. "Why don't you give it a try?"

"Would you — I mean, would you mind showing me how to do it properly? I always just slap it on, but you do it so well."

"Love to. Come and sit here where the light's better."

By the time Finn came home from school an hour later, Alice had been exfoliated, cleansed, and made up to Gabs' satisfaction (and her own astonishment).

"I don't believe I'm seeing this." Finn leaned in the doorway, watching them. "First my mother gets stoned in the park, and now she and a friend are painting each other's faces. Something to do with *War and Peace*, is it?" He sniggered. "*War paint*. Geddit?"

"Finn! Don't be so rude!"

"Oh, I don't mind." Gabs winked at Finn, and Alice wondered whether her flirtatiousness was deliberate or whether she simply couldn't help it. "Doesn't your mum look great?"

"She's okay. Would you — would you like a cup of tea?"

"Please. Isn't he just the sweetest?" Gabs said when Finn had gone to make the tea.

"Only when he thinks there's something in it for him," Alice said.

"What a shame I'm not ten years younger."

Alice thought it was a very good thing that she wasn't but forbore to say so. She was fond of Gabs — it was difficult not to be — but she wouldn't want her involved with Finn.

"Who — what was that dog I heard?" she asked as Gabs put the finishing touches to her face.

"That was a client." Gabs applied a final layer of mascara to Alice's lashes.

"You have a client who *barks*?"

"Yeah. That's what turns him on."

"And you don't mind?"

"Why should I? He's the one who's paying. It's his call."

"I still don't really understand why you do it, Gabs. There must be so many other jobs you could do."

"None that pay as well, though. And I quite enjoy it. It makes the clients happy, and I'm not hurting anyone."

"Except the wives."

"You sound like Father Cuthbert. Anyway, the wives never find out. It's not like you and your bloke. These guys don't *love* me. Some of them think they do, but it never lasts. They soon get over it. And it gives their marriages a little boost. It's a win-win, isn't it?"

"I suppose so."

"Each to her own, eh?"

Finn returned with a tray of tea (Alice didn't know they even possessed a tray), and the conversation turned to more mundane things.

"You got a girlfriend?" Gabs asked him.

"Nope."

"Good-looking boy like you — I'm surprised."

Alice gave her a warning look.

"Okay, okay." Gabs laughed. "I just hate waste."

"Is there anything else I can get you?" Finn asked. "A biscuit?"

"No biscuit, thanks. Have to watch my figure," Gabs said.

The cue for a compliment — had it been deliberate? — hung in the air but remained unanswered, and Alice was relieved. Apparently even Finn had his limits.

"What about you and Father Whatsit? How's the plan going?" Alice asked when Finn had left the room.

"Augustine. Father Augustine." Gabs sighed. "Not well. I've done all I can short of stripping off and showing him my assets."

"So you're giving up?"

"Oh no. I never give up."

"Why doesn't that surprise me?"

"Do I look that ruthless?"

"More — determined, I'd say. So, what are you going to do?"

"I'm going to bide my time. Not much else I can do, is there? But you mark my words, Alice. I'll get there in the end. I always do."

"What — always?"

"Yep. Always." Gabs lay back on Alice's bed and rested her head on her arms. "But for now, I've got other things on my mind."

"Like what?"

"My sister's pregnant."

"Your holy sister?"

"That's the one."

"Goodness!"

"Quite. It seems to have been a sort of virgin conception. You could say it was a miracle, but not quite the kind Steph usually goes for."

"Oh dear. What's she going to do?"

"The silly cow's going to have the baby."

"And you don't approve?"

"Nope. But it doesn't matter what I think." Gabs paused. "Did you ever think of — of not having Finn?"

"Oh yes."

"But?"

"I guess I was a coward. And by the time I really faced up to it, it was getting a bit late."

"And you don't regret it?"

"Sometimes." Alice laughed. "But no, I don't regret it. And as it turns out, it was my only chance of motherhood. I never really thought about children before I had Finn, but I think I'd feel — impoverished now if I'd never had a child."

"I'm not having kids," Gabs said. "Far too much hassle."

"Not even Father Augustine's kid?"

"Ah. Father Augustine's kid… That might be different. Especially if it had his eyes."

"Gabs, you're incorrigible."

"So I've been told."

Later on, when they were having their evening meal, Finn asked Alice why she and Gabs were friends.

"She's so not your usual type," he said.

"What is my usual type?"

"Oh, you know. A bit posh, interested in politics and things. Not sexy, like her."

As it happened, Alice wasn't particularly interested in politics, but she read the papers and watched Panorama, and that was probably what Finn meant. And it was true. Gabs certainly wasn't the kind of person she would have made friends with in the usual way, but circumstances had thrown them together, and on the whole, Alice was grateful. The evening in the park had been a bit of a disaster, but no one had forced her to smoke or to drink so much. In retrospect, it had been quite fun, although she wouldn't care to repeat the experience.

The following week, Alice had a date with Jay.

She had been dreading this, because by now Angela would have had her scan, and in spite of herself, she wanted to know all about it. It made no sense; it would be like poking a stick into a wound to see how much it would hurt, and she knew this was going to hurt a lot. But she also knew she had to do it.

They had been together for nearly an hour and were sitting chatting in Jay's car when she finally asked.

"Well? How was the scan?"

"You really want to know?" There was a mixture of anxiety and relief in Jay's voice.

"Of course I want to know. It's a big part of your life. You can't just keep everything about the baby — well, secret. After all, I tell you things about Finn."

"Well, it's the right size for the dates. All its organs appear normal. There are no problems."

"And?"

"And what?"

"What is it? Boy or girl?"

"Oh, Alice! It's a girl!" There was no mistaking the joy in Jay's voice. "I didn't know I wanted a girl until we found she was — is — a girl."

"But you know now?"

"Yes."

Alice thought miserably that, until now, she hadn't realised how much she *didn't* want this baby to be a girl. A baby girl; pink and frilly and vulnerable; twisting Daddy round her little finger. She imagined Jay with his daughter in his arms, carrying her on his shoulders, holding her hand on the way to school, comforting her over her first heartbreak, giving her away on her wedding day. Jay and his daughter. Whatever happened to Jay's marriage, his daughter would be there for keeps.

"Are you painting the nursery pink?"

"Well, as a matter of fact, we — oh, Alice! I didn't want to talk about this, but you did ask."

"Yes, I did ask."

"And now?"

"And now, as you've said so many times, we just carry on."

"I'm so glad you see it like that." Jay took her in his arms. "Thank you for being so generous, so, well, *accepting*. It'll make things — us — so much easier."

For you, thought Alice, returning his embrace. *It'll make things easier for you.* For herself, she felt only a dull sense of misery. For whatever Jay might say, things would never be the same again. How could they be? From now on, he would be juggling three women instead of two, and she knew who was most likely to be the loser.

"I expect you've got a photo. Of the scan," she said now.

"I think I have," Jay said. "They gave us each one at the hospital. But I'm sure you don't want to see it. After all, they all look the same at this stage, don't they?"

"No. I'll see it. I — I'd like to see it." After all, she might as well start now. In due course there would, no doubt, be other photos: baby photos, toddler photos, school photos. Perhaps if she saw enough of them, she would eventually become immune to the pain.

Jay got out his wallet and produced a grainy grey photo, and he was right. It looked more or less identical to every prenatal photograph Alice had ever seen. And yet she found herself examining it carefully. The dome of a head, a face half-hidden by a tiny arm, a curve of belly, miniature knees. Alice scrutinised the picture but could find nothing particularly significant. She handed it back.

"I told you," Jay said, replacing the photo. "They might have been scanning anyone's baby. I certainly wouldn't have known the difference."

"There's no need to sound like that," Alice said.

"Like what?"

"As though you couldn't care less. Jay, this is your baby. Your daughter. Of course you think the photo's special. How could you not?"

"Well, okay then. We do, but I don't expect anyone else to be interested."

We. There had been no "we" when Alice had had Finn. She remembered the photo of her own scan — the wonder and excitement with which she had gazed at it. But there had been sadness, too, because there had been no one to share it with, and her mother ("very nice, dear. Which way up is it?") hadn't been at all the same. She still had that photo stuck in an old medical folder somewhere. It hadn't seen the light of day in years, but Alice thought that when she got home, she would look it out and perhaps show it to Finn. Even at that early stage, his manhood had been in no doubt. That at least ought to please him.

"Are you all right?" Jay asked her. They had left the car and were walking along a canal bank. It was a beautiful summer's evening, and they had brought glasses and a bottle of wine.

"Yes."

"You don't seem yourself."

"Don't I?"

"No. Come on, Alice. It's the first time we've been able to spend an evening together for ages. Try to — oh, I don't know. Try to be a *bit* happy."

"I can't. I just can't. I'm sorry. I don't want to spoil our time together, but I've never been any good at pretending."

"Alice, darling. If it's the baby, it was you who started all this, asking about the scan, discussing the photo. I was quite prepared not to talk about babies at all."

"How can we not talk about babies when I'm sure you spend a lot of your time thinking about yours? Of course you're preoccupied with it; how could you not be? And if it's a big part of your life, then I have to accept it and share a bit of it. Otherwise our relationship isn't *real*."

Jay spread his jacket on the grass and sat down. "Why do you have to make everything so complicated?" he asked. "Why can't you just enjoy us — our relationship — and leave my home life out of it? I very rarely talk about it myself, but you keep bringing it up."

Alice sat down beside him, hugging her knees and looking out over the muddy brown water. A pair of swans glided serenely past, and she wondered whether these beautiful birds, which were supposed to mate for life, were ever tempted to stray.

"I'm not *making* things complicated; they just are," she said. "We can't take our time together out of its context and pretend that everyone and everything else doesn't matter."

"We've managed so far."

"We've never had to face anything as big as this before. Besides, you're a man. You can pigeonhole me neatly away when we're not together. With me, it's different. You — you *leak* into all the other areas of my life. I can't get away from you."

"Do you want to?"

"Yes, in a way. Then this wouldn't hurt so much."

Jay uncorked the wine and poured them each a glass, and for a while, they were silent. Eventually he spoke.

"Alice, the last thing I want to do is cause you pain. You know that. But with the best will in the world, it's inevitable. And I have no more control over this situation than you do." He rescued an insect from his wine glass and released it into the grass. "I want the baby — of course I do — because she's mine. My daughter. I can't *not* want my own child. But Angela… Angela's different." He sighed. "I wouldn't choose to spend the rest of my life with Angela. But now I have to. I have to stay on and make the best of things."

"Did you really feel you had a choice before?"

"In a way, yes. Before the baby, I had a — well, I had an escape route, I suppose. The fact that I could give up on my marriage if it really came to it made it possible to carry on. I've had patients who've told me they would never seriously consider suicide, but they know it's there if they ever need it. Of course, this isn't suicide — nothing like it — but it's the opportunity for a way out, a choice."

"You've never said any of this before."

"I've never felt like this before. I don't think I realised how much I needed that tiny element of control until I didn't have it anymore. But you —" he turned to look at Alice, and she was surprised to see that there were tears in his eyes — "you still have that choice. You could go — I certainly wouldn't blame you — and give yourself another chance, maybe find happiness with someone else."

Happiness with someone else. Briefly Alice considered what he'd said, and then shook her head.

"There is no happiness with anyone else. There can't be," she said. "It's you I love."

"Darling Alice, I don't deserve you." Jay pulled her down beside him and kissed her. "But I honestly don't know what I'd do without you."

When Alice got home that evening, Finn was watching a late-night film.

"I thought you were staying with Kenny," Alice said.

"He's been grounded."

"But *you* haven't."

"Same thing, with Kenny's dad."

"Poor Kenny." Alice had seen Kenny's father once — a great bull of a man, with the aggressive stance of an alpha male gorilla and, by all accounts, a temper to match.

"So," said Finn, "where've you been?"

"Does it matter?"

"Not really, but you're very late, and you've been crying again."

"I've got a bit of a cold, that's all."

"Not true." Finn swung his legs off the sofa and sat up. "You'll have to do better than that."

"It's complicated."

"Try me."

"Finn, no. I'm entitled to my life, and my — my secrets, if you like."

"Mum, I'm not stupid. I know you've been unhappy recently. I know you've got some weird new friends. And I'm pretty sure you've not read *War and Peace*. So, what's up?"

"As I said, it's complicated."

"I can do complicated. I'm not a kid anymore."

Alice sat down beside him. "I'm not sure you're ready for this kind of complicated."

"Don't you trust me?"

"Of course I trust you. It's just that there are some things you're better off not knowing."

"Does Trot know this — whatever it is?"

"Yes, he does."

"Well, then, you can tell me. I'm much more sensible than Trot."

"That's true." Alice laughed.

"Okay then. Are you going to tell me?"

Alice looked at Finn. He had grown a lot in the last six months. His profile had lost the softness of childhood, and he was already more man than child. He could be very mature when the occasion demanded it, and he could also be discreet.

"If I tell you some of it, will you let me leave it at that?"

"Have you told Trot everything?"

"No."

"Okay." Finn folded his arms.

"Right, then." Alice wondered for a moment whether she was being very unwise, but there was no going back now. "I've been — seeing a man for some time. It's not a relationship that will ever go anywhere, but I'm — I'm very fond of him. Sometimes it's painful. My 'weird new friends' as you call them are people I can talk to. They've got problems too — different problems — and it's good to be able to offload a bit."

"No *War and Peace*, then?" Finn seemed amazingly unfazed by Alice's revelations.

"No *War and Peace*."

"And no more pretending? No more — lies?"

"Definitely no more lies."

"I *thought* it was man trouble," said Finn with satisfaction. "Poor old Mum." He squeezed her shoulder, then stood up and stretched. "I'm going to make a sandwich. D'you want one?"

Gabs

Following the disastrous picnic in the park, Gabs had decided that enough was enough. She had little in common with Alice and Mavis, and they certainly hadn't been any help to her. When Mavis phoned to arrange the details of the next meeting (it would be her turn to host it), Gabs would make her excuses, and that would be that. She didn't need Alice and Mavis in her life, and she was pretty sure that the feeling was reciprocal.

Then came Alice's phone call. Gabs had been in a particularly good mood, and the idea of trying out make-up was irresistible. She had immediately forgotten her resolve never to see Alice again and had had a thoroughly enjoyable afternoon playing with Alice's very expensive samples and flirting with Alice's dishy son. She had been able to offload some of her worries, too, and Alice had proved to be a sympathetic listener. Perhaps the Basic Theology meetings could continue after all.

In the meantime, there was Steph.

Steph was fretting, and of course Gabs was the only person she could talk to. Gabs did her best to be understanding, but she still thought her sister was mad. She also thought it was high time that the ineffectual Clive was informed of his impending fatherhood.

"He needs to get used to the idea, too," she said as Steph was revisited by her breakfast for the third morning in succession. "Besides, why should you be the only one to suffer?"

"He'll be awfully upset." Steph rinsed out her mouth and dried her face. She looked terrible.

"Good," said Gabs. "You're upset. I'm upset. I guess now it's his turn, don't you?"

"I suppose."

"Right, then. You'd better phone him."

"Do I have to?"

"You have to. No time like the present. Where's your mobile?"

Gabs fetched Steph's mobile and watched her as she dialled Clive's number.

"What shall I say?" Steph whispered.

"Tell him you need to see him."

"What if he asks why?"

"Oh, for goodness' sake, Steph, give it here." Gabs took the phone from Steph. A man's voice answered.

"Is that Clive?" Gabs said.

"Yeah. Who wants to know?" The voice sounded jolly, with a hint of flirtatiousness. Gabs reckoned she'd soon put a stop to that.

"Steph's sister wants to know," she said. "Remember Steph? From church?"

"Yeah. I remember Steph. Course I do. You're the sexy sister, are you?"

"Not so fast, Romeo," said Gabs, thinking that Clive seemed to have grown up a bit since she last saw him. "Steph needs to see you."

"What about?"

"You'll just have to wait and see, won't you?"

"Will you be there?"

"I'll be there," said Gabs grimly.

"I'll come to your place, then, shall I?"

"You do that. Tonight if possible. Seven o'clock be okay?"

"Fine. I'll look forward to it."

Gabs rang off and handed the mobile back to its owner.

"How was he? What did he say?" Steph wanted to know.

"He sounded fine. A bit too fine, if you ask me. But he'll sober up soon enough when we tell him the good news."

"Oh, Gabs. Don't be too hard on him. He's really nice when you get to know him."

"I'm sure he is. And I'll be perfectly reasonable, provided he's prepared to face up to his responsibilities." Gabs patted Steph's shoulder. "Now don't worry. Put on a bit of slap, and get yourself off to work. We're both going to be late."

Today was one of Gabs' days for working for Care-at-Home, the agency that employed her, and she was looking forward to it. It was good to work with real people for a change, rather than the spoilt, wealthy clients who, it seemed to her, spent an unhealthy amount of time (and money) compensating for what they imagined to be their sexual deprivations. The elderly people she visited were always pleased to see her and good for a chat, and while Gabs was rarely able to stay long, she liked to feel that she left them in better spirits than when she arrived. Occasionally if the workload was light, she would style someone's hair for them or do their nails; Gabs understood how much this could mean.

"Hair's like a lawn," she told one woman as she put in a few heated rollers. "If the lawn's neat, you can get away with murder in the garden. Same thing with hair. If your hair looks good, the rest of you doesn't matter so much."

"Is the rest of me that bad?" the woman asked, but with a smile.

"The rest of you is just fine." Gabs gave her a hug. "This —" she waved the hairbrush — "is just the icing on the cake. Trust me."

That afternoon, Gabs had a meeting with her supervisor. Mrs. Grant was relatively new to the job. A stern, hatchet-faced woman, she ruled her little empire with a rod of iron, and was very much in the job for the money. She seemed to care little for her clients, and even less for their carers, and Gabs couldn't stand her.

"I've received a complaint," she said before Gabs had even had time to sit down.

"Oh yes?" Lesser mortals found Mrs. Grant terrifying. Gabs, however, did not.

"Yes." Mrs. Grant picked up a folder and opened it.

"Okay." Gabs leaned back in her chair and waited.

"Well, aren't you going to ask me what it's about?"

"You asked me here, so I guess you're going to tell me." Gabs inspected her fingernails. One of them was broken. Damn.

"Miss Kershaw phoned. She says you left her with wet hair."

"Oh, does she?" Miss Kershaw was an exceptionally difficult woman. She was always complaining, and usually no one took any notice. This was beginning to feel personal.

"Yes, she does." Mrs. Grant leafed through her file. Gabs knew that she was playing for time, waiting for some kind of reaction. But Gabs wasn't going to give her the satisfaction. "So, what do you intend to do about it?"

"I could pop back and dry it tomorrow?"

"Don't be impertinent, Gabriel."

Gabs stood up. "Look," she said, "you know and I know that that woman's an awkward old bat. I'm about the only person who'll go near her now, and believe me, I don't do it for love. If she doesn't want me around anymore, that's fine by me."

"She has a contract with this agency. We've agreed to see to her — her personal needs."

Gabs knew that Miss Kershaw considered her personal needs to be many and that she was also very rich. The agency would be most reluctant to lose her as a customer. Since Gabs was pretty well the only carer she would tolerate, the agency also needed Gabs.

"Okay. What do you want me to do? Grovel?"

"That will not be necessary. But I think an apology might be in order."

"No chance," said Gabs.

"I beg your pardon?"

"I said, no chance. I'm not apologising to that old bag."

"Really, Gabriel! That's no way to speak about a client!"

"Suit yourself," said Gabs cheerily. "But I've put up with more than my fair share of lip from that particular *client*, and if she doesn't like me, she doesn't have to have me."

"Just a word would be enough, I'm sure." Mrs. Grant was beginning to look desperate. "If you could just give her a quick phone call? I told her you would."

"Sorry, but no. I'm prepared to go on visiting her — and you should thank your lucky stars that I am — but that's it. No apology."

"I'm not accustomed to being spoken to like that by a member of my staff!"

"Well, that's tough. But if you're going to take notice of people like Miss Kershaw, I can't guarantee that you won't be *spoken to like that* again." Gabs grabbed her bag and made for the door. "I'll see you on Wednesday."

Game, set, and match to me, thought Gabs to herself as she walked down to the carpark (normally she favoured taxis, but for her agency work, her car — a bright pink mini — was essential). As she drove off, she felt almost sorry for Mrs. Grant. The poor old trout had probably been looking forward to giving Gabs a dressing-down, but had ended up practically begging her for that apology. Gabs knew that her dislike for Mrs. Grant was equalled only by Mrs. Grant's similar feelings towards her, and that if it had been any of the other carers, Mrs. Grant would have dealt with the complaint herself. This afternoon's interview had been intended as a show of strength, but it had backfired badly, and Gabs guessed that her supervisor wouldn't take her on again in a hurry.

When she got home, she found Steph cooking supper.

"Soufflé okay?" Steph asked, whisking egg whites in a bowl.

"Fine." Gabs would have preferred something more substantial, but she realised that Steph was trying to show her appreciation in the only way she knew — by cooking something complicated — and so it would have to do.

After their meal, Steph brushed her hair and put on some lipstick.

"He's the one who should be doing that," Gabs observed. "You have nothing to fear, you know."

"I don't think this shade would suit Clive," said Steph in a rare attempt at humour. She put down the lipstick. "Oh, Gabs. I'm so nervous. What on earth am I going to say?"

"D'you want me to handle it?" After all, she'd done all the 'handling' so far.

"Oh, would you? I know I'm a wimp, but I just don't know where to begin."

"You're not a wimp. You're just too nice — that's your trouble."

"But you will be — you will be…"

"Gentle with him?"

"Yes."

"I'll do my best. Depends whether he behaves himself."

Clive arrived promptly at seven. He too had apparently made an effort; his hair was carefully spiked and jelled, and he reeked of cheap aftershave.

"Well, hi," he said when Gabs let him in. "You're looking pretty good."

"This," said Gabs firmly, "is not about me. It's about Steph. I'm just here to support her."

"Why does she need support?" Clive dragged his gaze away from Gabs' bosom.

"You'll see."

Steph was seated on the edge of the sofa, looking nervous. She greeted Clive shyly, and he gave her a dutiful peck on the cheek.

"Okay. Sit down, would you?" Gabs said, feeling that she was dealing with a pair of tongue-tied teenagers. Clive sat.

"Right. We'll come straight to the point, shall we? Steph's pregnant."

There followed a very long pause, during which Steph went pale and then bright pink, and Clive stared at the carpet. Then he looked up.

"She can't be," he said. "Well, not by me, anyway."

"She is," said Gabs. "By you."

"But we haven't — we didn't — well, she just can't be."

"It was that evening in the car," Steph whispered.

"What evening in the car?"

"*You* know."

"Would you like me to remind you?" Gabs asked. Since he didn't reply, she went on to give such a detailed account of the events of the evening in question that by the time she'd finished, both Steph and Clive were crimson with embarrassment.

"Gabs, you didn't have to... well, go into so much *detail*," Steph said through tears of humiliation.

"Well, someone had to," Gabs said. "Now, Clive, what are you going to do about it?"

"How — how pregnant is she?" Clive asked.

"About two months."

"Can't she have something done?"

"Like what?" Gabs was enjoying watching him squirm.

"You know. An operation or something."

"It's called an abortion, Clive, and as a good Catholic yourself, I'm sure you'll understand that Steph won't do that."

"My dad'll kill me."

"Quite possibly. That's not Steph's problem. She has a dad of her own, who will probably provide the same service for her."

"Oh, heavens! Dad! I'd forgotten about him!" Steph said. "He'll go mad."

"I'll sort Dad out when the time comes. Now, Clive, the good news is that there's help at hand."

"What kind of help?"

"Well, it's not what you'd call a solution, but Father Augustine is prepared to talk to you both."

"You've told *Father Augustine*?"

"Yep. And he'll have a chat with you both. It'll be a start, at any rate."

"Do we have to?"

"Bloody hell! You're beginning to sound like Steph. And no. Of course you don't *have* to. You can sort the whole thing out on your own if you'd prefer to. But I think Father Augustine would be helpful."

"Was he — angry?"

"Just disappointed, I'd say."

"Oh." Clive fiddled with the frayed edge of the hole in his jeans. "So what do we have to do?"

"Make an appointment to see him."

"Yeah. Steph, would you…?"

"No," said Gabs. "I think you should, Clive. It's about time you did something. Steph has been spewing her guts up for the past couple of weeks, not to mention all the worry. It's your turn now."

"Shall I — shall I phone him now?"

"Why not?" said Gabs, wishing now that she'd volunteered to do it for him. For then she would have had an opportunity to speak to Father Augustine herself. "Here. Take my phone; the number's on it."

Steph and Gabs waited as Clive stuttered his way through what sounded like a very muddled conversation. When he'd finished, he looked relieved.

"He's ill," he said, handing back Gabs' phone.

"Who's ill?" Gabs asked.

"Father Augustine."

"Why? What's wrong with him?"

"I didn't ask."

No, thought Gabs furiously. *Of course you didn't ask. Because all you're concerned about is your own problems. The health of someone who's offered to help you is of no consequence.* She resolved to phone the presbytery herself at the earliest opportunity to find out a bit more.

"Well, did you ask to see Father Pat?"

"No. You didn't say anything about Father Pat."

"*This is not up to me!*" Gabs wanted to strangle him. "This is your problem. If Father Augustine's not available, then it will have to be Father Pat, won't it?"

"But Father Pat's so fierce," said Steph. "He'll be furious."

"No, he won't. He must be used to things like this." Gabs thought that Steph was probably right, but there was no point in worrying her further. "It's his job to help, and you've been a pillar of his church. I reckon he owes you one."

By the time Clive left an hour later, an appointment had been made for both of them to see Father Pat. Neither seemed to be very pleased about the arrangement, but at least it was a start, and Gabs, for one, would welcome someone else's input, even Father Pat's.

Later on, when Steph had gone to have a bath, Gabs phoned the presbytery. The housekeeper answered.

"Can you tell me how Father Augustine is, please?"

"He's comfortable."

This was hospitalspeak, and Gabs felt a frisson of alarm.

"Why? Where is he?"

"In the hospital."

"What happened? I mean, is it serious?"

"I'm afraid I can't tell you that."

"Was it an accident?"

"I can't tell you."

"Oh, for goodness' sake, woman, you can at least tell me how he is. That can hardly be breaking any confidences."

"If you're going to talk to me like that —"

"I'm not talking to you like anything! I just want to know! I'm — I'm his sister."

"Father Augustine is an only child. He has no sisters. And since you've been so rude and have also lied to me, I'm afraid I have to ring off."

And that was that.

For the next twenty-four hours, Gabs fretted and fumed. She tried phoning the hospital, but had no luck. No one appeared to have heard of a Father Augustine, and Gabs realised that his real name might be quite different. As to his surname, she had no idea what it was.

"You could try asking for the Catholic chaplain," said Steph, who was still in grateful mode. "He's bound to know."

"So he is."

Gabs phoned the hospital again. After a prolonged wait, in the course of which she had to press a lot of buttons and then listen to a rather piercing trumpet tune (was this really what the relatives of the sick needed to hear when they were anxiously awaiting news?), a man answered the phone.

"Are you the Catholic chaplain?" Gabs asked.

"I am."

"Well, I just want to know — do you have a priest in the hospital?"

"I am the priest in the hospital."

"No, I mean a sick priest."

"You want a *sick* priest?"

"I don't *want* a sick priest; I'm *looking* for one. He's — he's a friend. I want to know how he is."

"Now, you know I can't give out that kind of information. Unless of course you're the next of kin."

"I could be," said Gabs.

"What do you mean, you could be?"

"Well, I don't know whether he has any family, and if he hasn't, then I could be his next of kin, couldn't I?"

"My dear, it's up to the patient to say who's their next of kin. It's not up to me. And it's certainly not up to you."

"So you can't tell me how he is?"

"I'm afraid not."

"But you know who I'm talking about? I know him as Father Augustine."

"Not such a close friend, then."

"Well, no. But you know who I'm talking about?"

"I do."

"Okay. Just one question, then. Is he alive?"

The man laughed. "I think I'm allowed to say that he's alive. Yes. I think that would be acceptable."

"Not — not dying then?"

"Not as far as I know. Now, my dear, that's really all I can tell you, and I probably shouldn't have even told you that. If you really want to know how your — friend is, then I suggest you find his real next of kin and ask them."

"So that's it?"

"That's it."

Well, at least Father Augustine wasn't at death's door, and was therefore likely to leave the hospital at some stage. Gabs toyed with the idea of going to the hospital and trying her luck again, but decided against it. Besides, she didn't want to embarrass Father Augustine by pitching up when he was ill in bed. That would hardly be fair. And he'd be feeling particularly vulnerable in his pyjamas.

Father Augustine in pyjamas. Gabs sighed. Hitherto she had only seen him in his dog collar or his clerical robes, dressed for his job. But in pyjamas, he'd be just like anyone else — just a no-frills *man*. A no-frills and very sexy man. There was something about pyjamas that Gabs had always found particularly seductive, especially as nowadays so few men seemed to wear them. But she was quite sure Father Augustine would wear pyjamas. With stripes.

"Any luck?" asked Steph, who was being quite sympathetic considering her views.

"Well, I have it on authority that he's not dead."

"I'll ask about him when I go to Mass, shall I? Someone's bound to know."

"Please."

"Shall I do another soufflé for supper? Or would you like a quiche?" Steph seemed to have bought more eggs. What was it with Steph and eggs? Gabs wondered. Shouldn't it be coal?

"Steph, please, could we have something ordinary? I'm starving. I need junk."

Steph looked at her pityingly. "I don't know how you can," she said, "especially as you're supposed to be in love."

"Believe me," said Gabs, "being in love takes it out of you." She relieved Steph of the box of eggs she was holding and replaced them in the fridge. "What you need — what we both need — is fish and chips from the fish and chip shop. Have we any ketchup?"

Mavis

Clifford's voice on the phone was breathless with excitement. "Mavis? I've got some news. I've got to have to have an operation!"

"Why? What's wrong with you?"

"*You* know. It's my heart."

"Yes, but you've got all those pills and that little puffer thing."

"Ah, but you know that test I had at the hospital?"

Mavis certainly knew about the test. She also knew all the details, right down to which clothes Clifford had worn for the occasion and the consultant's name. "Yes?"

"Well, I've got three blocked arteries! Three! Can you imagine that?"

Mavis tried to imagine three blocked arteries, but all she could come up with were three little tubes stuffed with butter (she had always imagined cholesterol to look like butter). What were they going to do? Suck the butter out? No doubt Clifford was about to tell her.

"Yes," Clifford continued. "And I've got to have a triple bypass operation!"

Mavis knew very little about bypass operations — they always sounded to her like some kind of traffic complication — but she knew that lots of people had, and survived, them, so she took Clifford's news calmly.

"Oh dear," she said, hoping that that was the right response.

"You don't sound very worried," Clifford said.

"Well, neither do you." The awful cliché about 'the wonderful things they could do these days' flashed through Mavis's mind.

"I'd be worried if it were you."

"Thank you."

"Aren't you going to ask me all about it?"

"Of course." Mavis sat down and made herself comfortable. This was going to take time. "Please tell me what they're going to do."

"Well," said Clifford, "they kind of switch off your heart, and a machine takes over, and then they take veins from somewhere else…"

The account went on and on. Mavis was still wondering how Clifford was going to manage without those veins — after all, didn't one need all one's veins? — when he finally came to a halt.

"So, what do you think?"

"I think…" Mavis groped around for something useful to say. "I think it's just wonderful the things they can do these days."

"Yes, isn't it? And afterwards, I shall be in intensive care for a while."

Intensive care, Mavis knew, would be hypochondriac heaven. Every tiny ache and pain taken seriously; all those machines ticking and buzzing; all those drips and tubes; all that *attention*.

"What does Dorothy think?" she asked.

"Well, funnily enough, she doesn't seem particularly worried."

"Really?" Dorothy went up in Mavis's estimation.

"Yes. She's taken the news very calmly. Of course, she came along to see the specialist with me —" (of course) " — and asked a few questions, but she seems fine about it. To tell you the truth, I was a little bit hurt."

"Oh dear." Mavis pulled herself together. "Well, I shall be very concerned indeed. And of course, I'll miss you."

And the sex, she thought bleakly. She would certainly miss the sex. Was that very bad of her? For how long would Clifford be *hors de combat*?

"I thought you would," Clifford said.

"Will I be able to visit you?"

"Oh no. Family only, I'm afraid."

"Won't you mind that? I mean, won't you feel a bit sad that I can't see you?"

"Of course." Clifford didn't sound at all sad. "But I'm afraid it can't be helped. It won't be for long, unless there are complications."

Ah. Complications. We mustn't forget those. Mavis waited to be told about the complications, but apparently these could wait for another time.

"When are you having this done?" she asked.

"In a fortnight."

"So that gives you time to —" time to what? Put his affairs in order (Mavis had always rather liked that expression)? Buy new pyjamas? — "time to get ready," she finished rather lamely.

"Yes. And to see you. Of course I must see you before I go in."

"That would be nice." Mavis immediately felt better and regretted some of her less charitable thoughts during the course of this conversation. "Could we — are you all right to go to Dennis's?"

"I think I could manage Dennis's," Clifford said. "Provided we're careful."

After Clifford had rung off, Mavis sat and thought about what he had said and tried to analyse her feelings. Obviously she was concerned, but why didn't she feel more worried? There had been a time when she had had nightmares — literally — about something awful happening to Clifford, but since his retirement he had taken such exceptionally good care of himself that she could no longer imagine anything happening to him at all. Sometimes she felt that it was more than likely that he would outlive her, not least because she couldn't afford the expensive specialists and private hospitals favoured by Clifford and had to settle for whatever the NHS could give her.

Meanwhile, the weather was hot and humid, Maudie had had another disastrous pie-making session (three broken dishes, and it had taken Mavis two hours to clear up the mess), and the cat, possibly mistaking her for a visitor, had ambushed her one evening when she came home from work, necessitating a visit to the doctor for a tetanus injection. This move was ill-advised on the part of Pussolini, for Mavis had been so angry that she had locked him out of the house for twenty-four hours and refused to feed him.

"You can go and find your own supper," she'd yelled at him as he slunk snarling into the undergrowth at the bottom of the garden. "If you can catch me, then you can certainly catch a mouse. Dratted animal!"

A week after her conversation with Clifford, Mavis received a surprise phone call from Alice.

"Hi, Mavis. I wonder whether you could do me a huge favour?"

"Yes?" People rarely asked Mavis for favours, and a huge favour sounded ominous.

"I thought I'd do a makeover for an article I'm writing, and it occurred to me that you might be just the person."

"You're doing a what?"

"A makeover. You know. You get someone with —" Alice's voice trailed away awkwardly for a moment — "someone with a good face and complexion who doesn't wear much make-up, and you sort of transform them."

"Transform them how?"

"With make-up. I've got all these wonderful samples, and I could try them out on you. Then if it works out well, we might be able to do it properly and get a photographer down to take pictures, and you'd appear in our colour supplement. Gabs thought you'd be the ideal candidate."

"Gabs?" What had Gabs to do with all this? Had Alice and Gabs been meeting behind her back? Not just meeting, but discussing her appearance? Mavis experienced a stab of jealousy.

"Yes. You know what Gabs is like. She's really into make-up and stuff, and I'm not much good at it, and when I told her I needed a — a model, she said you'd be ideal. She said you had good bone structure and lovely skin."

"Gabs said that?"

"Yes."

"Oh." No one had ever praised Mavis's bone structure or skin, not even Clifford (but then he was usually preoccupied with other bits of Mavis). Was Alice telling the truth?

"That's quite a compliment, coming from Gabs," Alice said.

"Yes."

"Well?"

"Well what?"

"Will you do it? Come round here one evening and have a makeover?"

"I don't mind coming for this — this makeover thing, but I'm not sure about the photographer," Mavis said. She had never been comfortable having her photo taken, as she was never sure what to do with her features while it was happening.

"Well, never mind about that now. I could just find out what suits you, and then use it for my article. Gabs has already done me; I'm dark. It would be helpful to have someone who's fair."

Fair? Was she fair? Mavis scrutinised her face in the kitchen mirror. Certainly she had been as a girl, but now her skin was more sallow than fair, and her hair, which had been quite a nice dark blond, had turned to mouse streaked with grey.

"Mavis? Are you still there?"

"Yes. I'm not sure that I'm fair, though."

"Well, you're fairer than I am, and I'd really like to do you. Please? It won't take long."

"Can I bring Mother?"

"Of course you can. We always love to see her, and Gabs says she'll pick you both up."

"Gabs will be there too?"

"Gabs is going to be doing it. Believe me, Mavis, you don't want to be made up by me."

Mavis wasn't sure she wanted to be made up by anyone, but it would be an evening out, and if she could take Maudie there'd be no problems with finding a sitter.

"All right," she said, feeling rather reckless. "I'll do it."

On the evening in question, Gabs called for Mavis and Maudie promptly at the time they'd arranged.

"Ooh! A pink car!" Maudie said. "Are we going to confession?"

"Not today, Mother," Mavis told her. "Nice car," she added. "It's a very interesting colour."

"My sister calls it the tartmobile," Gabs said. "She thinks it's terribly vulgar. I love it."

When they arrived, Alice was waiting for them. She had set up a mirror on the kitchen table, together with rows of bottles and tubes and brushes. She went to make coffee (Mavis had rather been hoping for something stronger) while Gabs set to work. Maudie, meanwhile, was settled in front of the television, and the front and back doors were locked in case there was a repetition of her last escapade. Mavis was relieved to see that there appeared to be no sign of Alice's son. She had always felt awkward with young people, especially young men, and she didn't want this one watching her undergoing such a personal procedure.

"You know, you have got lovely skin," Gabs said, tilting Mavis's face towards the light. "You just need to look after it properly."

Mavis wondered whether she ought to feel offended at what could have been perceived as a criticism, but Gabs had such an artless manner that it was hard to take offence.

"What am I supposed to do?" she asked.

"I'll show you."

An hour and a half later, Mavis was transformed. Gone were the shadows under her eyes, the bushy eyebrows, the sallow complexion. When she looked at herself in the mirror, the face that looked back at her was the face of a stranger. She put up a hand to touch her cheek to make sure it really was her. Her skin felt soft and creamy and glowed a subtle pink. She ran her fingers along a newly plucked eyebrow. Long dark lashes fluttered beneath glimmering eyeshadow, and when she smiled, the smile was a pretty dusky rose colour.

"Goodness!" she said.

"Yeah. Great, isn't it?" Gabs said. "What do you think?"

"I — don't know." Mavis was used to her old face and her old skin. She wasn't sure that she had the personality to carry off this new look.

"I think you look fabulous," said Alice, who had been watching and taking notes.

"I feel a bit like those people on that television programme. Mother likes to watch it. You know the one. They whiten people's their teeth and give them plastic surgery, and they come out looking — artificial."

"But I haven't changed *you*," Gabs said. "That's *your* face and *your* features you're looking at. I've just brought out the best in you."

"I suppose so." Mavis wondered whether she was supposed to be grateful. So far, she wasn't making a very good job of it.

"I know," said Alice, "let's have a proper drink, and then you can have another look. I'm sure it will grow on you."

They all had several drinks, and Mavis began to feel decidedly better. The face in the mirror, pink with expensive blusher and cheap wine, was beginning to look a bit more like her own. Perhaps she could get used to it after all.

"Of course, you know what would help?" Gabs said.

"What?" Mavis was feeling decidedly nervous.

"If we coloured your hair. Not that there's anything wrong with the colour, but everyone does it nowadays." (Did they?) "We could put in some highlights. It would give your face a nice lift. You'd be amazed."

Mavis was beginning to think that she'd had as much amazement as she could cope with for one evening, but another part of her thought, why not? What had she to lose? It was years since she had changed the way she looked, and she'd hardly noticed that the same old foundation and hairstyle didn't look at all the same on Mavis at fifty-something as they had on Mavis as a young woman.

"Could you do it?" she asked Gabs.

"Sure. No problem. I do my sister's, and she's never complained. We'll fix a date."

"I think I'd like to get used to this makeover thing first," Mavis said, "if you'd show me how to do it myself."

The following day was Friday, and Mavis was taking a half-day off work and meeting Clifford for their final date before his operation. Determined to wear her new face for him, she spent a lot of time getting ready, carefully applying some of the samples Alice had given her. She went a bit wrong with the eyeliner, but managed to do the rest very satisfactorily, and when she had finished, she was pleased with the result. Clifford would be delighted. It would be a little good luck present for him.

But Clifford was very far from delighted.

"Mavis, what have you done?" he demanded when she opened the front door to him.

"What do you mean, what have I done?"

"Your face!"

"I was given some new make-up. Don't you like it?"

"No, I do not! It makes you look — you look *common*."

"Clifford, what a horrible thing to say! I go to all this trouble, and you insult me!"

"I didn't ask you to do it, and I certainly never wanted you to. I like you the way you are. The way you were, I mean. I liked the old Mavis."

"Well, I like the new Mavis, so I'm afraid you'll have to get used to it."

Hitherto, Mavis had always given in to Clifford where her appearance was concerned. It had been Clifford who had always said that he liked her the way she was, and so for his sake (and because she herself wasn't particularly bothered), she had never tried anything new. But she had had no idea that he would take such a violent dislike to what was, after all, just a bit of make-up. Not for the first time, it occurred to her that perhaps it was time she started pleasing herself.

And the old, chivalrous Clifford — what had happened to him? There had been a time when Clifford wouldn't have dreamt of speaking to her like this, but nowadays, he was becoming increasingly critical, and on one or two occasions, like today, he had been bordering on downright rude.

"It's those new friends of yours," Clifford continued. "I knew they were a bad influence."

In fact, Clifford knew very little about Gabs and Alice, but had always seemed oddly jealous of them. Mavis had long known that in the compartment of his life that he kept for her, there was no room for competition, and since she had few friends and was largely tied to Maudie, there had never been anything for him to worry about. But Alice and Gabs were new territory, for Clifford as well as for Mavis, and she knew he didn't like it.

"Are we going to stand arguing on the doorstep all afternoon?" Mavis asked, thinking longingly of Dennis's. Clifford's unpleasantness would have merited a sulk, but there wasn't time. He was going into the hospital next week. If they didn't make the most of this afternoon, she knew she would regret it.

"Well…"

"I'm wearing some…" She whispered something in his ear.

"Really?" Clifford looked pleased.

"Yes. Really."

"Just for me?"

"Of course just for you. Now, come on, let's make the most of this afternoon."

But the afternoon was not a success. For a start, Dennis had apparently paid one of his rare visits to the flat, and the bed, which they always left with clean sheets, had obviously been put to use for Dennis's own amorous couplings. Someone had drunk the bottle of champagne they'd left in the fridge, and Mavis's special device, which she'd inadvertently left behind last time, had been moved, its open box lying accusingly on the bedside table.

"Oh!" Mavis was quite overcome. "How awful!" She felt that she would never be able to look Dennis in the face again (she overlooked the fact that she'd only met him once and was unlikely to meet him again).

"Dennis is a man of the world," said Clifford, who had regained some of his good humour on the journey while he regaled Mavis with accounts of all the things that could go wrong after a bypass operation.

"I don't care what he is. That's not the point!"

"It is his flat."

"That's not the point, either."

"We'll book a hotel room, shall we?" Clifford said.

Mavis glanced at her watch. The nearest hotel, she knew, was some distance away, and she mustn't be late home.

"The car, then?" Clifford said, seeing her expression.

Mavis knew that this was generous of Clifford (perhaps he was trying to make amends?). They rarely made love in Clifford's car, and it had always been the venue of last resort. While it was a large car and the seats reclined, Clifford too was large, his build unathletic, and the exercise had rarely been worth the considerable discomfort it engendered.

And then there was the problem of finding a suitable parking place. Years ago, when they had been younger and more reckless, they had been discovered in a leafy lane by two young policemen, and Mavis had never quite recovered from the embarrassment of having to explain what she was doing (hadn't it been obvious?) while trapped between Clifford and the steering wheel with her knickers round her ankles. (Clifford, half-suffocated by Mavis when she reached across to wind down the window, had been unable to speak at all.)

"I know," she said now. "We'll go to my house."

"But what about your mother?"

"Mother will be fast asleep. It was her morning at the day centre, and it always tires her out. I think it's worth the risk."

But we all know what happens to the best-laid plans, and this one was no exception. Mavis and Clifford had barely settled themselves on Mavis's bed and Clifford had just finished unwrapping Mavis and was preparing to get stuck in, so to speak, when Maudie came into the room.

"Oh, there you are, Mavis," she said. "Shall we have a cup of tea?"

"Mother! Get out at once! This is *my bedroom*!" Mavis shot up in bed and pulled the covers round her.

"Who's that man?" Maudie asked, apparently unfazed by what she saw. "Would he like a cup of tea?"

"Mother, *go away*!" Mavis shouted.

"You'll catch your death like that," Maudie remarked, standing in the doorway. "So will your friend."

Mavis's friend, who appeared to have run out of patience, had disappeared under the bedclothes and was trying to struggle into his trousers.

"A fine to-do this is, Mavis." Clifford's voice was muffled by the duvet, but his anger was beyond doubt. "And me with my bad heart. You said she'd be asleep!"

"Well, as you see, she's not." Mavis too was angry — angry with herself, angry with Clifford, but most of all, angry with Maudie. Would she ever be able to call her life, never mind her home, her own? "Mother! *Go away now*!"

How long this situation would have lasted is anyone's guess, but it was at this point that Pussolini decided to join in the proceedings. Glimpsing Maudie's plastic bag trailing along the floor behind her, he went in for the kill, puncturing it with his claws. There followed an unseemly scramble, in the course of which Clifford made his escape, gathering up the rest of his clothes as he went; the cat, terrified by all the noise, fled through the open bedroom window, shattering one of Mavis's favourite ornaments; and Mavis, naked and disappointed, was left to deal with the mess.

"Oh, Mavis. You're crying. What's the matter?" said Maudie, bewildered by all the fuss.

"Everything," wept Mavis, scrubbing at the carpet with an old towel (the plastic bag had been half full). "Everything's the matter. And it's all my fault."

"Of course it's not, dear," said Maudie, stroking and patting Mavis's shoulder. "It was the fucking cat."

"The *what?*"

"The fucking cat, dear."

"*Mother!*"

"It's all right, dear. Everybody uses that word nowadays. I heard them on the telly."

"I think," said Mavis, sitting back on her heels, "that perhaps it really is time you went to confession."

The Fourth Meeting: August

It happened that the date that had been fixed for the next meeting was the day after Clifford's operation. Alice wondered whether Mavis would be feeling up to it, and said so on the phone to Gabs.

"Poor Mavis. She's bound to be worried. Do you think we ought to leave it for a few days?"

"Oh no. Let's take her out and give her a good time," said Gabs. "It'll take her mind off things."

"Do you think?" Alice wasn't sure.

"Yes. Trust me, Alice. What Mavis needs is a bit of fun."

"What kind of fun exactly?"

"How about a surprise?"

"I'm not sure." Mavis had never seemed to Alice to be the kind of person to enjoy surprises, particularly if the surprises were organised by someone like Gabs.

"Okay. No surprise, then. But we could take her into town for a meal, and then do a bit of shopping," Gabs said.

"Won't the shops be shut?"

"They stay open late on Fridays."

"But she mightn't want to do any shopping!"

"Alice, I'm disappointed in you. Of course she'll want to go shopping. Everyone loves shopping."

Alice herself was not particularly fond of shopping. She had neither the time nor the spare cash to do the kind of recreational shopping people seemed to indulge in these days. She shopped for necessities. She suspected that Mavis might well feel the same way.

"And then there's her mother," Alice said. "We can't really take her."

"True." Gabs considered for a moment. "I know. How about your Finn? Couldn't he sit with her? He seems a capable sort of guy, and it wouldn't involve much — just keeping an eye on Maudie and staying clear of that awful animal. Shouldn't be too difficult."

Alice tried to picture Finn supervising Maudie, plus plastic bag and feral cat. "I suppose it might work."

"Of course it'll work! I'll put it to him if you like."

"No, I'll do it." The less contact Finn had with Gabs, the better. "And then I'll phone Mavis, shall I?"

"Yeah. Okay."

When Alice phoned with their plan, Mavis sounded doubtful. "I'm not sure," she said. "It rather depends on how the operation's gone."

"But you won't know, will you?"

"I was trying to think of a way of finding out, but you're probably right."

"So it might be better to spend an evening with us rather than at home worrying. After all, there's nothing you can do, is there? And at least you can talk to us."

"Are you sure your son can manage?"

"He'll be fine." In fact, Alice wasn't at all sure, but provided the cat was locked out and Maudie was locked in, there wasn't much that could go wrong — nothing of a life-threatening nature, anyway. "We'll call for you at six, shall we?"

On the appointed evening, Alice and Finn arrived promptly at Mavis's house.

"This is so kind of you, Finn," Mavis said.

"S'all right." Finn had not been pleased with the arrangement and was in a thoroughly bad mood.

"Now, Mother should be all right. Just let her watch the television, but make sure she doesn't wander."

"Okay."

"And the cat. I've put him out. Make sure he stays outside."

"I quite like cats," Finn said.

"You won't like this one. He — he catches people."

"*Catches* people?"

"He pounces. And he scratches and bites. If he miaows to be let in, take no notice."

"Okay."

"Oh, and don't let Mother drink. She'll probably ask for a glass of wine, but it's not a good idea."

Finn looked disappointed.

"I've put some cans of beer in the fridge. Do help yourself. But Mother had better stick to tea. I'll show you where everything is."

The three women met up in a burger bar. This had been Mavis's idea; she'd never been to one before and said she'd like to try it. Alice had always disliked this kind of establishment — the food (damp little buns stuffed with grease and calories); the industrial-size cartons of cola; the spoilt, noisy children (Finn, in his time, had been as spoilt and noisy as any of them); and the mountains of cardboard and paper that accumulated as the meal progressed. But the idea of introducing Mavis to this palace of childhood pleasure was a novel one, and so she went along with it.

"Right. What's the plan?" Alice asked, mesmerised by Gabs, who was consuming a towering mountain of food with apparent ease.

"Up to Mavis," said Gabs through a mouthful of chips. "It's her shout."

"Mavis, what would you like to do next?"

Mavis was toying with the lone and tiny fragment of salad that had emerged from her burger, and looked anxious and unhappy.

"I don't know," she said. "I can't really think of anything at the moment. Except Clifford."

"Of course you can't," said Gabs. "We need to phone the hospital."

"But you can't do that," said Mavis. "You're not allowed to unless you're —"

"Next of kin?" Gabs grinned. "I know. I've had a next-of-kin-experience recently. But I have a plan. Do you know the number of the hospital?"

Mavis produced a piece of paper from her bag and handed it to Gabs. "I don't think you ought to," she said. "Really. It's not allowed."

Gabs looked at her pityingly. "Do you want to know how your Clifford is?"

"Of course I do."

"Well, then, leave it to me."

"But it's so noisy in here!"

"Never mind that. Hospitals are used to noise. What's his surname, by the way?"

"Watts."

After an inordinately long wait, in the course of which Gabs seemed to have had a virtual tour of the hospital, she apparently found someone to talk to.

"Hallo? Oh, I wonder whether you can help me. My name is Charlene Watts, and I'm phoning from Australia. I believe you have my brother — Clifford Watts — with you, and I was wondering how he's doing." There was a pause. "Yes, I know I should ring his wife, but she's not at home at the moment. And as you must understand, I'm awfully anxious about him. We're not on the phone here in the outback, and I've had to walk miles in the dark to a phone box. Yes. Yes, thank you. I'll hang on a minute." Gabs grinned at the others, giving them a thumbs up. "Hallo? Is he? Oh, that's wonderful news. Thank you so much. No, I won't phone again. I just wanted to make sure he was all right. And do excuse the noise. The wombats are mating. Goodbye."

"It's not night-time in Australia," said Alice, impressed not only at the string of lies, but also at the distinct Australian twang Gabs had conjured up for the occasion. "And I believe most Australians have telephones."

"Never mind that. I had to think of something." Gabs turned to Mavis. "He's comfortable, apparently. The op went well, and his progress is 'satisfactory'. He'll be transferred to a ward tomorrow."

"Oh, thank you. Thank you!" And Mavis burst into tears. "I didn't think I was that worried about him," she said as the other two escorted her out into the shopping mall. "I kept telling myself he'd be fine, and that anyway, there was nothing I could do, but that only made it worse." She wiped her eyes. "But he'll be awfully cross."

"Awfully cross with who?"

"With me. He'll guess that it was me, won't he?"

"But it wasn't!" Gabs said. "That's the whole point. You can say with your hand on your heart that you never phoned the hospital."

"And Clifford does have a sister," said Mavis. "I think she lives in Barking."

"There you are then. Barking, Australia — does it really matter? He'll be pleased that she phoned."

"But *Charlene*..."

"Sorry. It was all I could think of. I always fancied being a Charlene."

"And what exactly *is* a wombat?" Alice asked.

"I've no idea. Now —" Gabs took each of the others by an arm — "what we need is a spot of retail therapy. How about it, Mavis?"

"Oh, I'm not sure..."

"Alice?"

"Why not?" said Alice, who could see the mood of the evening rapidly degenerating unless someone rescued it. "I for one need some new jeans."

"Jeans!" Gabs clapped her hands. "Mavis, have you ever worn jeans?"

"Goodness, no."

"High time you did, then. And you've got the right figure."

"Have I?"

"Sure." Gabs hesitated for a moment. "I know. We'll all buy new jeans. I could do with some as well."

"But —" Mavis looked appalled.

"No buts. Just try some on, and you'll see."

"But Clifford... whatever will he say?"

"Never mind Clifford. Just for this evening, you're going to please yourself."

The jeans project turned out to be surprisingly successful. After several false starts, Mavis, reluctant and fearful and still fretting about what Clifford would say (by this stage, Gabs felt that if she ever had the misfortune to meet Clifford, she might well be tempted to strangle him, heart condition notwithstanding), had been persuaded into a traditional but unassuming dark denim pair, and had had to admit that they were very comfortable and she could wear them for "messing around". Gabs couldn't imagine Mavis messing around in anything, but getting her into the jeans at all had been a triumph, so she didn't enquire further. She and Alice had both found what they wanted, and when they emerged from the gloomy and very noisy cavern where they had made their purchases, Gabs suggested that what they all needed was ice cream.

"My mum always took me for ice cream after we'd been shopping for shoes," Gabs said. "She said buying shoes was so boring that we needed a reward. I always wanted bright red shoes, or patent ones, but I wasn't allowed them because of school."

"Well, you've certainly made up for it now," Alice remarked as Gabs teetered along on her impossibly high heels.

"Haven't I just? Now, about this ice cream."

"Oh, I don't think I could, after all that food," Mavis said.

"Then you can have a coffee. Come along, girls."

Over their ice creams (even Mavis succumbed to a small vanilla), Gabs told them about her abortive attempt to be Father Augustine's next of kin.

"Well, you managed pretty well tonight," Alice said. "Couldn't you have used similar tactics?"

"Didn't work," Gabs said. "They weren't having any of it. Anyway, he's much better now, apparently, and out of the hospital. Someone told Steph at church. It was a burst appendix. Poor love," she said dreamily, toying with a spoonful of crushed nuts. "I hate the idea of him going through all that on his own."

"But I'm sure he won't have been on his own," Alice said. "He must have family, and friends. And Father Whatsit."

"Father Pat? He's not the kind of person you need when you're ill," Gabs said. "He's always put me in mind of the Grim Reaper."

"Well, hasn't he got parents?"

"Oh, parents!" scoffed Gabs. "Not the same, is it? And certainly not if they're anything like my dad."

"What about God?" Mavis said. "Presumably he believes in God, so that must be a comfort."

"God," said Gabs, "is all very well. But sometimes you need something more."

"So, what are you going to do now?" Alice asked.

"I shall go and see him," Gabs said.

"Is that a good idea?"

"Probably not, but that's never stopped me before."

"How d'you know he'll be there?"

"I know he's been to a kind of retreat place to recuperate for a week, and now he's back at the presbytery but not allowed to work yet. Father Pat will be out a lot of the time, so he'll be on his own. The housekeeper has Wednesdays off, so it will have to be a Wednesday." Gabs spared a fleeting thought for Gerald, who had a preference for Wednesdays, but Gerald would have to wait. She'd let him do his 'Best in Show at Crufts' thing to compensate. Gerald would like that.

"You've certainly done your homework," Alice said.

"Yep. This is a golden opportunity. Mightn't happen again for ages. I can't afford to miss it, can I?"

"What exactly are you going to *do* when you visit him?" Mavis asked.

"Ah." Gabs spooned up the last of her ice cream. "I'll just have to play it by ear, won't I?"

"How romantic," murmured Alice.

"Would you really — I mean, how far would you *go*?" Mavis asked.

"As far as possible. Believe me, Mavis, having waited so long, I'd be mad not to, wouldn't I? But I should be so lucky."

"If you really loved him, would you be doing this at all?" Alice asked.

"I could say the same thing to you."

"True. But Jay doesn't have a vocation, does he?"

"Maybe not. But having you around isn't in his best interests with a baby on the way, is it?"

"As I've said before, I didn't go out of my way to seduce Jay. It just happened."

"Nothing," said Gabs, "just happens. You make it happen." She decided to change the subject. "How's his baby coming along?"

"It's a girl."

"Oh dear."

"Oh dear indeed."

"Makes it more real, doesn't it?"

"Yes. Before, it was just a — well, just an idea, I suppose. Now it — she — is a person."

"With a pink nursery?"

"How did you guess!"

"I hated pink when I was a kid," said Gabs. "My mum made me wear pink all the time when I was little, and all I wanted to do was wear shorts and climb trees."

"You don't look the tree-climbing sort," said Alice.

"Oh, I can climb trees all right. I just don't choose to do it anymore. No. Steph was the girly one. I was the tomboy. From tomboy to tart in such a short time," she mused. "I wonder how it happened."

"I thought you didn't like calling yourself — that," said Mavis, who still found the word difficult to say.

"I'm among friends, aren't I?" Gabs grinned. She would never have dreamed that she would become friends with people like Alice and Mavis, and yet it seemed to have happened almost without her noticing.

"We're an odd trio, aren't we?" said Alice, apparently thinking along the same lines. "I wonder whether we'll stay in touch after — well, after whatever it is we're trying to achieve has happened."

"You mean, after we've all returned to the bosom of the church and a state of grace?" said Gabs, who, for her own part, couldn't imagine anything less likely to happen.

"I never was a Catholic," Alice said. "Remember? I just came along to the meeting to write that article."

"Did you? Write the article, I mean?" Gabs asked.

"No." Alice laughed. "It was all a bit too near the bone."

"So, if you're not Catholic, what are you?"

"Oh, wishy-washy C of E, I suppose. Like most people."

"I always fancied being C of E," Gabs said. "It seems you can do what you like, and still say you belong to a church. No rules. No guilt."

"Well, you can always join," Alice said. "I'm sure they'd be delighted to have you."

"And that's why I never could."

"Like that guy who said he could never join a club that would have him as a member?"

"Exactly. Besides, it may be easy to join your church, but it's bloody impossible to leave mine. Ask any Catholic. We all want a priest on our deathbed. Confession, last rites, the works. So we have to hang on in there."

"Just in case?" said Alice.

"Definitely just in case."

"Groucho Marx," said Mavis, who had been rather quiet during this exchange.

"What?" Gabs asked.

"He was the man who said he'd never want to belong to a club that would have him in it."

"Well, good for Groucho Marx. Sounds like just my kind of guy. I'll join his club anytime."

"Groucho Marx," said Mavis, "is dead."

Mavis was having a rather difficult evening.

For a start, there was Clifford's operation, and now that she didn't have to worry about him quite so much (although she suspected that "comfortable" was a one-size-fits-all word relied upon by hospitals for anyone who was still breathing), she was still concerned about him. She was also anxious about the repercussions that might result from Gabs' phone call. It had been kindly meant, and Mavis was very relieved that Clifford had pulled through his operation, but he could be very suspicious, and he would certainly know that she had been involved in that phone call.

The burger had been disappointing. She didn't know what she had been expecting, but this most certainly wasn't it. The greasy food, the cheery bad manners of the clientele, and the noise had all conspired to convince Mavis that this would be the last time she patronised such an establishment. The other two had seemed quite happy — they were probably used to this kind of thing — but Mavis, who rarely ate out, decided that she much preferred to eat at home.

And then there were the jeans. The others had been so complimentary that she hadn't liked to say how she felt, but secretly Mavis wasn't at all sure about them. Certainly they fitted her well enough, and they were fairly harmless, but she felt that if she wore them, she would be pretending to be someone else; it would be like dressing up. She had always suspected that she didn't have what it took to be a jeans person, and now she was quite certain. There were some things she just couldn't do, like paint her toenails or wear her sunglasses on her head (Mavis had tried this once in a rare attempt to be cool, but the sunglasses kept slipping off, and so she'd had to give up).

She had also disliked the whole changing room experience. For a start, the unforgiving lighting and the wall-to-wall mirrors presented to Mavis images of her body that she had rarely seen before, thus damaging what little confidence she had. Those bulges round her middle, that little roll of flesh under her bra, those dimpled thighs… did she really look like that? She had always considered herself to be quite slim, but apparently she had been living under a delusion.

In addition to this, she was unaccustomed to sharing her nakedness — in this case, semi-nakedness — with anyone except Clifford, and she had found the presence of Gabs and Alice discomfiting. She hadn't expected them to join her when she was trying on the clothes, and had been very conscious of her ancient and rather shapeless bra and what she had once heard described as "bucket knickers". These had been in stark contrast to Alice's skimpy briefs and the strange, stringy little garment worn by Gabs (Mavis had decided that she would rather go without knickers altogether than wear anything like that).

Finally, there were the two "tops" Gabs had insisted on choosing to go with the jeans.

"But I've got plenty of — tops," Mavis had said, thinking of her drawers full of blouses and cardigans. She would never have referred to them as tops, but she supposed that was what they were.

"Not the right kind to go with jeans," Gabs had said, picking out a black T-shirt with an indecipherable logo on the front. "Try this."

"Isn't it a bit young?" Mavis had asked, hoping the logo wasn't something rude.

"T-shirts suit everyone," said Gabs.

In the end, she had settled for two fairly inconspicuous garments: a T-shirt with a picture of a butterfly, and another with the bewildering letters FCUK on the front. Mavis had no idea what the letters stood for, but they seemed harmless enough.

She had ignored Gabs' obvious amusement, since she was rapidly learning that Gabs was very easily amused.

In spite of all these difficulties, sitting eating her ice cream, listening to the other two chatting away, Mavis was grateful for their friendship. Shopping with friends might not have been a comfortable experience, but it had been a novel one (Mavis had never shopped with friends before), and she felt that, changing rooms notwithstanding, it was something she wouldn't mind repeating. Normally she shopped on her own, buying most of her clothes in Marks and Spencer (as often as not, not even bothering to try them on first), with no one to suggest or criticise. Occasionally she would take Maudie with her, but her mother was an unreliable companion. She would wander off when Mavis's back was turned, or unwittingly indulge in a spot of shoplifting. On more than one occasion, Mavis had had to return items she had found secreted about Maudie's person, with explanations and apologies, and it was not something she enjoyed having to do. Maudie's departing wits had taken with them many of the boundaries that govern normal behaviour, and if she saw something she liked, then she would simply help herself. Mavis never ceased to be amazed at the ease with which her mother managed to get away with these small thefts — on one occasion, Maudie had walked out of a shop carrying a large and very heavy brass ornament — and had come to the conclusion that the life of a shoplifter was a great deal easier than she would have imagined.

How Maudie would have enjoyed this evening! The burger, the ice cream, all the noise and the people — in fact, all the things Mavis had found difficult — would have been right up her mother's street. Maudie had always been a sociable person, who loved shopping and parties and what Gabs would have called "having a laugh". Mavis herself had taken after her shy, taciturn father. Even after all these years, she still missed him.

"I think it's time I was getting back," she said now. "Mother's usually in bed by now."

"Me too," said Alice. "Finn has lots of homework this weekend, and I've got some work to do."

"Righto," said Gabs, gathering up her parcels (how had she managed to buy so much in such a relatively short time? Mavis wondered). "Let's go."

"You didn't really like the jeans, did you?" Alice said to Mavis when they were alone in Alice's car.

"Well…"

"Oh, come on, Mavis! You don't have to be polite. I could see you weren't happy with them. But give them a try. They really do suit you, you know. And before you say it, you don't have to wear them for Clifford. Wear them for yourself. You might even come to like them."

As they drew up outside Mavis's house, Finn met them at the gate.

"I can't wake Maudie up," he said.

"What do you mean?" Alice asked.

"Well, I went to make her a cup of tea, and when I got back she was asleep, and I can't wake her up."

"She tends to drop off," Mavis said. "She gets very tired about now."

But when they went into the living room, it was obvious that something was wrong. Certainly Maudie was in her chair and she appeared to be sleeping, but her body was bent at an awkward angle, one arm hung loosely over the arm of her chair, and a ribbon of spittle hung from her open mouth.

"Oh, God!" Mavis ran over to her. "Mother? Mother! Wake up! Can you hear me? Wake up!" She shook Maudie's shoulders. "Come on, Mother. Please!"

"What's the matter with her?" Finn asked. "She's been fine all evening."

"Finn, dial for an ambulance," Alice said.

"But —"

"Do it *now*."

Finn left the room, and Alice joined Mavis at Maudie's side. "What do you think?" she asked. "Has this ever happened before?"

"No. Never. Oh, God! I should never have gone out. I should never have left her! Come on, Mother. Please wake up!"

"Mavis, whatever this is, it wasn't your fault. It was going to happen whether you were here or not."

"She's not — dead, is she?" Finn asked, coming back into the room.

"No. Of course she's not dead," Alice said.

"Was it — was it something I did?"

"Of course not. I'm sure she'll be fine. Did you phone for the ambulance?"

"It's on its way."

"Then go and make a cup of tea for Mavis. She looks as though she could do with one."

Mavis was stooping over Maudie, half holding her in her arms, weeping into her mother's faded blue cardigan. She remembered her last words to her before she left: "You'll be fine with Finn. You know Finn, don't you? I'll be back soon." But she hadn't been back soon. She'd been away for hours. And now Maudie had had this — this whatever it was, and she hadn't been *there*. She had always promised herself that if anything happened to Maudie, she would be there.

"Why did I leave her? Oh *why* did I leave her?" she wept.

"You left her because you were having an evening out with friends," Alice said. "You're a marvellous daughter to her, but you can't be with her every minute of every day. After all, you leave her to go to work, don't you?"

"That's different."

"Why? Why is it different?"

"I *have* to go to work."

"Well, sometimes you have to go out, too. To give yourself a break," Alice said. "Now try not to worry. She's breathing, she's got a good strong pulse, and the medics will be here any minute. Drink your tea. You're going to need it. You may be in for a long night."

"You've been so kind," Mavis sobbed. "So kind. Both of you."

"That," said Alice, "is what friends are for."

The ambulance arrived, and the ambulance men were kind and efficient and reassuring. They told Mavis that it looked like a stroke, and yes, of course she could come in the ambulance with Maudie.

"We'll follow in the car," Alice told her.

"Are you sure?" Mavis said. "It seems an awful lot to ask."

"You didn't ask, and yes, of course I'm sure. You need someone around. For you."

"But your work…"

"Never mind my work. This is more important."

"What about the cat? Oh dear. I'd completely forgotten about poor Pussolini."

"If ever an animal was capable of looking after itself," said Alice, "it's that one. Now, let's get going."

It was only when they reached the hospital that Mavis realised, with some surprise, that for the best part of an hour, she hadn't given so much as a thought to Clifford and his operation.

Part Five

Alice

During the mercy dash to the hospital, Alice noted that Finn's mood seemed to have improved greatly, and reflected that there was nothing like an emergency (someone else's emergency, naturally) to lighten the mood.

"There's no blue light," he complained as they tried to keep up with the ambulance. "No siren. Why isn't there a siren?"

Alice, who had been thinking the same thing, decided not to share her own conclusions: that being old largely cancelled out the emergency factor. Old people die — that's what they do. And if it's going to be sooner rather than later, what's the hurry?

"If it had been me, or even you —" (thank you, Finn) "— wouldn't they have had a siren?" Finn persisted.

"Quite possibly." Alice narrowly avoided a motorbike. "I have no idea what rules govern the use of sirens."

"It wasn't my fault, was it?"

"No. I've told you. Of course it wasn't your fault. You just had the bad luck to be there."

"Will she be all right?" Was there just the slightest hint of glee in Finn's voice?

"I've no idea."

"Are we going to stay at the hospital all night?"

"No. Yes. Possibly. How on earth do I know at this stage?"

"Just asking."

"Well, don't." Alice negotiated her way past a lorry. "I need to concentrate."

At the hospital, a very young-looking doctor examined Maudie (the fact that he looked so young probably said more about Alice's age than about that of the doctor). He told Mavis that yes, it did look as though Maudie had had a stroke. They would have to do tests, and they would know more in the morning. The best thing Mavis could do would be to go home and get some rest.

"Oh no," Mavis said. "I couldn't possibly do that. I'll stay with Mother."

"Would you like us to stay with you?" Alice asked. "I'm perfectly happy to, if that would help."

But Mavis said she would be all right. Looking at her pale, anxious face, the new (and still inexpertly applied) make-up smudged down her cheeks, Alice felt a surge of tenderness. Poor Mavis. She seemed so isolated, with her mother and the cat and that awful Clifford. Had she no other friends who could rally round? It appeared not. Alice promised to phone Mr. Strong in the morning to tell him that

Mavis wouldn't be in to work, and to contact a neighbour, who might be persuaded to feed the cat.

"Well, that's that," said Finn as they made cocoa on their return home in the small hours. He sounded disappointed, but what had he expected? An elderly woman suffering from a stroke was not the kind of thing of which TV medical dramas — the only kind Finn knew about — were made.

"That's that," Alice agreed.

"I'll never let you get like — well, like Mavis," Finn said after a moment.

"What do you mean?"

"Lonely. I'll — I'll look after you." Finn's voice was gruff, and Alice knew how hard it was for him to express emotion.

"Thanks, Finn. That's sweet of you." She gave him hug. "I'll bear that in mind."

But Alice's patience was about to be sorely tried, for the following week, there was a parents' evening at Finn's school.

"I think Trot should come this time," Alice told him.

"Why?" Finn looked up from his laptop.

"Why do you think?"

"He won't like it." Finn clicked on the mouse. The picture that came up (from where she was, it looked suspiciously like a pair of breasts) was quite definitely nothing to do with maths homework.

"Well, that's tough. He's your father, and it's time he played his part."

Finn was right. Trot didn't like the idea at all.

"But why, Alice? Why now? I thought you did all that sort of thing."

"*That sort of thing* being bringing Finn up, feeding him, putting up with his moods, clearing up after him —"

"Okay, okay. I get the message. But you were the one who decided to have him."

"*What?*"

"You had him."

"I can't believe you're saying this, Trot. We sorted all that out years ago, and it's hardly affected you at all. You've abrogated pretty much all responsibility for your son —"

"Oh. He's my son now, is he?"

"Yes. He's your son. As much as he is mine, as a matter of fact. I've never asked much of you, but I think it would be nice if you came along to the school to hear how he's doing. This is the beginning of his final GCSE year, and they want to discuss last term's reports. It's important. This is Finn's future we're talking about."

"You could always tell me what they say."

"I could, but I won't. If you want to know, you'll have to come with me."

"And what if I don't want to know?"

"Now you're just being childish." Alice sensed a hangover — Trot was always petulant after a heavy night — but decided not to say anything. "You ought to want to know. It's good for Finn if he thinks you're taking an interest."

"But I do take an interest! I took him fishing last weekend, and we went to that football match. I had an awful job getting the tickets, and they were bloody expensive. I —"

"Trot, these are all fun things. Now that Finn's nearly an adult, it's time you took an interest in his future. Fishing and football are all very well, but they're not going to equip him for a career."

"I didn't get any qualifications, and I'm doing okay."

"Yeah, right. No career, no regular income, no wife or family to look after. Come to think of it, you're in much the same position as Finn. The difference being that Finn is fifteen and you're… you're… well, a lot older." It occurred to Alice that she had no idea how old Trot was.

"I paint. I sold five pictures at that last exhibition."

"Five pictures! Well, I hope you're not going to let that change your life!" Alice finally lost her temper.

"You can be very nasty sometimes, Alice," said Trot.

"If you don't come to this parents' evening, you'll find I can be a lot nastier. You owe it to Finn. Come to that, I think you owe it to me. It's one evening, Trot. Just one evening. Surely you can manage that?"

In the event, Trot consented to give up his evening. He also managed to get himself invited to supper beforehand.

"How does he do it?" Alice asked as she prepared sausages and mash (no fatted calf this evening).

"Charm," Finn told her. "It's where I get it from."

But during the parents' evening, it transpired that charm wasn't the only thing Finn had inherited from his father. Their first interview was with Finn's form teacher, Mr. Langley.

"He's lazy, Mrs. Mayhew —"

"Ms.,' said Alice, not wanting anyone to think she was married to Trot, who nowadays sported a tatty little moustache and was wearing a very grubby pair of jeans.

"Ms. Mayhew. I apologise." Mr. Langley looked at Trot, and then glanced hastily away. "Finn's bright. He could do anything he wanted to if he was prepared to work, but not to put too fine a point on it, he's bone idle."

"I say!" Trot started to protest. "That's not fair! I know for a fact —"

"Shut up, Trot," Alice hissed. She had heard all this many times before and was having none of Trot's nonsense. Besides, it was high time that he was told about this other side of his son. It was one of the reasons she had asked him to come with her.

"It's difficult to know what to do," she said. "He'll spend ten minutes on his homework, and then say he's finished it. I've no way of knowing whether that's true. Or he'll tell me that he does work hard, it's just that I never see him when he's doing it."

Trot laughed, and Alice glared at him.

"I can read him the riot act if you'd like." Mr. Langley seemed a mild-mannered man, not the kind to read an effective riot act. Seeing Alice's expression, he smiled. "Oh, I can be quite scary if I need to be, but sometimes parents object. We have to be so careful nowadays."

"I shan't object," Alice said. "Scary sounds exactly what Finn needs. I'll be only too happy for someone to frighten him into doing some work."

"Well, *I* object —" Trot began, but Alice gave him a sharp kick under the table. She had brought him along to listen, not put in his two pennyworth.

It was the same story with all the other teachers. Finn was bright, but lazy. Alice had been told this on numerous occasions in the past, and she was at her wits' end. In the pub on the way home, she tried to explain to Trot what an uphill struggle it was, trying to make Finn do any work, but Trot just couldn't see it.

"If he really is that lazy — and I'm still not sure I believe all these people — then can't you just lock him in his room till he's done his homework? Should be simple enough," said Trot over his pint of bitter.

"Lock Finn in his room," repeated Alice, sipping her wine and trying to keep calm. "Now there's a brilliant idea. Lock him up with his iPod and his sound system and his mobile and —"

"You could take them away."

"Oh yes. So I could. I could empty Finn's room out and leave him alone at his desk. Brilliant, Trot. Thank you so much. Now why didn't I think of that before?"

"Can't be that hard," grumbled Trot.

"Okay. Why don't you have him for the weekend and see if you can manage it? You've been promising he can come and stay for ages, and now's your chance."

"But I was going to go out with some mates. It's all fixed."

"Well, unfix it and have Finn instead. He could do with some proper time with you, and I could do with a free weekend. I'll bring him round on Friday after school."

"With his bike? We can go for a bike ride."

"With his bike. *And his homework.*"

Alice had another reason for wanting a free weekend. Jay had told her that Angela would be staying at her mother's for a couple of days, and he wasn't on call, so for once they might be able to spend some proper time together. She wondered briefly whether she could risk asking Jay to come and stay, but dismissed the idea. It was more than probable that Trot would tire of his parental duties and decide to return Finn early, or Finn himself might pitch up on his own (it was only a half-hour bike ride away). Once again, they would have to go in search of neutral ground — something that had once seemed adventurous, even exciting, but which had long since lost its attraction.

Jay, however, had other ideas.

"We could rent a cottage," he said when Alice phoned to tell him she would be free.

"Could we?" She was doubtful.

"Why not? We're both off the hook for the weekend, and it would be nice to have somewhere that's ours, even if it's only for a couple of days."

"You mean play house?" The idea was certainly attractive.

"Exactly. We can cook for each other, and make love when we want to, and be totally private. What do you think?"

"I think it sounds wonderful."

Alice thought the idea of having a whole house to themselves — even a very small one — was very appealing. An affair was by its nature an all-or-nothing kind of thing. You were either together — in the same room or car, taking the same walk, eating the same meal — or you were apart. There was nothing in between. If they had a place to themselves, they would have space as well as each other's company. They would be able to conduct themselves like a normal couple. They wouldn't have to make the most of every minute, which could add pressure to an already difficult situation, since they would have two whole days together. If they were to have a row (and of course she hoped very much that they would not), there would be time to make it up afterwards. Making up after an argument is difficult if you've only got a short time in which to do it, and sometimes when she and Jay parted, it was on patched-up rather than friendly terms — explanations still wanting, apologies unsaid, both of them feeling ill-used and unhappy.

If she was going to be away for the weekend, Alice realised that she would have to tell Finn in case he needed to contact her at home. This proved remarkably easy.

"Are you going with the boyfriend?" Finn asked (he appeared to be texting his friends at the same time as talking to her).

"Yes. Yes, I am," Alice said.

"Great." Finn's thumbs moved over the tiny keyboard with astonishing speed, and Alice briefly wished he could apply himself as diligently to his schoolwork. "When will you be back?"

"Sunday afternoon. Is that okay?"

"Yeah. Fine. Trot and I are doing a bike ride with one of his mates."

"What about homework?"

"I'll have done it by then."

"Promise?"

"Promise." Finn grinned. "Trot says he'll give me a tenner if I have it all done by Sunday."

"That's bribery!"

"Yeah. Great, isn't it? You should try it sometime."

Jay found the cottage on a website. It wasn't ideal, being a bit farther away than they would have wished, and the setting — in the country, just, but near a large town — was not ideal. But as Jay pointed out, last-minute holidaymakers can't be choosers, and it was a great deal better than the alternatives. Alice found herself looking forward eagerly to what would be their first whole weekend together. It was something they had often talked of, even planned, but never quite managed — something, she suspected, that neither of them had ever really expected to happen.

But right from the start, it was apparent that things weren't going to go according to plan. Perhaps it was the heightened expectations, the pressure to enjoy themselves and make the most of an opportunity that might not come their way again. Locations and dates can be arranged — moods and emotions cannot — and from the moment they arrived at the cottage, Alice knew that she was in entirely the wrong frame of mind. She remembered feeling just the same one Christmas when she was a teenager. Her mother had made a huge effort, as always; the decorations, the meal, the tree were all perfect; Alice herself had received everything she could have wished for. And yet the imperative to have fun — to have a good time, to be nice to everyone, to enjoy every minute of the day — had proved too much, and she had ended up by spoiling it for everyone.

She felt exactly the same now, and while by her age, she certainly should have known better, within a couple of hours of their arrival, she found herself picking a quarrel with Jay.

"I said I'd cook dinner," she said when Jay announced that he would like to do the cooking. "I was looking forward to making you a meal."

"Well, that makes two of us." Jay laid fillet steak and asparagus, raspberries and cream out on the kitchen worktop. "There. A feast fit for a king!"

But Alice was annoyed. She had said that she would shop for their first meal; she had planned it carefully and enjoyed doing it. Jay had agreed to provide the wine, and perhaps some crisps and olives.

"I'm not keen on asparagus," she said, aware of how childish that sounded, but unable to stop herself.

"Everyone likes asparagus," Jay said, breaking off the spears and putting them in a saucepan. His calmness was infuriating.

"Well, I don't."

"Never mind. I can eat it myself."

This, of course, was entirely the wrong thing to say. Jay should have been apologetic; he should have realised he had been remiss in not consulting her first. He also ought to be concerned that while he was eating his bloody asparagus, Alice would be having to make do with salad. Alice was mature enough to know that she was being unreasonable and that she was risking sabotaging their precious weekend, but she was sufficiently infuriated not to care.

"I'll wash the raspberries, shall I?" she said in what she hoped were icy tones.

"Already done," said Jay cheerily, opening the champagne. "Come on, Alice. Have a drink."

"I don't feel like a drink." Alice did feel like a drink, and as Jay knew only too well, she always felt like champagne (who didn't?). But she continued to make her silly little stand. She seemed unable to stop herself.

"Alice, what is your problem?" Jay paused, glass in one hand, bottle in the other. "You seem determined to spoil this evening. What's the matter with you?"

"Nothing's the matter."

"Of course something's the matter. Tell me what it is, and we'll sort it out."

"I said, *nothing's the matter.*"

"Okay. If you're sure." Jay tasted the champagne and poured himself a glassful. Apparently he had decided to ignore her ill temper.

"Nice champagne?" Alice asked.

"Excellent. I thought I'd bring a really good one to celebrate our weekend together. A shame I'm going to have to drink it on my own."

"You're really going to do that, are you? Drink champagne on your own?"

"Well, if you won't join me, I'm going to have to, aren't I? Now that the bottle's open."

"I don't know how you can!"

Jay banged his glass down on the table. "You tell me that nothing's the matter. I accept what you say. And now, apparently, that's wrong too. What, exactly, am I supposed to do, Alice? Tell me how you want me to behave, and I'll do my best to oblige."

"I want you to stop controlling this — this *relationship.*"

"From where I'm standing, you're the one in control. You're the one hell-bent on spoiling our weekend. You're the one who's in a nasty mood. I'm not controlling anything!"

"Yes. Yes, you are. All this, everything we do, is controlled by you. You and your marriage. When we meet, when we can speak on the phone, the secrecy — everything. And now, when I plan to cook us a meal and have everything ready, you have to take control of that, too, and do it yourself. I'm not even allowed to cook for you. Everything — *everything* — is controlled by you."

"But it's you I'm doing it for." Jay sat down at the table and ran his fingers through his hair. "Alice, why now? We've had this kind of conversation time and time again, and now that we have a chance to spend a whole weekend together, you spoil it by bringing it all up again. I don't understand you, I really don't."

"No. You don't, do you?"

"Bloody women!" Jay finally snapped. "You're all the same!"

"*Women*? Do you mean the sainted Angela has moods, too? Oh dear. Poor Jay."

"Don't you bring Angela into this!"

"Oh no. I forgot. Angela must be protected at all costs, mustn't she? Poor, blameless Angela, with her — with her precious bump and her nice pink nursery!" And to her horror, she burst into tears.

"That," said Jay, "was unworthy of you." And ignoring the tears, he flung back his chair and left the room.

Alice had painted herself into a corner. She knew that she was being totally unreasonable. She knew she was being selfish and thoughtless and unkind, and that she had said some horrible things, entirely without provocation. Worst of all, she knew that if their weekend was to be saved from total wreckage, she had to be the one to do it. Jay had done everything he could to keep the peace; now it was her turn.

She opened the back door and stood for a moment on the step, taking in the night-smell of damp earth and leaves and grass. It was already dark outside, but a crescent moon hung suspended in the arc of the sky, as though from an invisible thread, surrounded by a flotilla of stars. Jay knew the names of many of them, and usually she enjoyed listening to him as he explained the different constellations.

She walked carefully across the tiny lawn, enjoying in spite of herself the feel of the turf beneath her bare feet and the cooling breeze against her cheeks. Looking up, she felt, as she always did, the unimportance of herself and of the world she inhabited in comparison with the hugeness of everything that lay beyond, and it made the pettiness of her behaviour seem even more trivial, stupid, *unnecessary*.

"I'm sorry," she whispered. "I wish I could take it all back. I'm so, so sorry."

"I know you are." She hadn't heard Jay come up behind her, and now his arms encircled her waist. "I know you are."

They stood for a few minutes in silence, watching the stars, listening to the soft sounds of the countryside. If she turned her head, Alice could hear the steady thump of Jay's heartbeats under his thin cotton shirt, and the soft sound of his breathing.

"That's Orion." Jay pointed. "See his belt across the middle?"

Alice nodded. "I really am sorry," she said. "Terribly sorry. I've no idea what got into me."

"Haven't you? Haven't you really?" Jay turned her to face him.

She shook her head.

"Things have been difficult for a while," Jay said.

"You mean, *I've* been difficult for a while."

"No, not just you. Us. The situation."

"You mean — the baby?"

"That too. I know how hard it must be for you, darling, but what can I do about it?"

"Nothing. There's nothing you can do. Nothing either of us can do."

Jay took her hand. "Let's go indoors. While the champagne's still cold."

Much later, as they lay together in bed, watching the thin curtains shifting in the breeze and listening to the distant hooting of an owl, Alice was filled with foreboding.

"It's nearly over, isn't it?" she whispered. "You and me. We can't go on for much longer, can we?"

There was a long silence, and then Jay sighed.

"I don't know, sweetheart. I really don't know. But just for now, let's try and live in the moment. Let's make the most of what we have."

"You're right." Alice moved more closely into his arms, resting her head in the curve of his neck. "Actually," she said, "asparagus is my favourite vegetable."

"I know." Jay laughed. "Why do you think I brought it?"

Gabs

Gabs' life was becoming complicated, and at the moment she could do without complications.

For a start, there was Steph. Steph, in fact, was becoming less of a problem since the dreaded visit to Father Pat, for contrary to everyone's expectations, Father Pat had been surprisingly helpful. He had praised Steph and Clive for "doing the right thing" (apparently choosing not to mention the fact that all this was because they had started off by doing the wrong thing) and being "good Catholics" (Gabs cringed).

"He was so nice, Gabs," Steph said. "You'd hardly believe it was the same man!" (Gabs didn't.) "He had lots of ideas and said that the baby might bring us closer, in which case we could get married."

"He *what?*"

"He said — he said that Clive and I might end up by getting married."

"Steph, if you marry that wimp, I'll never speak to you again."

"Well, it's unlikely; of course it is. But Clive is being very sweet at the moment."

Gabs tried to imagine Clive being sweet, and failed. "Well, it's your funeral," she said.

"Don't be like that, Gabs. I'm doing my best."

"I know you are, and I'm sorry, but the thought of my little niece or nephew being brought up by Clive…"

"It'll be Clive's child, whether he's there or not," Steph reminded her.

In fact, Clive had taken to coming round rather a lot, and while at first Gabs suspected it could well be because he wanted to chat her up again, he did seem to be genuinely caring where Steph was concerned, and that was no bad thing. At the very least, it meant that she wasn't the only one supporting her sister, and for that alone she was grateful. Their father, when Steph had finally told him her news, had been outraged, slamming the phone down before Steph had time to say anything more, and they hadn't heard from him since. So there was unlikely to be any support coming from that quarter.

Then there was Gabs' job at the agency. While Gabs and Mrs. Grant had — and probably nurtured — a thorough dislike for each other, Gabs did enjoy the work. She didn't need the money — her other activities took care of her needs more than adequately — but she loved the clients and would miss them were she to leave. But Mrs. Grant had a niece coming over from Australia, who was a trained nurse and was interested in working for the agency, and Gabs feared that this would be a perfect opportunity for Mrs. Grant to get rid of her. She had had the statuary three written warnings, so there would be nothing to stand in the way of her dismissal. It occurred to her that she could pre-empt any decision by resigning before she was sacked, but that would be giving in, and Gabs had never been one to give in easily.

Mavis, too, was becoming something of a responsibility. Since Maudie's stroke, she had taken to phoning Gabs up to talk about her worries and ask her advice.

"You know about these things," she would say. "What do you think?"

And Gabs would have to explain that she wasn't medically trained; she had clients who had suffered from strokes, but she wasn't qualified to advise on a particular case.

Maudie had regained consciousness and rallied a little, but she was unable to move her right side, and her speech was all but gone, and Mavis was beside herself. The doctors had told her that Maudie might recover some of her lost faculties, but she was old, and it had been three weeks now. Any recovery tended to happen early on, and the longer Maudie continued in this state, the less likely she was to recover much more.

Gabs had visited her twice — she was fond of Maudie and sorry for Mavis — but privately she didn't hold out a lot of hope. While Maudie appeared pleased to see her, she continued to stare at her strange new world with wild, bewildered eyes, as though seeking explanation where there were none. Her words — jumbled sounds, punctuated by little cries — were almost impossible to understand, and she gripped Mavis's hand in a pathetic attempt to prevent her from leaving.

"I know how hard it must be, but you have to start letting go," Gabs said over coffee in the hospital canteen. "Something was bound to happen sooner or later. She's old, Mavis. She can't last forever."

"But not like this." Mavis wiped away her tears with an embroidered handkerchief. "I never wanted it to happen like this."

"I know." Gab sighed. "Peacefully in her sleep, at home."

"How did you know?"

"Isn't that what we all want?"

"They're talking of her going into a home," Mavis said. "They can't keep her here much longer; they need the bed." She bit her lip. "I promised her that she would never have to go into a home."

"Mavis, you meant it at the time. But you can't look after her yourself. She's a heavy woman; she needs round-the-clock nursing. How would you manage that?"

"I could get help."

"Help's expensive, and it's never there when you need it. Where's the help in the middle of the night, or if she falls?"

"I suppose a home wouldn't have to be permanent," Mavis said. "Just till she's a bit stronger. I could tell her it was just for convalescence, couldn't I?"

"Yes. Give it a try. She might enjoy the company of other people. She does spend a lot of time on her own, doesn't she?"

On her way home, Gabs pondered Mavis's predicament and thanked her lucky stars that she was unlikely to find herself in the same position. Her mother had been dead for years, and her father had all but disowned her. Gabs wouldn't put it past him to demand filial duties of his daughters should the occasion arise, but she would have no hesitation in reminding him that he hadn't earned the right to expect anything from either of them. He had already told her that he had disinherited her (not that there was a lot to inherit); well, two could play at that game. And given his reaction to Steph's condition, he certainly shouldn't expect anything from her.

But the biggest problem facing Gabs was her campaign to win over Father Augustine. She had missed two opportunities because of a bad cold, but fortunately for her, he had suffered some kind of setback and was still off work. However, this situation couldn't last much longer, and if she was to succeed, she needed to do something this Wednesday. The housekeeper always went into town on her day off, and Father Pat took Mass in the local Catholic school on Wednesdays. This was Gabs' last chance.

Gabs had no idea what she was going to do or say if she were fortunate enough to find Father Augustine in and on his own, but she reckoned that love would show her the way. It was true that hitherto, love had never shown her anything, but then she had never been in love before. She felt — no, she *knew* — that when the time came, the right words would come, and anything that happened afterwards would follow naturally.

But the right words didn't come. Father Augustine was certainly in, and he appeared to be on his own, but what Gabs hadn't expected was Father Augustine in his dressing gown.

"Oh." For a moment she was lost for words. "Good morning, Father."

"Good morning. I'm afraid I have to ask you to go. I was about to have a shower. As you see, I'm not prepared for — for visitors."

"Oh, that doesn't matter. This will only take a moment." Gabs edged her way past him and into the hallway. "I brought you these." She handed him some very expensive chocolates. "I'm so sorry you've been ill."

"That's very kind of you." He took the chocolates. "But I really have to insist that you go. This is — this is quite inappropriate."

"Don't worry." Gabs shrugged off her jacket. "I'm in the caring profession. I'm used to people in dressing gowns."

"But I'm not. I'm not used to being seen like this." Father Augustine put the chocolates down on a chest and tried to usher Gabs toward the door.

"Oh, goodness. I feel a bit faint." Gabs sank into a chair. "Could I — could I ask you for a glass of water?"

"Yes. Yes, of course." Father Augustine hurried off to fetch the water, leaving Gabs to gather her wits and cobble together a plan B.

"Thank you." Gabs sipped her water. "I think I'd better put my head between my knees."

"Do you need a doctor?" Father Augustine enquired. From her upside-down position, Gabs noted that his legs were bare, and it looked very much as though he wasn't wearing anything under the dressing gown.

"No. No doctor. If I could just lie down for a minute? I'm sure I'll be fine."

"Oh dear." There was a note of panic in Father Augustine's voice. "I'm not sure where — oh dear!"

"A sofa, perhaps?" Gabs murmured. "Just for a few minutes?"

"A sofa. Yes." Still her host remained rooted to the spot. Gabs noticed that his legs were pleasantly hairy, his feet long and pale, the toenails neatly trimmed. Sensing that things were about to grind to a halt, Gabs tilted sideways, and Father Augustine gave an anxious little cry. "A sofa. Yes. I'll help you, shall I?"

"That would be kind."

Gingerly Father Augustine placed an arm under Gabs' and helped her to her feet. Together, they tottered down the hallway and into a small sitting room.

"I think I'm going again," Gabs said, leaning against him with her full weight.

Father Augustine strengthened his hold on her. By this time, he had both arms round her, and Gabs' head was resting against his shoulder as he tried to lever her across the room.

"You're — so — kind," Gabs murmured. Slowly, very slowly, she manoeuvred a hand through a gap in Father Augustine's dressing gown, resting it on his stomach.

Father Augustine started. "Please — please be careful," he said, trying to remove the hand.

But Gabs, feigning confusion, slid the hand gently downwards until she found what she was looking for, and let her fingers brush lightly against Father Augustine's groin. She was pleased to find that at least part of Father Augustine was pleased to see her, and she strengthened her hold.

"Oh, please. Please don't!"

Poor Father Augustine. He was obviously on the horns of a terrible dilemma. Either he let Gabs fall, or he continued the journey to the sofa, now horribly aware that she knew what was going on in his head.

"Please don't," he said again. "*Please.*"

Now, Gabs knew perfectly well that if she really loved Father Augustine — loved him in that altruistic, unpossessive way that is supposed to be true love (although she suspected that there was no such thing) — she should stop now. There was still time to rescue the situation, not to mention spare Father Augustine further embarrassment, but she too was reaching the point of no return. She knew — who better? — that in a sexual encounter, there often comes a "what the hell" moment — a point where judgement and ethics go out of the window, possible repercussions are forgotten, and raw animal passion takes over. In that moment, Gabs knew that if she went ahead, there would be problems, decisions, and pain for one or both of them, but she was beyond caring. She had planned and dreamed of this moment for so many weeks, there was no way that she was going back now, even if she could.

"Where's your bedroom?" she whispered.

"What?"

"Your bedroom. Where is it?"

"We shouldn't. We can't. Oh, please!"

"Yes, we can." Gabs stroked and caressed, and Father Augustine gave a little moan. "No one need know."

"Don't. Please, don't. Oh, God!"

"Your bedroom. Where's your room?"

"Upstairs. Oh, God!"

"Come on, then."

Her supposed faintness forgotten, Gabs half pushed half pulled Father Augustine up the stairs and into the only room whose door was open.

"This one?" she asked.

"Yes. Oh, please don't. Oh, God forgive me!"

Gently Gabs pushed Father Augustine back onto the bed, and undoing his dressing gown, she set to work on his body with all the skill born of years of practice.

"Oh dear. Oh, God!" Father Augustine's voice was despairing, even if his body no longer resisted her attentions.

"Just let it happen," Gabs whispered. "For once in your life, just do what comes naturally; do what you want to do."

"But I can't. I can't!" He tried to cover his crotch with his hands, but Gabs gently moved them away.

"You have a beautiful body," she said, looking down at him. "Just beautiful."

And it was true. Father Augustine's body was slim and pale, his chest dusted with just the right amount of hair, his hips firm and narrow. Gabs felt a surge of tenderness when she saw the thin red scar running down the side of his stomach, the marks left by the stitches still clearly visible. Gabs looked at his cock — magnificent, erect, and strong — and was overwhelmed with pity. It was surprising that that poor neglected member hadn't wasted away over the years, tucked away out of sight, forbidden any kind of pleasure. There could be no guilt-free sex for a priest, for even that of a solitary nature was frowned upon by the church. But she would make up for all those wasted years; she would show him what his body was made to do, and she would make sure that he enjoyed it.

"Please. Please don't," Father Augustine moaned, trying to sit up. "Please."

But Gabs took no notice and set to work with her fingers and her tongue until he was rendered speechless.

"That's better," Gabs murmured. "That's much better." She undid her blouse and drew his hand inside, guiding his fingers to her nipple, which stiffened under their touch. He gave a gasp, but he didn't remove his hand, and Gabs was encouraged. She was almost there. This longed-for moment was just minutes away.

"We shouldn't — oh, God!" said Father Augustine again.

"Shhh," Gabs said, as though she were soothing a small child. "Just let yourself go. Leave everything to me. It'll be fine. Everything will be fine."

Very slowly, she removed his hand from her breast and drew it down her body, stroking it over the smooth skin of her belly and hip, brushing it against her pubic hair, and finally settling it between her legs, guiding him to the right place, hearing her own small gasp of pleasure as his fingers, which had taken on a life of their own, began to caress her.

After a few more moments, she carefully manoeuvred herself on top of him, and lifting her hips, she guided him inside her. "There," she whispered. "Isn't that what you want? Doesn't that feel good?" She rocked her body slowly back and forth, making the most of the moment, gazing down into Father Augustine's eyes, in which she could see what appeared to be a mixture of terror and amazement. "Just take your time," she said. "Take your time. Enjoy this moment, my darling. I'm doing this for *you*."

Poor Father Augustine. He didn't hold out for long. How could he? After (presumably) years of celibacy, it was a wonder he'd managed to hang on at all, and when he came, it was with a cry that was so fierce, so agonised, that Gabs was frightened.

"It's all right." She slid carefully off him and tried to put her arms around him. "It's all right, darling. Everything's all right."

"No, it's not." Father Augustine's normal voice appeared to have returned. "I've done a terrible thing." He sat up and grabbed his dressing gown, wrapping it tightly around himself. "A terrible, terrible thing."

"No, you haven't. You've done a natural thing. A good thing." Gabs tried to stroke his hair, but he pushed her hand away.

"May God forgive me." He held his head in his hands. "May God forgive me for the terrible thing I've done. And I've taken advantage. I've taken advantage of a young woman."

"No, you haven't." This was not at all the reaction Gabs had expected. "Of course you haven't. If anyone's taken advantage of anyone, it was me. I took advantage of you, if you want to put it that way."

"But I'm a priest. I should be able to control my passions." To Gabs' horror, she saw that there were tears in his eyes. "I've let everyone down. My church, my vocation, you…"

"You haven't let me down!" Gabs sat down on the bed beside him. "And I have no regrets. What we did was — beautiful. How can you regret that?"

"This — what we did. It belongs in marriage. That's where it belongs. Nowhere else."

"It belongs to people who care about each other! You care about me, don't you?"

"I care about God. My life belongs to him."

"But God can't give you — this. What we've just had."

"Sex is a gift from God, but not like this; and not for me." He was weeping openly now, but although Gabs longed to comfort him, something prevented her. "Oh, what am I going to do? I shall have to go away!"

"Yes. Yes! We'll go away. Together." Gabs felt a surge of hope. "We'll start a new life together. We can —"

"No. No! I can't be with you. I can't see you again. I can never see you again."

"Why ever not?"

"*I'm a priest!*"

"But you don't have to be a priest forever. You can leave the church. We can get married, have children, live wherever you like. You can be a normal *man*!"

"No. You don't understand." He stood up. "Please go now," he said. "Please go, and — and don't come here again. Please don't come here again."

"Don't make me go!" Gabs too was near to tears. "Please don't make me go."

"I can't — make you go. But I'm asking you. If you care for me at all, please go. Go now."

"All right. If that's really what you want."

"It is. And I'm sorry. I'm so sorry for what I did. It was unforgivable."

Afterwards, Gabs had no idea how she managed to get home. She must have driven (she had borrowed a friend's car as it was less conspicuous than her own), but she had no memory of that journey. She had no memory, either, of finishing the bottle of wine in the fridge, of having a shower, of putting her crumpled clothes in the washing machine. When Steph got in from work hours later, Gabs was sitting in a chair, staring into space. She didn't know how long she had been there, nor did she care.

"Gabs? What on earth's the matter?" Steph put down her bag of groceries. "What's happened?"

"Happened?" Gabs tried to remember what had happened, and then immediately blocked it out of her mind again.

"Yes. Happened." Steph crouched down beside Gabs' chair. "Something's happened. Has somebody hurt you? One of your — clients? Tell me, Gabs. You have to tell me!"

"Something's happened," Gabs repeated, but the words were meaningless to her.

"Yes. Something's happened. Now tell me what it was, Gabs. You have to tell me. Have you been — raped?"

"Not raped."

"Well, what, then? Are you hurt?"

"Not hurt."

"*What has happened?*" Steph gave her a little shake. "For crying out loud, Gabs. Tell me!"

Gabs looked up into Steph's face — into her sister's kind, anxious face — and the awfulness of the morning's events came flooding back to her, and she started to cry.

"Heavens, Gabs. It must be pretty bad. You never cry!" Steph said, putting her arms around her. "Come on. You know you can tell me anything. Anything at all."

"Not this," said Gabs through her sobs. "Not this."

"Yes. This. Especially this. Whatever it is."

"You'll be furious. And it's what I deserve."

"Why should I be furious?" There was a moment's silence, and then Steph's voice dropped. "Oh, heavens. It's Father Augustine, isn't it?"

Gabs nodded.

"Gabs, what have you done? Tell me what you've done!"

"It was awful. Awful." And Gabs burst into tears again. "It was the most awful thing, and it was all my fault. Oh, Steph — you should see him. He's so ashamed. So desperately ashamed. And he *apologised*. To me. I think I've done him terrible harm, and he's taken the blame himself."

"Yes. He would." Steph's tone was icy.

"Whatever you feel about me, it can't be worse than how I feel about myself."

"Well, I suppose that's something."

"Please, Steph. Please try to understand."

"Oh, I understand. You seduced a good, kind, trusting man. You did it in cold blood —"

"Not in cold blood! I love him!"

"No, you don't. You were thinking only of yourself. Well, it seems that you got what you wanted, and now you've got what you deserve." Steph picked up her bag of groceries and took them into the kitchen, closing the door behind her, leaving Gabs on her own.

And for perhaps the first time in her life, Gabs knew what it was to feel shame.

As she sat in her chair, watching the dusk gathering outside the uncurtained window, listening to the sounds of Steph banging about in the kitchen, a final thought came to her, hitting her like a body blow.

"I never kissed him," she wept, overwhelmed yet again by what she had done. "I never even kissed him!"

Mavis

Four weeks after her stroke, Maudie had made little improvement, and Mavis was beginning to realise that she would have to arrange some kind of permanent care for her. The hospital had done all they could, and now it was time for her to move on. They needed the bed, the sister told her; it was time for Maudie's care to be passed on into other hands.

Mavis knew that what she was told was true; she could see that Maudie — unable to walk, speak, or feed herself — was using up valuable resources. But she also knew that her mother was being gently edged out into the twilight world of care for the elderly — the care of those for whom the medical profession had given up and for whom, in any case, there was probably little time left. Had Maudie been younger or of more value to society (a Judi Dench, perhaps, or a Queen Mother — one of those national treasures for whom exceptions could be made), no doubt more efforts would have been expended on her behalf. But she was an ordinary woman who had led an ordinary life; she was of little consequence to the world she had inhabited for almost ninety years, and when her time came, that world was unlikely to miss her.

But Mavis already missed her. She missed her terribly. She missed the sound of her voice and the shuffle of her slippered feet around the house; she missed the daytime television programmes, the unnecessary trips to confession, and the demands for "just a little glass of wine, Mavis. Just a small one." She even missed the occasional forays into the kitchen for purposes of pie-making, because at least they demonstrated that her mother still had life in her, that she still had things she wanted to do, however inconvenient the consequences for Mavis herself. And she resented those who appeared to assume that she would be relieved that she no longer had to personally care for her mother.

"You'll have more time to do what you want," a well-meaning neighbour said. "You won't be so *tied*."

But while Mavis had initially feared for her own independence when Maudie had moved in with her, she had come to enjoy having her around and had never thought of her as a tie. Apart from the inevitable restrictions it placed on her relationship with Clifford, she had neither regretted nor resented her mother's presence, for Mavis remembered the kind, funny, outgoing person Maudie used to be, and she was grateful to have had such a woman as her mother.

The hospital recommended a nursing home. It was conveniently placed, within walking distance of Mavis's house, but it was basic. Maudie had only a few thousand pounds in savings, so there was no money for the posh or the private.

But the staff were kind, on the whole, and Maudie's shared room looked out onto the garden. It could have been worse.

Maudie, however, hated it.

"Bad!" she yelled every time Mavis went to visit her, using one of the few words still at her disposal. "Bad!"

"But what's bad, Mother? What is it that's bothering you? Look! You've got a lovely room, and nice — what's your name, dear? Ivy? — Ivy over there to share it with you."

"Bad!" persisted Maudie, thumping the table with her good hand. "*Slumpish.*"

"What?"

"Slumpish. Bad slumpish."

"Look, I've brought you a bottle of wine. Matron says you can have a small glass before your supper."

Maudie eyed the wine and shook her head.

"Slumpish," she said, although she accepted a small glass. "*Muffkin.*"

Mavis was at a loss as to what to do. She visited Maudie every day, bringing her small treats and trying to help her with her speech (which only seemed to get worse), but Maudie remained unhappy. The small television in her room didn't work properly, and the one in the day room — which appeared to be on all the time — was turned down so low as to be inaudible. She didn't like the food, and she couldn't communicate with her fellow inmates (most of whom were as confused as she was). It was altogether a very distressing situation.

The only thing that seemed to bring Maudie any pleasure was Gabs' visits. Gabs wasn't able to visit her often, but Maudie was always delighted to see her.

"Bad!" she would cry. "Bad *girl!*" And she would smile her new, lopsided smile and hold out her one functioning arm for a hug. Mavis tried not to feel jealous — she herself rarely enjoyed such a welcome — but Gabs told her that this was always the way. The misery and the complaints were kept for the nearest and dearest, since they were the most likely to take them to heart. She, Gabs, was a mere outsider, and therefore not a rewarding target for emotional outbursts.

Mavis wasn't the only one missing Maudie, for Pussolini — that most self-centred of animals — was pining.

"Are you sure?" Mavis asked the vet when she phoned for his opinion. "He doesn't seem the type to pine."

"You'd be surprised," the vet told her. "I've even known a horse to pine for its owner. That's unusual, I grant you, but cats are domestic animals, and they become very attached to people. This one obviously loved your mother."

"What can I do?" Mavis asked, looking at the new, subdued Pussolini, who was making his way unsteadily back to Maudie's room (the only place where he would settle). "At this rate, he'll starve to death."

"Give him food he can't resist," said the vet. "Chicken, perhaps, or some nice fish. There'll be something he will eat. You just have to find out what it is."

But Pussolini refused to try the chicken and spat out the fish. All he would take was milk, and that had to be warmed before he would drink it. His temper hadn't improved — he still snarled and spat at Mavis — but the spirit had gone out of him, and the snarling and the spitting were half-hearted, mere echoes of the sounds he used to make. Mavis toyed briefly with the idea of taking him to visit Maudie, but immediately dismissed it as impracticable. The last time she and Maudie had tried to get him into his cat basket, there had been an epic battle, necessitating a visit to the hospital for antibiotics (and in Mavis's case, stitches). It was not an experience worth repeating, and in any case, the inevitable parting at the end of the visit would only serve to cause further distress.

And then there was Clifford.

Clifford had made a good recovery from his operation, but was still milking his condition for all it was worth, and Mavis was running low on sympathy. She had heard detailed accounts of everything that had happened, from the moment Clifford entered the hospital ("with four new pairs of pyjamas. Four, Mavis! Because Dorothy says *you never know*") until the day he left it (with, apparently, only two pairs of pyjamas, because the hospital had managed to lose the other two), and while she tried to show an interest, she had to admit, if only to herself, that the whole thing was becoming deeply boring. They had only managed to meet once, since Clifford still wasn't allowed to drive, and that had involved two bus rides and a long walk in the pouring rain. Much as Mavis had been looking forward to seeing him, she couldn't help wondering whether it had all been worth it just for the pleasure of holding Clifford's hand and listening to Clifford's interminable accounts of his medical adventures. Afterwards, she realised that he hadn't even asked her how she was, merely commenting on her new hair colour (courtesy of Gabs). Needless to say, he hadn't approved. As for Maudie, his only comment had been that she had "had a good innings". Mavis had always disliked this particular expression, because it seemed to her that when one was missing someone, the length of their innings was irrelevant. When she came to think of it, Clifford himself had had a reasonable innings, but she doubted whether he would like to be reminded of it.

Mr. Strong, too, had been causing her problems. His appearance wasn't the only dapper thing about Mr. Strong; he led a dapper little life and ran a dapper little business, and didn't like either being interrupted. Hitherto, he had been quite accommodating where Mavis's mother was concerned, but apparently this accommodation didn't stretch to lengthy hospital visits, and when initially Mavis had wanted to spend much of her time at Maudie's bedside, he had not been at all understanding.

"But why?" he had asked. "Why do you need to be there so much? She's in the hospital, and the nurses will look after her. You have a job, Mavis. Responsibilities. I'm disappointed in you."

The disappointment was mutual, and Mavis told him so. She had worked loyally and conscientiously for many years, and felt that she was owed a little flexibility in what was, for her, a crisis.

"I have no other family," she told him. "If it were my husband, you would understand, wouldn't you?"

"Of course." Mr. Strong had a grey little wife and understood about marriage. "That would be different."

"Why? Why would it be different?" Mavis wanted to know.

"I am my wife's next of kin."

"Well, I'm my mother's next of kin."

"Marriage," said Mr. Strong, "is a special case."

"Well, my mother's a special case," Mavis said. "She's been a wonderful mother to me, and I'm not letting her down now."

"But you tell me she's confused. She probably doesn't even know you're there."

"She does sometimes, and besides, that's not the point. *I* know I'm there. And that's what matters."

"Well!" said Mr. Strong, who was not used to confrontations. "You may have to consider how much you care about your job, Mavis. There are other people out there who would jump at the chance to work for me."

But Mavis was not going to succumb to threats, nor did she believe that there was anyone at all out there who would want her job. She knew that she was invaluable to Mr. Strong; that when it came to menswear, she had an eye for colour and style; that she was good with the ditherers and the last-minute present buyers; and that Mr. Strong would be very foolish indeed to get rid of her. She also knew Mr. Strong's little ways, of which there were many, and she knew his customers. Mr. Strong could posture and protest all he liked; she was pretty sure that her job was safe.

And if it wasn't? Gabs had once told her that there was more to life than "slaving away in a silly little shop," and while Mavis had been quite offended at the time, now that she thought about it, she reckoned that Gabs had a point. She might not be irreplaceable, but neither was her job. She had a little savings; she could afford to buy time to look around and take stock (not Mr. Strong's kind, either). She would try to do her job as well (and as regularly) as she could, but whatever happened, Maudie would come first.

But now at last there was good news, for Clifford had been given the all-clear and was allowed to drive once more.

"I'll come over to your house, shall I, Mavis? Now that we shan't have any interruptions from your mother."

Mavis didn't like Clifford's tone but had to agree that the idea was a good one. Dennis had now more or less taken up permanent residence in his flat, and even if he were not there, Mavis would always worry that he might suddenly appear, like the man in *Brief Encounter*. Besides, she was still embarrassed about the discovery of her device and annoyed about the missing champagne. As it was, Clifford could come over on her day off, and she would make a nice lunch for them both.

At first things went smoothly. Clifford was in good form and seemed gratifyingly pleased to see her. He had brought wine and flowers, and even complimented Mavis on her appearance (compliments had been in short supply recently). He was pleased with the lunch (Mavis had prepared all his favourite things), and when he showed her his scar, she was suitably impressed.

"That cat doesn't look too well," Clifford remarked as Pussolini tottered through the dining room. "Are you feeding him enough, Mavis?"

"Of course I'm feeding him. It's just that he's not eating. He's pining for Mother."

Clifford shouted with laughter. "Pining? That cat pining? I don't think so," he said.

"Well, he is. The vet said so."

"In that case, that's a good thing, isn't it? He's a horrible animal — you've said so yourself often enough — and if he manages to starve himself to death, that'll be one less thing for you to worry about."

"Mother loves him."

"But she's never going to see him again, is she?" Clifford helped himself to more cheese. "She need never know."

"Are you expecting me to lie to her?"

"No need to lie. Just don't tell her."

"So you're suggesting that I watch him slowly starve and do nothing about it?"

"You don't have a lot of choice, do you?" Clifford picked out his teeth with a cocktail stick, a habit Mavis abhorred.

"He drinks a little warm milk."

"A little warm milk! For goodness' sake, Mavis. He's a *cat*! Why go to all that trouble for a cat? Especially that one."

"I've become fond of him," Mavis said, realising that in a funny way, it was true. The house often felt terribly empty these days, and it was good to come home to something alive, even if that something was only an evil, pining cat.

"Well, you've certainly changed your tune."

"Maybe I have. But I get lonely, living by myself."

"Well, if that cat stops you from feeling lonely, you've certainly got a problem," Clifford said.

"I don't suppose you've ever been lonely, have you?" Mavis asked him.

"Probably not."

"Then you've no idea what it's like."

"I can imagine what it's like."

"I don't think you can. Any more than I can imagine what it's like to have — to have heart surgery."

"That's different," Clifford told her. "You can have no idea what it's like being put under an anaesthetic and not knowing whether you will ever come round."

"I've had an anaesthetic —"

"Ah, but not one like this. Can you imagine what it's like saying goodbye to your family, being wheeled away from them, not knowing whether you'll ever see them again?"

Mavis did in fact have a pretty good idea since Clifford had described this experience to her so many times that she knew the story by heart.

"I can put myself in your shoes, yes," she said. "I just sometimes wish that you could put yourself in mine."

"I don't like the sound of all these accusations."

"I'm not accusing you of anything. It's just that I've done my best to imagine how difficult it must have been like for you in the hospital, having a major operation. But you never seem to understand what it's like for me, living here on my own, visiting Mother, looking after the cat, having Mr. Strong going on at me all the time because I need time off."

"Mavis, do I detect a hint of self-pity?"

There are few things more infuriating than having someone accuse you of a fault that they themselves have in abundance, and Mavis could feel herself becoming seriously angry.

"It takes one to know one," she said, throwing caution to the winds.

"And what's that supposed to mean?"

"It means that you — I — both of us have spent a lot of time feeling sorry for you, but I can't remember a time when you have ever shown any sympathy for me."

"So," said Clifford, buttering himself another biscuit (should he really be having this much cholesterol?), "our reunion is to be turned into a discussion of my shortcomings, is it?" He put cheese on his biscuit and took a bite.

"No, of course not. And I'm sorry. It's just that I've missed you, and I suppose I wanted you to know how miserable I've been without you."

This was not entirely true, but Mavis knew that it was up to her to rescue the situation, which was, in the end, of her own making. If she could focus on Clifford and his illness and his joyous return to good health rather than telling him about her own problems, all would be well.

But then, was this right? Was it honest to conduct a relationship with reference to the feelings of only one of the parties involved? Her relationship with Clifford had become increasingly lopsided over the past few months, and if it carried on in this way, there would eventually be nothing in it at all for Mavis. She had always tried to be unselfish and considerate, but she had her limits, and Clifford was certainly doing his best to test them. It occurred to her that nowadays, she seemed to spend all her time looking after other people. Her mother, the cat, Clifford; even Mr. Strong had sometimes needed emotional support. When the little grey wife found a breast lump, when someone crashed into his new car, when the cleaner took three days' takings from the till, and then did a runner all the way to New Jersey — all these had been occasions for Mavis to lend him a sympathetic ear. But who did this for Mavis? To whom could she turn when things went badly? Certainly she used to be able to depend on Clifford, but not anymore. Clifford was far too busy looking after number one to pay more than glancing attention to any of her problems.

Mavis wondered how Dorothy was coping and whether she was feeling the same.

"How's Dorothy?" she asked now, pouring coffee.

"Fine. Why?"

"Oh, no reason. It's just that all this must have been worrying for her, too."

This was the right thing to say.

"Yes. Of course she was worried. I mean, she was bound to be, wasn't she? After nearly forty years of marriage. But Dorothy's very strong. Actually, I did expect just a little more support from her, but she encouraged me to be independent, to do things for myself. I don't think," Clifford added, stirring cream into his coffee, "that Dorothy would have made a very good nurse."

"Good for Dorothy!"

"What do you mean?" Clifford looked at her suspiciously.

"Oh, just that it's always good to encourage independence, isn't it? You must have been pleased that she was so encouraging."

"Ye-es. I suppose so." Clifford put down his coffee cup and wiped his mouth on his napkin. "Mavis, shall we go to bed?"

Mavis beamed at him. She had redeemed a dodgy situation and would get her reward after all.

"I thought you'd never ask."

The following night, Pussolini died. He died without fuss, curled up on Maudie's bed, as though he had finally given up waiting for her return. When Mavis lifted his fragile corpse, it felt like a tiny bag of bones. It was hard to imagine that this little scrap of a cat had once been so large and so full of life and energy and sheer animal vitriol. She dug a hole under the lilac tree and buried him, wrapped in Maudie's old flannel nightie, for which he had always had a particular fondness.

When she had finished, Mavis went indoors for a solitary wake of tea and biscuits. Sitting at the kitchen table, feeling the silence of the empty house closing in around her, she wept. She wept for Pussolini and his miserable last few weeks; she wept for poor Maudie, who had loved him so much and who would never know of his passing (she had to admit that in this instance, Clifford had been right); and she wept for herself.

For the first time in her life, Mavis felt entirely alone.

The Fifth Meeting: October

Since Alice, Gabs, and Mavis had now got to know one another so much better, further official meetings seemed unnecessary. However, they had promised one another that they would keep them up for a year, and so an October get-together was to be arranged.

"What are you all doing this time?" Finn asked Alice. "Is it your turn to sort it?"

"I've lost count. But I don't mind doing it."

"Can I come?"

"No."

"Why not? I like them. Especially Gabs." Finn grinned.

"That's one of the reasons why not. Besides, you wouldn't want me tagging along when you're out with your friends, would you?"

"You wouldn't want to come."

"True."

"Well then."

"The answer's still no."

"Okay. But what are you going to do?"

"Well, I think it would be nice to include Maudie."

"Is she allowed out?"

"She's not a prisoner. Of course she's allowed out."

This idea had in fact only just occurred to Alice, but as she was an honorary member of the group, it seemed somehow mean to leave Maudie out. She phoned Mavis and put the idea to her.

"I don't know." Mavis sounded doubtful. "She's awfully confused. And heavy. She's put on a lot more weight."

"She's been awfully confused for ages. It might do her good. As for being heavy, with three of us we ought to be able to manage."

"But she hasn't been out at all yet."

"Then perhaps it's time she did. Are you all right, Mavis? You sound a bit low."

"I've just buried the cat."

"Oh, I am sorry."

"Thank you. Everyone else seems to think I should be pleased to be rid of him, but I'm not."

"Of course you're not. He might have been a bugger, but he was part of your family. And at least he had a personality. He wasn't one of those bland, boring lap cats."

"That's true." Mavis laughed. "Someone once tried to pick him up and put him on her lap. I thought he was going to kill her."

"Quite right, too." Alice hesitated. "Was Clifford nice about it?"

"No. Not at all."

"I'm sorry." Alice privately thought that Clifford sounded quite awful, but was wise enough not to say so. "All the more reason for an outing, then. For you and for Maudie. Where do you think she'd like to go? Where would she choose if she could?"

"The zoo. She loved going to the zoo. She said seeing all those animals was like travelling, but without the bother. But I don't think there's a zoo near enough."

"There's that big country house. It's got a safari park. Even better than a zoo if you want to travel."

"Don't the monkeys climb all over the cars? I've heard they do awful damage."

"That's part of the fun. Finn used to love it when he was little. We can take my car. It's so old it won't mind the monkeys, and I don't think we'd all fit into that pink thing of Gabs'."

Alice needed cheering up, and the idea of taking Maudie to a safari park would certainly help. When she phoned Gabs, it sounded very much as though Gabs could do with cheering up, too.

"What's the matter?" Alice asked.

"Don't ask," Gabs said. "Long story."

"Long stories can be shortened."

"Not this one. And not over the phone."

"Okay. Well, we're thinking of taking Maudie to the safari park."

Gabs thought this was a great idea.

"I'm just a bit concerned about the lifting," Alice said. "She'll need heaving in and out of the car, and she's awfully heavy. In the home they have a hoist thing."

"That's because of fucking health and safety. Nurses are wimps these days. They're not allowed to lift a cup of tea without getting help. Leave it to me. We'll manage. I haven't yet found anyone I can't lift."

"Are you allowed to? Lift people at work, I mean?" Alice asked.

"What do you think?"

"Okay. Silly question."

"We can bring a picnic, and have it in the car."

"No dope, though." The thought of drug-induced euphoria in a smallish car surrounded by wild animals was not an attractive (or safe) one.

"Absolutely no dope."

October can be one of the loveliest of months, and so it was on the day of the outing: a golden day of warm sunshine and gently falling leaves, spiced up with the lightest of breezes. The three women collected Maudie from her home, where Gabs' offers of help were dismissed as she was winched into the car by a terrifying machine and several care assistants ("What a load of bollocks," muttered Gabs), and they were off.

At first, Maudie was subdued and appeared bewildered by the sudden change of scene after her lengthy incarceration, but after a while she became chatty and cheerful, and while no one could understand what she was saying, it was good to see her looking more like her old self. She was wearing some rather peculiar clothes, which Mavis said were not her own (clothes in the home appeared to be interchangeable among the residents), but she added that since Maudie didn't mind what she wore, there was no point in making a fuss.

They had chosen a weekday, so the safari park wasn't crowded, and after they'd bought their tickets and a bag of animal food, they were able to drive straight in.

At the sight of the first animal (a hippo), Maudie was completely carried away.

"Bad!" she cried. "Oh, *bad!*" She waved and laughed and tapped on the car window. "*Bad!*"

"They're not bad, Maudie," Alice said. "They're nice hippos. Can you say hippos?"

"I wouldn't worry," Mavis told her. "These days, everything's bad. It doesn't mean anything."

Giraffes and deer stuck their heads through the car window, and Maudie fed them from her bag of food, dropping bits all over the floor of the car and even popping one or two into her own mouth. By the time she'd finished, her hand and clothes were covered with animal slobber, and she appeared to be in seventh heaven.

"Bad. Slumpish!" she cried, trying to pat the nose of a strange stripy creature with a runny nose. "*Slumpish!*"

"Well, this was certainly a good idea," Alice said. "She's having a wonderful time."

When they reached the monkey enclosure, they closed the car windows, as instructed, and drove slowly through, oohing and aahing over the babies and laughing at their antics as they slithered over the roof of the car and tried to dismantle a wing mirror. No one noticed Maudie opening the window, possibly because everyone assumed she was incapable, and it may have been open for several minutes before disaster struck.

It is amazing how quickly cute and cuddly can turn into ferocious and terrified, but that's what happened when a large and very obviously male monkey managed to get into the car.

"Bad!" yelled Maudie as it landed on her lap. "Bad, bad, *bad*!"

Bad indeed. The monkey, which had been confident and very much at home outside the car, became a reluctant and very angry passenger inside it. Immediately there was pandemonium, while the monkey flew round the interior of the car like a whirlwind, ricocheting off laps and shoulders and windows, shrieking and chattering, biting and scratching.

"Bloody hell! What do we do?" cried Gabs as she tried to detach two small and very sharp hands from her hair.

"Food! Give it some food!" cried Mavis.

"I think it's beyond food." Gabs gave their guest's shiny red bottom a slap. "Get out, you fucking animal! *Get out*!"

"Let's open all the windows," Mavis said.

"No. Because then they'll all try to get in. Ouch!" The monkey tore at Alice's shirt. "Get off, you little shit!"

More monkeys, attracted by the noise, were gathering on the bonnet of the car. Their friend, desperate to join them, thumped and scratched at the windscreen, screaming monkey obscenities. Maudie was beside herself with what appeared to be a mixture of fear and delight, and Alice was having one of those moments where you know everything will probably be all right in the end and that you will dine out on this story for years, but in the meantime your mind has entered a state of paralysis.

Fortunately, just when it seemed that the situation could only get worse, the monkey finally realised how it had got in, and made a swift and noisy exit, peeing on Maudie's lap as it went and leaving the occupants of the car frightened and exhausted.

"For God's sake, close that window, somebody!" Gabs was the first to recover. "And to think I used to think monkeys were rather sweet!"

Alice leaned across Maudie and wound up the window.

"Fucking animal," said Maudie, loudly and clearly. "Fucking, fucking, fucking!"

"*Mother!*" said Mavis.

"Never mind that. Blame me, if you like," Gabs said. "Besides, she spoke! She actually said something that meant something."

"And she's right. It was a fucking animal." Alice brushed herself down. "Is everyone okay?"

Considering the malevolent mood of the monkey and the sharpness of its claws, they had got away lightly. Everyone had acquired a few superficial scratches, and Gabs had a rip in her T-shirt, but otherwise there was little harm done.

"I think," said Alice, starting the engine, "that I've had enough of monkeys for one day. Bears, anyone?"

Back in the carpark, they mopped Maudie up as best they could, but she was sticky from animal saliva, very dishevelled, and thanks to the monkey's parting gift, she smelt terrible.

"Oh dear," said Mavis, scrubbing at Maudie's skirt with a tissue. "What will they think back at the home?"

"They'll think she had one hell of a good time, and that's what matters," Gabs said, laying out a rug on the grass beside the car. "Mavis, they're paid to clean her up, so let them do it. Chill out, will you?" She produced a bottle of wine and some glasses. "Wine, anyone?"

"Should we?" Mavis asked, sitting down and getting out several neat Tupperware containers. (Gabs might have known that Mavis was a Tupperware person. She herself favoured plastic bags.)

"Yes," said Gabs. "We certainly should. Heaven knows, we've earned it. Besides, we always have wine."

"Bad?" Maudie held out her hand. "Oh, bad!"

"Of course you can have some, Maudie." Gabs poured her half a glass. "There you go."

Gabs was in a quandary. She was longing to tell the others about her disastrous meeting with Father Augustine, but was pretty sure they would disapprove. On the other hand, who else could she talk to? Steph was still barely speaking to her, and there wasn't anyone else.

"I need to talk," she said. "Please."

"Fire away," said Alice. "After all, that's what we're here for, isn't it?"

"You're not going to like this," Gabs said. "Either of you."

"Oh," said Alice, putting down her glass.

"Yes. Oh."

"You haven't!"

Gabs nodded. "I'm afraid I have."

"How?" Mavis asked after a moment. "How on earth did you manage it?"

So Gabs told them. She spared them some of the details, but otherwise she gave them a pretty accurate picture of what had happened.

"So there it is. I've told you. And please don't be furious, because Steph has been giving me a hard time ever since it happened, and I know I'm in the wrong, I know what I did was awful, and no one can be angrier with me than I am with myself. But I can't turn the clock back."

"Would you?" Alice asked. "If you could?"

"Oh yes. A hundred times, yes. I never thought I'd be saying this, but it was the worst, most selfish, stupid, thoughtless thing I've ever done in my life."

"Goodness," Alice said. "This isn't like you, Gabs."

"You mean I'm incapable of remorse? That I plough my way through people's lives making them miserable and not giving a damn?"

"Of course not —"

"Because you'd be right. On this occasion, anyway."

"So what now?" Mavis asked. "How is — Father Augustine?"

"He's gone."

"Gone where?"

"I've no idea. I suppose he must have told the powers that be what happened, and he's probably been despatched to a monastery on a remote Scottish island to live on bread and water and beat himself with twigs."

"Really?" Mavis asked.

"No, of course not. But they'll have sent him somewhere to teach him to mend his ways; and they weren't his ways, they were mine. The fault was all *mine*." Gabs grabbed a handful of tissues from her bag and wiped her eyes. "And the worst thing of all is that that he wrote me a letter and *apologised*! He insisted that it was his fault, and he actually apologised. To me." She buried her face in her hands and wept openly. "I loved him, you know. I loved him so much!"

"Gosh, you really did, didn't you?" Alice moved closer and put her arm round Gabs' shoulders.

Gabs nodded. "Yes, I did. I'm not sure that I really loved him... before. I lusted after him to such an extent that I think I interpreted it as love. But now..." She stifled a sob. "After the way he's behaved, the way he *was* with me... I don't think I've ever met such a good person. I mean really, truly *good*." She blew her nose. "And of course I shall never see him again. Or probably anyone like him." She started to sob again. "Oh, what shall I do? Whatever am I going to do?"

"You might," Alice said after a moment. "Meet someone like him, I mean. You're still so young, Gabs. You've got time." Her voice sounded wistful.

"Have I? Have I really? I don't think so. I've been round the block so many times, Alice. I've met so many men. Okay, so most of them were just out for what they could get, but I have met one or two good ones as well. But never anyone like him. There — there just isn't anyone like him."

"Would you want to — to be with anyone like that? Anyone — well, that good?" Mavis asked.

"You mean, I could never be good enough for him."

"No, that's not what I meant."

"Well, you'd have a point. I'm not good enough. Not nearly good enough. But I could change. I *would* change. I've never wanted to change before — never really seen the need — but he's shown me what I might be. He's made me realise that I could be a — well, a better person. And I'd like to be a better person, for him. I'd do anything — *anything* — for him. To make him happy. But of course, now I'll never have the chance." She plucked at the grass and then wiped her hand on her jeans. "And I'm worried about him. How he is. How he's coping. I've put him in this — this terrible situation, and I can't do anything to help him out of it."

"He'll be all right," Alice said. "He's got his God, and I'm sure there'll be good support for him. This kind of thing must happen quite often." She squeezed Gabs' shoulder. "And you'll be all right too, one day. Not yet, maybe. But one day."

"Yeah, I guess." Gabs wiped away tears. "But I'll never be the same again."

"Is that a bad thing?"

"Probably not. But I would have liked to change *for him*. There isn't anyone else to change *for*. I know that sounds silly, but no one else really cares how I am. My friends think my lifestyle's a bit of a laugh, and of course Steph disapproves. But no one really *cares*."

"We care, don't we, Mavis? Not in a judging kind of way, but because it would be good if you could be really happy. And I can't believe that your lifestyle, as you put it, makes you happy."

"Ah, but the money does," said Gabs, with the glimmer of a smile.

"Gabs, you're incorrigible!"

"Yeah. That's my trouble, isn't it?"

"Bad," Maudie said through a mouthful of doughnut. "*Bad!*"

"Oh, Maudie, if you only knew." Gabs got up and rescued half a sandwich that had become stranded on its journey down Maudie's substantial bosom. "If you only knew. Anyway, enough about me. How are you, Alice?"

"Pretty bloody," Alice said. "Jay and I had this weekend together, and I practically ruined it. If Jay hadn't been so understanding, it would have been completely wasted. Bugger, I think that's my mobile." She got up and retrieved her bag from the back seat of the car.

The others waited as Alice spoke on the phone. Evidently the news wasn't good.

"I'm so sorry," she said, beginning to gather up her things. "I have to go. Finn's had an accident."

"What kind of accident?" Mavis asked.

"He's in A & E. They think he's broken his arm."

"Heavens! Is he okay?" Gabs asked.

"They say he is, but they've been trying to get me for the last hour, and I didn't hear my phone. Apparently Trot's with him."

"Well, that's something," Mavis said.

"You don't know Trot. He's no use at all in an emergency." Alice paused. "I'm afraid that means you'll all have to come with me, because of the car. But at least it's on the way back to Maudie's place. Is that okay?"

"Of course," said Gabs, who had an appointment with Gerald later on and had not been looking forward to it (things had moved way beyond Best in Show at Crufts, and she would be glad of an excuse to cancel him).

"Let's go, then."

They arrived at the hospital half an hour later, and after some discussion, Alice went on ahead while Gabs and Mavis commandeered a wheelchair for Maudie, who appeared to be sound asleep. This could take some time, and they could hardly leave her in the car.

When they caught up with Alice, she and Finn were waiting for Finn's arm to be plastered. Trot had apparently gone in search of tea.

"How's it going?" Gabs asked.

"Painful," said Finn, nursing his arm. "Fractured radius."

"How did you do it?"

"I fell off a radiator."

"How on earth…?"

"Don't ask," said Alice, who was obviously not in the best of moods.

Finn pulled a face at Gabs, who winked at him.

"Bad," remarked Maudie, who had woken up.

"Too right," said Finn.

"Slumpish."

"I'll say."

Trot appeared with two polystyrene cups of tea. He too brightened when he saw Gabs.

"Well, hi," he said. Then he turned to Alice. "You took your time," he said.

"I didn't hear my mobile."

"Good job I had mine, then."

"There's no need to look so smug, Trot. I think this must be the first time you've ever actually had to be on medical standby, and I'm sure you did an excellent job."

"Fucking animal," said Maudie, yawning.

"*What?*" Trot handed tea to Finn.

"Don't mind Mother," Mavis said. "She doesn't mean it."

"Oh yes, she does. We had an — incident with a monkey," Alice said. "It got into the car in the safari park."

"I wish I'd been there!" Finn said.

"No, you don't," Alice told him. "Believe me, no one needs a monkey in the car."

"I have to make a phone call," Gabs said. "I'll be back."

She went out into the carpark and dialled Gerald's number. He would be cross and disappointed, but it couldn't be helped. She rarely let her clients down — it was bad for business — but this was unavoidable.

Gerald's phone was switched off, which was a relief, so she left him a message. The Gerald thing was getting out of hand, and it was really time to call it a day, but the money was good and she knew he'd be terribly upset if she were to discontinue their meetings. Last week, he had actually proposed to her, and for a brief moment, Gabs had had a nightmarish image of herself walking down the aisle in her wedding dress, with Gerald padding along beside her wearing his diamond-studded collar and lead, all panting tongue and dangling balls. Of course, it wouldn't really have been like that. When he wasn't with Gabs, Gerald was a chartered accountant who played golf on Saturdays and lived a perfectly respectable life. Most of them did. But even if she wanted to marry him — even if he gave up his dog act altogether — she would never be able to see him as anything else.

As she walked back towards the hospital, Gabs wondered why it was that she had never received a proposal from a *normal* man. It wasn't as though she never met any. But such proposals as she had had included one from a divorced brain surgeon with a predilection for sheepskin rugs and high heels (he wore the heels), and a wannabe dairy farmer, who pretended to milk Gabs' substantial breasts into a galvanised iron bucket. Hardly husband material, even for someone as unconventional as Gabs.

She took a small mirror out of her bag and inspected her face. She looked a mess — all puffy eyes and streaks of mascara — but for once, she couldn't have cared less. She looked at her watch and decided she probably had time for a quick fag.

Mavis was having a most unsettling afternoon. She had been genuinely terrified by the monkey incident (unlike the others, she didn't find monkeys particularly cute, and she was quite sure they were riddled with fleas); she was upset at the state of Maudie, and the fact that she would be returning her to the home too late for tea; and she was also disappointed that she hadn't had the chance to discuss the Clifford situation. But she told herself that no doubt another meeting could be arranged, and in any case, Finn was more important.

Looking at Finn and Alice, and their easy, bantering relationship, Mavis found herself wishing that she too had a son. Not a daughter. She wouldn't have wanted a daughter. But a son — someone who would depend on her but upon whom later on she could depend; someone who would make her laugh (for Mavis could see that Finn had a good sense of humour); someone who was *family*. Maudie's illness had brought home to her the fact that without her mother (and if she didn't count a distant cousin in New Zealand), she was without any kind of family. She imagined a future of solitary Christmases and holidays with single-room supplements, and an eventual old age without anyone who would care enough to make sure that she was well looked after. No one really loves me, she thought, except Mother. No one at all.

Of course, Clifford loved her in his way, but she could never come first in his life, and he certainly wouldn't be able to take care of her if she were unable to care for herself. She wasn't sure that Clifford was capable of taking care of anyone; he had become too self-centred. She tried to imagine him looking after Dorothy if she ever needed it — Clifford hefting Dorothy into those giant knickers; Clifford buttoning blouses and doing zips-ups — and she couldn't see it happening. Once, when she had broken her wrist, Clifford had tried to help her to dress after their lovemaking, and she had wondered that a man who had on many occasions managed to undo a bra with one hand couldn't manage to do it up again with two.

"You all right, Mave?" Trot asked her. "You look a bit thoughtful."

"It's been that kind of afternoon." Mavis smiled at Trot. He had a kind face, even if he was a bit scruffy and called her Mave. She thought that Alice could do a lot worse than marry him, especially since they had a ready-made family in Finn.

"Read *War and Peace* yet, have you?" he asked her.

"Don't worry," Alice said. "Trot knows the score. He just likes teasing people."

"As a matter of fact, I have," Mavis told him.

"Good, is it?"

"Long."

"Ah. I thought as much."

At this point, Finn rejoined them, his arm plastered in a fetching shade of red.

"They let you choose the colour," he told them. He seemed to have cheered up.

"At least it's your left arm," Alice said. "You'll still be able to do your homework."

Finn scowled at her.

"Give the poor guy a break," Trot said.

"Just for tonight, then." Alice patted Finn's shoulder. "Right. Home everyone. We'll take Maudie first."

"Can I help?" Trot asked.

"You could take Finn, and give him something to eat."

"Sorry. Got a date."

"Then why offer?" Alice asked him.

"It's what you do, isn't it?"

"Only if you mean it. So I suggest you cancel your date and look after your son. We won't be long."

Trot grumbled and complained, but he took Finn with him, and the others piled back into Alice's car. Mavis marvelled at the ease with which Gabs managed to manhandle Maudie into the front seat, barely waking her in the process (Maudie, exhausted by what had been a long and eventful day, had gone back to sleep), before settling herself beside Mavis in the back.

By the time they reached Maudie's institution, it was after nine o'clock, and there was much unlocking and unbolting of doors before a nurse eventually came to meet them.

"Maudie's in the car," Alice told her. "Could we have a wheelchair, please?"

"You'll need the hoist."

"We can manage without the hoist," Gabs said. "You get the chair and leave it to me."

"But we have to use it. Because of health and safety."

"Bugger health and safety. And I don't *have* to do anything. I'm nothing to do with this place."

"Well, there's no need to talk to me like that!"

"We're all tired," said Mavis, who could see things getting out of hand. "It's been a long day."

The chair was fetched, and the sleeping Maudie was moved into it with amazing ease, considering Gabs' diminutive size. Even the nurse seemed impressed.

She wasn't quite so impressed when she had had a proper look at Maudie.

"Oh dear," she said. "What have we been doing?"

"*We*," said Alice, "have entertained a monkey in the car, had a very sticky picnic, and spent three hours in A & E."

"Oh dear. What's happened to her clothes?"

"Monkey pee," Alice told her.

The nurse looked at her suspiciously. "Has she had anything to eat?"

"Since lunch? Two bags of crisps and a bar of chocolate."

"Oh dear."

"There wasn't anything else. And perhaps you could stop saying 'oh dear' and help us get her to her room."

While Mavis admired the way Alice spoke to the night nurse (she herself would never have dared to be so bold), she felt that she should be the one to take charge. After all, she was Maudie's daughter.

"I'm sorry she's in such a state," she said. "I did phone to say we'd be late."

The nurse's expression softened. "Yes, I got the message. Well, you'd better come along."

"What, all of us?" Mavis asked.

"Well, I haven't got time to put her to bed; I've got the hot drinks and the medicines to do."

"And I have a wounded son to get home to," Alice said.

"That's not my problem."

"But Maudie is?" Alice told her.

"It's all right," said Mavis hastily. "I'll get her ready for bed and get a taxi home. You two go. I'll be fine."

"I'll stay," Gabs said. "It'll be quicker with two of us. And," she added, as the nurse was still hovering, "we shan't be needing any hoist."

In Maudie's room, Gabs whipped off Maudie's clothes and gave her a quick wash while Mavis looked out a clean nightie (someone else's, naturally, but that seemed to be par for the course).

"There," Gabs said. "Good as new." She cleaned Maudie's dentures and put them on her bedside table, then levered her into bed and tucked her in. "Time to go." She kissed Maudie's cheek. "Bye, Maudie."

Maudie opened one eye. "Fucking animal," she said.

In the back of their shared taxi, Mavis had an overwhelming desire to weep. She was exhausted, she was worried about Maudie, and she couldn't see any end to an existence that seemed to be fraught with difficulties.

"You okay?" Gabs asked her.

"Not really."

"Poor Mavis." Gabs put an arm round her. "Things aren't easy for you at the moment, are they?"

"I shouldn't bother you with my problems. You've got enough of your own."

"We've done my problems," said Gabs. "It's your turn now."

"Well, it's just that there doesn't seem to be anything to look forward to. I know that sounds ridiculous. I'm not a child. I should be able to live without — treats and nice things happening."

"We all need treats," Gabs said. "Even tiny ones. Little pegs to hang our lives on, give them a lift." She passed Mavis a tissue. "What about Clifford? He being any use?"

"Not a lot. He's too preoccupied with his own problems."

"But he's okay now, isn't he?"

"Yes. Yes, he is. But d'you know, I think he'd almost rather that he wasn't. He likes to be the centre of attention, and now that his operation's over, the attention's died down a bit. I think he misses it."

"He sounds to me like a selfish bastard," Gabs said. "He seems to walk all over you."

"Sometimes it does feel a bit like that." For a brief moment, Mavis wondered why she hadn't leapt to Clifford's defence. "But he never used to be like this. He's changed since he retired. He can still be very kind, very sweet."

"But not at the moment."

"No. Not at the moment."

"Which is when you need him, isn't it?" Gabs got out a packet of chewing gum and put a piece in her mouth. "Stops me thinking about the ciggies," she explained. "Want some?"

"No, thanks."

"Mavis, why do you stay with him?"

"I keep asking myself that," Mavis said. "And I don't really know."

"Is it because there isn't anyone else?"

"I suppose that's part of it. And we go back a long way."

"He's a habit, then."

"In a way. And I do love — well, I'm very fond of him. Most of the time."

"Who are you trying to convince?"

"Myself, I suppose. And then there's — there's the sex."

"Good, is it?"

"Well, it was. But now Clifford likes to choose what we do — because of his heart, he says — and I don't always like it."

"What is it he wants exactly?"

Mavis blushed and whispered something in Gabs' ear.

"Mmm. You're right." Gabs popped another piece of gum in her mouth. "A lot of women wouldn't do that. There's more to you than meets the eye, Mavis."

"But I suppose it's better than nothing," Mavis said. "If Clifford and I finished, would I ever have any kind of — physical relationship again?"

"Course you would. There are plenty of blokes out there, Mavis. You've got lovely eyes and nice boobs. You underestimate yourself."

That night, after Mavis had got home, Clifford phoned. She told him about the outing to the safari park, but he didn't seem particularly interested, merely remarking that they had been "very stupid to let that old woman open the car window."

"And how've you been?" Mavis asked him, biting her tongue.

"Well, I've had this pain in my leg, and I'm a bit concerned. I've got a friend who knows about these things, and he says it could be something called *intermittent claudication*. I looked it up, and I've got all the symptoms."

Mavis sighed. It had been a very long day, and all she wanted was a hot bath and her bed. She listened for a few more minutes, and then very gently, almost apologetically, she replaced the receiver.

She was surprised to find that she hardly felt guilty at all.

Part Six

Alice

As soon as Alice heard Jay's tone of voice on the phone, she knew that Angela had had her baby. On the surface, his greeting was the same as usual, but she knew him too well not to hear the undercurrent of excitement.

"Angela's had the baby, hasn't she?" she said.

"How did you know?"

"Call it feminine intuition."

"Ah."

"Well, aren't you going to tell me all about it?"

"Oh, Alice. I didn't know how to do this. I thought of asking to see you and telling you face-to-face, but —"

"Like giving someone bad news, you mean?"

"No. Of course not. But I knew it was going to be difficult."

"You mean, you knew *I* was going to be difficult," said Alice, knowing that that was exactly what was already happening. She was overcome with sudden nausea, and sat down on a kitchen chair.

"Not at all. But I can imagine how you must feel."

"Can you?"

"I've a pretty good idea."

"Well, tell me. Tell me how I feel, Jay, and then I won't have to go to the bother of finding out for myself."

"Alice, *please*."

"I know, I know. I'm sorry, really I am. And I'm being pretty ungenerous, too. So do tell me about it. I want to know; of course I do."

"Well, she went into labour yesterday afternoon. The baby was born early this morning."

"And you were there?"

"Of course I — yes, I was there. She wanted me there."

As she questioned Jay, Alice knew that she was pouring salt into her own wounds; it was almost as though she were trying to get all the pain out of the way quickly. For naturally, Jay would have been there. Nowadays, wasn't it rare for fathers not to be present at the births of their children?

Apart from a formidably businesslike midwife, there hadn't been anyone with her when Finn was born. She had asked her mother whether she would like to be present when her grandson came into the world, but her response ("No thank you, dear. I'll see you both when you're all tidied up") had been unequivocal.

"And everything went all right?" she asked now.

"Everything went fine. Angela was very — no, you don't need to hear that. She had a good labour, and we've got our daughter."

"And she's beautiful."

"Of course. We think so, anyway."

Oh, how that "we" seemed to cut into her, like a knife. Before the baby, Jay had rarely referred to himself and Angela in that way, and Alice had managed to persuade herself that they weren't really a couple at all — or if they were, it was in name only. The baby had changed all that.

She pulled herself together. "What are you going to call her?" she asked.

"Arabella."

"Oh." Alice hated what she thought of as frilly names, and Arabella was not without frills.

"Not your kind of name, I know, but Angela likes it."

"And you? Do you like it?" It was an unnecessary question, but Alice wanted to know.

"It's — okay. I'll get used to it."

Alice felt a small tingle of pleasure. If Jay had been the one to choose the baby's name or if he had been more enthusiastic about what they had called her, she would have found it even more hard to bear.

"So, I guess congratulations are in order."

"Congratulations would be nice."

"Oh, Jay, I do congratulate you. Of course I do. It's wonderful news, and you must be so thrilled."

But Alice knew that her good wishes had come too late and that Jay was hurt. How could she do this to him? On this, which must — or certainly should — be one of the happiest days of his life, how could she not be happy for the man she was supposed to love? And yet she was overcome with misery, not just because Angela was probably at this moment holding Jay's baby in her arms, but because she, Alice, was such a nasty, jealous person that she hadn't even been able to act as though she were happy for him.

"You'll be able to have bonfire birthday parties," she said now, trying to remedy the situation.

"What?"

"You know. Children's birthday parties can be a nightmare, but as hers is so near to Guy Fawkes, she'll be able to have fireworks."

"I suppose she will."

But the moment was lost. Alice had had her chance — and goodness knows, she had had enough time to prepare for it — and she had blown it.

"So — I expect you've got lots to do?"

"Yes. Yes, I have."

"Goodbye, then."

"Goodbye, Alice."

For a long time, Alice sat on at the kitchen table, gazing out of the window at the leaden sky of a dank November morning. She didn't cry — as far as Jay's baby was concerned, she had done all her crying weeks ago — but she felt a bleak emptiness that she had never felt before. She knew that her behaviour had been unforgivable and that Jay must be angry as well as hurt. But she also knew that even had her congratulations been fulsome and sincere, it wouldn't really have changed anything. She had known — they had both known — that the writing was on the wall. Their relationship had weathered all kinds of storms; there had been rows and misunderstandings in abundance. But they had never had to face anything as big as this, and Alice knew that there could only be one conclusion. How odd that something as small, as innocent, as a newborn baby should be the one unsurvivable obstacle to a relationship that had once seemed indestructible.

But if Alice thought she had reached rock bottom, there was more to come.

"Trot and I want to talk to you," Finn told her over their lunch of sandwiches.

"That sounds very portentous." Alice pushed away her plate, deciding she wasn't hungry.

"If you're not eating that, can I have it?"

"Be my guest. So what's this all about?"

"Best to wait till Trot comes," said Finn through a mouthful of sandwich. "He'll be here at teatime."

"And wants feeding, I suppose."

"Thanks, Mum. He said you'd offer."

"Did he now?"

"Yeah."

"I don't trust you two."

Finn grinned. "Trot and me are perfectly trustworthy."

"Trot and *I*."

"What?"

"Oh, never mind."

Trot turned up promptly at five. Alice thought he looked ill at ease and wondered what on earth he was up to.

"Could I have a beer?" he asked.

"Of course. We'll all have one." Alice fetched three cans from the fridge. "Now, what's this all about, Trot? I hope it's not one of your silly games."

"No silly game," said Trot, opening his can and taking a long swig.

"What, then?"

Trot and Finn exchanged glances.

"It's like this." Trot put down his beer and leaned forward in his chair. "I never had a gap year."

"It seems to me that your whole life has been one long gap year," Alice remarked.

"I never had a gap year," Trot continued, ignoring her. "And Finn would like one, wouldn't you, Finn?"

"Too right," said Finn.

"So, we thought we might have one together."

"When?" asked Alice, with a feeling of foreboding. "When exactly were you and Finn thinking of taking this — this break from your labours?"

"Well, the thing is —" Finn began.

"When, Finn? Just tell me. When? Not a difficult question."

"After — after my GCSEs. More beer, anyone?" Finn made to get up.

"Finn, sit down. What on earth are you talking about? Of course you can't take a gap year after your GCSEs. What about A Levels? You'll have two more years before you can even think about gap years."

"He doesn't want to do A Levels," Trot said. "Not yet, anyway."

"He doesn't want to do A Levels," Alice repeated. "What a mature decision. He's not yet taken his GCSEs, and he's already decided, has he?"

"Well, yeah." Finn looked uneasy.

Alice took several deep breaths. This was not a time to lose her temper. "And whose idea was this — this *gap year*?" she asked.

"Mine." Trot and Finn spoke together, then looked at each other and giggled.

"It was your idea, Trot, wasn't it?"

"Well, not exactly. We were discussing it, and Finn said he wanted to travel, and I've always wanted to, and it seemed like a good idea. It'd be safer with two of us," he added (the only sensible thing he'd said so far).

"I really don't want to do A Levels, Mum. I've never wanted to. I've told you and told you, but you won't listen."

"If he gets good GCSEs, he'll be fine," said Trot, who as far as Alice was aware knew nothing at all about the importance of further education (and was also living proof that a disregard for qualifications was no guarantee of success in life).

"Let me get this straight," Alice said. "Finn is going to do his GCSEs, and then the two of you are just going to — to bugger off round the world. Is that it?"

"That's about the size of it," Trot agreed.

"And has anyone discussed this with Finn's teachers?"

"Naturally we wanted to talk to you first," Trot said piously.

"How kind."

"Yes, well, you are his mother."

"And you, Trot, are his father. You're supposed to be encouraging him to make the best of himself; you should be considering his interests. As it is, I suspect you just want a companion for your silly adventures. You want to sacrifice Finn's future for your own fun."

The argument continued through tea, with Alice becoming increasingly cross and frustrated, and Finn and Trot — who had obviously made some kind of pact — being sweetly reasonable — thus, as they presumably saw it, putting Alice firmly in the wrong.

After their meal, Kenny called round, and he and Finn went up to Finn's room together, leaving Trot and Alice alone.

"What really annoys me," Alice said, "is that you two seem to have been planning this — this *escapade* for some time, without a word to me."

"Can you wonder?" said the new, reasonable Trot. "We knew this was how you'd react."

"Who are you really doing this for, Trot?" Alice asked.

"For both of us. I want to travel; Finn wants to travel; we'd both like someone to do it with. Going together seems the obvious solution."

"And you can't wait until he's finished school?"

"He'll have finished school."

"You know what I mean. Till he's eighteen."

"Look." Trot leaned forward, his hands clasped between his knees. "How's this for a deal? If Finn works really hard and gets good GCSEs, and if he still wants to leave school and travel, then that's what we'll do. But if he changes his mind and decides he wants to stay on, then he does that. Seems fair, doesn't it?"

"And if he fluffs his GCSEs?"

"Then we'll have to cancel our plans, and he'll have to go back and take them again."

"Promise?"

"Promise."

"And you won't put any pressure on him?"

"Not if you won't."

"You'll encourage him to pull his finger out?"

"Yes."

"And if he decides to go back and do his A Levels after this little jaunt, you won't stand in his way?"

"Absolutely not. Why should I? Alice, I know you think I'm irresponsible, but I do have his best interests at heart."

"Who's going to pay for all this? Travel isn't cheap."

"I've got a bit saved up. I've got one or two things I can sell, and I'll adapt the van so we can sleep in it. And we can work if necessary. If we live simply, it shouldn't be too expensive. In any case, that won't be your problem, Alice. I don't expect you to pay for this."

After Trot had gone, Alice gave the idea some more thought. She still didn't like it, but she had to admit that it wasn't quite as mad as it had seemed at first. Finn had never really liked school, and while he was bright enough, he would never be particularly academic. A year away just might help him to think again about his future. It would give him a chance to get away from school and home and see things from a different perspective, and then he could go to college and take his A Levels the following year if he wanted to.

But what would she do without him?

As Finn was growing up, she had become increasingly aware of the brevity of childhood and hence the relatively short time for which she had him to herself. She would never have another child now; Finn had been her one chance of motherhood. Last week had seen his sixteenth birthday. Those sixteen years had flown by, and now, if this plan went ahead, her time with him would be over by next summer. He would come back, of course, and would probably be living at home again, but it wouldn't be the same. Things would never be the same again.

Once more, she was consumed with fury at Trot, who was planning to steal from her the final precious years of Finn's childhood. Trot, whose input had been minimal, was now cashing in on all her hard work — on everything she had done to help Finn to become the person he was — and taking him off as a companion for his globetrotting. She knew that Trot loved Finn, but he was also self-centred in the way that people who live alone sometimes are. He had never had to consider anyone else's needs as other than secondary to his own, and while he would certainly do his best to ensure Finn's safely, that was about all she could expect from him.

The next time she saw Jay — a brief, snatched meeting, for Jay had other responsibilities at the moment — Alice told him about the gap year idea.

"Is it such a bad idea?" he said. "I always wished I'd had a gap year."

"But not at this stage. Not before A Levels," Alice said, wishing they had found somewhere more salubrious than a roadside greasy spoon.

"Well, what does he want to do? As a career?"

"He's no idea."

"So he doesn't know what qualifications he'll need, does he?"

"Maybe not. But surely it would be better to start off with at least some qualifications? A Levels, at least?"

"Not necessarily."

But Alice knew that Jay was having trouble concentrating. He looked exhausted, and there was something that looked suspiciously like baby sick on the shoulder of his sweater. She decided to change the subject.

"How's the paternity leave going?" she asked.

"Tiring."

"Nights?"

"We take it in turns."

"Not — not breastfeeding, then?"

"Angela didn't like the idea."

No, thought Alice. Angela wouldn't. She felt a tiny surge of triumph. Finn — poor fatherless (at the time) Finn — had at least had the best in that department, for Alice had breastfed him for nearly a year. That this was as much due to laziness and poverty as anything else was something Alice chose to ignore. She liked to think of herself as something of an earth mother, who had happily sacrificed her figure and her sleep for the good of her baby. In fact, Finn had been a good sleeper, and Alice's breasts had recovered nicely, but at least she had taken the risk. *She had put her baby first.*

"How is the baby?" Alice asked.

"She's fine. Screams rather a lot, but I guess that's what babies do."

"Finn didn't scream much."

"Well, lucky you."

This was not going well, but then, how could it? Each of them had preoccupations in which the other played no part, and both were too tired to make much of an effort.

"Have you any photos?" Alice asked.

"Of the baby?"

"Who else?"

"I may have." Jay got out his wallet. "I didn't think you'd want to see them, so I didn't bring any."

Alice both did and didn't want to see photos of Jay's daughter. One part of her was curious, but the other felt (illogically) that if she never saw a photo, then it would be almost as though the baby didn't really exist. She could continue in her present state of semidenial.

"Oh, I have. There's just one." Jay took out a small photograph. "But I'm afraid it's got —"

"Angela in it," Alice finished for him. She had never seen a photo of Angela before, and oddly, this was harder than seeing the baby, who could, in this photo at least, have been anyone's newborn child.

She examined the photograph. It was obviously taken just after the birth, for the baby was swaddled in a towel and Angela still wore a hospital gown and an identification band on her wrist. Her hair was tousled, and her eyes were shadowed with exhaustion. But there was that smile (Is there any other smile like it?) of the new mother — triumphant, exultant, disbelieving (Is this really mine? Did I produce this miracle myself?) — as she gazed down at the tiny face and still-damp, dark hair of her new daughter.

"I'm sorry," Jay said. "I didn't want you to see this one. It — it..."

"Brings it all home?"

"Yes."

"But it — she's there, Jay. I can't keep pretending you don't have a wife and child." She hesitated. "She's very pretty."

"The baby?"

"Well, yes. But you can't see much of her in this picture. I meant Angela."

"I suppose so."

"You don't have to pretend, Jay. She is pretty. And it must be nice to — well, to have a pretty wife."

Jay took the photo from her and replaced it in his wallet.

"Pretty doesn't seem important somehow," he said. "But yes, Angela's pretty. And she's nice. And I think she will be a good mother. Is that enough for you?"

Alice swallowed hard (I won't cry. *I won't*). "I suppose the hardest thing is — that you have a photo of them both in your wallet. That you carry her — them — around with you. Ridiculous, isn't it?"

"Well, that's what you do, isn't it?" Jay said wearily. "People ask to see a photo, and that's what they expect. Especially people who know us both."

A waitress came round with a none-too-clean cloth and wiped their table.

"We haven't finished yet," Jay said. "And we'll have two more coffees, please."

The waitress shrugged, and went off to fetch the coffee, leaving the table wet and smeary.

"I don't think I'll have any more coffee," Alice said, getting up from her seat. "I ought to get going."

"Pressing engagement?" Jay managed a smile.

"No pressing engagement. Just that we — this — isn't going too well, is it? And perhaps we'd better leave things for a few days. To give us both time to think."

"No." Jay caught her arm. "Don't go. We need to talk. We can't leave things — well, like this."

"I thought you were in a hurry."

"This is more important." Jay picked up his jacket. "Let's talk in my car."

In the car, Jay took Alice's face between his hands and forced her to look at him.

"Alice, have you any idea — any idea at all — how hard all this is for *me*? I know it's awful for you. We've discussed that, and I've done my best to understand how you must feel. But it's just as difficult for me."

"How can it be?" Alice tried to look away again.

"It just is. In a different way, but it is. Of course the baby's wonderful, and I know I'm going to be besotted with her, but it's you I want to be with, to spend my life with, to grow old with. You're the one. You'll always be the one."

"You've never said it like that before."

"No, because there wasn't any point, was there? It would only have made things harder for you. But I sometimes wonder whether you realise how much I love you. How much I *need* you. How do I get it into your stubborn little head how much you mean to me? What do I have to *do*?"

"Oh, Jay! I don't deserve you." Alice gulped back the tears that were threatening. "I've been such a cow recently, and you've taken it all on the chin."

Jay took her in his arms. "Darling, let's not play the blame game," he said. "And let's not waste any more time over recriminations or guilt or any of that stuff."

"Because we haven't much? Time, that is." Alice's voice was muffled against his chest.

"I don't know." Jay kissed the top of her head. "I honestly don't know. In a way, it's up to you. I think I can carry on like this, especially if the alternative is losing you altogether. But is it fair on you?"

Sitting back in her seat, Alice gazed out of the car window. The lorry drivers were leaving now, climbing into their cabs, shouting their farewells. A dog (a stray?) sniffed about among the debris by the rubbish bins. The sky darkened with the threat of rain. She sighed.

"I just don't see how it can work," she said. "It's not fair on you, either. You, Angela, or the baby. You have a family now. You'll want to do the right thing by them. I'm the — the outsider. I'm the one who has to go."

"Don't make any decision yet, Alice. Please. Give me — us — a chance." He took her hand in both of his and held it against his cheek. "Can we see how things go? This — situation is unknown territory. It just may be easier than we think."

"We'll see how things go, then."

But driving home, Alice knew — as she had known for weeks — that there was no decision to make. She and Jay had no future together, and it wasn't so much a matter of what would happen as when. In a way, a short sharp ending would be so much easier than all this pretending and procrastination, but still she couldn't bring herself to make that final break.

That evening, Alice reached an all-time low. Quite apart from her problems with Jay, Finn was away for the night with a friend, and the house echoed with emptiness. She missed the clatter of his feet up and down the stairs, the ringing telephone, the thump-thump-thump of his music vibrating through the house. This is how it's going to be, she thought. Gap year or no gap year, one day I shall be on my own, and this is how it will feel.

When the telephone did ring, she jumped.

"Hi," said a cheery voice.

"Hi, Trot."

"Thought you could do with a bit of cheering up."

"What makes you think that?"

"You've seemed pretty down recently, and the gap year thing — well, the timing wasn't too great. I'm sorry."

"That's okay."

"So, shall I come round? I've got some cheap plonk."

"Do you ever have any other kind?"

Trot laughed. "You know me so well."

He came round with his plonk, and Alice made beans on toast for them both.

"So, tell me," said Trot when they'd finished eating and Alice was fetching another (much nicer) bottle of wine, "what's up?"

"It's the baby," Alice told him. "Jay's wife's had her baby, and things aren't — well, they're becoming very complicated."

"I'll bet." Trot poured more wine.

"To put it in a nutshell, the end is in sight, although I don't think either of us is ready to accept it yet. Jay says it's up to me, and I suppose it is, but it's so hard."

"Oh dear."

"I love him so much — I *need* him so much. How am I going to manage without him? What am I going to do?" Alice blew her nose and took several deep breaths. "But I'm not going to cry."

"Cry away if it helps," Trot said.

"No. No more crying, Not yet, anyway."

"How can I help?" Trot asked after a moment.

"You can't. Not really. No one can."

"I can listen." Trot made himself comfortable on the sofa. "I've been told I'm quite a good listener."

So Alice, fuelled by wine and sympathy, poured out all her unhappiness of the past few months, while Trot, who really did seem to be listening most attentively, continued to refill their glasses and make all the right noises.

"So there you have it," Alice said when she'd finished. "One big problem; one simple solution. I just can't bring myself to make the break."

"No need to just yet," Trot said. "In the meantime, why don't you come to bed with me?"

"*What?*"

"Don't look so shocked. You need comforting, and sex is the best comforter I know. Plus, we have done it before."

"But I don't remember anything about that!"

"Neither do I. Does it matter?"

"But — what about Jay?"

"This has nothing to do with Jay. Besides, he sleeps with his wife, doesn't he? That baby must have come from somewhere."

"But we were drunk last time!"

"Well, we're not exactly sober now, are we?"

"That's true." Alice looked at Trot, who was freshly shaven and wearing clean jeans and sweatshirt, and felt a sudden flicker of suspicion. "Trot, did you plan this?"

"Not exactly plan, no. But I thought it might be rather nice. For both of us. And for old times' sake. Why not?"

"I suppose I ought to be angry."

"Why? You can always say no." Trot finished off the last of the wine. "So, what do you think?"

Alice looked at Trot. He was certainly not unattractive. He had nice eyes and a very endearing smile, and everything about him was comfortably familiar. And while she wasn't particularly bothered about the sex, just at that moment, she could imagine nothing nicer than a strong pair of male arms around her.

"No strings?" she asked after a moment.

"Absolutely no strings," Trot said, pulling her to her feet.

Alice stumbled against him and giggled. "Can you have a one-night-stand if you can't even stand up?"

"Course you can." Trot took her in his arms and kissed her. "That's better. Now all we have to do is pick up from where we were — how many years ago, was it?"

Gabs

Gabs hated November. It seemed to her the bleakest, most hopeless of months, with all the nice weather behind you and nothing to look forward to except Christmas. She and Steph usually spent a dutiful Christmas with their father, but since Steph's dramatic fall from grace, this year they might get away without it. They might even have a nice Christmas together, just the two of them — provided of course that in the meantime Steph had managed to climb down from her high horse and forgive Gabs.

Steph seemed to have taken Gabs' treatment of Father Augustine personally, and while her anger had abated, she had taken to treating Gabs with a cool contempt, which was, if anything, worse.

"What about Christian love?" Gabs demanded after a particularly unpleasant exchange.

"What about righteous indignation?" countered Steph.

"That's all very well, but you're not the injured party. And *he* didn't bear any grudges."

"Father Augustine," said Steph, "is a particularly good man."

"I'm not disputing that. I know he is. But isn't it time you moved on? It's done. It's in the past. There's nothing I can do to change things. If I crawled all the way to Rome on my hands and knees, I couldn't put the clock back."

"I know." Steph sighed. "I'm just — disappointed, I suppose."

"What, disappointed in me?"

"Yes."

"Oh, come on, Steph! You know me. You should have got over being disappointed in me years ago."

"But this was different."

"I know. But can we *please put it behind us*? I've paid a bigger price than you'll ever know for what I did, believe me. I've been to hell and back recently. I never thought I had a breakable heart, but I have. And it's unbearably painful. I need you, Steph. I really need you. Not to forgive me or condone what I've done. Just to be — well, my sister, I suppose. To be *there*.' She paused. "I think you need me, too."

"Well, you have been very supportive," Steph admitted. "I don't know how I'd have managed without you."

"Well, then?"

"But there's Clive."

"Ah. Clive."

Clive had been another bone of contention, for while Gabs continued to disapprove of him, he and Steph seemed to be getting on rather well, and while they certainly weren't sleeping together (perish the thought), they appeared to be, if not an item, then something very like it.

"Okay. How about this? You try to forgive me for Father Augustine, and I'll do my best to like Clive. How would that be?"

"It would be a start."

After that, things began to improve. Gabs made a real effort with Clive (although for the life of her, she couldn't see what Steph saw in him), and the subject of Father Augustine was finally dropped.

But Gabs continued to think about him, to dream about him, to long for him. Oddly, her longing was no longer physical; it was more a craving to be part of his life, to meet him, speak to him, even just look at him. Gabs' view of men was on the whole a jaundiced one, for she often saw them at their most depraved. The men she met in the course of her work could be self-serving, disloyal, and greedy. Some were merely pathetic, but they rarely aroused her sympathy. But in Father Augustine she had seen, perhaps for the first time in her life, real integrity, and it had had an enormous effect on her. Here was a man who seemed able to put his own needs entirely to one side; to sacrifice what might have been for what he felt called to do, with no guarantees or even necessarily any expectation of happiness. His was a life of service and dedication, and this was something Gabs had never come across before.

Then there was the shame. Hitherto, Gabs had been quite comfortable in her own skin. She knew she had her failings — didn't everyone? — but she also knew that she was intelligent and caring. She never deliberately harmed anyone, and she was a good and loyal friend. She even managed to justify her activities with her clients by reasoning that if it wasn't her, it would be someone else, and she was providing a useful service. She knew for a fact that what she did helped to keep some marriages going, for if it were not for her, many of her clients would almost certainly have left their wives. She injected into their lives the spice their marriages lacked, leaving the wives (poor innocent cows) to have the babies, wash the socks, and put the meals on the table.

But her encounter with Father Augustine had changed the way she saw herself. What she had done had been little short of wicked, and his integrity had only served to show up her lack of it. For the first time in her life, Gabs didn't like herself. Where before she had seen resourcefulness, now she saw only opportunism; what she had liked to think of as a spirit of adventure she now realised was selfish risk-taking. As for her entrepreneurial skills, they were no more than greed. Skill didn't come into it.

But if Gabs was beginning to see herself in a different light, she wasn't going to change overnight. This was partly due to apathy — she was just too miserable to care — and partly because it was hard to know where to start. When she confided this to her sister, Steph was surprisingly helpful.

"Why not start with little things?" she suggested.

"What do you mean?"

"Well, how about that difficult old woman you go on about? You could start by making an effort with her."

"I do make an effort!"

"Do you?"

"Sometimes."

"Well, make a bigger effort."

So the next time Gabs visited Miss Kershaw, she agreed to cut her toenails. This may not sound like a major breakthrough, but for Gabs it was, partly because she had a thing about feet and partly because she had an even greater thing about Miss Kershaw.

"Careful! Careful!" screeched her patient as Gabs hacked away at the horny misshapen extremities, which, she thought, would have been better served by a farrier.

"These — are — tough," said Gabs between gritted teeth.

"That's because they've been left too long," said Miss Kershaw.

"And whose fault is that?"

"Not mine. I can't be expected to reach all the way down there."

"Well, it's not mine either," said Gabs, coming up for air.

"Yes, it is. I asked you last time."

"What about the chiropodist?"

Miss Kershaw sniffed. "I don't get on with her."

"Is there anyone you do get on with?"

"What?" Fortunately Miss Kershaw was rather deaf.

"Nothing," muttered Gabs, returning to her task. "There. All done." She put down her scissors and got up from the floor.

"You've missed a bit."

"No, I have not."

"Yes, you have."

"How about — how about I paint them for you?" Gabs asked. "I've got some nice polish in my bag."

"But it's November!"

"So?"

"So who's going to see them?"

"You are," said Gabs. "And I am. And anyone else who comes to see to you."

Hearing no further objections from her client, Gabs set to and did a really nice job, transforming the unpleasant yellow talons that were Miss Kershaw's toenails with a nice shade of cherry red.

"Isn't that better?" she said when she had finished.

"Hmm." Miss Kershaw removed her reading glasses and scrutinised her new red toes.

"Don't like it," she said. "Horrible colour. Makes me look like a tart."

Gabs grinned. "Miss Kershaw, take it from me: you will never, ever look like a tart."

"I still don't like them. Clean it off again."

"No time, I'm afraid," Gabs said, biting her tongue. "You'll just have to live with them."

"Well! How dare you speak —"

But Gabs was already out of the door.

So much for good deeds, she thought sourly as she got into her car and started the engine. Perhaps she wasn't quite ready for that new start after all. The little acts of kindness as recommended by Steph were of little value if they benefited neither the recipient nor herself.

Later that afternoon, she had an appointment with Gerald, and she had finally decided to tell him she was calling it a day. Since his unsuccessful proposal, Gerald had been difficult and demanding, as though determined to ensure that Gabs paid for her folly in refusing him, and Gabs had had enough.

"I don't understand why you won't marry me," he kept saying. "I'm rich, we get on — what's the problem?"

And try as she might, Gabs couldn't convince him that she was never going to change her mind.

"I don't want to get married," she told him. "Not to you; not to anyone."

"All girls want to get married," Gerald told her.

"Not this one. Besides, there's — there's someone else."

"You never told me that!"

"Well, it was none of your business, was it?"

"Are you going to marry him?" Gerald demanded.

"I've told you. I'm not going to marry anyone."

"So, you're still free!"

"Gerald, I am not *free*, as you put it, and I don't want to marry you. For the last time, *I don't want to talk about this anymore!*"

So Gerald had taken to a new and rather alarming police dog act, in which he chased Gabs round the room and tried to bite her ankles. It was amazing how quickly this rather plump little man could scurry along on his hands and knees, and he had surprisingly sharp-looking teeth.

"Police dogs don't actually bite," Gabs had objected last week, when he had very nearly caught her. "They just hang on to people's clothing."

So Gerald had torn her skirt, and Gabs had been very angry. This week, she was going to tell him that enough was enough. He would either have to hang up his collar and lead, or find someone else to play his silly games.

When she told him, to her distress, Gerald actually wept.

"What shall I do without you?" he said. "Our meetings are the high point of my week."

"Ditch the dog thing, and I'll keep on coming," Gabs said. "I don't mind the firing squad or the traffic warden, but the dog thing has to go."

"But that's my favourite," Gerald said. "That's why I need you. You do it so well."

Gabs wrote a name and telephone number on a piece of paper and handed it to him. "Try this girl," she said. "I'm sure she'll do it for you."

"Is she — is she as pretty as you?" Gerald asked.

"Much prettier," Gabs said. "And she loves dogs."

"May I have a goodbye kiss? Just one?"

"No. Certainly not."

"You're a hard woman," grumbled Gerald, putting on his Y-fronts.

"Good job you're shot of me, then, isn't it?"

Getting rid of Gerald was a weight off her mind. She would miss the money, and the lobsters and champagne, but otherwise she was very glad to see the back of him, dangling balls and all. Now she decided she would ditch the cabinet minister, who was about to write his memoirs (notwithstanding promises of anonymity, Gabs was wary of memoirs), and she would have reduced her client list and hence a little of the culpability attached to her occupation. Steph was desperate for her to give it up altogether, but Gabs reminded her that it was she herself who had suggested she improve her life in small stages.

"Besides," she explained that evening over supper, "I need the money."

"You don't," Steph said. "You've got all that money in the bank, and you've said yourself that you earn enough from the agency."

Gabs told her about Mrs. Grant's Australian niece, who had now arrived in England complete with work permit and was standing in the wings just waiting to step into Gabs' shoes.

"If Miss Kershaw complains about her toenails, I've had it," she said.

"*What?*"

"Oh, never mind."

Fortunately Steph didn't press the point, as she had preoccupations of her own. Over the past months, she had become transformed from horror-stricken hard-done-by virgin to obsessive mother-to-be. Some people are said to be all heart; at the moment, Steph was all womb, and her world currently centred round that wonderful organ and its (apparently) miraculous occupant. She had long since given up alcohol (she had never drunk much anyway), she would only eat organic food, and if anything came out of a tin or a packet, she would discard it at the whiff of an E-number. She and Clive went to antenatal classes, where she apparently learnt to breathe and Clive learnt to rub her back (Gabs thought the classes were a rip-off, and told her so), and the flat was filling up with baby magazines, baby clothes, and baby furniture.

"This is getting ridiculous," Gabs said one evening when she came home to find the tiny hallway blocked by a large cot and a baby car seat. "Where are you going to put all this stuff?"

"I'll put it all away," Steph said, "when I've made space for it."

"And doesn't a car seat need a car?" Steph was neither a driver nor a car owner.

"Well, I thought…"

"No. *Oh* no. Not in my car. No baby seat in my car, Steph."

"Why? Why not?"

"Bad for business."

"You can always take it out."

"So this is for occasional use only?"

"Of course. And look." Steph produced a neat little set of wheels. "It converts into a pushchair. Isn't that great?"

"Great."

"And there's this little cover you put over it when it rains. And you can also —"

"Steph, you're becoming awfully boring. Can't we talk about something else?"

"Well, you did ask."

"So I did. What's for supper?" (Having cut down her hours, Steph was now in charge of the housekeeping.)

"Actually, Clive's here. He's brought steaks."

"Good for Clive!" The presence of Clive might just be outweighed by the prospect of steak.

"He only brought two," said Steph, and blushed. "He wasn't thinking," she added.

"Now there's a surprise," said Gabs, who was tired and hungry.

"But he's painting the box room," Steph said.

"Well, fancy that."

The box room was another cause of ill-feeling. Since the flat belonged equally to Gabs and Steph, having been bought with money left to them by their mother, the box room too belonged to them both. Given time, Gabs would probably have offered it to Steph as a bedroom for the baby without being asked, but Steph had, as it were, helped herself without consulting her sister, and was doing it up accordingly. It was already full of baby impedimenta, for Steph's route to work led her past a new baby shop — a softly lit pastel cave, full of all the things a canny retailer knows a baby can't possibly need but its mother will find irresistible. This week alone, Steph had bought a doll-size pair of soft leather booties, a tinkly mobile, and a handmade wooden rattle — all, as Gabs pointed out, priced in inverse relation to their usefulness.

"And what colour is he painting *our* box room?" Gabs enquired. "Let me guess. Yellow?"

"Well, yes. It's a nice pale shade of lemon. You'll like it, Gabs."

"Does it matter what I like?"

"Of course it does."

"Anyway, why the obsession with yellow? Wouldn't it help if you found out the gender of this baby?" Gabs could imagine few things more infuriating than the hospital staff knowing something about her own unborn child that she did not. "Then at least you could colour code it accordingly. Actually, I can't see the point of the whole pink and blue thing; after all, you wear blue, and Clive has at least one pink shirt. It isn't as though people need to be reminded whether their baby's a boy or a girl."

"That's not the point."

"Well, what is the point?"

"You just can't dress a baby boy in pink. It would look ridiculous. And as for its sex, we don't want to know yet. That's all. We want it to be a surprise."

"How can it be a surprise? It will be either a boy or a girl. That's hardly a surprise. Now, if you were to give birth to a badger cub, say, or a vampire, that would certainly be a surprise. But —"

"Oh, for goodness' sake, Gabs! Will you just leave it? Clive and I want to find out when it's born, and not before." Steph hesitated. "You can have my steak if you like. I'll have an omelette."

"Oh, don't mind me," said Gabs. "You two just stay here and enjoy your steaks and do yellow things in the box room. I'm going to get a takeaway."

She put her coat back on and slammed out of the flat. She had had enough of Steph, of babies, of miserable old people and difficult clients. For two pins, she would dig out her passport (presuming she could find it) and just take off. But of course, she couldn't do that, because like everyone else, she had responsibilities.

Parked outside the Indian takeaway, she decided she wasn't hungry after all, so she started up the engine again and drove off. She had no idea where she was going, but she needed to be on her own, and the car was the best (and safest) place. No one bothered her in the car, and since she had left her mobile at home, no one could reach her, either. This, she thought, as she narrowly avoided a motorbike, is rock bottom. She had felt low before, had even once or twice been depressed, and following the death of her mother, she had experienced real grief. But she was of a naturally happy disposition, and as a rule, things rarely got her down for long.

But since Father Augustine, everything had changed. Quite apart from her misery, she had started assessing her life, and had found it wanting in almost all departments. What had she achieved? Where was she going? Where would she be in, say, ten years' time? She had no idea. She had money saved, but for what? She had never had ambitions or made plans; her relationships had been brief and unsatisfactory; she had no proper career and no prospects. She didn't want to be like Steph — the two of them were far too different — but at least her sister had a career and now a baby to plan for. She had a *future*. Gabs couldn't see that she had any future at all.

Outside it was bitterly cold — one of those dank, foggy, November nights that presage the miseries of the winter to come. Gabs pulled into a lay-by, leaving the engine running so that she could turn up the heating. She fumbled in the glove compartment for a cigarette, then switched on the radio. Someone was playing a sentimental song about love and loss, which, Gabs thought, just about summed up her own life at the moment. Whoever it was that said it was better to have loved and lost than never to have loved at all was talking bollocks. The pain simply wasn't worth it.

After a while, she stubbed out her cigarette, wrapped her coat tightly around her, huddled down in her seat, and closed her eyes. Sleep. That was what she needed. Sleep. But sleep wouldn't come, and besides, the car needed a new battery, and it was more than likely that the heating would go off. What would become of her then? If she were asleep, she would probably die of hypothermia. Gabs was certainly miserable, but she didn't want to die. Not yet, anyway.

And if she did, would anybody care? Steph would, of course. Her sister might be angry with her, but she also needed her. Her friends might miss her. As for her father, he would certainly be surprised, but would he actually mind? Probably not. Come to think of it, since Gabs hadn't made a will, he would most likely inherit her substantial savings. This would no doubt please him enormously (he was a feckless alcoholic), so this seemed a fairly good reason for not dying.

After spending some time sitting brooding and smoking, Gabs eventually returned home in the small hours, cursing as she tripped over the cot and the car seat in the dark, and waking Clive, who was asleep on the sofa. The flat was still redolent of grilled steak, and Steph and Clive had not washed up after their meal, leaving the sink full of dirty dishes.

"Bloody hell!" Gabs crashed around in the kitchen, throwing plates in the dishwasher and making as much noise as possible. "Does no one around here think of anyone but themselves?"

"Well, you obviously don't." Clive rose up from among the cushions on the sofa. "Waking everyone up like this!"

"By everyone, I suppose you mean you?" Gabs paused with a saucepan in her hand. She was sorely tempted to batter Clive over the head with it.

"Well, yes. I've got work in the morning."

"You also have a home to go to. You don't *have* to stay here. What you seem to forget is that this is my flat as well as Steph's, and you are trespassing on *my* hospitality!"

"Gosh! Steph said you were being moody!" Clive sat up carefully, covering his crotch with his hands (although he was wearing boxer shorts, and Gabs doubted whether there would have been much to cover if he had been stark naked).

"Did she now?"

"Yes, she did. And it's hard for her, in her condition. She needs looking after."

"And I suppose I don't? Does it occur to anyone that occasionally — just occasionally — I wouldn't mind a bit of consideration, too?"

At that moment, a door opened, and Steph emerged, yawning.

"What's going on?" she asked. "Has something happened?"

"Your little friend here is objecting because I've come home to *my* flat and am tidying up *my* kitchen after your little feast," Gabs told her.

"*Our* kitchen," Steph said. "And I was going to do it in the morning."

"Yeah. Right." Gabs banged down her saucepan in case she should be tempted to use it. "And I suppose it didn't occur to either of you that it might be a tad depressing for me to come back and find the place in this filthy state? When you've had all evening to sort it out?"

"What's the big deal?" Clive pulled a sweater over his thin, coat-hanger shoulders.

"The big deal," Gabs said, "is that I'm tired, and I'm miserable, and this — this *mess* is the last straw."

"Steady on, Gabs." Steph put out a hand, but Gabs pushed it away.

"No. I won't steady on. I've had enough of you. Both of you. I've had enough of my home being — being *invaded*. You've got a room, Steph, and it's big enough for two, but oh no. Clive has to sleep on the only sofa in the only living room because you're not bloody married! How ridiculous is that? Meanwhile, the rest of the flat is full of Clive's things and baby stuff and fucking yellow paint. I'm surprised you haven't taken over my room as well!"

"Now you're being ridiculous!"

"Is this all because of that priest?" asked Clive, who had found his trousers, and with them, apparently, his confidence.

Gabs turned to Steph. "You *told* him! I can't believe you told him!"

"Well, of course I told him. We're together. We tell each other things."

"But that was confidential! I trusted you, Steph. *I trusted you!*"

"I think I should be going," Clive said, edging towards the door. "Leave you two to sort things out."

"You do that, Clive. You get the fuck out of my flat and go home to mummy. I'm sure she'll look after you."

"Gabs, how could you? How could you speak to Clive like that?" Steph demanded when Clive had left.

"Quite easily, actually. He had it coming."

"No, he did not. He was my guest, and he had every right —"

"Oh, shut up, Steph. Please, please, just shut up." And Gabs sat down and burst into tears. "I don't know what to do," she sobbed. "I just don't know what to do. Oh, Steph, whatever am I going to do?"

"About what? Do about what?"

"About my life, Father Augustine — oh, everything. It's all such a mess." She looked up at Steph. "And I'm sorry if I was rude to Clive, but he's here all the time, and I can't talk to you properly, and I haven't anyone else at the moment. I feel so — so lonely."

"Well, if you treat people like this, I'm not surprised you're lonely."

"I know, I know. I've been horrible."

"You certainly have." Steph was evidently not in forgiving mode.

"And I suppose now you'll tell me that my problems are all of my own making."

"Well, aren't they?"

"Yes. Yes, of course they are! But d'you think that makes it any better?" Gabs looked at Steph, with her pink furry slippers and her smug little bump, and just for a moment, she hated her. "But of course, you wouldn't understand that, would you?"

"A sister who has sex for money and then sets out to seduce an innocent priest? No, I don't understand. I don't understand at all."

"And you're so bloody perfect, aren't you? Even though you had sex with a man you didn't love and are having his little bastard!"

"How dare you! How dare you talk to me like that!" Steph placed her hands protectively over her stomach.

"That's right," Gabs said. "We mustn't let Junior hear naughty language, must we?"

"Gabs, *how can you?*"

"Oh, shut up, Steph. Just shut the fuck up!"

Gabs got up and took herself off to her room, slamming the door behind her. There, she threw herself face down on the bed and howled into her pillow, pulling the duvet over her head to muffle the sound. Life was awful. Everything was awful.

The grief, the isolation, and the sheer misery were, quite simply, unbearable. How on earth was she ever going to get through this?

Eventually she must have fallen asleep, for the next thing she knew, it was morning, and Steph was standing in the doorway holding the telephone.

"Didn't you hear this?" she demanded.

"Obviously not. What's the time?"

"Just after seven." Steph switched on the light. "Gabs, look at the state of you!"

Gabs peered at her reflection in the mirror. The face that looked back at her was streaked with mascara, the eyes bruised with exhaustion, the hair a tangled mess.

"Your concern is touching," she said.

"Never mind that. Just take this call, will you, and then I can get back to sleep. If you remember, I had a rather disturbed night."

"Who is it?" Gabs asked.

"It's that Mavis person. Why couldn't she phone you on your mobile? Here." Steph threw the phone onto the bed and disappeared back to her own room.

"Hello?" Gabs began to peel off her clothes with her free hand. They reeked of cigarette smoke, and she was badly in need of a shower.

"I'm so sorry to disturb you," said Mavis. "But I just had to talk to someone."

"Oh." Gabs tried to gather her wits. "Why? What's happened?"

"It's Mother." (Who else?) "She was taken into the hospital last night, and I've been there with her ever since. She's had another stroke. Oh, Gabs. She looks much worse this time. Whatever shall I do?"

Mavis

Mavis knew that Maudie was frightened. Her one good hand — not so good now — made tiny fluttering movements, like those of an injured bird, and the sounds that she made were the cries of a distressed child. Her face was frozen into immobility, but her eyes, bright with life and fear, seemed to beg for help.

"Please, can she have something?" Mavis asked the sister. "Something to make her less — afraid."

The sister patted her shoulder and told her not to worry. Maudie's movements were random. They didn't mean anything. "And if we did give her drugs, they would mask any improvement," she added.

"But you said there probably wasn't going to be any improvement," Mavis reasoned. "So what harm can it do?"

"I think it's best to leave these decisions to the doctors, don't you?"

Mavis felt small and patronised and utterly helpless. She wished very much that Gabs were still with her, but Gabs had had to go to work.

Mavis thought it likely that this kind of situation brought out the best in Gabs; she had an insouciance, a strength, a *capableness* that made her seem far older than her years, and she had the knack of getting things done. Although she had looked exhausted ("man trouble; don't ask"), it was Gabs who had argued until Maudie had been moved from a trolley in A & E into a proper bed in a ward, Gabs who had demanded a comfortable chair for Mavis, and Gabs who had found her a welcome cup of tea. And when one of the nurses had asked whether Gabs was her daughter, Mavis had been rather pleased. Gabs' occupation apart (and even that seemed less important now that they knew each other better), Mavis would have been rather pleased to have her as a daughter.

The following morning, Maudie had a scan, and the doctor told Mavis that she had suffered "a massive brain haemorrhage".

"We'll just keep her comfortable," he said, his eyes already wandering towards his next (and probably more interesting) patient, and even Mavis knew that keeping someone comfortable was hospitalspeak for having reached the end of the road. Maudie wasn't going to get better; she didn't even have to ask.

"Can't you give her something?" she asked again. "She seems so frightened."

The doctor consulted Maudie's chart, and then shook his head. "I'm afraid not. And it wouldn't make any difference. Stroke patients are often like this. It doesn't mean anything."

So Maudie was no longer Maudie; she was a stroke patient, behaving the way stroke patients behaved. When tears leaked from Maudie's eyes, that too was apparently normal.

"Stroke patients do cry a lot," the staff nurse told Mavis. "It doesn't mean they're unhappy. They just get emotional."

"What's the difference?" Mavis asked.

The nurse smiled. "When you've been doing this job as long as I have, believe me, you'll realise that this is all par for the course."

Since Mavis was never going to do the nurse's job, this seemed a ridiculous thing to say, besides being particularly unhelpful. Maudie was a stroke patient, and stroke patients were miserable; therefore Maudie must be miserable. Well, Mavis didn't know anything about other stroke patients, but she wasn't going to sit by and see her mother suffer. There had to be something she could do.

When Gabs called in later on to see how things were going, Mavis told her what had happened.

"It seems that they're quite happy for her to suffer like this," Mavis said. "I can't bear it, Gabs. I just can't bear it. I promised her I'd always make sure that she was all right, and now she really needs help, there doesn't seem to be anything I can do for her. They're just — leaving her. Nobody seems to care. It's as though she doesn't matter."

"Oh, she matters all right. Our Maudie certainly matters." Gabs thought for a moment. "Leave this to me, Mavis. I'll sort it."

"You won't — you won't make a *fuss*, will you?"

"If that's what it takes, I'll certainly make a fuss. But don't worry, Mavis. It'll be my fuss, and if anyone gets into trouble, it'll be me. You wait here."

She went off, and returned ten minutes later with a young doctor in tow.

"You see, Doctor, we really need to do something to relieve her suffering," Gabs said. "We hate to see her like this."

The doctor dragged his eyes away from Gabs' bosom. (Didn't he see enough bosoms in the course of his work?)

"I'm sure we can do something," he said.

"Oh, that's so kind of you," Gabs simpered. "My godmother was always such a *strong* woman" (godmother?) "and we hate to see her like this."

"I'm sure you do." Briefly, the doctor's gaze found its way back to her bosom. Gabs caught his eye and winked at him, and he blushed. "Yes. Certainly. I'll see what I can do," he said, and scurried off with Maudie's chart.

"How do you do it?" Mavis asked when he'd gone.

"Do what? Oh, the man thing, you mean?"

"Well, no. I didn't mean that. But that, too."

"I vowed that I'd try and change," Gabs said, "after — after what happened. But somehow I can't help myself, even when I'm feeling miserable. It's like a reflex. 'Born to flirt,' Steph says, and I suppose she's right." She sighed. "Change is a darned sight harder than you think."

"Oh, I know."

"Do you?" Gabs asked. "Do you want to change, Mavis?"

"Doesn't everyone? In some way or another? I'd love to be more assertive, for a start. Like you. Get things done. Not be afraid of authority."

"What's to be afraid of?"

"I don't know. Not being liked, perhaps. I've always been afraid of not being liked."

"I couldn't give a damn," said Gabs. "What people think is their problem."

"That must be wonderful."

The doctor returned with promises of a nurse with an injection to calm Maudie down. He looked embarrassed and kept his eyes firmly on Maudie.

"Poor lamb," said Gabs when he'd gone again. "I know what he needs. Quite nice-looking too."

"I thought you were going to change," Mavis said.

"Wasn't it Saint Augustine who wanted to change, but not yet? I guess I'm a bit like that. It's a kind of work in progress," Gabs said. "Right. I'm off. Oh, by the way, I phoned your Mr. Strong to tell him you wouldn't be in. He wasn't very pleased."

"Mr. Strong is rarely pleased," said Mavis.

"He said that he'd probably have to bring in his wife."

"Oh dear." Mrs. Strong was thought by some to be suffering from early dementia. She occasionally 'helped out' in the shop, but Mavis thought that this was more therapy for Mrs. Strong than help for Mavis, since she tended to put everything away in the wrong places and give the customers too much change. Mention of bringing in Mrs. Strong was a threat, albeit a veiled one.

But Mavis no longer cared. "Bugger Mr. Strong," she said boldly. "He can stew for all I care. He's been precious little support to me, and if I lose my job, well, I'll probably live."

"Good for you, Mavis," Gabs said. "You tell 'em."

"Thank you. Thank you so much." Mavis touched Gabs' hand. "I don't know what I'd have done without you."

"Don't mention it. Besides, you've done me a favour. I was having a bit of a crisis, and you've helped take my mind off things."

Maudie appeared to settle after her injection, and when she seemed to be sleeping peacefully, Mavis called for a taxi home so that she could have a bath and something to eat. She also phoned Clifford to tell him what had happened.

"Oh dear. And we were going to meet up tomorrow, too," Clifford said. "How disappointing."

"Is that all you can think about?" asked Mavis.

"Well, I'm sorry about your mother, Mavis. Of course I am. But we knew this was going to happen, didn't we?"

"Did we?"

"Yes. She's old. She was bound to have another stroke sooner or later. Perhaps better sooner, all things considered."

"And you know all about strokes, do you?"

"Well, I did do some research on the internet."

"Oh yes." That would have been the time when Clifford had had a headache for several days and had taken it upon himself to diagnose the problem. In the end, he had decided it was a brain tumour, but the stroke was very much in the running, as was something terrifying called a 'subarachnoid haemorrhage'. Clifford had taken to the idea of the subarachnoid haemorrhage. Mavis had not. (Dorothy, apparently, had laughed and told him not to be so silly.)

"Clifford, have you any idea how unkind you sound?"

"Not unkind at all. Practical. I'm being practical, Mavis. Facing reality. And I think you might find it helpful if you could do the same."

"What I would find helpful would be some support, some understanding."

"Yes. Yes of course." Clifford seemed to pull himself together. "Perhaps I could fetch you from the hospital tomorrow, and we could have an early dinner together."

"That would be nice. Thank you."

But the evening was not a success. For a start, Clifford declined to come up to the ward to see Maudie, which Mavis had thought might help him to understand her situation a little better.

"Oh no, Mavis. It's a little too soon, I'm afraid."

"What do you mean, too soon?"

"It — it brings everything back," Clifford told her.

Mavis thought that hospital visits would be just up Clifford's street, and as for bringing everything back, well, since he spent much of his time doing just that, what was the problem?

But no. The new, sensitive Clifford couldn't cope with Maudie in her hospital bed (Mavis privately thought that he couldn't be bothered to make his way up to the fourth floor, even though there was a perfectly satisfactory lift), and so they met downstairs by the reception desk.

"You look pale," Clifford said, kissing her cheek.

"I'm just tired," Mavis said. "I haven't had much sleep."

"You must get your rest," Clifford said as they made their way to the carpark.

This sounded promising, and so Mavis told him about her two nights sitting by Maudie's bed and how difficult it was to sleep in a chair.

"No one sat by my bed," Clifford said.

"Well, I suppose in intensive care, you have so many nurses you don't really need anyone."

"That's not the point." Clifford opened the car door for her. "It was the fact that no one *wanted* to sit by my bed. If you'd been my wife, you'd have been at my bedside, wouldn't you, Mavis?"

"Well, yes. I'm sure I would." How was it that nowadays, Clifford managed to turn all conversations back to himself?

"If only we'd been younger when we met," Clifford sighed, driving off down the road.

"I *was* young," Mavis reminded him.

"Well, yes. But you know what I mean. I think we'd have made a good couple." He paused. "I could still leave Dorothy, you know."

Mavis looked at him, surprised. "It's a long time since you've said that," she said.

"Well, I still mean it. And I'm sure Dorothy could manage without me."

Mavis too was pretty sure that Dorothy could manage without Clifford, but she didn't say so. More to the point was the fact that she was beginning to realise that she too could probably do without Clifford. It had taken some time for her to realise this, for Clifford had been around for so long that he was an intrinsic part of her life. Clifford's phone calls, their meetings, their little anniversaries (Clifford was good at marking these), the visits to Dennis's flat — these had all been woven into the fabric of her life, and for years she had thought that they were essential to her happiness, but now she wasn't so sure. Clifford's self-absorption had become burdensome, his conversation increasingly dull, and as for the sex, that too appeared to be dwindling in frequency, as well as in any pleasure it brought to Mavis. Perhaps Clifford's libido was wearing off with age, but such lovemaking as they managed was so restricted by boundaries pertaining to Clifford's physical problems that Mavis often thought that it was hardly worth their while bothering at all. By the time they had waited for Clifford's little blue pill to work and he had been settled comfortably, with pillows in all the right places, it was often nearly time for him to go home. As for Mavis's little device, that hadn't seen the light of day (or anything else) for weeks.

"Well?" said Clifford now.

"Well, what?"

"What about me leaving Dorothy?"

"Oh no," said Mavis at once.

"What do you mean, no?"

"Just what I said. It would never work. It might have worked once, but not now. No. We're much better off as we are."

"Are you saying I should have left Dorothy before?"

"I'm saying nothing of the kind. I'm just saying that it's too late, Clifford. For both of us. Besides, there's Mother."

"But she's dy— she's not going to get better, is she?"

"I don't know. But I'm not going to start planning a life without her."

Clifford drove on in silence. Mavis hoped very much that he wasn't sulking. Clifford's sulks always took time, and she was anxious to get back to the hospital.

After a few more miles, they found a pub that promised GOOD FOOD, and Clifford pulled in.

"Will this do?" he asked.

"Fine," Mavis said. She hadn't had a proper meal for two days and was quite hungry.

But the food, despite its promise, wasn't particularly good, and Clifford was annoyed and complained. The waitress got upset, the manager was defensive, and at the end of an unpleasant ten minutes, neither party was satisfied.

"I wish you wouldn't do that," Mavis said when they were safely back in the car. "The food wasn't that bad, and it wasted our evening."

"I don't believe in settling for second best," Clifford told her.

"If you eat at a random pub, that's a risk you have to take," said Mavis.

"But honestly! Salad with fish and chips! And *grated carrot!*"

Back at the hospital, Clifford accompanied Mavis as far as the entrance, where they encountered Gabs.

"Oh, hi!" Gabs greeted Mavis with a hug. "I've been looking for you. You must be Clifford." She held out her hand. "I've heard so much about you."

Clifford was obviously torn between admiration of Gabs' legs (which were sandwiched between the tiniest of skirts and a pair of scarlet calf-hugging boots) and annoyance at her knowing who he was. The struggle was brief, and the legs won.

"Hello," he said, taking her hand.

"I'm Gabs."

"Gabs is one of my best friends," Mavis said.

"Oh." Clifford had difficulty in concealing his astonishment.

"Yeah. You wouldn't think it, would you?" Gabs grinned.

"Well…"

"You don't have to say anything." Gabs turned to Mavis. "I went up to see her. I think she recognised me, but it's hard to tell. Poor Maudie. I'll go back up and wait for you, shall I?"

When Gabs had gone, Clifford turned to Mavis.

"You never told me about — her."

"I told you I had new friends; I just didn't describe them."

"But really, Mavis. She isn't your type at all."

"How do you know what my type is? Gabs is kind and generous, and I don't know what I'd have done without her."

Clifford bridled. "You know you can always turn to me. You don't need — people like that."

"People like what? How dare you, Clifford! How dare you insult a friend of mine — someone you don't even know! Especially when you could hardly take your eyes off her."

"That's rubbish!"

"D'you know, Clifford, I don't care. I don't care what you think of my friends or whether or not you enjoy ogling their — assets. I've got more important things on my mind. I'm going up to see Mother now." She paused. "Do you want to come? No — of course you don't. It brings back all those painful memories, doesn't it? Well, I mustn't keep you. Goodnight."

In the lift, Mavis felt a surge of something like triumph. While she was both hurt and angry, and what she had said to Clifford had probably been very childish, he had had it coming. Since his operation, everything — *everything* — had been about him: his health, his problems, his needs. Gabs, too, had had her problems, and yet she had managed to put them aside for Mavis — something no one else had done in years. Gabs might be a "bad girl," but in the essentials, she was good in a way that Clifford would never be.

When she reached the ward, Maudie was awake.

"Hello, Mother." Mavis sat down and took her hand.

"She's trying to say something," Gabs said.

"Mother? What is it? What do you want?"

Maudie mumbled and coughed, and shook her head in frustration. Her eyes were fixed on Mavis's face, as though pleading with her to understand what she was trying to say.

"I don't know. I can't make it out. Gabs, can you?"

"What is it, Maudie?" Gabs said, leaning over her. "What can we do to help?"

Tears trickled onto Maudie's pillow as the mumbling became more frantic.

"Perhaps she wants a priest," Gabs whispered to Mavis. "Has she seen a priest?"

"Oh, goodness! I never thought. Mother, would you like to see a priest? Would you like — confession?"

Maudie's lips twitched as though she were trying to smile, and her face seemed to relax.

Late as it was, the Catholic chaplain was sent for. He was reassuringly elderly, and seemed pleasant and sympathetic.

"Shall we — may we stay?" Mavis asked.

"Let me talk to her on my own for a few minutes. Just a few minutes. Confession is private, as I'm sure you know." He smiled. "She'll be all right; don't worry."

"She may not understand," Mavis said.

"Never mind. That doesn't matter."

The curtains were drawn around Maudie's bed, and Mavis and Gabs waited outside, listening to the soft murmuring of the priest's voice.

"There." The priest finally emerged. "I think she understood. I've given her the last rites, and absolution. She's settled now."

"Did she — did she say anything?" Mavis asked.

"It was rather odd, actually. I couldn't hear properly, but I think what she was trying to say was 'bad' something. Could it have been 'bad girls'?"

Gabs and Mavis looked at each other and smiled.

"Yes. It could have been," Mavis told him.

"Well, she certainly doesn't seem to have been a bad girl. Perhaps her mind was wandering."

"Perhaps it was."

The priest nodded, packing his things away in a small black bag. "Whatever it was, she's sleeping now. She's at peace."

Maudie never regained consciousness. The doctors said she must have suffered a further stroke, but Mavis preferred to believe that the chaplain's visit had, as it were, given her permission to go. Her small sins forgiven, her poor exhausted body anointed, Maudie was ready to be with the God she had worshipped so faithfully all her life.

Mavis was at her bedside until the end, and wondered at the smallness — the *unimportance* — of her mother's life and of her death. Her passing would go largely unnoticed, as though the world she had lived in had closed gently over her, leaving only the slightest of ripples to show where she had been. And yet she had made her contribution: she had lived a good life, been a loving wife and mother and a loyal and entertaining friend.

Some lines of a poem came to Mavis — something she had learnt at school and that she had always remembered: lines about another small, unimportant woman, who had lived, like Maudie, "among the untrodden ways," but who had nonetheless been deeply missed when she died.

"But she is in her grave, and oh,
The difference to me!"

"Oh, the difference to me," Mavis whispered, gazing at that still, beloved face. "*Such* a difference!"

And sitting by the bed, still holding her mother's hand in her own, she buried her face in the counterpane and wept.

The Funeral: December

Finn wanted to go to Maudie's funeral.

"I've never seen a funeral before," he said.

"It's not the Tower of London or *Star Wars*," Alice objected. "It's not something you *have* to see. There'll be enough funerals in the future, believe me."

"But I want to go to this one." Finn spoke with his mouth full. Why was Finn always eating? What was *wrong* with him?

"It's not as though you knew her that well," Alice said.

"I found her when she got lost, remember?"

"You helped to find her."

"Same thing."

"Look, Finn. A funeral is — personal. Mavis is terribly upset. It needs sensitivity."

"I can do sensitivity." Finn poured himself another bowl of cereal. "I liked Maudie. She was good fun."

"Well, that's the first sensible reason you've given."

"And Trot wants to come, too."

"Oh no. *Oh* no." If Alice suspected Finn's motives, she suspected Trot's even more.

"Trot rescued you all that time," Finn said. "You'd probably still be rolling around in the park if it wasn't for Trot."

"Now you're being ridiculous. Look. If you promise to behave and if Mavis doesn't mind, you can come. Oh — and if you can find something suitable to wear. You can't go to a funeral in jeans."

"Why not?"

"Finn, I'm warning you."

"Okay. No jeans." Finn drank the last of his milk from the bowl. "Great. I'll go and tell Kenny."

Alice herself wasn't looking forward to the funeral. It was the last thing she needed at the moment. Last week she had finally said goodbye to Jay.

It had been one of those increasingly rare occasions when Jay had been able to get away for an evening, and as soon as they had arranged it, she had known that that night had to be the night. She couldn't put it off indefinitely, and the time had come to bite the bullet. There would never be a good time, just perhaps a least bad time, and she had wanted to do it properly; she didn't want rushed goodbyes in some dingy pub or car park.

"Come to the house," she'd said to him.

"Are you sure?" Jay had sounded surprised.

"Yes. Finn's staying with a friend. We won't be disturbed."

Jay had brought flowers, as though he knew what was coming, and for perhaps the first time ever, they seemed awkward with each other, like two shy strangers. Alice poured wine, and they sat talking about small, safe things: Alice's job, a patient of Jay's who had had a bad reaction to his treatment, even the weather. But while they chatted, all Alice could think of was that this was it. This was the last time she would sit beside Jay, feel his hand in hers, smell the faint smell of soap and hospitals on his skin, hear his voice.

"Why do you keep looking at me like that?" Jay asked later on as she prepared supper.

"I'm just — taking you in. I don't want ever to forget what you look like."

"Why would you do that?"

"Because — because this is it, Jay." Alice put down her glass. "The last time. This has to be the last time."

There was a long silence, then Jay looked away and nodded. "I know," he said.

"How do you know?"

"The way you sounded on the phone, the way things have been going recently. And now, the way you look this evening. That top I've always loved, my favourite perfume." He ran his fingers through his hair. "I just know."

"I'm sorry," Alice said. "Oh, Jay! I'm so sorry."

"No. I'm the one who should be sorry. I've — got you into all this."

Alice came over and put her arms around him. "We got ourselves into this. Both of us. And I have no regrets. No regrets at all."

"Really?"

"Really."

"Oh, Alice, I don't — didn't — deserve you, deserve the time we've had together. You've been so good about everything, so accommodating, so…" He gave a small, helpless gesture. "You've just been — amazing."

"Jay, I've been an absolute cow recently, as you well know."

"That too." They both laughed. Jay picked up his glass, and then replaced it on the table. "Can we — may I make love to you? For the last time?"

"For the last time," Alice repeated. "How sad that sounds."

She had often wondered what happened to the sex lives of people who were properly together — married couples, people who had lived together for years. Did the sex gradually fizzle out as they grew older, until they were left just holding hands because they hadn't the energy to do anything more? Or were they aware that the last time was just that: a final episode in a lifetime of sexual encounters? And did they miss it, or did they accept it as inevitable? Of course there was much more to marriage than sex, but because she and Jay had had so few opportunities, sex had acquired a greater importance than it might have had they been married.

That night, they made love with a passion verging on desperation, as though they were trying to cram into that one hour all the years of lovemaking that would be denied them in the future and afterwards. Alice buried her face in Jay's neck and wept.

"Don't cry." Jay stroked her hair. "Darling Alice, please don't cry."

"I can't help it. I know what we're doing is the right thing, but it's so hard. *So hard!*"

"I know." There were tears in Jay's eyes, too. "I guess this is the price. We knew we'd have to pay it one day. This is our — well, our day of reckoning, I suppose." He attempted a laugh, but the laughter sounded flat and hollow, and Alice realised that she would probably never hear him laugh again.

For a long time, they lay holding each other, talking quietly. *I shall never forget this evening,* Alice thought. *I want to remember every last detail.* Jay's pale blue shirt (now discarded on the floor); the five o'clock shadow on his cheeks, because he'd rushed over straight from the hospital; the fact that he'd been wearing odd socks (had he noticed? Probably not. Alice knew that he often got dressed in the dark to let Angela sleep in after being up with the baby); the enormous bouquet of roses and freesias (her favourites); the smoked salmon that neither of them had been able to eat. Like a series of precious photographs, she wanted to preserve it all, for while she knew the memories would cause her pain, she also knew that what she and Jay had had together would always be an important part of who she was, and she didn't want to forget even the smallest detail.

"I — slept with Trot," she said suddenly. (Where on earth had that come from?)

"When?"

"The other week. I'm so sorry."

Jay sighed. "It doesn't matter. Sweetheart, it really doesn't matter. It can't spoil what we've had, and besides, we all need a bit of comfort."

"That's what Trot said."

"Wise man."

"I wouldn't say that." Alice laughed. "Trot may be many things, but I'd never call him wise."

"But I do envy him," Jay said. "Because he'll go on being a part of your life. He'll be able to see you whenever he likes."

"Well, he is Finn's father."

"That's what I mean." He turned to kiss her. "Darling Alice, what am I going to do without you? How am I going to — to *be* without you?"

"You'll be all right. We — we'll both be all right. Eventually," Alice said.

"But not yet."

"No. Not yet."

Jay pulled her closer into his arms. "The worst thing will be missing you so much but not being able to talk to you about it. Not being able to share it with you."

"I know."

"Do you think — I mean, could we keep in touch? Just occasionally? Just so that I can make sure you're all right."

"I'll be all right. And no, I don't think we'd better keep in touch. It'll only make things worse. For both of us."

"A clean break, then?"

"A clean break. It's the only way. For us. And for — for your family."

Jay's family. For the first time that evening, Alice realised that she hadn't asked about the baby, and Jay hadn't mentioned her. It was as though for this one evening, they had both agreed to shut the rest of the world out, leaving the two of them to say their farewells undisturbed.

"I want you to go now," she said, moving out of Jay's embrace. "Before we have any more time to think about it."

"What — right now? Just like that? You really want me to go without — without a proper goodbye?"

"I'd like you to go right now. Quickly, please. I'm going to go and have a shower, and when I come out, please — just don't be here. I'm not going to say goodbye. I can't bear it."

Jay took her face between his hands and gazed at her for a long moment, then kissed her gently on the lips. "If that's what you want. I guess the very least I can do is to do this the way you want."

"I don't *want* any of this," Alice said, fighting back more tears, "but I can't think of any other way."

And that was how they had done it — the clean break. Afterwards, Alice wondered whether they should have managed it differently; whether she should have seen Jay to the door, or at least waited until he'd gone before she had her shower. But the idea of watching his departure — of waving him off, seeing him drive away down the road — would have been even worse than returning from the bathroom to the empty bedroom and the rumpled sheets and the smell of him lingering on the pillow.

Trot had guessed what had happened and was being very supportive — in some ways, a little too supportive.

Ever since they had been to bed together, he had assumed a different relationship between them. He had taken to phoning more often, and not just to speak to Finn, and had even suggested a weekend away together.

"It was fun, wasn't it, Alice? You enjoyed it? Why not a repeat performance?"

"That's hardly a romantic way of putting it," Alice had told him.

"No. But you know what I mean."

"Trot, we've slept together twice. Just twice. I have no recollection of the first time, and my memory of the second is pretty hazy."

"Then let me refresh it," Trot said.

"No, Trot. Maybe one day, but not now. Not yet. I'm not —"

"Ready?"

"Yes. That last time was — fine. Perhaps even what I needed. And I really value your friendship. But I love Jay. I think perhaps I'll always love him. Not seeing someone doesn't stop you from loving them. I only wish it did. Things would be so much easier."

Trot sighed. "Such a shame. You've got a beautiful body, Alice."

"Thank you, kind sir. But that's hardly a basis for relationship."

"Maybe not. But it's a start."

But Alice wasn't ready for a new start of any kind. She needed time to herself, to lick her emotional wounds and to grieve both for what had been and for what could never be. Trot could — and did — continue to be a good friend; someone who understood the situation and someone she could talk to. But that was all. Maybe one day — who could tell? — there might be a future for them together, but Alice would rather be on her own than settle for second best. Besides, Trot was still determined to have his gap year, with or without Finn, and Alice doubted whether she was sufficiently important to him to be allowed to get in the way of his plans.

Alice and Gabs had been doing a lot of rallying round since Maudie's death, for Mavis really didn't seem to have anyone else. There had been vague talk of distant relatives who might or might not come to the funeral, but otherwise Mavis seemed very isolated. Alice was grateful to be able to concentrate on someone else's problems for a change, but she did wonder how anyone as basically nice as Mavis could find herself so alone, and she privately blamed Clifford. It seemed that Clifford had stolen not only Mavis's body, but her whole life as well. At least Alice had never allowed Jay to do that (to be fair, he would never have wanted her to). And she had Finn as well as her many friends. In that, compared with Mavis, she could count herself lucky.

It had been agreed that Alice would drive Mavis to the funeral. Mavis had said that she didn't fancy travelling in "one of those big black shiny things," and Alice had sympathised. Once — only once — she had had to travel in one herself, on the occasion of her father's funeral, and it had struck her as particularly cruel that at a time of such distress, one should have to parade one's grief so publicly. People in the street had stopped and stared as the cortège made its stately progress through the town, and one old man had removed his cap and bowed his head in respect.

She agreed with Mavis that the anonymity of an ordinary car was far better, and Alice's car was nothing if not ordinary. Gabs had offered hers, but even she had understood that if Mavis wished to be inconspicuous, a bright pink mini was not the answer.

Mavis was much exercised over the matter of the food for "afterwards".

"Mother always said there should be 'funeral meats,'" she said. "What *are* funeral meats?"

"I've no idea," Alice said.

"Do you think ham sandwiches would do?"

"I think ham sandwiches would be fine." After all, it was a funeral, and ham was meat. "I'll do them if you like. And egg and cress. They usually go down well." Alice herself was of the view that cress was tickly and tasteless and served no useful purpose except, perhaps, when grown by children on blotting paper for fun, but most people seemed to like it.

"Oh, would you?"

"Of course. How any people are you expecting?"

"Well, that's the trouble; I've no idea. Mother did have a lot of friends, but many of them have died, and those that are left are old and pretty frail. I'm not sure they'll want to turn out in this cold."

"Never mind," Alice said. "Finn will hoover up any leftovers."

"I'll make a cake," Mavis said. "Or do you think little cakes would be better?"

"Funeral fancies," murmured Gabs, "or perhaps coffin and walnut?" But fortunately Mavis was out of earshot.

Gabs herself was bringing wine.

"Wouldn't tea be more suitable?" Mavis had asked.

"Tea *and* wine. In this weather, we're going to need it," said Gabs. "Don't worry. My treat."

Alice could see that Mavis was puzzled at the idea of alcohol at a funeral being a treat, but on this occasion, she was with Gabs. She reckoned that by the time Maudie was safely interred, they would all need something stronger than tea.

Now, getting ready to go, Alice wondered whether she should have bought something black. Mavis was quite conventional, and she had forgotten to ask what would be appropriate. The nearest she had was a dark navy coat, so that would have to do. She had always wondered that the characters in television soap operas, many of whom were supposed to be strapped for cash, invariably turned out to funerals kitted out from head to foot in black — shoes, hat, the lot. She found an old pair of black boots at the back of her wardrobe and dusted them off.

Finn was wearing his suit. It had been bought for a wedding a year ago, and he appeared to have grown several inches since.

"Oh dear," Alice said, looking him over and tweaking a cuff. "You've grown."

"Yeah." Finn grinned. "That's what kids do. We grow. I told you you should have let me wear jeans."

"Perhaps we should have borrowed one from Trot."

"Trot hasn't got a suit. He doesn't believe in them."

"Now why doesn't that surprise me? Well, you'll have to do, I'm afraid. But you can't wear those trainers."

"I've only got my school shoes. I can't wear those!"

"Oh yes, you can."

"But, Mum —"

"Finn, shut up and do as you're told. I'm tired, and we're going to be late. I haven't got time to argue."

Gabs avoided funerals. They always reminded her of her mother's funeral — of her thirteen-year-old self sobbing at the graveside, fearing for her beloved mum in that cold, dark earth, and fearing even more a future without her. Her father had been so drunk he had had to be half carried from the churchyard, and she and Steph had clung to each other like the Babes in the Wood.

"What'll we do?" she had whispered to her sister on the journey home. "What'll become of us?"

"We'll survive," Steph had told her. "That's what we have to do. And we'll look after each other."

They had been doing just that more or less ever since. Their father had become drunker (how dare he drown sorrows that she knew to be no more than crocodile tears?), and the sisters had become closer. And they had indeed survived.

Gabs too was unsure what to wear to Maudie's funeral. She had a black leather skirt, but it was extremely short. She had a long skirt, but it was an Indian patchwork affair, with sparkly bits and gold beads dangling from the belt.

"What do you think?" she asked Steph.

"Haven't you anything else?"

"Nothing more suitable."

"You call those suitable?" Steph walked round her as though she might look different from behind. "Borrow one of mine. It's going to be a long time before I can fit into any of them again myself."

"Wig?" asked Gabs.

"Absolutely no wig. Don't be ridiculous."

"Maudie liked me whatever I wore, and she quite admired my wigs," Gabs said. "I think she was one of the few people who didn't judge me."

"But you said she was mad!"

"Only a bit mad. But she was pretty canny." Gabs picked out a pale grey cashmere skirt. "Can I have this one?"

"I suppose so. But don't spill anything on it."

Driving to the funeral, Gabs wondered whether life could get any worse. She had been fonder of Maudie than she liked to admit, and certainly more than she could tell Mavis; after all, Maudie had belonged to Mavis, and so it would be inappropriate for her to exhibit too much grief. But there had been something decent about Maudie — something genuine, loving, *kind*. Gabs hadn't experienced much kindness in her adult life, and she had been attracted to Maudie's warmth and Maudie's embraces, which always smelled of lavender water and mothballs (did anyone really use mothballs anymore?). She was going to miss her.

Then there was Steph's engagement. She still found it hard to believe that her sensible sister had actually consented to marry Clive, but there it was. The happy couple had celebrated with something sparkling (non-alcoholic, of course), and Steph now sported a (cheap) diamond ring and had already accumulated a stack of wedding magazines.

"What are you doing with these?" Gabs had flicked through the magazines. They all looked the same: Barbie-doll girls in white dresses — from slinky, via prim Jane Austen, through to meringue — plus advice on everything from make-up to marquees. "Are you really going to — to *dress up* for this?"

Steph sighed. "Oh, Gabs, you know I've always wanted a white wedding. I know it's pathetic, but I want it to be the one thing I do *properly*."

"Of course you do." Gabs had relented. "Poor old Steph. And you haven't even got a mother of the bride to wear a posh hat and be proud."

"No, but I've got you. I thought — I thought you might be a bridesmaid?"

"Did you now?" Gabs tried to imagine herself in a long conventional frock carrying a posy of something bridal, and failed. On the other hand, what had she got to lose? "Oh, go on then. Why not? But no peach, no aqua, and no yellow. I look terrible in yellow. When's this going to happen?"

"I thought in the spring. The baby will be a couple of months old, so I should have my figure back."

"If not, I've got an amazing corset you can borrow. I'll lace you into it. You won't be able to breathe, but you'll look stunning."

Privately, Gabs blamed Father Pat for all this. How dare he coerce Steph into a lifetime of misery and boredom just in the interests of God and respectability? And yet it could be that Steph would be happy with Clive. She had always been undemanding, and Clive did seem genuinely fond of her. Stranger things had happened.

Of course, one of the problems was that Gabs was jealous — not of the marriage (perish the thought), but of Clive's place in Steph's life. Hitherto, it had always been Gabs and Steph against the world. Now she feared that if she didn't toe the line, it could well become Steph and Clive against Gabs. If this was to be avoided, she would have to embrace her new brother-in-law in every sense, and while she might come to accept that Steph liked — even loved — him, he would never be her kind of person. When she had had time to get used to the idea of the baby, she had rather liked the idea of its presence in the flat; she could even see herself sharing it (and thus being absolved of any need to have one herself). But Steph's marriage would make her superfluous. She might be required for babysitting purposes, but otherwise she would just be an aunt (such an ugly, old-maidish kind of word, she had always thought). As for the flat, things were going to be pretty cramped, and she couldn't imagine them all getting on together for long. She could probably afford to buy Steph out and find somewhere else, but she didn't really want to. Clive, needless to say, had no place of his own, and in her less charitable moments, it had occurred to Gabs that this might have played some part in his decision to marry Steph.

It was a bright cold day — not one of those wet, windswept funeral days you so often see in films — and Gabs cheered up a bit. She had filled the boot of the car with wine, plus a couple of bottles of champagne; whatever else she might feel about today, it would be nice to see the others and do a bit of catching up. But when she saw Mavis, she was shocked.

Mavis was pale, and she had lost weight. Her clothes seemed to hang off her, as though they too were grieving, and when she came over to greet Gabs, her eyes were brimming with tears.

"Thank you so much for coming," she said as Gabs embraced her.

"Did you really think I wouldn't?" Gabs asked.

"No. No, of course I didn't. It's just that you've been — you've been so kind."

Gabs muttered something about that being what friends were for, and took Mavis's arm. "Is Clifford coming?"

"I don't think so. He said it wouldn't be — appropriate."

"Oh, did he?"

"And he didn't really know Mother."

But he knew you, thought Gabs furiously. How could this pompous, selfish man, who over the years had taken so much from Mavis, not make this little effort when she most needed him?

"Perhaps you're right," she said now.

The interior of the church had the familiar smell of damp and incense hat always took Gabs back to her childhood Sundays, when she and Steph were marched off to Mass, washed and scrubbed and thoroughly uncomfortable, and instructed by their mother to "behave yourselves, don't pick your noses, and make sure to hand over *all* your collection money" (Gabs had been known to secrete some of hers in her sock). There seemed to be quite a good turnout, although as Mavis had predicted, many of them required the assistance of Zimmer frames and sticks, and there was at least one wheelchair. Gabs wondered what it must be like, getting to a stage of life where funerals outnumbered other more cheerful rituals, and you knew that before long it would be your own turn. She looked at the row of cotton-wool heads in front of her and wondered what they were thinking. Was there some relief in knowing that yet another person had beaten them to it, that at least they were *still alive*? Or were they all wondering whether they would be next?

The priest was brisk and businesslike, and the requiem mass for Maude Winifred Wetherby was soon over. A short address was given about Maudie's life, her regular church attendance, and her numerous good works in the parish. But none of these related to the Maudie Gabs had known, and she felt sad. Mavis had said that she might say a few words if she felt able to, but apparently she did not, and so the real Maudie went unacknowledged.

Afterwards, Gabs joined Alice and Finn as everyone gathered at the cemetery for the burial.

"Do you think they've ever dropped anyone?" Finn asked as the funeral directors made their way down a grassy slope to the graveside with Maudie balanced precariously on their shoulders.

"No. They're used to it," Alice told him.

"But what if they did?"

"Well, it would be a bit undignified, I suppose."

"How do we know it's really Maudie in there?" he persisted. "It could be anyone, couldn't it? It could just be a pile of bricks."

"Why would anyone want to bury a pile of bricks?"

"Or stolen goods," said Finn, warming to his subject. "Then they could come back later and dig them up."

"Finn, will you please stop asking silly questions."

"But —"

"Shut up, Finn. I mean it."

Finn turned to catch Gabs' eye, and she winked at him. Such a shame he's so young, she thought. In a couple of years, he's going to be quite a looker.

The coffin was lowered into the grave, and Mavis was handed a small lump of earth. She looked helplessly at Gabs.

"You throw it in," Gabs whispered. "On top of the coffin."

"Why? Why would I want to do that?"

"I've no idea, but it's what you do. Tradition, I suppose."

"Can I have some?" Finn asked.

"For the last time, Finn, *shut up*," Alice said, "or you can go and sit in the car."

"I only asked."

"Well, don't."

Mavis threw her lump of earth, which scattered over the lid of the coffin, obscuring the shiny brass plate that bore Maudie's name.

"That's it," Mavis said after a respectful silence had been observed, and people began to talk in subdued voices. "She's gone. Mother's gone."

Weeping, she turned away and began walking slowly back towards the road and the parked cars. Gabs wondered briefly whether she should go and join her, but realised that just for the moment, Mavis needed to be alone.

Right up until the last minute, Mavis had hoped that Clifford might come to the funeral, but she should have known better. He had told her that he wouldn't be coming, and Clifford prided himself on being a man of his word, especially when that word involved an arrangement convenient to himself. Now, she felt hurt and disappointed and angry. Over the years, she had made fewer and fewer demands of him, and this was really such a small thing to ask. He need only have attended the service and then gone home. She wouldn't have expected him to stay on afterwards — just perhaps to say a few words to her before he went.

In the carpark, Gabs caught up with her.

"So he didn't come," she said, taking Mavis's arm.

"No. No, he didn't." Mavis was grateful for Gabs' understanding. "I knew he wouldn't."

"But you hoped."

"Yes, I hoped. I seem to do a lot of hoping."

"Poor Mavis. Let's get you home."

Mavis looked at the pink mini and hesitated for a moment.

"Oh, why not?" she said, waving to Alice to show her what she was doing. "I'd like to go with you. I'm fond of Finn, but he does ask a lot of questions."

The mini attracted some strange glances, but Mavis decided she was beyond caring. She had just said her last farewell to the only person who truly loved her, and she would have been happy to travel in a tank had that been the only available means of transport.

"It went well, didn't it?" Gabs said.

"I suppose so. But it wasn't really *Mother*."

"I know what you mean. But funerals rarely are, are they? They never seem to do justice to the person who's died."

"Mr. Strong didn't come, either," Mavis said.

"Did you expect him to?"

"Not really, but it would have been nice if he'd shown that he cared just a little. After all, I've worked for him all these years, and he met Mother several times. But I suppose he's still annoyed with me."

This was an understatement, for Mr. Strong, in a particularly unkind moment, had actually totted up the amount of time Mavis had taken off work during Maudie's illness, and had been outraged at the result of his research. That the illness had proved terminal had done nothing to ameliorate his anger ("after all, you didn't *know* she was going to die, Mavis, did you?"), and neither had the activities of Mrs. Strong. Mr. Strong had unwisely brought in his wife to help while he was away for the afternoon, and this good lady (and she was a good lady — just a very bad shopkeeper) had contrived to lose half a day's takings and three pairs of socks.

"All that *money*, Mavis," he had told her when relating this sorry tale. "And the socks. How did she manage to lose three pairs of socks?"

"Perhaps she gave them away," Mavis had suggested. After all, stranger things had happened when Mrs. Strong was in charge.

"Now you're being ridiculous."

"Is there any other explanation?" Mavis asked.

"Theft. Yes, theft, Mavis. Someone stole those socks *from under my wife's very nose.*"

This conjured up such an extraordinary image (Mrs. Strong being particularly well-endowed in the nasal department) that Mavis, who was exhausted to the point of hysteria, had actually laughed. It was this, she suspected, that had proved the final straw in their relationship, and she was pretty sure that her days at the shop were numbered. For even if Mr. Strong wished to keep her on, Mavis wasn't at all sure that she wanted to work for him anymore.

The wake back at the house was attended by a respectable number of people, many of them neighbours, and Gabs and Alice helped Mavis serve them with tea and sandwiches. When everyone had left, Mavis suggested they open the wine (nobody had wanted it after all), and the others gladly agreed. The next day being Saturday, Finn had been collected by Trot, who was taking him home for the night, so the three of them were on their own.

"Thank goodness that's over," Mavis said, battling with a champagne cork. "I've been dreading today."

"Of course you have. Here — let me do that." Gabs took the bottle from her. "You fetch some glasses."

They toasted Maudie in champagne, and when that was finished, they toasted her in red wine.

"What will you do now, Mavis?" Alice asked. "Your life's going to be very different, isn't it?"

"I'm not sure." Mavis had been giving the matter some thought. "I shall stay here, of course. I've lived here all my life. But I might find another job."

"What about travel? Had you thought of that?" Gabs asked.

"I've always been a bit nervous of going abroad," Mavis said. "All that business with tickets and customs and weighing your luggage. I went to Paris once, and my suitcase went to Madrid." She felt considerably more cheerful and ever so slightly drunk. "No, I'm not sure about travel."

"What about Clifford?" Alice asked.

"*What* about Clifford?"

"I suppose you wouldn't want to be away from him for too long?"

"Ah. I didn't tell you, did I?"

"Tell us what?"

"I left Clifford a message saying that if he didn't come to the funeral, that was it. That I wouldn't be seeing him again."

"You *what*?"

"Yes. I wasn't sure I meant it at the time, but now that he hasn't turned up, I feel so angry that I may very well stick to my word."

"Did he reply?"

"Yes. He left me a message saying the living were more important than the dead — the living presumably meaning him. But he seems to have forgotten that I'm not dead. I'm living, too. And I'm — well, I used to be important to him."

"Wow. You have come a long way," Alice said. "But shouldn't you wait a bit? At least until you're a bit more… well…"

"Sober?" Mavis suggested. "I was perfectly sober when I left that message."

"He'll be very surprised, won't he?" Alice said.

"Yes. Very. I've made threats before — lots of them — but I've never carried them out."

"And you're really going to carry out this one?"

"Yes. I rather think I am." Mavis topped up her glass.

"Well, good for you," Gabs said. "I think he's treated you shamefully. The fat, selfish brute."

Mavis had forgotten that Gabs had met Clifford, and there had been a time when she would have taken exception to this description of her lover, but now she found herself agreeing.

"He is a fat, selfish brute," she said. "Nowadays, I'm no more to him than a — a kind of plaything. He uses me to while away the time when he's not on the golf course or — or googling his spleen."

"So you could go travelling if you wanted to," Gabs said. "There's nothing to stop you, is there?"

"I suppose not. Oh, I don't know. I'll have to see."

"I know!" Alice put her glass down. "I've had an idea. Let's *all* go travelling!"

"What do you mean?" Gabs asked.

"Well, if Trot carries out his threat and takes Finn off on a jolly after his GCSEs, I'll be free. Gabs — you could be free, couldn't you, if you wanted to? And then, Mavis, you could come with us, and we'll sort out all the tickets and things."

"Brilliant!" Gabs said, spilling wine on the cashmere skirt. "I'm up for it if you both are. Steph doesn't need me anymore, and as for Mrs. Grant, she can stuff her job."

"We'll *all* go on a gap year!" Alice said.

"A gap year?" Mavis looked puzzled.

"It's really a young thing, but anyone can do it. You just — take off, and see what happens. It'll probably be more of a gap six months, but it'll be the same kind of thing."

"You mean, work our way round the world?" Mavis asked.

"Who said anything about work? I could certainly work my way round the world. No problem." Gabs smirked. "But with the greatest respect, I doubt whether you two could. No, we aren't going to work. We're going to have fun."

The three of them spent the next couple of hours fantasising about riding on elephants and buying exotic souvenirs in souks until Gabs and Alice decided it was time to phone for taxis home.

"We're far too drunk to drive," Gabs explained, knocking over a chair as she made her way to the lavatory. "We can collect our cars tomorrow."

"You could stay here," Mavis said, but immediately regretted it. There wasn't much room for visitors in her small house, and she wasn't ready to contemplate the prospect of anyone sleeping in Maudie's bed.

"No." Alice picked up her handbag. "We'll go now and leave you in peace. You've had quite a day, and I expect you're ready for your bed. Will you be all right, Mavis?"

"Yes, I'll be fine."

But when they had gone, Mavis didn't feel fine at all. All the euphoria induced by the wine and the company dwindled away, and a great wave of loneliness swept over her. Of course there wouldn't be any travelling, any 'gap year'. It was all a silly dream. In fact, now that this year was over, she doubted whether Alice and Gabs would want to keep in touch with her anymore. In the meantime, she would have to grovel to Mr. Strong to keep him sweet, and she would work among the socks and ties until it was time for her to retire.

What had she to look forward to? As she brushed her teeth and put on her sensible brushed cotton nightdress, Mavis contemplated a bleak future: a future without Maudie, without Clifford (and in a way, even now, Clifford might be better than nothing), and with few friends. She found that she even missed Pussolini. At least he had been *there*; he had been a living presence — albeit a malevolent one — in the house. But she wouldn't get another cat. Whatever happened, she wasn't going to become that cliché: the lonely old woman with a cat. A dog, perhaps? Mavis knew nothing about dogs, but she didn't fancy having to pick up their nasty little doings and take them home in a plastic bag. At least Pussolini had had the decency to bury his in the garden.

When Mavis checked her mobile, she found there was a message from Clifford. For a moment, she hesitated. It wasn't too late to go back. Clifford hadn't expected her to keep her threat, so she could back down without losing face. But then she was reminded once again of Clifford's recent lack of consideration, his self-obsession, his *unkindness*; and she deleted the message without even reading it.

The next morning, Mavis awoke with a splitting headache. As she cleared away empty cups and glasses, the curled remains of ham sandwiches, and the empty wine bottles (had they really drunk all that?), she tried to push away the tide of gloom that kept threatening to envelop her. She must pull herself together. It was the day after her mother's funeral; of course she was miserable. How did she expect to feel?

It was nearly lunchtime when Gabs and Alice arrived in a taxi. They seemed very excited and were carrying a pile of maps and brochures.

"We've come to cheer you up," Gabs announced, dumping her burden on the table. "We've come to make plans."

"What plans?" Mavis asked, wondering whether she should put the kettle on.

"Gap year plans."

Hazy memories of the last night's conversation began to surface in Mavis's aching brain. "Oh," she said.

"You're going to love this, Mavis," Gabs continued. "We've been working it all out. It'll be expensive, but if you can manage it, so can we. Have a look here." She opened out a map. "We can either fly direct to, say, Australia, and then make our way back. Or we can get the Eurostar and then travel by train across Europe." Gabs' finger (black nail polish) moved rapidly eastward across the map. "Then there's this train we can take down through Yugoslavia, and if we cross to Turkey here, we can —"

"Hang on a minute, Gabs," Alice said. "Let the poor woman get her head round the idea. Could we have some coffee, Mavis?"

An hour and several cups of strong coffee later, the plan was taking shape, and even Mavis was becoming excited. They would have to wait until after Finn's exams, of course, but then they really could take off for six months.

"It sounds almost too good to be true," Mavis said. "But it's going to be awfully expensive."

"We've thought of that," Gabs said.

"Yes." Alice put down her coffee cup. "I've been putting money aside for Finn if he goes to university, but as he seems determined not to, I thought I might spend some of it on myself. I might even persuade my newspaper to pay me to write about it, although I doubt whether they'll pay my expenses. They could decide to get rid of me altogether, but I can always do some freelancing when I get back."

"I'm okay for money," Gabs said, "so there's just you, Mavis. Do you think you could manage it?"

"Well…" Mavis thought for a few minutes. "Mother did have a few thousand in her building society account, and I have some savings. But it seems a bit — well, frivolous to spend it on a holiday."

"It's not a holiday. It's an *experience*," Gabs said. "And knowing Maudie, I'm sure she would have been delighted for you to do this. It's an adventure, Mavis. It'll be fun. When did you last have fun?"

Now that she came to think about it, Mavis realised that fun wasn't something that had played much part in her life. Certainly she had had fun as a girl, but not as much as most of her friends, to whom fun tended to mean boys and parties. Mavis hadn't been very successful with either boys or parties. When she had first got together with Clifford, they had certainly had fun; they had had secret picnics and small intimate celebrations, and they had laughed a lot. But since his retirement, Clifford had become increasingly serious and had shown little interest in anything that might be construed as fun, not least because, as he frequently explained, he was unwilling to do anything to compromise his health. Fun, it would seem, carried risks that he was not prepared to take (although Mavis was unsure as to what those risks might be).

Now, she looked at Gabs and Alice — at their anxious, expectant faces, at the maps and the leaflets and the sheets of notes in Gabs' untidy handwriting — and she knew what her answer would be. How could it be anything else?

"All right. I'll do it," she said, feeling very brave and not a little reckless.

The other two breathed a sigh of relief.

"Oh, that's great!" Gabs hugged her. "You won't regret it."

"In that case, we ought to drink a toast," Alice said.

"Yes! A toast!" said Gabs.

"Haven't we all had enough?" Mavis was still nursing her headache.

"Just a tiny one." Alice found the dregs of a bottle of wine and divided it between three glasses.

"To our gap year!" she said.

The others clinked their glasses.

"To our gap year!"

Epilogue: A Year Later

On a bright August afternoon, the bishop had conducted a service to bless the new font in Father Cuthbert's church, and the two men were enjoying tea and cake in the presbytery garden.

"What happened to that little group of yours, Father?" the bishop enquired.

"The... er..."

"Basic Theology Class?" Father Cuthbert suggested.

"Yes. Yes, of course. Basic Theology." The bishop chuckled. "There were one or two rather intransigent members, as I recall."

"Well, it's odd that you should mention it, Your Grace, because I received a postcard yesterday morning."

"A postcard?"

"Yes. I have it with me." Father Cuthbert fumbled in his pocket and brought out a crumpled picture postcard showing a foreign-looking shepherd herding three sheep through a gateway. The bishop turned the postcard over. The card bore an Israeli postmark, and the message simply said: "Three lost sheep returning to the fold," followed by three scrawled signatures.

"I wonder what it means," Father Cuthbert said.

"Oh, that's quite clear, Father," said the bishop with a smile. "Your three — *lost sheep* have seen the light, and it looks as though they are paying a visit to the Holy Land. A little pilgrimage, you might say. How satisfactory. Well done, Father. Well done!"

Father Cuthbert cast his mind back and recalled the faces of Gabs, Alice, and Mavis. Had these three women really repented? Could it be true? Being a realist, he had his doubts, but he decided that on this occasion it would be best if he kept them to himself.

"Thank you, Your Grace. Thank you very much," he said. "Another cup of tea?"

BOOK THREE: RUTH ROBINSON'S YEAR OF MIRACLES

Prologue

My Uncle Eric is telephoning the zoo to ask how many Thomson's gazelles a lion can eat in a fortnight.

Uncle Silas is stuffing a weasel on the kitchen table by candlelight (we have a power cut).

A respectful knock at the front door heralds the arrival of yet another minibus full of pilgrims hoping for a miracle.

Outside it is raining — a typical, nasty, dank November drizzle — and a piglet is trying to get in through the cat flap.

In the midst of all this, I am trying to cobble together something for our supper (the weasel is being prepared for posterity rather than for consumption).

I pause to take stock.

Six months ago, I had a regular job, a monthly salary and a comfortable flat to go home to.

How on earth have I got into all this?

Part I: Summer

In the first three months following conception, the embryo develops from a single cell into a tiny recognisable human being. By the end of that time, it will measure up to 10cms in length and weigh about one ounce. Its head is almost half the size of its entire body, it has begun to move independently, and it will have fingernails and toenails. All its major organs will be in place.

Chapter One

Many women the wrong side of thirty-five seem to want a baby but not necessarily a man. I am on the wrong side of thirty-five, and all I ever wanted was the man. But it seems that I have got the baby instead.

I sit on the lavatory and cry. How many other women all over the country are also at this moment sitting on the lavatory and crying, either because they are pregnant or because they are not? The pregnancy testing kit is uncompromisingly positive. Good news, it seems to say. You're going to have a baby!

But I don't want a baby, I sob. I never wanted a baby. I don't even like babies! And I've always been so careful. Besides, aren't I supposed to be past my childbearing best? There seems to be a proliferation of articles and programmes about the ticking of body clocks and the folly of women who Leave It Too Late. My body clock has kept a tactful silence for as long as I can remember, and apart from the monthly (and expected) reminder that I am not pregnant — that one more disappointed egg has gone unfertilised to its tiny grave — I have never given it a thought. But I have made one slip; one tiny slip; and now this. A cruel reminder that behind every sexual act between fertile couples of opposite sexes there lurks a baby waiting to be conceived.

I flush away the evidence and wipe my eyes. Maybe the test is wrong. They can be wrong sometimes. And I don't feel pregnant. My stomach is still washboard flat, my breasts small and firm, and I don't feel in the least bit sick. How can a silly little strip of paper be right when my body (not to mention my head) is in denial?

But I am not stupid. I know how these things work. And my oh-so-reliable period is a week late. Barring accident or interference, I am going to have a baby.

It couldn't have come at a worse time. The orchestra in which I play the violin has recently had to make cuts, and as a lesser player in one of the back desks, I have been 'let go', as they kindly put it. This was a blow indeed, although not entirely unexpected, and to cheer myself up, I planned to award myself a belated gap year on the strength of a small legacy from my grandmother. And why not? I have no responsibilities, my mortgage is small and my life my own. My good friend Mikey — solid, dependable and reassuringly gay — was going to accompany me. We were going to scuba dive in the Red Sea, trek at the foot of the Himalayas and visit Petra. We had it all worked out. My small bedroom is littered with atlases and brochures, phrase books and useful telephone numbers. I was going to let my flat (the contract is already signed; a nice young Norwegian couple would look after it and feed the cat as well) and go off with a rucksack and my violin on my back (Mikey took issue with the violin, but as I explained, I wouldn't dream of going anywhere without it. I could always lock it up in a safe somewhere if we did anything really exotic). I was going to be free from the constraints and expectations of the world of work. I was going to have an *adventure*.

I spend a sleepless night worrying about my new and unwelcome condition. I know life isn't fair, and I've never expected it to be, but do I really deserve this? I've always tried to be responsible, such relationships as I have had have nearly all been long term and monogamous, and I have always practised safe sex. Except this once. Just the once.

His name is Amos (his parents, like mine, are religious) and he is an old friend; a big bearded trombonist with hands like shovels and arms made to hug. I needed a hug — so, it seemed, did he — and this is the result.

Do I tell Amos? Over my second cup of Horlicks, I ponder the question, and decide that I shall not. Amos has his own problems; he has endured a recent and very messy divorce, and he too has lost his job (violinists are not the only ones getting the push). Besides, I know that whatever happens this will tie me to Amos, and I'm not sure this is something either of us will want. This is my pregnancy; my problem. Especially since I told Amos that I was on the pill (by that stage we were in a state of reckless undress, and lying seemed a much easier option than waiting for Amos to 'pop to the chemist', as he had kindly offered to do).

By four fifty-three am, having worked my way through the prospect of keeping the baby and, fleetingly, the possibility of having it adopted, I consider taking advantage of the Woman's Right to Choose. It is not something I have ever given much thought to since I never expected to find myself in this position, but now it seems the least unattractive of my alternatives. I sit up in bed and switch the light on. Yes! I am a woman, and I shall choose. My gap year isn't lost; it's merely postponed. I feel faint stirrings of hope, thinking with satisfaction that with a bit of luck they are the only stirrings I am going to feel, for I shall have an abortion. After all, it's a small procedure at this stage, neither I nor my unborn child will feel a thing, and in a week or so I will be back to normal. Fortunately, Mikey and I were leaving it until the last minute to book our tickets (Mikey likes nothing better than a bargain), so I can allow myself a little leeway. I'm sure the Norwegians can make alternative arrangements for a couple of weeks, and then everything will be back on track.

A week later, having persuaded two doctors that this unwanted pregnancy will seriously compromise my sanity, I am sitting in the waiting-room of the clean, clinical building where I shall be divested of my little problem. I decided to go to a private clinic because they could see me at once, and I thought I would be unlikely to bump into anyone I know. My gap year fund is shrinking by the minute, but I have some savings which will help. Mikey (who had to be told, for obvious reasons) has insisted on coming with me. Mikey is being unusually silent.

'Are you all right?' I ask him, thinking that really it should be the other way round. 'You're being very quiet.'

'I feel quiet.' Mikey turns the pages of a glossy magazine.

'What's up?'

'Nothing.' He examines the price of a very expensive country mansion, and whistles through his teeth.

'Are you sure?'

'Quite sure.'

'You're behaving like a woman,' I tell him.

'What do you mean?'

'That's what women do. They say nothing's wrong when it is, and then get cross if no-one tries to get to the bottom of the problem.'

'Okay.' Mikey puts down his magazine. 'I don't think you should be doing this.'

'Doing what?'

'The abortion.'

'*Now* you tell me! Anyway, it's not your baby, so it's none of your business.'

'It is my business. You've made it my business.'

'No I haven't!'

'Yes you have.'

A passing nurse gives us as funny look, and it occurs to me that of course she assumes that Mikey is the baby's father.

'You insisted on coming with me. I didn't make you. I didn't even ask you.'

'You had to have someone.'

'No I didn't!'

'Yes you did. No-one should go through something like this alone.'

'So you accept that I'm going through with it?'

'I know you mean to. But Ruth, have you really considered what you're doing?'

'Of course I have.' This is not entirely true. I have tried hard to push the whole baby thing to the back of my mind and look upon this in the same way as I would a visit to the dentist.

Mikey reaches into his pocket and takes out a small booklet. On the cover is a joyously pregnant woman, her hands smugly clasped round her bump. Inside are graphic illustrations of foetal development.

'Look at this.' He jabs a finger at a picture of a seven-week foetus. 'Eyes and little arms, and a heart.'

'So?' The foetus looks like a cross between a seahorse and a new-born rabbit.

'So, it's a human being.'

'Hardly.'

'You know what I mean.' Mikey sighs. 'It has all the potential to be a person. It could be a brain surgeon or a nuclear physicist or —'

'A chimney sweep?'

'That too.'

'Mikey, I can't. Apart from anything else, I can't let you down. We fly in a fortnight —'

'Not necessarily. And anyway, a baby is more important than cavorting around the world with me.'

'Mikey, please. This is hard enough as it is.'

'Is it?'

I hesitate. If I'm honest, this hasn't been hard at all. Apart from when I found out, I've been in very successful denial. It annoys me that Mikey is disturbing my comfort zone and putting unwelcome thoughts into my head.

Mikey wheels out his trump card.

'I would give anything — *anything* — to be a father,' he says. 'But I never shall be.'

'You could be.'

'No I couldn't. I shall never be able to have straight sex, and I certainly have no intention of looking for a willing woman and a turkey baster. I've accepted my lot. Perhaps you should accept yours.'

'Mikey, you're not being fair.'

'Neither are you.' He returns to his magazine, and we maintain a sullen silence. The minutes tick by.

'Miss Robinson?' A starched nurse comes into the waiting room. 'Would you come this way, please?'

I stand up and pick up my bag. Mikey looks up from his magazine, but he doesn't say anything.

'Good luck?' I prompt him.

Mikey shakes his head.

'There's nothing good about this,' he says. 'But — be safe.'

Fifteen minutes later, I am lying on a trolley awaiting my turn on what I imagine to be some kind of surgical conveyor belt. I am wearing one of those backless hospital gowns, and I feel naked and defenceless. I have been given an injection to help me relax, but all it's done is make me feel strange and floaty and very slightly sick. I wish very much that I was anywhere but here.

I must have dozed off, because through a drug-induced haze, I can see my small seahorse/rabbit hovering somewhere near the ceiling. Perhaps I have had the operation, and my little embryo is having one of those out-of-body experiences on its way to the hereafter, only with me watching it rather than the other way round.

It reaches the window, where it scrabbles hopelessly for a few moments, and then it slithers down in a streak of pink ectoplasm and disappears.

I wake up as the trolley begins to move, and for a few moments I rather enjoy the sensation of being transported somewhere; of other people taking charge and of everything being out of my hands. Someone is pushing me with brisk, business-like footsteps. Soon, all this will be over. I open my eyes, and the ceiling (palest cream, with little decorative swirls. You don't get those on the National Health) moves backwards above me. We go round corners and someone opens and closes doors. I begin to drift again.

'No. *No*!'

Who was that? The voice sounds panicky and very close. Very like mine, in fact.

'No what?' Another voice, soothing and female. The trolley rumbles on its way.

'No!' This voice is quite definitely mine.

'It'll soon be over, dear. Just you relax.'

'NO!' I clutch the edges of the trolley and try to sit up. 'Let me off! Let me out of here! I want to go home!'

The trolley comes to an abrupt halt.

'You've signed the consent form, dear. Everything's arranged. Mr. Buxton is waiting for you.'

'Bugger Mr. Buxton! I just want to go home. You can't keep me here against my will!'

'If you're going to talk like that, I'm sure we don't want to keep you at all.' The voice is stern, like that of a very cross nanny. 'I'll have to go and speak to Mr. Buxton.'

A minute later, a masked face is leaning over me. I can tell from its eyebrows that it is not pleased.

'Now then, Miss Robinson. What's all this about?' Mr. Buxton's voice is that of a busy man who is not used to having his day disrupted.

'I want to go home.'

'You mean you've changed your mind?'

'I suppose so.'

'Well, have you or haven't you? We haven't got all day. We talked this through —' up to a point — 'and you had counselling —' five minutes with a rather bored nurse — 'You've had every chance to think about your decision.'

My eyes fill with sudden tears. Oh, where is the smooth-talking, kindly Mr. Buxton of three days ago? What has happened to the gentle fatherly figure who "understood how hard these decisions are" and who offered me his support, whatever I decided? I didn't need him then, when I felt strong and determined and grown up. I need him now, when I am confused and unhappy and vulnerable. But that Mr. Buxton seems to have been left behind in his consulting rooms, together with his smart charcoal suit and spotted bow tie, and the peaceful watercolours of lakes and fields and woods on his dove grey walls.

'Well,' he continues, 'if you've changed your mind, then that's that. But of course, there will still be a fee to pay. Someone else could have had your appointment.'

His voice goes on, calm but reproachful, but I am no longer listening. I imagine my little seahorse/rabbit drifting away from its window and snuggling back into my womb, where it belongs. There is the ghost of a smile on its round featureless face, but the smile is grateful rather than smug.

'Your partner is waiting for you,' a nurse tells me, as she helps me dress and collect up my things.

'He's not my partner,' I tell her, emerging from the changing room.

'No,' says Mikey, who loves this kind of situation. 'I bat for the other side. Can't you tell?' He minces towards us, holding out his hand for my bag. 'What made you change your mind?'

'Not you, if that's what you were hoping,' I tell him, rather unkindly.

'I was hoping nothing of the sort.'

'No. I'm sorry.'

'That's all right.' He pats my knee.

'I just — well, I just couldn't do it. That's all.' I hesitate. Should I tell him about my vision (if that's what it was)? No. Better not. 'You were right. I hadn't really thought about it. I hadn't thought what it *meant*. And when I was lying there waiting, I knew it wasn't for me. Maybe for other people, but not me.' I feel unutterably tired, and just want to get home.

'You won't regret it,' Mikey says.

'It's okay for you to say that.'

'I mean it. And I'll be godfather.'

'Oh, would you?' Mikey would make the perfect godfather, and for a moment, I feel quite excited.

'I'd be honoured. I shall buy it lovely presents for its birthday, and take it to the zoo.'

I have a vivid mental picture of Mikey, hand-in-hand with my seahorse/rabbit, looking at camels and monkeys, and I giggle.

'I don't know what they gave you in there, but we need to get you home,' Mikey says sternly. 'Before you become hysterical.'

Chapter Two

A week later — how things can change in a week! — things are not looking good. Since Mikey has managed to persuade me that the gap year must at the very least be postponed, I'm sure that with a bit of luck I'll be able to stay on in my flat, take on some violin students and make some kind of living for myself and the seahorse/rabbit. The Norwegians will understand. After all, this is an emergency.

The Norwegians do not understand. Neither are they nearly as nice as they once appeared to be. They tell me, in impeccable English, that they have rights. I have signed a piece of paper. My flat — *my* flat — is theirs for the next twelve months.

I explain that something has cropped up, and I have nowhere to live. The Norwegians tell me that they also have nowhere to live, and that where I go is my problem. They are moving in on Tuesday. Please can I make sure that the flat is clean and that I have defrosted the fridge.

Couldn't they make it Thursday? I plead. Even Wednesday? No, they could not. The Norwegians have made nice tidy little Norwegian plans, and these plans include moving into my flat on Tuesday. It appears that they are still prepared to do right by the cat, for that is in the agreement, but not to give me even one extra day, which is not. If I ever get to go on my gap year, I shall definitely not visit Norway.

In desperation, I ring round my friends. Surely someone, somewhere, will take me in, if only temporarily. I shan't take up much room, and I promise to play my violin very quietly. I can even busk until I get some students. But everyone seems to have some reason or other why they can't put me up. Of those who might have been able to have me, two friends are having marriage problems, one is moving house herself, and another is about to have twins. As for my orchestra friends, they are mostly poor and living out of suitcases, quite apart from worrying about their jobs. It would be churlish to add to their problems.

Feeling desperate, and very sick (the morning sickness has now kicked in with a vengeance) I reach the bottom of the accommodation barrel and find my parents. I shall go and spend the night with them, and break my news to them as gently as I can. It's not something I am looking forward to.

Now, perhaps I should explain about my parents. They are nice enough people, but they are stuck in a nineteen fifties time warp; an age when nice girls got sensible jobs (teaching, nursing, social work; that kind of thing) and then married, had children and led unblemished lives of dedicated domesticity, after which they went trustingly to their reward (they are also strict Evangelical Christians). My parents are undoubtedly good people — they give generously to charity, help (if not actually love) their neighbours, and lead generally blameless lives — but there is a lack of joy or humour which I find very hard to take in all but the smallest of doses. My childhood was bordered by strict rules and narrow boundaries, and as an only child, I was very lonely. Sundays — for me, the worst day of the week — were days of mind-numbing boredom, involving two church services, plus Sunday school, and I was not permitted to do anything which could be called work. Occasionally, I would sneak out with my violin and practise in the garden shed, but if I was discovered, retribution inevitably followed, so it was rarely worth the bother. Sundays apart, approved friends were allowed to come and play, but not stay overnight, and parties were regarded with suspicion. I remember our annual holiday (a fortnight by the sea) as dull and uneventful; a cliché of Englishness, with my father dozing in a deckchair and my mother doing nothing more adventurous than paddling discreetly at the water's edge. We ate cheese and tomato sandwiches and Penguin biscuits and drank stewed tea from a flask, and I was allowed the occasional ice-cream, but on the whole, I would infinitely have preferred to have stayed at home.

I am a mystery and a disappointment to my parents. My musical ability is something they seem to see as a threat rather than a gift; the pursuit of hedonism rather than of art. True, they paid for my violin lessons, clapped politely at school concerts, and when I was awarded a place at music college, they didn't exactly stand in my way, but neither did they encourage me.

'Are you sure, Ruth? Are you quite sure?' my mother said, when I finally left to take up my place. 'It seems such a — such a *risky* way of life.'

'Quite sure, Mum. I've never been surer of anything.'

For how could I explain to her that music was my world, my life? That music flowed in and through me like the air I breathed, and that I could no more live without it than I could transform myself into the kind of daughter they wanted?

No-one understood where my musical ability had come from. My mother played the piano a little, and my father sang (badly) in the church choir, but otherwise, apart from light music on the radio and Songs of Praise on a Sunday evening, music played no part in their lives. A great uncle was reputed to have been a reasonably proficient cellist, but by the time I knew him he was old and arthritic, his days of music-making long gone, together, sadly, with his memory.

But worse by far than the idea of living at home is the prospect of telling my mother and father that I am pregnant. For a start, I know for a fact that they still believe me to be a virgin; they have always taken my word for it that when I go on holiday with a boyfriend we sleep in separate rooms, and that any man staying at my flat occupies the sofa. My fall from grace is going to come as a dreadful and most unexpected blow.

In the event, their reaction is worse than even I could have anticipated. I have read about people turning pale, but I have never actually seen it happen until now.

'Oh, Ruth! How could you do this to us?' My mother exclaims, after a few moments' horrified silence.

'Mum I haven't done anything to *you*. If I've done anything to anyone, I've done it to *myself*.'

'What will people think?' My father joins in. He has not gone pale so much as red. He does a good line in what he sees as righteous indignation, citing Jesus among the moneylenders as his example, and he is very, very angry. 'Have you thought about our reputation?'

'This isn't about you.' I too am getting angry. 'It's about *me*! Do you think it's easy for me? Do you think this is what I want?'

'I don't know —'

'No. You don't know. You know very little about me, as it happens. You've never really understood me, have you?'

'We've tried —'

'No, you haven't! You've never tried. You've never tried to *know* me. My music, my friends, *my* way of life — all of it. You treat me like a — like some kind of foreigner!'

'What on earth can you mean?' My mother seems to be recovering herself. 'We've given you everything you need. We've cared for you, loved you —'

'Have you? Have you really? Isn't loving someone all about accepting them for what they are? Years ago, you created a mould, and you've been trying to fit me into it ever since. But it doesn't work that way. I know I'm a disappointment to you, and I'm sorry about that. Believe me, at the moment I'm a disappointment in myself. But there have been so many times when I've needed you — needed your support — and you haven't really been there for me.' I know I'm being unfair, but having got going, I'm finding it hard to stop. All the anger and disappointment over the years seem to be coming to the surface in an unstoppable tide. 'I am who I am, Mum. I try — as you do — to live my life as best I can. But I'm different. Different from you. Can't you understand that?'

'Oh, we understand that all right. You're most certainly different from us.' It's my father's turn. 'We understand that in spite of every opportunity, in spite of a good Christian upbringing, you can go and behave like this. It seems we've been wasting our time all these years.'

'Dad, I'm thirty-six years old! You finished bringing me up years ago. What I do now is my responsibility, not yours. Besides, it's the *twenty-first century*. Things have changed. You mightn't like it, and of course you're entitled to your opinion, but nowadays there's no stigma to being a single parent. No-one *minds* anymore.'

'Well, they should mind. They should. It's a disgrace, that's what it is. I've always said so, haven't I, Rosemary?' (turning to my mother). 'But I never thought anything like that would happen in this family. I never thought it would happen to us.'

'*It's not happening to you!*' I yell. 'It's happening to me! My baby, my life, *my disgrace*, if you like. All mine. You don't have to have any part in any of it if you don't want to. You can disown me if it makes you feel better.'

'There's no need to be silly, Ruth. Of course we wouldn't disown you,' my father says. 'We'd never disown our own flesh and blood.'

The argument rumbles on, to the exhaustion of all parties and the benefit of none. The divide between my mother and father and myself is as wide and as deep as it ever was, and it seems that none of us has the power to change it. There have been occasions when I would genuinely have liked to be what my parents want me to be — for a start, it would have made life so much easier — but with the best will in the world, it could never happen. Years ago, I even wondered whether I could have been adopted, but my dark hair and eyes (my mother's) and stubborn chin (my father's) have long since put paid to that theory.

'Well, I'll go and put the cocoa on,' says my mother, when everything has been said that could possibly be said, and I have enraged them even further by refusing to divulge the paternity of my unborn child. 'Would you like some, Ruth?'

Cocoa? At a time like this? But for my parents, their routine is a lifeline second only to God, and it would take more than their daughter's downfall to prise them away from their bedtime cocoa (half milk, half water, with one teaspoon of sugar).

'No thanks. I think I'll just go to bed.'

I give them each a dutiful kiss, and go upstairs. Maybe Mum and Dad will see things differently in the morning.

Chapter Three

Breakfast at my parents' house is a dignified affair. Not for them the dripping tea bag dredged from its mug, the burnt toast eaten on the hoof. The table is laid with a white cloth, tea is brewed under its smug knitted tea cosy, and neat triangles of toast stand to attention in the toast rack (my parents are the only people I know who own — never mind use — a toast rack). Most families that I know come down to breakfast in relays and grab what they can find, but in my parents' house we are expected to breakfast together (cereal and toast on weekdays; a boiled egg on Sundays). As I unfold my table napkin and wait for my father to say Grace, I imagine days or even weeks of these breakfasts and this atmosphere (today, an enveloping thick grey blanket of reproach and disappointment), and resolve to find myself somewhere to rent as soon as possible. True, it would be convenient to stay on here, at least until I have enough students to enable me to make some kind of living, but it would be at the expense of the sanity of all concerned, and hence simply not worth it.

But in the event, the decision is taken out of my hands.

'Your mother and I have been talking.' My father butters a small piece of toast, looks at it for a moment as though it might be in some way unclean, and then puts it carefully in his mouth. 'Haven't we, Rosemary?'

My mother nods unhappily.

'And we think it best if you don't stay here.'

'What?' This is something I hadn't expected.

'Yes.' He continues, as though I hadn't spoken. 'Best all round, really.'

'How can it be best?'

'We have our reputation to think of. It may sound old-fashioned to you, Ruth, but the church is very important to us. People respect us. Look up to us, really. Your mother teaches at Sunday School; I still preach the occasional sermon. And then there's the Youth Group. What kind of example would it be if we had — if you — well, if people saw you living here?'

'You mean — you mean you're actually throwing me out? Like a Victorian father? Is that what you're doing?' I am incredulous. I didn't think even *my* father would do anything like this. I am fortunate indeed that he's not a Victorian father, for if he were, no doubt it would be the workhouse for me.

'Well of course we're not. We can't throw you out if you don't live here, can we, even if we wanted to? We're just saying that it would be — awkward if you lived here at the moment. We're asking you to find somewhere else to live.'

'But surely I can stay just until I find somewhere to rent? After all, I don't look pregnant. No-one need even know. And I'll pay my way.'

'It's not about money, and it doesn't matter that you don't look — well that things aren't obvious. People will ask questions, and we'll have to tell them the truth.' Ah. The truth. Far be it for me to stand between my parents and the truth. 'I'm sorry Ruth, but there it is. This problem is not of our making.'

Looking at my father, his heightened colour, the way he is stabbing at the butter, I can see that he's still very angry, and I know what all this is about. I'm being punished. I've been a bad girl, and this is my punishment; to be banished from my parents' house. It may well have something to do with what people think, but it's got a lot more to do with how my father feels.

'And the baby? Are you going to disown that, too?'

'We'll have to cross that bridge when we come to it.' My father holds out his cup for more tea.

'My baby isn't a bridge to be crossed! It's a human being; your grandchild. None of this is the baby's fault. "Suffer the little children —"'

'Please don't try quoting Holy Scripture at me, Ruth. Especially out of context. As I said, we'll have to see.'

'What about you, Mum? What do you think?' I see my last straw, and grasp at it, but without much hope.

'I'll do as your father says, naturally.' My mother looks uncomfortable. 'It's probably best that you go away. Just for the time being.'

'And the baby?'

'As your father says, we'll — we'll see.'

I am filled with sudden rage. Hitherto, I have dwelt on my situation rather than my unborn child. My baby, to whom I have yet to give more than a few glancing thoughts since my visit to the clinic, suddenly becomes enormously important, and for the first time in my life, I feel I am not alone in my battle against my parents. I now have someone on my side. It may be tiny — still at the seahorse/rabbit stage — but it is mine. We are a unit. My baby and I against the world. I feel empowered and protective and — yes — even maternal, and I smile, in spite of myself.

'This is nothing to smile about, Ruth.' My father dabs at his mouth with his napkin, and then folds it neatly and replaces it by his plate. 'However, just to let you know that we want to do right by you, we have an idea.' He pauses to make sure he has my full attention. 'We thought you might go and stay with the twins for a while.'

'Applegarth's huge. They've got plenty of room,' my mother offers.

'Yes,' my father continues. 'I'm sure they'll be glad to help.'

Why on earth should they be glad to help, when my parents are not? But it's an interesting idea.

My uncles — my mother's elder brothers — are identical twins. Eric and Silas have remained unmarried, and have always lived together, occupying their parents' old home, a huge rambling Victorian house in the middle of nowhere, together with a menagerie of animals and a chaotic amount of clutter. They are gentle eccentrics, devoted to each other and all living things. They have never, as far as I know, made any kind of living, existing comfortably on their inheritance (my grandfather made a lot of money in wool. Needless to say, my mother has divided most of her share between her church and various charities) and such food as they are able to grow themselves. Although nowadays I see little of them, I have always been fond of my uncles, seeing them as the most human (and by far the most interesting) members of my small family. However, I'm not at all sure how they will feel about having their disgraced niece thrust upon them at short notice.

'When were you thinking of asking them?' I say, folding my own napkin in an attempt at insouciance.

'I already have.'

'But it's only half-past eight!'

'They get up early to do the milking.'

Milking? 'And?'

'They're thinking about it.'

'I'll bet they are.'

'They're ringing back at eleven.'

'And you didn't think to consult me before you did this?'

'No. I didn't.' My father stands up, drawing a line under our conversation. 'Since you are so irresponsible, and that is putting it kindly, as to get yourself into this — situation, you can't really expect us to trust you to make a wise decision as to what to do next.'

By half-past eleven, the expected phone call still hasn't come, and my father is pacing up and down the hallway looking at his watch and tutting like the White Rabbit (although of course, unlike the White Rabbit, it is not he who is late). My father hates unpunctuality, and although he has known his brothers-in-law all these years, and they have never considered time-keeping to be a priority, their behaviour never fails to surprise and infuriate him. Accepting other people's modi vivendi is not my father's forte.

It is twelve fifteen when the expected phone call finally comes, and my father shuts himself in his study to take it. Lingering in the hallway outside, I hear little of what he says, although such words as 'shame' and 'waste' and 'disappointment' give me a taster of the tone of the conversation. When he finally emerges, it is not without an air of triumph.

'All settled,' he says, his relief palpable. 'They're happy to have you for as long as you need to stay, and there are no neighbours to gossip, so they have nothing to worry about on that score.'

Eric and Silas have always seemed to me to be the last people on earth to worry about gossiping neighbours — or anything else, come to that — but I let it pass.

'I don't believe they're churchgoers,' he continues (he knows very well that they aren't), 'but I'm afraid that can't be helped.'

'What a shame,' I murmur.

'What was that?'

'Nothing.'

Two days later, I have finished clearing out my flat, packed up those things I want to take with me, said a fond (and unreciprocated) farewell to the cat, and am on my way. The Norwegian invasion is just hours away, and I don't trust myself not to tell my new tenants all the things which are still fuelling my indignation. Suffice it to say that I hope the boiler makes its early-morning howling noise (an occasional but very alarming occurrence) and that the neighbours throw one of their more boisterous parties. After their uncharitable behaviour, the Norwegians do not deserve any consideration from me.

My father drives me the forty miles to my uncles' house (I sold my car to help pay for the gap year). It is not a comfortable journey.

'So,' he says, after about fifteen minutes. 'What plans do you have?'

Plans? I haven't had time to plan anything, and my parents seem to have taken care of my immediate future.

'Well…' I hesitate.

'I thought as much.' The car veers violently to the left. 'You haven't given this much thought, have you, Ruth?'

'I need time,' I tell him lamely.

'You don't have much time.'

'I believe these things take about nine months,' I say, in a weak attempt at humour.

'Not funny, Ruth.'

'I never said this was funny.' My father's not the only one feeling angry. 'But it's happening. It's a done deal. I'm having a baby. Lots of people have babies, and yes —' because I know what's coming next — 'many of them are out of wedlock. Dad, it's not the end of the world!'

'It's the end of your reputation.'

I can't believe I'm hearing this. 'I'm a *violinist*, Dad. My reputation — such as it is — rests on my musicianship, not on my virginity!'

'Well, really!' The car screeches to a halt at traffic lights.

'I'm only saying what you're thinking.'

'I think we'd better end this conversation before one of us says something we regret,' my father says, as the car starts up again.

And I think he's right. Looking at his stern profile, his neat collar and tie, his highly polished shoes, I find it hard to believe that this man is related to me at all. Parents are supposed to love their children unconditionally, but where my father is concerned, this seems to be very much in doubt.

Will I love the seahorse/rabbit unconditionally? Only time will tell.

Chapter Four

We arrive at my uncles' house late, since my father has had to stop the car twice for me to be sick. My copious vomiting took place without comment from either of us, which was probably just as well. My father has never felt comfortable with illness of any sort.

It always amazes me that the open countryside inhabited by my uncles can exist so near to relative civilisation. It is hard to believe that these sweeping hills and wide skies and lack of any neighbouring habitation are a mere three miles from a respectably-sized town, but so it is. The house itself, known as Applegarth, is situated at the end of a rutted track. It is well-built but run down, with a wilderness of a garden adjoining a paddock occupied by what look like several broken-down agricultural implements and a variety of livestock. Eric and Silas call it a smallholding. My father calls it a mess.

'What would their dear mother say?' he mutters, as he drives cautiously round bumps and through puddles. 'She was so fond of this place.'

'I expect Silas and Eric are fond of it too, in their own way,' I say.

'In that case, they should look after it.' My father stops the car so that I can get out to open a gate, causing several chickens to run squawking into the bushes. 'I suppose that's what you call free range,' he remarks. 'It's a wonder they don't get stolen or run over.'

'They're more likely to be eaten by foxes here,' I point out.

When we reach the house, Eric and Silas greet us on the doorstep.

'Welcome, welcome!' They kiss me and shake my father's hand. 'Come on in. We've made soup.'

'Ruth probably won't have any. She's got an upset tummy.' Dad has obviously decided not to acknowledge the cause of my indisposition. He scrapes something unpleasant off his foot and then, after hesitating for a moment, takes of his shoes.

'I'm fine now, and I'd love some soup.' I deposit my case in the entrance hall, and look around me. Coats and caps hang several deep on hooks inside the porch and some, having given up the unequal struggle, are lying in heaps on the floor. There are wellingtons and walking boots, sticks and galoshes, and even a rifle propped up casually in a corner.

'Is that safe?' Dad asks, indicating the rifle.

Silas (or Eric) laughs.

'It's not loaded. And we only use it for rabbits.'

'How comforting,' my father mutters.

In the large kitchen, every available surface is occupied with clutter. There are unwashed pots and pans, old newspapers, tools, clothes and bags of animal feed. A large dog is sleeping by the very grimy Aga and two cats are curled up on the draining board. Something which could be soup is bubbling away in a kind of cauldron. It smells interesting.

'I'll have to say no to the soup,' Dad says, backing away nervously, as though he might catch something. 'Rosemary's expecting me home.'

I know this isn't true since today is Mum's day for doing meals-on-wheels, and I'm surprised. Dad glances at me, and there is mute appeal in his eyes. He looks out of place and rather pathetic standing there in his stockinged feet, and I take pity on him.

'Yes. She did tell him to hurry home,' I say. My father looks at me suspiciously, and I smile at him. 'Mustn't keep her waiting.'

'No. No. I'd best be going.' He hesitates for a moment. 'Thank you for having Ruth.'

'No problem.' Eric/Silas grins. 'It'll be nice to have a woman around the house.'

I walk back down the track to open the gate for Dad, and he winds down the car window.

'We've done the right thing.' He hesitates. 'Take care of yourself.' This is the nearest he gets to an endearment, and I'm touched.

'You too. Love to Mum.'

As I watch the car making its cautious way back down the track, its usually gleaming paintwork now generously splattered with mud, there's a lump in my throat. Poor Dad. While I find his attitude hard to understand, I am his only child, and such a disappointment. Perhaps families are destined to disappoint each other; all those expectations, those cosy stereotypes, those impossible hopes. How can anyone begin to live up to them?

Back at the house, Eric and Silas are glowing with good cheer. They introduce me to the dog ('we call him Mr. Darcy') who opens one eye in acknowledgement, and the cats, who appear to have no names and who ignore me. The soup ('Nettle and rabbit. Don't worry — it's much nicer than it sounds!') is delicious, and I have two helpings. Afterwards, we eat early cherries from the garden and slices of rather stale bought cake, after which I'm taken on a tour of the grounds.

When I was a child, I used to stay regularly with my uncles. My parents' apparent ambivalence about the domestic set-up was countered by their need to pursue various church activities for which at the time I was considered too young. Since my only grandparent lived two hundred miles away, Eric and Silas were the obvious people to have me, and they were always more than willing. They didn't put themselves out or make any special arrangements; they simply absorbed me into their way of life, treating me as an equal (and expecting me to behave like one), and

I adored my visits. Free from any injunctions to keep my clothes clean, wash my hands before meals or go to bed at seven, I ran wild (as much as one little girl on her own can do such a thing). I helped with the animals and the cooking, I climbed trees and paddled in the stream and rode the one-eared donkey in the orchard before returning home with a healthy suntan, scratched and bruised knees, filthy clothes and a head full of interesting information. I may not have known where human babies came from, but the provenance of piglets and kittens was no longer a mystery to me, and if my parents objected, there wasn't much they could do about it. As I once heard Silas explaining to my mother, 'The child sees what she sees. It's only nature.' And they had to put up with it.

The grounds surrounding the house haven't changed much, although the quantity of livestock has increased. There is now a pretty doe-eyed jersey cow, two goats, some sheep and several pigs, including a very pregnant sow called Sarah. There are also at least two dozen chickens, four beehives, some ducks in a very muddy pond and a peacock. The peacock just arrived one day, I'm told, and is ornamental rather than useful. A selection of ramshackle sheds and outhouses provides shelter for the animals, and while their surroundings leave a lot to be desired, the animals look well-cared-for.

The garden is a riot of flowers, weeds and vegetables, all coexisting in apparent harmony. There are cabbages and nettles, broad beans and nasturtiums, roses and tomatoes. The white bells of bindweed can be seen flourishing among the raspberry canes and there are fruit trees and brambles in the orchard.

'It's like the *Secret Garden*,' I say, as I pick my way across this jungle while Mr. Darcy, who has woken up and joined us, chases exciting smells among the bushes.

'Yes. It's a bit of a mess,' admits Silas/Eric.

'Oh, I didn't mean that.'

'We don't mind.' He pauses, 'One day we'll have to sort it all out, but we always seem to run out of time.' They both laugh, as though at some private joke. 'I hope you'll be able to put up with us.'

Back at the house, I feel a bit like Snow White entering the home of the seven dwarfs. She didn't *have* to do all that cleaning (although with a merry band of Disney rabbits and birds to help her she seemed to make light work of it), but I can understand why she did it. I have a feeling that I shall have Snow White urges before I've been here long, for while I'm not a particularity tidy person, I think I'll find it hard to live in this chaos. Will my uncles mind if I do a bit of tidying up? I'll leave it a day or two before I suggest it, since I would hate to do anything which implied criticism of my hosts.

'Oh, you've brought your violin with you!' Eric/Silas cries, as we re-enter the house. 'How lovely! We've got an old piano, but we can't play it. Silly, isn't it? But you will play for us, won't you, Ruth? We love a bit of live music, don't we, Silas?'

His brother nods and smiles, and I notice again the slight dimple in Silas's chin and the way Eric's eyebrows sweep up at the corners, and resolve to make sure that from now on I shall remember who is who.

When I am shown up to my room, I find that I have been promoted from the tiny attic bedroom I slept in as a child to the big front bedroom, with its heavy dark furniture, worn carpet and ancient brocade curtains.

'We were born in this room,' Silas tells me, as he brings up my suitcase. 'In this bed, actually.'

The bed is huge, with an elaborately carved headboard and great sunken mattress which dips alarmingly in the middle. It has probably hosted the couplings and births of whole generations of my mother's family, and I try to look enthusiastic.

'We thought about buying a new mattress,' he adds. 'But I'm told the this one's quite cosy.'

The mattress certainly turns out to be cosy, for once I've given up any attempt to climb out of the dip in its middle, I find that it envelops me like a womb, and that first night I sleep better than I have in weeks. It occurs to me that it would have been very hard to keep up even the most severe of marital disputes if the protagonists had to retire to this bed afterwards, because close — not to say intimate — physical contact must be unavoidable if both parties were to get any sleep. Maybe all beds should be like this, in the interests of domestic harmony.

When I awake the next morning to the sounds of birdsong and the insistent crowing of a cockerel, I wonder whether I shall ever have someone to roll into a dip with me; someone to cuddle up to at night and laugh (or cry) at the day's happenings; someone to share my life, and be a father to the baby. Even Snow White got her man in the end, and with very little effort on her own part. I, however, am unlikely to find myself a prince (or anyone else, come to that) so long as I remain hidden away in this outpost of civilisation.

I determine that at the earliest opportunity, I shall start looking for a more permanent place to live.

Chapter Five

When I come down to breakfast, I find that my uncles have already eaten, and I am invited to help myself to 'whatever takes my fancy'. At the moment, nothing much takes my fancy, especially as the idea of trying to find something edible amid the chaos is more than a little daunting (Eric and Silas appear to have breakfasted on the remains of the soup).

'Goat's milk,' they advise, when I explain about the morning sickness. 'It never fails.' *How on earth do they know?* Silas pours me a generous glassful.

The milk is obviously fresh as it's still warm, and as I struggle to swallow it, I wonder why the thought of milk warmed by a goat is so much less appetising than milk warmed in a saucepan. It's somehow too intimate, like sitting on a seat recently occupied — and warmed — by a stranger. Maybe it would help if I were acquainted with the goat in question. But wherever the milk came from, it appears to do the trick, for while I'm still not up to breakfasting on soup, I eat two slices of bread and honey and some of yesterday's cherries.

'There.' Eric and Silas regard me with satisfaction, as though I am a child who has finished up her greens. 'Not so bad, was it?'

I agree that it wasn't bad at all, and also have to admit that I'm feeling considerably better.

'Would you mind if I did a bit of — well just a little bit of tidying up?' I ask them. 'Just so that I feel I'm doing my bit.'

My uncles roar with laughter.

'She wants to sort us out,' says Eric. 'That'll be a job and a half. But help yourself if it makes you feel better. Just don't throw anything away.'

I try not to feel offended. After all, my offer was intended to help them, not me. I shan't be staying for long, so it's not my problem if my uncles want to live like pigs.

Three hours later, I am totally exhausted, but I've found (and cleaned) most of the kitchen floor and some of the surfaces. Things which are obviously rubbish are piled in one corner; things which may be of some use in another. The washing machine (Snow White may have found her prince, but she didn't have a washing machine) is whirring merrily away, and the cats have gone out into the garden to sulk as I've removed their cosy little nest of old jumpers from the draining board. When Eric and Silas come in for lunch, I have found bread and cheese and pickled onions, and laid them out nicely on the table.

'Goodness.' Eric goes over to the sink to wash his hands. 'You didn't have to do this, you know. You're our guest. Besides,' he adds, 'Blossom comes in tomorrow.'

'Blossom?'

'Our cleaner. She doesn't really do much housework —' I'll say she doesn't — 'but she needs the money, and she's magic with the animals. That's really why we keep her on. We couldn't manage them all and the garden on our own.'

Blossom. I imagine a lovely cuddly woman with a wide welcoming bosom and equally wide smile; someone I can talk to, and maybe even someone who will know something about babies, even if she's lacking in the cleaning skills department. I look forward very much to meeting her.

How wrong can I be.

When Blossom arrives next morning, she turns out to be a small skinny woman, with eyes like darting black beads in a face taut with disapproval.

'What's all this, then?' she asks, before she's even taken off her coat.

'Our niece has come to stay,' Eric/Silas tells her (I still can't tell them apart from behind). 'Blossom, meet Ruth.' He disappears into the garden, leaving Blossom and me to get acquainted.

'How do you do?' I hold out my hand.

'Hmm.' Blossom ignores the hand. 'How long you staying?'

'I don't really know. Not long. Just until I find somewhere else.'

'What have you done to the kitchen?'

'I tidied it a bit.'

'Hmm. They won't like that.'

'They didn't seem to mind. And at least we can find everything now.'

'They could find everything before. That's the way they like it. I don't interfere in the kitchen.' (Now there's a surprise.)

I try to overcome the temptation to ask what it is that Blossom actually does, and wait to see. She fetches brooms and brushes from under the stairs, and clears a kind of runway through the clutter in the hall, thus giving easier access to the stairs, various doorways and the downstairs lavatory. The coats and caps she leaves where they've fallen, presumably because she isn't tall enough to replace them. She shakes the doormat, polishes the door knocker, and then repairs to the kitchen to make herself some coffee. She doesn't offer me any, so I make my own.

'Where do you live?' I try to make conversation.

'Village.' Blossom slurps her coffee, and adds more sugar.

'How do you get here?'

'Bike.'

'And — your husband?' I notice her wedding ring. 'What does he do?'

'Dead.' Blossom wipes her mouth on the back of her hand.

'Oh, I'm so sorry.'

'Don't be. Miserable bugger, he was.' There is the ghost of a smile. 'Well rid of him.'

'And — children?'

'Son. And daughter. No better than she ought to be.'

'Oh dear.' I suspect that in Blossom's book that probably applies to me, too. 'Do you see much of her?'

'Nope.' Blossom gets up from the table and deposits her empty coffee cup in the sink. I notice that she doesn't wash it up. She picks up a bucket and opens the back door. 'You expecting?' She turns, her hand still on the door handle.

'Yes. Yes, I am. How did you know?'

'Can always tell.' Blossom looks pleased. 'Knack,' she explains.

'Oh. That's — handy.'

'Can tell you the sex, and all.'

'Really?'

'Stand up and turn around.'

I do as I'm told.

'Boy,' she says, and goes out into the garden, banging the door shut behind her.

'How did you get on with our Blossom?' Silas asks when they come in at lunch time.

'I don't think she likes me very much.'

'Don't mind Blossom. She doesn't like anybody.' He laughs at my expression. 'You're wondering why we have her, aren't you?'

'Well, it did cross my mind.'

'Sometimes we ask ourselves, don't we, Eric? I suppose she's become a habit. And she doesn't chatter or expect us to look after her.'

'How on earth did she come to be called Blossom?'

'She doesn't look much like a Blossom, does she? I believe it was one of those baptismal mix-ups — a deaf priest, a mother who didn't like to point out a mistake. Something like that. Her father was Welsh and wanted her to be Blodwyn, but it wasn't to be.'

'She told me my baby would be a boy.'

'Then that's what it'll be. Blossom's always right.'

'How does she do it?'

'I've no idea.' Silas cuts himself a slice of bread. 'She says it's a knack, but she won't tell us her secret. She does it with piglets, too.'

'What, all the sexes?'

'No, but she can tell us how many there will be. She says Sarah's going to have thirteen, and she'll be right, give or take a piglet or two. Thirteen's a lot, though, poor old girl. Sarah's getting on a bit. We may have to drown a couple.' He butters his bread. 'I might stuff one,' he adds thoughtfully.

'*Stuff* one?'

'It's a hobby.'

'Stuffing things?'

'Taxidermy. I'm teaching myself,' he says, through a mouthful of bread and cheese. 'I've never done a piglet. It might be rather fun.'

'Do you — stuff things too?' I turn to Uncle Eric.

'Good Lord, no. Not my kind of thing at all.'

'No. He's much too busy disproving Noah's Ark,' Silas says.

'Noah's Ark?' This conversation is becoming weirder by the minute.

'The Creationist theory,' Eric says. 'Noah and the Ark; animals going in two by two; all that. Some people actually believe it. Every word of it. So I'm doing some research.'

'Gosh. My parents wouldn't approve of that at all,' I laugh. 'Do they know?'

'Certainly they know. And you're right. They don't approve. But there's not a lot they can do about it. Your father asked me "not to pollute your mind with my theories", but I said you were old enough to decide for yourself.'

'To be honest, I haven't given it a lot of thought,' I said. 'Well, not since I left home, anyway.'

'Well, do. It's very interesting. I started with Adam and Eve. That bit was quite easy.'

'And the talking serpent and the apple?'

'Ah.' He looks pleased. 'It wasn't an apple, for a start. You have another look at your Bible. There's no mention of an apple. Just the fruit of the tree of knowledge. It could have been an apricot, or a fig.' He cuts himself more bread, and offers me a slice. 'I like the idea of mankind being seduced with a fig. They're so much more sexy than apples. We've got a marvellous fig tree in the garden.' He takes a large bite of his bread. 'There's nothing to say it was an apple.'

'I never thought of that.'

'People don't. And then there's Jonah and the whale. If you look at the physiology of whales, you'll find that Jonah would have been destroyed by its gastric juices within twenty minutes, and that's if he could find any air to breathe while it was happening. He certainly wouldn't have lived to tell the tale.'

'And Noah?'

'Don't get him started,' Silas says, peeling a rather mottled banana. It reminds me of the hide of a giraffe, but maybe that's the Noah's Ark effect.

'Noah's the best of all,' Eric says. 'At least, it's the most interesting — and by far the most impossible. Just imagine. All those creatures, all that fodder, all the extra animals to feed to the carnivores, all that mucking out. Quite impossible. Pass the pickle, please. But I'm having this discussion with a — friend, and he wants proof, so I'm going to prove it.'

'How?'

'Research, Ruth. Research. He wants facts and figures; he shall have facts and figures.' He smiles at me. 'You can help if you like.'

'I think I'd better not. My parents would never speak to me again. Besides,' I add carefully, 'isn't it possible that someone's done all this before.'

'Done all what before?'

'Disproving the Ark. You could look it up on the internet and find out.'

'We haven't got a computer. Besides, I'd like to do it myself. It makes it more fun. Computers may be wonderful things, but I think they tend to make people lazy.'

'You're probably right.'

We finish our lunch, and I make coffee.

'Give us a tune, then,' says Silas.

'What, now?'

'Why not?'

So I get out my violin and tune it, after which I play them a Bach gavotte. I realise with dismay how out of practice I am, and resolve to put in at least two hours every day. My uncles, however, are delighted, and applaud enthusiastically.

'That was wonderful, Ruth,' Silas says. 'I'd no idea you were so good.'

'Not good enough, though.' I put my violin back in its case. 'You have to be exceptional to get anywhere these days. I didn't even manage to stay in the back desk of the seconds in a third-rate orchestra.'

'But you love it.' It was a statement rather than a question.

'Oh, yes!'

'Well then. How many people find — and do — something they really love? That's what matters.'

'What about you? Do you both love what you do?'

My uncles exchange glances and smile.

'I think we've always been happy,' Eric says. 'We love this place, our animals, our way of life. We're very lucky to be able to do it.'

'And you — get on?' For a moment, I wonder if I have overstepped the mark, but they don't seem to mind.

'We have the odd tiff, but yes. We get on,' Silas says. 'We've never been apart for more than a night or two. People think we're odd, but then I suppose we *are* a bit odd. It doesn't bother us what other people think.'

'I don't think it's odd. I think it's wonderful,' I say with feeling. And I mean it. To live your whole life with someone you really care about, doing something you love; what more could anyone ask?

'What will you do now, Ruth? What are your plans?' Eric asks.

Oh dear, that question again.

'I don't know. I still haven't got used to the idea of the baby yet. But I won't be under your feet for long, I promise. I'm going to start looking for a place to rent, and then get myself some pupils and start teaching.'

'But we thought you were staying here,' Silas says.

'Is that what Dad said?'

'Well, no. But we assumed you would. As you've nowhere else at the moment.'

'I couldn't possibly —'

'Why not? We've got plenty of room, and you're more than welcome.'

'But my teaching. What about that?'

'There must be people around here who need violin lessons. You could advertise.'

'Well ... you're awfully kind.' It's certainly an attractive proposition. On the other hand, I don't want to take advantage of my uncles' generosity, and with no mobile signal or internet (the house is surrounded by thick woodland) I would be terribly cut off. 'Can I think about it? In the meantime, I'll pay my way, and do what I can to help.'

'You think about it, then. No hurry.' Silas picks up his plate and dumps it in the sink. 'But you're very welcome.'

So it would seem. And if this particular Snow White has to wait a little longer for her prince, then the way I'm feeling at the moment, it seems a small price to pay.

Chapter Six

As the weeks go by, I find it hard to believe that I have ever lived anywhere else. It seems to have taken me no time at all to settle into my uncles' way of life, and almost for the first time in my life, I feel truly at home. Even Blossom seems to have accepted me as a member of the household, and while never overtly friendly, she condescends to exchange a few brief words — Blossom's words are nothing if not brief — when she stops for coffee. Of course, I loved living in my flat, but (unless you count the cat) I have never had anyone to share it with, and living with Eric and Silas has made me realise how much I enjoy being with other people. Even at home with my parents before I went to college, I used to feel lonely, because there was so much about me that they didn't understand.

'You've already practised once today, Ruth,' my father would say. 'Do you really need to start doing it again? That bit sounds fine to me.'

'I just need to get this phrase right. Just ten more minutes.'

'If you must,' he would sigh. 'But I can't see what another ten minutes is going to do.'

'Dad, you've never liked Bach, so you wouldn't understand.' He wasn't the only one to get irritated.

'Too many notes. Far too many notes.' And thus, arguably the greatest composer who has ever lived would be briskly dismissed.

Here, I feel accepted and perhaps even loved, and my music is actively encouraged. My uncles have no expectations of me, nor I of them, and in the relaxed, comfortable atmosphere of this shambolic house, I believe that I am becoming a nicer person. I enjoy having to consider the needs of other people; to fit in with their routine and their way of life. I like helping around the house and garden, and I have accomplished skills which I could never have dreamed of. Not only have I learnt that it's perfectly possible to live happily without wanting to tidy up every five minutes, but more usefully, I have learnt to milk a goat, skin a rabbit, and make delicious soups and salads out of ingredients I have hardly ever seen, never mind eaten, before. As for the internet, which I once thought essential to any kind of civilised life, I no longer give it a thought.

'Just stretch out your middle finger,' Eric says now. He is measuring my forearm with a rather frayed tape measure. 'By the way, you're looking much better.'

'Am I?'

'Oh, yes. You looked thin and pasty when you arrived. The fresh air must be doing you good.' He puts down his tape measure. 'I make it nineteen inches.

Damn. It does seem to vary. Silas's was twenty inches. And it's meant to be eighteen. Eighteen doesn't seem very much somehow.'

'Very much for what?'

'A cubit. It's supposed to be the measurement from the elbow to the middle finger. Noah measured his Ark in cubits.'

'Why?'

'God told him to.'

'God doesn't seem a measuring sort of person, somehow.'

'I know what you mean.' Eric makes notes on a piece of paper and refers to a battered Bible on the kitchen table. 'I think I'll make it eighteen inches, which fits nicely into yards. It's much easier if we can do it all in yards.'

'We?'

'Well you're helping now, aren't you?' He makes more notes. 'The Ark had to be three hundred cubits long, so that's — let me see — about a hundred and fifty yards. Not nearly big enough. I can see that already.'

'Wouldn't it have been easier for you to start with the size of the Ark, rather than the habits of the animals?' I ask, for Eric has already done some research into the diets of a variety of species.

'In a way, but the animals are more fun, so I shall alternate.'

'But if you can see straight away that there isn't room for them all, then that's that, isn't it?'

'Oh, Ruth, Ruth. We have to *prove* it. We need *proof*. Facts, figures, that sort of thing. We've got to show him *exactly* why there isn't enough room. And we've not just got to tell him how impossible it all is, but how ridiculously impossible. We've got to blow him — and his Ark — right out of the water.'

'Oh. I see.' I hesitate for a moment. 'Who's "he"?'

'Well, as a matter of fact, it's your father.'

'Oh dear.'

'Yes. Oh dear indeed. But I didn't know you were coming when we had our — discussion, and I don't want to give up on it now.'

'I can see that.'

'If you don't mind, that is.'

'Oh, I don't mind at all. Dad thrives on this sort of thing. And if anyone can provide a successful argument in favour of all those animals living in even the tiniest of Arks, then my father's your man.' I watch Eric leafing through his Bible, making notes and chewing his pen. 'Is it all right if I go now?'

'My dear girl, of course you may go. I've kept you too long as it is.'

He does have a point, for quite apart from routine house and animal duties, I've already spent an hour on the phone to the zoo trying to get answers to a list of questions ranging from whether zebras eat hay to the gestation of the rhinoceros.

The man at the zoo is kindly and tries to be helpful, but he is bewildered by all these questions.

Upstairs in my room I get out my violin and warm up with some scales. I'm not doing nearly enough practice, but without a goal, much of the incentive has gone. I shall never be a soloist, and now not even an orchestral player. So what (or who) am I playing for? My pupils? Even if I manage to get any, they won't mind whether I practise or not. My public? Unless you count Eric and Silas, I don't have a public. Myself? As I watch my fingers moving up and down the fingerboard, I remember practising these same scales for the exams I did as a schoolgirl, and my parents even then questioning the point of all that work. And I can see my small, furious, foot-stamping self trying to explain.

'It's for me, me, me! *I do it for me*! I love it. Can't you see? Can't you *hear*?'

But all they could see was that their daughter was wasting hours of her time (and quite a lot of their money) doing something which they saw as trivial; a hobby perhaps, a pastime, but certainly not a career which would earn any kind of living. They didn't like the sound that I made and couldn't fathom why I enjoyed making it, and even the high marks I achieved in my examinations (invariably with distinction) failed to impress them. It was as though I had burst into another language and expected them to converse with me. It was totally foreign. *I* was totally foreign.

I put down my violin and sit on the bed. Over the years, I have devoted thousands of hours to my music; hours of scales and exercises, of pieces and studies, and once, gloriously, a violin concerto with a full orchestra. They have been hours of toil, hours of weeping frustration but also moments of indescribable pleasure. Am I going let all that hard work go, just because I have no immediate goal? I told Eric and Silas that I love what I do, and of course it's true. But like every love affair, my relationship with the violin is going through a rough patch; a period when it might be tempting to let it go, at least for the time being. Is that what I really want?

I pick up my violin again, running my fingers along the grain of the wood, feeling the smooth polished back, stroking its familiar ribs and surfaces. I bought it with money left to me by a godfather, and it's old and quite valuable. Far better musicians than I shall ever be have owned and played this instrument, and I often wonder who they were, how they came by it and how or why they passed it on. Maybe one day it will pass into the hands of my own child — my son, if Blossom is to be believed — and he in his turn will give it to one of his own children. Or perhaps he will sell it. Who knows? But one thing is certain. So long as I can play, I will. Not for audiences or even for money, but, as I told my parents all those years ago, for me. Because I have to. Because, quite simply, it's what I do. I stand up and riffle through a pile of music, then I take out one of the Bach unaccompanied suites and painstakingly start to practise the first movement.

'Any phone calls?' I ask, when much later I come downstairs for a cup of tea (with no mobile signal, I'm now dependent on the landline).

'None for you,' Silas says. 'Don't worry. Someone will reply sooner or later.'

'But I really need to be earning now,' I say, getting milk from the fridge. 'I put the advertisement in ten days ago.'

'It's probably the wrong time of year, August. Who needs violin lessons in August?'

He's right, of course. I should wait until the autumn and the new school year. But my savings are beginning to dip alarmingly, and while I've long since said goodbye to any hope of a gap year, I'm going to need things for the baby. Eric and Silas have said they're quite happy to keep me, but I value my independence. Besides, it would be wrong to take advantage of their generosity.

'I shall busk,' I say, pouring boiling water onto a teabag. 'I shall take my fiddle and go into town and busk. Someone's bound to throw me a coin or two if I wait long enough. I did it on the underground when I was at college. There were three of us together at the bottom of the escalator at Paddington Station.' Oh, happy days. 'I did all my Christmas shopping one year out of my busking money.'

'What on earth did your parents say?' Silas asks. He is examining his latest acquisition, a dead squirrel, on the draining board.

'I didn't tell them. They would have been appalled. They would have considered it to be no better than begging, and the thought of their daughter begging on the streets would probably have finished them off. But they got very nice presents that year.'

'Good for you.' Silas sounds abstracted. 'This is amazing.' Tenderly, he lifts up his squirrel to show us. The squirrel doesn't look dead at all, merely surprised (as well it might). 'Not a mark on it, and it must have been knocked down. I shall enjoy doing this.'

'Is busking legal?' Eric asks.

'I'm not sure now. I'll phone the police and find out.'

Ten minutes later, after an interesting telephone conversation with someone official at the police station, I have discovered that busking comes under the Vagrancy Act of 1824.

'Very old-fashioned. Like being hanged for sheep-stealing,' I tell Eric (Silas is still preoccupied with his squirrel).

'Does that mean you can't do it?'

'Apparently I might get by on the grounds of providing "street entertainment".'

'Does that mean you have to have an audition?'

'Heavens, no. But I might be inspected by someone from the Town Centre Management Team, whatever that is. I could take Mr. Darcy with me, if you'll let me. People might be able to resist me, but they'll melt when Mr. Darcy does that reproachful thing with his eyebrows.'

'Are you fit to hang around street corners with your violin?'

'Perfectly fit,' I assure him. 'It'll do me good.'

'And the baby?'

'It'll do him good, too. It's never too early to start enjoying music.'

And while I've no idea whether the seahorse/rabbit has developed anything in the way of ears yet, I'm sure that I'm right. Bring on the council official and the generous, music-loving punters. I can't wait to begin.

Chapter Seven

But before I can commence my busking career, there are medical matters to attend to.

Now I have to admit that I had entirely forgotten that pregnancy is regarded not so much as a natural event as a medical condition fraught with hazards, and that a variety of investigations is required to ensure that nothing awful is happening either to me or to the baby. It was Silas who pointed this out, and Silas who took me down to his GP in his muddy Land Rover. All was apparently well, as far as the GP could tell, but I am apparently due for my twelve-week scan.

'Yes. It's important to check up on things after the first trimester,' says Silas, who has been looking things up in his book.

'Trimester?' I ask him.

'Three months. It comes from the Latin,' he informs me kindly. 'Pregnancy is divided into three trimesters, and each one —'

'Yes. Thank you, Silas, I think I get the message. And the doctor gave me this booklet. I can read up all about it.'

'My book has diagrams.'

'So has the booklet.' I pat his hand. 'Don't worry. From now on, I promise to keep myself fully informed.'

I have never had a scan before, and envisage myself being posted into one of those long dark tubes for a lonely and claustrophobic half-hour or so, but apparently this scan is quite a simple procedure, and I will be able to see what's going on. Now I come to think of it, I have seen friends coming hot foot from their scans, proudly sporting grainy and (to me) completely unrecognisable photos of their unborn offspring. Hitherto, I haven't paid much attention to scans, but now that it's time for mine, I'm rather looking forward to it.

So, it would seem, are my uncles.

'I think I should go with her,' Silas says.

'What, you mean come in and watch?' I'm not at all sure about this.

'Why not? I believe people are allowed to bring their partners, and you don't seem to have one, so I can come instead. To support you,' he adds, although even I can see that he is desperate to see what goes on (Silas is a terrible hypochondriac, and has a hypochondriac's fascination for all things medical).

'What about me?' Eric says. 'I think I should come too.'

'Of course you can come too,' Silas says. 'We'll all go. And we can go to the pub for lunch afterwards.'

'Hang on a minute,' I say, with the uncomfortable feeling that my life is being taken over. 'This is my scan. I think I should be the one to decide.'

'You need us to drive you there,' Silas reminds me.

'That's not fair!'

'No. Of course it's not. All right then. We'll take you and wait in the car while you have it.'

'With nothing to do,' says Eric.

'And these things always take hours.'

They both look at me, their expressions so ridiculously alike that I can't help laughing.

'Okay. You can both come. But don't blame me if you're not allowed in. And please don't do anything embarrassing.'

'Would we!'

'I don't know, but I have a feeling you might.'

But while it has occurred to me that one or other of my uncles might well do or say something inappropriate, I never considered the affect that two identical elderly men would have on a waiting-room full of pregnant women and their partners. There are the double-takes, the whispers, the covert and then not-so-covert glances, and the outright stares. I wish with all my heart that Eric and Silas could have worn different clothes, or brushed their hair in different ways, or at the very least, sat at opposite ends of the room. But no. Here they sit, side by side, reading old copies of *Woman's Own* and pausing occasionally to beam at their audience.

'Do you have to do this?' I whisper to Eric, who is sitting beside me.

'Do what?'

'Play to the gallery.'

'I can't think what you mean.' He turns to the problem page ("Is my partner two-timing me?" screams one of the by-lines. More than likely, I think sourly).

'You know exactly what I mean.'

'My dear Ruth, if you're born with a handicap, you might as well make the most of it.'

'It's not a handicap!'

'No, but it might as well be, the way people behave.'

'I believe you're enjoying this.'

'And why not? You must admit, it's quite fun.'

'I would have thought you'd have tired of this kind of fun by now.'

'That's what our mother used to say. But you don't have to sit next to us if you don't want to.'

'You're behaving like children!'

'She said that, too.'

Fortunately, at this stage a white-coated young woman calls out my name.

'Miss Robinson? Come this way, please.'

Eric and Silas put down their magazines and get up to follow me (more stares and whispers. Maybe everyone thinks I have twin sugar daddies).

'Are you coming with her?' The young woman looks dubious. 'Both of you?'

'We'll explain when we get inside,' says Silas. 'You see,' he continues, once the door is closed behind us, 'we're her next of kin.'

'What, both of you?' she says again.

'Oh yes. Can't you see the family likeness?' (There is no family likeness.)

'Well, maybe just one of you, if that's all right with Miss Robinson.'

I open my mouth to say something, but Eric gets in first.

'It's a bit delicate,' he says. 'You see, until six months ago, we were conjoined twins. Up until then, obviously we'd never been apart at all. And we — well, we still find it hard.' I swear I can see tears in his eyes.

'You were operated on that recently? Surely it would have been in the papers. That sort of thing is always on the news.' Apparently my white-coated friend isn't as gullible as Eric had hoped. She looks them both up and down, as though searching for a missing leg or the remains of a shared arm.

'Oh, no newspapers.' Eric looks shocked. 'Patient confidentiality,' he says, tapping the side of his nose. 'We managed to keep it out of the papers. We still walk with a limp,' he adds.

The technician is obviously baffled. As for me, I'm furious. They have obviously done this before. This routine is well-rehearsed, and they've got it off so pat and their delivery is so convincing that in the end they are both given permission to stay. Eric winks at me, but I ignore him. They may be able to get round officialdom, but it's going to take a lot more to get round me. I consider sending them both out, but I feel suddenly vulnerable, and would appreciate their company even if I haven't yet forgiven them.

But all our differences — if that's what they were — are forgotten when the scan begins and we see the monitor.

'Look.' The technician points to the screen. 'There's its heart beating, and there's an arm ... and another. See there. It's kicking.'

'Oh. *Oh.*' Silas appears lost for words. He and Eric exclaim and coo over this tiny apparition as though they alone are responsible for its existence, while I am totally bemused. True, there is something swimming about on the screen, bobbing gently in its warm watery world, and I can just about see a beating heart and something which might be a limb. But they are the heart and the limb of a seahorse/rabbit, not anything which resembles a human being, and I feel cheated and disappointed. It is like showing people round one's own haunted house, and being the only one who can't see the ghost.

'Oh, Ruth! You are *so* clever! Look what you've made!' Eric says, and this time there are real tears in his eyes. 'I don't think I've ever seen anything so wonderful.'

'Is it all right? There's nothing wrong with it, is there?' Silas asks.

'Everything looks fine, although of course she'll have another scan at twenty weeks.'

'Excuse me,' I hear myself say, 'but this is my baby.'

'Of course.' The technician smiles at me. 'I'm so sorry. But your friends —'

'Uncles,' says Silas.

'Uncles, then. Well they like to talk, don't they?'

'They certainly do,' I say with feeling. But of course, now that I have her attention, I can't think of anything else to say.

'Boy or girl?' Silas ventures.

'Boy of course,' Eric says.

'Would you both please shut up,' I say, and turn back to the technician. 'Can you tell the sex yet?'

'Blossom's never wrong —'

'*Please*, Eric. Can you tell?'

'Too early, I'm afraid. But of course your Blossom has a fifty percent chance of being right.'

'She wouldn't like to hear you say that,' mutters Silas.

Just for a moment, lying on this couch with my tummy exposed and these two mad people having their discussions across my body, I think of Amos; big, generous Amos, with his beard and his smile and his kind brown eyes, and for a moment, wish that he was sitting here beside me, holding my hand. But he doesn't even know about the baby. What kind of a father would he have made? I wish I had been able to tell him about it, for now I know that we really have managed to create a new life, even if to me at least it bears little resemblance to a human being, I feel as though I have stolen something from him, albeit unwittingly. His genes, his input, are alive and apparently well inside my body. All those weeks ago, I exercised my "right to choose" when I decided to go ahead with my pregnancy, but Amos was never given any choice at all.

In the pub over a ploughman's and best bitter (Eric and Silas) and a cheese and tomato sandwich and orange juice (me) my uncles get out their grainy photos (they managed to persuade the technician to give them one each) and coo over them together, pointing out to each other features which even I know to be invisible at this early stage. But they apologise to me very charmingly for their behaviour in the hospital, and of course, I forgive them.

For quite apart from anything else, where on earth would I be without them?

Part II: Autumn

By the end of the second trimester, the foetus weighs between one and a half and two pounds. The skin has thickened, the lungs are developing well and hearing and taste have developed. Eyebrows and eyelashes are present, although the eyes themselves may still be closed. A pattern of sleeping and waking may be detected, and there are periods of intense activity. At this stage, the baby has an 85% chance of survival outside the womb.

Chapter Eight

It is decided that my day for busking should be Wednesday.

Wednesday is the day for the farmers' market in town, and Eric and Silas have a small stall. They sell goats' milk, eggs, honey and rich Jersey cream, plus such vegetables as have managed to fight their way to maturity through the forests of weeds (there are always many more than I would have thought possible, but Eric and Silas claim to have green fingers). I am quite sure that the cream and the milk are illegal, since the sale of such things is controlled by a raft of agricultural legislation, but Eric and Silas have little regard for rules and regulations, and they have loyal customers who can be depended upon to keep their mouths shut. Their 'dairy produce' is kept, literally, under the counter, the surface of which is spread with respectably legitimate vegetables and flowers. Legal considerations apart, their stall is always popular, although I suspect that this owes as much to the novelty of their twinned state as the quality of their produce.

Wednesday, say Eric and Silas, is the best day for me to start as they can give me a lift, and also keep an eye on me. I think this seems a very sensible idea. Blossom, however, does not.

'What do you need looking after for? Big girl like you.' This is a long sentence by Blossom's standards and I detect more than a hint of jealousy.

'Well, I think it's very kind of them,' I tell her.

'No better than begging,' she sniffs, wielding her broom as it ploughs its familiar route through the week's clutter to the bottom of the staircase.

'I'm not begging, Blossom. I'm earning money. I'm playing for people. And if they like it, they'll pay. If not, they don't have to. It's perfectly straightforward.'

'My Kaz wouldn't.' Kaz is the errant daughter.

'Well, Kaz probably can't play the violin.'

'Wouldn't want to. Nasty scratchy thing.' Blossom takes a swipe at a spider's web.

'Well, thanks, Blossom.'

Blossom's bony backside quivers with disapproval as she stops to pick up some piece of debris.

'Don't you like music, Blossom?' I ask her.

'Nope.' She drops her findings into her dustpan.

'None at all?'

'Nope.'

'Would you like some coffee?'

'Make me own.' She squashes a spider and sweeps up the remains.

'You do that.'

Trying to talk to Blossom when she's in this kind of mood is pretty well impossible, but I refuse to let her dampen my spirits. I feel cheerful, and for the first time in three months, I feel well. Gone is the nausea and the exhaustion, and my tummy is still relatively flat, even if there is someone living inside it. Besides, I am looking forward to playing to an audience again, even if it's only an audience of short-tempered shoppers, and I have my music planned. There will be some Bach, for the more discerning, and some jolly Irish pieces I once played with a dance band, and a virtuoso little number by Paganini (almost impossible, but will anyone notice the mistakes?).

It is the day before my street début, and I am playing through my programme in the kitchen, where Eric is measuring out the plans for the Ark on huge sheets of graph paper, and Silas is finishing off his squirrel. The squirrel, once so squirrel-looking, now looks very dead and rather shapeless, and its tail refuses to stand up in the usual perky squirrel way.

'That sounds great,' says Silas, half-way through a piece, but I can tell he's not listening properly. He whistles through his teeth as he withdraws the stuffing from the squirrel's tail (wire wrapped in some kind of cotton) and unravels it. 'I shall have to start again,' he says. 'And squirrels are supposed to be easy.'

I decide not to say anything. I have never understood the point of taxidermy; of killing a perfect, beautiful animal and then taking hours and hours trying to make it look perfect and beautiful (and alive) again. Admittedly Silas doesn't do any killing — most of his specimens are found by the roadside, and only a minority of those are suitable, the remainder being squashed beyond recognition — but it still seems a pointless occupation. No doubt in the hands of an experienced taxidermist, the finished article might be considered very fine, but nothing dead, however well stuffed, can look as beautiful as it did when it was a living breathing creature.

And it's all such a palaver. There are the tools and the chemicals and the stuffing materials, not to mention the copious notes which Silas has made on his several visits to Nigel, the local expert, and which are now strewn around the kitchen. Silas's manual tells him that he should be able to do a squirrel from start to finish in a couple of days; Nigel, being kinder, says give it a week. So far, it's taken him nearly ten days, and all this work to produce something which looks like a cross between a guinea pig and a monkey.

I put down my violin.

'It looks very — fat,' I say, eyeing Silas's hapless victim.

The squirrel squints defiantly back at me through its new shiny glass eyes, its empty tail hanging limply at its side.

'Do you think so?' Silas pauses. 'It doesn't really look like a squirrel any more, does it?' he adds forlornly.

'Well...'

'It's a good effort,' Eric says, but even to me, his tone is ever so slightly patronising.

'Oh dear. Nigel said to beware of over-stuffing. He said that was the commonest beginner's mistake. But I thought a squirrel ought to be nice and plump. Bugger.' Silas runs his hands through his hair, and the nice plump squirrel/guinea pig/monkey topples over onto its side. 'Perhaps I should concentrate on the badger.'

Eric and I agree that this is an excellent idea, not least because the hide of the said badger has spent the last two days floating in a mixture of noxious chemicals in the only bathtub. Both Eric and I are longing to be able to use the bath (although I suspect that like me, Eric's not sure about using a receptacle which has recently played host to such a grisly occupant).

'The badger might be easier,' Silas says, cheering up a bit. 'A bit more to get hold of. The squirrel was very fiddly.'

'Very fiddly,' Eric and I agree.

'What shall I do with this?' Silas holds up his squirrel.

'Finish the tail, put it down to experience and give it to Blossom,' I suggest. Blossom has been quite complimentary about the squirrel and it's her birthday next week.

'Good idea.' Silas looks relieved. 'I could tie a ribbon round its neck and it might look quite festive.'

'Very festive.' I hesitate for a moment. 'If I play through the rest of my programme again, could you tell me what you think?'

'Sorry, Ruth. Yes, of course.' Silas puts aside his squirrel and sits down, folding his hands in his lap. 'Play on. I'm listening.'

This time, they both listen attentively, and as usual, applaud enthusiastically when I've finished. I'm not sure that my uncles are the most discerning of audiences, but no-one could say they aren't encouraging.

'Very good. Very good indeed,' Silas says. 'Isn't it amazing that a few pieces of cat gut and some horse hairs can make a sound like that.'

I can see that he's still in taxidermy mode, but he does have a point. I wonder, not for the first time who first decided to try this particular combination — wood, gut, horse hair — for music-making, and pay silent tribute to them. Whoever it was must have been a genius.

We all stop what we are doing, and start to get ready for market day tomorrow. Eric and Silas have to prepare the produce for their stall, and I must look out something suitable to wear. I'm not sure what the dress code is for street musicians, but respectable poverty seems safe and easy, so I settle for a pair of old but clean jeans and a Save the Dolphins tee shirt (after all, everyone loves dolphins, don't they?).

On Wednesday morning, I feel quite excited. At last I can take a bath (the badger is drying out in the kitchen; Eric kindly let me have the first go, but not before he'd scrubbed the bath thoroughly with disinfectant, muttering darkly about badgers and TB). Do I wear make-up? I decide not, but I have washed my hair and I tie it back in a neat ponytail. Mr. Darcy, who has settled himself comfortably in his usual place by the Aga, is not pleased to be disturbed, and has to be dragged out to the Land Rover, growling and complaining. It's a bit of a squeeze, what with the sacks of vegetables, the pots and jars of dairy produce and several buckets of early chrysanthemums, and I sit squashed between my uncles with my violin on my lap and Mr. Darcy lying across my feet. But physical discomfort apart, it's a beautiful morning, the sun is shining, and there should be plenty of punters. It seems a promising start.

When we arrive at our destination, Eric and Silas park me outside Boots, and go off to sort out their stall. I set out my music and tune my violin, placing its empty case invitingly open for any contributions. Mr. Darcy lies beside me looking appealing. He has that doggy knack of resting his chin on his front paws and raising his eyebrows one at a time, rolling his eyes tragically at passers-by. If my playing doesn't do the trick then Mr. Darcy's theatricals can hardly fail.

But I have forgotten how hard busking can be. It's not just the lack of eye contact or even the being ignored, but the way people take a kind of detour round the busker, leaving an arc of empty pavement in a relatively crowded street, as though it's contained by an invisible fence.

'You need some change.' Eric has returned to see how I'm getting on. 'Here.' He empties the contents of his pockets into the violin case, leaving a respectable collection of coins, some keys and a grubby handkerchief. He retrieves the handkerchief and the keys, and shakes the money about a bit. 'See if this'll do the trick.'

I thank him, and play on. Sure enough, the coins begin to arrive, among them some pounds and even one five-pound note, and my confidence grows. I smile as I play (I remember this used to help in my student days) and gradually I begin to enjoy myself. One or two people even stop to talk, to ask about the music and make a fuss of Mr. Darcy and generally pass the time of day. A man from the greengrocer's offers Mr. Darcy a bowl of water and an elderly woman buys me a sandwich in a plastic wrapper and says something about homelessness being a disgrace (do I look homeless?). The church clock strikes one o'clock, and I decide to take a break.

And it is then that I see Amos.

At first, I think it's just someone who resembles him, but this is unlikely. Amos is huge; six feet five and broad-shouldered, with a particular loping walk. He has his back to me, and must be twenty yards away, but when he turns, it is Amos's face, Amos's beard, Amos's familiar furrowed brow distantly reflected in a shop window. I feel a swell of joy and of longing, for while I haven't given a lot of thought to Amos over the past weeks, suddenly I know that of all my friends he is the one I most want to see. I want to see him and feel him and talk to him, and most of all, I want to tell him about the baby. He may not be pleased — in fact I'm pretty sure he won't be — but I've decided that he has a right to know and to choose whether or not he wants anything to do with his child.

Amos begins to move away again, and I am faced with a dilemma. He is walking fast, and I know that I'll never catch him up carrying a violin case and leading a reluctant dog. On the other hand, I can't leave them unattended. The violin is my most precious possession, and Mr. Darcy can't be depended upon not to go walkabout if I leave him. For a moment, I hesitate, and in that moment, Amos quite simply disappears. One minute he is striding away up the street, and the next, he has vanished. I decide to abandon my patch and go after him. Clutching my violin and dragging Mr. Darcy on his lead, I hurry up the street, peering into shops and down alleyways, vainly calling Amos's name, and attracting some very odd glances in the process. But to no avail. My mission is hopeless; Amos could be anywhere.

I lean against a wall to get my breath back, and tears roll down my cheeks; tears of disappointment and frustration and, yes, tears of longing. Because something lost acquires many times the value it had before, and it would seem that I have just succeeding in losing Amos. Of course, it's quite ridiculous to get so upset. When I awoke this morning, nothing could have been further from my mind than Amos, but now that I have seen him — so nearly missed him — it seems unbearable that I've been unable to speak to him.

And it was such a coincidence. What is Amos doing in this little market town? I believe that he has an aunt in Wiltshire, so he could be visiting her, but even then it's amazing that our paths should so nearly have crossed. I could look the aunt up, but of course I don't know her name. I could phone Amos, but he's recently changed his mobile number, and I don't even know where he's living at the moment, or where his parents live.

Suddenly the day has lost its shine. Even the fact that I have managed to earn nineteen pounds and forty-six pence (not at all bad for a morning's work) fails to lift my spirits. As I return to my post and share my sandwich with Mr. Darcy (who perks up considerably), I ponder my situation. And by the time the church clock strikes two, I have made a decision.

Somehow, I am going to find Amos.

Chapter Nine

Amos and I go back a long way, and our relationship has always been one of comfortable familiarity rather than of intimacy. We were at music college together, where we did all the usual student things; rag weeks, beer-drinking contests in The Bell, wild parties and giggling trials of a range of 'illegal substances'. When I think back to my student days, I wonder why anyone put up with us at all, but then maybe they too had enjoyed their years of reckless irresponsibility.

And of course, we played our music. The one thing we were all passionate about was our music, and we spent long hours in cramped practice rooms playing our scales and studies. Amos's preferred practice room was adjacent to mine, and to this day I believe that one of the reasons I have tended to play too loudly is all those hours trying to drown out the sound of the trombone. Once, only once, I knocked on his door and asked whether he could tone it down a bit.

'Tone it down?' Amos roared, appearing in the doorway like Moses delivering the ten commandments. '*Tone it down?* What do you think this is?' He waved his instrument at me. 'A bloody harmonica? You get back to your scraping and I'll do my blowing, and may the best man win.'

I never complained again, and soon afterwards we became friends.

We laughed at each other's jokes (Amos could be very funny) and cried on each other's shoulders. We advised each other on matters of the opposite sex and commiserated when things went wrong (which they frequently did). Amos weaned me off what he called 'silly drinks' (Bacardi and coke, snowballs and Avocaat) and introduced me to the delights of Merrydown cider and best bitter, and we even briefly shared a flat. Free from the complications and pitfalls of sexual attraction (we had long since agreed that we were not each other's type), our friendship lasted happily throughout our student days, and while there have been times when we have had little contact with each other, we have always kept in touch.

Amos is far more gifted than I, and I envied him his musicianship, which he seemed to take for granted. While I had to work hard to pass my exams (college examinations were a far cry from the ones I had taken at school), Amos seemed to sail effortlessly through his. While I panicked and lost sleep, Amos remained calm and optimistic.

'It's just an exam,' he used to tell me. 'Just a silly little exam.' And he would clock up yet another distinction.

But the world outside college was tough and competitive, and when we left, Amos struggled as much as I did to find work. He did some jazz, and some teaching, and even spent a season playing in a dance band on a cruise liner, while I spent three years playing in a string quartet, which eventually folded through lack of funds (and, I suspect, talent), taught on the peripatetic circuit, and did a few more run of the mill jobs while 'resting' between musical engagements. My parents tempered their disappointment with quiet triumph. Hadn't they always said that my chosen career was a perilous one? I did my best to ignore them. In the meantime, Amos and I drifted apart.

It was the orchestra which brought us together again.

New, young and enthusiastic, for a while the orchestra did fairly well under its prize-winning youthful conductor (another colleague from college days). We worked hard, travelled long distances, and accepted pitiful salaries to make it work, but in an age when even the best orchestras struggle for money, it was doomed. After a difficult two years, our conductor reluctantly decided to down-size from full symphony orchestra to chamber group, and since there is no room in such an ensemble for second-rate violinists or even first-rate trombonists, Amos and I found ourselves out of a job.

At about the same time, Amos and his wife of eighteen months decided to divorce. I had always had my doubts about Annabelle (so, he told me afterwards, had Amos), but had never voiced them. Annabelle was willowy, glamorous and fiercely intelligent, but utterly unmusical. Having done everything she could to mould Amos into the kind of husband she wanted (if she didn't like beards, trombones, or beer, why on earth had she married him?), she found herself a sleekly pin-striped financial wizard and settled cosily with him into the gleaming chrome and glass and leather of his riverside flat. This didn't prevent her from trying to take Amos for everything she could get (he had practically nothing, so her efforts were fruitless), and the experience left Amos disillusioned and miserable.

'It's not that I still love her,' he confided to me in the pub, on that last evening together. 'It's just that everything's turned so *nasty*. She doesn't want me. I don't want her. Period. Why can't we leave it at that? What's wrong with "irretrievable breakdown"? Few things could be as irretrievably broken down as our marriage. But no. She wants to cite "unreasonable behaviour".'

'Hers or yours?'

'Mine of course.'

'What unreasonable behaviour?' I asked him.

'Good question.' Amos sipped his pint. 'Something about noisy practising and chicken curry and socks —'

'*Socks?*'

'I like brightly-coloured socks and she hates them. Hardly grounds for divorce.'

'Couldn't you have worn more subdued ones?' I ventured.

'Ruth, you're missing the point.'

'Which is?'

'The woman is totally unreasonable. Another beer?'

'Please.'

Amos pushed our empty glasses across the bar and nodded to the barman.

'No mention of her adultery, of course,' he continued. 'Now that *is* grounds for divorce. But, oh dear me, no. I'm not allowed to drag her precious "private life" through the divorce courts. So it's back to me and my curries and my socks.' He sighed. 'I never asked for all this unpleasantness, but it seems that it goes with the territory. I just want to get the whole thing sorted as painlessly as possible. Not a lot to ask, really.'

I agreed that it wasn't.

'Thank God we didn't have a kid.'

'Did she want one?'

'No. Annabelle's career means far too much to her.'

'And you? Did you want children?'

Amos gazed into this beer glass, as though searching for an answer.

'Yes. Yes, I think I did. Well, I did once, anyway. But marriage to Annabelle soon put paid to that.'

'But with the right person?' I persisted.

'Ah. The right person.' Amos grinned. 'With the right person it might be quite a different story. Yes. I think with the right person kids would be fun.'

How ironical that only a couple of hours after this conversation took place we were destined to make our own baby.

Of course, the baby would never have happened if Amos hadn't invited me back to his flat for coffee.

'You're too tipsy to go home yet,' he said, steering me out of the pub and down the road (I had driven up to see him). 'You need coffee, and plenty of it.'

But the coffee failed to make much impression, so Amos suggested that I should stay the night.

'You can have my bed and I'll sleep on the sofa,' he said.

His words hung in the air like something unfinished, as though waiting for one of us to deal with them. I looked at the sofa. It seemed about half the length of Amos; it was even too short for me. Amos caught my glance and smiled at me. I smiled back. I noticed for the first time that he had very sexy eyes (how come it had taken me so long?) and Amos obviously found something he rather liked about me. He took my hand.

'On the other hand...' he said.

'On the other hand,' I replied.

We both laughed, and suddenly, we were in each other's arms, tearing at each other's clothes like a pair of teenagers. Within minutes, the floor was littered with shirts, jeans, socks (including fluorescent green ones) and underwear, and we were hot-footing it to the bedroom.

Amos was a good lover; gentle and considerate as well as passionate; and despite the effects of several pints of beer (usually death to my libido) I found myself responding in a most satisfactory manner. Afterwards, I lay with my head on his chest thinking fondly of the importance of old friends and wondering why on earth we had never done this before.

'We make a good team, don't we?' Amos said, stroking my hair as we drifted towards sleep.

'Mm.'

'Shall we do this again some time?'

I laughed.

'Why not?'

I could feel him smiling in the darkness.

'Why not indeed.'

But when we parted company the next morning, we made no plans for a repeat performance. Amos had his divorce to worry about, together with the question of where the next pay cheque was coming from, and I had my gap year. But we promised to keep in touch, and meet up again "some time".

'I'll send you a postcard,' I told him as we kissed each other goodbye.

'Send me lots,' Amos said, 'One from every destination.'

'I'll do that,' I promised.

But we had both forgotten that Amos was having to move out of his flat and didn't yet know where he would be living, and neither of us could have known that the piece of paper upon which I'd written down his new mobile number had already been left behind, mislaid in a tumble of bedclothes.

By the time I reached my car that morning, I had already lost Amos.

Chapter Ten

For a few days following my near-encounter with Amos I feel low and dispirited. I am troubled by disturbing dreams, in one of which my poor little seahorse/rabbit (in my thoughts and dreams, it is still a seahorse/rabbit; never the grainy grey foetus of my scan) is weeping inconsolably. 'I want my daddy, I want my daddy,' it cries. I pick it up and try to hold it, but it slithers from my grasp and disappears, and when I awake, I too am weeping. In another dream it has packed up its belongings and is leaving.

'Where? Where are you going?' I cry.

'To find my father,' it tells me, bundling up its possessions in one of those red spotted handkerchiefs you read about in fairy stories. 'You are not enough.'

You are not enough. And of course, it is right. When I come to think about it, I have never been enough; not a good enough daughter, not a good enough violinist, and now apparently not a good enough mother, even though my baby is not yet born.

Is Amos the answer? Quite probably not, since however good a father he might prove to be, he wouldn't make up for my own shortcomings as a mother. And supposing he were to turn out to be a better parent than me; how would I cope with that? What would it be like to bear and give birth to a child, and then have someone else come along and cope better than I could? But even I know that parenthood is not a competition — rather, a team effort — and as Amos said all those months ago, he and I make a good team. I decide to put all thoughts of the baby on hold for the time being. After all, I have over five months before I have to meet my problems head on, as it were. Anything can happen in five months.

Fortunately, my broodings are interrupted by the activities of Sarah, that paragon of motherhood, for the following week she gives triumphant birth to her family of piglets.

This takes place in her shed, with Blossom in attendance and the rest of us admiring from a distance. Apparently Blossom is the only person Sarah will allow to come near her when she is farrowing, opening an evil piggy eye and giving a warning grunt when anyone else threatens to approach, and Blossom is in her element. As each slippery pink piglet arrives, Blossom wipes it with a handful of straw and hands it to its mother for approval, announcing the sex and condition as she goes.

'Male. Nice weight. Another male. Good. Little female. Bit weak.' And so on.

And they keep on coming. Nine, ten, eleven. The atmosphere in the shed becomes tense, for how will Blossom react if she has been wrong, and there are more or fewer than thirteen? Blossom hates being wrong (it does occasionally happen),and has been known to sulk for a week.

But no. On this occasion we are safe, for after the thirteenth piglet, Sarah gives a sigh and opens both eyes, and we all applaud. Thirteen it is. Once again, Blossom is vindicated.

To my surprise, there is no further talk of drowning and stuffing excess piglets, but there is one tiny runt, and Silas decides to rear it himself.

'Won't work,' says Blossom. 'Be dead by morning.'

The piglet is dead by morning. Poor Silas has stayed up with it all night, feeding it and rubbing its tiny body to try to keep it warm, but to no avail. When I come downstairs for breakfast, I find him in tears.

'Oh, Silas! Whatever's the matter?'

'My piglet. It died.'

'I'm so sorry.' I make him tea and give him a hug. 'Perhaps it was for the best.'

'Perhaps.' Silas blows his nose on an enormous handkerchief.

'And this sort of thing must have happened before.'

'Lots of times. But you never get used to it.'

'And — you can stuff it?'

'There is that.' He pauses. 'Except that it would be a bit like stuffing a friend.'

A friend? A newborn piglet he's known barely twelve hours, a *friend*? One of the many things about my uncles which never fails to amaze me is their emotional involvement with animals which are largely bred to be eaten. In the short time I have lived with them, they have personally despatched several chickens and ducks, and sent a pig and a beautiful billy kid to slaughter, and on every occasion Silas has shed tears. Once, when I asked him about it, he replied that it was 'the least he could do', but I think the real answer is that he simply can't help it. Eric's approach is more pragmatic, but he too hates killing things, although once the animals have been butchered into neat little meaty packages, both brothers are perfectly happy to eat them. I decide that if it is ever my misfortune to come back as a farm animal, I would like to belong to Eric and Silas. Their animals may end up in the pot, but they live happy lives and are much loved.

'Told you,' says Blossom, when she turns up after breakfast to check on her patients and Silas tells her his news.

'Careful what you say,' I whisper. 'He's really upset.'

'Silly old fool,' says Blossom cheerfully, disregarding the fact that the silly old fool has been extremely good to her, and moreover that Eric and Silas are probably the only people in the world who would employ her. 'Soon get over it.'

Meanwhile, Sarah and her brood are doing nicely. When I pay her a visit, I marvel at her serenity and at the neat little row of babies suckling from her recumbent form.

'How do they each find a teat like that?' I ask Blossom.

'Each have their own,' she says.

'And do they stick to it?'

'Course.' She eyes me pityingly. 'Don't know much about animals, do you?'

'Well, no. But I haven't had much opportunity.'

Blossom smirks.

'Not got the hands for it,' she tells me.

'What do you mean?'

'Look at them. Long white fingers.' She sniffs. 'Never make a farmer.'

I take my long white fingers — *violinist's* fingers, I console myself — and retreat to the house. I have learnt not to join battle with Blossom. She may be a woman of few words, but she has a knack of winning any argument.

The whole household seems cheered by the arrival of the piglets. Silas, having come to terms with his bereavement, is making his plans to restore his piglet to the glory it never achieved in its brief lifetime, and Eric has made progress on his ark.

'Noah's ark isn't just impossible, it's totally ridiculous,' he tells me. 'Even if you only have a few dozen species it quite simply wouldn't work. All that fodder. All that prey.'

'*Prey?*'

'Of course. Mice and rats for the foxes and things, small deer for the big cats. That sort of thing. Of course, mice and rats wouldn't be too much of a problem. I could breed those pretty fast.'

'You?'

'Well, Noah, then. But other bigger mammals have quite long gestation periods, and only produce one baby at a time. So there would need to be a lot of those, just to keep everything fed.'

'Couldn't you just breed thousands of mice?'

'I thought of that, but there still wouldn't be enough. So as I was saying, instead of simply disproving the Ark as measured in Noah's cubits, I've decided to prove how big it would really have to be, instead. At the moment, with the figures I've got, it would need to be about the size of the Isle of Wight.'

I picture the Isle of Wight as a neat lozenge off the south coast, but have no idea how big it is.

'As for the number of people needed to build it, not to mention the wood and the time it would take, I'm not even going to go into that.'

'Is all this effort really worth it?' I ask, amazed that a simple argument with my father can have given rise to all this industry. 'After all, you admit yourself it's only theory.'

'Never dismiss theory, Ruth. It can be quite fascinating.'

'He loves a project,' Silas tells me. 'With a bit of luck, this'll keep him amused for years.'

I look at Eric, bent over his graph paper.

'Perhaps you should have been an academic,' I tell him.

'I would love to have gone to university,' he agrees.

'Then why didn't you?'

My uncles exchange glances.

'It was me,' Silas says. 'I failed my exams. I spent some time in hospital with rheumatic fever, and never really caught up with my school work. I tried to make Eric go without me, but he wouldn't.'

'Do you regret it?'

But even before he replies, I know the answer. Quite apart from their mutual dependence, Eric and Silas are not the kind to waste time on regrets.

That afternoon, Mikey pays us an impromptu visit on his way down to the West Country. Mikey and I have been keeping in regular touch, and I am delighted to see him.

'I couldn't go past without calling in to see how you are,' he says, giving me a hug.

'You the father?' Blossom, who never bothers with introductions, is hovering with her empty dustpan.

'No. I'm gay. Can't you tell?' Mikey grins at her.

'Can't say as I can.'

'Ah well. Can't win 'em all.' He follows me through to the kitchen. 'What's up with her?' he asks me.

'Blossom? She doesn't like visitors. She barely tolerates me.'

Mikey laughs.

'And how's my godchild?'

'Fine. Everything's fine.'

'And the identical twin uncles? How are they?'

'Come and meet them.'

Eric and Silas take to Mikey immediately, and he to them, and after we've been out to visit Sarah and her family, we spend a companionable hour drinking gooseberry wine (apple juice for me), and chatting, while Blossom clatters mutinously up and down the hallway, eavesdropping. Mikey admires Silas's badger (which is nearly finished and stands in the corner of the kitchen looking like an ageing Master of Ceremonies), listens carefully to Eric's plans for his Ark without showing any signs of surprise, and generally makes himself agreeable. I had forgotten what delightful company Mikey can be.

'What's happened to your gap year?' I ask, as I see him out. This is something which still preys on my conscience.

'I've shelved it for the time being. Besides, I've — met someone.'

'Oh, Mikey! How exciting!'

'Yes. It's a bit soon to get excited, but I'm very happy.' He takes my hands in his. 'And you? What about you, Ruth? Are you happy?'

I hesitate.

'Yes. Yes, I am on the whole.'

'But?'

'But — well, I suppose I'd like someone, too.'

'Anyone in mind?'

'Well...'

'The baby's father perhaps?'

'Perhaps.'

'But you don't want to talk about him.'

'I do and I don't.' I sigh. 'It's — complicated.'

'Isn't it always?'

'I suppose so. But I've never had a baby with anyone before, so this is a first for me.'

'Do you — I mean, how do you feel about him?'

'I honestly don't know. We've been friends — good friends — for years, but the sex was a one-off. We've never had that kind of relationship. It was always straightforward.'

'And now it's not.'

'Now it's not even a relationship, because I have no idea where he is.'

'Oh dear.'

'Yes. So I haven't any chance of finding out how I feel about him, if that doesn't sound too weird.'

'Not weird at all.' Mikey pauses. 'But you'd like to find him?'

'Yes. Yes, I would. For a while, I wasn't sure, but now I really want to at least get in touch. To tell him about the baby.'

'Someone must know where he is,' Mikey says. 'Nowadays, it's very hard to just disappear.'

'You'd think so, wouldn't you? But Amos has a thing about technology and the internet. He has the most basic mobile, and hates computers. He never does social media. So he's not traceable the way most people are. Besides, he has a vengeful ex-wife who's after his assets, and he's trying to hide from her. He was never going to be easy to find.'

After Mikey has gone, I go up to my room and sit on my bed, gazing out of the window at the view of ramshackle sheds and untamed vegetation. Speaking to Mikey, I have finally put into words what I've been feeling for a while, especially since that fleeting glimpse in town: whatever it takes, I'm going to try to find Amos.

I reach for up my address book and start leafing through the pages. Someone somewhere must know where he is.

Chapter Eleven

In the course of the next two days, I manage to contact several people, none of whom have any idea where Amos might be. He has apparently mentioned another cruise ship, in which case he could be anywhere in the world, and also "taking time out", which could mean much the same.

But before I have time to be seriously disappointed at what is essentially non-news, something happens to turn our household completely upside-down, and take our minds off anything but the matter in question.

It is all Blossom's fault.

Perhaps I should first explain that Blossom is a fully paid-up rosary-carrying Roman Catholic. Not for Blossom the twice-yearly trip to the confessional; she apparently goes to both Mass and confession every week.

When Silas first told me I was completely stunned. 'Blossom in confession! I wonder what she says?'

'So do we.'

'Probably not a lot as she never admits she's in the wrong,' I say, rather unkindly.

'There is that.'

'But still.'

'As you say. But still.'

To be fair, Blossom doesn't talk about her faith much, but it does go some way to explain her attitude to my condition and to the behaviour of Kaz. I'm not at all sure what it is that Kaz does to incur her mother's disapproval, but knowing Catholics — and I know quite a few — it's almost certain to have something to do with sex. I have often thought that the Catholic church would be much happier if there were no such thing as sex; if instead of having babies, people simply divided in two, like those micro-organisms we studied in biology at school. Clean, simple and straightforward, with no messy relationships or the 'impure' thoughts and deeds to which my Catholic friends felt obliged to confess.

I wonder why it is that Blossom's religion has apparently failed to make her a nicer person, but as Silas and Eric point out, she might be a lot worse without it. Silas, ever charitable, says she could well be trying very hard, and have found that this is as far as she can get on her spiritual journey, but I remain convinced that Blossom is a deeply unpleasant person, and that not much can be done to change her.

Be that as it may, it is a very different Blossom from the one we know (if not love) who bursts into the kitchen on a wet Monday morning after feeding the hens.

'Dear Lord! Oh, dear Lord!' she collapses into a chair.

'What? What's happened?' Eric asks her. 'Are you hurt?'

'Dear Lord. Oh, Holy Mother of God.' There are actual tears in Blossom's eyes. Eric gives her a little shake.

'Come on, Blossom It can't be that bad.'

'Bad? Oh, not at all. Not bad. It's a miracle. A miracle in this house. Praise the Lord!'

'Miracle? What miracle?' Silas joins in.

'The blessed Virgin Mary. In the hen house.'

'You mean — you mean you've had a vision of some sort?' says Eric carefully. 'Is that it?'

'No, no. It's still there. Oh, praise the Lord!'

'Are you saying that the — the Blessed Virgin is in the hen house?'

'No. Yes. Well, sort of.'

'Tell us, Blossom. Take your time.'

'Oh, Holy Mother! Bless us all.' Blossom crosses herself. We all wait.

'She's there. She's right there on the wall. I saw her clear as I'm sitting here.'

'On the wall.' Silas repeats the words thoughtfully. 'Where — where exactly on the wall?'

'It's not her herself, of course —' well, there's a relief — 'but her image. With stars.'

'With stars. My goodness,' says Eric.

'Come. Come and see!' Blossom leaps to her feet and pulls at Silas's hand. 'All of you. Come and see.' She scurries out of the back door and leads the way along the muddy path to the hen house.

The hen house is the oldest of the outbuildings, having been made many years ago by my grandfather. Rather unusually, it is constructed from oak, since, as Eric explained to me, that was the only wood which was to hand at the time. Everyone has always agreed that a lovely piece of oak like that is wasted on the hens, but it has stood the test of time and of many generations of birds, and Eric and Silas are very attached to it. They used to hide in it as boys, and my poor mother once spent a terrifying afternoon in it when her brothers locked her in. It is, in short, a part of family history.

When we catch up with Blossom, her eyes are fixed on the side of the hen house and she appears to be in some kind of trance. I follow her gaze, but can see nothing unusual. I wonder whether you have to be a Catholic to see these things (after all, they always seem to appear to Catholics). Agnostics like myself probably don't stand a chance.

'There. There she is.' Blossom rouses herself and points. 'There. The Blessed Mother herself. And — stars.'

We all look. After a minute, Eric and Silas move closer.

'Well — I think I can see something,' Silas says, but he sounds a bit doubtful. He fishes in his pocket for his glasses, and peers more closely.

'What? What can you see?' Blossom cries.

'It could be — yes, it looks a bit like a figure.'

'Yes! Yes! Oh, thanks be to God!' Blossom clasps her hands and lifts her gaze heavenwards.

'Hang on a minute, Blossom. Maybe we need to calm down a bit.' Silas says. 'We mustn't jump to conclusions.'

'Can I have a look?' I ask.

Eric and Silas move back, and I join Blossom.

'There! There she is,' Blossom says, pointing a grubby finger.

Sure enough, in the grain of the wood it is possible to make out a vague figure; tall, wearing a kind of long garment, with what could be outstretched arms.

'I see what you mean,' I say.

'And stars? Can you see the stars?'

There is a circle of speckles round the head of the figure. Certainly, with a bit of imagination, they could be taken for stars.

'I think I can.'

'There! Told you! Even Ruth can see her.'

Even Ruth. Thank you, Blossom.

Eric and Silas carry out another inspection, and agree that there certainly is something that looks a bit like a figure.

'But even if it is a person, how can you tell who it is?' Eric asks.

Blossom looks at him pityingly.

'The Blessed Virgin likes to appear. That's what she *does*.'

This seems true enough. I have read of Virgins appearing, variously, on hillsides, in skyscapes and even on pieces of toast. Why not on the side of our hen house?

It is a strange phenomenon that once you see a figure or an object in a piece of wood (or in anything else, come to that) it becomes impossible not to see it. I myself have found the head of a fox and a lop-sided dragonfly in the knotted wood of the bathroom floor, and there are lots of faces in the floral material of the curtains in my old bedroom at home. Thus the curtains are no longer flowery, but peopled with little pink and white strangers, and whichever way I look at them, I can't turn them back into flowers.

So it is with Blossom's Virgin. Now that I have seen her, I can't *not* see her. She is there. And the more I look, the more Virgin-like she becomes. I fancy I see features, hair, even a veil. The outstretched arms bless, the tiny stars twinkle. I am almost convinced. I try looking away, and then looking back again, but she is still there. I can almost imagine that the garment she is wearing is blue. Whatever happens, from now on every time I look at the hen house, I too will see the Virgin Mary.

'I'll phone Father Vincent. That's what I'll do,' Blossom says.

'What can he do?' Eric asks.

'Father Vincent will *know*.'

Father Vincent doesn't know. When summoned to inspect Blossom's miracle, he seems far more concerned about the mud on the route to the hen house and the lively and unwelcome attentions of Mr. Darcy than the possibility of any miraculous manifestation.

'Hm.' He stands at the side of the hen house, looking thoughtful.

'Well? Well, Father?' Blossom is almost skipping up and down in her excitement. I am amazed, not only at Blossom's unusually high spirits and the sudden loosening of her tongue, but also by her demeanour. I have never seen Blossom showing respect for anyone before, but she is almost grovelling in her behaviour towards Father Vincent.

Father Vincent puts on his spectacles and leans down, rubbing his chin thoughtfully.

'Hm,' he says again.

We all wait. It would appear that without Father Vincent's imprimatur, Blossom's miracle isn't a miracle at all, so a lot hangs on his verdict.

'You can see her, can't you, Father? There she is, bless her, with all those little stars.'

'Well...'

'Yes? Yes, Father?'

'I suppose it could be. Just could be. But it's very hard to tell.'

'Perhaps we should pray, Father? Shall we pray?' Blossom makes as though to kneel down in the mud.

'No need to kneel,' Father Vincent says hastily. 'We can pray standing here quietly.'

Father Vincent and Blossom stand for several minutes with their eyes closed, and once again, we all wait. When they open their eyes, I find that I'm holding my breath, as though their verdict is of great importance.

'It is the Blessed Virgin, isn't it, Father? Please say it's her!' Blossom says.

'It's not for me to say whether or not this is the Blessed Virgin.' Discreetly, Father Vincent wipes his shoes on a clump of grass.

'Who then?' I ask, unable to contain my curiosity. 'Who decides what's real and what isn't?'

'We need a miracle or two,' says Father Vincent. 'Yes. That's what we need. A miracle.'

'What sort of miracle?'

'A healing, perhaps. Yes. A healing would certainly help.'

I cast about in my mind for someone who needs healing.

'Sarah has a touch of mastitis,' Eric suggests.

'Sarah?' Father Vincent turns to him.

'Our sow.'

'Oh, no. Not a sow. That would not be appropriate.' Father Vincent sighs. I feel that he is not really entering into the spirit of the occasion. 'I'll need to talk to the bishop.'

Even I know that people like bishops are busy and take a long time to answer things, and as we all troop back into the house for a cup of tea, I feel quite sorry for Blossom. After all, does it really matter whether her Virgin is real or not? If it makes Blossom happy (and it would seem that it does) then where's the harm?

But despite her disappointment, Blossom seems strangely cheery, stirring Father Vincent's tea for him and getting out chocolate biscuits and even cracking a little joke or two. I have the distinct feeling that Blossom is up to something, and I wonder what it can be.

In the event, I don't have long to wait.

Chapter Twelve

Two days later, Blossom turns up with two strange men who, she says, wish to pay their respects to the Virgin. She will escort them herself, she tells us. She knows how busy we all are (Does she? Blossom never seems to have any idea what anyone else is doing, and cares even less, but we let it pass).

But on Friday, we find out who Blossom's friends were.

MIR-*EGG*-LE OF THE HEN HOUSE! screams the headline in the local paper, together with what appears to be a craftily airbrushed photograph of Blossom's Virgin and a half-page article about Blossom herself:

'*Local farmer, Blossom Edgar, has discovered what is believed to be a manifestation of the Blessed Virgin Mary ingrained in the wood of her hen house*', it begins.

Blossom a *farmer*? *Blossom's* hen house? Even Eric and Silas are indignant.

'Well, really, Blossom. This is a bit much. You could at least have asked us,' Eric says.

'You'd have said no.' Blossom is unrepentant.

'Yes. We almost certainly would have.'

'There you are, then.'

'But Blossom, this is our house and our hen house. We should be the ones to decide whether we want to be invaded by the press.'

'Should be pleased.' It would seem that Blossom has returned to monosyllabic mode.

'Well, we're not.'

'Too late,' says Blossom with a hint of triumph.

'Well, yes. In this case, it is too late. But please don't let anything like this happen again.'

'Oh well. I suppose there's no harm done,' Silas says later when Blossom has gone home. 'And she's had her moment of glory.'

But the following week, the first pilgrims arrive.

'Where is she? Where's the Blessed Virgin?' The two women who appear at the front door are breathless with excitement.

'I'm afraid this is private property,' I tell them. 'And in any case, the — the manifestation has to be verified. It may take some time.'

'Oh, we don't mind about that,' one of them assures me. 'We can make up our own minds.'

'But this is still private property. I'm afraid I can't invite you in. It's not my land. And the owners are out.' Eric and Silas have gone to the feed merchant in town.

'If it is the Blessed Virgin, then you have no right to keep her to yourself. This kind of thing belongs to everyone.' She turns to her companion. 'I'm right, aren't I?'

'Well...' The other woman looks uncertain.

'Of course I am,' she continues. 'It'll be round the back. We don't need to trouble you, and we won't be any bother. Just ignore us.'

And before I have time to think of a reply, she has taken her companion's arm and led her round the back of the house towards the outbuildings. They look harmless enough, and as it's pouring with rain, I decide to leave them to it, although I keep a watchful eye from the kitchen window.

When Eric and Silas return, I tell them about our visitors.

'Probably just a one-off,' says Silas. 'I don't expect we'll be bothered again.'

But how wrong can you be. The next day, there are two small parties, and the day after that, four. Blossom, who has had two days off, is delighted when we tell her what's been happening.

'A shrine,' she says ecstatically. 'A shrine in our own garden!'

'No, in *our* garden, Blossom,' Eric says. 'We've already told you, this is our garden, not yours. And the hen house is ours too. You have no right to invite all these strangers round as though you own the place. It really is too much!'

I have never seen either of my uncles angry before, but obviously the very real threat posed to their privacy is having its effect.

'Didn't invite them,' says Blossom mutinously. 'Just came.'

'Yes, because of that stupid article in the paper. Blossom, you knew this would happen, didn't you?'

'Might have.'

'Of course you did. I have a good mind to take the hen house to pieces and destroy that panel. I can always make another.'

'Can't do that. It's holy. It's a *shrine*.'

'Just you watch me.'

'Your dad's hen house? Turn in his grave.'

'He'd get over it.'

Eric and Blossom glare at each other for a moment, then Blossom appears to change tack.

'I'll sort it out. See to the visitors. Won't know they're there.'

'I don't know.' Eric looks doubtful, as well he might. 'They'll disturb the animals. And then there's the security risk, too.'

'Leave it to me,' says Blossom.

'I still don't think it's a good idea. What do you think?' He turns to his brother.

'Let's give it a few more days, and see what happens,' says Silas, whose mind is on other things. He has found a particularly pleasing specimen by the roadside on the way home and is obviously longing to deal with it. 'This may all die down.'

But the pilgrims keep on coming. They arrive in cars and on foot, and they traipse up and down the garden, creating a mud bath as they go. To be fair, they are on the whole respectful and apologetic, they don't make much noise and they come and go quite quickly, but they are there. And someone has to be around to oversee the proceedings.

A week later, when an entire minibus full of pilgrims has made its way up the track, my uncles are at their wits' end.

'The trouble is, they'll come whether we let them or not,' says Silas. 'And the idea of people creeping round the house in the middle of the night to pay homage to our hen house, and disturb the hens, is not a pleasant one.'

'Creosote,' says Silas. 'We'll creosote the whole hen house, and that will be that.'

'We can't. Creosote's illegal. Cancer risk or some such nonsense,' Eric tells him.

'Paint, then. We'll paint it.'

'Seems a pity. It won't fit in with the other outbuildings.'

I open my mouth to suggest that nothing other than total squalor would fit in to the chaos of tumbledown sheds which comprise my uncles' domain, but then I close it again.

'Wood preservative, then,' says Eric.

'Won't it show through?' I ask.

'Shouldn't do. And it could do with a spot of weatherproofing, anyway. This way, we'll kill two birds with one stone.'

'Or chickens.'

'This isn't funny, Ruth. We have a real problem here.'

'Sorry.'

'You can help. It shouldn't take long.'

The following day, Eric drives into town and returns with several large tins of very dark wood preservative, and by the evening, we have the whole job done. The hen house looks very smart, standing out among the other more ramshackle outbuildings, but more to the point, there is no sign of the Virgin. Several disappointed visitors have had to be turned away, and there is now a large sign on the gate to the effect that the Virgin Mary has "disappeared".

'Which is true enough,' says Silas, 'even if she needed a little help. After all, if these manifestations can appear, then presumably they can disappear. I'm going back to my fox.'

Neither Eric nor I are going to argue with him. The fox in question has been with us now for two days, and is beginning to smell.

'What do you think Blossom will say?' I ask Eric, as he and I mix feed for the pigs.

'She'll be furious. Apart from anything else, she hates not having her own way.'

'We did do the right, thing, didn't we?'

'Of course we did.' Eric laughs. 'You're not turning Catholic on us are you? It's a bit late for that.'

'No. But you must admit, it was odd. It really did look like — well, like *something*. A bit more than a few knots in the wood, anyway.'

'I reckon Blossom's Father Vincent will be relieved,' Eric says. 'He didn't seem at all keen on the idea of a shrine on his patch, and I can't say I blame him.' He slops pig feed into a trough. 'It seems to me that miracles are a lot more trouble than they're worth.'

But if Eric thinks miracles are trouble, they are nothing compared to Blossom's reaction when she comes to work the next day and finds out what we've done. Shocked silence gives way to hysteria, followed by a torrent of vituperation. What we have done is apparently worse than blasphemy, worse than the blackest of mortal sins. Not only have we looked a spiritual gift horse in the mouth, we have outraged God Himself with our behaviour. We are worse than heathens and idolaters, and are, all three of us, condemned to eternal hell fire.

'Goodness!' says Silas, when Blossom has slammed out of the back door to have another look at our handiwork. 'I didn't know Blossom even knew half those words. She's a dark horse, and no mistake.'

'Why do you let her talk to you like that?' I ask them, more surprised at my uncles' reaction than by Blossom's behaviour, which was more or less what I had expected (Blossom's vocabulary is all there when she chooses to use it, as I've discovered to my cost).

'We don't "let" Blossom do anything. She's a law unto herself.' The plans for Eric's Ark are spread all over the table, and he's engrossed in designing an enclosure for some of his reptiles. He doodles with his pencil and rubs his chin. 'Do crocodiles eat snakes?'

'I've no idea.'

'Ring the zoo and ask, Ruth. There's a pet.'

Chapter Thirteen

Within a week, the drama of the hen house and its apparition has died down. One or two visitors still knock on the door to enquire about the whereabouts of the Virgin, but most people appear to have accepted her disappearance, and life returns to normal. Blossom's attitude remains unforgiving, but as Eric remarks, we can live with that. She never was a little ray of sunshine, so the fact that she's sulking is barely noticeable, and if her efforts with the duster and the vacuum cleaner are even less effective than before, her devotion to the animals remains intact. Even Blossom can't blame the animals.

Meanwhile, my own attention returns to my burgeoning pregnancy. With all the recent goings-on, not to mention my preoccupation with finding Amos, I have given scant thought to the development of the baby, but it would seem that my attention is not required for it to flourish quite satisfactorily. It continues to grow steadily, and of course I continue to grow with it.

My feelings towards it are ambivalent. While I am happy to acknowledge the miraculous nature of pregnancy and childbirth, I am not quite so happy about the way I am being taken over. Accustomed to having my body to myself, I find that there are times when I resent having to share it with someone else; someone who will grow and stretch, making me grow and stretch too; someone who plans to requisition my breasts for feeding purposes, and to that end is already causing them to balloon out of all proportion to the rest of me (I have always been rather proud of my small, neat boobs). And it's not just my body that I have to share. Presumably I have to share my nutrition as well, and common sense tells me that the baby will get first pick of everything — food that *I* have eaten, for *me* — leaving me with such organic leftovers as are not required for its further development. Add to all this the tiredness and the mood swings, and the fact that neither the baby nor I are allowed to mitigate them with a soothing glass or two of wine, and there are times when I feel more than a little hard done by.

None of this is helped by the involvement of my uncles. Ever since the scan, they have taken a proprietorial interest in my condition, volunteering to take me into town for my check-ups and on occasion entertaining perfect strangers with accounts of my progress. The grainy photographs still play a part in all this, one of them currently occupying the mantelpiece (together with a handful of baler twine, the latest electricity bill and several empty rifle cartridges), but I find that my own enthusiasm for my condition diminishes in inverse relation to that of my uncles. It is as though the baby has become their property rather than mine, and while I know that it needs all the friends it can get, I find myself resenting this. I am tired of being asked how I am feeling (tired), whether I have felt the baby moving (no) and whether I'm feeling excited about it (no, no, *no!*).

And then there is Silas's particular interest in all things medical.

In my experience, there are two kinds of hypochondriac. There is the anxious, neurotic am-I-going-to-die-of-this kind, and the interested, isn't-this-fascinating kind. Silas's hypochondria is of the second variety. Hence, while he anticipates — seems almost to want — investigations and operations, he appears unafraid either of them or of the possible outcomes. Not for Silas the gloomy contemplation of death and disease; more the dispassionate absorption of the scientist. Silas is deeply interested in the workings of his body, and sees illness, real or imagined, as a challenge; a problem to be solved rather than an unpleasant experience to be endured. I personally feel that it is no coincidence that Silas has taken to taxidermy. When he has no preoccupations with his own body, he can concentrate on trying to restore those of his hapless subjects. In many way, Silas would have made a very good doctor.

The *Book of Family Medicine*, his favoured bedside reading, is a well-thumbed volume to which he has frequent recourse. Its fragile pages are worn, many of its paragraphs underscored, with comments in the margins in Silas's spidery handwriting, and he is happy to dispense its advice to anyone who might require it. He also possesses an ancient stethoscope, courtesy of a medical friend (although I think it unlikely that he has any idea what he's listening for) and a DIY blood pressure machine. Since I joined the household Silas has self-diagnosed, variously, a brain tumour, appendicitis and a duodenal ulcer. These have all subsided within a few hours — before medical help could be sought — but have been as real to Silas as the genuine article. In many ways it's a good thing he doesn't have access to the internet, which can be a rich source of medical misinformation (and misleading suggestions) to people like Silas.

Silas's hypochondria extends to the rest of the household — a kind of hypochondria by proxy — and this can be tiresome. His book has a large section on Pregnancy and its Complications, and I find him reading it covertly when he thinks I'm not looking.

'How's the blood pressure, Ruth?' he asks me this morning. We are in the kitchen together, where Silas is putting the finishing touches to his fox.

'Fine.'

'How do you know?'

'Well, it was last time.'

'Should I — would you like me to check it for you?'

'No, thanks.'

'It'll only take a minute.'

'*No*, thanks.'

'Just to set your mind at rest?'

'My mind is at rest. Or it would be, if people would just leave me alone.'

'I'm sorry, Ruth.'

'No, *I'm* sorry.' I feel suddenly ashamed. 'I know I'm being ungracious and horrible. But Silas, I just want to forget about the baby. I've got ages yet before I have to think about it properly, and I want to enjoy the time I've got.'

'Don't you want the baby?' Silas says, after a moment.

'I don't know. I really don't know. At first, I didn't. Then I did. And now I'm not sure.'

'What's not to be sure about? You're young, you're healthy, even if you won't let me take your blood pressure. You seem to have made your decision. But Ruth — you seem to be ignoring the baby. You won't talk about it, plan anything. You're just — drifting.'

All this is true. After my vision — hallucination, dream, whatever it was — at the abortion clinic, I knew I wanted the baby. Or at least, I didn't want to do away with it. I would have the baby; decision made. But I never really thought beyond that point, especially since my failed attempts to find Amos. It's as though there is a wall in front of me, and I can't think about what lies beyond it. For the time being, life is comfortable; I'm with people I love and who care about me; I have plenty to keep me busy. I daren't even try to look beyond that wall for fear of what I might see.

'You could have it adopted,' Silas says. 'Plenty of people do.'

'Do they?' In my experience, people no longer have their babies adopted. It seems that everyone, from penniless teenagers who are seeking to give meaning to their lives to wealthy celebrities (who are probably doing the same) is having babies out of wedlock. It's the cool thing to do. Having your baby adopted is uncool. It is also, strangely, something I have barely considered.

I try to imagine myself handing over the seahorse/rabbit to a pair of delighted and grateful strangers. I think of the freedom I would regain and the glow of a good deed (selflessly?) done. My parents would be freed from their impending disgrace, I would be able to go on my gap year, and if Mikey would be minus a godchild, I'm sure he could live with that. After all, this isn't about Mikey, it's about me, not to mention that delighted and grateful couple, who even now could be out there somewhere grieving over their childless state.

Then I examine the other side of the adoption coin; the guilt, the emptiness, the now pointless stretch marks and other scars of childbirth, and the milky breasts waiting for someone to feed. And then the years of wondering and imagining, and eventually the waiting for that knock on the door, when a grown-up and reproachful teenager may well accost me to ask why I didn't want him; why I *gave him away*.

And Amos. Okay, so he doesn't know about the baby — may well never find out about it — but supposing he does ('You gave away a baby? *Our baby*? Oh, Ruth! How *could* you!')? What on earth would I tell him? Having stolen half a baby from him (albeit unwittingly), do I have the right simply to give it away?

'Well?' Silas is still looking at me. 'It's a possibility, isn't it? But you need to make up your mind, Ruth.'

'No.' I sigh. 'No adoption.'

'You're sure?'

'Quite sure.'

'Well, then.'

'Well then what?'

'Ruth, you know we're happy to have you here for as long as you like. We love having you around, and the baby will be welcome, too. But it's not much of a life for a young woman, stuck out here in the sticks with two old men. Or for a child, come to that. You need to make — plans.'

'I've rather liked not making plans. Apart from my job, I've never really been a planning sort of person. I've tended to — well, to let things happen.'

'So I gather.'

'But I suppose you're right. I ought to plan *something*.' I gaze out of the window. In the lemony light of a late-summer sunset, Eric is leaning on the three remaining bars of what used to be a five-barred gate admiring the livestock; Mr. Darcy is rolling in a patch of what could just be mud, but is probably something worse; one of the cats is carefully peeling a pigeon on the lawn. None of them appears to have — or need — plans. 'What would *you* do, Silas?'

'What would I do?' Silas stands back to admire his fox (really quite fox-looking). 'I think I might start by making my peace with my parents.'

'But I never wanted to fall out with them in the first place!'

'I know that.' Silas tweaks a foxy ear. 'But I also know your mother is pretty miserable about this situation. It wouldn't take much to talk her round.'

'Do you think?'

'I know.'

'How do you know?'

'We talk. From time to time. You forget; she's our sister.'

'I did try phoning Mum. I rang her last week.'

'And?'

'She sounded a bit strained. Not herself. But I think Dad was probably there too, and she never says anything that would upset him. I didn't dare mention the baby. One step at a time, I guess.'

'Well, maybe the next step is to go and see her. It's always better, face to face.'

'You're right. I'll do that. I'll go next week.'

'Good girl. You can borrow the Land Rover.' Silas regards his fox thoughtfully. 'You know, this fox reminds me of someone.'

'I know — Blossom!' When I come to think about it, the fox does bear a startling resemblance to Blossom.

'You're right.' Silas grins. 'Better not tell her.'

'Mum's the word.'

'And talking of mums —'

'Okay, okay. I'll go and see her. I've already said I will.'

But in the event, it turns out that my visit is not necessary after all.

Chapter Fourteen

The knock at the front door is timid; almost apologetic.

'Was that the door?' Eric asks.

'I'll go and see,' I tell him.

'It's probably the man about the llamas,' Eric calls after me (this is a very long story, and I won't go into it now). 'Tell him next week. Definitely next week.'

But it's not the man about the llamas.

'Mum!' My mother is standing on the doorstep holding a small suitcase and a collection of bags. 'What are you —'

'Can I come in?' Mum pecks me on the cheek. She looks tired and drained.

'Of course. Of course you can come in. Here, let me take your bags.' I usher her into the hallway. 'Eric! Silas! It's Mum!'

'Rosie! How lovely to see you! This is a nice surprise.' Silas gives her a hug. 'What brings you here?'

I'd forgotten that my uncles call Mum Rosie (my father always uses her full name), but looking at her now, small and vulnerable beside her big — in every sense — brothers, I can see that she could be a Rosie.

'I need — I need to speak to Ruth. Is that all right? For a few minutes.' She turns and then starts as she catches sight of Silas's fox. 'Gracious! What's that?'

'Oh, don't mind him.' Silas drapes a tea towel over the fox's head. 'There. Now he can't see you.'

'Is he — is he —?'

'Dead?' Silas laughs. 'Oh yes. Very.' He turns to Eric. 'We'll make ourselves scarce, shall we?'

When they've left the room, I make coffee, and Mum and I sit together at the kitchen table. She seems ill at ease, twisting a flowery handkerchief in her fingers, her eyes darting round the room as though expecting more foxes to creep out of the woodwork.

'How — how are you, Ruth?'

'Fine. I'm fine.'

'And — the baby?'

'Fine too, as far as I know.'

'You look well.'

'Yes. Thank you.'

There is a pause in which Mum stirs sugar into her coffee (she doesn't normally take sugar).

'This is difficult,' she begins. 'I've got something to tell you. Not good news, I'm afraid.'

'Dad? Is it Dad?' I feel a frisson of fear.

'No. Well, yes. In a way. Oh, Ruth —' she turns to me, and there's a kind of desperation in her eyes — ' I've left him. I've left your father.'

'You've *left* him?'

'Yes.'

'When did this happen?'

'This morning. Well, things have been difficult for a while. They came to a head last night, and we had a row. We've never had a row before. Not a real one.' Mum looks as though she still finds is hard to believe. 'I couldn't get through to him how I felt. He just wouldn't listen. So after I'd washed up the breakfast things, I — I left.'

'But why? How did all this start? You two have always seemed such a — *couple*.'

'It's — complicated.'

'Tell me. You have to tell me, Mum. If I'm to understand.'

'Yes.'

'Come on.' I reach across and take her hand. 'Just tell me. It can't be that difficult.'

'Oh, Ruth! I can't — I couldn't —' And she bursts into tears.

I let her cry for a few minutes, awkwardly patting her shoulder, wondering how best I can help her.

'It was — it was about you.' She blows her nose. 'Oh, Ruth — I couldn't bear it. Not knowing how you were, not having anything to do with the — with the baby. I just couldn't bear it.'

'But you know I'd have come home any time. You only had to say.'

Mum shakes her head.

'Your father.'

'Dad.' Of course. My father has never been one to go back on a decision, particularly one involving matters of morals (or, as in my case, the lack of them). I was brought up to believe that the man was the head of the family, and therefore Always Right (my father is a fervent follower of the teachings of St. Paul), and it took the outside world and a good dose of common sense to teach me that this was by no means always the case. It could be that my mother is at last beginning to see the light.

'He didn't want you to come home. He didn't even want me to see you. Well not yet, anyway. He loves you, Ruth, in his own way. He really does. But —'

'On his terms?'

'I suppose so. Yes. And he really didn't know how to deal with this — with this situation.'

'No. I can see that.' I drink my coffee, which is cooling rapidly. 'What's he doing now?'

'Painting the fence.'

'*Painting the fence?*'

'He thinks I'll be home to cook his dinner. But I won't, Ruth. I won't. I can't take it anymore. I've had enough.'

'Do you — do you love him?' I ask, after a moment.

'I did. I certainly did once. But I don't know any more. Being married to him was a habit. Our life together is a habit. I care about him. Of course I do. And I'd never wish him harm. But I want more than that. Before it's too late. I know what I've done is wrong — leaving him like this — but you're my daughter. My only child. This — baby could be my only grandchild. I may not get another chance.'

'And God? What about God?' I know this is cruel, but I genuinely want to know. I feel that all my life I've come second to God, as far as my parents are concerned. Is my mother really willing to compromise her beliefs for me?

'God. Yes.' Mum fiddles with her teaspoon. 'I think there's room for Him, too. Somewhere. But maybe my God isn't the same as your father's any more. Can you understand that?'

I have always thought of my father's God as the God of the Old Testament; a God who often seemed to me more concerned with battles and sacrifice and punishment than forgiveness and love.

'Yes. Yes, I can.' I stand up and look out of the window, where I can see Eric and Silas hovering at a tactful distance, pretending to be busy. 'So what are you going to do?'

'That's the other problem. And you may not like this either, Ruth. But I thought I might ask if — well ask whether I could stay here. Just for a while. Until I've got myself sorted.'

'Oh.' Of course I don't like it. I don't like it at all. I was more or less compelled to come here, and at the time I didn't really want to. Now, it would appear that my mother wants to gatecrash my comfortable new life and join in. 'Well...'

'I knew you wouldn't be pleased, Ruth. And I can understand how you must feel, after what — well, after what your father and I have done. But I've nowhere else to go.' She spreads her fingers in a little lost gesture, and I feel sorry that I ever made her feel unwelcome. Poor Mum. Trapped in a life where she is bound to my father and God (probably in that order), she has never had time to make a life of her own. She hasn't had a job since I was born, and such friends as she has are from the church or the voluntary organisations to which she belongs. They are all nice enough, but I think it unlikely that any of them would stand by her in this crisis.

'Of course I don't mind. It would be good to have you here, though it's not exactly what you're used to.'

'I know that. Silas and Eric have always lived in a bit of a muddle, but they're family. My family. We used to be — well, we were very close before I got married, but — but —'

'Dad didn't really approve of them?'

'Something like that. I think he likes them. Well, he hasn't anything against them, anyway. But he doesn't understand them. Their way of life, the fact that they've never really had proper jobs, the way they've turned their back on God.'

'I think if Dad took the trouble to get to know them better, he'd be surprised. They're good people, which is what really matters, and they've been wonderful to me.'

'I knew they would be.' For the first time, Mum smiles, looking almost pretty. I've never thought of my mother as pretty, but when I come to think of it, I haven't often seen her smile. 'I knew we could trust them to look after you.'

Of course, when she asks them, Eric and Silas both say they are delighted to have Mum for as long as she likes. She can have the room she slept in as a child. It will need a bit of a tidy (this, I happen to know, is an understatement), but they're sure she'll be comfortable.

'We thought it might come to this, one day,' Silas tell me some time later, when a large pile of assorted junk has been moved from Mum's room and she's has taken her things upstairs. 'I probably shouldn't say this to you, Ruth, but we never thought the marriage was — quite right for her. Not that we have anything against your father,' he adds, glancing at his brother, 'but they seemed so — unsuited somehow.'

'How, unsuited?' I ask him.

'Well, your mum was quite a girl when she was young. She had lots of boyfriends and she liked a good time. Your father...'

'Wasn't so much one for a good time?' I suggest.

'I suppose you could say that. But he was serious and steady, and maybe that's what your mum needed. And after all, it seems to have worked so far, doesn't it? And may well do again.'

'Do you think she'll go back to him?' I ask him.

'I've no idea. Perhaps she needs a bit of time to — well, to find herself. Sort herself out. But there's no hurry. We're happy to have her.'

When Mum comes downstairs some time later, she has changed and freshened up, and looks more in control.

'Would you like a guided tour?' I ask her.

'Yes. That might be a good idea,' she says. 'Then at least I can be of some use.'

I find her a pair of old wellingtons and we walk round the garden and outhouses. I introduce Mum to Sarah and her fast-growing family, and she admires some new fluffy chicks and a beautiful Jersey calf. She makes no comments about the state of the place, and I'm grateful; for seeing things as it were through her eyes, I can't believe that Silas and Eric have managed to function so well for so long in all this chaos. I refrain from telling her about the Virgin of the hen house; it's too soon for anything quite so outré. My parents see Roman Catholics as idolaters; unworthy to be called Christians, and under no circumstances to be trusted. Visions of the Virgin are most certainly to be avoided at all costs.

'Well, that's it,' I say, as we end up back at the house. 'What would you like to do now?'

'I think,' says Mum, 'I'd better phone your father. To tell him he'll have to cook for himself this evening.'

Chapter Fifteen

'Who's this, then?' Blossom demands, when she comes in the next morning.

'This is my mother. Mum, this is Blossom.'

'How do you do?' says Mum.

'Humph.' Blossom, ignores my mother's outstretched hand (I'd forgotten to warn Mum about Blossom). 'How long you staying?'

'Well, I'm not sure...'

'Where you sleeping?'

'She's sleeping in her old room,' I say, for the pleasure of seeing Blossom's reaction.

'What old room?'

'The little one on the top landing.'

'I slept in it as a child,' Mum adds.

'Relation then, are you?'

'I'm Eric's and Silas's sister. Ruth's mother, as she said.'

Blossom regards her stonily for a moment, and then hauls the vacuum cleaner out from the cupboard under the stairs, and plugs it in.

'Can't stand here chatting,' she says. 'Work to do.'

'We weren't chatting, Blossom. I was introducing you to my mother.' Just this once, I've been unwise enough to let Blossom's rudeness get to me.

'Can't hear you,' yells Blossom above the roaring of machinery. Something rattles up the tubing, and Blossom switches it off and stoops to investigate.

'I said that I was just trying to introduce you to my mother,' I repeat.

'Well, met her now, haven't I?' Blossom pokes about in the vacuum cleaner's innards and retrieves half an old toothbrush (an item much favoured by Mr. Darcy as a toy) and stows it away in her apron pocket, then switches on again. I can see we're not going to get anything more out of Blossom, and Mum and I retire to the kitchen.

'What an — odd person,' says Mum.

'Oh, she's odd all right. Goodness knows why Eric and Silas put up with her. But she'll be okay now she's met you. Just ignore her. She's upset because she likes to feel she's in charge of this place, and she hates surprises.'

But Blossom has only just started. She follows poor Mum round the house, ensuring that whatever job she is about to do, Mum's in the way. She skins a freshly-killed rabbit under Mum's nose (quite unnecessarily, as Silas usually does that sort of thing) and she flatly refuses to spring clean Mum's room, although Eric asks her very nicely.

'No time,' she says.

'You've got another two hours yet,' says Eric reasonably. 'It shouldn't take that long.'

'Take more'n that.'

'No it won't. Not if you start now.'

Blossom eyes Eric beadily.

'Bad back,' she says. 'Done enough cleaning for today. Do the pigs.'

'What bad back?' asks Silas, the medical expert.

'Personal,' says Blossom going out and slamming the back door behind her.

'How can a bad back be personal?' asks Mum, puzzled.

'Blossom's bad back can be anything she likes,' says Eric wearily. 'If she's got one. Which I very much doubt.'

'Why doesn't she like me?' Mum asks.

'I suspect you're a threat,' Eric says. 'Ruth was bad enough — another woman around the house, and all that — but now there are two of you, she probably sees it as two against one.'

Poor Mum. Her visit has not got off to a good start, and there is more to come, for the next day, Mikey pays me another visit. He says he is 'just passing' again, but I suspect there's more to it than that, for he seems strangely excited.

Mum hasn't met Mikey, and as far as I know has never met any gay person. She's not so much homophobic as homo-ignorant (if there is such a thing), and given Mikey's exuberant lack of tact, I anticipate trouble.

At first, things go well enough. Mikey greets Mum very nicely, doesn't ask embarrassing questions as to the whys and wherefores of her visit, and there is a safely general discussion round the kitchen table when he joins us all for lunch. But I can see that he is bursting to say something, and after half an hour, he can contain himself no longer.

'Oh, Ruth! I've been dying to tell you. You know that new partner I was telling you about? We're in love!' he tells me (and of course, everyone else).

'That's great, Mikey.' I try making warning signals, but Mikey is oblivious.

'Yes. It all happened so quickly. We're going on holiday together.'

At this stage, I try to reach Mikey's foot with mine to give him a kick under the table, but he's too far away. I look despairingly at my uncles, but neither of them seems to have noticed the impending danger.

'How lovely for you,' Mum beams. 'What's her name?'

'Gavin. *Gavin.*' The word rolls off Mikey's lips as only a lover's name can; smoothly, adoringly, and (to most people) indisputably male.

'What an unusual name for a girl!' cries my mother, still completely in the dark.

I make one last, desperate attempt to reach either Mikey's love-glazed eyes or his foot, but it's too late.

'Oh, Gavin isn't a girl; he's a man,' Mikey tells her. 'Can't you tell? I'm —'

At last my foot reaches its target and administers a sharp blow to Mikey's ankle, and he finally shuts up. But of course, the damage is done. I have never seen anyone blush the way Mum does when she realises what Mikey's saying; what Mikey *is*. Even the tips of her ears seem to go puce. She looks at me despairingly, and I realise that of course she has no idea what to do. She has no rules for this kind of situation, and Mum lives her life by rules. My father isn't there to give her guidance, and she hasn't the confidence to trust any reaction of her own. She is almost certainly torn between politeness, horror and a deep and unspeakable embarrassment, and I feel desperately sorry for her.

'Mum, why don't you go and put your feet up?' I suggest. 'You must be tired. I know you didn't have a very good night.'

She gives me a grateful look and practically scampers from the room. A few minutes later, Eric and Silas wander off to inspect a leaky roof, and Mikey and I are left on our own.

'Oh, *Mikey*! How could you!' I am furious with him.

'How could I what?'

'My mother's never come across a gay person before. She didn't know where to put herself!'

'Perhaps it was time she did.'

'Did what?'

'Meet a gay person.'

'Oh, don't be so ridiculous.' I begin collecting up the lunch things. 'Mikey, my mother is a complete innocent. She lives under the thumb of my father and thinks and believes what he thinks and believes. In my father's book, gay people are beyond the pale.'

'How sweet,' Mikey murmurs.

'No. Not sweet. Just ignorant. But they are basically good people, and they are *my parents*.'

'Am I supposed to be sorry?'

'It would be a start.'

'Okay. I'm sorry.'

'Not good enough.'

'I really am sorry, Ruth.' He kisses my cheek. 'Will that do? But I'm so happy, and I wanted you to be happy for me.'

'Of course I'm happy for you. I'm delighted for you. But next time you have a piece of news like this, please spare my mother. She's having a hard time at the moment, and she can do without you and your love life.'

'Okay. Understood.'

'That's all right, then.'

'So can I tell you about Gavin now? Please, Ruth. Just five minutes.'

Mikey spends the next half-hour telling me about Gavin while we do the washing up together, and I listen, because Mikey is a good friend and I really am happy for him.

'So,' he finishes. 'Now tell me about you.'

'There's not much to tell, really. I'm fine, and the baby's fine. But the bad news is that my mother seems to have left my father.'

'Goodness!'

'Yes. I'm sure it's not permanent, but still, it's all a bit messy.'

'And you're caught in the middle.'

'Well not really, because my father hasn't been in touch. Mum only arrived yesterday.'

'And she's now trespassing on your patch.'

'Well, I'm glad she feels she can come here, of course I am.'

'But you were comfortable as you were. The three of you, and that ghastly Blossom.'

'Yes. Does that sound awful?'

'Not awful at all. It's perfectly natural. You've settled in so happily here — it all seems so *right* — and of course your mum being around is bound to make a difference.'

'It does a bit.'

'And still no man?' he asks me.

'I'm hardly likely to find one round here, am I?'

'No. I suppose not. But what about the baby's father, Ruth? Is there no chance of your making a go of it with him?'

'I don't even know where he is.'

'Mm. That could be problematic.' Mikey stacks plates neatly away in a cupboard. 'Are you ready to talk about him yet?'

'Oh, why not?'

So I put away my tea towel, and tell Mikey about Amos. I tell him about our long friendship, Amos's divorce and the night we spent together. I tell him about the comforting familiar *hugeness* of Amos, his sense of humour, his warmth and his kindness.

'And — I miss him,' I end lamely. 'I never thought I would, and if it weren't for the baby, I probably wouldn't be giving him a thought, but I really, really miss him.'

'Anyone would think you were in love with the guy,' Mikey remarks after a moment.

'Can one fall in love with someone when they're not there?'

'I don't see why not. After all, you seem to know him pretty well. And I'm sure having a baby with someone must make a difference.'

'Yes. Yes, it does. And of course, that's another thing. The baby.'

'What about the baby?'

'I've done nothing about it. I can't think about it or make plans for it or anything. I'm just — stuck. Eric and Silas say I should start making decisions about the future, but I can't *see* a future. Not with a baby. I know I decided to keep it, and I've no regrets about that, but it doesn't seem real, somehow. I just see myself living here for ever with my bump, milking goats and arguing with Blossom and playing my fiddle to bored shoppers.'

'You could give the baby to me. I'd love to have your baby.'

'That's a thought.' For a moment, I have a vision of the seahorse/rabbit being carried off into the sunset by Mikey (and probably Gavin as well. Why not?). It would be loved and cared for by someone I know, and I could have visiting rights. The perfect solution all round.

But while Mikey is undoubtedly half-serious, the baby wouldn't have a mother, and I'd like it to have a mother. Besides, now that my own mother is joining in I am no longer the only person involved. Mum is clearly preparing for — even looking forward to — her role as a grandmother, so I can hardly give her grandchild away. It seems that the Woman's Right to Choose ends once the pregnancy is under way; after that, other people enter the equation, with their own hopes and expectations, and it's hard to ignore them.

'You'd make a lovely dad, Mikey, and it's tempting. But I have to go ahead with this. I'll manage somehow.'

'Then at least find Amos.'

'I've done everything I can think of. He just seems to have vanished.'

'People can't do that. Not with the internet, and mobiles, and CCTV.'

'Amos can. He hates the internet, and likes people not knowing where he is. It's a kind of pride thing with him, being invisible. Plus, he's hiding from his ex.'

'I could still try to Google him for you.'

'Other friends have tried, but no luck so far. But I'd love you to have a go, if you don't mind.'

'Of course I will. There can't be that many trombone-playing Amoses. He should be pretty easy to find.'

'Even Amos Jones?'

'Especially Amos Jones.'

'You're a star.' I give him a hug.

'And still a godfather?'

'Certainly still a godfather,' I assure him. 'I can't think of a better one.'

Chapter Sixteen

All things considered, my mother has settled into the household surprisingly well. She appears unfazed by the chaos, seems to enjoy the animals, and is obviously deeply fond of Eric and Silas. It's as though the three of them have picked from where they were when they were children, and it's lovely to see Mum laughing once more.

Of course, not everything delights her, and she finds Silas's taxidermy hard to understand.

'I wouldn't mind so much if they looked the way they're meant to,' she confesses to me. 'But they all look so — odd. Not at all the way they must have when they were alive. That badger looks more like a small bear on its way to a fancy dress party than a real badger.'

'Silas over-stuffs them,' I tell her. 'He can't help himself. He gets an animal just right, and then he can't resist adding a little bit more stuffing, and ruins the effect. He also puts in the wrong eyes.'

'The *wrong eyes*?'

'Yes. He has to send away for the eyes. He got a batch of dogs' eyes by mistake, and he can't bear to waste them.' Which of course explains the reproachful doggy gaze of several ill-matched animal faces. 'Mr. Darcy can't stand it. He doesn't like the taxidermy thing any more than we do, but it's the eyes that really get to him. I think he takes it personally.'

And then there's Eric and his researches. Poor Mum is torn between curiosity and her long-held fundamentalist beliefs. I can see that she is longing to look at Eric's plans (which have now had to be moved into what is optimistically known as the study because they've outgrown the kitchen table), but has misgivings because of her loyalty to Dad and her church.

'Oh, go on, Mum. What harm can it do?' I ask her. 'You can carry on believing what you've always believed, and still have a look at Eric's Ark. It's really very interesting.'

So Mum spends an hour on her hands and knees with Eric poring over his plans, while he explains at length about carnivores and herbivores, which animals can co-habit and which must be kept apart, and the amount of excrement they will all produce in a day (which, Eric explains cheerily, can all be chucked into the sea, because if there's one thing Noah has plenty of, it's sea).

'I thought you didn't believe in Noah,' Mum says, perhaps glimpsing a tiny opportunity for Eric's salvation.

'I don't. This is all theory.' Eric rolls up his plans and stows them carefully away in an old chest out of Blossom's way (Blossom has no time for Eric's researches, and given half a chance is more than capable of hoovering up all his hard work). 'Don't worry, Rosie.' He pinches her cheek. 'I'll be okay. You don't need to believe in a great boat full of animals in order to be saved.'

Every evening, my father phones, and Mum speaks to him for about five minutes. She is reluctant to tell us what he says, but he is apparently coping well.

'The church are all praying for us,' she tells me.

'I bet they are,' mutters Silas, mixing chemicals in the sink.

'But he keeps asking when I'm coming home. I don't know what to do, Ruth. I've never been in this situation before. What do — what do people do?'

'I've no idea. But you're doing okay, Mum. And at least you're able to think things through without anyone putting pressure on you.'

'I suppose so.'

'Do you miss him?' I ask her.

'I don't know.' Mum rolls out pastry for a pie she's making (she's "earning her keep" as she puts it by doing much of the cooking). 'I ought to miss him, oughtn't I? After nearly forty years. I certainly ought to feel — well, something more than this.'

'I don't think oughts count when it comes to feelings. After all, you can't help what you feel, can you? It's what you do that counts.'

'And what I'm doing is wrong. I made vows, Ruth. Important vows. I believed — believe in them. And now look at me.'

Poor Mum. I don't think there are any divorced or separated couples among her sheltered acquaintance, so this is unknown territory for her. I often wonder how people like my parents survive the mores of our post-modern world. They behave like lost time-travellers from a bygone age, expecting everything to be as it used to be — as it ought to be — unable to accept or understand change. I'm sure my father is more worldly-wise than my mother, and that he has succeeded in protecting her from the more shocking aspects of the twenty-first century. They rarely watch television, and newspapers are carefully rationed. They have what Dad calls the "wireless" (who still uses that word?), listening to the news and the occasional church service, and such books as they read are all about the Bible or the joyous "witness" of those who have seen the light. There are a few children's books left over from my childhood (*Peter Rabbit*, *Barbar the Elephant*, *What Katy Did*, *Little Women*; safe, clean stories with happy endings), but that's about it. Matters sexual were never discussed, and such information as I had was gleaned from the rather clinical sex education lessons at school, and ill-informed friends (you can't get pregnant if you have sex standing up; that kind of thing. My friend Molly Wilkins put this theory to the test, and soundly disproved it).

'But I'm not going back. Not yet,' Mum says now. 'I'm not ready.'

I think it's the first time I've heard Mum say what *she* wants to do. It occurs to me that she's spent her whole life doing things for other people or because other people have told her to do them. Things are certainly changing.

The next day's post brings news from Mikey. He has Googled Amos, and come up with some interesting, if ancient, snippets, under the following headings:

'*Young trombonist wins prestigious prize*' (*The Times*, May 1990). Typical.

'*Student leads demonstration against regime in Zimbabwe*' (*Daily Mail*, February 1994). Also typical.

'*Gifted jazz-player survives window fall*' (*Daily Telegraph*, April 1999). Ditto. Amos is accident-prone. He puts it down to his height, but actually he's incredibly clumsy.

'"*His playing made our holiday,*" *wrote Enid Horton, who enjoyed one of our musical cruises last year*' (Cruise brochure, Summer 2000).

There are various other bits and bobs; extracts from local newspapers, concert reviews, a mountaineering accident and, strangely, a brief appearance on a TV cookery programme, but nothing which can be of any use in actually tracking Amos down. The last mention is two years ago, and since that, nothing. It would appear that Amos hasn't just disappeared from the face of the earth; he's vanished from cyberspace, too.

Mikey is sympathetic in his accompanying note, and says he's "sure Amos will turn up sooner or later". It's the sort of banality lovers delight in; the world they inhabit is so blissful (if in the long run, so removed from reality) that they feel it incumbent upon themselves to spread the bliss around by trying to convince the rest of us that our worlds, too, will reach this pinnacle of perfection, if only we wait long enough.

I am more disappointed by Mikey's letter than I would have expected. I have faith in Mikey, and I had really hoped that he would come up with something more concrete. Each Amos-related disappointment is harder to deal with than the last, and this time, I find myself close to tears.

I wander outside to find someone to talk to. Mum and I are getting on pretty well, considering our different predicaments, but I don't think either of us is ready yet for an Amos conversation.

I run Silas to ground in the greenhouse, where an amazing array of plants is managing to flourish among the broken flower pots and the weeds which have managed to negotiate the spaces left by several broken panes.

'It smells wonderful,' I tell him, as I am hit by a blanket of warm moist air, redolent of sun and soil and tomatoes.

'Mm. Doesn't it.' Silas straightens up and smiles at me. 'What's up, then?'

'How do you know there's anything up?'

Silas taps his nose. 'I can always tell. Baby okay?'

'As far as I know.'

'Made any decisions yet?'

'I've been trying to find its father.'

'Good for you! Any luck?'

I shake my head. 'Not yet. Mikey's been on the case, but Amos seems to have disappeared.'

'Amos. You never told us he was called Amos. Well, that's certainly a good name for anyone's father.'

'Yes. Even Dad would — might approve.'

'So what next?' Silas ties up a drooping frond of something with a piece of string.

'I don't know.'

'Have you talked to your mum yet?'

'Not yet. I guess she's got enough problems of her own at the moment.'

'It might take her mind off them. Give her a chance, Ruth. I think she really does want to help, but doesn't know where to begin.'

'Has she said so?'

'She doesn't have to.' He puts away his string and wipes his hands on the seat of his trousers. 'You forget. We've known her a lot longer than you have. People don't change that much.'

'I will talk to her. Soon.'

'That's good.'

I'm grateful for the way my uncles lead but never coerce me. Their advice is often good, but they never either assume I'll take it or put pressure on me to do so. It's just there; an offering, nothing more. And because of the generous undemanding spirit of the offer, as often as not, I accept it. I remember all the times my father gave me "advice", and how I frequently refused to take it on principle, although it wasn't all bad. It might not have been given in the way Silas's is, and was often couched in the terms of a command or a criticism, but perhaps I should have given him some credit. He was probably only doing what he thought was right.

I pick a tiny bright red tomato and put it in my mouth.

'Would you have liked children, Silas?'

'Yes and no.' Silas seems unsurprised by my question. 'Yes, because it's one of the most wonderful things anyone can do, and no, because it's such a huge responsibility. And I never met the right person to have them with.'

'Did you — have you — I mean —'

'Have I ever had a girlfriend? On yes. When we were younger, Eric and I had quite a few. But the twin thing got in the way, and in any case, none of them worked out. In the end we settled for what we have, which is more than many people manage.'

Later, we make our way back to the house together carrying baskets filled with bright red tomatoes and yellow peppers and glossy aubergines the colour of bruises. They look almost too beautiful to eat, and certainly much too good to part with, but they have to go, for tomorrow is market day.

I must go and practise my violin.

Chapter Seventeen

A few days later, just when life seems to be settling down a bit, there is another major interruption in the form of the reappearance of the Virgin of the hen house.

'She — it — can't be back!' Eric says in disbelief, when a triumphant Blossom announces these unwelcome tidings.

'See for yourself.'

'You must have done something, Blossom. This is certainly your doing.'

'Rain did it.'

'It couldn't have. That was perfectly good wood preservative. It's guaranteed waterproof.'

'Suit yourself.'

Eric and Blossom glare at each other.

'I will suit myself. And I'm certainly not going out in the rain to look at all this nonsense,' Eric says.

'Shall I go and look?' My curiosity is aroused.

'Fine, Ruth.' He lowers his voice. 'But please don't encourage her.'

I put on wellingtons and an old raincoat and trudge down the garden behind Blossom.

'There!' she says, when we reach the hen house. 'Told you.'

Sure enough, Blossom's miraculous image appears to have made a come-back. There it (she?) is, outstretched arms, little stars and all. If anything, the image is even more lifelike than it was before.

'How...?' I am astonished.

'Rain,' Blossom says again. And she's right. I don't know what substance it was that we used to paint the hen house, but it has completely washed away, leaving the oak pale and pristine, if a little wet, and Blossom's Virgin as good as new.

Blossom crosses herself, and risks a rare smile.

'Can't keep *her* away,' she tells me. 'If she wants to appear, she'll appear. No stopping her.'

Mystified but oddly fascinated, I make my way back to the house. There's no sign of Eric or Silas, but Mum has just returned from taking Mr. Darcy for a walk (Mr. Darcy neither likes nor needs walks, but it's all part of Mum's idea of being useful). They are both soaked to the skin.

'What's going on?' she asks me. 'Eric won't say, but something's happened, hasn't it?'

'Sort of.' How do I tell my fervently anti-papist mother that there's a religious apparition on the premises?

'Well?' Mum takes off Mr. Darcy's lead (an unreliable structure concocted from baler twine) and dries him with an old towel.

'It's like this.' Very carefully, trying as much as possible to spare Mum's feelings, I explain about Blossom's faith and Blossom's apparition.

'It's idolatry,' says Mum, after a shocked silence. 'That's what it is. Idol-worship. I wonder Eric and Silas put up with it.'

'They don't. They've done their best to get rid of it. But when you come to think about it, it's pretty harmless.'

'Harmless? You call this *harmless*? Ruth, what can you be thinking of?'

'Mum, you don't have to have anything to do with it. It's between Eric and Silas and Blossom. It's their hen house and her apparition. And look at it this way. If this is actually going to put a smile on Blossom's face, isn't it worth it?'

Mum still looks unhappy.

'I don't like it,' she says. 'This — kind of thing. It's not right. It's evil.'

And try as I might, I can't persuade my mother that Blossom's Virgin need have nothing to do with her. Mum's now part of the household, albeit temporarily, and apparently she feels that she will be in some way contaminated by its presence.

'What would your father say?' she keeps repeating

'Don't worry. Eric and Silas will probably paint over it again, and we can forget all about it,' I tell her. 'Would you like to see it?'

'No. Oh, no. Certainly not. I wouldn't — couldn't look at it. That wouldn't do at all.'

Meanwhile Blossom, sensing the strength of Mum's feelings, does her best to make things worse by praising the Lord and crossing herself, and telling us all how good the Holy Mother is to visit us again like this, when we have gone out of our way to get rid of her.

'It can't stay,' Eric tells her, when he's been out to have a look for himself. 'That stuff they gave us was useless. We'll have to get something stronger. We're not going through all that miracle business again.'

'Can't get rid of her,' Blossom says. 'Not twice.'

'Three times if necessary,' says Eric. 'Blossom, let me make this absolutely clear. These are our grounds, and they are home to our animals. We are not having strangers tramping about visiting our hen house. It's quite out of the question.'

'It does look quite — well, quite real,' I venture. 'Have you looked at it properly? You have to admit, Eric. It's more than just a bit of wood grain and a few scratches.'

'Whose side are you on?' he asks me (Eric is not in a good mood today).

'Well, yours, of course. But all the same...'

'No, Ruth. Absolutely no. It's got to go, and there's an end to it.'

Blossom sulks and curses and bangs about the house until Silas tells her to take the rest of the morning off and go home.

'Can't. You'll do something to her.' Blossom gets out a mop and bucket and starts sloshing soapy water round the kitchen floor.

'So what are you going to do? Stand guard by the hen house?'

'Might do.'

'Blossom, I'm not asking you. I'm not even telling you. I'm *ordering* you to go home and cool down. Come back tomorrow and we'll talk about it. We can't do anything about it before tomorrow, anyway, and we certainly can't have a sensible conversation when you're in this kind of mood.'

After Blossom has clattered off on her ancient bicycle, leaving the kitchen floor awash with suds and her mop lying across the hallway, Mum asks Silas what he's thinking of.

'Why do you let her speak to you like that?' she asks him. 'You should get rid of her. You can't just hang on to her because you're sorry for her.'

'Sorry for her? Sorry for Blossom?' Silas roars with laughter. 'No-one needs to be sorry for Blossom, I can promise you. And there's no need for us to get rid of her. That's just Blossom's way. She'll calm down soon enough.'

'You're too soft. Both of you. That's always been your trouble.'

'Maybe. But Blossom suits us.'

'You mean, you suit Blossom. No-one else would employ her.'

'Probably not.'

'You two are impossible.'

'That's what you love about us.' Silas pats her on the head. 'Now, I'm going to ring up the hardware shop and complain about that preservative. There must have been some mistake.'

The following morning, Blossom turns up early. Her mood has clearly improved, and she is almost polite to Eric and Silas.

'Got an idea,' she tells them, as she washes up the breakfast things without being asked (Blossom never does the washing-up).

'Oh, yes?' Eric says.

'Move the hen house into the back field.'

'Move the hen house? Who's got time to move the hen house, even if we wanted it moved?'

'Our Lazzo.'

'Oh yes?' Lazzo (short for Lazarus, so called because he nearly died as a baby) is Blossom's son. She rarely mentions him, and appears to have as little time for him as she has for Kaz, but apparently he has his uses. 'Well, even if he would, why should anyone move the hen house? It's perfectly all right where it is.'

'Visitors,' explains Blossom.

'Ah. Visitors. But there won't be any visitors because there won't be anything for them to see once we've painted over it.'

I wait for Blossom to explode, but she has obviously changed her tactics.

'Shame,' says Blossom. 'Should be pleased. It's a sign.'

'Yes. A sign that that dratted hardware place sold us the wrong stuff. And as you know, we're *not* pleased. Not at all pleased. We just want to be left in peace to get on with our lives.'

But Blossom's not going to let Eric and Silas get away quite so lightly. She has it all worked out, she tells them. If the hen house is moved to the back field (which is more thicket than field), together with its occupants, then a separate track can be made which will bypass the house and garden, and any visitors can come and go without disturbing anyone.

'What about the hens?' Silas asks.

'Be fine. Leave them to me.'

'And how do we control the number of visitors?'

Blossom wheels out her trump card.

'Tickets.'

'*Tickets?*'

'S'right.'

'And do you imagine that we're all going to take it in turns selling tickets so that people can view our hen house? Do you think we've got the *time?*' Silas is becoming seriously angry.

'Church,' says Blossom. 'Church'll do it.'

'Oh, will they!'

'I've asked.'

'You had no right!'

'No harm in asking.' Blossom breathes on a glass she's drying and polishes it. 'He said yes.'

'Who said yes?'

'Father Vincent.'

'Oh, him.'

Blossom goes on to explain that Father Vincent is quite happy for the parish secretary to distribute tickets. Not for money, of course; that wouldn't be right. But it would limit numbers, and there would be strict visiting times.

'You've given this a lot of thought, haven't you?' Silas asks wearily.

'Yep.' Blossom polishes another glass, and holds it up to the light.

'Why, Blossom? Why are you doing this?'

'For Our Lady,' says Blossom piously.

Eric and Silas look at each other.

'I suppose we could look into it,' Eric says. 'Just look into it, mind. No promises.' Eric is currently preoccupied with the dietary habits of snakes, and is anxious to defuse the situation so that he can return to his researches. 'And of course, we'll have to speak to Father Vincent.'

'If — *if* we decided to go ahead with all this, how much would your Lazzo charge for his — relocation activities?' Silas asks.

'Wouldn't charge,' says Blossom.

'What, nothing at all?'

'S'right. Do it instead of penance.'

I know a bit about Catholics and their penances. With a bit of luck, Lazzo might even get time off purgatory, as well. If he's anything like his mother, he could probably do with it.

'We'll need to phone Father Vincent,' Silas says.

'You do that.' Blossom puts away the last of the crockery. 'Going to do the pigs.' She goes out of the back door, closing it quietly behind her.

'Goodness!' says Silas. 'If that's what Blossom's Virgin does for her, it's almost worth it.'

'Hmm. I want to know what Father Vincent has to say,' Eric tells him 'I have a feeling we haven't heard the whole story.'

After a lengthy telephone conversation, Eric informs us that we've been seriously misled.

'Reading between the lines, I suspect that Father Vincent agreed to Blossom's suggestion in order to get her off his back. It was late last night, and he says he'd "had a little drink or two". He did admit he'd said yes to something, but he can't remember what. Most unwise.'

'Did you explain?' Silas asks.

'Yes. To be honest, I don't think Father Vincent's too bothered about Blossom and her Virgin. I get the feeling he'd probably agree to anything. But apparently, he has a very accommodating secretary, and he says that she'd probably agree to give out tickets. Provided it doesn't take up too much of her time.'

Listening to this exchange, I build up a picture of an idle parish priest, fond of a tipple, and a poor overworked secretary, who'll probably be less than enthusiastic about all this. I may of course be wrong.

'What's happening?' Poor Mum, who is also listening, is looking more panic-stricken by the minute.

'Nothing. Yet.' Silas smiles at her. 'And certainly nothing for you to worry about.'

'People aren't going to worship this — this *thing*, are they?' she asks.

'Of course not,' says Eric, who I'm sure has no idea what they're going to do. 'And nothing's been decided yet, in any case.'

'I could help,' I say, after Mum's left the room, for I've been thinking. 'I could oversee things; make sure no-one steps out of line.'

'Oh, not you too, Ruth. I thought you of all people would understand!' says Silas.

'Of course I understand. It's just that I have a feeling you're going to give in anyway, so we might as well do the thing properly.'

'And that includes the church and tickets?'

'It could do. But not every day, of course. If we restrict visitors to certain times, then surely there's no harm in it. And if things don't work out, or people become a nuisance, we can always paint over it again.'

The truth is, despite the fact that I'm enjoying my new life, I still have time on my hands. I do my bit to help, and there's my weekly busking, but Blossom's Virgin offers new possibilities, and it would be something else to take my mind off the future.

'Are you prepared to do this? Because we certainly haven't got time.'

'Yes. It might be fun.'

'Don't let Blossom hear you say that.'

'I think Blossom will agree to anything, if you let her keep her Virgin.'

'I'm not sure I want Lazzo around the place,' says Eric. 'Can he be trusted?'

'I've no idea.' I know even less about Lazzo than my uncles do. 'But you could say you'd like to meet him first.'

'I suppose we could.'

Lazzo turns up later in the afternoon. He's not at all what I expected, for while he's not especially tall, he's built like an army truck, with a wide moon of a face, short thick legs and hands like shovels. Taken all together, his appearance would be terrifying if it were not for the mild, almost childlike expression in his eyes, which are so pale as to be almost colourless. It's hard to believe that Lazzo ever issued from the womb of anyone as tiny as Blossom, but this must have been the case (and of course, he was premature. Perhaps Blossom's body, as uncompromising as Blossom herself, expelled him as soon as he'd outstayed his welcome). On reflection, I'm grateful that I shall never have to meet Lazzo's father.

'Come to help,' says Lazzo, leaning his (Blossom's) bike against the wall. It would appear that he has inherited his mother's way with words.

We invite him indoors and ply him with tea (strong, four sugars) and biscuits (seven custard creams) after which we all repair to the hen house to see what would need to be done.

Lazzo inspects the hen house and its possible destination, strokes the hens (he must have his mother's way with animals, because the hens would normally run a mile rather than be stroked), and gives his stubbled chin a thoughtful rub.

'Okay,' he says.

'You'll — you would do it, then?' Silas asks him.

'No prob.'
'And the run?'
'Yeah.'
'You'll need help.'
'Do it on me own.'
'It's very heavy.'
'Take roof off. And nesting boxes. Be fine.'
'And you'll be careful? It's very old, and we're — fond of it.'
'Yeah.'
'If you're sure, then.'
'Sure. Do a path, too.' Lazzo gives us a surprisingly sweet smile.
'And what about pay?' Eric asks him.
'Nope. Mum says not.'
'Are you sure?'
'Yeah.'
'Do you always do what your mum says?' Silas is obviously as curious as I am.
'Better that way.' Lazzo laughs, and we join in. I'm beginning to warm to Lazzo. 'Start tomorrow?'

Eric and Silas exchange glances.

'Start tomorrow,' they agree.

It would seem that Lazzo has got the job, and Blossom has clocked up an important victory. The Virgin of the hen house is here to stay.

Chapter Eighteen

Blossom is in triumphant mode. She practically dances round the house with her duster, and even comes in on her days off. She also smiles.

Surprisingly, this is neither a pretty nor a welcome sight. Blossom smiling is not like other people smiling. There is none of the open friendliness one might expect from a normal person; none of the acknowledgement by one well-intentioned human being of the common humanity and good will of another. Blossom's smile has something sinister about it; a touch of the I-know-something-you-don't (or perhaps in this instance, I'm-up-to-something-you're-not-going-to-like).

'I wish Blossom would stop smiling,' my poor mother says. 'I don't like it.'

I know she feels threatened by Blossom and that her feelings are compounded by this new and terrifying smile, but there's not a lot we can do about it. We can hardly tell Blossom to stop. As for my uncles, they have other preoccupations than the newly-smiling Blossom. Eric has just arrived at the knotty problem of insects ('they're small, of course, but there are so *many* of them'), and Silas has found a dead whippet.

'I've phoned the police, and no-one knows anything about it,' he says wistfully. 'I'll never get another chance like this. I need to get started on it soon.'

'What did the police say?' I ask him.

'They said I'd better wait, but I can't. They don't understand. It's beginning to smell. And Eric won't let me to put it in the freezer.'

'Is it like when you find money?' I ask him.

'How do you mean?'

'If it's not claimed within a certain period, then you can keep it.'

'Probably, though I don't suppose they get many people wanting to keep other people's dead dogs.'

'The owners might be quite grateful,' I suggest. After all, a stuffed whippet has got to be better than a corpse. 'You could stuff it, and then if someone claims it, drive the car over it so that it looks run over again, and let them have it back. They mightn't notice the difference.'

'Do you think?' His face is so boyishly hopeful that I can't help laughing.

'Oh, why not?'

'I'll get started, then?'

'I would. No time like the present.'

Meanwhile, Lazzo is labouring away at the task of moving the hen house. He appears to be incredibly strong, and a very hard worker once he gets going. His triceps bulge and the veins in his neck stand out as he lifts huge sections of timber, and if glimpses of buttocks and an expanse of hairy stomach are less than attractive, then we can always look the other way. I trot to and fro with mugs of strong tea and doorsteps of bread and cheese (Lazzo's size is matched only by his enormous appetite) and Mr. Darcy watches adoringly from the sidelines. He brings Lazzo his ball and his old rubber bone, and the tattered bedsock he sleeps with at night, and even the treasured half-toothbrush. He lays them all at Lazzo's feet, then lies down in the long grass, his chin on his paws, following Lazzo's every move with soulful brown eyes. I'd give a lot to be adored the way Mr. Darcy adores Lazzo.

Blossom's attitude towards her son is to ignore him.

'Best left,' is her only comment, when I mention his presence.

'You must be proud of him,' I venture. 'He's an amazing worker.'

'Humph.' Blossom shrugs.

'Who does he work for normally?'

'Doesn't work.'

'Why not?'

'On benefit.'

'Why?'

'Special needs.' Blossom turns on the vacuum cleaner, her chosen way of terminating a conversation, and I am left to ponder the special needs of Lazzo.

If you discount tea and sandwiches, Lazzo's needs seem to be few, and certainly not particularly special. Is there something about Lazzo we ought to know, I wonder? Or is he — or more likely, his mother — pulling a fast one? And if so, how does Blossom reconcile that with her faith? The next time I bring Lazzo his tea, I scrutinise his face for clues, but can find none. I would have thought that someone like Lazzo would be eminently employable.

'Do you have — another job, Lazzo?' I ask him as he leans against a tree trunk drinking his tea.

'Nope.'

'Why not? You seem — very capable.'

'Not allowed.'

'Why not?'

'Born premature,' explains Lazzo, posting a fist-sized sandwich into his enormous mouth.

'But wasn't that rather a long time ago?' For few people must resemble a premature baby less than Lazzo does.

'Yeah.' Lazzo grins. 'But Mum says I've got special needs.'

'And have you?'

'Used to have fits,' he says, swallowing a huge piece of sandwich. I watch in fascination as it makes its journey down a neck so thick that it could be an extension of his head. It's a bit like watching a snake swallowing an antelope (I saw this once on a television programme).

'And do you still — have fits?' I know I'm being impertinent, but Lazzo intrigues me.

'Nah. Well, little ones.'

'What kind of fits?'

In reply, Lazzo rolls his eyes and slobbers a bit, shaking his massive frame like a tree in a gale. I try to stand my ground.

'Epileptic, then?' I suggest, after a moment. I have an epileptic friend who manages to hold down a very high-powered job with no apparent difficulty.

Lazzo nods, and loads his mouth up with another sandwich.

'Can't you have tablets?'

'Forget to take 'em.' As he speaks, I can see clumps of bread revolving in his mouth like cement in a mixer.

'What about your mother? Couldn't she remind you?'

'She'd be cross. Thinks I take 'em.'

'So what do you do with them?'

'Sell 'em.'

'*Sell* them?'

'Yeah. Got a mate gets high on my tablets.' Lazzo laughs. 'Do him more good than me.'

'And — the benefit people. Won't they catch up with you?'

'Haven't yet. Do a little fit for 'em when they come round. Soon gets rid of 'em. People don't like fits.'

'I can imagine.' If I were a benefit person, I'd soon make myself scarce if I had the misfortune to witness Lazzo doing his special needs act.

'So you just — stay at home?'

'S'right.'

'How do you get on with your mother?' I've been dying to ask him this.

Lazzo laughs. 'No-one gets on with Mum.'

So it's not just us, then. Well, I suppose that's something.

'That must be difficult. How do you manage?'

'Just take no notice.'

'And — Kaz?'

'She's all right. Never in, though. Pole dancer.'

'Really?' I've never met anyone who's related to a pole dancer. Though I'm not sure why Blossom disapproves of her daughter. After all, pole dancing is perfectly above board, isn't it?

'Good money,' Lazzo explains, picking his teeth with a piece of straw.

'I'll bet.'

Lazzo looks me up and down appraisingly. 'Should give it a go,' he suggests with a grin.

I make a mental note to try not to become over-familiar with Lazzo. He has a certain charm even though he may be a little odd, but no doubt he's equipped with the usual complement of hormones and urges, and if there were to be any sort of struggle (perish the thought) there's no doubt as to who would — literally — come out on top.

As though to drive the point home, half an hour after this conversation, the baby takes the opportunity to remind me of my responsibilities by delivering its first unmistakeable kick. I've been told to expect 'flutterings' or feelings I might mistake for indigestion, but this is a proper kick; faint, to be sure, but almost certainly delivered by a tiny foetal foot. It may be that there have been other movements, and in my state of semi-denial I have failed to notice them. I shall never know. Whatever may or may not have happened, I now have unequivocal proof that the baby is, quite literally, alive and kicking.

Chapter Nineteen

'I can go with her. I'd like to go with her. And she said after last time she didn't want us both again, so only one of us can go.'

'What about me? It was my idea.'

'But I know more about this sort of thing than you do. I promise I'll bring back a full report.'

'Anyone can bring back a full report. Ruth can do that.'

'True. But it makes sense for it to be me. I've read all the books, and I know what questions to ask.'

'Lend me the books, and I'll know what to ask, too. Anyway, the hospital staff are the people in the know. *We* don't have to know anything at all. And I'm sure they'll be delighted to explain.'

I listen in fascination as Eric and Silas argue over the lunch table as to which of them is to accompany me to my twenty-week scan. I've never heard them argue before, and while this is a relatively amicable discussion, there is an undertone of stiff-necked determination on both sides.

'May I say something?' I ask at last.

'Of course. Go ahead, Ruth,' Eric says.

'This is my scan, right?'

'Of course.'

'And I'm insured to drive the Land Rover now?'

'You know you are.'

'Then I can go to the scan on my own. And I can bring back — how did you put it? — *a full report* myself. That way, no-one needs to feel left out, and you can both stop this silly argument.'

Their faces fall into identical expressions of surprise and disappointment, and I can't help laughing.

'I'm sorry, Ruth,' Eric says, after a moment. 'I suppose we just forgot, well, forgot...'

'That I was here?'

'Something like that.'

'Well, it's a good thing I am here. And presumably I have the casting vote.'

'But it seems such a waste,' mourns Silas. 'It's so interesting, and you're allowed to take someone. I'll never get an opportunity like this again.' He makes it sound like a wasted theatre ticket.

'Yes. But I can hardly choose between the two of you, can I? So it's fairer to have neither of you. No-one will be pleased, but no-one will be disappointed.'

'We could toss up for it,' Silas suggests.

'I don't think so.'

'Ruth?' I'd forgotten my mother was there.

'Yes, Mum?'

'I'd love — I'd really love to come with you. If you'll let me.'

'Oh, Mum! Of course I'll let you. I'd love to have you with me. You're the obvious person. And we can go for lunch afterwards.'

Eric and Silas stand down gracefully (after all, they can hardly take issue with my mother accompanying me to the hospital), and after extracting promises of photos and answers to the list of questions Silas has compiled, they go out to do something unpleasant to a goat.

'Did they really both go with you to your last scan?' asks Mum over the washing-up.

'Yes. They were an absolute pain.'

'I'm sure they were. But Ruth — was it appropriate for them to, well to see you like that?'

'Like what?'

'With no clothes — *down there*.'

'It was a knickers-on affair; all perfectly dignified,' I assure her. '*Down there* was all covered up, and just the tummy showing. But in any case, I don't think I'd want them again, and certainly not both together. They were very sweet, but they wouldn't let me get a word in edgeways. And they did their double act in the waiting room and made an exhibition of all of us. I'm not going through that again.'

'They used to do that as little boys.'

'Well, it's probably all very sweet with little boys, but with elderly men, it's excruciating.'

'I can imagine.' Mum folds her tea towel and hangs it up. 'Ruth?'

'Yes?'

'I'm — I'm so glad I came. Not glad about leaving Dad, of course, but glad I'm here now, seeing you like this. Being — well, being with you.'

'I'm glad too.'

'But I'm worried about your father.'

'Why? He's okay, isn't he?'

'Up to a point.' She sighs, twisting her wedding ring round on her finger. 'But he's not used to looking after himself, and — well, it is my job. I know that's an unfashionable view, but it's all I've ever done since we married. Looked after the house and Dad, and you of course, when you were at home. Dad worked hard before he retired, and I saw it as my role to support him. I still do.'

'Did you enjoy it?'

'Enjoy what?'

'Being — well, a housewife, I suppose.'

'Yes. On the whole, I did. But that's another thing. I'd like to do something else as well; I'd like to be *good* at something else. Something different. Before it's too late. Does that sound odd?'

'Not odd at all. Isn't that what most of us want? To do something really well? That's certainly how I feel about my violin, and although I'll never be as good as I'd like to be, at least I've given it my best shot. What sort of thing would you like to do?'

'I don't know. I'm not creative, or musical, or anything like that, but there must be something I could do. Something new. Something *different*.' Mum sits down at the table, and rests her chin in her hand. 'I may have been quite a good wife, but I wasn't really a very good mother, was I?' she says after a moment.

'Well, you looked after me beautifully. I had a — good childhood,' I say carefully.

'But I never tried to understand you. I thought I did, but now, when I see you with Eric and Silas, so relaxed, so *easy* — I feel I must have got something wrong. And the violin.' She sighs, and pulls at a strand of her neatly permed hair. 'I knew it meant a lot to you, but I didn't understand why. When I hear you playing now, and see how much Eric and Silas enjoy it, and the encouragement they give you...' her voice tails away. 'I should have been the one to encourage you, even if I don't know much about music. It was as much a part of my job as looking after you. But I didn't know. I never really understood. And now I suppose it's too late.'

'I don't think it's ever too late in relationships,' I tell her. 'Provided both people want things to change. I don't think I'm really the daughter you wanted, am I? And it's not your fault I'm the way I am. Take the music. In some ways, I'd prefer not to want to be a musician. It leads to so much heartache and disappointment. Life would have been so much easier if I'd wanted to be — a chartered accountant, for instance. A nice safe profession, with far less scope for failure and a good income. And Dad would have been thrilled.'

'He would, wouldn't he?' We both laugh.

And of course, all this is true, provided that in the fullness of time Dad was able to walk me down the aisle in my white frock and hand me and my virginity over to a suitable young man (maybe another chartered accountant. Why not?), after which I would "settle down" and keep house for him and any offspring we might have. And the whole cycle would begin again. A little dull and predictable, but safe, and oh, so respectable.

'And I'm to blame, too,' I say now. 'Instead of ranting and slamming doors, I could have sat down with you and explained things properly. I could have tried to understand you, as well as the other way around.'

'You did get pretty angry,' Mum says. 'But we were the adults.'

'Well, now I'm an adult too, and we — well, you and I, anyway — can start to understand each other.'

'Don't make the same mistakes with — with your baby,' Mum says now. 'You've got the chance to make a better job of it than I did, and a clean slate, even though you've got no — there's no —'

'Father?'

'Yes.' She hesitates. 'Who was he, Ruth? What was he like?'

I recognise that she's been working up to this question, and I admire her courage, for it can't have been easy. Mum and I have never really confided in each other, and this is uncharted territory.

'Well, he's nice,' I begin lamely. 'A musician. A very good one. Much better than I'll ever be.'

'And — oh, Ruth, I really need to ask you this. Is he — is he married?'

I shake my head. 'He was, but his wife found someone else and he's now divorced.'

I note the little intake of breath at the D word, but Mum doesn't comment.

'Do you still see him?' she asks me.

'No. We've lost touch.'

'That's a shame.'

'Yes. Yes, it is. It's funny, really. We've never played a big part in each other's lives, and yet now I really miss him. I haven't even had the chance to tell him about the baby, and he ought at least to know that. Then it would be up to him what he did about it. If anything. And before you ask —' for I can see the question trembling on Mum's lips, almost begging to be let out — 'I might even marry him, if he'd have me. Not just because of the baby, but because he's a good man, we've lots in common, and I think we'd be good together. But we'd have to see about that.'

'He can't have just — disappeared.'

'That's what I thought. But it seems that he has. Disappearing is what he does. He'll probably turn up sooner or later, but we could be talking months or even years. I've tried to track him down, but I think he must be abroad.'

'Does he have a steady job?'

'I've no idea.' I laugh at Mum's expression. 'Musicians and steady jobs don't necessarily go together. As you and Dad kept telling me, it's risky business.'

And for the time being, we leave it at that. I realise afterwards that Mum and I have covered more ground in the last hour than we have in the past ten years, and I'm grateful to her for initiating the conversation. If it had been left to me, would we ever have talked like this? I doubt it. My mother has the courage that I lack, and I feel new respect for her. In many ways, she is a much better human being than I can ever hope to be, and while I disagree with many of her principles, she has certainly lived by them. It is to my shame that this could never be said of me.

The scan takes place the next day, and while the baby certainly appears to be more baby-like than it was last time, and Mum 'oohs' and 'aahs' over tiny fingers and toes, a waving arm, a 'dear little face' ('I believe it's got your nose, Ruth.' Has it? How on earth can she tell?), I still fail to experience any of the wonder and delight I'm supposed to feel.

'Aren't you at all excited, Ruth?' Mum whispers, when the technician disappears for a moment to fetch something. 'I'd no idea it would be as amazing as this. We never had this sort of thing when I was expecting you.' She seems to have forgotten the unfortunate provenance of her foetal grandchild in her wonderment at the combined miracles of nature and modern technology.

'Of course I'm excited,' I tell her (what else can I say?).

'Do you want to know the sex of your baby?' The technician has returned.

'No — yes — I don't know.'

'Silas does,' Mum reminds me.

'Well, it's not his baby,' I snap, and am instantly sorry. I give her hand a squeeze. 'Yes, okay. Why not?'

'A boy,' we're told. 'Were you hoping for a boy?'

'I — don't mind. But Blossom will be pleased.'

'What's Blossom got to do with it?' Mum asks.

'Blossom reckons she can always tell. She told me weeks ago that it was a boy.' It would have been nice to be able to confound Blossom, but now it seems that even that small victory is denied me.

We go through Silas's list of questions, and receive patient (and on the whole, satisfactory) answers. No, the baby doesn't appear to have any congenital defects or chromosomal abnormalities, although there are no absolute guarantees. Yes, it is the right size for its gestation, has all the right bits and pieces in the appropriate places and the degree of its activity is normal. It probably weighs about a pound (only a pound? That's less than half a bag of sugar. I try to imagine a pound of baby, and fail) and its various measurements are to scale.

As we emerge later on into pale autumn sunshine, I feel an overwhelming sense of loneliness, and suddenly I ache for the big, comforting presence of Amos; for the feeling of his arms around me, his clean man-smell, his comfortable chest, even the tickle of his beard against my cheek. I imagine him seeing in our baby all the things I don't yet seem able to see, and telling me what a clever girl I am (isn't that what new fathers are supposed to say?). We would walk hand-in-hand across the road to the pub for lunch, and he would have his usual pint of bitter (in a jug with a handle) and I would sip my tomato juice, and we'd get out our new photos of the baby, and admire them together. Best of all, we would be a *couple*; a couple sharing *our* baby.

Mum has been better company than I could have hoped for (or deserved), but it's Amos that I want with me now. I imagine his delight at the prospect of a son, his dreams of taking him to football matches (Amos loves football. Who will take the seahorse/rabbit to watch football if it hasn't got a father? Every child deserves at least one parent who understands the off-side rule), helping with maths homework, running in fathers' races on school sports days, and in the fullness of time, teaching it to drive. How will I manage to do all these things on my own? How do single parents *cope*?

'Are you all right, Ruth?' Mum asks me.

'Something in my eye,' I tell her, fumbling in my bag for a tissue.

Despite our new improved relationship, I'm still not ready to tell Mum how much I long to find Amos.

Chapter Twenty

It has taken Lazzo nearly a week to complete his labours with the hen house, and the project is almost finished. A large patch has been cleared in the back field, with a rough path leading to it from the main track, and the hens are comfortably installed in their new surroundings. The Virgin side of the hen house is exposed, with the rest — including the nesting boxes — fenced off by the run, so that the hens are spared the worshipful activities of their visitors. As Silas says, whatever the hens may or may not be, they are certainly not Roman Catholics. As it happens, they seem to have suffered very little from the upheaval, and I put this down to Lazzo. He has a quite extraordinary way with animals, reminding me of Dickon in *The Secret Garden*. Cows come up to him to be stroked; Sarah, who normally eschews any physical contact, allows him to tickle her tummy; the cats — usually so haughtily independent — fawn all over him; and poor Mr. Darcy is completely besotted.

'How do you do it?' I ask, as Lazzo and I sit together on a log contemplating his handiwork. Lazzo is holding a chicken on his lap, gently ruffling its feathers with a very dirty thumb, while Mr. Darcy lies adoringly at his feet.

Lazzo looks down at the chicken.

'Dunno,' he says.

'Have you always been good with animals?'

'S'pose. Had a hamster when I was five,' he offers, as though this is some kind of explanation.

'And?'

'Cat got it.'

'Oh.' I don't seem to be getting anywhere. 'Have you ever thought of working with animals?'

'Never thought of working.'

We both laugh. I have grown fond of Lazzo. Apart from his appraising glances and the occasional suggestive wink, he has been on the whole civil, sensible, and fun. He has a good sense of humour, and his company is undemanding. He appears to be perfectly self-sufficient, comfortable in his own skin, and content. While Blossom may have been a pretty awful mother, she must have got something right.

'What do you want to do? In the future?' I ask him. 'There must be something you'd really like to do.'

'London Zoo,' says Lazzo promptly.

'What, work there?'

'Just go.'

'Have you never been?'

'Never been to London.'

'Then I'll take you,' I promise him. 'One day, I'll take you to London Zoo.' I bend down to pull Mr. Darcy's ears. 'But what else? You must have some kind of — ambition?'

'Nope.'

'Would you like to — get married?' I venture, realising that this is possibly a tactless question.

'Mum says no-one'd have me.'

'She can't be sure.' I feel a surge of indignation on Lazzo's behalf. How dare Blossom pass judgement in this way? How can she possibly know?

'Says I'm too lazy. Got a point.' Lazzo grins, and pats my shoulder. 'Fine as I am.'

And he's probably right. It's so easy to attribute to other people one's own hopes and aspirations; to decide that they can't be happy because their lot isn't what one would want for oneself. In a way, I envy Lazzo. He appears to have everything he wants, plus his childlike ability to live in the present. A doorstep of bread and cheese, a can of beer, a sunny day, the rough lick of a cat's tongue on his hand — Lazzo appears to get his pleasures from simple things. I can't imagine him agonising over past mistakes or future plans; wanting things he can't have or worrying about what people think of him. Lazzo is what he is, take it or leave it. One could learn a lot from Lazzo.

Now that the business of relocation has been dealt with, the small matter of the Virgin has to be addressed, together with the imminent advent of her admirers. But when I mention the subject to Blossom, it would seem that everything's in hand.

'All sorted,' she tells me, her beady eyes challenging me to interfere with her plans.

'What about the tickets?' I ask her. 'You said it would be a tickets-only affair.'

'Done,' says Blossom.

'What do you mean, done?'

'Church.'

Blossom's minimalist means of communication can be absolutely maddening. Sometimes I want to take her by her shoulders and shake the syllables out of her until there are enough of them to constitute a proper sentence.

'What about the church?'

'All in hand.' Blossom reaches for the switch on the vacuum cleaner, but I turn it off at the wall.

'Blossom, we need to know. We need to know who's coming, when they're coming, and how many. You can't just make all the decisions off your own bat.'

Eric and Silas are out, and Mum is washing her hair. Blossom and I are on our own.

After a lot of cajoling I manage to acquire a few basic facts. A small committee from the Catholic church has apparently visited the hen house (how come we didn't notice? It's not as though small committees are a normal part of the landscape) and have given their seal of approval. Someone has volunteered to print tickets on their computer, and Father Vincent has given his blessing (I'll bet he has. I suspect Father Vincent will do anything for a quiet life). Visitors will be admitted on two afternoons a week. A large notice has been made for the gate (we now have a separate path leading to the hen house), giving the days and times when the Virgin is receiving visitors, and Father Vincent is donating a padlock out of the church petty cash.

'You could at least have checked with Eric and Silas,' I tell her.

'Did. Weren't listening,' Blossom tells me. 'Eric on the phone; Silas stuffing something. Often don't listen,' she adds. 'Not my fault.'

I know very well whose fault it is. Blossom has a habit of raising awkward subjects when she knows they are least likely to be heard, and then interpreting silence as agreement. Whatever may be said about Blossom, she's not stupid.

'Oh, well. I suppose that's okay,' I concede. 'Two afternoons should be manageable. How will people know about it?'

'Parish magazine. Told them start next week.'

It would appear that Blossom has thought of everything.

When Eric and Silas return, they agree that we should be able to accommodate visitors on two afternoons a week, although, as I suspected, they were unaware that they had already agreed to the arrangement.

'So long as you take charge, Ruth. You said you would,' Silas reminds me.

'If Blossom lets me, I'm happy to be in charge.'

'She'll have to do as she's told,' Eric says.

'Blossom,' I remind him, 'never does what she's told.'

'Well the two of you will have to work things out together. Silas and I haven't the time.'

Working with Blossom proves to be easier than I had anticipated, largely I suspect because she is so keen for the project to work and knows that as Eric's and Silas's representative, I have the power of veto. After the first week, Eric and Silas agree that the project has given rise to very little trouble. Visitors arrive at the appointed times, bearing their tickets, and on the whole they behave nicely. They come in twos and threes, reverent and respectful, murmuring in low voices, sometimes praying, and Blossom, Lazzo and I take it in turns to oversee things.

The Virgin herself looks if anything more lifelike than she did before she was moved. Her outline is sharp and well-defined, her robe flowing, the stars — and they really do look like stars — form a halo round her head. I find myself wondering whether Blossom might have touched her up a bit when we weren't looking, but everything is true to the original grain of the wood. Even Blossom can't interfere with nature. Blossom herself maintains a small vase of flowers beneath the apparition, and while these are regularly consumed by Sarah and her brood, they add to the hen house a touch of the roadside shrine which reminds me of a long-ago Austrian holiday.

Do I believe in the Virgin of the hen house? Once I would have said categorically that I did not, but now, I'm not so sure. I've never been the kind of person who looks for (or wants) signs or miracles, but I have to admit that this is, if not miraculous, then certainly a rare kind of curiosity. Mum watches me anxiously, and I know she harbours a secret fear that I shall "go over to Rome" (I heard her confiding as much to Silas), but I certainly have no intention of doing that. Not for me the trips to the confessional, the collection of indulgences and the weekly attendance at Mass; I had far too much religion when I was a child to be tempted back into any kind of church. But I have a growing respect for our pilgrims; for their apparently unquestioning faith and their readiness to accept proof of the existence of God, while having no actual need of any such proof. And I envy them. It must be wonderful to be able to place oneself in the hands of a deity, and trust that everything will be taken care of.

Eric and Silas take little interest in the Virgin. Now that they know that their chickens are safe and that Blossom is being kept sweet, they apparently feel they can get on with their lives. Silas is still working on his whippet ('I think it's my best yet, Ruth. I do hope no-one wants it back.' Since it no longer bears any resemblance whatever to a dog, never mind a whippet, I think he can rest assured that this is unlikely to happen). And Eric's researches are becoming increasingly complicated.

'Take the bettong,' he says at breakfast.

'What's a bettong?' Mum asks.

'A small Australian marsupial.'

'How interesting.' Mum reaches for the marmalade.

'And the possum,' Eric continues. 'And the wallaby, and of course the kangaroo. And all the other marsupials. I'd no idea there were so many of them. Would Noah have taken two of all of them, do you suppose?'

'You don't believe in Noah,' I remind him.

'That's not the point, Ruth.'

'No. Of course not. Sorry.' I have a vivid mental image of kangaroos (and bettongs) leaping over the side of the ark into the boiling waves. 'Can kangaroos swim?'

'Why?' Eric looks at me suspiciously.

'It doesn't matter. No. I'm sure Noah would have taken just two kinds of marsupials. A big one and a small one.'

'Ah.' Eric looks relieved. 'It's just that all the working out takes *so much time*. I've given up with all the insects. I'm keeping those to a minimum. Not that they take up much room, but there are literally millions of them.'

'I know.' I have the flea bites (courtesy of the cats) to prove it.

'Sad about the marsupials, though. I liked the sound of the bettong.'

'Something would probably have eaten it.'

'Ruth, I wish you wouldn't persist in treating this whole thing as a joke.'

Mum excuses herself and gets up from the table. Ark conversations always make her uncomfortable.

'And bees,' Eric continues (he loves it when we pay attention to his research).

'What about them?'

'Big problem, bees. Did you know that without bees, life on earth would die out in two years?'

'Then you'd better take more than two.'

Eric looks at me in exasperation.

'Of course there'd have to be more than two. But how would they survive, without flowers?'

'Don't they hibernate in the winter?'

'Yes. But the flood didn't subside until the 'tenth day of the tenth month'. It would be difficult to persuade a hive — or even several hives — of bees to sleep for ten months.'

'Pot plants? You could take lots of pot plants.'

'Now you really are being silly.'

'Yes. I doubt whether the Noah family would have the time to look after pot plants as well as everything else.' I myself have never managed to keep even one pot plant alive, and I don't have an Ark full of animals to take care of. 'So without the bees, the whole thing falls apart?' I ask him.

'You're missing the point, Ruth. What I'm trying to do is not so much prove that Noah *didn't* build his Ark, as showing exactly how big and how much of everything there would have to be, and therefore he *couldn't* have done it. I'm designing an Ark which could take everything, but showing that it would have to be far too big to be remotely possible. So we have to have bees, even if it means an even bigger Ark.'

'Bigger than the Isle of Wight?'

'Quite possibly.'

'Ah.' I start clearing away the breakfast things. 'I think I ought to get going,' I tell him. 'And it seems clear that you've got a few more calculations to do.'

Chapter Twenty-One

Meanwhile, Mum is still fretting about Dad.

'How does he seem when you speak to him?' I ask her.

'Not too bad. But he keeps asking me when I'm coming home. He doesn't seem to understand that I can't. Not yet, anyway.'

'And you've told him that?'

'Yes.' She hesitates. 'Ruth?'

'Mm?'

'Would you do me a favour?'

'Of course.'

'Would *you* go and see him? Just to make sure he's looking after himself?'

'Mum, of course he's looking after himself. The reason he's usually no good in the house is that you do everything for him. He's perfectly capable if he's got no-one else to wait on him. Why don't you go and see for yourself? You don't have to stay.' But even as I speak, I know that my mother can't do as I suggest. I know as well as she does that if she goes back, she'll stay there. My father has such a hold over her that she would never be able to, as it were, leave him twice. It's a miracle that she's managed to do it at all.

'Okay,' I tell her. 'I'll go. Just this once, mind.' I'm still smarting from Dad's treatment of me. 'I'm not making a habit of it.'

'Thank you. And I won't ask you again, I promise.'

I set off the following morning in Mum's car, feeling like Little Red Riding Hood, with my basket of eggs and cream (courtesy of Eric and Silas) and a casserole and a cake from Mum. Silas is desperate for me to take his whippet ('see if he thinks it's real, Ruth. I haven't tried it on anyone new') but whatever I feel about Dad, I wouldn't go so far as to subject him to that.

There are long delays on the motorway and a diversion, and the journey takes me twice as long as it normally would. When I arrive at my parents' house, I am not in the best of humours.

Neither is my father.

'Your mother said you'd be here in time for lunch,' he says, without preamble, as he whisks me through the front door (presumably so that prying neighbours are spared a glimpse of my shameful new shape). 'Lunch is at one o'clock in this house, as you well know.' There seems to be a lot of smoke, and a strong smell of burning. The smoke alarm is ringing merrily in the background.

'Sorry. The roads were horrendous.' I wipe my feet carefully on the doormat and make as though to kiss him, but he backs away as though fearing an attack, covertly eyeing my bump.

'Well, the lunch is ruined now.' He leads the way into the kitchen, and I resist the temptation to tell him that a delayed meal doesn't have to be a burnt one.

The kitchen table is laid for two, and on the side is a baking tray containing four sad little black smoking bundles.

'What is — was it?' I ask.

'Sausages.'

'Anything else?'

'Mashed potato.' He lifts the lid off a saucepan, revealing a grey viscous mass which could once have been potato. I also notice a recipe book opened at "Braised Sausages with Onion Gravy". I decide that it would be pushing my luck to enquire about the gravy.

'We could go to the pub?' I suggest. 'My treat.'

Dad looks shocked.

'You know my feelings about pubs, Ruth,' he says. 'Anyway, this food is perfectly edible. Waste not, want not.' (This is one of his favourite mantras.)

'We wouldn't have to waste it. I could take it back with me for the pigs. They'd love it.'

This is not the right thing to say, and I am given a short lecture on my lack of gratitude and my shortcomings as a guest.

It is one of those meals where you have to concentrate all your energies on forcing the food down while trying hard to think of something else. As I swallow crunchy morsels of sausage (my father has contrived to burn them so thoroughly that there is barely any sausage at all remaining inside the crisp carbon shell) I try to imagine that they are pork scratchings, potato crisps, peanut brittle — anything crisp and delicious. Anything but burnt sausage. There is no alcohol to anaesthetise the taste buds, and the potato is if anything worse than the sausages. Mercifully, there is ketchup, and I smother my food with that.

'I thought you didn't like ketchup.' Dad says.

'Craving,' I explain, patting my bump. 'With some, it's coal. With me, it's ketchup.' In a way it's a pity I don't crave coal, since burnt sausages might well be the next best thing.

'No pudding, I'm afraid,' Dad says, when we've finished. 'I'm not much good at that sort of thing. But I've got some fruit.' He produces a bowl with three freckled bananas and a rather tired bunch of grapes. There's a fly sitting on the grapes (will there be flies on Eric's Ark?). Dad shoos it away.

'No thanks. I'm fine.'

'Coffee, then?'

'Coffee would be great.'

As Dad fusses over cups and percolator, we make small talk: Dad's allotment, the people at church, the weather.

'And — your mother?' he asks eventually. 'How's she?'

'Fine, She's fine.'

'She should be here, you know. With me. That's where she should be.'

'Do you miss her?'

'Miss her?' Dad looks puzzled. 'Well, yes. Of course I do. But it's more than that. People — talk.'

Ah yes. How could I forget? People talk.

'I expect they'll get over it.'

'First — you, and now your mother,' Dad continues, as though Mum and I have been playing a game of tug-of-war with his reputation. 'It's very difficult.'

'It's been difficult for all of us,' I say evenly.

'Has it? Has it really? You and your mother seem to be having a wonderful time cavorting about in the country.'

'Actually, we're working very hard.'

'So you've got her working, have you? Looking after all of you? I bet you have. I should think Eric and Silas are delighted to have your mother running around after them.'

'She's not running around after anyone. She's just doing her bit.' I spoon sugar into my coffee. 'We both are.'

'So when's she coming back?'

'You'll have to ask her that.'

'Well, I'm asking you.'

'Dad, I don't know when she's coming back. Mum's a grown woman. She makes her own decisions.'

'But she sent you here, didn't she?'

'She wanted to make sure you were okay.'

'And what will you tell her?'

'That you seem to be coping pretty well.'

For I have a feeling that all is not as it seems. When I went to fetch milk from the fridge, I noticed half a shepherd's pie neatly covered with cling film, a whole cooked chicken and what looked like a compote of dried fruit (so much for there being no pudding). Either Dad is a better cook than he lets on, in which case the burnt sausages were some kind of ruse, or he's being fed by someone else.

'You had a visitor,' Dad says now.

'A visitor? When?'

'It must have been a couple of weeks ago. A man came looking for you.'

'What sort of man?'

'Big bearded chap. Looked a bit like a tramp. He said he was a friend of yours.' Dad pours more coffee. 'Carrying some kind of instrument. A trumpet or something.'

'A trombone?'

'Could be. It was in a case.'

Amos! Dad has found Amos! Or rather, Amos has found Dad. I don't have any other big bearded friends, and Amos never goes anywhere without his trombone. I remember that I once gave him my parents' address, and he's obviously kept it.

'Oh Dad, that's wonderful! What did he say? What did you tell him?' I can hardly contain my excitement. 'How did he seem? Was he well?'

'I've no idea. I didn't ask him. He appeared to be well enough. He was only here for a few minutes. Seemed to think you were abroad — a gap year, I think he said — and asked if we'd heard from you.'

'You told him where I was, of course?'

'I did no such thing. Chap looked most unsuitable.'

'Someone came looking for me, *and you didn't tell him where I was?*'

'No. I just told him you'd gone away.'

'So he could still think I'm abroad?'

'Quite possibly.'

'Dad, you had no right! You had no right to send him away without telling me!'

'It's not my responsibility to put you in touch with strangers who turn up on our doorstep. He could have been anyone.'

I am so angry, I'm shaking. How could he? How could Dad have taken it upon himself to send Amos away like this?

'You might at least have phoned me to let me know, then I could have decided what I wanted to do. Have you any idea what you've done?'

'The responsible thing, I should hope.'

'You've sent away the father of my child. That's what you've done. I've been looking for him for weeks, and you've sent him away without even telling me!'

'Well, I'm telling you now.'

'But it's *too late*! How am I supposed to find him now? Did he leave an address?'

'He said something about going abroad. Yes, I'm sure that was what it was. He said he was going on a cruise. It's all right for some,' he adds sourly, which is rich coming from Dad, who doesn't approve of holidays, and certainly wouldn't dream of going on a cruise himself. 'Going on a cruise, when he has — responsibilities.'

'He won't be *going* on a cruise. He'll be *working* on a cruise. He's a musician. He has a living to earn. As for the responsibilities, he can hardly be accused of neglecting them if he doesn't know anything about them, can he?'

'You mean — you mean he doesn't know about — about your condition?'

'That's exactly what I mean. And now he may never know, thanks to you.'

'If you go around behaving like an alley cat, then you have only yourself to blame,' Dad tells me. 'Don't you start blaming me.'

'*How dare you!*'

'The truth hurts, doesn't it?'

'I can't believe you're saying this! And you call yourself a Christian!'

'It's *because* I'm a Christian —'

'*No*. No, Dad. You're not a Christian. Christianity is about love and forgiveness and tolerance, and —'

'If you're such an expert, how did you manage to get yourself into this mess, Ruth? You tell me that.'

'*This is not a mess!*' I yell at him. '*It's a baby!* My baby. And it's your grandchild too. Like it or not. Nothing I say or do can change that. And if I'm trying to do the right thing by finding Amos and making some kind of life with him, then you should be with me, not against me.'

'I think you should go, Ruth. Before you say something you regret.' Dad gets up from his chair, and prepares to see me out. He is calm and unruffled, glowing with churchy self-righteousness, and at this moment, I really hate him. I can't believe that a couple of hours ago I actually felt sorry for this lonely man and his burnt sausages; that I was touched by the promise (albeit unfulfilled) of onion gravy. Now, I can't wait to be on my way.

'Don't bother to see me out,' I tell him. 'I know the way.'

'That's all right, then.' He gives me the pitying look of one who is looking down on a sinner from the cosy perspective of the moral high ground. 'Give my regards to your mother.'

'You can give her your — *regards* — yourself.' Regards? After forty years of marriage? No wonder poor Mum's had enough. 'And it might just help if you were to do the phoning from time to time, instead of leaving it all to her. *If you want her back.*'

As a parting shot this is unworthy of me, and I experience a brief moment of shame. After all, Dad is on his own; he has no-one to complain to or take his side, for he's got far too much pride to confide in anyone outside the family. On the other hand, he's scuppered what I currently see as my one chance of happiness, for as far as Amos is concerned, I too could be anywhere. We could chase one another round the world until kingdom come, and never find each other. And since Amos was merely trying to look me up, probably on the off chance, and is unaware of the urgency of the situation, from now on, any real effort is going to have to come from me. By now, he has probably forgotten all about me, and is happily bobbing about on the ocean waves playing smoochy dance music to rich, over-fed tourists.

On my return journey, a lorry driver winks at me as we stop alongside each other at traffic lights. He has a beard and a kindly face, and his big, capable-looking hands rest lightly on the steering wheel. He reminds me of Amos.

I cry all the rest of the way back to Applegarth.

Chapter Twenty-Two

When I arrive back, tired and disillusioned (I had set out willing to bury hatchets and offer at least one small olive branch), Mum is naturally anxious to know how things went.

I am closely questioned as to the cleanliness of the house (not bad at all), the welfare of my father (ditto) and whether he is eating properly. I answer to the best of my ability, while trying to keep my tone positive.

'I'm not sure about his cooking skills,' I tell her, 'but he's certainly getting food from somewhere.'

'You make him sound like a stray cat.'

'Same kind of thing.' I am entertained by the idea of Dad eating saucers of scraps left out on people's doorsteps.

'Really, Ruth!'

'Sorry. But he's missing you, and sends his love.'

'Are you sure? Are you sure that's what he said?'

'Certain.' After all, I can hardly pass on the chilly "regards" Dad wanted me to relay, and my little lie is unlikely to be discovered.

Mum looks pleased.

'Perhaps he's coming round after all.'

'Well, you were the one who left,' I remind her.

'Yes. But I meant coming round to the idea of you. And the baby.'

'Well, I suppose he might be. But I wouldn't count on it. Not yet, anyway.' It would be unkind to raise her hopes. 'You know Dad and his principles. It takes a lot to make him change his mind.'

Mum sighs. 'Well, I suppose there's no hurry. Provided Eric and Silas don't mind putting up with me.'

'You know they love having you,' I tell her. 'So do I,' I add, and find to my surprise that it's true. It's been good having Mum around, and while we're not yet exactly confidantes, we're becoming increasingly comfortable with each other.

The following afternoon is a hen house afternoon, but there is no sign of Lazzo, whose turn it is to do hen house duty. Eric and Silas are out seeing a man about a pig and I was hoping to have a few uninterrupted hours of violin practice (Mum, needless to say, is having nothing to do with Virgins or hen houses). It is a warm for late October, and I am sitting in the garden rehearsing all the things I'd like to say to Dad (I'm still smarting from the Amos incident), when the phone rings. I run indoors to answer it. It is Blossom.

Blossom on the telephone is something else. At least when you have her face to face, you can fill in some of the gaps by trying to interpret her expression, but listening to her disembodied voice is like trying to unscramble a foreign language.

'Laz fitting,' she says, without preamble.

'*What?*'

'Our Laz. Fitting.'

'Fitting? Fitting what?' Carpets? Soft furnishings? What is Blossom talking about?

'*Fitting.* Like he does. You know.'

'Oh. You mean Lazzo's having fits?'

'What I said, isn't it?'

'Is he okay?'

'Course.' Pause. 'Won't be coming in.'

'Can you come then, Blossom? We've got a lot on.'

'Can't. Busy.'

'Oh dear.'

'Kaz coming instead.'

'That's kind of her.'

'Not kind. Told her to.'

'Oh. Right.' I spare a thought for Kaz. Supervising pilgrimages is hardly compatible with Kaz's professional calling and I open my mouth to say something appreciative, but Blossom has already rung off.

Fifteen minutes later, Kaz arrives.

I'm not quite sure what I was expecting, but whatever it might have been, Kaz isn't it. She is amazingly like Blossom, and yet totally different, for while following her mother's template, Kaz manages to be beautiful. It is as though someone had taken Blossom and airbrushed out her age and her imperfections, to make, literally, a new woman of her. The eyes which appear black and beady in Blossom, are dark and luminous in Kaz. Blossom's small bony body becomes toned and celebrity slim in Kaz, and Blossom's sharp features and pointed chin give an elfin, Peter Pan look to her daughter.

That Kaz contrives to be beautiful is all the more astonishing since she appears to have gone out of her way to deface the gifts with which nature has endowed her. Her dyed-blonde hair is scraped back in an untidy ponytail, and a variety of studs and rings pierce her eyebrows, ears and lips, while two tiny snakes are tattooed around her wrists. All this is set off with knee-length laced leather boots, a skimpy top and a faded denim skirt which just about covers her bottom. The effect is electric.

'Sorry I'm late,' Kaz says, giving me a radiant smile. 'Bloody bike had a puncture. Laz was supposed to fix it, but he forgot. He's a lazy bugger.'

'Oh, that's okay,' I say weakly, trying to imagine how anyone can ride a bike in a skirt that short.

'I'm Kaz,' she says, unnecessarily.

'Hi. Good to meet you.'

'You must be Ruth.'

'Yes. Yes, I am.'

'Expecting, I see,' remarks Kaz, patting my bump. 'I was expecting once,' she adds.

'Oh. What hap— I mean, what did you do?'

'The usual.' Kaz sighs. 'I couldn't keep it. I hadn't any money. Besides, Mum said she'd kill me if I had a baby. I was only fourteen.'

'I thought Catholics were against abortion?'

'They're against murder, too, but that wouldn't have stopped Mum from killing me. She's what you might call a pick and choose Catholic. And she didn't pick my baby.'

'How did you feel about that?'

'A bit sad, I suppose, but I was only a kid. And in our house, we do what our mum says. It makes life easier.'

'I can imagine.'

Kaz grins. 'You don't like Mum much, do you?'

'Well ... she's very good with the animals.'

'Don't worry. I don't like her much, either.'

'Then why do you live at home?'

'I guess I'm too lazy to move out.'

We both laugh. I'm warming to Kaz. She's bright and funny, and unlike her mother and brother, she actually speaks in whole sentences.

'Did she tell you about my work?' Kaz asks.

'Lazzo did mention something about it.'

'Well, for the record, I'm not what you probably think. Mum thinks pole dancing is the same as lap dancing.'

'Isn't it?' I know nothing about either.

'Not at all. We don't touch the clients, and they're not allowed to touch us. Sex is strictly off limits. But I'm in demand, and I get good tips.'

'I'll bet you do.' I would imagine that most men would give a great deal to spend an evening watching Kaz. 'How — I mean, what do you actually do?'

Kaz slips off her shoes, and grasping the edge of the door, shimmies effortlessly up and down it.

'Bit like that, but with a pole,' she says. 'It doesn't really work with a door.'

'Goodness!' I'm impressed.

'What's your feller do?' Kaz asks, picking a splinter out of her hand.

'I don't really have a — feller,' I tell her.

'You must have once.'

'He's — disappeared.'

'Buggered off, has he? Typical.' Kaz fumbles in the top of her boot and brings out a packet of cigarettes. 'Mind if I smoke?'

'Go ahead. No, he didn't bugger off exactly. We just — lost touch.'

And I find myself telling Kaz all about Amos. She's a surprisingly good listener, and it's a luxury for me to have someone to confide in. Eric and Silas are very sweet, and Mum does her best, but Kaz is nearer my own age, and has no personal involvement in either me or my baby.

'Tricky,' she says, when I've finished.

'Yes.'

'And you really want the baby?'

'I've thought about it a lot, and while I'm certainly not desperate for a baby, I don't *not* want it.'

'And you don't fancy being a single mum.'

'Not really.'

'Me neither,' says Kaz with feeling. 'But then I don't really fancy being a mum of any kind. Not after seeing the mess Mum made of me and Laz.'

Actually, I think Blossom's children have turned out remarkably well, but maybe they have arrived where they are through their own merits rather than because of anything their mother did.

'Ok. Let's get to work.' Kaz stubs out her cigarette on the heel of her boot. 'Where's this hen house of yours?'

In the course of the afternoon, eleven people come to pay their respects to the Virgin.

'All barmy,' says Kaz, when the last of them have said their farewells and driven off into the dusk. 'Quite barmy.'

'You don't believe in any of this, then?' I ask her.

'Good lord, no. Do you?'

'Well, I'm not a Catholic.'

'And you think I am?'

'I suppose I assumed you must be a Catholic of sorts.'

'According to Mum, I'm beyond the pale. No pearly gates for me,' says Kaz cheerfully.

'Is that what *you* think?'

'I don't know.' Kaz lights up another cigarette. 'I think I believe in God, or something like God. But not this miracle stuff.'

'But you must admit it looks very convincing.'

'Not bad,' Kaz says. 'But it would have to be all-singing all-dancing and glorious technicolour to convince me.'

We walk back towards the house together.

'Cup of tea?' I ask her, as we arrive in the kitchen.

'Got anything stronger?'

'We've got nettle wine or —' I examine a smudged label — 'parsnip brandy.' These are the only bottles which are open. I hesitate to broach a new one, even for Kaz.

'Blimey.' Kaz looks impressed. 'Let's have a go at the parsnip stuff, shall we?'

'Why not?' I know I shouldn't be drinking, but surely one little glass won't hurt the baby?

The parsnip brandy nearly takes the skin off the back of my throat, and even Kaz has a brief choking fit.

'Wow!' she says, when she can speak again. 'Where did that come from?'

'I think Eric made it. He likes experimenting.'

'It's the kind of drink,' Kaz says, after a few minutes, 'where you have to have more in order to appreciate it.'

'I see what you mean,' I say, as the kitchen revolves slowly round us (I'm not used to alcohol). 'You sort of get used to it, don't you?'

'Certainly do. Bloody, hell! What's that?' Kaz has caught sight of the whippet.

'It's a stuffed whippet,' I tell her.

'Get away! What is it really?'

'It really is a stuffed whippet.'

'A stuffed whippet! Now I really have seen everything.' Kaz begins to laugh. 'A stuffed whippet!'

Kaz's laughter is so infectious that I begin to laugh too. Within a few minutes, we're both helpless.

'Stuffed Whippet ... whipped stuffit ...' By now, Kaz is crying with laughter. 'Oh my goodness!'

It is at this moment that my mother decides to put in an appearance.

'What on earth's going on?' she asks.

'Stiff whuppet,' Kaz explains.

'*What?*'

'Dog thingy.' Kaz waves a hand in the direction of the unfortunate whippet, and collapses in another fit of giggles.

'This is Kaz,' I say trying to affect an introduction through my tears. 'We've — we've had a little drink.'

'So I see.' Mum is not amused. 'And what about the baby?'

'He's had a little drink too,' says Kaz.

For a briefly sober moment, I realise that I may have made a mistake.

'I'm surprised at you, Ruth,' Mum continues. 'Look at the state of you!'

'My fault,' says Kaz cheerily. 'It was my idea.'

'But Ruth's a responsible adult. She's perfectly capable of deciding for herself.'

There is something about a completely sober person trying to be sensible when it is far too late for sense that is totally irresistible. Kaz and I howl with laughter.

'Really, Ruth! You're drunk!' says Mum.

'Lighten up, mate. It's not the end of the world.' Kaz offers her glass to Mum. 'Here. Have a little drink. Do you good.'

'I am not your mate, I don't drink, and I think it's time you were going.'

Oh dear.

'Can't ride a bike like this,' says Kaz. 'Fall off,' she explains.

'You came on a bike?'

'They all come on the bike,' I tell her.

'Not all together,' Kaz says. 'It's the family bicycle.'

Fortunately, at this point Eric and Silas return. They seem to know Kaz, and are quite unfazed by what's going on.

'I see you've been trying the parsnip brandy,' Eric says. 'What did you think of it?'

'Excellent,' says Kaz. 'Very — very tasty.'

Eric looks pleased.

'Yes. I thought it was rather good. Silas hates it. Have you tried it, Rosie?'

'No, I certainly have not.'

'Well, never mind.' He turns to Kaz. 'I'd better run you home, Kaz. The bike can go in the back of the Land Rover.'

After Kaz has gone and I have sobered up a bit (giggling isn't the same on your own), Mum asks me about Kaz.

'She's Blossom's daughter,' I explain.

'Ah.'

'What do you mean, *ah*?'

'Well that explains it, doesn't it?'

'Explains what?'

'Her behaviour.'

'Mum, Kaz is nothing like Blossom. She is nice and intelligent and kind, and she's *young*.'

'What's that supposed to mean?'

'I spend all my time here with you and Eric and Silas. And that's fine. But sometimes it's nice to talk to someone my own age.'

'She's hardly your age, Ruth.'

'Well, someone nearer my age, at any rate. My friends are all over the place, and I hardly ever get to see them. Sometimes it's nice just to let go and — be silly.'

'Well, you certainly managed that.' Mum is still in shrewish mode. 'What does she do, anyway? For a living?'

'She's a pole dancer,' I tell her.

'But that's disgusting!'

'That's what Blossom thinks, but pole dancing is perfectly respectable.' I try to remember what Kaz told me. 'They never touch the customers, and the customers aren't allowed to touch them. It's a bit like — like the ballet, really.'

'That's not what I've heard,' says Mum, who having made up her mind about Kaz seems reluctant to change it. 'I just hope she's not trying to persuade you to do anything like that.'

I think I'll stick to my busking. I know my limitations.

Chapter Twenty-Three

November is heralded by the typical cold dank conditions I always associate with this most unpleasant of months. Gone are most of the colours and the fruits of the autumn, and we tramp to and fro over ground thick with a mush of mud and fallen leaves. Most of the chickens have stopped laying, one of the goats has lost her kid ('wrong time of year,' said Silas glumly), and despite our best efforts, such vegetables as have survived are rotting faster than we can gather them in the damp conditions. I have had to give up my busking as I find standing around in the cold so tiring, and while I know it was the right decision, I resent having had to make it for reasons beyond my control.

I have always hated November, not least because I loathe fireworks. When I was about five, I was invited to a fireworks party, where a nasty little boy chased me all over his garden with bangers. That, coupled with the horrifying image of someone who looked very much like his father being incinerated on the huge bonfire, instilled in me a terror I remember to this day. I managed to unfasten the gate and run home, crossing two roads on the way, and was eventually discovered hiding in the tool shed, weeping with terror. I had nightmares for weeks afterwards. To this day, I cannot see the point of fireworks. If I want to look at something pretty, I can find it in flowers and scenery and art. If I want surprises, life provides plenty of those without any need for the artificial kind. And I do not enjoy sudden loud noises.

Neither do Eric and Silas's animals.

You would think that out here in the country, November 5th would pass virtually unnoticed. Not so. There are a couple of houses not far away, both with children, and both apparently hell-bent on commemorating Guy Fawkes and his nefarious activities. Fortunately, Eric and Silas have managed to persuade them to restrict their celebrations to the night in question (in recent years Guy Fawkes, like Christmas, has tended to spread itself over several days), so that some precautions can be taken. But with the best will in the world it's impossible to persuade a cow that unexpected bangs and bumps and showers of coloured stars aren't cause for consternation. While the neighbouring households are no doubt oohing and aahing as they fire their rockets and burn their effigies and eat their hot dogs, for us it's all hands to the pump, trying to offer consolation to the livestock.

We have locked up such animals as we can, but I suspect that for some, this merely compounds their misery. Inside the house, Mr. Darcy is beside himself with terror, the cats are hiding in Mum's bed, and Sarah, that most independent of animals, has managed to escape from her shed and get into the house, where she has taken refuge in the larder, her anxiety betrayed by the trail of terrified little turds she has left in her wake.

Fortunately, Lazzo has come round to help, and has been a tower of strength, visiting sheds and outhouses, stroking and comforting, and ending up on a kitchen chair with Mr. Darcy shivering in his arms and a can of beer in his hand.

'Noisy,' remarks Lazzo, as another shower of sparks lightens the sky outside the window.

'D'you think fireworks are getting louder?' Eric asks, of no-one in particular. 'I'm sure they never used to make so much noise.'

'It probably just seems like it.' Silas pours himself some nettle wine (we are having our own party of sorts. I, needless to say, am back on the wagon). 'It'll pass.'

'Should that pig be in the larder?' Mum is much exercised by the mess (not to mention the smell) which has accompanied Sarah's visit.

'She always spends Guy Fawkes in there,' says Eric.

'Is it — hygienic? I mean, a pig in a larder...'

'Probably not.' Eric grins at her. 'But it hasn't done us any harm yet.'

Mum moves her chair nearer the door. 'If you say so. Though I don't know what Brian would say.' (Brian is my father.)

'Then don't tell him,' Silas says.

Mum looks uncomfortable. I'm pretty sure that she still tells Dad most of the things that go on in this household, for old habits die hard, and I wonder how long she can hold out before the inevitable climb-down and return home. I know she's not happy, suspended as she is between two very different lives; torn between her loyalty to my father and her feelings for me, not to mention her hurt at the minimal effort Dad has made to retrieve her. But what can she do? Poor Mum. With the best will in the world, she'll never really fit in here. It's too far removed from everything she's used to. But having made what is — for her — a very courageous move, will she fit back into her old life again? Only time will tell.

A few days later, all of our minds are taken off our individual worries by a more serious matter.

For some time now, Silas has been researching the long-term effects of rheumatic fever, and we haven't taken a lot of notice. After all, health issues have always been a major source of fascination for Silas, and most of the time there is little for the rest of us to concern ourselves with. And if he's been a bit tired of late, perhaps a little breathless, then these things happen at seventy-four, don't they?

'Mitral stenosis,' says Silas, reading from his medical book. 'I think that must be it. I seem to have all the symptoms.' He applies his stethoscope to his chest and listens attentively. 'But I can't hear anything. Damn.'

'Do you know what you're supposed to hear?' I ask him.

'Not really.' Silas sighs. 'I've read about heart murmurs, but I've never heard one, so I don't really know what I'm looking for.'

'Perhaps you should let the doctor check you out.'

'Oh no. Well, not yet, anyway. People don't usually drop dead from mitral stenosis.'

'Are you sure?' It certainly sounds impressive enough to be fatal.

'Quite sure,' Silas assures me. 'This kind of thing can rumble on for years. And my blood pressure's fine.'

'Good.'

'And I'm not a bad colour.' He examines his reflection in the hall mirror. 'Or maybe just a little cyanosed. What do you think, Ruth?'

'What's cyanosed?'

'Blue. Pale. It's caused by lack of oxygen.'

I examine Silas's face. 'You look okay to me.'

'Mm. I'm not sure.' He examines his hands. 'It can affect the extremities, too.'

Silas's hands are so dirty I don't think it would much matter what colour they were, but if Silas reckons his fingertips are a little blue, he may be right. After all, he's lived with them for long enough.

'Are you sure you shouldn't go to the doctor?' I ask him. 'I'll take you.'

'Maybe eventually, but there's plenty of time yet. This was bound to happen sooner or later.'

'Was it?'

'Oh yes. Rheumatic fever does this. It goes away for years, and then the effects come back to haunt you in later life.'

And he goes on to give me a detailed explanation. He uses words like haemolytic streptococcus and carditis, sub-cutaneous nodules and erythema marginatum, mitral regurgitation and aortic stenosis. This kind of vocabulary is meat and drink to Silas; to me, it's double Dutch.

'Gosh. All that,' I say weakly, when he's finished.

'Yes. It's a nuisance, but so interesting, don't you think, Ruth?'

'I suppose so.'

'We are fearfully and wonderfully made,' Silas tells me cheerfully.

'Yes.'

'I'm going to do the pigs now.'

'Take care.'

A week later, Silas collapses. One minute, he is standing at the kitchen table putting the finishing touches to his latest victim (a weasel; Silas has always wanted a weasel, and has been wildly excited ever since he found it); the next, he's lying on the floor, looking very pale and rather surprised.

'Silas? Silas! Are you all right?' I'm completely panic-stricken. I've never seen anyone pass out before, and have always been queasy when it comes to medical emergencies. I also have no idea what to do.

'Yes. Yes, I think so.' Silas tries to sit up.

'No. No. Stay where you are. You mustn't move.' Somewhere in that tiny section of my brain which stores my minuscule knowledge of things medical there is the strict injunction *not to move the patient*. Or is that just in the case of accidents? And what about the recovery position? What is it, and should I put Silas in it now? I have always wondered about the expression 'in a flap', but now I understand, because my hands seem to be making involuntary fluttering movements as I panic and dither, and Silas lies obediently on the floor, waiting for me to do something helpful.

'Fetch Eric,' Silas tells me.

'Yes. Yes, of course. Eric.'

'He's fixing the bedroom window.'

'Bedroom window. Yes.' I look down at Silas. 'Can I — should I —'

'Fetch Eric. Please, Ruth.'

'Yes. Yes, of course.'

I fly upstairs and fetch Eric. Together we arrive back in the kitchen, where Silas is still lying on the floor.

'Well, now.' Eric creaks down into his knees and places a hand on Silas's forehead. 'Mm. You are a bit sweaty. What exactly happened? And how are you feeling?'

'I had some kind of syncope attack —' *syncope attack?* — 'and I'm feeling a bit — woozy.' Silas takes his own pulse. 'Atrial fibrillation,' he tells us, after a moment.

'Translate,' Eric orders. 'This is no time to show off your medical knowledge, Silas. Ruth and I are worried.'

'I've fainted, and I'm having palpitations,' Silas explains. He looks calm and untroubled, and the unworthy thought occurs to me that Silas is enjoying this. He now has a real illness with real symptoms. He will be able to spend hours poring over his grisly book analysing his condition.

'Can you sit up?' Eric asks (no recovery position, then).

'I think so.' Carefully, Silas sits up. The colour immediately drains from his face. 'Better not.' He subsides onto the floor again.

Eric places a folded jacket under his head. 'Dial 999, Ruth. I think we need help,' he tells me.

Burly ambulance men arrive, cheery and reassuring. They ask Silas lots of questions before levering him onto a stretcher and into the ambulance. Eric and I follow in the Land Rover, leaving a note for Mum, who is at the hairdresser's. Eric is pale and quiet, and we don't speak, although I long to offer some kind of comfort and also to ask whether he's suffering any of Silas's symptoms. I've read about twins suffering identical pains even when they're miles apart; is Eric's pallor due to some psychic twin response, or is it simply anxiety?

At the hospital, there is a lot of waiting around. Silas is offered an injection for the pain.

'I haven't got any pain,' he objects.

'For your distress, dear,' the nurse tells him.

'I'm not distressed.'

'It'll calm you down.'

'I'm perfectly calm.' But in the end, Silas agrees to the injection because, as he says, he's always wanted to know what diamorphine ('you'll know it as heroin, Ruth. Highly addictive') feels like. And it can't do any harm, can it? Personally, I think it's Eric who could do with the injection, but no-one's asking me.

Much later, when Silas has had a variety of tests and seen at least three doctors, they tell him he has 'a little problem with a heart valve'.

'Mitral stenosis. I told you,' says Silas.

'Well, yes. It could be.' The doctor looks disappointed. Even I know that doctors don't like patients to use medical-speak. There is a strict boundary between the medical practitioner and the layman, and Silas has crossed it.

'Rheumatic fever,' Silas explains, his words still slurry from diamorphine. 'When I was, when I was...'

'Seventeen,' Eric says.

'That's right.' Silas smiles. 'Seventeen.'

'We'll have to keep you in,' the doctor tells him. 'For observation and more tests.'

'Valve replacement?' Silas asks, his face bright with anticipation.

'It's much too early to say.'

'But I might have to have one?'

'It's possible.'

'Pig or titanium?' Silas asks (what *is* he talking about?).

'That would be for the surgeons to decide. If it becomes necessary. But that's a long way off at the moment.'

'Goodness,' I say to Eric, when much later we have said our farewells and are on our way home, leaving Silas cosily tucked up in bed. 'You'd think he was enjoying it.'

'He is enjoying it.'

'How can he?'

'Silas loves to be ill. He's always been like that.'

'Yes, but this is his *heart*.'

'So much the better,' says Eric grimly.

'He must be mad!'

'He is.'

'Poor Eric. You must be awfully worried.'

Eric attempts a smile. 'Of course I am.'

'And you can't share that with Silas.' Eric and Silas usually share everything.

'Quite.'

I put my hand on Eric's knee. 'You've got us. Mum and me. I know it's not the same, but at least you're not on your own.'

'No. I know. Thanks, Ruth.'

We get home to chaos. Mum, who's been keeping in touch by phone, has been trying to cope with Blossom, who's been called in for emergency animal duties. The argument they have been having has evidently turned nasty, and Sarah has taken advantage of the situation by coming in through the open back door and helping herself to an unattended bag of groceries, while Mr. Darcy is chasing a chicken round the living room.

'She can't tell me what to do,' Blossom tells us mutinously.

'I haven't been telling her to do anything,' says Mum, who is very close to tears.

'Have.'

'No, I haven't. I just asked you — *asked* you — if you would mind seeing if there were any cabbages left.'

'Not my job.'

'But surely in an emergency that doesn't matter?'

'Don't need cabbages in emergency.'

'It's not for the emergency! It's for *dinner*!'

'Perhaps you'd better finish the animals and go home,' Eric suggests to Blossom.

'Done 'em,' says Blossom.

'Well, it doesn't look like it. Sarah's in the kitchen, for a start.'

'Not my fault. *She* left the door open.'

'I did not!' Mum cries.

'Did.'

'Enough!' Eric's patience has finally run out. 'Blossom, would you please put Sarah to bed, and catch that dratted chicken before Mr. Darcy does. Then for pity's sake, go home. We've got enough troubles without all this.'

Chapter Twenty-Four

Silas spends several days in hospital, and is in his element. He has a whole range of tests, and talks of, among other things, unpronounceable blood tests, an echo something-or-other, and an ECG. I have just about heard of the ECG, but everything else is shrouded in mystery. We have travelled to and fro fulfilling Silas's requests for, among other things, clean pyjamas, chocolate, nettle wine and the medical bible. Eric refuses to bring in the stuffed whippet (Silas apparently promised to show it to the nurses) and has to take the wine home (no alcohol allowed), but manages to smuggle in a tiny stuffed mouse "to compensate the nurses for their disappointment".

Poor Eric is exhausted. He and Silas have rarely been apart, and he seems somehow depleted without his brother. I know he's not sleeping well, and the journeys to and from the hospital are both time- and energy-consuming, involving as they do a thirty-mile round trip plus the obligatory search for a parking place and the trek along miles of dismal hospital corridors. Mum and I take it in turns to accompany him, but he won't hear of us going without him, and I know that he is fulfilling his own needs as much as Silas's. As for his Ark, that's had to be put on hold, and I know he misses it. The Ark has become Eric's treasured hobby, fuel for his brain (not to mention his imagination), and perhaps the only thing which might have taken his mind off his worries. I too miss the Ark; I miss the curious questions and conversations to which it gives rise, and my even more curious dialogues with the people at the zoo as I assist Eric with his enquiries. I have developed quite a cosy relationship with one of the curators, who rashly invited me out on a date, although we have never met. I reluctantly declined out of loyalty to Amos and the seahorse/rabbit.

Meanwhile, the rest of us are desperately short-handed, and Lazzo and Kaz are brought in to help. Kaz is currently short of work, and Lazzo has nothing better to do, so it suits everyone (except, of course, Blossom).

The weather continues to be bleakly unpleasant, and the increase in my size is slowing me down. The only person/thing which appears to be thriving is the Virgin, whose followers are growing by the day and who I swear is getting more and more life-like. Eric I know has had more than enough of her and thinks it's time we called it a day (the hardware store has promised him a preservative which is guaranteed to cover up pretty well anything, supernatural or otherwise), but when he mentioned this to Blossom, she threatened to withdraw not only her own services, but those of her family as well, and as she very well knows, we can't do without them.

In addition to all this, Mum is beginning to pine.

'I miss him, Ruth, I really miss him,' she admits to me, as she slices vegetables for the evening meal. 'I know he's awkward, and I don't expect you to understand, but I — I'm *used* to him.'

'Then go home, Mum. Go back to him,' I tell her. 'I'll understand.'

'I can't.' She pushes her hair out of her eyes, weeping onion-tears. 'He told me I had to choose, and I've chosen you. You and the baby. I can't go back on that now. In any case, he mightn't even have me.'

'Oh, he'd certainly have you.'

'Do you think so?'

'I know so.' I crunch a piece of raw carrot. 'What does the minister say?' Mum has joined a kind of house church in the nearby town, and seems to derive some comfort from the support it offers.

'He prays with me, of course. He's been very kind, but I know he thinks I ought to go back to your father.'

'Then go back. You can still see me. It's not as though I've emigrated. And when Dad sees the baby, he may change his mind.'

'I don't think so. He's so obstinate. He always has to be *right*. He'll never climb down, even if he secretly wants to. Besides,' she says, chopping celery, 'I'm needed here. Eric and Silas are my brothers, and I'm all the family they've got. It's the least I can do, to help out in this crisis. They've always been so good to me.'

I gaze out of the window. Through the drizzle, I can make out Eric's stooping figure bent over some ancient piece of machinery, and I fight back sudden tears. Eric is miserable, Mum is unhappy and guilt-ridden, the animals, those most reliable barometers of emotional climate, are restless and jumpy, and I am suffering from backache and indigestion. And there is still no sign of Amos.

'Ruth? Are you okay?' Mum looks up from her vegetables.

'Yes. No. I don't know. Everything's suddenly — horrible.'

'I know what you mean.'

'I just wish something *nice* would happen.'

Two days later, something nice does happen in the form of another surprise visit from Mikey.

'Oh, Mikey! Am I glad to see you!' I practically leap into his arms.

'Hey! Hang on! You nearly knocked me over! What's all this about, then?' Mikey laughs as he disentangles himself and kisses me warmly on the cheek.

I sit him down and tell him about Silas and how worried we all are and how miserable life has become since his admission to hospital. I tell him about Mum, about Blossom (who is now ruling not just the roost, but the house, and just about everything else, and loving every minute of it) and about the abundance of unwanted pilgrims. I tell him that I shall be thirty-seven next year and life is passing me by, that my violin-playing has deteriorated so badly that no-one will ever want me to play for them again, and that I still haven't managed to find Amos. And I finish by bursting into tears.

'Oh dear.' Mikey pats and soothes and makes sympathetic noises.

'I know I'm wallowing,' I say, when I can get the words out, 'but just for once — for once —'

'It's good to have a wallow?'

'I suppose so. Yes.' I take the not-very-clean hanky Mikey has offered and blow my nose.

'I've brought Gavin to meet you,' Mikey says, when I've calmed down a bit. 'But maybe now's not the best time.'

'Why? Where is he?'

'In the car. I thought I'd make sure it was a good time before bringing him in. Just as well, as it happens.'

'Oh, do bring him in. Please. I'd love to meet him.'

'Are you sure?'

'Quite sure. Just give me a minute to mop up.'

Five minutes later, Mikey introduces me to Gavin.

In my time, I have come across many attractive men, but I have never met one I would describe as beautiful. Gavin is beautiful. He is tall and slim and blond, with completely even perfectly-formed features, the bluest eyes I have ever seen, and the kind of smile that bathes you in warm sunshine. For a moment, I'm completely lost for words.

'Ruth? *Ruth!*' Mikey wrenches me out of my trance. 'This is Gavin.' His pride is so transparent that I almost laugh.

Gavin smiles, and holds out a hand.

'Yes. Sorry. Hi.' I shake the hand, which (of course) is warm and firm and smooth. 'I'm so sorry you had to wait all that time in the car.'

'Not at all.'

'Ruth's my oldest friend,' Mikey says (am I? I'd no idea. The thought of being Mikey's oldest friend is ridiculously cheering).

'Any oldest friend of Mikey's has to be a pretty good friend of mine,' says Gavin, with another radiant smile.

'Tea? Coffee? Er — mulberry wine?' I ask them, examining the label on the currently open bottle.

'Tea, I think. We're sharing the driving,' says Gavin.

Sharing the driving. It sounds so cosily domestic I want to weep.

For few minutes we make small talk; the household, the animals, my violin-playing, Gavin's job as an estate agent. This seems a terrible waste, but I resist the temptation to ask him whether he's ever thought of a career on the stage or perhaps as a model, as I'm sure he's been asked this many times before. But I bet he sells a lot of houses.

The back door opens and Kaz comes in. She stops short, and takes a long, astonished but practised look at Gavin.

'Fucking hell!'

'*Kaz!*' I feel instantly ashamed, although strictly speaking, Kaz is nothing to do with me.

'Sorry. But you have to admit he's a bit of a stunner.' Kaz appears unabashed by the fact that the stunner is almost certainly within earshot. She crosses the kitchen and holds out a hand. 'Hi. I'm Kaz.'

Gavin introduces himself, and they chat for a moment or two. Gavin tries to bring Mikey into the conversation, but Kaz ignores him, for she is doing what she obviously does best. Kaz is flirting.

Now of course, I've seen people flirt, many times. I have flirted myself, and enjoyed it as much as anyone. But I have never seen a professional at work.

Kaz is a professional.

I watch in admiration the lowered eyes followed by the coy Princess-Diana peep through the lashes; the tilt of the body which reveals just enough décolletage; the pout of the lips and the little-girl voice. This is a new Kaz; one I haven't seen before. Hitherto the only men around here have been Eric and Silas, who are obviously too old for this kind of treatment. The pilgrims, Kaz has told me more than once, have their minds on other things, and aren't worth the bother. Unfortunately, she appears to be unaware that Gavin is also not worth the bother, if for an entirely different reason, but I'm unable to catch her eye.

Mikey, unintroduced and ignored, is enjoying all this hugely, and he returns my despairing glance with a wink.

Eventually, Gavin manages to affect an introduction. 'Kaz, have you met Mikey?' Mikey and Kaz nod to each other.

'I'm Gavin's partner,' Mikey says, dropping his tiny bombshell with impressive insouciance.

Kaz pauses for a moment, then shrugs and laughs. 'Well, that was a waste of time, then, wasn't it?' she says, returning to her normal spiky self. 'Worth a try, though,' she adds with just a hint of wistfulness.

'Certainly worth a try,' says Gavin graciously. 'And I'm honoured.'

'You're welcome. Can I have some of that wine?' Kaz reaches for the bottle. 'I reckon I've earned it. I've finally got the hang of that bloody goat. Milking a goat,' she says, to no-one in particular, 'is a bit like sex. Once you get going, it's difficult to stop. It's sort of — compulsive.'

I have never felt that milking a goat is remotely like sex, and since over the past few months I've had a great deal of the one and none at all of the other, it is difficult not to feel just a little sour.

'I'll bear that in mind,' I mutter to her, 'next time I —'

'Milk a goat?' Kaz grins at me.

'Something like that.'

But generally, it's been a very pleasant visit, and culminates with a tour of the hen house. It appears that Gavin is a lapsed Catholic, and is especially intrigued by the Virgin. I have met lapsed Catholics before, and have always been puzzled at their extraordinary loyalty to a church which, by definition, has let them down in some way. At least one friend of this persuasion (or perhaps it should be dissuasion) has told me that while she doesn't attend Mass any more, she will certainly require the services of a priest on her death-bed, and most Catholics won't hear a word against the Church they have (if only temporarily) deserted.

'It's the gay thing,' Gavin tells us, as we toil up the muddy path. 'I know God doesn't mind about it. He's much too broad-minded. But the Catholic Church is terribly hung up on sex. Always has been.'

'Then join another church; one which is as broad-minded as God.'

'Oh, I couldn't do that,' Gavin tells me.

'Why ever not?'

'Because it's the One True Church,' Kaz pipes up with a wink. I imagine Kaz has long since passed the lapsed Catholic stage on her journey to her present state of cheery godlessness.

'Not exactly,' Gavin says. 'It's just that a Catholic is what I am.' He negotiates a puddle, splashing his immaculate trousers. 'You know when you have to fill in those hospital forms, and they ask you your religion?'

'Yes.'

'Well, I always put RC. I simply can't imagine putting anything else.'

'And if you're dying, you'll want a priest to come with one of those little bottles of oil?'

'Oh, definitely. Little bottles of oil are de rigueur.'

'And last confession?'

'Definitely last confession.'

'Will you have to confess to being gay?'

'God knows I'm gay. He's fine about it.' He pats me on the shoulder. 'Don't worry about it. I certainly don't.'

But lapsed or not, Gavin is impressed by the Virgin of the hen house.

'This is amazing,' he tells Mikey. 'Why didn't you tell me about it before?'

'It's just a few scratches.' Mikey is not only an atheist; he also has no imagination. 'I didn't think it was really worth mentioning.'

'Mikey, this is more than a few scratches.' Gavin squats down to examine it more closely. 'It really does look, well, it looks...'

'Virgin-like?' I suggest.

'Yes.' Gavin agrees. 'I'm not usually one for signs and miracles, but this is something else.'

'Well, the punters certainly think so. They come in their droves.'

'Any miraculous cures yet?' he asks with a grin.

'None that we know about.' I straighten Blossom's vase of flowers (hideous plastic violets from the pound shop, as Blossom has given up trying to stop the animals from eating real ones. This has not, however, deterred the goats, who have paid an illegal visit and eaten several).

'And what does the local priest say?'

'Not a lot. He has as little to do with it as possible. I think he's the drinking, delegating sort.'

I think of Father Vincent, who hasn't been near us in weeks, and once again, I wonder what he really thinks about all this. His secretary continues to churn out tickets, and the pilgrims keep on coming, but Father Vincent keeps a very low profile. Father Vincent may be lazy, but he's certainly not stupid.

Later on, as Gavin and Mikey get into their car, bickering affectionately about whose turn it is to drive, and whether they should take the bypass, the baby performs a fluttering tap dance inside me.

'Don't worry,' I tell it, as I walk back towards the house. 'Sooner or later your daddy will come and find us.'

And then perhaps I too will have someone to bicker with and argue over the map-reading. I give a sigh. Seeing Mikey and Gavin has been lovely, but I envy the cosiness of their coupled state.

I hope my turn will come soon.

Chapter Twenty-Five

Silas is ready to come out of hospital. They have "stabilised" his condition, but apparently not cured it. Silas tells us that the only permanent cure lies in an operation, and seems disappointed that his condition's not considered serious enough to merit one for the time being. But never mind. He has a wonderful range of new tablets — heart tablets, water tablets ('not water tablets. *Diuretics*,' says Silas, who hates to be patronised) and blood-thinning tablets with a name which even Silas has trouble remembering.

Eric fetches him home.

It is only now, seeing the newly stabilised Silas, that I realise how ill he must have been. It's a long time since I confused him with his brother — in fact, now, I wonder that anyone could confuse them at all — so I have become accustomed to seeing him as an individual. And if he's been a bit paler and thinner than Eric, then I assumed that was the way it's always been. But since he's been in hospital, Silas has put on weight and his colour's improved, and he looks, literally, a new man.

We all tell him how well he looks, but his feelings about this are obviously ambivalent. While he appears to feel fitter and stronger, I know that he hankers after the attention and the drama which accompanied his admission to hospital, and we are not allowed to forget that he has been 'very ill, you know, Ruth. Very ill indeed.' Yes, Silas. We know.

Although he's anxious to get back into the swing of things, we try to prevent him from overdoing it. Light duties only, we tell him, and point him in the direction of his half-finished weasel. In this, he's more than happy to comply, and while the weasel has suffered from being abandoned at a crucial stage, Silas doesn't appear to mind. As he tells us, very few people know what a weasel looks like anyway, so if this one deviates a little from what nature intended, it's unlikely that anyone will notice. Meanwhile, Lazzo stays on to help, but we can no longer count on Kaz. She's being taken on by a new club, she tells me, and she has acquired a small car, so she no longer has to rely on buses and trains. She's happy to lend a hand when she can, but we mustn't rely on her.

'A mobile dancer is a busy dancer,' she tells me cheerfully, as she drives round to show us her new wheels. 'The manager won't pay for taxis, and I can't afford them.'

Kaz has painted her car buttercup yellow and decorated it with neat turquoise daisies.

'What do you think?' she asks me.

'Well, it'll certainly stand out,' I tell her.

'That's what I thought. You can borrow it if you like,' she adds.

'That's kind of you, but I think the Land Rover is more — me.'

'You're probably right.' Kaz climbs back into her car and winds down the window. 'Well, I'm off to see a man about a pole.'

'Good luck.'

'Who needs luck?' Kaz shouts, as she bounces off down the track.

Sometimes I wish I had Kaz's confidence.

It would appear that during the winter, my uncles' activities die down, and they enjoy a period of relative quiet. They close their market stall, selling what little produce there is to private customers, who come and collect it themselves. I have no idea what they live on, since even in the summer, their income from what they sell wouldn't even heat the house, but then this has always been a bit of a mystery. I know they have various investments from their inheritance, and Eric at least enjoys dabbling on the stock market, so I assume most of their income comes from that.

Outside home, their needs are few. They rarely travel anywhere, and as far as I can see, never take holidays. Most of their clothes are falling apart, but then as Silas says, what does it matter? Hardly anyone sees them and they certainly don't mind what they look like. They do occasionally buy new shoes and wellingtons, and they make a monthly trip to the barber's; a filthy establishment, cluttered with old newspapers and magazines, with unsightly heaps of greying hair in every corner and a ceiling stained yellow by bygone years of cigarette smoke. Here Lennie, a wizened man of indeterminate age, dispenses haircuts and gossip for a fiver a time. Eric and Silas consider this excellent value, and wouldn't dream of going anywhere else.

Mum and I both pay our way, but my savings are dwindling rapidly, so I return to my busking, but on different days now that Eric and Silas no longer have their market stall, driving myself and sometimes travelling further afield to give myself (and the punters) a change. Mr. Darcy, who has his own fan club, now loves these outings, so I still take him with me, and while I'm finding it all increasingly tiring, in my present situation, needs must. My burgeoning pregnancy attracts plenty of interest, not to mention increased revenue, and people come up to chat and give advice. I've even made one or two friends.

Mum, however, hasn't changed her views since I was a busking student, and while she sometimes lets me borrow her car, she doesn't hesitate to tell me what she thinks.

'I don't know how you can stand there in the street like that, with everyone looking at you, Ruth,' she tells me.

'But that's the whole point, Mum. I'm a performer. That's what performers do.'

'An orchestra is one thing,' she persists (that's not what she said at the time), 'but hanging round street corners collecting *money*.' She gives a delicate little shudder. 'It doesn't seem right.'

'I don't hang around anywhere, and I don't *collect* money. People pay me. I'm not pretending to be homeless or even particularly poor. And if my playing gives people pleasure, and they're prepared to pay, what's the problem?'

'I don't know what your father would say.' This, as always, means she knows exactly what Dad would say, as do I. What Dad would say in almost any circumstance is usually entirely predictable.

But the phone call we receive from him two days after this conversation isn't predictable at all. The call brings tidings of unexpected disaster, for apparently Dad has had an accident with the chip pan, and the resulting inferno has succeeded in destroying two thirds of the house.

Mum, needless to say, is beside herself.

'The house burnt down. Our home. *Burnt down*.' She is inconsolable. 'And chips! Your father's never made chips in his life. He doesn't even like chips!'

'Is he all right? Is he hurt?' I want to know.

'Oh, yes yes. He's fine. But *the house*. And *chips*. What was he doing making chips?'

I recognise the preoccupation with chips as some kind of displacement anxiety, and it's probably fulfilling its purpose, for isn't it better that Mum should worry about my father making chips than the fact that she's probably lost almost everything she possesses?

'Of course, he must come here,' says Eric at once.

'Oh, could he?' Mum says. 'He's nowhere else to stay. He's had offers from the church, of course, but I don't think he'll want to take them up. He hates to be *beholden*.'

'Of course. He's more than welcome.' This is nice of Eric, since my father has never been especially polite to my uncles, and wouldn't have relished having either of them to stay.

'I haven't mentioned it to him yet. I hope he'll agree to come,' Mum says. 'He can be so — well, he may not want to...'

'I think he'll come,' I tell her, because of course this is the perfect excuse for Dad to bring about a reconciliation without the necessity for a climb-down. In a way, for my parents' relationship (if for nothing else) it's a win-win situation.

Sure enough, Dad accepts the invitation, but typically refuses all offers of transport (both Eric and I offer to fetch him), insisting on driving himself. When he arrives a few hours later, subdued and bedraggled, I am shocked at the change in him. Gone is the confidence and the self-control; the air of pious sobriety. He looks somehow shrunken and vulnerable, like the little old man he will no doubt one day become. He is unshaven, and wearing a dirty cardigan with the buttons done up unevenly, and funnily enough it is this which I find most touching.

'Dad!' I give him a hug, and for once he barely resists. 'Are you all right?'

'A little shaken, of course. But no real harm done.'

'That's good.' I take his small suitcase, wondering what can be in it. Does he still have any clothes, or did they all go up in flames?

Mum comes into the hall to meet him. She looks shy and awkward, her hands twisting together in front of her as though involved in some private battle of their own.

'Brian.' She starts to walk towards him, and then seems to think better of it.

'Rosemary,' Dad says, but makes no move towards her.

'Tea?' I ask quickly, hoping to oil the wheels of this very awkward reunion. 'I'm sure you could do with a cup of tea, Dad.'

'Yes. Thank you. Tea would be very nice.' My father follows me into the kitchen. 'Where are Eric and Silas?' He sounds apprehensive.

'They're outside with the vet. They may be a while,' I tell him.

He looks relieved. 'Oh. Right,' he says. 'Nobody — nothing too ill, I hope?'

'Just a couple of castrations.'

Mum blushes, and I feel a wave of exasperation. She has lived here for some weeks now, in the course of which there have been a number of births and a variety of couplings, none of them particularly discreet and one or two in full view of the house. Will she never get used to the idea of sex?

'Well,' says Dad, some time later, as he sits at the table stirring his second cup of tea. 'We are very blessed.'

'How do you make that out?' I ask him.

He turns a reproachful gaze on me.

'The Lord has been good to us, Ruth. Our home is almost destroyed, and yet no-one has been hurt. Yes. The Lord has been very good.'

Mum nods her agreement, although she is still red-eyed from crying.

This is one of the things I shall never understand about my parents' faith. Their home of nearly forty years almost razed to the ground, many if not most of their possessions destroyed, and here they are, praising the Lord; the same Lord, presumably, who could have stopped the fire if he'd had a mind to. It seems to me that my parents' God cannot lose; he gets all the credit when things go well, and none of the blame when they don't. This is not the right time to raise the matter, but I would dearly like to hear how they can explain this (to me) extraordinary dichotomy.

'How much — how much is — gone?' Mum asks now.

'Well, the kitchen, obviously,' Dad says. 'And most of the rest of the ground floor. Upstairs, things are a bit better. The fire only managed to get as far as Ruth's room. The rest is more or less undamaged.'

'Is my room — completely destroyed?' I ask carefully.

'Pretty well,' says Dad, reaching for another biscuit (his spirits seem remarkably improved). 'But you didn't use it much, did you? And there was only a lot of old stuff from when you were a child. Nothing you'll miss.'

Nothing you'll miss. How typical of Dad that even now he's incapable of putting himself in anyone else's shoes; of trying to understand a situation from any viewpoint other than his own. I feel a sudden ridiculous surge of grief as I think of the room which I slept in all my life until I left home, and which is still officially mine; the room which was my refuge in times of trouble, where I nursed my teenage sulks and (oh, delicious danger!) shared my first bumbling kiss with the minister's son while, through the floorboards, we could hear the faint sounds of our parents' voices as they prayed together in the room below.

Of course, all the stuff I really need has long been removed, but there are all those other things; all those bits and pieces of my childhood. The swimming certificates and posters on the wall, and the rosette I won in my brief equestrian career (it was for fourth place, and there only were four competitors, but I carried that rosette round with me for weeks). Then there are the books; among them *Heidi*, *The Wind in the Willows*, *the Secret Garden*, and my favourite of all, *Charlotte's Webb*. The baby might have enjoyed those. There was the patchwork quilt stitched by my grandmother, the only person who I felt really understood me. She and I used to call it the "crosspatch quilt" because I could never remember the word "patchwork". I remember her arthritic fingers stitching away at that quilt while she told me about her early married life and my mother's childhood. There was a particular patchwork square — pale blue brocade roses — which I remember especially because it was a one-off, and she was sewing it the day her beloved cat was run over.

And then there were the drawers full of mementoes: my first tiny pink ballet shoes, my music certificates, old school books, letters and photos; and the usual dross of foreign coins, broken pencils, buttons, ancient pots of dried-up cosmetics, hair clips and odd earrings. Someone once said that everyone has a broken wristwatch in a drawer. I had two.

'Of course, I got in touch with the insurance people straight away.' Dad is still talking. 'They're getting back to me tomorrow. I gave them this phone number. I hope that's all right?'

'Of course,' Silas says. 'And now perhaps you'd like to get yourself settled? Will you be sleeping — I mean, where would you like to sleep?'

'Oh, with Rosemary of course.' Dad appears unfazed by the question. My mother's opinion obviously doesn't count, but she nods her acquiescence.

As I carry Dad's suitcase upstairs and find extra pillows and towels, I wonder what kind of reconciliation my parents will have (I assume they will be reconciled. It must be hard to stay separated in the same bed). Will they talk things through? Touch each other? Make love? Like most people, I find the idea of my parents' sex life hard to envisage, but there's no reason why they shouldn't still have one.

I shall probably never know.

Part III: Winter

During the third trimester, the baby's eyes open, the bones develop fully and the lungs mature. The movements become more forceful and the baby gains several more pounds in weight in order to reach an average birth weight of between seven and eight pounds. The soft downy hair (lanugo) which covers its body falls off, and the baby learns to suck. At thirty-eight weeks the baby is considered to be full term, although the normal gestation is forty weeks.

Chapter Twenty-Six

I feel absolutely huge. Everyone tells me I am not, but I have never been pregnant before — never had to share my body with anyone else in this extraordinary way — and as I cart my little passenger around, in and out of cars and through the small openings of sheds and outhouses; as I lever myself out of the depths of my uncles' saggy sofa and have to abandon yet another favourite garment that refuses to do up, I feel cumbersome and clumsy and also deeply unattractive.

I recall with puzzlement the comments of pregnant friends, who "couldn't wait for the baby to *show*" and can no longer remember a time when mine didn't. What was it like to do up belts, wear a bikini, have a waist? I have bought several smock-like garments at the market, and have let out my jeans on a piece of elastic, and wonder at the proudly pregnant bellies of girls who seem happy to walk around with their bumps completely naked and their belly buttons turned inside out (at least mine hasn't done that yet).

My father has been with us for a week now, and despite this overwhelming evidence, is still obviously in a state of denial where my pregnancy is concerned. Since he never refers to it, it's become the elephant in the room (or perhaps I have become the elephant in the room; I certainly feel like one). Occasionally he will refer to a time 'when you're better, Ruth', as though having a baby were some kind of illness, but otherwise he manages to pretend it's not happening. Dad has always had this knack of ignoring the embarrassing or the distasteful, and at the moment he's surpassing himself.

'What does he say to you, Mum?' I ask my mother, but she just shakes her head.

'He doesn't talk about it.'

'What, not at all?'

'Not at all.'

'And what happens if you mention it?'

She gives a helpless little shrug.

'You mean, you don't mention it?' I'm not surprised, but I do feel a bit hurt.

'Well, no. I can't, Ruth. He's so worked up about the insurance people and the fact that he can't get hold of anyone when he wants to. There's no point in worrying him further.'

And I suppose this is true enough. Dad spends long hours on the phone, keeping a meticulous note of every minute he spends, and leaving money in a little pot on the window sill, getting increasingly impatient with whoever he's talking to, and giving a running commentary to anyone who'll listen.

'They're playing that tune again. Greensleeves, isn't it? You'd know it, Ruth ... oh, here we go. "This call may be recorded for training purposes". Whatever for? They presumably know what *they're* saying, and *I* haven't said anything yet. My call is very important to them. Well, I should hope so. "If you know the extension, then dial the number now". Well, I don't know the extension; why should I? Are these people stupid? Now I've forgotten what I'm supposed to press next. I'll have to go back to the beginning.' And more change rattles into the pot.

My parents seem to have slipped back into their marriage as though it had never been disrupted, but maybe this can be explained by the fact that neither of them has had to step down or lose face in any way. My father had to have somewhere to live, and this was the obvious place, and Mum hasn't moved at all. She is still here with me and Eric and Silas. So perhaps this has satisfied both parties. They are kept busy, travelling back and forth between Applegarth and home in an attempt to rescue such belongings as they can from the ruins of the house. I accompany them on one of these forays, but my room is so badly damaged that all I can find among the still-smoking rubble are the remains of a very singed teddy bear, half a dolls' house and a rusty horse shoe. They are not much to remember my childhood home by but better than nothing, and I put them tenderly in a cardboard box to take back with me. I have no idea what I'm going to do with them, and for once, my parents don't ask. Perhaps the three of us, briefly united in our loss, are prepared to make allowances for such small shows of sentiment.

Otherwise, Mum keeps busy with her domestic chores and Dad with his negotiations over matters of insurance and house repairs. They attend Mum's new church together, and seem surprisingly comfortable with one another. I know that Dad is uneasy about Silas's taxidermy activities, and thinks that it's all 'most unhygienic', but since this isn't his house, he can't really say much. As for Eric and his Ark, Dad avoids this entirely, although I can see that Eric is longing to update him with his progress. There is more than an element of mischief in this, because Eric, armed with his dossiers of what he considers to be irrefutable facts, senses victory (he has a lot to learn about my father) and hankers after a little taste of it now. But Dad isn't going to fall into that trap, so the Ark has joined the baby and become another no-go area. As for the Virgin of the hen house, no-one mentions that. No doubt Dad will find out about it, but I think we all hope it will be later rather than sooner.

Meanwhile, Mikey calls in with news of Amos. I am enormously excited.

'Tell me! Tell me, Mikey! Where is he? What's he doing?'

'Hold on. Not so fast. The news isn't all good,' Mikey warns me.

'Why? What's happened? He's not had an accident, has he?'

'No. As far as I know, he's fine. I tracked him down to a cruise in the Caribbean, but apparently he's had a row with the conductor and disembarked on Barbados. No-one's heard from him since.'

'A row? What sort of row?'

'I've no idea. They're pretty pissed off with him, though, so I didn't like to ask too many questions.'

'Oh, Amos! How *could* he!' I'm very close to tears.

'Well, he didn't know did he? About the baby, I mean. As far as he's concerned, he's his own man. He can do what he likes.'

'But I need him. I need him *now*. Not in six months or a year or whenever it is he's planning on coming home.'

'Of course you do,' Mikey soothes.

'And now it could be ages before he appears again.'

'That's possible,' Mikey agrees. 'But he's bound to come back to England pretty soon, isn't he? There can't be that many jobs on Barbados for itinerant trombone players, and presumably he has a living to make.'

'I suppose so.'

'You've decided that you do love him, then?' he asks me, after a moment.

'I don't know. I can't really know until I see him, and even then, *he* mightn't love *me*.'

'Of course he'll love you,' Mikey says. 'If I were straight, I'd certainly love you.'

'Oh, Mikey. What am I going to do?' I wail.

'You'll just have to be patient. You've still got — how many months?'

'About three.'

'Three more months to find him. A lot can happen in three months. And I'll carry on looking. I've got a friend who's got a brother in Barbados.'

'How big is Barbados?' I ask him.

'I've no idea. It doesn't sound big, does it?'

I agree that Barbados doesn't sound that big. Quite small, really. And Amos is very hard to miss.

'What a nice young man,' my father remarks, when Mikey has gone (they met for just three minutes). 'Now, that's the kind of young man you want, Ruth. Steady and sensible. Yes. Just what you need. Better than that bearded fellow.'

Oh, Dad. If only you knew. But I decide not to tell him about Mikey's sexual preferences as I think he's had enough shocks for the time being. And it's no good reminding him that Amos is the father of my child. Dad remembers what he wants to remember, and he certainly doesn't want to remember that. Mikey apparently has assets which Amos doesn't have, and my father has never trusted beards.

The house, which was so tranquil when I arrived, is beginning to feel rather full. It's not that my parents take up much room; it's more that everyone is suddenly having to be awfully careful how they behave. It wasn't so bad when it was just Mum; she was becoming relatively relaxed and was even learning to fit in. But with the advent of my father, things are more difficult. My uncles have the patience of saints. They put up with Grace before meals, temper their language, and try to conceal the more earthy aspects of life at Applegarth. But I feel the strain on their behalf, and I also feel responsible. Had I not been here in the first place, my parents would no doubt have found somewhere else to stay — after all, don't insurance companies pay for hotel accommodation in circumstances such as this? — and Eric and Silas would have been able to carry on their untroubled existence without interference.

But if the house feels full, it is about to become more so.

Exactly ten days after my father's arrival, Kaz falls out with Blossom. No-one manages to get to the bottom of what exactly happened (although a man called Angus and a fifty-pound note come into it somewhere), but there it is. Another crisis, and yet another homeless person.

You would think it was impossible to fall out with Blossom, since no-one is ever, as it were, *in* with her. But apparently the fragile relationship between mother and daughter, having reached breaking point, has finally snapped, and Blossom has turned Kaz out of the house.

'It won't be for long.' Kaz stands on the front doorstep at midnight in the pouring rain, her car parked in the mud behind her. 'But at this time of night ... I couldn't think of anywhere else to go.'

'Have you no friends who could put you up?' I ask her (being the only one still up, I answer the door).

'Not really.' Kaz heaves a rather large suitcase into the hallway. 'Most of my friends are dancers like me, living in digs or with their parents. They haven't got room.' She grins at me from under her dripping fringe through eyes sooty with rain and mascara, and I wonder yet again how, whatever the circumstance, Kaz always manages to look ravishing. 'Any chance of a drink?'

'Whatever have you got in that case?' I ask her some minutes later, as we sit in the kitchen drinking (sloe gin for Kaz. Tea for me).

'Oh, you know. Clothes, make-up. Stuff for work. Don't worry, Ruth.' She pours herself another drink. 'I'll make it okay with the boys —' this is Kaz's preferred name for Eric and Silas — 'and I'll even do extra hen house duty. In this weather you should be glad of me.'

'My father's here, too,' I remind her.

'You leave him to me,' Kaz says. 'Trust me. He'll be a pushover.'

Sure enough, when Dad meets Kaz at the breakfast table the next morning, after the initial surprise, he appears completely won over. She does what I think of as her class act; not exactly flirting, but demure and deferential, with just a little touch of the Princess Diana thing she does with her eyelashes. She listens with rapt attention to everything he has to say, and is most sympathetic about the insurance people.

'You're so right,' I hear her say. 'These people have got you just where they want you, haven't they? I've no time for them at all.' (I am pretty sure that Kaz knows nothing at all about house insurance, and cares even less).

'What an — interesting girl,' says Dad, when Kaz goes out to help with the animals. 'In spite of all those rings and things; a most interesting girl. And so sympathetic, too. I have to hand it to you, Ruth. You've made some very nice friends since you've been here.'

Eric and Silas don't appear quite so pleased at the sudden appearance of their new guest, but they take the news stoically.

'Oh well. She can always sleep in the attic,' says Eric. 'So long as she doesn't intend to entertain any gentleman friends.'

When I relay this information to Kaz, she laughs.

'He needn't worry. My boyfriends wouldn't touch this place with a bargepole,' she tells me. I've met one or two of them, and they tend to be of the posh, moneyed variety; wealthy young men who spice up their dull lives by paying to watch girls like Kaz.

'You don't sound very grateful.'

'Of course I'm grateful. I've a lot of time for the boys, bless them. But would you want a romantic liaison in this tip of a place? I think not.'

I can imagine nothing I'd like better, but Kaz wouldn't understand.

Chapter Twenty-Seven

With the onset of winter, interest in the Virgin of the hen house begins to ease off a little, and I think we are all relieved. For while she has been less trouble than we anticipated, hen house duty on dark wet afternoons is something we can all do without, and while we have restricted the number of afternoons to two, it is still a commitment.

'Couldn't we pack the whole thing in for the winter?' I suggest to Blossom. 'After all, there aren't that many visitors now, and the weather's awful.'

'Nope.' Blossom gives me one of her looks.

'Just for a couple of months?' I can't believe I'm begging favours from someone who, when it comes down to it, is just a hired hand. But this hired hand is in a very powerful position, and she knows it, for without her, Eric and Silas would find it almost impossible to cope.

'Nope.' The look becomes dangerous. Blossom is preparing to make trouble.

'Blossom, we've got a lot on. Whoever's looking after things, it's always a disruption. Silas still isn't a hundred percent. He needs a bit of peace and quiet. And Mum and Dad don't approve —'

'Not my problem.'

'No. Maybe not. But *you* don't have to live here.'

'Wouldn't if you paid me.'

The idea of paying Blossom to live with us is laughable, but I'm in no mood for humour. I decide to try another tack.

'Well, just until the new year, then. How would that be?'

Blossom pauses, as though to consider.

'Think about it,' she concedes.

'That would be great.'

'Let you know Thursday.'

I'm too relieved to enquire as to the significance of Thursday. The prospect of even a few weeks without the tramping of strangers past the garden is too good for me to wish to endanger it by pushing my luck any further.

But I shall never know whether Thursday would have brought the anticipated reprieve, for I am not the only one who has been making plans.

The very next day we receive an unexpected visit from Mikey and Gavin. This is not unusual, as Mikey frequently calls in on his travels, and I'm always pleased to see him. But he doesn't often bring Gavin with him, and has never before brought Gavin in a wheelchair.

'Oh, dear. What's happened? Have you broken something, Gavin?' I ask, when Gavin and his wheelchair have been unloaded from the back of Mikey's car.

'We've come to visit your Virgin,' Mikey tells me.

'What are you two up to?'

'We're not up to anything. It's just that Gavin's decided to return to the Catholic Church and he wants to see it again.'

'But what's wrong with him? Is there something the matter with his legs?'

'You'll see.'

It's a relatively warm Saturday afternoon, the first sunshine we have seen for a couple of weeks, and there is a good gathering of pilgrims admiring the Virgin, praying and taking photographs. They draw back respectfully when they see the wheelchair, and Mikey parks his charge in front of the Virgin, where he and Gavin bow their heads apparently in prayer.

I am puzzled. Hitherto, Mikey has shown little interest in our Virgin, but perhaps Gavin, in returning to his faith, has managed to take Mikey with him. After all, it's quite possible. I'm sure that Mikey would dance barefoot on hot coals if Gavin asked him to, he is so besotted. On the other hand, why haven't they explained the wheelchair? Surely Gavin hasn't suddenly been struck down by some grave and unmentionable disease? Mikey and I have never had any secrets from each other. I would hate to think that he didn't feel he could trust me after all these years.

Meanwhile, people gather round the wheelchair, asking questions. What's wrong with Gavin? Has he always been unable to walk? If he's looking for a miracle, maybe he should try Lourdes. Someone's aunt came back from Lourdes cured of a tumour. People exchange views and experiences of Lourdes, and the gathering becomes something of a party.

Then quite suddenly, Gavin leaps from his wheelchair, flinging out his arms as though about to embrace some invisible giant.

'A miracle! It's a miracle! I can walk!' he cries, hugging Mikey and turning to the other visitors. 'Look, everyone! Oh, praise the Lord! I can *walk*!'

'Crippled from birth —' it is now Mikey's turn — 'and will you look at him now? Just look at him! He's walking with the best of us. We came looking for a miracle, and here it is. A miracle! Much better than Lourdes,' he adds tactlessly (I'm pretty sure that Mikey knows nothing at all about Lourdes).

Together, they pirouette round the wheelchair, while their fellow-pilgrims give little cries of astonishment and joy. A couple fall to their knees in thanksgiving, someone murmurs Hail Marys, while the rest gather round and ply Gavin with questions. What does it feel like? Has he really lived his life in a wheelchair? Did he have any kind of vision? Did the Virgin move? *Did she speak to him?*

But the performance is over. Gavin and Mikey reward their audience with radiant smiles and handshakes all round, before running off toward the house murmuring about having to make phone calls and letting Gavin's dear mother know the good news (Gavin's dear mother, I know for a fact, died when he was eleven).

'How could you, Mikey? *How could you?*' I demand, when we get back to the house. 'That was in the most appallingly bad taste.'

'It was fun, though, wasn't it? You have to admit, Ruth, it was a laugh.' Mikey tries to put his arm round me.

'It was not a laugh.' I push him away. 'It wasn't fun, either. Not for anybody else. What about all those poor people? They think they've just seen a miracle, and it was just you two making fools of yourselves. And of them. It was an unforgivable thing to do.'

'Oh, get a life, Ruth. Whatever's happened to your sense of humour?'

'My sense of humour is perfectly intact, thank you. I just don't happen to think it's amusing to play tricks on vulnerable people.'

'We're sorry,' says the newly-healed and now subdued Gavin. 'We really didn't mean any harm.'

'Oh, don't apologise to her, Gav. We haven't done anything wrong.' Mikey is unrepentant. 'Ruth's just in a bad mood.'

There are few things more infuriating than being told you're in a bad mood when, basically, you are not. It comes second only to being told that 'it must be the wrong time of the month' (at least he can't say that to me at the moment).

'Right. That's it. Go.' I point to the door. 'Just go.'

'What? No cup of tea?' Mikey looks astonished.

'No cup of tea. No cup of anything. Remember, I'm in a bad mood. You said so yourself.'

'But I didn't mean —'

'*Just go*, Mikey, would you? And take that bloody wheelchair with you.'

After they have gone, I find that I am shaking; shaking with anger, but also with disappointment and hurt. I thought I knew Mikey better. It's true that he has always enjoyed the odd practical joke, but he has never to my knowledge done anything so lacking in consideration for other people's feelings. But apparently I have misjudged him. It's tempting to blame the Gavin effect, but at least Gavin had the grace to apologise. I have to conclude that the whole thing was Mikey's idea.

My parents have been out for the afternoon with Eric and Silas, bonding over an ancient stone circle (this has been a pleasing development, as hitherto there has been little socialising between them), and they return just as Mikey and Gavin leave.

'Couldn't they stay?' Eric asks (Eric is fond of Mikey, who is always interested in Ark-related developments).

'No. They had to go.'

'Oh, what a shame.'

'I'll tell you about it later.'

When I finally get Eric and Silas on their own, I tell them about the "miracle", but they are disappointingly unperturbed.

'Oh well. No harm done,' says Silas, examining a dead frog (frogs are a new departure; advanced stuff, so I'm told, and in short supply in the winter, so Silas is pleased).

'You think so?' I ask him.

How little my uncles know about the power of miracles! For word spreads rapidly, and before we know it, we are inundated with visitors, with and without tickets. They come at all times of the day, and occasionally even at night, carrying torches. Thursday, the day of Blossom's decision, comes and goes unnoticed, for there is now no question of closing the hen house; more, the problem of how to manage what is rapidly becoming a crisis.

'Of course, it's trespass,' I say. 'It's your land. Surely there's some law to protect you.'

'Nowadays, the law seems to be more on the side of the person breaking it,' says Silas, who knows a man who was prosecuted for chasing a burglar with a sawn-off shot gun. 'We'll ask Blossom. She may have an idea.'

Blossom is typically unhelpful, but does refer the problem to Father Vincent, who pays us another visit accompanied by his new curate, with Blossom in the unlikely role of mediator.

'Oh, I say! That really is amazing.' The curate, who appears a great deal more impressed by the Virgin than Father Vincent, crosses himself. 'She looks so — *real*. And they say there's been a healing as well?'

'No. No healing. Just a practical joke,' I tell him.

'But I've spoken to witnesses. People who were there at the time. They said there was this man in a wheelchair —'

'The man in the wheelchair was perfectly able-bodied. He was an accomplice in a particularly cruel trick.'

'Ah.' The curate looks disappointed. He is young and fresh-faced and eager, and I feel sorry to have to disappoint him. 'But if it helps more people with their faith, surely that can't be bad.' He turns to Father Vincent for assurance.

'Faith built on deception isn't faith,' says Father Vincent firmly. 'Let's go back to the house and talk about it.'

I know from my brief acquaintance with Father Vincent that he is hoping to be offered a drink, and he's not disappointed. Over mulberry wine (just a cup of tea for the curate, who's driving) we discuss the problem.

'You could donate the hen house to the church,' the curate suggests (we have been invited to call him Father Ambrose, which seems a terribly portentous name for someone so young).

'No room,' says Father Vincent, pouring himself more wine.

'And what about the hens? It's their home,' says Silas.

'Don't they mind all these visitors?' Father Ambrose asks.

'Strangely enough, they don't. I think they're getting used to it,' I tell him. 'In any case, they run around all over the place during the day time, so they only use it at night and for laying.'

'Electric fence?' says Father Vincent. 'For the visitors, not the hens, of course.' This is not a very Christian suggestion, but I think the wine is beginning to take effect.

'Someone would sue,' says Eric gloomily.

'We could try to get more volunteers from the church to supervise, and maybe collect money for some kind of cause,' I suggest. 'At least that would do some good.'

'What cause?' Eric asks.

'Chickens.' Blossom who has been silent for some time, speaks up.

'What do you mean, chickens?'

'Rescue chickens.'

'Rescue what chickens?' Eric is becoming irritated.

'Battery.'

'I don't think a chicken charity would be appropriate for Our Lady,' says Father Vincent. He has difficulty with the words 'chicken charity', and I'm relieved that Father Ambrose is doing the driving.

'God's creatures,' says Blossom piously.

'No doubt. But a human charity might be more — appropriate,' says Father Ambrose.

'Both, then.'

'It's certainly a thought,' says Silas. 'If we can — police things properly, and Eric and I don't have to do too much. It might be managed.'

'Leave it to me,' says Father Ambrose, who is obviously much taken with the whole Virgin project. 'Would you let me — organise it?'

'We'd be absolutely delighted,' Silas assures him. 'If you're sure you've got the time.'

'There are some things one has to make time for,' Father Ambrose assures him earnestly. 'It will be a privilege.'

'The path's in a terrible state,' says Eric, after we have all had time to digest Father Ambrose's proposal. 'All those people tramping about have churned it up badly.'

'Gravel,' says Blossom.

'Expensive,' counters Eric.

'Lazzo knows someone.'

'Does he, indeed?'

Eric's suspicion may be well-founded.

'Legit,' Blossom pre-empts him.

'Not free, though,' says Silas.

'Good as.'

So after a lot of discussion and almost two bottles of mulberry wine, the decision is made. Lazzo will get a load of good-as-free gravel from his contact and reinforce the path with it. Father Ambrose will recruit more volunteers from the church to take over hen house duty and try to control the numbers by means of strict notices and more official-looking tickets, and we'll give it a try.

'Just a month's trial, mind,' says Eric, and Silas nods agreement. 'If that doesn't work we'll have to resort to something drastic.'

'What's drastic?' Kaz blows into the kitchen and helps herself to a glass of wine.

'It's a long story,' I tell her.

Kaz eyes Blossom suspiciously. 'If it's anything to do with Mum, I'd say no if I were you.'

'Too late,' says Blossom triumphantly.

And I'm afraid she's right.

Chapter Twenty-Eight

Within a week, Father Ambrose has taken over responsibility for the Virgin of the hen house, and things have improved enormously. Lazzo has laid down his gravel, collecting boxes have been put in place (Battery Rescue, the chicken charity, to appease Blossom, and Oxfam for those pilgrims who prefer human beings to chickens), and some very official-looking reusable tickets have been produced. Pairs of volunteers, complete with shiny badges, supervise the hen house during agreed opening hours, and on the whole, the punters are co-operative.

December is if anything worse than November. There is no Christmas-card frost twinkling in the trees; no bright sharp wintry mornings; and not a trace of snow. There is just more rain and more mud, dark afternoons followed by nights of penetrating cold. The house is not what you'd call cosy, since the heating system is erratic and the rooms are large with high ceilings. I have always wondered about high ceilings. Why is it that big houses built before the luxury of central heating invariably have these lofty rooms, where (presumably) what little heat there is rises ceiling-wards to hover unhelpfully above the heads of those it is intended to keep warm, while the draughts sweep unchallenged under the ill-fitting doors?

And then there is the prospect of Christmas.

Out of a sense of duty, I have always tried to spend Christmas at home with my parents. This is another of the many downsides of being an only child: without me, my parents will not have a family Christmas, since (apart from Eric and Silas) they have no other family to have it with. Our Christmases are never the jolly occasions enjoyed by other families. There are no crackers and paper hats; none of the drinking and merrymaking enjoyed by so many of my friends. We all go to church, after which my mother cooks a capon since, as she points out every year, there's no point in roasting a whole turkey for just the three of us. (For my own part, I have never been entirely sure what a capon is, except that it is a sort of inferior turkey substitute which only appears at Christmas, having undergone some kind of intimate operation). After lunch, we gather by the startling bright green plastic Christmas tree (Woolworths, circa 1980) to listen to the Queen and exchange presents.

When I was small, I always had a Christmas stocking, although there was never any pretence as to the existence of Father Christmas, since my father considered it 'wrong to tell lies to a child'. Nor for me the visit to Santa's grotto in the local department store, the excitement of waiting for a festive old man to clamber down the chimney, or the carefully prepared sherry and mince pies set out on the hearth. It was made absolutely clear to me from the start that Father Christmas was a myth, together with the munificent tooth fairy who frequented the homes of my more fortunate friends. If I have anything to do with it, the baby is going to believe in Father Christmas until it's at least eighteen, and will make a small fortune from the teeth placed under its pillow.

As I trudge back and forth with buckets of animal feed, I wonder what Christmas will be like here at Applegarth. My parents are still staying despite knowing full well that the insurance people are willing to pay for accommodation (I suspect that removal to an hotel would be seen to constitute some kind of climb down on the part of one or other of them); the rift between Blossom and Kaz has, if anything deepened, so Kaz is still living here; and Lazzo, who apparently misses his sister, is spending increasing amount of time with us, although he still goes home to sleep. If things carry on like this, I foresee a very full house at Christmas, not to mention a disconcerting clash of customs and beliefs.

But two weeks before Christmas, we receive a visitor.

It seems to be my lot to find unexpected visitors on the doorstep, but this is probably because I am nearly always in. My parents are increasingly out, seeing people about repairs to their house or attending prayer meetings with their new church friends, and Eric and Silas never answer the door if they think someone else is around to do it. As for Blossom she rarely answers doors at all, as she says it is not in her job description.

The man on the doorstep is middle-aged, lean and rather good-looking, with nice eyes and an anxious smile.

'My name is Kent Riley. I'm looking for my father,' he tells me, fending off the advances of Mr. Darcy.

'Your father?'

'Yes. Ridiculous, isn't it? At my age, I mean. It's taken me ages,' he adds, and I notice that he looks frozen.

'You'd better come in.' I hold the door open for him, 'although I'm not sure you'll find your father here.'

'Well, it's worth a try.' Mr. Riley takes off his muddy shoes and looks round the hallway with interest, as though expecting to be presented with an identity parade of missing fathers. 'I never met him, you know.'

'Oh, didn't you?'

'My mother wouldn't even tell me who he was.'

'Your mother?'

'She died six months ago.'

'Oh. I'm sorry.'

'That's all right.'

'Who is — your father?'

'I'm not sure. But I think his name was Purves, and I know he lived here.'

'Ah.' Purves is the surname of Eric and Silas, and they have lived here all their lives. I take a couple of deep breaths. Eric? Silas? Eric or Silas a *father*? Surely not.

'You don't have another name for — your father?' I say, leading the way to the kitchen. Silas's frog is spread-eagled on the kitchen table. I quickly cover it with a tea towel.

'No. My mother used to get so upset at the thought of my getting in touch with him, that I gave up asking her about him. After all, I've done okay without a father so far. But she left me a letter at the solicitor's saying that I might find my father at this address. So I thought I'd come and see if — well, if he's still alive.'

While we are having this conversation, my thoughts are spinning. What do I do? Silas mustn't be upset at the moment, as it's bad for his heart. My parents certainly shouldn't be involved due to the private nature of the business in hand. Kaz would certainly say something tactless. This leaves Eric.

'I'll just fetch my uncle,' I say. 'He might be able to help.'

Eric is very preoccupied with the problem of bamboo shoots and pandas, and is reluctant to leave his investigations.

'Can't you see to this man, Ruth?' he asks me, looking longingly at his charts and notes.

'No, I'm afraid I can't. This is a personal matter, and nothing to do with me. I probably shouldn't even know about it,' I tell him.

'Oh, well. If you're sure.'

'I'm sure.'

Eric greets our visitor, and offers him a drink.

'I think perhaps I ought to be going.' I edge towards the door.

'No, no, Ruth. Do stay.' Eric pours a cloudy liquid into glasses (the label has come off the bottle. I hope it's not weed killer).

'But this may be private,' I tell him.

'Nonsense,' says Eric. 'Now.' He turns to Mr. Riley. 'What can I do for you?'

'It's complicated.' The man looks desperately round him, as though searching for some kind of assistance. 'Is your name — Purves?'

'Yes. Eric Purves.' Eric tastes his drink and then holds his glass up to the light. 'Parsnip, I think. Yes, I'm sure this is the parsnip. Not at all bad, as I recall.'

'Well, I think you might be my father.'

'Ah.' Eric puts down his glass. He appears amazingly calm. 'What makes you think that?'

Mr. Riley explains about his mother, the mystery of his paternity, and the letter.

'I'm so sorry to bother you with all this, particularly after all this time. It must come as quite a shock to you. But you see, I really need to know.'

'Of course you do.' Eric pauses. 'And who — who was your mother?'

'Mary Riley. She never married, so if you knew her, that would have been her name.'

'Mary Riley,' Eric muses, as though mentally going through a check-list of past lovers. 'Yes. You know, I think there was a Mary Riley. It was a long time ago, of course. A very long time ago.'

At this moment, Silas comes in. He greets Mr. Riley cheerfully, and then starts hunting for his frog.

'I'm sure I put it down here somewhere,' he says. 'Ruth, have you done something with my frog?'

'Silas, I think you'd better listen to Eric,' I tell him.

'Yes. Silas, Mr. Riley thinks I'm his father.'

Mr. Riley is still apparently reeling from the identical twin effect, and I can't help feeling sorry for him. After all, there are just so many shocks someone can be expected to cope with in one afternoon. I refill his glass, hoping this might help.

'And are you?' Silas asks. 'Oh, here it is!' He recovers his frog from under the tea towel and places it on the draining board.

'I suppose I could be,' Eric says. 'He's Mary Riley's son.'

'Mary Riley, Mary Riley.' Silas says thoughtfully, 'Oh, *that* Mary Riley! I remember. She was a lovely girl. Nice sense of humour.'

I hope her son has inherited the sense of humour, for I have a feeling he's going to need it.

'So, what do you think?' Mr. Riley looks pathetically from one to the other.

'Well, we both *knew* Mary Riley,' says Silas carefully.

'Oh yes. We both knew her,' Eric says. 'Quite well, actually.'

'How well?' Mr. Riley has decided to be blunt.

'Very well.' Silas and Eric exchange glances.

'What, both of you?'

'Both of us.'

'You mean you shared — relationships?'

'Oh, not always,' Eric tells him, 'By no means always. But sometimes, when one thing ended, another would begin. You know how it is.'

'Are you saying — are you saying that either of you could be my father?'

'I think we're saying it's possible.' Eric refills everyone's glasses. 'What did you say your name was?'

'Kent. Kent Riley.'

'Why Kent?'

'My mother said I was conceived in Kent.'

'Surrey.' My uncles speak in unison.

'I beg your pardon?'

'Not Kent. Surrey. If it — you — were anything to do with us, it was definitely Surrey,' says Silas.

'Perhaps she thought that Kent Riley sounded better than Surrey Riley,' says Eric.

There follows a discussion about Kent and Surrey, and what Mary Riley might or might not have been up to in either county.

'You don't sound very surprised by all this,' Mr. Riley says, after everyone has decided that Kent is on the whole prettier than Surrey.

'Oh, I think we're surprised all right,' Silas says, 'but nothing's been proved yet, has it?'

'No. We need proof,' says Eric.

'Well, I've no problem with that,' says Mr. Riley (Kent, I suppose we should call him, especially as it looks as though he may be family).

'Of course, if you can prove that one of us is your father we'll have to share you,' says Silas.

'Why's that?'

'Shared DNA. Our DNA is identical, so while we might find out that either of us could be your father, we wouldn't know which one.'

'Oh. Oh dear.'

'Why? Does it matter?'

'I don't know. I hadn't really thought about it. I'd resigned myself to having no father at all, and now it looks as though I may have two. It takes a bit of getting used to.'

'And we had resigned ourselves to having no sons at all, and now we'll have to make do with half each,' says Eric, who has overdone the parsnip wine and is becoming pink-faced and merry. 'Have you any children?' I think this is greedy of Eric. Isn't a son enough, without expecting grandchildren as well?

'No. I never married.' No-one points out that it is just been shown only too clearly that marriage is no prerequisite for the fathering of children.

'Oh well. Never mind.'

'I don't, most of the time,' Kent says, 'but I think I'd like to have been a father.'

'It's not too late.' Eric laughs. 'Look at us! We never expected children, and now it looks as though we might have one after all!'

While this discussion is going on, it occurs to me that Eric and Silas may not be the only ones to have discovered a new relation, for I may be about to acquire a cousin. Never having had a cousin before — never really having had much in the way of family at all — I am very pleased with this idea.

'Mr. Riley — Kent — what do you do?' I ask him. 'For a living, I mean.'

'I'm a piano tuner.'

There follows a long, interested silence.

'Not — not a blind piano tuner?' asks Silas.

'Certainly not a blind piano tuner. Many of us can see perfectly well.'

Eric and Silas are clearly disappointed, and I feel enormously sorry for Kent. He has more than likely just found two possible fathers, and already he has proved to be a disappointment.

'Well, I think it's wonderful,' I tell him. 'We can play duets.'

I think of the poor neglected piano in the room next door. Our new-found relation may be just the person to bring it back to life.

Chapter Twenty-Nine

It is decided that what with the approach of Christmas and the amount of work generated by the extra care needed by the animals in this most unforgiving of seasons, any DNA investigations can wait until the new year. But our new relation seems here to stay, at least for the time being.

Meanwhile, it transpires that whatever Mary Riley may have been up to in her lifetime, she contrived to save quite a lot of money, all of which she left to her only son. Kent is now what he himself calls 'a free man'. His piano tuning days are over. He has let his mother's house, and bought himself a nice little caravan, which he has fitted up with all mod cons. With this in tow, he intends to tour the country, looking up friends (and putative fathers) and visiting those towns and cities he has never managed to see before. Kent says that he has 'done' abroad, and that it is wildly overrated. It's time to reacquaint himself with the country of his birth. He admits that he was sad to leave his piano behind, but his inheritance wouldn't stretch to a caravan large enough to accommodate it.

Needless to say, Eric and Silas have invited him to stay on 'so that we can all get to know each other', so the caravan is now parked behind the outhouses, and Kent is rapidly becoming one of the household. I'm delighted, my parents are slightly puzzled and Blossom is indignant ('too many people,' she complains, although Kent keeps well out of her way). Kaz is another story.

When she first meets him, she's polite enough, but after a day or two, she begins to show a suspicious amount of interest in him.

'This Kent person,' she says casually, while we are seeing to the pigs. 'He's rather nice.'

'How, *rather nice*?' I ask her.

'Quite sexy, actually.' Kaz bends over the bucket of swill she's mixing.

'Oh Kaz, you can't!'

'Can't what?'

'You know perfectly well what I mean. For a start, he's too old for you. And anyway, aren't you seeing someone else at the moment?' For these days, it's hard to keep up with Kaz's love life.

'Oh, him. He's boring. I was giving him up anyway. No. I think it's time for someone more mature.' She winks at me.

'Kaz, you can't just *use* Kent because you want someone more mature. Hasn't the poor guy had enough shocks for the time being?'

'What's got into you, Ruth? I'm not using anyone, and Kent is a grown man and can make his own decisions.' She looks at me thoughtfully. 'You know, I think you're jealous!'

'Don't be ridiculous!'

But in a way, she's right. Having found this new almost-relation, I'm oddly reluctant to share him. Silas and Eric, as putative fathers, are different. But Kaz has no claim on Kent, and I want to keep it that way.

'Well, nothing's happened yet,' says Kaz peaceably, as we return to the house. 'We'll just have to see, won't we?'

My parents have been given just as much information about Kent as Eric and Silas consider they need; they have been told that he is the son of an old friend ('true, in a way') and that he has come to visit. Further information will be forthcoming if the DNA results prove to be positive. As Silas points out, there is no point in shocking them unnecessarily. Both my uncles agree that my mother might well be pleased to have a nephew, but the circumstances (not to mention the confusion) surrounding his provenance might prove more difficult to explain, never mind accept.

I am in a seventh heaven, for at last I have someone to make music with. While I clean up the piano, digging out everything from spiders' webs to old socks and even a dead mouse from its dusty innards, Kent does his best to tune it.

'I don't think I can bring it up to concert pitch without breaking strings,' he tells me. Fortunately, I am not blessed with perfect pitch, so I can just tune my violin down a fraction and we are ready to go. The piano is more honky-tonk than Steinway, but any piano is better than no piano, and I for one am not complaining.

Kent proves to be an excellent pianist. I am unsurprised — I have come across many piano-tuners who are similarly gifted — but my uncles are amazed. Like many people, they have hitherto regarded piano tuners as second-rate musicians (if they can be counted as musicians at all), but Kent rapidly wins them over, and he and I entertain everyone with an evening of Mozart and Beethoven.

Even my parents are impressed.

'He plays very well. For a piano tuner,' I hear Mum say to Dad.

In addition to his music, Kent adds a great deal to the running of the household. He's an excellent cook, bachelor-tidy in his habits, and good with the animals. He takes an interest in Silas's taxidermy, and even assists Eric with his researches (although I suspect that he considers them to be a waste of time).

As I watch him stooped over some task, or see his long fingers moving over the piano keys, I become increasingly convinced that he is indeed the son of Eric or Silas. In addition to the physical resemblance, he even shares some of their mannerisms. The way he shakes his head when he's puzzled; the occasional amused lift of an eyebrow; the sound of his laugh. All these remind me of Eric and Silas. And while I was initially unsure as to whether having a son would be a good thing for my uncles, I've now been completely won round. I think that Eric and Silas are beginning to feel the same, for while they accepted Kent's arrival with equanimity, I know they must have been disturbed by it. Now, it is as though they have always known him. He is, quite simply, part of the family.

I am not the only one to have noticed a resemblance.

'Family, is he?' Blossom asks me, after Kent has been with us a week. It's a question which she's obviously been longing to ask, and the waiting's finally got too much for her.

'He's the son of an old friend,' I tell her. 'She died recently.'

'Hmm.'

'What do you mean, hmm?'

'You know what I mean,' says Blossom. '*You know.*'

But now something happens to take my mind off life at Applegarth, for I have news of Amos. I've alerted everyone I can think of (friends, friends of friends, colleagues from the orchestra, even a dentist we once shared in London) and finally someone from the orchestra has received a postcard from Barbados, and has thoughtfully forwarded it to me. Palm trees and blue skies adorn the front, but on the back, the news isn't good.

Having a wonderful time in this amazing place. The people are so friendly that I feel as though I've come home. Even found a band to play in. May stay here for ever! December in England seems a very long way away. What's there to come home to?

ME! I want to tell him. There's me to come home to, and our baby! Oh Amos! Please come home!

But my tears fall uselessly onto the postcard, trickling across the sandy beach and the palm trees and smudging the ink of Amos's handwriting. He has nice handwriting, and it occurs to me that I have never seen it before. There has never been any reason for us to correspond. And now, when there is every reason, I have no address to write to. Supposing Amos really does decide to stay on? Supposing he never comes back? He has always had a penchant for dark-skinned women. He could well settle down with a Caribbean wife and a brood of tawny children, with never a thought for (or come to that, any knowledge of) the child he's left behind. Perhaps, in years to come, my son and I will voyage across the sea and try to find him. But of course by then it will be too late. We shall merely be an embarrassment; a cruel reminder of the life he's tried to leave behind.

I suppose I could try writing to the British embassy in Barbados. Do embassies concern themselves with such domestic matters? Almost certainly not. Perhaps I should go to Barbados now to search for him? But I haven't enough money, and I wouldn't know where to start. Also, the idea of travelling, once so attractive, has become daunting to me in my pregnant and vulnerable state, and the prospect of running the gauntlet of airports and queues and the complications of foreign officialdom on my own is not one I relish. I need my family and friends; I need continuity; I need to feel *safe*. Spinning across the world in search of Amos doesn't sound at all safe, especially as it is more than likely that I wouldn't find him. Briefly, I wonder whether Mikey would come with me. But Mikey is still sulking in the aftermath of the wheelchair episode, and in any case, it wouldn't be fair to take him away from Gavin at this early stage of their relationship. I shall just have to continue waiting, and see what happens. I wish most fervently that I had never seen that postcard. My friend meant kindly in sending it to me, but it has done nothing to raise my spirits.

'What's up, Ruth?' Kaz has come into the kitchen to make herself some coffee.

I tell her about the postcard. Kaz already knows about Amos, and has been on the whole sympathetic.

'Mm.' Kaz pours hot water into a mug. 'Are you sure you really want this guy?'

'No. Not absolutely sure. But I think I do.'

'Better to have no man than the wrong man,' Kaz tells me.

'Do you think you'll get married one day?' I ask her.

'I might, if I could find someone like Kent,' she teases. I decide to ignore her. 'But probably not. The only married couple I've ever had anything to do with were my parents. They were a nightmare together.'

'What was your dad like?'

'Oh, mousy, hen-pecked. A miserable little man, he was. Though I blame my mum.'

'Did she make him very unhappy?' I have often wondered about Blossom's marriage.

'She certainly did. But then, he asked for it. He was such a wimp. And he wouldn't fight back.'

'Why didn't he leave her?'

'Search me. She told him to often enough.'

'Wasn't she at all upset when he died?'

Kaz laughs.

'Not at all. At least no-one can call Mum a hypocrite.'

'And Lazzo? Was he — close to your father?'

'No. In any case, Lazzo wasn't Dad's.'

'Ah.' I was wondering how it was that the combination of a mousy little man and Blossom had managed to produce anything as large as Lazzo. 'How does she reconcile that with her faith?'

'I told you before. Mum's selective when it comes to her faith. She takes the bits she wants, and discards the rest.'

'How handy.' I pause for a moment, envying Kaz's ability to look ravishing whatever she happens to be wearing (today, dirty dungarees, an old flat cap belonging to my uncles and a torn trench coat). 'Who was Lazzo's father?'

'No idea.' Kaz spoons sugar into her coffee, and props herself against the sink.

'Does no-one know?'

'Mum probably does, but she's not telling, and Lazzo doesn't seem to care. I'm glad she had him, though. He's a good lad, is our Lazzo.'

'Yes. He's wonderfully straightforward, isn't he.'

'Heart of gold,' Kaz agrees.

'And is Lazzo a Catholic?'

Kaz laughs. 'Well, he was an altar boy when he was little, but he ate all the communion wafers and was dismissed. Sacrilege, they called it, and Mum was furious. But I think he was just hungry, poor kid. Our Laz was always hungry. But no. He's not really a Catholic any more, though Mum does sometimes try to drag him to Mass.'

After Kaz has left the room, I ponder on the subject of God. Do I believe in Him? I was force fed with so much religion as a child, that I used to think that I had been put off for life, but of course God and religion are not necessarily the same thing. Thinking about it now, I decide that I probably do believe in something like God. Wide night skies, an expanse of sea, the music of Bach, the poetry of Shakespeare — they all seem to come from something beyond a mere coincidence of genes or particles. But they also seem to me to have little connection with the petty rules and regulations and the repetitive hymns, often sung to the accompaniment of a guitar, which are the life blood of the church attended by my parents. These prettify and reduce God, like the paintings of Holman Hunt, making Him small and ever so slightly sickly. My God, if I have one, is huge and powerful and mysterious.

But then, what right have I to belittle a faith which gives so much comfort, and in which my parents have invested so much of their lives? Isn't it possible that we are all right, in our different ways?

I wander outdoors and make my way up to the hen house. A weak winter sun is shining on the Virgin, making her appear even more lifelike than usual, and someone has placed a bunch of Christmas roses on the ground beneath her. I envy the pilgrims their faith. It would be wonderful to believe that our Virgin really is a divine sign, and that the real Virgin Mary is still alive and well and doing good in the world.

You know what it's like, I tell her. You didn't exactly plan your pregnancy, either, did you? You must have had a pretty difficult time. Please help me to cope.

And please, if you have any influence at all, help me to find Amos.

Chapter Thirty

Christmas at Applegarth is very different from any Christmas I've experienced before. The house is as full as ever, and Lazzo joins us for the day (Kaz tells us that Blossom doesn't do Christmas, and probably won't even notice her family's absence). The turkey — an ill-tempered bird of enormous proportions who has spent the last few months chasing us round the garden and biting our legs — has been despatched and prepared, Mum has made a Christmas cake, and a real Christmas tree stands in the hallway, decked out with decorations which go back to my uncles' and Mum's childhood. Numerous dusty bottles of wine are brought up from the cellar, their labels washed off for identification purposes, and everyone has Christmas stockings.

'What, all of us?' Mum asked, when she was told what was to happen.

'All of us,' Silas told her. 'Eric and I always give each other a stocking, but as there are so many of us, we thought we'd all draw lots and do each other's.'

I draw Kaz, and wonder what on earth I can put in it, for Kaz has a mind of her own when it comes to matters of taste. But in the event, she is thrilled.

'I've never had a stocking before,' she tells me, as she unwraps little parcels of chocolate and bath essence and some rather naughty knickers from the market. 'I always wanted one as a kid, but Mum said no.'

'Didn't you get presents?' I ask her. 'You must have had something?'

'Money usually. And maybe some sweets. Nothing much else, though. If I have kids, they're going to have stockings just like this one.' She pops a Malteser in her mouth. 'What about you, Ruth? Will you give your child a Christmas stocking?'

'Oh, yes. I should think so.' It occurs to me that the baby should probably have one next year, but what does one put in the stocking of anyone so small? I know nothing at all about babies. Do they eat sweets? Play with toys? *Do* anything? No doubt I shall find out.

My parents pay lip service to the stocking ritual (Mum has drawn Lazzo, and Dad, Silas), but I can see their hearts aren't in it, and they hanker after the kind of Christmas they are used to. After a meal which is more mediaeval banquet than traditional Christmas lunch, they make their excuses, and drive off to spend the rest of the day with some of Mum's new friends from church. In a way I'm pleased, for at least they are united in their discomfort at the goings-on at Applegarth. I feel for my mother's situation, but I would hate my parents' split to be permanent. Maybe it's something to do with the perversity of my generation, for while we aren't necessarily too bothered about marriage for ourselves, we nonetheless expect out parents to stay securely within its boundaries.

After they have left, everyone else continues to make inroads into the homemade wine, until Eric and Silas fall asleep in their chairs. Kaz, who is by now very drunk indeed, is draped across the table singing Jingle Bells, one pert little breast attempting to escape from the confines of her strappy little top. Kent, who says he needs some fresh air, is feeding the chickens. As for Lazzo, he is still admiring the contents of his stocking. Mum's efforts have been unimaginative — among other things, sweets, socks, and a keyring — but she couldn't have had a more appreciative recipient. Lazzo has unwrapped all the little parcels, and arranged his gifts in a neat row. I can see he's longing to open some of the sweets, but doesn't like to spoil the appearance of his arrangement.

'Go on, Lazzo. Have one. That's what they're for,' I urge him (although after the excesses of lunch time, I personally can't imagine ever wanting to eat again).

Lazzo picks up his packet of sweets and turns it over in his hands. Then he puts it back in its place.

'Have one of mine.' I take pity on him.

'Ta.' Absently, Lazzo takes a handful of toffees, which vanish without apparently any need for chewing on Lazzo's part. 'Never had presents like this,' he tells me, picking up his keyring and stroking it.

'Have you got some keys you can put on it?' I ask him.

'Nope.'

'What, none at all?'

'Nope.'

'How do you get into the house when you go home?'

'Key's under a stone.'

'Oh. Would you like a key?'

Lazzo's face brightens, and I forage in my bag and find an old front door key from a long-ago flat, wondering why it is that people never get around to throwing away old keys. Carefully, Lazzo attaches the key to his keyring, then holds it up for me to admire.

'Perfect,' I tell him.

Lazzo nods happily. His capacity for finding pleasure in small things never fails to amaze me, and I feel oddly humbled. Here is someone who has never (as far as I know) experienced much in the way of parental love and appears to have very few possessions, and yet he appears perfectly content with his lot. I have heard Lazzo swear, certainly, and he has a very colourful vocabulary in that department, but I have never heard him complain. Whatever he is doing, he gives the impression that that is the thing he wants to be doing above all else. He may not be particularly clean (I notice that among Mum's gifts there is a large can of cheap deodorant) and his table manners are appalling, but he is gentle and courteous and, in his own way, chivalrous. I don't think it would be an exaggeration to say that I have grown to love Lazzo.

'What's your mum doing today?' I ask him.

'Bed,' Lazzo tells me.

'What, all day?'

'Yeah. Always does.'

'What about church?'

'Midnight.'

Of course. I'd forgotten that that was what Catholics do at Christmas. It always seems to me to be a very sensible arrangement; get the formalities out of the way as early as possible, and then get down to the serious business of celebrating.

'So she's all by herself?'

'Doesn't mind.' Lazzo helps himself to another half dozen toffees.

'Did she — give you anything? A present?'

Lazzo laughs.

'Nope. Says I get board and lodging. Shouldn't expect anything else.'

'Do you mind?'

'Nope.' Lazzo finishes up the toffees.

'Did you give her anything?'

'No money.'

This is true enough, for Lazzo never appears to have any money. Although Blossom has cautioned against it, my uncles insist on paying him something for the work he does for them, but I know for a fact that he hands it all over to his mother. She feeds him and buys his few clothes, and if he did have money of his own, he'd probably spend it unwisely.

'Got fags off our Kaz,' he offers.

'That's nice.'

'Yeah. Five hundred. Keep me going.'

'They certainly should.'

By now, Kaz appears to have passed out. Lazzo carries her into the sitting room and deposits her on the sofa, where she lies snoring gently. One of her arms dangles over the edge like that of Chatterton in his famous portrait, and her right breast has finally broken free of its moorings, its rosy nipple pointing triumphantly towards the ceiling. Most people in this situation would look dishevelled and decadent. Kaz simply looks beautiful. Nonetheless, I cover up the rogue breast with a coat, for while Lazzo doesn't appear to have noticed, I would hate to embarrass Kent on his return.

By seven o'clock, everyone is beginning to recover, and we receive a Christmas visit from Mikey and Gavin, who come bearing gifts and forgiveness.

'I think I've sulked for long enough to make my point,' says Mikey, giving me a hug.

'I think you have.' I return his embrace. 'But I'm afraid I haven't bought you a present. I didn't know you were coming.'

'Neither did we. It was a spur of the moment thing. We were going to have our first Christmas on our own, but we got bored and decided we needed a party, so we've come to see you.'

'But we're not having a party.'

'You are now.' Mikey fetches bags from the car, and unpacks pork pies and crisps and nuts and Christmas crackers, and yet more drink. 'There! A party! Now, where's the corkscrew?'

When my parents return at eleven, they find Mikey's party in full swing, with a drunken game of charades in progress. Kaz and Kent, together with several cushions, are under an old raincoat pretending to be a camel, with Gavin, his head covered with a tea towel, as its Arab owner and Lazzo some kind of tree. Mikey and I are doing the guessing, but Silas, who is supposed to be on our team, is asleep, and Eric is fretting because he's realised that he hasn't accounted for camels on his Ark, and is wondering whether he needs to have dromedaries as well, or will the camels do for both?

'You don't hear much about dromedaries, do you?' he says. 'Camels, yes, but not dromedaries. What do people do with dromedaries?'

'I've no idea,' I tell him.

'Camels drink a lot,' he murmurs. 'Oh dear.'

'It would seem,' says my father, taking off his coat, 'that everyone has been drinking a lot.'

This strikes Mikey and me as terribly funny, and we roll on the sofa, crying with laughter. Eric merely looks hurt. Both halves of the camel collapse on the floor, Silas wakes up with a start, and the tree wanders off into the kitchen to look for more beer.

All in all, I think you could say that it's been a very merry Christmas indeed.

Chapter Thirty-One

It is now January (if anything, even worse than November, with its grey twilight days and penetrating cold), and everyone is tired and grumpy. Meanwhile, I have commenced ante-natal classes.

After two sessions, I've decided that nothing can be quite so smug as a room full of cosily pregnant women lying on cushions on the floor doing their breathing exercises, each cocooned in a warm blanket of reproductive self-satisfaction. While I thought I would welcome the opportunity to talk to women of my own age and in the same condition, I had no idea of the self-centredness of pregnancy, and after two coffee breaks' worth of conversation about backache and breastfeeding and Braxton-Hicks contractions, I long for talk of anything but babies. What do these women actually *do*, apart from being pregnant? Have they lives, jobs, interests? It would appear not, or at least not at the moment. Right now, their lives centre round their bumps, the wonder of what's inside those bumps, and most importantly of all, how it's going to get out (we are all first-timers. Presumably second-time-round mothers are too busy to bother with all this, or maybe they feel they already know enough. I envy them).

Of course, Silas wanted to come with me, but fathers' evening (the only time when men are invited) doesn't happen until later, and in any case, I don't think it would be appropriate. In the absence of a genuine father, I have been invited to call on the services of a "birthing partner", but so far, I've decided against it, since there doesn't seem to be a suitable candidate. Silas, who is dying to be chosen, is out of the question, my mother (the obvious choice) seems unsure, and Kaz, who has volunteered for the part, is not in my good books.

For Kaz is beginning to make headway with Kent.

She hasn't told me so. In fact, she hasn't told me anything at all, but I can tell from her demeanour that something has happened. She sings as she goes about her work, volunteers to do the most unpleasant of jobs and has even made her peace with Blossom, although she continues to live with us. I know for a fact that she has dumped the "boring" boyfriend, and since the latest club didn't work out after all, she's short of work, and living here she has little opportunity to meet anyone else.

Kent, too, has changed. Always a cheerful person, he now literally glows with happiness, and nothing is too much trouble. On several occasions I have intercepted covert glances and smiles between the two of them — the kinds of secret smiles particular to lovers — and wherever possible he and Kaz contrive to work together. Kaz has been teaching Kent to milk the goats, and I've even caught her giving him what appeared to be a pole dancing demonstration in the garden, using a long-abandoned telegraph pole by the hedge.

'What on earth is Kaz doing?' Eric asks, as we watch from the kitchen window. 'She's going to hurt herself if she tries to climb that thing. It's probably rotten by now.'

'She's not trying to climb it. She's — dancing with it.' I know my voice is tight with hostility, but just at the moment, I can't help it.

'Now I've heard everything!' Eric has never understood the pole dancing thing. 'Don't you go trying anything like that, Ruth. You could do yourself serious damage.'

'I wouldn't dream of it.'

At this moment, Kaz begins to swing effortlessly by one arm, her head thrown back, legs stretched out at an impossible angle, looking as ravishing as ever despite her torn shirt and filthy jeans while Kent watches, apparently mesmerised. Suddenly, I'm overwhelmed with jealousy. I know this is nasty of me; they are both free and single, and they are both people I'm fond of. I should be pleased for them. But up until now — notwithstanding a possible relationship with Eric and Silas — Kent has been *my* friend; my almost-relation. He's been the person I play music with; the one who really understands and shares my passion. And now it seems as though he's found an altogether different, more exciting kind of passion; something I can't share in at all. And I don't like it. Besides, I'm the one who needs a partner, not Kaz. Until recently, Kaz has had putative lovers beating a path to her door, while I, with my impending motherhood, have no-one at all.

After two weeks of this, I can't stand it any longer.

'Kaz, how *could* you?' I ask her, as we muck out the pigs together. Kaz is doing most of the work since my size (which to me appears colossal but which I'm told is quite normal) prevents me from doing much in the way of bending.

'How could I what?' Kaz pushes Sarah out of the way with the handle of her shovel (Sarah hates her home being disarranged, and always makes herself as unpleasant as possible).

'Kent.'

'Ah.'

'Yes. Ah.'

'Well, what's it to you?' She stands back and wipes her hands on her jeans.

'I — I'm —'

'Jealous?'

'Of course not!'

'I wouldn't blame you,' Kaz says. 'He is rather gorgeous, isn't he?'

'Not particularly.' I'm in no mood to collude in this kind of conversation. 'Anyway, when did it all start?'

'I suppose — inside the camel.'

'*What?*'

'You know. At Christmas, when we were playing charades, and Kent and I were a camel. Under a rug. We — kissed.'

'How romantic.' If I wasn't so cross, I'd laugh.

'Yes. It was rather. I was going to tell you, but I knew you'd be like this.'

'I'm not being like anything. It's just — I don't like seeing him being taken advantage of.'

'Ruth, no-one's taking advantage of anyone. We just — like each other. We get on.'

'But you've got nothing in common!'

'Oh yes we have.' Kaz winks. 'More than you think.'

'Have you — well, have you —?'

'Not yet. No. But we probably shall.'

'And you've got a cosy little love nest waiting for you in the caravan, haven't you?'

Kaz closes the door of the sty and leans against it. 'Ruth, do you have to be like this? I thought we were friends.'

'Yes. No. I don't know.' And to my horror, I burst into tears. 'I'm sorry. I really am. It's just that I'm fat and tired and unlovely, and you're young and beautiful, and — and I feel so alone!'

Kaz puts her arms round me and pulls me into a hug, and for a few minutes we stand there in the drizzle as I sob into her shoulder and she pats my back and makes the kinds of soothing noises that Lazzo makes for the animals.

'Come on,' she says, pushing me gently away. 'It's freezing out here. Let's go back into the house and I'll make us some tea. And Ruth?'

'Yes?'

'Don't tell the boys about — about me and Kent yet, will you? It may come to nothing, and it's early days.'

I promise that I won't.

Later on in bed, I am awakened by the activities of the baby, who seems to be playing football with my liver, and my thoughts turn again to Kaz and Kent. Maybe it's not so bad after all. Neither of them seems to have had it easy so far, and don't they both deserve a little happiness? If Kent turns out to be my cousin, and he and Kaz stay together, then Kaz will be a kind of cousin, too, and I've always wanted more relatives. Kaz would make a good relative; maybe even the next best thing to a sister. She's kind and funny and loyal. I reflect that I could do a lot worse.

As I rearrange my pillows and turn onto my back, I conclude that my problem is that I'm now surrounded by couples. Eric and Silas have each other, as do Mum and Dad. Even Sarah has what might be called a gentleman visitor, who is delivered from time to time from the back of a very dirty truck and stays just long enough to guarantee another litter of piglets. I have only met him once, and he is if possible even more ill-tempered than she is, but none the less, he is her mate (although no doubt the mate of many others, besides), and he seems to do the business to the satisfaction of both parties. I'm the only one who's alone.

Mikey has heard from his contact in Barbados, who has made a few enquiries but come up with nothing in the way of news of bearded trombone players, or indeed any trombone players at all. It seems that Barbados is bigger than I had imagined, and any search for Amos would be of the needle and haystack variety. Amos may even have already tired of it and left. As I drift off to sleep, I dream of Amos and me running towards each other across a palm-fringed beach, like a Caribbean Cathy and Heathcliffe.

'Ruth! Ruth!' Amos calls, but his voice and image become fainter and fainter until I find myself alone, and when I awake again, my pillow is damp with my tears.

Chapter Thirty-Two

It's becoming increasingly apparent that Silas is unwell again. He is breathless and pale, tires easily and complains of swollen ankles and palpitations.

'I think it's come back,' he tells us, leafing through his health bible. It is a new one, which Eric gave him for Christmas since the old one was falling to pieces. It was not something Eric wanted to buy, since he had had more than enough of the last one, but he had to agree that Silas would only fret without what he sees as an essential aid to living. The new book is big and shiny and up-to-date, illustrated with the kinds of photographs that most people would do a great deal to avoid, and Silas loves it.

'Look.' Silas jabs a finger at a diagram of a heart valve. 'That's what it's supposed to look like. I think mine must be shot to pieces.'

'But you don't know what your heart looks like,' I object. 'How can you possibly tell?'

'I can feel it.' Silas places a hand on his chest. 'It's fibrillating again. The valve just isn't working properly. Look, Ruth.' He shows me a picture of a non-functioning valve. 'That's what's happened to it. I think I'm in mild heart failure.'

He goes on the explain about "mitral regurgitation" and "oedema" and says that this almost certainly means he should have an operation.

'Anyone would think you wanted an operation,' I object. 'No-one *wants* operations.'

'Well, of course I don't actually *want* one,' Silas says, just a little too cheerfully. 'But if I have to have one, then so be it.'

'You should see the doctor anyway,' Eric says. 'You need a thorough check-up.'

'All in good time, all in good time,' Silas says, opening his book again. 'I want to make quite sure I know all the facts before I start seeing doctors again.'

'But the doctor will know all the facts. *You* don't have to,' I object.

Silas regards me gravely over the top of his spectacles.

'You can't be too sure,' he says. 'And it's my body. I think I should be the one to decide what to do with it.'

Since none of us can argue with that, we have to leave Silas to get on with it, but I know that poor Eric is terribly worried, and I feel for him. In matters of his own health, Silas, usually the most thoughtful of men, can be very inconsiderate, for surely he, more than any of us, should understand how Eric is feeling.

'You must be awfully worried,' I say to Eric, when we are alone together.

'Of course I am. But what can I do?' He is currently preoccupied with the subject of koala bears and eucalyptus, and for once I'm grateful for Eric's Ark, because at least it's something to help keep his mind off his brother. 'He's so stubborn. It would be easier if he didn't enjoy all this so much. He's having a wonderful time with that bloody book of his. I wish I'd never given it to him. It only encourages him.'

'He would have bought it for himself anyway,' I remind him. 'You know what Silas is like.'

'True.' Eric puts down his pen. 'Did you know that the koala bear is a marsupial? Isn't that interesting?'

The following day, Silas collapses at the lunch table. As we once again await the arrival of the ambulance, Eric curses himself for not doing something sooner. It should never have come to this, he says wretchedly. We should have bundled him into the car and shipped him off to the doctor with or without his permission. If anything happens to Silas, he tells us, he will never forgive himself. Mum, too, feels responsible; even I feel responsible. In fact, it seems to me that everyone feels responsible except the patient, who is lying serenely on the kitchen floor issuing instructions through lips the colour of damsons.

'Don't talk, Silas,' Eric tells him, 'You're just tiring yourself out.'

'Take — my — pulse,' whispers Silas.

I take his pulse. I can barely feel anything, and what I can feel is thin and thready and very irregular.

'What — is — it?'

'Difficult to tell. A bit irregular.'

Silas nods. 'As — I — thought.' He smiles, and I find myself actually feeling angry with him. How could he? How could he be so cheerful when everyone else is so worried? Doesn't he spare a thought for Eric? For Mum? Apparently not. Silas is doing what he does best; he is Being Ill. And don't we all enjoy doing what we do best?

In hospital, Silas has all the tests he had last time, and is fully vindicated. His mitral valve has become virtually useless, and he needs a new one.

'There,' he says, sitting up in bed and talking through a plastic oxygen mask. 'I was right all along.'

'So you were,' says Eric, who is by now paler than Silas.

'They say they're going to operate as soon as possible,' Silas tells us. 'I'm not sure what kind of valve they're giving me. Apparently the organic ones are very good, but the metal ones last longer.' I notice that his bible has managed to get into the hospital with him, and sits proudly on his bedside locker beside a bowl of fruit and the stuffed frog, which Silas considers to be his finest work. The nurses do not like the frog, and the words "bacteria" and "cross-infection" have been mentioned, but no-one has had the heart to remove it. 'They can sometimes repair valves, but mine has gone too far.' He pauses for breath. 'I — told — you — so,' he adds, 'only the other day. Didn't I tell you,' he pauses again, panting through the steady hiss of oxygen, 'it was shot to pieces?'

Silas's operation is scheduled for the following week. We are told that if it is left any longer, there is a risk of his condition deteriorating so much that he will be unfit to undergo surgery at all. In the meantime, he has further tests, and is given drugs to "stabilise his condition". He looks terribly ill, but remains in good spirits, enjoying all the attention and making notes on everything pertaining to his illness and its treatment. As for the rest of us, we have been warned that Silas is a very sick man, and that while his chances are good, we must take into consideration that he is no longer young. While I think we have all managed to work this out for ourselves, it is not comforting to have it spelt out by someone in the know. Sometimes I wish that the medical profession would keep their more disappointing thoughts to themselves.

Poor Eric is beside himself with worry, and is unable to concentrate on anything, and Mum isn't much better. I also feel very sorry for Kent, who having only recently discovered that he has two fathers, is now having to come to terms with the fact that he may end up with just one (and a broken one at that, for who can imagine Eric without Silas?). Dad, on the other hand, is coming into his own, and while his offers of leading us all in prayer are politely declined, his support is very welcome. He makes telephone calls, does shopping, and drives people to the hospital to visit Silas. He even feeds the chickens. While I'm sure he does all this with the best of intentions, I also feel it must help to take his mind off recalcitrant insurers and unreliable plumbers, for work on the house is only just getting started, and my father is not a patient man.

The day of Silas's operation is one of those extraordinary January days when spring decides to put in a fleeting, tantalising appearance; a brief reminder that winter isn't here to stay, and that whatever else is happening, there's light at the end of the seasonal tunnel. There are snowdrops in the garden, and the first hints of birdsong, the sky is a pale, washed blue, and the air is fresh and fragrant. As we drive to the hospital for our vigil (for it's unthinkable that we should not be in the building while Silas has his operation), I think we're probably all feeling the poignancy of the contrast between our own emotions and the beauty of the world outside.

I have always thought that waiting is one of the hardest things we have to do in life. Whether it's waiting for exam results, or for the longed-for phone call from a lover, or even for something relatively unimportant like the arrival of a visitor, it seems to have a paralysing effect. I can never get down to anything when I'm waiting. It's as though life is put on hold, and nothing can move forward until the thing which is awaited has happened and I am released once more into activity, whatever form that may take.

It's like this today. Eric requested that Mum, Kent and I should accompany him to the hospital, and here we all are in the Relatives' Room, which is bland and perhaps purposely characterless, with its pale walls and its fawn-upholstered chairs and its jug of plastic roses. Waiting. I can almost hear the time ticking by, although the clock on the wall makes no sound, and while there is plenty we could be saying, we all seem lost for words. There are magazines on the table, but none of us has touched them, and I have brought a book, but couldn't think of reading it. I am praying to the God I don't really believe in, Mum is almost certainly doing the same, Kent is standing by the window studying the distant view of the car park, and Eric is sitting on the edge of a chair, as though at any moment he may be required to leap up and do something. I have paid two visits to the coffee machine outside to purchase plastic cups of something warm and murky, and a nurse has popped in a couple of times to see if we're okay. Otherwise, the silence ticks by virtually uninterrupted. I don't think I have ever known time pass so slowly.

After two hours and fifty-five minutes (yes, I've been counting. I'm sure everyone's been counting), a doctor arrives in blue theatre scrubs. I think we all immediately know that something is wrong.

'Yes?' Eric jumps to his feet. 'How is he? What's happened?'

Very carefully, the doctor closes the door behind him and turns to face us.

'I'm afraid there's been — a complication,' he tells us.

'A complication? What complication? How is he? What's happened?' Eric lets rip with a barrage of questions.

'I'm afraid —'

'Yes? Yes? Come on! Out with it! *What has happened to Silas?*' Eric grabs hold of his sleeve. 'Tell us. You have to tell us!'

'I'm trying to tell you.' Gently, the doctor disengages himself from Eric's grip. 'The operation itself went well, and the new valve is functioning nicely. But unfortunately your brother — he is your brother isn't he? — suffered a haemorrhage during surgery. He lost a lot of blood very quickly, and while we replaced it as fast as we could, his blood pressure fell dangerously low. There is the possibility of —'

'What? The possibility of what? What's going to happen to him?'

'The possibility — just the possibility — of brain damage.'

Time stops ticking. For a few moments, life itself seems to stand still. In these few moments I know that whatever happens, I shall never forget this day, this moment, this horrid little room, which seems suddenly redolent of all the grief, all the tragedies, all the bad news which has been released within its walls. I shall remember Eric's mismatched socks, just visible beneath his trousers; the stain — coffee? — on the carpet, shaped rather like a map of Italy; the hideous roses, with their faded plastic petals; the single leafless sapling outside the window; the tiny vapour trail of a distant aeroplane across the ice-blue sky.

And the sound. The first sound which breaks the silence. The soft, heartbreaking sound of Eric weeping.

Chapter Thirty-Three

The next few days are an agony of waiting, punctuated by the mundane tasks needed to keep ourselves (not to mention the animals) alive and give some semblance of normality. Ordinary everyday jobs like cleaning my teeth or washing up the dishes take on a strange irrelevance; I keep stopping to ask myself what I'm doing them *for*. What does it matter if dirty plates stack up on the draining board, or my toothbrush goes unused for a couple of days? Who *cares*? I suppose I have been fortunate. Up until now, I have never had any kind of brush with tragedy. I recall with equanimity the long-ago death of my grandfather; he was old, and I scarcely knew him. When I was about twelve, the family cat was run over, and I did shed tears over him. But this is so much bigger, its potential for grief so much greater. I have grown to love my uncles dearly, and my sadness is compounded many times over by that of Eric, who is quite distraught. Silas is being kept sedated to "give his body a rest", and the extent of any damage won't be known until they withdraw the drugs and let him wake up. Eric spends his days sitting by Silas's bed in the Intensive Care Unit, among the forest of tubes and drips and the beeps and sighs of the machinery upon which Silas now depends, and his nights pacing up and down in his room, which is next to mine, sometimes weeping, sometimes listening to the BBC world service on the radio. I hear him going downstairs at two and three in the morning to make cups of tea, his footsteps slow and apologetic and infinitely weary.

'Are you all right, Eric?' I join him in the kitchen, unable to bear the idea that he is down here suffering on his own while everyone else is asleep.

Eric looks up. He seems mildly surprised.

'Oh, Ruth. What are you doing down here?'

'I came to see you.'

'Ah.' He pauses, kettle in hand. 'Cup of tea?'

'Please.' I sit down at the table. 'Eric what can I do to help?'

He sits beside me, nursing his mug between his hands. 'Nothing. There's nothing anyone can do. That's the trouble.' He manages a pale smile. 'You see, we've never been apart before.'

'What, not ever?'

'Not ever. Well, maybe a night or two here and there, but never longer than that. As children we did everything together, and we've lived together ever since. There's been no need to be apart.'

'Oh, Eric. I'm so, so sorry.' I'm unable to think of anything else to say, because of course there's nothing anyone can say. All I know is that Eric's heart is breaking, and however much we may want to help him, he is beyond our reach, in a world of his own.

'I can't think of anything else, do anything else. I can't even be anything else. All I am is Silas's brother. Waiting.'

Waiting. That word again. Eric is suspended between the chance of hope and the expectation of grief, and for the time being at least, has come down on the side of grief, and in his state of suspense (which when I think about it now, takes on a whole extra meaning) is totally disabled.

I take his hand and rub it gently between my own. It feels terribly cold, but I doubt whether Eric is aware of it. He's probably been pacing about for ages in his unheated bedroom. He hasn't even bothered to put on a dressing gown. I get up to fetch a coat from the hall, and put it round his shoulders.

'You'll catch your death,' I tell him, 'And then what use will you be to Silas if — when he needs you?'

'I suppose we always assumed we'd die together,' he says, and I know that he hasn't heard a word I've been saying. 'Silly, isn't it? But we were conceived together, born together, went to school together. We even started shaving on the same day. There wasn't much to shave, but we shaved it off anyway with our dad's old razor. And we felt so proud. Real men, we told each other. Not boys any more. *Men*.'

'I've often wondered what it must be like to be a twin.' I stir sugar into my tea, which is much too strong.

'And I've often wondered what it must be like not to be one. To be an individual, unique, entirely different from everyone else. As children, we were always being compared with each other. Our school reports, exams, team games.' He sighs. 'We both hated games. We were the ones to be picked last for team games, but it was still a competition to see which of us would be picked the very last. Usually no-one knew which of us they were picking anyway, as they could never tell us apart.'

I know that not all twins — even identical ones — are as similar as this; some in fact contrive to be quite different. There were identical twins in my class at school who went to considerable lengths to make themselves as individual as possible, even to the extent of wearing their school uniforms in different ways. Few needed (or indeed, dared) to confuse them. But it seems that Eric and Silas have always delighted in their similarity and the confusion it causes, and don't appear to need to establish their individuality, although it's certainly there for anyone who takes the trouble to get to know them.

'He's still alive, you know,' I say, after a moment. 'They say there's a chance he'll make a full recovery. You told me so yourself.'

'Yes. But when I see him lying there, he looks so — so *not Silas*, somehow. Almost as though he's already gone.'

'I don't think anyone looks their best when they're unconscious,' I tell him gently.

'No. You're right.' He pulls the jacket more closely around him. 'I suppose I was always the pessimist. I left the optimism to Silas. I mean, look at the way he approached this operation. Anyone would think he was going on holiday.'

'Yes. He'd have been so interested in all this, wouldn't he? It seems such a waste that he's not awake to — I don't know — to *enjoy* it.'

'Yes. He would have loved it, wouldn't he? All the attention; all those drugs and machines and things. I've been keeping notes, you know.'

'What notes?'

'A kind of diary. What happened when; which doctors came to see him and what they did and said. That kind of thing. In case ... well, for when he gets better.'

'That's such a nice idea, Eric. He'll love it.'

Eric smiles, as though for a brief moment he's actually forgotten the seriousness of Silas's condition, then I watch his expression change as reality kicks in again.

'Oh Ruth. What would I do without him? Or if he's damaged; if he's unable to speak or understand. How will I bear it?'

I give Eric a hug. 'I think you have to do the "one day at a time" thing,' I say. 'I've always hated that expression, but there's no other choice, is there? We have to — oh, I don't know — keep the home fires burning for Silas. For when he comes home. Whatever condition he's in. There's not a lot we can do for him at the moment, but we can do that.'

'You're right, Ruth. Of course you are. And I found this amazing hare on my way back from the hospital this afternoon. He's never done a hare before. You don't often see them near the road, do you? But this one's enormous, and absolutely perfect, although it must have been knocked down.'

'It sounds wonderful. What — what have you done with it?'

'I put it in the freezer. Double wrapped. Right at the bottom. Underneath Dorothy.' (Dorothy was a daughter of Sarah's, who having proved to be barren has recently been despatched and butchered into neat little packages). 'She'll never find it there.'

We exchange complicit smiles. Mum accepts most of the things which go on at Applegarth, but draws a line at Silas putting his specimens in the freezer where we keep the food. I don't suppose even she would object under the present circumstances, but Eric's right. It's better that she shouldn't find out.

There is the sound of footsteps coming down the stairs, and Mum joins us in the kitchen. I notice for the first time that she seems to have aged since Silas's illness.

'What are you two doing?' she asks, surprised.

'Tea and sympathy,' Eric tells her. 'Like some?'

'What, tea or sympathy?'

'Either.'

'A bit of both, I think.' Mum puts her arms around Eric and for the first time I notice how alike they are. I suppose that because of the twin thing, I've never considered that my mother might resemble her brothers, but now I see that she shares their eye colour, and her expression — one of sadness and concern — is very like Eric's.

We sit round the table together talking softly, trying to reassure each other that "everything will be all right". While I join in, I still wonder why it is that people always say this to each other in times of crisis, as though defying fate to deal the blow they fear, while as often as not it's perfectly obvious that things are very far from all right, and moreover, are unlikely to become so.

There's a knock at the back door, and I unlock it to find Kent, wearing a coat over his pyjamas.

'I saw the kitchen light on. Is everything okay?'

'Well, nothing's new, if that's what you mean.' I fetch another mug from the cupboard.

'I'm not — intruding?' He takes off his boots and places them side by side on the doormat.

'Of course you're not. Come and join the party.'

Poor Kent. One of the family, and yet not one of the family, this must be so hard for him. Mum still doesn't know his full story, although I think she may have her suspicions, and Dad certainly knows nothing. And while I'm sure he must have told Kaz about it, his real position, whatever that might be, is as yet unknown and unacknowledged. He must be in an emotional no man's land at the moment, but is too sensitive and thoughtful a person to draw any kind of attention to himself.

'Can I do anything?' he asks now.

'No. No-one can do anything. That's the trouble,' Eric says. 'The not doing anything.'

'Who's not doing anything?' Kaz wanders into the kitchen, ruffled and bleary-eyed, her skimpy nightie ill-concealed beneath a kind of giant cardigan. She and Kent exchange one of their glances, but I no longer mind. Now is not the time for petty jealousy.

'All of us,' I tell her. 'For Silas.'

'Well, we can cheer up for a start. Silas would hate all this.' She stifles a yawn, and treats us to one of her infectious smiles. 'While there's life, and all that. What you all need is a drop of this in your tea.' She fetches a bottle of brandy left over from Christmas, and pours a generous measure into everyone's mug (except mine). 'Warm you up,' she explains. 'It's freezing in here.'

Only Kaz could get away with such inappropriate jollity, and I could hug her for it. Her good humour (fuelled, I suspect, by the effects of love) infects us all, and soon everyone's mood improves. Eric even manages a laugh, and Mr. Darcy, who has been sleeping by the Aga, wakes up and thumps his tail on the stone floor.

'That's better,' says Kaz with satisfaction. 'Tomorrow's another day.'

'Tomorrow's already here,' I tell her. 'You ought to get back to bed, Eric. You need to get some sleep, or you'll be in no fit state to go and see Silas.'

But as the clock in the hall strikes the hour, the telephone rings. For a few seconds we sit staring at one another, frozen into immobility. Time seems to stand still. I hear my heart thumping in my ears, and am aware of everyone holding their breath, as though waiting for something to happen.

Then Eric clears his throat.

'Answer that, could you, Ruth?' he says, and I notice that his hands are shaking. 'I don't think — I don't think I can bear to.'

Chapter Thirty-Four

Pneumonia. Such a pretty word, I've always thought; a girl's name, perhaps, or some kind of flowering shrub.

But of course, in reality, not pretty at all. Potentially deadly. I believe they used to call it "the old man's friend" because it often provided merciful release from some lingering painful illness, or perhaps from a life which had outlived both comfort and purpose. *But not Silas!* Not Silas's life. Not after all he's already been through.

'How?' Eric asks. 'How did he get pneumonia in here? He should have been safe. *We thought he'd be safe!*'

'He's a very sick man. You have to understand that.' The doctor looks very young, exhausted, ruffled from sleep.

'We know he's a sick man. But we didn't expect him to get even sicker.' Eric is beside himself. '*How — did — this — happen?*'

'Please sit down. The nurse will make you some tea.'

'*I don't want tea.* I've done nothing but drink tea for days now. Tea isn't the answer!'

'Sit down, Eric.' Mum pulls gently at his sleeve. 'Sit down and listen to what the doctor has to say.'

Eric crumples into a chair, and the doctor explains. The pneumonia has developed suddenly and rapidly; Silas's resistance is lowered due to his illness; they are doing all they can. He talks of x-rays and antibiotics, of more drips and further tests. Silas's chances are not good, but he is "holding his own". The next couple of days will be crucial.

Afterwards, when the doctor has gone, Eric sits with his head in his hands.

'I don't know how much more of this I can take,' he says to no-one in particular.

'You have to, Eric. You just have to,' Mum tells him. 'For Silas. We'll go and see him, shall we? I'll come with you. You stay here, Ruth, and phone home. Everyone will be wondering what's happening. It's not fair to keep them waiting.'

I go outside to use my mobile, and phone Applegarth, where Kaz, Kent and Dad are waiting for news, then I fetch myself coffee from a machine. I feel exhausted beyond any tiredness I have ever felt before. The baby has reduced (hardly the right word, but I can't think of another) me to a lumbering elephant of a woman, and as I cart my exhausted body and its small passenger back to the relatives' room and find myself a chair, I wonder how it is that many women go back and do the whole pregnancy thing over and over again, ending up sometimes with three, four or even more children. For whatever I may feel about my own child, now or when I get to meet it, I know for a fact that I shall never want another. I'll have done my bit; I shall have replaced myself on the planet, and formed the next link in the family chain. I certainly don't need to do it again.

It's funny how thoughts of my imminent motherhood, occasional at the best of times, have gone out of the window since Silas's illness. The baby is there, and presumably it will eventually emerge (apparently in about five weeks' time), but I have put it to the back of my mind. I have received a reproachful phone call from the midwife enquiring as to why I'm no longer attending her classes, but it seems self-indulgent to spend time huffing and puffing on a cosy nest of cushions while the rest of my family are going through all this. No doubt when the time comes, I'll push the baby out. People do it all the time. Apparently, it's impossible *not* to push babies out when the time comes. So why all the fuss?

For the moment, all that matters is that Silas should get better. It may be that a part of me is only too willing to be relieved, if only temporarily, of thoughts of the future, or simply that I am still maintaining a degree of denial. I shall never know. What I do know is that if Silas recovers, I shall be willing to cope with anything. I will go to ante-natal classes every day if required to do so; I'll be a model mother and even a model daughter; I'll even sacrifice any hopes of seeing Amos again, if only Silas will get better. Please, Silas. Please, please, *please* get better.

'Are you okay?' A nurse comes into the room, and I realise that I've been crying.

'Yes. Yes, I'm all right.'

'Well, you don't look it.' She closes the door behind her. 'Are you his daughter?'

'No. He's my uncle.'

'You're close, are you?'

'Yes. I suppose we are.' I'd never thought about it before. 'I live with him — them.'

'That must be hard. Especially with a baby on the way.' She touches my hand. 'When's it due?'

'Due?'

'The baby.'

'Of course. The baby.' I push my hair out of my eyes and blow my nose. 'About a month, I think.'

'Not long to go, then.'

'No.'

'Can I get you a cup of tea?'

'Please.'

Tea again. Where on earth would we be without tea? I suppose the French and the Italians have coffee on these occasions, but what about, say, the Americans? What do they drink in times of crisis? Iced tea, perhaps, at least in the summer. I've read about iced tea, but never actually tried any. Iced tea, lemon tea, herbal tea… My thoughts drift and swirl, and I see people — lots of people — drinking tea;

Japanese women cross-legged on the floor, sobbing as they pass round tiny decorated cups; people queueing by the huge shiny urn used by one of Mum's women's groups; I see teapots, kettles, tea bags, tea leaves. The seahorse/rabbit appears and tells me it hates tea, and why can't I give it milk like a normal mother? *Normal mothers* don't give tea to babies, it tells me. Why can't I behave like a normal mother? It fades away, weeping, and now I am in a boat going to look for Amos. The boat is operated by pedals, but my feet won't reach them and there's no-one around to help. I panic as the boat begins to quiver and tremble, as though tossed by a succession of tiny waves.

I wake up whimpering to find Mum gently shaking my shoulder.

'Ruth? It's all right, dear. Don't cry.' She touches my cheek. 'Come on. It's time to go home.'

'Why? What's happened? How's Silas?' The anxiety of my dream is still with me. 'He hasn't died, has he?'

'No. He hasn't died. He's — stable.'

'Hospital-speak,' I tell her, now fully awake, and I think of all those other hospital clichés: "as well as can be expected," "fighting for his life" (how can anyone who is seriously ill *fight*?), "comfortable". It's almost as though hospital staff are issued with a list of words and phrases which are supposed to give comfort but which fool nobody. 'How is he really?'

'Unconscious, of course, but they say his chest is a bit clearer. Eric's staying on. I'm going home to have a bath and a nap. I'll come back later.'

'What about me? When can I see him?'

'Well, I suppose you could pop in quickly now. Just for a couple of minutes. We'll ask.'

I've hardly been inside the Intensive Care Unit up until now, leaving the visiting to Mum and Eric. It's a strange place, with an atmosphere and rhythm of its own, isolated and apart like a womb; a world within a world. Staff move around in theatre scrubs, speaking softly, attending to the recumbent forms around them. They look smoothly efficient, more like technicians than nurses, but then I suppose in these circumstances efficiency is more important than the touchy-feely nurses of my imagination.

I remember Eric describing his brother as looking '*so not Silas*', and he's right. It's hard to connect the still figure beneath the clinical white sheet with the Silas I know. This figure breathes — in-out, in-out — fluids are dripped in and others drain away, but everything is mechanical; everything is *not Silas*. Eric is sitting beside him holding his hand, but his eyes are closed, and we don't disturb him.

'Let's go.' Mum whispers, as though we are in church.

I nod, too choked to speak, and together we tiptoe from the room. As we leave the building and make our way to the car park, the grey wintry sky threatens rain, bleak skeletons of trees reaching out towards it as though in supplication. Like those other memories of the day of Silas's operation, I know that whatever happens, I'll always remember these things; this sky, these trees, the echoing of our footsteps along the deserted walkway; even the car park, which is half empty. Only the workers and the wounded and the families of the seriously ill visit hospitals at night.

We drive home together in silence. Dad and Kent have gone back to bed, but Kaz has stayed up to wait for us, and is dozing in a chair. Wordlessly, she gets up and holds out her arms to me, and I stumble into them.

'Oh, Kaz,' I sob. 'He looks so *awful*.' Kaz's arms scarcely reach around me now, but the closeness of her and the familiar smell of her perfume (something expensive; a gift from a boyfriend?) is infinitely comforting.

'I've made porridge,' she tells us.

'*Porridge?*' Mum looks puzzled.

'Porridge,' says Kaz, 'is what you need. With brown sugar and lots of cream.'

'Porridge? At a time like this?'

'Especially at a time like this.' Kaz fetches bowls and spoons, and a big jug of cream from the fridge. 'Comfort food,' she explains. 'Plus, you need something to soak up all that tea.'

'How did you know about the tea?' I ask her.

Kaz laughs. 'I'm right, aren't I?'

'Spot on.'

'Well, then. Be good girls and eat up your porridge. It'll do you good.'

Chapter Thirty-Five

To add to our troubles, we have a chicken crisis.

Somewhere, somehow, news of our chicken charity collecting box has been translated into an appeal for actual chickens. It is probably a simple case of Chinese whispers; after all, the leap from chicken charity to chicken sanctuary is a relatively small one. But whatever its provenance, in the course of the past couple of weeks, we have found ourselves suddenly inundated with unwanted chickens. There are rescued chickens, hen-pecked chickens, neglected chickens and even a few happy healthy chickens. There are also two vicious cockerels, and, oddly, a small white duck.

'Chickens are us,' remarks Eric, in a rare moment of humour. 'And they aren't even laying. What on earth are we going to do with them all? And those half-naked ones — they must be freezing.'

'We could knit them little jackets,' says Kaz.

'Not funny, Kaz,' I tell her.

'No. Sorry.'

'But at least we can eat one of those cockerels before they eat each other.'

The bird in question is duly despatched and casseroled, leaving his fellow to take out his fury on Mr. Darcy and any human being who comes his way. Meanwhile, the cockerel in residence — an unassuming, harmless little bird called Henry, who has been in sole charge at Applegarth for years and has successfully fathered generations of fluffy yellow offspring — becomes withdrawn and depressed, and the resident chickens, who all know each other and have their place in the pecking order (what else?) are confused and disrupted by so many uninvited guests. There isn't room for them all in the hen house, so at night such newcomers as we can find are rounded up and herded into a small leaky shed. The rest have to fend for themselves and run the gauntlet of the neighbouring foxes. It is not a happy situation.

Fortunately, food isn't a problem, for pilgrims come bearing offerings of corn and scraps (perhaps since the Virgin herself is not in a position to accept gifts, it's felt that the chickens might like to do so on her behalf), but the sheer numbers of chickens are becoming a considerable problem. Chickens escape into the road and are run over; chickens leak out into the fields and outbuildings and even into the house; chickens roost in the greenhouse. There seem to be chickens everywhere.

'How about a sort of chicken exchange?' suggests Kaz, having discovered another feathery corpse in the driveway. 'Like a bring and buy, only chickens rather than white elephants.'

'So long as the buy outnumbers the bring,' says Eric. 'We certainly don't want any more chickens.'

'I'll organise it,' Mum says suddenly. 'Why don't you leave it to me?'

We all look at her in surprise. Mum has never shown much interest in the livestock, and has tended to avoid the chickens because of her feelings about the Virgin (Mum still has problems with the Virgin, and Dad won't discuss the matter at all).

'Well, if you're sure,' says Eric.

'I'm sure. I need a project. Something to keep my mind off, well, you know.'

We know. And Eric gratefully accepts Mum's offer. She spends an afternoon making a large sign to the effect that chickens may be collected and taken away, provided the prospective owners check with her first and guarantee a good home.

'What's a good home?' I ask her.

'Oh, you know. A decent run, food and water. That kind of thing.'

'How do you know people won't just take them home and eat them?'

'That's a risk we'll have to take.'

'Pick your own chicken,' Kaz muses. 'Well, it's certainly a novel idea. What are people going to take the chickens home in?'

'That's up to them,' Mum says. 'They'll have to bring a cage or something.'

'How are they going to catch them?' I ask her. 'It's not like picking strawberries. Strawberries keep still. Chickens don't.'

'That's up to them, too. But I suppose we could make a sort of net. Perhaps Lazzo would make one. He's good at that sort of thing.'

'How are we going to stop people taking *our* chickens?'

'They'll have to be shut in the run for the time being.'

'They won't like that.'

'I'm afraid that's tough,' says Mum. 'They've had it too good for too long. It's time they were — contained.'

So our chickens are padlocked into their run, which has sole access to the entrance to the hen house, while their new friends are left the freedom of the garden. It doesn't seem a very fair arrangement, but as Mum says, for the time being, there's nothing else for it. And when all's said and done, they are only chickens.

But the chickens are not used to being restrained in this way, and, encouraged by Henry, set up a considerable racket in their attempts to escape from their prison, while the new, free-range chickens tease and provoke them from the other side of the wire mesh.

'Told you,' says Blossom, who didn't actually tell us anything but hates anyone other than herself having ideas where the animals are concerned.

'Well, what would you do?' I ask her. 'Have you a better idea?'

'Nope.' Blossom chases an invading chicken out of the back door. 'Not my business.'

'Well, if it's not your business, then perhaps you'd best keep your ideas to yourself.'

This is not like me, for as a rule I go to great lengths to be polite to Blossom, but since Silas's illness she has been quite impossible. Eric, ever charitable, says it's probably because she misses him, and I suppose he could be right, but a bit of support wouldn't come amiss. Blossom knows the score; she must see how we're all struggling to keep going; and yet she continues to be if anything even more ill-tempered than usual.

'What is the *matter* with your mother?' I ask Kaz, having tripped over the flex of the vacuum clear which has been left out in the middle of the kitchen.

'Search me.' Kaz is doing her make-up, peering into a tiny mirror propped on the window sill (she's filling in for another dancer tonight, although she's "scaling down" her professional activities as Kent apparently isn't happy about them).

'She's being so *nasty.*'

'That's Mum,' Kaz agrees, applying plum-coloured eye shadow with a tiny brush.

'But why? Why is she so thoroughly unpleasant all the time? What's her problem?'

'You know —' Kaz applies the finishing touches to her eyelashes and puts away her mirror — 'I've been asking myself that ever since I could think, and I've never come up with an answer.'

'How on earth did you survive? As a kid, I mean.'

'Dunno.' Kaz shrugs. 'Just got on with it, I suppose. And I had Lazzo. I'd never have survived without our Laz. And Dad. Dad wasn't much use, but at least I could talk to him. And he was in the same boat as Lazzo and me.'

'Three against one?'

'Yep. Although the one always came out on top.'

'I'll bet.'

'There. How do I look?' Kaz stands up and runs her fingers through her hair (which she's recently dyed pink).

'Fabulous. As usual.'

'Ta.' Kaz grins. 'Hope the punters feel the same way.'

'Oh, they will. If they've got any sense.' I hesitate. 'How's — how's it going with Kent?'

'I thought you didn't approve.'

'I don't — didn't. But then I realised I was being selfish, and you were right. I was a bit — well, jealous.'

'I told you.'

'Okay, no need to gloat.'

'Sorry. That wasn't very nice of me, was it? Poor Ruth. You need to find your Amos, don't you?'

'Yes. Oh, yes!' I feel again the familiar ache of loneliness, which sees to increase with my size. 'But you still haven't answered my question. How's it going?'

'Great. It's going really great. He's so kind. You know, I don't think I've come across many really kind people. Plus, he's good looking, and sexy —'

'Too much information, Kaz. I get the picture.' I hesitate. 'Kaz, would you — would you marry him?'

'It's a bit early for that! But d'you know, I think I might. And then, just think — I'd be family, wouldn't I? I'd love to be part of this family.'

'So he's told you about — about Eric and Silas.'

'Yep. I think it's really cool to have two dads, and I think he's coming round to the idea, too. And I'd have two fathers-in-law!'

'I never had you down as the marrying kind.'

'Me neither.'

'And your mother would have to wear a hat!'

We both laugh. 'She wouldn't come,' Kaz tells me. 'Whatever the circumstances, she'd find a reason not to come. Mum hates weddings.'

'But surely, *your* wedding —'

'Especially my wedding. Trust me.'

'Well, you'd have all of us. Lazzo could give you away. Oh — and I'll help you choose the dress!'

For what could be more fun than dressing Kaz up as a bride? She could get married from Applegarth, and we might even have a marquee (provided enough uncluttered space could be found). Despite my initial reservations, I find myself feeling quite excited at the idea.

'Hold on a minute, Ruth. We're not quite there yet! But thanks for being — nice about it.' Kaz picks up her bag. 'Gotta go. See you later.'

As Kaz's car rattles off down the driveway, scattering chickens in its wake, I realise that for a whole five minutes or so I have managed not to think about Silas. But now reality kicks in with a thud, and I feel my spirits sink. Weddings — celebrations of any kind, come to that — are off-limits at the moment, and may be so for some time to come.

I fetch a bucket and start mixing pig feed.

Chapter Thirty-Six

Despite the gloomy prognostications of the doctors, Silas continues to hold his own. He isn't exactly better, but he's no worse, and a note of optimism creeps into the household.

Poor Eric is worn out with his vigils, refusing to take a day off, and must have lost nearly a stone. He looks almost as ill as his brother; more so in a way, because there is an artificial glow to Silas's skin which has nothing to do with his condition but which gives an appearance of health. No-one would confuse the two of them now; they don't even look like brothers, never mind twins. The GP has given Eric pills to help him sleep, but I don't believe he takes them, preferring to remain on permanent alert in case he's needed at the hospital. His Ark plans remain rolled up in a drawer; he hasn't touched them since Silas's operation. And while I'm still pursuing a bit of research for him on the subject of birds (and believe me, if the mammals are complicated, the birds are many times more so), I haven't liked to update him on my progress. The Ark, like so much else at Applegarth, is going to have to wait.

Meanwhile, I have had some news. A postcard has arrived for me at my parents' address from Amos, and while there's not a lot on it, it's still news. Amos is apparently on a ship on his way home, together with a small Caribbean band he founded while in Barbados. He has had a "great time" and tells me that the trombone goes "amazingly well" with steel drums (I can't imagine it, but where music's concerned, Amos is usually right). He will be arriving back in England "soon", and hopes "to meet up some time".

The casual note of the postcard is not cheering. "Soon" isn't nearly specific enough for me, and no-one wants to "meet up some time" with the man they love (or even the man they think they might love), but never mind. Amos is alive, and is not staying in Barbados for ever, and this has to be good news for me. Of course there is no return address, and since he hasn't given me the ship's name or company, I can't contact him that way. But it would seem that some time in the not too distant future, I may be seeing Amos. I only hope it's sooner rather than later, for whatever I may feel, the baby won't delay its arrival just to accommodate its parents.

'Is that the chap with the beard?' asks my father, who has obviously read the postcard.

'That's the one,' I tell him.

'Hmm.'

'What do you mean, hmm?'

'Looked untrustworthy.'

'Dad, just because he has a beard —'

'Not just the beard.'

'What, then?'

'He had shifty eyes.'

I think of Amos's lovely brown eyes (more lovely and more brown with absence, of course) and despair. It could just be that no-one's good enough for his little girl, but I immediately dismiss the thought. It would be lovely if this were the case, but simply not Dad. He's not the *my little girl* type. No. Beards and shifty eyes notwithstanding, he doesn't approve of my condition, and therefore by association the person who put me in it. I just hope that Amos doesn't rock up at my parents' house only to find signs of the recent conflagration and no-one to enlighten him as to my whereabouts, for the reconstruction works are not going well, and the house is still in a pretty sorry state, although piles of bricks, some scaffolding and a cement mixer are all signs of hope for the future.

But of course, if Amos should experience a momentary fear that my parents and I have all perished in the blaze, he can always ask the neighbours. Now there's an idea! I shall get my mother to leave a note with the people next door to the effect that if anyone comes looking for me, they should contact me at Applegarth. I am delighted with this idea, and plan to put it in motion forthwith.

Lazzo comes into the kitchen.

'Nice postcard,' he remarks.

'Yes, isn't it.'

'Lots of sea.'

'Yes. There is quite a bit.' The postcard is in fact almost entirely sea, with one tiny island in the distance and what might be a palm tree.

'Made the net,' he continues, pulling a packet of cigarettes from his pocket and looking at them longingly (he's not allowed to smoke in the house).

'Net?'

'For the chickens.'

'For the — oh yes. Well done.'

'See it?'

'Yes please.'

Lazzo brings in a complicated construction consisting of a long wooden pole with what looks like a wire tent on the end.

'There.' He puts it down on the floor.

'Goodness!'

Lazzo grins at me. 'See it work?'

'Oh — right. Yes of course.'

We go out into the garden, Lazzo wielding his net, and search for chickens. Typically, they all seem to be hiding, but at last he spies one behind the greenhouse, and sets off in surprisingly rapid pursuit. There is a lot of squawking and flapping, plus one or two choice expletives from Lazzo, and the chicken is brought back for my inspection. It looks ruffled and very cross, but otherwise in good shape.

'Why, that's great, Lazzo. Really ingenious. I just hope the pilgrims can run, because the chickens certainly can.'

'Do it for them,' says Lazzo, beaming (he loves praise, I suspect because it's in pretty short supply at home).

'You aren't always here,' I remind him.

'Mobile.'

'Oh, yes.

Lazzo has recently acquired a mobile, and is completely wedded to it. I've no idea whom he phones, and why, especially since he is a man of such very few words, but he spends a lot of time labouring over misspelt text messages, experimenting with ring tones and playing its various electronic games. The fact that there's no reception here causes him much frustration. When I have had occasion to phone him on it from the landline, he seems unsure how to reply, and there's usually a lot of huffing and puffing, peppered with little clicking noises, before I actually get him to hear what I have to say.

'You mean you don't mind us phoning you to come and catch chickens?' I ask him.

'S'right.'

'Ok then, that's what we'll do. You can be chief chicken-catcher.'

Lazzo beams again, and while it occurs to me that perhaps I should have asked Mum first, since this is now her project, I'm sure she won't mind. Running fast after chickens is not what my mother does best, and I think she'll probably be delighted to have someone else do it for her.

Eric returns from the hospital earlier than usual to tell us that the doctors are planning to start reducing the dosage of some of Silas's drugs and try taking him off the ventilator.

'I'm not sure I want them to,' he says. 'In a way, I prefer not to know. As things are, there's still hope. But if they take him off the drugs and he doesn't regain consciousness, well, that's it then, isn't it?'

'Not necessarily,' says Mum. 'It could take time, couldn't it?'

'I think if he's going to get better, it'll happen quite quickly.'

'Is that what they said?'

'More or less.'

'When are they starting?' I ask him.

'Tonight, after his consultant's been round. I'll go in first thing tomorrow, of course.'

'Do you want anyone with you?' Mum asks him.

'Would you come, Rosie?'

'Of course.'

'D'you mind keeping an eye on things here, Ruth? We'll — we'll keep in close touch.'

'Of course I don't mind. I'd be happy to.'

Following Eric's news, the waiting seems to intensify for all of us, and once the routine evening jobs are done, none of us are unable to settle to anything. Mum tries to make a cake, but omits some vital ingredient and has to throw the whole thing away. Eric paces to and fro like a lost soul. Poor Kent, still on the periphery of the family, retires to his caravan "to give us space". And I try to practise the violin, an activity which has become increasingly difficult of late because of the tiredness induced by my pregnancy. Only Dad is gainfully employed, bullying the builders who are trying to rebuild the house. Of course, I don't know this for sure, but from the conversations he relays back to us, it sounds to me very much like bullying. The builders are either the laziest men on the face of the earth (Dad's perception) or have the patience of saints (mine).

The following morning, Mum and Eric leave early for the hospital. I busy myself around the house, hindered by Mr. Darcy, who senses trouble and follows me round like a shadow, and by Blossom and her vacuum cleaner. After I've tripped over the flex for the third time, I finally lose patience.

'Blossom, please, please would you look where you're going with that thing? Someone's going to do themselves an injury.'

'Their look-out,' Blossom says. She looks a bit pale even for Blossom, and I noticed that she didn't have a biscuit with her coffee earlier on (always a bad sign).

'Are you — are you all right, Blossom?'

'Course.' Blossom turns away, but not before I detect what look very like tears in her eyes.

'Are you — worried about Silas?'

'Might be.' She sniffs and blows her nose on a tattered Kleenex.

'He'll be all right, you know, Blossom. I'm sure he will.' I put a hand on her arm, realising that it's the first time she and I have ever had any kind of physical contact.

'Better be. The old bugger.' There's the ghost of a smile. 'Taken flowers up to the Virgin,' she confides. 'Some nice early daffs. Said a prayer for him, too.'

'Well, that was kind.' I feel quite exultant, having finally found the soft side of Blossom, but realise it would be dangerous to push my luck any further. 'Would you like another cup of coffee?'

'Wouldn't mind,' says Blossom graciously. 'Any biscuits?'

The morning drags. Every time the phone rings, I jump, but so far it's been a man about a blocked drain, a wrong number, and Dad fretting about the right sort of bathroom tiles. Did Mum say blue patterned, or plain? He can't remember. At the moment I can think of few things I care about less than bathroom tiles, so he gets pretty short shrift. I reflect that my father has ill-timing down to a fine art. At midday, we receive a brief bulletin with the news that Silas has been taken off the respirator and is breathing on his own, but is still unconscious. Is that good news or bad? No-one seems to know.

Kent and Kaz join me for lunch, but none of us is very hungry, and my half-hearted attempt at artichoke soup goes virtually untouched. A couple of pilgrims/chicken-lovers turn up asking for chickens, and after an unseemly scuffle involving half a dozen people and a great many chickens (Lazzo isn't answering his mobile) we manage to capture five, plus, incidentally, the white duck. The duck is given a reprieve and the chickens set off in the back of a very posh Volvo, where they can be seen hurling themselves against the rear window in a flurry of feathers as they depart down the drive (the putative owners having forgotten to bring a receptacle). The minutes and the hours tick by.

At five thirty-four, the phone rings again. I leap to answer it, treading on Mr. Darcy's tail and knocking over a lamp.

'Oh, Ruth!' Mum sounds beside herself.

'Yes? What? What is it Mum? Is Silas all right?'

'Oh Ruth.' Mum is sobbing now.

'Please, Mum! *What's happened?*'

'Silas. It's Silas.'

'Yes?' Of course it's Silas! Does anything or anybody else in the world matter at the moment?

'He's — Oh, Ruth! — he's asking for his frog!'

'His frog? What frog?' For a moment, the significance of Mum's news escapes me.

'*His* frog. You know. The stuffed one. Oh, Ruth, isn't it wonderful? *Silas is asking for his frog!*'

'Yes. Yes of course.' My fuddled brain struggles with images of Silas and frogs, and a myriad other questions. Then the significance of what she's saying finally hits home. 'You mean he's conscious? He's talking? He's *okay?*'

'Yes! That's exactly what I mean. You can't imagine what a relief it is —' do you want to bet? — 'and Eric is, well, Eric's —'

'Pleased?'

'Not just pleased. He's *so* relieved. I don't think I realised how desperate he's been until Silas spoke to him.'

'Oh, Mum! That's fantastic!'

'Isn't it? Of course, he's got a long way to go still, but it really looks as though he's on the mend at last.'

'What are you doing now?'

'I think we'll stay just a bit longer, then we'll come home. I believe Eric might actually sleep tonight.' She pauses. 'Ruth?'

'Yes?'

'What *did* we do with that frog?'

Chapter Thirty-Seven

Silas is being a terrible patient. He has been home just five days, and is driving us all up the wall.

'It says in my book...' are the words we are learning to dread, for Silas's bible has something to say on every tiny symptom, and Silas would have us know everything it has to say.

I have to admit, I'm disappointed. I was looking forward to looking after Silas; a Silas who would depend on us for his care, a Silas who would be sweetly undemanding, a Silas who would — dare I say it — be *grateful*. I imagined him lying on the sofa in the sitting-room swathed in blankets, sipping sweet tea or delicious home-made soups, taking little walks at times convenient to the rest of us, getting better every day (of course) but doing it without causing any trouble.

Not so. Silas is very far from grateful. He is restless and bored, tapping his way round the house (he's been persuaded to use a walking stick until he's a bit steadier on his feet) interfering and generally making his presence felt. I know I'm not the only one to dread that tap-tapping, and the demands which accompany it, for the rest of the household too are becoming irritable and fractious.

'What does he want *now*?' Eric sounds exasperated at the imperious tinkle of the little bell Silas keeps by his bed. 'I've only just been up to him. He's had his breakfast, he's got the newspaper and the telephone. I've re-filled his hot water bottle. What else can he possibly want?'

'I'll go,' I tell him. 'You stay here and finish your coffee.'

When I enter his room, Silas is sitting up in bed with his reading glasses perched on the end of his nose, consulting his book.

'I think I'm getting a rash,' he tells me. 'It says here —'

'Oh, Silas! Not that book again! Why don't you put it aside for a bit and read something else? How about a nice cheery thriller?'

'It says here,' Silas continues as though I haven't spoken, 'that a penicillin allergy usually begins with a rash. I think I must be allergic to penicillin.'

'You've been on penicillin for ages. Surely it would have shown up before now?'

'Not necessarily. It says here —'

'Let me have a look at you.'

Silas pulls up his pyjama top to reveal a pink, healthy chest (healthy, that is, if you ignore the large scar running across it).

'It looks fine,' I tell him.

'It itches.'

'You're probably too hot. It's awfully stuffy in here. Shall I open a window and let some fresh air in?'

'Gracious, no!' Silas looks shocked. 'I might catch a chill.'

Even I know that catching chills from open windows is more old wives' tale than fact, and I suggest to Silas that he looks up "chill" in his bible.

'You're not taking this seriously,' Silas tells me.

'Silas, we've done nothing but take you seriously recently. We've worried ourselves sick, we've thought of little else, but —'

'Really? Have you really?' Silas looks pleased.

'Yes. Really. But now you're on the mend, and of course we're all delighted, and we'll do anything for you within reason. But we've got other things to think of as well.'

'Yes. I see what you mean.' Silas looks chastened, and I fear I may have overdone it.

'But we don't mind. Of course we don't. We all love you, and we still worry about you,' I assure him, anxious not to give the wrong impression. 'You're our priority at the moment —'

'Oh good. Well then, about this rash —'

'Silas, that's not a rash! Trust me. I know about rashes. I used to be allergic to all sorts of things as a child. You could say I'm something of an expert on rashes. And you *haven't got a rash*.'

'It's still very itchy.'

'It's probably dry. All that time in hospital with that central heating. It's probably dried your skin out. And no —' as Silas reaches for his book again — 'you don't need to look up dry skin. I'll give you some baby lotion. I use it myself. It's quite harmless, and very soothing.'

'Then could you —'

'Yes. I'll put it on for you.'

Half-an-hour later, Silas has been anointed and reassured, and is mercifully asleep. I know he should be up and about — we've been told he needs to keep moving, and much of the time he's only too happy to oblige — but it's such a relief to have him out of the way, that I leave him. He's got the rest of the day to potter round the house, and for the time being, we can get on with our chores.

'Now you've got an idea what it will be like when you've had the baby,' Mum says, only half-teasing. 'You have to get on with things while they're asleep, otherwise nothing gets done.'

Ah. The baby. There's apparently only about three weeks to go before it's due to make its entrance (or rather, its exit), and I've still hardly done anything about it. I've bought the basic necessities with help from Mum and generous contributions from Eric and Silas, but I haven't made any plans. I'm booked into the local hospital for the actual birth, and my uncles have said I can come back here afterwards, but that's about the sum of it. Mum keeps trying to encourage me to think about the future, and even Dad has enquired as to "what I intend to do" after the baby's arrival, but I simply don't know. Like a rabbit caught in headlights, I can't see beyond the moment. I still can't imagine a baby, or myself as a mother. Friends phone to ask how I am, Mikey is beside himself with excitement, Mum is knitting mountains of fluffy little garments, even Kent is excited; but for me, despite indigestion, backache, exhaustion and all the bounding activity that goes on inside my bloated body, the baby still has no reality.

I humour Mum by returning to my ante-natal classes, but I appear to have missed quite a lot, and I still find the sessions boring. Mum, who has put her squeamishness to one side and agreed to be with me for the birth, has started accompanying me, and learns how to rub my back, operate the gas and air and encourage my deep breathing. I find all this bewildering, but Mum is fascinated, and so I let her take over, reasoning that so long as one of us knows what to do, things should be okay.

'What are you going to call your baby, Ruth?' she asks me. 'Have you thought of any names?'

And of course, I haven't.

'How about Lucy for a girl? After Grandma?'

'But it's a boy. Blossom said so, and they told me at the hospital.' Is Mum too in denial? I know she would like a granddaughter, but she can't change the baby's sex just by calling it Lucy. If only life were that simple!

'A boy, then. What about a boy's name?'

'Malachi.' The name comes to me suddenly. 'I shall call it — him — Malachi.'

'Oh.' Mum looks both surprised and disappointed. 'Why? I mean, why Malachi?'

'He was a prophet.'

'I know he was a prophet, but you don't have to name your child after a prophet. There are lots of other good biblical names. John, Matthew — that's nice — Joseph, Peter —'

'No. Malachi.' Malachi, son of Amos, although I don't say this to Mum. The name pleases me. It's unusual, and has a nice ring to it.

'What would people shorten it to?' Mum asks.

'I've no idea. Does it have to be shortened?'

'People always shorten names.'

'They lengthen mine.' This is true enough, although my parents rarely call me Ruthie.

'He mightn't like it.'

'He mightn't like any name I choose. The whole thing's a bit of a gamble, isn't it?' It occurs to me what a huge responsibility it is naming a baby; giving it a label which it has to carry for the rest of its life, and which might not suit it when it grows up. I recall a schoolfriend — large and plain and lumpen — who had been given the name of Grace. Her parents couldn't have known how unsuitable the name would turn out to be, but in the end, they weren't the ones who had to live with it. At least Malachi doesn't give rise to any particular expectations (except perhaps a beard, and a penchant for seeing into the future). And it is undeniably dignified.

But Mum has gone on to speculate about second names (presumably in case the first one is rejected), and I let her get on with it. Four weeks still seem a long way away. Anything can happen in four weeks.

In the event, several things happen.

The first is a devastating raid by a fox, in which a great many of the immigrant chickens perish, together with the white duck.

'Bloody, bloody thing,' rages Eric, gathering up the tattered corpses. 'I can understand it taking just one. One is reasonable. Even a fox has to eat. But all these! All this waste. It's just been killing for the fun of it.'

'Isn't that what foxes do?' I ask him.

'Yes, but that doesn't make it any less infuriating.'

'They weren't really our chickens, were they?'

'That's not the point. And your poor Mum's terribly upset.'

This is true, for Mum has been taking her duties as chicken custodian very seriously, and now she blames herself.

'I should have locked them all up,' she mourns. 'I had a go, but some of them refused to be caught, and it was so cold last night that in the end I gave up. But it was wrong of me. I was being lazy. I could have caught them if I'd tried harder.'

'Mum, chickens are stupid things. It's not your fault if they decide to stay out all night. They know the score. There's a cosy shed there for them if they want it. You did your best.'

'And we can't even eat them.' Eric says. 'That blasted fox has mangled them to bits. I've a good mind to go out with my gun and see if I can catch him. He's bound to come back for more.'

'And if you shoot him carefully, I could stuff him.' Silas has joined us in the kitchen. 'See if you can get him through the ear. Yes. That would be a good place. The ear. You're a good shot, Eric. I'm sure you could do it. That'd preserve the pelt, and would be a nice clean kill.'

'That's thoughtful of you, Silas.' There's an edge to Eric's voice. 'Anything else I can shoot for you while I'm out there? An owl perhaps? A bat?'

'No. Just the fox.' Silas seems impervious to Eric's tone. 'Though a bat would be wonderful,' he adds wistfully. 'I wonder whether anyone has ever stuffed a bat?'

The next thing to happen is the disappearance of Mr. Darcy. One minute he is happily rolling in chicken manure (which of course we have in abundance, and which is his preferred emollient), and the next, he has completely vanished.

'It's so unlike him,' Eric keeps saying, as we hunt through sheds and outbuildings, whistling and calling. 'He's never done anything like this before. He's such a *home* dog.'

'And lazy,' suggests Kaz.

'That too.' But I can tell from Eric's tone that we shouldn't speak ill of the disappeared.

Mr. Darcy isn't a hunter, nor does he go out in search of the opposite sex. He's never been known to fight, and he doesn't go near the main road. He's a stay-at-home dog, occasionally a guard dog, if he can be bothered, but not a wanderer. The whole thing is a mystery.

Hitherto, I have taken Mr. Darcy for granted. He and I get on well enough, he's been a great asset for my busking, and has given me welcome companionship on windy days outside the pound shop, not to mention a talking point for the punters. He is not a creature of beauty, being a strange mixture of collie, terrier and several other rare and not-so-rare breeds, but he is unique. If he resembles anything at all, it is the result of one of those children's games where you add little bits of different animals to make an entirely new species. I would be happy to bet that there is no other dog on the face of this planet who looks like Mr. Darcy.

'Do you have a photo?' I ask Eric.

'There might be one somewhere.'

'We could make a poster.'

'But where would we put it? We're miles from the town. He can't have made his way there on his own.'

'Unless he's been stolen.'

Eric gives me a pitying look. 'Much as I love our dog, I think it very unlikely that anyone would want to steal him.'

'He could be shut in somewhere.'

'That's what I'm afraid of.'

Lazzo, who can eat up the miles like a giant in a fairy story, goes off on foot to search farther afield, and Silas, who needs to be kept occupied, is given the task of phoning such neighbours as there are to make enquiries and to ask them to look in their sheds and garages. Blossom crashes around with her vacuum cleaner, berating us all for our inattention (were we supposed to mount a round-the-clock guard against the possibility of anything happening to Mr. Darcy?), and the rest of us try to get on with our lives. But the ancient chipped dog bowl, the smelly blanket by the Aga, the dog hairs all over the furniture, the half-toothbrush — these are poignant reminders, and we all find it difficult to settle to anything.

A day later, we receive a further blow when Dad, attempting yet again to supervise jobs about which he knows nothing, falls off the roof of his house.

'Everyone keeps telling me how lucky I am,' he says, as he lies in hospital with concussion and three cracked ribs. 'Falling off a roof is not lucky.'

I know what he means. If you don't fall off a roof, no-one tells you how lucky you are, but if you do, then you are apparently lucky not to have killed yourself or at the very least, sustained life-threatening injuries, and people don't hesitate to remind you constantly of your good fortune.

'I'd like to know how they'd feel,' Dad grumbles. 'It's not funny. Falling off a roof.'

The faith and the optimism which carried him through the fire seem to have deserted him, but I suppose even Dad has his limits. It's been a horrible six months for him by any standards; he has a disgraced daughter, he's lost his home, nearly lost his wife, and now this. I think he's entitled to be fed up. Mum stays with friends so that she can visit him, and after two days' observation he's allowed out.

Of course, he comes back to Applegarth — where else can he go? — where he and Silas bond over their medical problems and get on remarkably well. Dad is introduced to Silas's book, and together they pore over it, looking for *complications*. Dad thinks the book is wonderful. He would like a copy for his birthday, he tells us, but Mum is not amused, and says that one hypochondriac in the family is quite enough.

Meanwhile, the weather is appalling — cold and sleety, with an icy north wind — and the heating breaks down. As I lumber up the garden carrying buckets of pig feed, with motherhood just a fortnight away, I wonder what else can go wrong. I also wonder — selfishly, no doubt, but perhaps with just a little justification — when it will be my turn to have some attention, because at the moment, I'm a bit short on it. As I lean over Sarah's door to fill her trough, I shed tears of exhaustion and self-pity, getting nothing for my troubles but a surly grunt and an evil look from one piggy eye.

'Sarah,' I tell her, 'you should count your blessings. You have no idea what a lucky woman you are.'

Chapter Thirty-Eight

Eric has shot the fox. He had to get up long before dawn, but he finally got it, and has returned in triumph.

'But you shot it through the head,' Silas protests. 'Look what a mess you've made of it! I said aim for the ear. The ear would have been perfect.'

'It may surprise you to know,' says Eric, who is cold and hungry and very tired, 'that my priority wasn't to provide you with a specimen. My priority was to kill the fox in order to protect the chickens. And that's what I've done.'

'Well, I think it's an awful shame,' says Silas sulkily. Silas has had a good night's sleep, breakfasted on hot porridge with brown sugar and cream, and is cosily wrapped up in the new dressing gown Mum gave him for Christmas. I sense trouble.

'If you think that I'm going to sit around on a freezing night trying to get in exactly the right position to shoot a fox through the ear — the *ear*, for goodness' sake! — then you're very much mistaken. Besides. You've already done a fox. Why do you need another one?'

'I wanted a pair. I thought we could have one on either side of the fireplace.'

'Over my dead body!'

'Over *your* dead body? *I'm* the one who's nearly died!'

'And don't we all know it!'

'What's that supposed to mean?'

'It means,' says Eric, peeling his gloves off hands which are blue with cold, 'that I've had enough of your illness. It means that there are other people in this house besides you. Ruth, for instance —' oh, please don't bring me into it! — 'who's exhausted; Rosie, who's been working her socks off; Lazzo and Kaz. Blossom, too. Brian, who's had a nasty accident. And Kent. You are not the only person who needs looking after.'

'I never asked to be looked after! I'm up and about, doing my bit ' —

'You're up and about interfering, and quoting that bloody book at everyone —'

'You gave me *that bloody book*, as you call it.'

'And you asked for it!'

Mum, Kent and I listen in astonishment. I have never heard my uncles exchange so much as a cross word, but it would seem that when they get going, they can argue with the best of us.

'I think I'll be going.' Kent edges towards the door.

'Me too. I've got the chickens to feed.' Mum joins him.

'That's right! Abandon us, why don't you?' shouts Silas.

'Well, I don't think you need us at the moment,' Mum tells him. 'You seem quite capable of fighting without any help from anyone else.'

'WE ARE NOT FIGHTING!'

We leave them to it. There is no point in trying to intervene, and although it can't be good for either of them, we should have seen something like this coming. Eric and Silas have been under considerable strain, not helped by a houseful of people. Accustomed to a peaceful life on their own, the past few months must have taken their toll, and I can't help feeling partly responsible.

'Still arguing, are they?' Blossom who has been hovering outside the kitchen door, looks pleased.

'I've no idea.'

'Sounds like it.'

'Well, if it bothers you, you can always do a spot of vacuuming. That should drown them out.'

'Telling me my job, are you?' Blossom bridles.

'I wouldn't dare,' I assure her.

The argument rages for some time, and is followed by a sulk. I thought I knew a bit about sulking, having been something of an expert when I was in my teens, but my sulks were nothing compared to that of Eric and Silas. The sulk hangs over all of us like a malevolent grey blanket, rendering the atmosphere indoors even more depressing than the cold and the mud outside.

'They used to do this as children,' Mum tells me. 'They could keep it up for days.'

'But they're usually so close.' I find their behaviour puzzling.

'It's because they're so close. They know exactly how to annoy each other.'

'But how can they annoy each other if they're not saying anything?'

'I've no idea. But it seems to work.'

'How did — does it end?'

'One of them apologises.'

'That doesn't look very likely at the moment.'

'You'll see.'

Eric is researching water buffaloes, and Silas is looking something up in his bible. They are both pretending to be happily occupied, but even I can see that they're miserable.

But in the event, the row between Eric and Silas is overtaken by a bigger and more serious altercation when two days later, Dad and Eric fall out over Eric's Ark.

To be fair, Dad has done his best to avoid the issue, aware, presumably, that it would be bad manners to pick a quarrel with someone who has been such a generous host. But Eric, still sore from his argument with Silas, finally gives in to the temptation to taunt Dad with his findings, and Dad, who is having serious problems with a recalcitrant electrician, falls into the trap.

'For a start, there's the weight of water,' I hear Eric saying, as I come into the sitting room.

'What do you mean, the weight of water? What's the weight of water got to do with it?' Dad asks.

'The weight of the rainwater; enough water, remember, to reach the top of Everest. It would sink the Ark before it had even started.'

'But it says in the Bible —'

'Never mind what it says in the Bible. The Bible story is a myth.'

'It most certainly is not!'

'It has to be. Because the whole story is nonsense.'

'How dare you —'

'Quite easily, actually.'

'If the whole story is nonsense, how come you're spending so much time going into it all? You tell me that!'

'I'm doing it to prove *how much* nonsense it is. I've given it the best possible chance; I've spent hours doing research. You ask Ruth. She's been helping me —' thank you, Eric — 'and I can tell you, there never was an Ark. There couldn't have been. Some kind of boat, perhaps, with some chickens, a goat, a few bits and bobs. Enough to keep a family going for a while. But not a whopping great Ark full of animals. It's a preposterous idea.'

'They found the remains on Mount Ararat. How do you explain that?'

'They found the remains of something, but it's by no means clear it was an Ark.'

'Of course it was the Ark! The Bible says —'

'No, no, *no!*' Eric is almost hopping with frustration. 'You can't keep saying that. It's a cop out! Think, man. *Think.* Question it, think round it, use your common sense!'

'Well, really. I didn't come here to be insulted!'

'No. You came here because you burnt your house down.' Oh dear. 'And when I try to explain to you the extensive research I've been doing, you completely dismiss it.'

'Well you're dismissing the Bible. The word of God.'

'The *story* of God, more like. Take the water buffalo.' Eric ploughs on, regardless of my father's indignation.

'Take *what?*'

'The water buffalo. It's just one example. How do you expect that to survive on the Ark? You tell me that.'

'I don't know anything about water buffaloes.'

'Exactly! And I don't suppose you know anything about lemurs, or wildebeest, or humming birds or spiders —'

'I don't have to know all about these things to believe what the Bible says.'

'So if the Bible says black is white, you'd believe that?'

'Now you're being ridiculous.'

'No. *You're* being ridiculous. You can't just abandon your common sense and your reasoning because of what the Bible says. Work it out. Think about it. Like I have.'

'Well, I think all this — *work* you've been doing is simply destructive. You're trampling all over beliefs people have held dear for generations. You have no right —'

'I have every right. I'm a scientist —' steady on, Eric — 'and I look at things logically.'

'Well you seem to have spent an awful lot of time trying to prove what you think you already know.' Dad indicates Eric's charts and notes. 'I'm surprised you haven't got more important things to do.'

'I'm doing it because I want to show not just that the whole thing is ridiculous but just *how* ridiculous it is. I'm not just telling you you're wrong; I'm *proving* it.'

'Well you haven't proved anything to me.'

'That's because you're not listening. You've decided what you want to believe, and you refuse to look at what's staring you in the face. It's rubbish. All of it. Rubbish. The Ark, the animals, the Noah family — just eight people, remember, to look after all those hundreds of creatures. That in itself is a bit far-fetched, *and* they had to catch them all in the first place — whichever way you look at it, it's a logistical impossibility.'

'You're enjoying, this, aren't you?' says Dad, after a moment.

'Of course I am. It's fascinating. I shall be quite sorry when I've finished.'

'I mean the argument. You're enjoying arguing with me, questioning my beliefs.'

'Well —'

'There! I told you! You're just doing this to annoy me. Admit it.'

'Of course I'm not. Do you really think I would spend months on a project just in order to annoy you? But to prove you wrong — now that's a different matter. I would certainly do it to prove you wrong. You and anyone else who takes the Bible literally. When we had that — discussion last year, I decided that I'd go into the whole Ark business, and I'm grateful to you, I really am. It's been fascinating.'

'Don't you patronise me,' says Dad, clambering back onto the high horse from which Eric has just about managed to dislodge him.

'Oh, don't be so pompous, Brian. It doesn't suit you.' It does, but I've got enough sense not to intervene. 'Come and have a drink. We've just opened some rather nice turnip wine. You must try it.'

'You know I don't drink.'

'Silly me,' mutters Eric.

'You said it,' counters Dad, and drawing himself up to his full but not very substantial height, he takes himself off to bed.

'Wasn't that a bit naughty, Eric?' I ask him, when Dad has left the room.

'Probably.' Eric grins. 'But he's so easy to wind up. And we were going to have this discussion sooner or later, weren't we?'

'You call that a discussion?'

'Oh, come on, Ruth. Don't you go all disapproving on me. Come and have a little taste of the turnip wine. I'm sure just a little taste won't hurt the baby, and I hate drinking alone.'

Chapter Thirty-Nine

The following morning, all rows and sulks are forgotten, for Kent has received the result of his DNA test.

'Well, that's it,' he says, looking rather stunned.

'Yes? What did they say? What's the result?' Silas asks him. 'Come on. Don't keep us in suspense.'

Kent folds his letter and replaces it carefully in its envelope. 'It's — positive.'

'Wonderful! That's wonderful isn't it, Eric?'

'Wonderful.'

'Wonderful,' echoes Kent, studying his letter.

'Well, aren't you pleased?' Eric asks him.

'Yes, of course. Of course I'm pleased. It's just that it's a bit of a shock. I knew it was possible, otherwise I wouldn't have come here in the first place, but after all this time it seemed such a long shot, and I'd prepared myself for disappointment.'

I think I understand what Kent must feel. I too always expect the worst, and try to prepare myself for it. The down side of that is that I'm not ready for the good news when it comes. Kent apparently feels the same.

'I'd already been wondering what to do if the answer was no,' he continues. 'After all, you wouldn't have wanted me hanging around here if I wasn't your — if I wasn't related, would you?'

'Yes we would!' my uncles speak together.

'A "no" result wouldn't have made you a different person, and we've loved having you around,' Silas adds. 'In a way, this doesn't change anything, does it?'

'It does for me,' Kent says. 'It gives me a whole new view of who I am. It takes a bit of getting used to.'

'Come and feed the pigs with me,' I suggest, sensing Kent's mixture of feelings. 'A breath of fresh air is what you need.'

'That is one seriously nasty animal,' Kent says, five minutes later, as we lean over the door of Sarah's shed.

'Isn't she? But I'm fond of her in a funny way. She's certainly a character.'

The character looks up at us, her jaws slobbering swill, giving us the evil eye as only Sarah can.

'What's to be fond of?' Kent asks. 'I don't get it.'

'Not a lot.' I laugh. 'I suppose it's because she's part of Applegarth, and believe it or not, she's a wonderful mother.'

'I can think of mothers I'd rather have.'

'Speaking of mothers...'

'Yes.' Kent sighs. 'Well, mine was a character, too. She was a pretty good mother on the whole, but she put herself about a bit, too.'

'Just as well for you that she did,' I remind him.

'True. I suppose in a way she couldn't help herself. She was so pretty. Even in old age, she had these amazing blue eyes, and a nice pair of legs, and a kind of twinkle. She was giving the milkman the glad eye right up until the day she died. Everyone loved her.'

'Do you miss her?' I ask, after a moment.

'Oh, yes. Of course I do. For years, there were just the two of us. She never had a live-in lover. She said it was because of me, but I think she wanted to keep her options open.'

'Or maybe she just didn't find the right man to live in with.'

'That's possible, too.'

'And now, this.' I bring the conversation back to the matter in hand.

'And now this,' Kent agrees. 'I know I must seem ungracious. Ungrateful even. It's just that I really had prepared myself not to be their son — doesn't that sound odd? *Their* son? — and was already making plans. And now — well, I've got a lot of catching up to do. There's so much I want to ask them. Family things, personal things. Things I haven't dared to ask before. Up until now, I've tried to keep a bit of a distance. I didn't want to get too attached to them and — all this. Now, they're family, and everything's different.'

'And you've got a cousin.'

Kent squeezes my shoulder and smiles; Eric's (or is it Silas's?) smile.

'I've got a cousin,' he agrees. 'And a rather lovely one at that.'

'Thank you, kind sir.' With my enormous bulk it's a very long time since I felt lovely, and although I'm sure Kent's just being kind, I can't help feeling pleased.

'Not at all. I've always wanted a cousin. Mum was an only child, so I was a bit short on family.'

'Me too.' I hesitate. 'Kent — I'm really pleased about, well, about you and Kaz.'

'She's told you, has she? I didn't think anyone knew.'

'I'm a woman, Kent. Women notice these things.'

'And — the others?'

'No-one's said anything, so I don't think so. But you both look so happy it's a bit hard to miss!'

'I've never felt like this about anyone before,' Kent confides. 'But — and you mustn't tell Kaz I said this — I've thought long and hard, and I've decided there can't be a future for us.'

'What? Why ever not? You're not already married, are you?' Because if Kent has a secret wife hidden away somewhere, I'm going to be seriously angry with him.

'No. Nothing like that. It's — our ages. I'm too old for her, Ruth. I'm nearly twice her age. It wouldn't be fair.'

'Isn't that for her to decide?'

'She says it's not a problem, but while it's fine now, what about the future?'

'In my experience, the future rarely turns out the way you expect it to. Just look at me! Besides, Kaz is a big girl. She knows what she's doing.'

'And I know what I'm doing,' Kent says sadly. 'And it's not right, Ruth. It's not fair. But please don't say anything to her. It's up to me to break it off. And I will, when the time's right.'

'Then is it fair to — to keep on with the relationship at all if you're going to end it?'

'Probably not. I suppose at first I thought it would run its course, and things would sort themselves out. But now it's getting serious, and I don't know how to stop it.' He sighs. 'I'll have to tell her soon, but, well…'

'Not yet?'

'Not quite yet.'

'Well, it's up to you of course, but it'll break her heart.'

'I know. Oh Ruth, what have I got myself into?' He leans his elbows on the door of the sty and rubs his face in a way that is so reminiscent of Silas that I wonder that we ever needed that DNA test at all.

We stand for a few minutes watching Sarah wolf down the last of her breakfast and snuffle round her trough for the remaining fragments.

'She goes free range when the weather's okay,' I tell him, thinking it's time we changed the subject.

'What a terrifying thought!'

'No, actually she's all right when she's out. She just hates being cooped up.'

'I can imagine.'

We turn back towards the house.

'May I ask you something?' I have a burning question, but am not sure whether or not it's the right moment.'

'Ask away.'

'Do you mind — I mean, does it matter to you which one is your father?'

'Funnily enough, no it doesn't. They are so much two of a kind, even if I knew, I think I'd see them both in the same light. It might be a little awkward when it comes to my introducing them to people — and I'm longing for them to meet some of my friends — but no. I honestly don't mind not knowing. In a way, it makes it all more interesting.'

'What's going to be really interesting is telling Mum,' I tell him.

'She must suspect something like this.'

'Oh, yes. But Mum is a great one for burying her head in the sand. If something is hurtful or distasteful, or if it doesn't come up to her exacting standards, she tries to ignore it. Mum doesn't do confrontation. Dad, on the other hand, weighs right in and tells everyone what he thinks. There's nothing reticent about my father.'

'I've noticed.'

'And I don't think he suspects anything because, apart from anything else, he's terribly unobservant. He won't have noticed how like Eric and Silas you are.'

'Am I really?'

'Oh yes! Can't you see it?'

'I think I've been trying not to. But yes. A bit. I can see I'm a bit like them, but probably more like Mum.'

We have just reached the house when a very smart car creeps cautiously up the drive, and a very familiar dog jumps out. He is wearing a new posh collar, and there is a well-dressed woman following him and carrying a matching lead.

'*Mr. Darcy!*' I hold out my arms, and Mr. Darcy leaps into them, licking my face and covering me with mud. His feet may be muddy but his fur is clean and fluffy, and he smells sweetly of lemons. Someone has given Mr. Darcy a bath. 'Where have you been, you bad dog? We've been so worried!'

'Oh dear.' The woman totters through the puddles in her unsuitable shoes, looking embarrassed. 'I did hope he wasn't yours as we've rather fallen for him.'

'But where did you find him?' I push Mr. Darcy down, and he turns his attentions to Kent.

'I think he must have come back with us in the car when we collected those chickens.'

'But he's been gone nearly a week!'

'Yes. Well, we've only just realised what must have happened. We never saw him get into the car or get out of it. As far as we were concerned, he just turned up. We phoned the police —'

'So did we!'

'Well, they weren't much help. Anyway, we thought he must be a stray. He was awfully hungry.'

'Mr. Darcy is always hungry,' I tell her. 'But he definitely belongs here.'

'Yes. I can see that. Oh dear. What shall I tell the children?'

'You could buy them a puppy?'

'That wouldn't be the same at all. Tiger — we called him Tiger. Don't you think it suits him? — is house-trained, you see, and has such lovely manners.' Tiger? *Lovely manners?* Perhaps this is the wrong dog after all. But the little tear in his left ear, the lop-sided wag of the tail, the beetling eyebrows — these are all Mr. Darcy. He looks a little sheepish, as well he might, but there is no mistaking his identity.

I briefly consider inviting our visitor in, but this is Kent's day, and besides, at the moment I don't think I can face another lot of explanations, plus the identical twin effect (this woman looks the susceptible type), so I wave her politely on her way.

'Does he often go off with people like that?' Kent asks.

'He loves riding in cars, but he doesn't usually hijack other people's.'

'Oh well. No harm done, and he's home, which is the main thing.'

Back in the kitchen, Mr. Darcy receives a rapturous welcome from my uncles. Even Blossom can't hide her relief.

'Decided to come back then, did you?' she asks him, wiping mud off his paws with an old towel. 'Dratted animal. Don't know when you're well off.'

'We can have a double celebration!' says Silas.

'What double celebration?' Blossom demands.

'Oh dear.' Silas turns to Eric.

'She'll have to know sooner or later.'

'Yes. But know what, exactly?'

'We've just discovered I'm a relation,' Kent says. 'Isn't that good news?'

'Son, more like,' says Blossom.

'Well, yes. Possibly.'

'Whose?'

'I'm afraid that's personal,' says Eric quickly.

'Yes. Personal,' echoes Silas.

'Personal, my backside.' Blossom, sniffs. 'Got a right to know,' she adds.

'No, Blossom. You haven't. Not yet, anyway,' Eric says. 'This is a private family matter.'

'Ruth know, does she?'

'Yes.'

'Humph.'

'Ruth's *family*,' Silas tells her. 'It's only fair that she should be told.'

Blossom gives me an evil look. While she seems to have little use for her own family, she hates to be reminded that she's not a member of ours.

'Oh come on, Blossom. Surely you understand,' Eric says.

'Only been here five minutes,' Blossom says, presumably referring to me.

'She's still family,' Eric says.

'Been here years, I have,' Blossom retorts.

'That's true. And we're very grateful.'

'Grateful!' scoffs Blossom.

'And you get paid,' Silas reminds her.

'Paid! Paid, indeed!' Blossom slams out of the back door.

I've no idea what Blossom means by this, but she is clearly not pleased. I dread to think what she'll do next, for Blossom does an interesting line in revenge, and I don't fancy the idea of anything like that being directed at me.

'What will you tell Mum?' I ask, after she's gone.

'That's what we've been wondering,' Silas says. 'But we think it'll have to be the truth.'

'A version of the truth,' Eric adds.

'Yes. We've decided to tell her that Kent is Eric's. That'll be one shock less for her to cope with. I'll be his uncle,' he adds. 'I'm quite happy to settle for uncle. In public, anyway.'

'Good luck, then.'

'Yes. I think we're going to need it.'

In the event, Mum takes the news pretty well, although she's undoubtedly shocked. I think she has hitherto believed her brothers to be dedicated celibates, and to have incontrovertible evidence of a sexual liaison, however long ago that might have been, is going to take a bit of getting used to. But she does agree that Dad need not know, at least for the time being, and she seems quite pleased to have a nephew.

Two days later, I come across Blossom in the hallway. She has a knowing glint in her eye, and I sense trouble.

'Had a visitor,' she tells me, switching off the vacuum cleaner and folding her arms.

'Who, me?'

'S'right.'

'Well, who was it?' I take off my coat (I have just returned from the clinic).

'Big feller.' Blossom is watching my reaction, eking out her news and enjoying every minute of it.

'Yes?' I feel a frisson of fear. I suspect that Blossom's revenge has already taken place, and is going to be more wounding than even she could have anticipated.

'Beard,' says Blossom. 'Trumpet thingy.'

'Amos.' I can't believe it. I can't bear it. *Amos*. So close, and now gone. 'What did you tell him?' I try to keep my voice even. 'Where is he now?'

'Told him I'd never heard of you. Told him you don't live here.' Blossom is actually smiling. 'Went away.'

'*Blossom!* How could you? How dare you? *You had no right!*' I grab hold of the front of her pinafore and give her a little shake. 'It was a wicked, wicked thing to do!'

Blossom pulls herself free. 'Don't you touch me!'

'When was this? How long ago?'

'Two hours, about. Didn't notice.'

'Have you *any* idea what you've done?'

Blossom shrugs.

'You've turned away the father of my baby, that's what you've done. I've been trying to trace him for months and now I may never find him!'

'Not my problem.'

'But *why*? Why did you do this? What have I ever done to you?'

Blossom mutters something about my morals, and babies out of wedlock.

'And what about lying?' I counter. 'That's okay, is it? It's all right to tell lies to a total stranger? Lies about something which is none of your business?'

'Seems nothing's my business nowadays,' says Blossom mutinously.

'Just because Eric and Silas don't want you to know all about their private lives, you decide to take it out on me? That's not fair, Blossom, and you know it.'

'Done, now. Too late to do anything about it,' says Blossom.

'Did he leave a phone number? An address? Anything at all?'

'Nope.'

'And you didn't think to ask anyone else? Eric or Silas? My mother?'

'Out.'

'What, all of them?'

Blossom smirks, and I can see that she's lying, although I haven't any proof.

'Well, I think what you've done is unforgivable. I've tried to get on with you, Blossom. I've put up with your rudeness and your moods, and this is all the thanks I get.'

'Your problem.' Blossom switches on the vacuum cleaner again. 'Nothing to do with me,' she yells above the noise.

'Quite. It was *nothing to do with you*.' But of course, Blossom can no longer hear me.

It would seem that our little chat is now over.

Chapter Forty

Kaz finds me weeping at the kitchen table.

'Hey! What's up? Bad news at the clinic?' Kaz sits down and puts her arm round my shoulders.

'No. Your bloody mother.'

'Oh dear.' Kaz hands me a roll of kitchen towel.

'Oh dear indeed.' I blow my nose. 'Sorry to talk about her to you like this, but she really is a cow of the first order.'

'Tell me about it.' Kaz sits down beside me. 'So what's she been up to this time?'

'She's been "up to" turning away Amos.'

'Your bloke?'

'Well, he never will be now, will he? Blossom told him no-one here had ever heard of me.'

'Oops.'

'He turned up — he actually came here looking for me. I left this address with my parents' neighbours so that if he ever came looking for me, he'd know where to find me. I was out, and it had to be your mother who answered the door. Blossom *never* answers the door. Talk about sod's law!'

'God, I'm sorry Ruth. Didn't he leave a message or anything?'

'No. Because as far as he's concerned, I don't live here, do I? I suppose I'm lucky she didn't tell him I was dead while she was about it.'

'I knew she was upset with you all, but not that upset. Oh dear. I'm so sorry, Ruth. I really am.'

'It's not your fault.' I tear off more kitchen roll and wipe my eyes. 'But oh, Kaz! What am I going to do? Amos finding me here was my last chance, and now it's gone. And so has he. He won't come back here again.'

'He mightn't have been the right one for you. You said so yourself.'

'Yes. But *I* wanted to decide. *My* decision. Not bloody *bloody* Blossom's!'

'I can see that.' Kaz strokes my hair. 'Is there anything I can do?'

'Not really. An itinerant trombone player ought to be easy to find, particularly that one, but apparently not. Amos seems to have this knack of disappearing.'

'How was the clinic?' Kaz changes the subject.

'Oh, fine. The midwife said about ten days to go.'

'That's good, isn't it?'

'You know, Kaz, I don't really care. I'm so tired, there's been so much going on, what with Silas's illness and everything. I've hardly had time to think about babies.'

'Ruth, you have to. It's ridiculous to say you haven't had time to think about the baby. The truth is that you don't want to think about it.'

'That's not fair!'

'Isn't it? You've had nine months to think about it, and you hardly ever mention it. It's almost as though there isn't a baby at all. You decided to keep it. You've had all your scans and things. Now you have to start planning for it. Looking forward to it, even.'

'You sound like my mother.'

'That's a good thing, isn't it? You need a bit of bossing about. You need someone to look after you.'

'I need Amos.' The tears start again. I imagine Amos's big arms around me, Amos telling me everything's going to be all right, Amos at my side while I give birth to our child, Amos bringing me flowers, and being proud. 'I need him so much, Kaz. You've no idea how much.'

'I can imagine.' Kaz pauses for a moment. 'Well, we'll just have to find him.'

'How? How are we going to find him?'

'Let's start with your friends. We'll phone them all up and see whether anyone has any idea of where he is.'

'But I did that ages ago.'

'Yes, but that was when he'd gone abroad. Now that he's back, you've got more chance of finding him. He must be somewhere, for goodness' sake! Someone must know where he is.'

I fetch my address book, and together Kaz and I go through it. Of course, many of my friends don't know Amos, but the musical world is a small one, and my friends from college and from the orchestra prove to be more help than I had anticipated. There have been several recent sightings of Amos, who has apparently been doing the rounds, looking up old friends. No-one seems to know where's he's living, or even to have his phone number, but Amos is apparently very much around, and looking for work in the London area.

'That's a start,' says Kaz, when we call a halt for a cup of coffee.

'London's a big place,' I remind her.

'Yes. But it's a lot nearer than Barbados, and you've left plenty of messages. I bet he'll get in touch soon. Just you wait.'

I am not good at waiting, although given the amount of practice I've had recently I certainly ought to be. But I have no choice. If Amos gets any of my messages, I'm pretty sure he'll be in touch, but there's no guarantee that it'll be soon. As for the baby, Kaz and I discuss this at length and we both decide that it would be best that he shouldn't know about it at this stage. As Kaz says, it might scare him off, and that's the last thing I want to do.

'Though I don't think Amos is the kind of person to be scared off by a baby,' I tell her. 'Or anything else, come to that.'

'Why take the risk?' Kaz asks me.

'Good point. He'll have to know some time, but perhaps not yet.'

Fortunately, at this point we are interrupted by several pilgrims who wish to adopt chickens, and since Lazzo is currently suffering from flu and Mum is out helping Dad choose kitchen units, the job falls to Kaz and me. Neither of us is good with Lazzo's chicken-catching device, so it takes us an inordinate amount of time to trap three particularly scruffy specimens (it seems the fox chose all the better-looking ones).

'But I wanted the ones with the little furry trousers,' their putative owner objects. 'These aren't nearly so pretty.'

'Little furry trousers are all very well,' says Kaz, nursing some nasty scratches, 'but they don't lay well.'

'Are you sure?' The pilgrim/chicken-lover looks dubious.

'Quite sure. Trust me. And these have all been blessed. By a bishop.'

'Have they really?' The woman looks impressed. I notice that she is carrying a rosary. Kaz says the religious ones are always the most gullible.

'Of course. You've no idea what a difference it makes. Now, take them home and enjoy them.'

'Kaz, really! You're almost as bad as your mother,' I tell her, as we return to the house. 'Blessed, indeed!'

'Well, I had to get rid of her somehow, and there's no way I'm chasing little furry trousers all over the garden. Little furry trousers run very fast indeed. Only Lazzo can catch them, and I'm not even going to try.'

'And is it true that they don't lay well?'

Kaz laughs. 'I've no idea.'

Today is not supposed to be a day for visits to the Virgin, but we receive three more lots of visitors before dark. Two are regulars, and know their own way around, and the third has brought a rather splendid pair of Rhode Island Reds.

'My son gave me these for Christmas,' he tells me. 'My wife died in the summer, and the children think I'm lonely. But I'm not sure chickens will help.'

I agree, wondering what kind of people could conceivably imagine that chickens would be an antidote to grief. A dog or cat might at least be company, but chickens?

'I'm sure we'll find them a good home,' I tell him, and then, because I feel sorry for him, I invite him in for a cup of tea. By the time I've heard his story of long years of caring for a wife gradually disabled by dementia ('the long good-bye, they call it,' he tells me) I feel ashamed for feeling so sorry for myself earlier on. After all, I'm still fairly young, I'm fit, and as Kaz points out, no-one has died. I resolve to pull myself together and start being responsible, beginning with an inventory of the pitifully small collection of equipment which awaits the advent of the baby.

'Two vests won't be enough,' says Kaz, watching me.

'Then I shall buy more.'

'And nappies. You've forgotten those.'

'Nappies, too.'

'You'd better hurry up. Time is not on your side.'

'Right. Tomorrow I shall go out and buy vests and nappies.'

'That's my girl,' says Kaz. 'I'll come with you. And we can go to that new little café that sells wonderful cream slices.'

'Aren't I big enough already?' I ask her.

'No-one,' says Kaz, 'is ever too big for a cream slice.'

Chapter Forty-One

But during the vest/nappy-buying expedition, Kaz appears to have preoccupations of her own.

'Kaz? What's up?' I ask her, when we adjourn for coffee and cream slices. She looks pale, and she obviously hasn't slept, and I suspect that the news isn't good.

'I've slept with someone.'

'Kent. Yes. You said you were going to.' My heart sinks. For if they've slept together, breaking up will be so much harder.

'No. Someone else.'

'Goodness.' I put down my cup. 'But why, Kaz? And who?'

'An old friend.' Kaz fiddles with her teaspoon.

'Let me get this straight. You're supposed to be having a — thing with Kent, but you've gone and slept with an *old friend*! What on earth were you thinking of?'

'Long story.'

'Good thing we've got plenty of time, then.'

'You're not going to make this easy for me, are you?'

'Nope.' Though given Kent's feelings about the future, this may be one solution.

'I was — upset. Kent and I had this horrible row, and I needed cheering up.'

'I see. So the cure for a lovers' tiff is to dash out and find a replacement?'

'Oh Ruth, it wasn't like that at all.'

'Well, what was it like?'

'He's got this thing about his age, and I don't think it matters, and we had this argument, and it kind of — well, it got out of hand. I said some horrible things.'

'And he did, too?'

'No. Kent never does anything horrible. That's the trouble. He's so bloody *nice* all the time. He just goes all quiet and sad, and then I feel awful and make things even worse.'

'So let me get this straight. You were horrible to Kent, who didn't deserve it, and then you went off and slept with someone else. What a brilliant move!'

'Actually, he was the one who "went off". He said he needed to be alone, and he went back to his caravan, and I was upset, and I went to see Gary. Gary and I go back a long way. We just had a few drinks, but one thing lead to another. And Ruth, I'm so, so sorry. I feel terrible.'

'It's not me you should be apologising to.'

'I thought you'd — I thought you might understand. After all, isn't that what got you into your present mess in the first place?'

'Oh, no. *Oh* no. You're not comparing this — what you've done with my situation. I am not in a mess, as you so kindly put it. I may have made a mistake, but I didn't plan to get pregnant, and I did not let anyone down. Amos and I are — were — free agents. No-one else got hurt.'

We sit glaring at each other, while tears trickle down Kaz's cheeks and drip onto the checked tablecloth.

'Look, let's not fall out about this.' I decide that one of us had better rescue the situation before it escalates further. 'We need to decide what you're going to do.'

'I'll have to tell Kent, won't I?'

'Will you? Won't telling him make things worse?'

'I don't know,' Kaz says wretchedly. 'Oh, Ruth, what am I like?'

'Well, you're kind and funny, and — and bloody impossible!' I can't help smiling. 'But if you really love Kent, I'd leave this for the moment. It might make you feel better to tell him, but it certainly won't help the situation.'

'Mm.' Her hair is rumpled, and there are streaks of mascara down her cheeks, but she still manages to look as stunning as ever. 'Ruth, do you think — do you think twenty years older is too old?'

I've been thinking about this ever since my conversation with Kent, and I'm not sure. 'Yes and no. I think it's more a matter of you being mature enough to take on someone of his age. Running off and sleeping with someone else as soon as the going gets tough isn't a mature thing to do, is it?'

'I'll never do it again. If he stays with me, I swear I'll be faithful. I really will.'

'Well in that case, if I were you I'd go home and apologise nicely for the things you said, and try to discuss the situation as calmly as you can. I'm sure he'll listen if you can keep your cool. Then ask him to give you — you and him — a bit more time. After all, there's no hurry, is there? No-one's going anywhere.'

'Would you have a word with him?' Kaz pushes her plate towards me.

'If I get the chance, I will,' I promise, finishing off Kaz's cream slice and thinking that if I go on like this, I'm going to have one very fat baby.

The next day, I find myself alone with Kent in the orchard.

'About you and Kaz,' I begin.

'Has she been telling you about her — our row?'

'*Her* row, I think it was.' I laugh. 'Yes, she has. Kent, she really loves you. I know she's young, but could you give her a chance? I don't think Kaz has had much love in her life, and maybe someone like you is exactly what she needs.'

'I just feel that I'll be — taking advantage of her, I suppose.'

'Trust me. No-one takes advantage of Kaz,' I tell him. 'She's young, and she can be stupid, but she's also pretty canny, and I reckon she's been looking after herself most of her life. It's love that she needs.'

'Maybe. I'd love it to work out. She's a special girl, Ruth. Not just pretty. There are lots of pretty girls around. But few as — as special as Kaz. Perhaps you're right. Perhaps we should give it a bit more time.'

By now, the news of Kaz and Kent has got out, and everyone seems to know (everyone, that is, except my parents, who have a blind spot where such goings-on are concerned). Silas and Eric, those most accepting of men, seem quite happy about the situation, if a bit surprised. But Blossom is furious.

'Dratted girl!' she says, sending a tsunami of soapy water across the kitchen floor. 'Anything in trousers. Always been like that. Takes after her father.'

From what I've heard, nothing could be further from the truth, but there's no point in saying so.

'Don't you want her to be happy?' I venture.

'Happy? Humph.' Slosh, swipe. 'She wants to be *happy*, does she? I'll give her happy!'

She flings down her mop and slams out into the garden.

So it seems that yet again, the focus is on other people and their problems. Just as I have got Kaz on side and excited about the baby, her attention is lost to more pressing problems. And while I am still not as excited as I probably ought to be, I quite enjoy the excitement and the attention of others. For the first time since I came to Applegarth, I feel very much alone, and if I am honest, frightened. For whatever my feelings about it, the baby is going to come *out*, and it's going to hurt. That much I know. I've paid scant attention to the ante-natal classes, and I am ill-prepared for the rigours of childbirth. I have at least one friend who's sworn that she's "never going through that again", and has stuck to her word, enjoying her daughter but flatly refusing to have any more children. I have never been particularly good with pain, and Mum, while supportive, can be squeamish. Supposing she faints? Supposing we *both* faint? It won't be much of a welcome for a baby who didn't ask to be born and wasn't even wanted in the first place.

I wander into the sitting room and find Eric, who is preoccupied with the problem of humming birds. For it is not only bees and other insects that need flowers, he tells me. Humming birds do, too.

'But surely God wouldn't have expected Noah to have more than just two birds, and they could have been anything. Robins are nice and easy. How about robins?'

'No. The Bible says two of "every kind of bird, every kind of animal and every kind of reptile". So you can't get away with just robins. I've had to leave out a lot; it would take more than a lifetime to deal with every single species. But I've dealt with quite a few. Owls, eagles, ostriches — you've no idea, Ruth. It's incredibly complicated.'

I realise that the more complicated it becomes the more Eric enjoys it, but have enough sense not to say so.

'So you see, we'll have to have a garden, or even a small park, for all the creatures which can't do without living plants. At this rate, the Isle of Wight is definitely going to be too small. Perhaps something the size of Gibraltar.' He rubs his head. 'How big is Gibraltar?'

'I've no idea. Eric, you can't have a park on a boat. The soil would rot the boards and fall through.'

Eric sighs. 'Ruth, you're missing the point, like everyone else. I thought you at least understood. Of course it's not possible. At least, not possible on an Ark. But on a structure the size of Gibraltar — whatever that is — and reinforced with concrete (I must ask someone about that) it might be possible. Or maybe I could line the foundations with plastic.'

'They wouldn't have had concrete in those days,' I remind him. 'Or plastic.'

'I know, I know. That's not the point, either.' He jots down a note to himself. 'Come to think of it, I believe there's a cruise ship with a small golf course,' he says thoughtfully.

'Is there really?'

'I believe so.' He folds up his charts. 'Ruth, are you all right?' He pats my bump. 'Not long to go now.'

'So everyone keeps telling me.'

'It won't be so bad, you know.'

'What? The baby? Childbirth? The — my — future?'

'All of them.' He holds out his hand, and draws me down beside him on the sofa. 'You'll be all right, you know. And we'll do anything we can for you. You'll always have a home here, if you need one.'

'I know.' I squeeze his hand, and my eyes fill with tears. 'Kent's so lucky.'

'Why? Why is he lucky?'

'To have you — you and Silas — as his father. Fathers, I mean.'

'You have a good father, Ruth. And he does care, you know.'

'Perhaps he does, but at the moment I want to *feel* that he cares.' I look down at our linked hands. 'I don't think my father has so much as touched me since I was a small child.'

'People have different ways of showing affection. Some just aren't the hugging kind.'

'I suppose you're right.' I lift Eric's hand and hold it against my cheek. It is rough and chapped from working outside in all weathers, but the feel of it is infinitely comforting, and I realise that what I miss more than anything else at the moment is physical contact with another human being.

'He's a fortunate man, your Amos,' Eric says, as though reading my thoughts. 'I hope he does come and find you soon, and discover that for himself.'

'Oh, so do I, Eric. So do I.'

I gaze out of the window, where a wintry dusk is already draining away what little daylight we've had. Somewhere out there, perhaps not very far away, is Amos. I wonder what he's doing at this moment; whether he's playing his trombone, perhaps having a pint in a pub with a friend, driving somewhere in his dreadful old car, making a curry (Amos makes good curries). If I believed in telepathy, I'd send him a message. As it is, I just have to hope that one of the smattering of messages I've left all over the country reaches him soon.

Chapter Forty-Two

March comes in like the proverbial lion. A biting east wind whisks the last few brittle autumn leaves round the frozen garden and penetrates under doors and the edges of ill-fitting windows. The animals huddle in their sheds, and we huddle indoors, wrapped in as many layers as we can lay hands on. I look like a Russian doll; as though within each layer of clothing there lies another, smaller woman, similarly clad. Mum, who has never been good with the cold, suffers terribly from chilblains, and Silas, who still hasn't regained all the weight he lost during his illness, feels the cold more than usual. He is banned from outdoor duties, although he protests that he is fine, and that the 'fresh air will do him good'. Eric points out that it's more likely to kill him, and fortunately the medical bible agrees, so Silas has to do as he's told. He takes comfort from the corpse of the hare, recovered from beneath the frozen remains of Dorothy. We all hope that the stuffing of this unfortunate animal will keep him amused until the warmer weather arrives. The only people unaffected by the cold are Lazzo, who strides back and forth, often in his shirtsleeves, seeing to the animals, and Kaz and Kent. Having for the time being at least resolved their differences, they appear to have recaptured their initial glow, and this seems to be enough to keep them happy, if not exactly warm.

The baby is late. I never expected it to arrive on time, considering that after so long in the womb, it should be allowed a little leeway. I have never understood how babies can be late. I can see that early could be a problem; even I know that premature babies are bound to be underdeveloped. But late? It seems to me more than likely that each baby comes in its own time, and that that time varies from baby to baby.

But the midwife disagrees, and mutters about weight loss and something called 'placental insufficiency'. I know that the reason I have lost weight is that indigestion prevents me from eating as much as I normally would, but the midwife, a busty bossy woman, doesn't listen. I tell her it's my body; she says what about the baby? I say it's my baby, too; she says I'm being selfish, and threatens to have it induced. I ask whether this can be done without my consent. She reluctantly admits that it can't. Well, then.

I sit around and wait. Because of my size and accompanying exhaustion, I was relegated some time ago to light duties — feeding the hens, helping Mum with meals, a spot of hen house duty — but now everyone insists on treating me like an invalid, and I'm hardly allowed to do anything at all. I read and try to play the violin, but my attention span is so limited that I can't concentrate on either. My sleep is disturbed by the activities of the baby, who appears to have no notion of day or night, and by bad dreams. I have a recurring nightmare in which the baby refuses to come out — in fact never comes out — and I get bigger and bigger as the years go by.

'He's a man now, you know,' says the midwife, who is still apparently in attendance. 'He's started shaving.'

The idea of a fully-grown man living inside me and actually *shaving* is so horrendous that it invariably wakes me up.

These days, I hardly recognise Kaz. Gone is most of the ironmongery which used to adorn her face, her hair is returning to its natural colour (a pleasant shade of honey) and she's trying to give up cigarettes (Kent hates them).

'Though it's bloody difficult,' she tells me, as we shiver together outside the back door while she has a smoke. She's down to seven a day, and rations them carefully so as to get the most out of them. 'If you've never smoked, you don't know how wonderful it is. That first long pull of smoke into your lungs — there's nothing like it.' She removes what is now a minuscule stub from between her lips, gazes at it wistfully for a moment, and then screws it carefully into the ground with her heel. 'Let's go in and get warm.'

We wake the next morning to snow. When I look out of the window, the garden and the fields beyond are carpeted in white. The roofs and corners of the outbuildings are rounded and softened by snow, making them resemble gingerbread houses, and the branches of the trees are bent low under its weight. There isn't a breath of wind.

Perhaps there's still something of the child in me, for I never fail to be excited by snow. The magic white light, which seems to glow on the walls even before you've opened the curtains; the softness of the silence; the treat of being the first to make footfalls in virgin snow. Of course, as a child, I had snowballs and snowmen to look forward to, and I think I can say I've grown out of those, but there is still something special about waking up to snow, especially when, as today, it is totally unexpected.

But it would appear that I'm the only one excited by the snow, for downstairs, everyone is grumbling. Snow means more work, of course. It needs to be negotiated or shovelled away; such animals as are still allowed out during the day will have to be kept in, which means more mucking out; everything takes twice the time when you have to tramp through snow.

'Blossom won't be in,' says Eric wearily.

'Why?'

'She never comes when it snows. Says the bike won't work.'

'Well, she may have a point.'

'She may. But I think the real point is that she doesn't like snow.'

But Lazzo turns up, full of good cheer, and between us all (for once, my offers of help are accepted) we get the jobs done. By lunch-time, the snow is pock-marked by trails of footsteps, crossing and re-crossing each other, and my excitement has evaporated as quickly as it arrived. My fingers are stiff with cold, my feet are numb inside my wellingtons, and I know without looking that my cheeks have turned an unattractive shade of purple. Maybe snow isn't so much fun after all.

But after lunch, Mikey and Gavin turn up.

'We've come to help you make a snowman!' Mikey says. 'To cheer you up.'

'What a ridiculous idea.' I'm no longer in the mood for snowmen. 'Haven't you got a job to go to?'

'It's Saturday.'

'Oh. I'd forgotten.'

'Come on, Ruth. It's your last chance to be a kid before you're a mother.'

'You think?'

'I know.'

So we make a snowman. Kaz and Kent join in, and when it's finished, I have to admit that it's the best snowman I've ever seen. It — he — is huge (Mikey made the finishing touches with the help of a stepladder), and sports a rather fetching trilby hat and a moth-eaten dinner jacket.

'There. Don't you feel better now?' Mikey brushes snow off his jacket and beams at me.

'You know, I think I do.'

'I said you would. It brings out the child in you.'

'That's actually what I'm waiting for.'

'So you are!'

We all howl with laughter, while my father, who doesn't do fun in any form, watches us pityingly from the sitting-room window and Mr. Darcy runs round and round in circles, dizzy with excitement. A lone pilgrim, waiting for someone to attend to her, watches in astonishment, and Eric and Silas applaud from the back doorway.

Today has turned out to be a good day after all.

Chapter Forty-Three

Late in the evening, the wind gets up again, and before long it's howling round the house and down the chimney.

'It's snowing again. Already drifting,' says Kaz, letting in a blast of ice-cold air as she comes in from checking on the animals. 'Bloody hell, it's cold. Put the kettle on, someone. I can't move my fingers.'

Kent obliges, and Kaz peels off several layers and then goes to warm herself by the Aga.

'I think they forecast a blizzard,' says Eric mildly.

'Now he tells us,' mutters Kaz.

'Well, what would you have done about it?' Eric is scribbling madly at the kitchen table, making notes from a textbook. 'D'you know what? I forgot all about the dodo!'

'What about the dodo?' Kent asks.

'It would have been on the Ark.'

'But it's extinct,' Kaz objects.

'It wasn't then, though, was it?' I can tell from Eric's tone that he was hoping someone would say this.

'Well, no. But do you have to have it?' I ask him. 'After all, you've left out other birds, haven't you? Why not leave out the dodo?' I have a ridiculous mental image of a pair of dodos waddling up the gangplank into the welcoming arms of the Noah family.

'Because it's important. The fact that it's extinct could mean it's quite old —'

'Or quite careless.'

'I wish you'd take this seriously, Ruth.'

'How can anyone take dodos seriously?'

'It nests on the ground, so it will have to be kept separate in case someone treads on its babies.' Eric makes another note. 'Apparently it wasn't very bright.'

'Now there's a surprise,' murmurs Silas.

'What did you say, Silas?'

'Nothing.' Silas has nearly finished his hare, and is enormously pleased with it, although apparently hares' eyes are hard to get hold of. 'Will rabbit's eyes do, do you suppose?'

It is at this stage, in the middle of the dodo/hares' eyes discussion, that two things happen at once. All the lights go out and my waters break.

'Bugger!' I stand shocked into inactivity, warm water trickling down my legs and seeping into my socks. What do I do next?

'It's only a power cut, Ruth. Not to worry,' says Eric, foraging in a drawer for candles and matches.

'No. It's the baby. I think it's started.'

There is a stunned silence (which, when I come to think about it, is odd, since it's what everyone seems to have been waiting for).

'Where's Rosie?' Silas asks, after a moment.

'She's gone up to bed. She was feeling a bit under the weather. Do you think you can hang on, Ruth?'

The idea of hanging on to a baby who has decided to be born is so ridiculous that I laugh.

'No,' I tell him, 'I don't think I can hang on. Or rather, I don't *know* whether I can hang on. I've never done this before. But don't disturb Mum yet. This will probably take ages.'

'Not a good night to have a baby,' Silas remarks, going over to the window and drawing back the curtain. Frenzied snowflakes are hurling themselves against the darkened window. They appear to be going up rather than down.

'Thank you, Silas.'

'Oh, I'm sorry, Ruth. But I'm sure you'll be ok. It says in my book —'

'Silas, this is not the time for your book. I need proper help. I think I should phone the hospital.'

'Yes. Yes, of course.' Silas sounds disappointed. 'Can I ring them for you?'

'I think I'd better speak to them myself.'

But it isn't only the power lines that have come down, and the phone is dead.

'Mobiles. Has someone got a mobile?' Kent asks. Kent himself doesn't use a mobile, and knows very little about them.

'No signal here,' Eric says. 'No-one can use a mobile from Applegarth.'

'We could try,' says Silas.

We try. Three mobiles attempt to phone the hospital, and fail.

The first pain rises like a wave in my stomach. It isn't too bad, but I think it means business. I look at the circle of helpless faces round the candlelit kitchen table, hoping someone will say something helpful.

'I'll drive her to the hospital. Get your things, Ruth,' says Kaz. 'And for God's sake, wrap up warm.'

'In that case we really do need to fetch Rosie. Brian, could you go and tell her? She'll need some warm clothing,' Eric says.

Dad, who has been standing helplessly in the background, seems only too pleased to have something to do, and hurries off upstairs, while I pack a small suitcase (this should have been ready weeks ago, but somehow denial got in the way, so I've probably left vital things out).

Ten minutes later, Kaz, Mum and I totter unsteadily out into the blizzard, together with Kent, who's coming as extra support. The snow is falling fast, blown in all directions by a wind which is threatening to become a hurricane, stinging our faces in icy gusts and forming steep drifts all over the garden. We scoop the snow off Kaz's car, our hands already numb with cold, and climb in. With four adults and a suitcase, the car seems very full, and fulfils my worst fears by refusing to start.

'We'll have to take the Land Rover,' Kaz says.

'Are you insured for it?' I ask.

'Ruth, this is an emergency. Insurance doesn't come into it.'

'I'll drive if you like,' Kent offers.

'Please.'

Kent fetches the keys, and we all pile in. By now, I'm so cold that it's somehow ceased to matter. I sit hunched in the front passenger seat, my arms wrapped around my stomach, waiting for the next pain. It comes in a gentle crescendo, but is still easily bearable. I'm beginning to wonder what all the fuss is about. So far (weather conditions notwithstanding) this is proving to be a doddle.

We make our way cautiously down the driveway, through drifts of snow, the windscreen practically obscured by a billion snowflakes which dance and dazzle in the headlights.

After about ten yards, the Land Rover comes to a gentle halt. Kent revs the engine, but nothing happens. He gets out to have a look.

'There's a huge drift,' he tells us, 'and a massive tree's come down. We won't be able to get out, even if we manage to clear the snow.'

His voice is practically drowned out by the wind, but his meaning is clear. We're stuck.

'Is there another way round?' he yells.

'No.' I know this for a fact. The track is the only route through the thickly wooded coppice which separates Applegarth from the road. Silas and Eric have discussed plans for a 'back way', but these have never come to fruition. To all intents and purposes, we're stranded.

'Oh dear, oh dear.' Mum's gloved hands make little flapping movements. 'What are we going to do?'

'First things first. We need to get Ruth back into the house,' Kaz says. 'She's frozen.'

'Can you walk?' Kent asks me. 'Because the car is well and truly stuck now.'

'I think so.'

'Come on, then.'

With Kaz and Kent on either side of me and Mum still fretting behind us, we begin to walk back to the house. We are facing into the wind, which is so strong we can almost lean on it without falling. It hurls the snowflakes into our frozen faces, snatching away our breath, as we stumble over the hidden ruts, pausing as I have another, stronger contraction. Although it's such a short distance, it takes us about fifteen minutes, and by the time we reach the house, we're all exhausted.

'Well, you said you loved snow. You've got snow,' remarks Kaz, as we stumble in through the back door, bringing with us a strong gust of wind and yet more snow.

Eric and Silas fuss over us, as they help us out of our wet coats and gloves. When we're more or less settled, Eric makes a big jug of cocoa (at least the Aga is still working). I am still shivering, despite the rug around my shoulder and the hot water bottle on what's left of my lap. Up until now, it's all been a bit of an adventure, but now reality has set in and I'm beginning to feel seriously frightened.

'It'll be all right,' Eric says. 'The baby probably won't be born for ages, and by then the phones will be back on.'

'You think?' I wish I shared his optimism.

'Well, I certainly hope so. And anyway, people give birth all the time, don't they? In many parts of the world, they just get on with it on their own.'

'At the edges of paddy fields,' I finish for him.

Another bigger contraction tightens my stomach and makes me gasp. I have a feeling this is not going to be such a doddle after all.

'Perhaps she should go to bed?' Kent suggests (it seems that already I'm becoming a third person; a helpless victim, incapable of being spoken to directly).

'No. She's better up and about, as long as she feels like it.' I can tell that Silas has his bible on his knees, and is referring to it surreptitiously under the table.

'Don't we need boiling water?' Eric says. 'I'm sure I've read somewhere that we need lots of boiling water.'

'I always wonder what they want all that hot water *for*,' Kent muses. 'They never seem to use it; they just get it ready.'

'The hot water's a myth,' says Silas. 'But we'll need sterile scissors — now, those *will* need to be boiled — and some kind of string or thread to tie the cord.' He brings his book out of hiding and lays it on the table. 'And of course a clean sheet or towel to wrap the baby in. But first we have to clear the baby's airway. Well, that makes sense, doesn't it?'

I give Kaz a despairing glance. I don't want my predicament medicalised by Silas and his book. I don't like his plans for what "we" are going to do. What I need is sympathy, and cosseting, and someone who knows what they're doing. I'm very much afraid that if someone doesn't do something soon, I'm going to cry.

'She will be all right, won't she?' Dad asks. He suddenly looks small and vulnerable, and even in my present parlous state, I feel oddly touched.

'Of course she is.' Kaz takes control. 'Ruth, how about a nice hot bath? It'll warm you up, and while you're having it, I'll put some clean sheets on your bed, and a fresh hot water bottle. It's going to be pretty cold up there without the central heating. And then I think you should try and get some rest.'

'I'll give you a hand.' Mum is obviously desperate to be of some help.

'Oof!' Another contraction. Everyone watches in awe, as I sit it out. I've forgotten my breathing exercises (puff? pant? a bit of both?) and for the first time, I wish I'd paid more attention.

'A bath would be lovely. Thank you, Kaz,' I say, when I can speak again.

'Was that painful?' Silas asks. 'It shouldn't hurt that much at the beginning. It should —'

'Silas, I think you should shut up. And please put that bloody book away!' Eric says.

'I'm only —'

'Trying to help? Well, you're not helping at all. You take Ruth upstairs, Kaz. Shout if you need anything.'

The bath is soothing — even the contractions are less painful in warm water — and it is with some reluctance that I get out.

'How often are you having the pains?' Kaz asks, bringing me clean pyjamas.

'You sound like Silas,' I tell her.

'No, I think it's important. If they're really frequent, it means the baby's well on the way.'

'And what would we do about it?' I ask her.

'Good point.'

'You arrived quite quickly,' Mum tells me. 'For a first baby.'

We look at each other in the flickering candlelight, and I think it's at this point that we all realise the awful truth. I am almost certainly going to give birth here, at Applegarth, with no medical help whatsoever.

'We'll manage,' says Kaz, after a moment.

'Course we will.'

'And we'll both stay with you.'

'Yes. Please do.' I hesitate. 'Kaz?'

'Mm?'

'You're not squeamish are you?'

'No.'

'Not ever?'

'Not ever.'

'Have you ever — fainted?'

'Certainly not.'

'And you, Mum? Will you be okay with all this?'

'Of course I will,' says Mum, smiling bravely.

'Good.'

'I'll move my mattress into your room and sleep here,' Kaz says. 'We'll leave the candle alight, just in case.'

'Shouldn't I be the one to stay with her?' Mum asks.

'You've not been feeling too good, have you, and we're going to need you later,' Kaz says. 'We'll call you if anything happens. And Ruth, you should get some sleep if you can. I think it's going to be a long night.'

Strangely, I do get some sleep. The contractions ease up a bit, and I'm able to doze in between. Towards dawn, the wind drops, to be replaced by an eerie stillness. In the white glow reflected from the snow outside, I can see the outlines of furniture, and Kaz curled neat as a kitten under her duvet on the floor beside my bed. I wonder whether it's worth going downstairs to see if the phones are working yet, but decide against it. Having got nicely warm, I'm reluctant to leave my bed. Besides, since no-one can get to us through the snow, there's not much point in making phone calls. It's not as though anyone can deliver my baby over the phone.

I feel another contraction, and manage to breathe my way through it quite satisfactorily. Kaz turns on her back and begins to snore gently. Once more, I drift off to sleep.

Chapter Forty-Four

The baby means business.

I have been awake now for nearly an hour, and the contractions are getting stronger and a good deal more painful. There is none of the stop-start nonsense of last night. This is for real.

The news on my bedside radio (mercifully battery-operated) tells of storms and drifts all over the country. As usual, the British weather has been met with total astonishment by the British people, and everything has ground to a halt. There are people stranded in cars and trains, and sheep marooned in fields. All over the country, schools will be closed, and in Nottinghamshire, a woman has given birth in a village hall.

'At least this isn't a village hall,' says Kaz, returning from the kitchen with a tray of tea.

'There might be a doctor in a village hall.'

'And there might be an audience of several hundred. You wouldn't want that.'

'I suppose not.'

'How's it going?' Kaz wraps herself in her duvet, and sits on the edge of my bed.

'Painful.'

'How painful?'

'Pretty painful. Bearable, though.' I lever myself further up the bed.

'Should we fetch your mum?'

'No. Let her sleep for the moment, and I'll see how it goes.' I shiver. 'Gosh, it's perishing in here. The poor baby will freeze to death before it's even taken its first breath.'

'No it won't. Kent's lit a fire in the sitting-room, and you can lie on the sofa.'

'Where's Silas?'

'Doing the animals with Eric. But he's been looking things up in his book and he's dying to come and interfere.'

'Please don't let him!'

'What do you take me for?' Kaz grins. 'He wants to know how often your contractions are coming.'

'What did you tell him?'

'I said I'd no idea.'

'Good girl.' I wrap my hands round my mug of tea. 'And Dad? Is he okay?'

'I think he's praying. He said it was the only thing he could do. He's awfully worried, Ruth.'

'Poor Dad.' I could do with his prayers right now. 'I had this awful dream that the baby died and Silas insisted on stuffing it.'

'I wouldn't put it past him.'

'Neither would I. Are the phones back on?'

'No chance.'

'Bugger.'

'Bugger indeed.'

Another big contraction begins, and I almost spill my tea. I pant my way through it.

'Wow,' says Kaz, impressed. 'That was serious, wasn't it?'

'Just a bit.'

'You know, I thought I wanted children, but now I'm not so sure.'

'Thanks, Kaz.'

'You're welcome.' She puts down her mug. 'Let's get you downstairs before the next one.'

She helps me into my dressing gown, and down the creaking staircase. There seem to be a lot more stairs than there used to be, and I have to stop half-way for a breather.

In the sitting-room, a fire is blazing. Kent has pulled up the sofa and made it up with blankets and pillows. It looks quite cosy.

'Welcome to the delivery suite.' Kaz helps me on to the sofa and covers me with several blankets. 'I'll go and fetch some towels. We'll need towels. Breakfast?'

I shake my head as another wave begins. 'Please — keep — everyone — out. Ouf! And I think — it's time — to call Mum.'

Minutes later, Mum comes hurrying down, full of apologies. 'I was awake half the night, and then I must have dropped off. How's it going, love?'

'A bit — painful. But — I'm — managing.'

She sits down beside me. 'I won't talk. I'll just sit here quietly. But you tell me if I can do anything.'

The morning progresses slowly. Kent has set off on foot to see if he can tunnel his way out of Applegarth and find some kind of help, and Eric and Silas are busy seeing to the animals while Dad makes seemingly endless cups of tea for everybody. Meanwhile, Kaz, Mum and I are left to our own devices, with Mum rubbing my back and giving me sips of water, and Kaz timing my contractions.

'Every five minutes, regular as clockwork,' says Kaz, after what seems several days rather than a mere morning.

'What does that mean?'

'Didn't you listen to *anything* they told you?' Kaz says in exasperation. 'If I were having a baby, I'd want to find out everything I could.'

'Bully for you.'

'I don't understand you, Ruth.'

'I never asked you to.'

'Ruth dear — Kaz is only trying to be helpful,' Mum says.

'Well, it's not helping.'

Somewhere at the back of my mind there stirs a memory of being told about a stage in labour where women tend to lose their tempers and swear. Is this it?

Perhaps not.

'Sorry, Kaz,' I squeeze her hand.

'Me too.' She rearranges my pillows. 'This baby thing is exhausting isn't it, and I'm not even the one having the baby.'

Silas pops his head round the door, his face barely visible above a brightly-coloured muffler.

'Silas, you're supposed to knock,' says Kaz sternly.

'I'm so sorry, I just wanted to know —'

'Every five minutes,' Kaz tells him.

'Ah. That means —'

'Silas, we know what that means —' we don't — 'so please leave us to get on with it. Everything's fine.'

'Are you sure?'

'Quite sure.'

'Is Kent back?' Mum asks him.

'No. I think he'll be some time,' Silas says. 'The drifts are about eight feet deep in places.'

I spare a thought for Kent, who certainly isn't anything like eight feet deep, and hope he'll be all right. It would be awful if he were to give his life for me and my unborn child.

The time and the contractions tick by. The pain gets worse and more frequent, but I do my best not to make any noise, for I am uncomfortably aware that Silas is waiting somewhere nearby for an excuse to come and help.

'Mum, I need to push,' I gasp.

'Aren't you supposed to hang on a bit?'

'I — can't — hang — on!'

'Then perhaps you'd better go ahead, dear. I'm sure your body knows what it's doing.'

I push. It feels as though my whole body's trying to turn itself inside out, but nothing happens.

'Do you think I ought to — have a look?' Mum asks me, after several more fruitless and exhausting pushes.

'Please.'

Mum has a look.

'Oh, my goodness! I can see its head!'

'What, all of it?'

Kaz joins her, and they both peer under the blanket. 'Just the top,' she says.

'Hair?'

'Possibly. Gosh this is so exciting!'

'I'm — glad — you — think — so.' Another big push. I feel utterly drained. Whatever happens, this baby is going to be an only child.

'I think it helps if you put your chin on your chest,' Kaz says. 'And then push. I've seen it on the telly.'

'*Fuck off!*' The pain is overwhelming. All this pushing is going to kill me. 'Fucking, fucking baby!'

Mum makes a tutting noise, and despite the pain, I experience a wave of irritation, but Kaz wisely shuts up, and we all wait for the next contraction.

'Aaaaaaah!' This is a big one, accompanied by a searing pain.

'Oh, Ruth! Its head's out,' Mum tells me.

'Wow! This is amazing!' Kaz says.

'What — happens — now?' I lie back on my pillows, panting.

'Another push?'

'Here goes.'

The next push is a bit easier, and the one after that is accompanied by another sharp pain and a rather satisfying slither. There's a brief silence followed by a yell of protest.

The seahorse/rabbit has arrived.

'He's here. Your baby's here! Oh, Ruth! He's *beautiful!*' Tears are running down Mum's cheeks as she very carefully lifts up something slippery and howling, wraps it in a towel and hands it to me.

I look down into the face of my son. After a few moments, he stops crying, opening navy blue eyes beneath a slick of wet dark hair and gazes at me critically.

'Will I do?' I ask him softly.

'Oh, Ruth! Of course you'll do!' Kaz gives me a big hug. 'This is the most exciting day of my life. Congratulations!'

'Darling, you were amazing,' Mum says. 'Just amazing.'

I unwrap him and we all count his fingers and toes, wonder at his tiny fingernails, his neatly-drawn eyebrow and feathery lashes and his 'dear little knees' (Kaz's words). It is amazing that a year ago he didn't exist at all, and yet here he is, absolutely perfect in every way. A home-made human being.

'Could you — could you ask Dad to come in?' I ask Mum, after a few moments.

'Are you sure?'

'Yes. I'm sure.' Because now I want both my parents with me to share in this miracle.

Dad tiptoes into the room in his socks and approaches the sofa carefully ('like the shepherds in the stable,' as I afterwards say to Kaz).

'Oh, Ruth,' he says, very gently laying a finger on the baby's head. '*Ruth!*' And to my astonishment, I see that there are tears in his eyes.

An hour later, I am sitting up with my baby in my arms and we are drinking his health in elderflower champagne. The placenta (which had been completely forgotten in all the excitement) has been delivered, and in a moment of post-natal magnanimity, I even let Silas cut the cord with his newly-boiled scissors. Altogether, it's been something of a joint effort, and everyone seems inordinately proud, both of themselves and of me.

You read about childbirth (at least, most women do); you read about the different stages and what happens when and what you're supposed to do; you even read about the pain. Nobody, however, tells you about the afterglow.

I think now of all my favourite moments — performing a concerto with an orchestra; getting my diploma; the best possible sex; being in love (not necessarily the same thing) — but none can compare with this. At this moment, there is no-one and nothing in the world but me; me and this perfect little human being (how could I ever have thought of him as a seahorse/rabbit?). I never expected to feel like this; I didn't even know it was possible. But I believe that now — this moment — is the nearest I have ever been to perfect happiness.

'Hey!' I cry, to no-one in particular. 'I did it! *I did it!*'

As though in response, there are muffled footsteps outside and we hear the front door opening. There's the sound of raised voices, and a kind of scuffle, and a few moments later, Amos bursts into the room followed by Kent. They both look very cold and very wet, and Kent at least looks very cross.

'I'm so sorry, Ruth. I couldn't stop him. He wouldn't let me explain,' Kent says. 'I met him outside. He said he'd had an urgent message and needed to see you at once.'

'So you *do* live here!' Amos beams at me. 'When I came before, that weasily little woman said she'd never heard of you, and told me to go away. I only just got your message, and tried to phone, but I couldn't get through. What's the matter? Has something happened? Are you ill? It's taken me hours to get here. I had to abandon the car and —' he stops short. 'Whatever have you got there?'

'It's a baby.'

'*A baby?*'

'A baby.'

'Whose baby?'

'Your baby.'

'*My* baby?'

'Our baby.' I hold out our son to show him. 'Amos, meet Malachi.'

Epilogue

Six months later

I love September; still summer, but with a hint and promise of autumn, and (today at least) warm sunshine.

Malachi is sitting on a rug on the grass chewing at a biscuit with his one tooth. He catches my eye and smiles (Amos's smile), biscuity soup leaking down his front. Indoors, Amos is practising with all the windows closed (the neighbours are not fans of the trombone) and keeping an eye on his vat of home-brew (he has been picking up tips from Eric and Silas).

We've been living together in my flat ever since the Norwegians left, and things seem to be working out pretty well. We're neither of us in any hurry, but I think we are both hoping for a future together. Amos is a wonderful father, which considering he had no time at all to get used to the idea is pretty amazing. We argue frequently, laugh a lot, make love whenever the baby allows us to, and perhaps most importantly of all, are the best of friends. We both do a bit of teaching and Amos plays in a small jazz band. We get by.

My mother adores Malachi, and manages to ignore the fact that Amos and I aren't married, referring to Amos as her son-in-law. Since she and my father left Applegarth to move back into their renovated home, she has been much happier. I think this is in no small part due to her chickens.

While Mum was at Applegarth, she became very attached to her feathered charges, and she's started keeping rare breeds of chickens in the orchard. She has some pretty feather-footed bantams and some speckled Sussex hens, and some others with peculiar names which I can't remember. She's thinking of showing some of them, and she also sells their eggs.

'But we don't need the money,' Dad objects.

'That's not the point,' says Mum.

'Then you might as well give the eggs away.'

'That's not the point, either.'

Mum has discovered that having a saleable skill has its own value, which has nothing to do with making money and everything to do with self-esteem. Dad, who has enough of both, wouldn't understand.

My father still struggles with the whole baby thing. On the one hand, I know he's proud that he was one of the first people to see Malachi, but on the other, he's still upset at my unmarried state. However, he finds an increasing number of excuses to visit us (he's 'just passing', he's returning something I lent him, he's planning a surprise for Mum's birthday), and may even eventually forgive me for having a child out of wedlock. Sometimes, I hear him singing the baby tuneless little ditties when he thinks I'm not listening, and Malachi, who's a forgiving soul, gives every appearance of enjoying them.

Other things have been happening, too. Mikey and Gavin have had their union legalised, and have bought a tiny cottage together. They appear to be blissfully happy, and Mikey still finds time to visit his new godchild. Meanwhile, Kaz and Kent appear to have sorted out their differences and seem very settled and happy, living together in the caravan. Kaz has given up pole dancing at Kent's request, and has joined a local taxi firm, which she says she enjoys enormously ('I get great tips, Ruth!' I'll bet). She hasn't told Kent about her fling with Gary ('you were right, Ruth'), and they have no immediate plans for the future, but I hope and believe that they'll stay together, not least because I'm deeply fond of them both.

We keep in close touch with Applegarth, and have paid my uncles several visits. On these occasions, Blossom, who appears to consider that she's back in charge, is almost friendly, although I suspect that she's always relieved to see us go. Silas is fully restored to health and has recently stuffed a tortoise ('so hard to get hold of, Ruth, a dead tortoise. And so generous of the zoo'). Eric has almost finished his work on the Ark and is already looking around for another project to take its place. But I'm glad Kent and Kaz are around to keep an eye on things, especially as my uncles aren't getting any younger. They deserve a bit of looking after, and who better to do it than a newly-discovered son? Lazzo goes round most days to help. He loves Applegarth and the animals, and seems to ask for nothing more (although I'm still planning the promised visit to London Zoo).

And the Virgin of the hen house? I'm afraid the news there isn't so good, due to a recent incident involving a new initiative and a wild boar.

Eric, inspired by his researches into pig varieties, took it into his head to put Sarah to a wild boar instead of her usual mate.

'Nice gamey meat,' he explained. 'And the piglets will be so *interesting*.'

Now, Sarah has many idiosyncrasies, one of which is a refusal to conduct her couplings anywhere other than on her own territory, so the boar, kindly (and, I suspect, illicitly) loaned by a contact at the safari park, was duly delivered to do the business. So far, so good.

Unfortunately, before the happy couple could consummate their union, Sarah's visitor escaped, and came barrelling down between the outhouses and across a field 'like the wrath of God' (Silas's words), scattering sundry chickens and piglets in his wake. Upon being challenged by Lazzo with a broom handle, he made an about turn, and charged straight into the side of the hen house, impaling himself by his tusks and instantly demolishing all traces of the Virgin.

As Eric said afterwards, it is as though she had never been there at all.

A NOTE TO THE READER

Thank you for taking the time to read this collection. The first book, *Cassandra's Secret* is very loosely based on my own wonderful but eccentric mother and some of my own experiences. While some of the behaviour of Cassandra's mother is hers alone, my own mother did (for example) buy me those royal blue knickers. I have never forgotten the humiliation of having to wear them for PE every week. But we had some wonderful spring picnics picking primroses when I should have been at school. I wish she could have been here to read this book.

The second book is *Women Behaving Badly*. Friends are important to everyone — dare I say, especially to women — and this novel was originally going to be about a friendship between three "ladies who lunch". But ideas change, my own Catholic background (not to mention, Catholic guilt. No-one does guilt quite as well as the Catholics) intervened, and these three very different women emerged. They may well have lunch together, but their behaviour is very far removed from that of the ladies I'd originally had in mind. But we all find friends in unexpected places, don't we?

The idea for the third novel, *Ruth Robinson's Year of Miracles* arose out of all sorts of things: among others, my love of motherhood, music, and the countryside, and my affection for quirky eccentric people (my own family is full of them). The idea for the apparition of the Virgin came from markings which resemble a figure in the grain of an old blanket chest we use as a coffee table. The image is still clearly visible, stars and all (to me if to no-one else!).

If you have enjoyed reading this collection, I would be really grateful if you could write a review either on **Amazon** or **Goodreads**.

In the meantime, I love to hear from readers, and your comments are always welcome. I can be contacted via my website at **www.francesgarrood.com**

You can also follow me on Facebook at **FrancesGarroodAuthor.**

Sapere Books is an exciting new publisher of brilliant fiction and popular history.

To find out more about our latest releases and our monthly bargain books visit our website:
saperebooks.com

Printed in Great Britain
by Amazon